VISION AND DESTINY

The Dream fell away, and from the deserted Thrones of the World, Rising Sun saw his Vision. It would be with him always. Eventually, it would change his World forever, for in that frozen moment, Rising Sun received his first true sight of the gift and curse of his inheritance. He saw the World that encompassed the world he'd always known, the World that was greater than the world, the World that he now irrevocably inhabited. His curse and his power was to know the difference between them. Yet to know that greater World was to weep for it, and for the lesser world within it.

"Ah!" he moaned. "Ah! Ah!" As for the first time he beheld the last mammoth. . . .

THE LAST MAMMOTH

THE LAST MAMMOTH

MARGARET ALLAN

A SIGNET BOOK

SIGNET
Published by the Penguin Group
Penguin Books USA Inc., 375 Hudson Street,
New York, New York 10014, U.S.A.
Penguin Books Ltd, 27 Wrights Lane,
London W8 5TZ, England
Penguin Books Australia Ltd, Ringwood,
Victoria, Australia
Penguin Books Canada Ltd, 10 Alcorn Avenue,
Toronto, Ontario, Canada M4V 3B2
Penguin Books (N.Z.) Ltd, 182–190 Wairau Road,
Auckland 10, New Zealand

Penguin Books Ltd, Registered Offices:
Harmondsworth, Middlesex, England

First published by Signet, an imprint of Dutton Signet,
a division of Penguin Books USA Inc.

First Printing, July, 1995
10 9 8 7 6 5 4 3 2 1

*This is for Desmond Mong Seng Tan
Still all the right reasons . . .*

"Whenever a thing changes and quits its proper limits, this change is at once the death of that which was before."

—LUCRETIUS

"All changes, even the most longed for, have their melancholy; for what we leave behind us is a part of ourselves; we must die to one life before we can enter into another!"

—ANATOLE FRANCE

"You cannot step twice into the same river, for other waters are continuously flowing."

—HERACLITUS

BOOK ONE

STAIRWAY TO HEAVEN

"And when you gaze long into an abyss the abyss also gazes into you."

—FRIEDRICH NIETZCHE

CHAPTER ONE

1

The Green Valley, 17,953 B.C.

It took four strong men to hold the naked boy down.

The man with the knife took the boy's penis in his left hand and pulled on it, stretching out the foreskin. The boy gasped, but managed not to scream.

The man waved the knife at him ferociously. "Father Snake comes for you! Father Snake comes to eat you! Father Snake wants your little-boy snake for his own!"

The boy moaned. Sweat glistened through the smoky smudges on his cheeks. His terrified gaze sought the eyes of the man with the knife, but found no mercy there. The man brandished the knife again, leaned down, and screamed into the boy's face: *"Now you will die! Now the Great Father Snake will eat the head of your little-boy snake!"*

I didn't know it would be like this, the boy thought.

"Close your eyes," said the man with the knife.

The boy stared dumbly into the man's face. Drums thundered in his ears. It was almost impossible to think, let alone hear anything, with the wild, eerie howl of the bull roarers—carved pieces of wood whirled at the end of leather thongs—wailing in his ears. Firelit shadows capered across the soot-caked ceiling of the men's Mystery House, the shapes elongated and terrifying.

The boy's lips moved, but nothing came out. The face of the man with the knife—white-painted, red-toothed, perspiring—pressed closer, until the hot stench of his breath assaulted the boy's nostrils. *"Close your eyes and don't open them or your father will die, your mother will die!"*

The boy screwed his eyelids shut. In the confusing dark, he suddenly recalled his mother's words of the morning. Only a few hours before, now so long ago. A lifetime ago, it seemed.

"I know you are the bravest boy in the Green Valley."

But he didn't feel like the bravest boy *now,* did he? No, not in the steaming, shrieking dark, with the knife at his balls, the fearful moans of his fellow boy-journeyers filling his ears, and the Great Father Snake hissing for his blood, gnashing his viper teeth at the tender flesh of his penis!

The boy bit his lip as the men gripped him tighter. Rough fingers twisted at his foreskin, stretching it even farther. Bolts of agony thrummed in his heaving belly.

No, not so brave *now.* But he didn't open his eyes.

The flame-shot twilight of the Mystery House quivered with renewed fervor as the door opened and an awesome figure ducked inside. It might have been a man, but in the gloom, with the costume of dry, rasping snake skins draped about its shoulders, and the bleached bison skull concealing its features, it was hard even for those who knew that figure to be sure it was fully human.

The Shaman approached the log where the boy was pinned like a rabbit for the skinning. He shuffled along in a complicated dance that made the snake skins hiss against each other. In his left hand was a rattle fashioned from the skull of a large snake, filled with smooth stones, which he shook in rhythm with the movements of his feet. He held a knife chipped from red crystal in his right hand, and as he came up to the boy, he made sharp striking motions with the blade.

He raised both hands above his head, and the drums and bull roarers abruptly fell silent. Now only the arid scrape of his snake skins filled the silence. He saw the boy tense his body, saw his belly tighten in sharply defined ropes of muscle. But he was pleased to see the boy's eyelids, though quivering faintly, remain tightly shut.

Now another man came up behind the man who held the boy's penis, and grasped that man around the waist, as if to hold him steady. The snake man saw that all was ready, and he leaned forward and spat, first on each of the boy's eyelids, then on his lips, and finally on the head of the boy's penis.

"Great Father Snake is here now!"

The drummers pounded a single beat.

"Great Father Snake releases your little-boy snake from its protection, so that it may see the World with a man's single eye!"

Now the snake figure rattled the stone-filled skull once, like the warning shake of a viper, and then gestured with his crimson knife. The man who grasped the boy's penis gave it a final twist. Then, with a single stroke he sliced away the boy's foreskin.

The boy arched his back. Sweat ran in glittering streams from his face, his chest, his belly. But his eyelids never opened, and he didn't cry out.

The snake figure stamped his right foot, and the drums began again. The knife man raised the small bit of bloody flesh and shook it, spattering red drops across the boy's stomach. He tossed the piece of skin into the fire, symbolizing the death of the boy-flesh. Then he and his compatriot stepped quickly out of the light, to await the next boy who would ride the log.

The Shaman shook his rattle. "I name you Rising Sun!" he shouted.

The four men who had held the boy down now lifted him up. "Open your eyes, Rising Sun, for you are a boy no longer!" they chanted in a single voice.

"Open your eyes and see as a man sees. Speak your manhood name! Look through the eye of the one-eyed snake!" With these words they carried him quickly from the circle of light and set him down in the shadows. Another figure approached, knelt, and applied a dressing of unguents to the boy's penis.

The boy seemed weak and dazed. He opened his eyes, but his expression was staring and empty. The four men, who were his uncles, patted and soothed him, and wiped the sweat from his body with pieces of softly cured bison hide. The boy watched as another squirming, naked figure was lifted from the ground and carried to the smooth log.

The drums pounded. The bull roarers howled.

The boy smiled at last. The pain in his groin was fading as the magical salve did its work.

"My name is Rising Sun," he whispered. "I died as a boy. Now I am reborn a man."

He spoke the truth. But not all of it.

CHAPTER TWO

1

"Is he the One To Come? That's the question we must deal with now," said the Shaman Gotha.

White Moon bowed her head. She and her mate, Morning Star, were the two youngest of the group of four seated on log benches inside the Spirit House, and they had streaks of gray in their dark hair.

The Shaman was still sturdy and strong, but the twin braids that fell to his waist had turned the color of the winter steppe. Wolf, Chief of the Three Tribes and the eldest present, had no hair at all. Brown liverish splotches covered his bald dome and marked his wrinkled face. His black eyes twinkled with a lively intelligence that belied his advanced age, and a bit of the boy he'd once been still showed in the wry grin he offered at the Shaman's question.

"I thought you'd know the answer to that. After all, you went with my sister, Great Maya, into the Void and saw the Gods depart."

Gotha nodded. "I did. And so did the Keepers." He inclined his head toward Morning Star and White Moon. "But what we saw and heard there doesn't fully answer the riddle." He arched his eyebrows, and Morning Star and White Moon shook their heads in agreement.

White Moon said, "The Turtle spoke of a Gift, a

Promise, and a Test. I think the Gift was the Stone Re-
joined, and the Promise was of the One To Come. The
Turtle said the One To Come would descend from the
Keepers of the Stones, Morning Star and me. But the Tur-
tle didn't tell us who, or how, the Promise would enter the
World."

She shrugged. "I have many children. Rising Sun is
the eldest, but he has six brothers and four sisters. It
could be any of them, I guess. Whether it is Rising Sun,
I don't know."

Gotha rubbed his chin. "The Turtle prophesied a Test,
as well. I think that is how we are to know when the One
To Come is among us."

Morning Star said, "But we don't know what the Test
is. Just that it will be. How are we to know it?"

Wolf looked troubled, as he always did when he
thought of the departure of the Gods. "We don't have the
Great Spirits to guide us anymore. Only the Spirits of
the World, and they have no answers." He glanced at
Gotha. "Or have you Dreamed of anything, Shaman?"

"No. The World Spirits speak to me, the Spirits of
wind and lightning, water and the land, and all the lesser
Spirits, too, but this matter is beyond them. It belongs to
the Turtle, and the Turtle doesn't speak to me." He moved
his shoulders slightly. "Even if the Great Ones were still
with us, They were never to be trusted." He smiled
faintly. "The Gods loved Their tricks."

They nodded thoughtfully; all of them, in some way or
another, had endured the capricious whims of the Great
Departed Ones.

Gotha pursed his lips. "Is there anything you've noticed about Rising Sun that might give us a hint? I know
the boy well, but you are his father and mother. I'm told
that Great Maya demonstrated her extraordinary powers
as a child, and that both the ancient Shaman, Magic, and
the Root Woman, Berry, knew of them."

Moon and Star looked at each other. "He is a good
boy . . ." Morning Star replied. "I think he will be a
good man, sturdy and strong."

"He loves animals," White Moon said. "He gets that
from his father, I suppose."

Morning Star's facility with beasts of all kinds, both great and small, was well known. The talent had provided him with mighty rank among the hunters of the Three Tribes. He was the acknowledged master of hunt magic, greater than the Shaman Gotha himself.

"Yes, he loves animals," Gotha agreed, "but I haven't seen any special talents beyond affection and patience. He doesn't seem to have your power, for instance."

Morning Star sighed. The lack sorely disappointed him. Rising Sun seemed so normal. If only he'd shown a spark of something, *anything,* their decisions might be easier. But while Morning Star could soothe even a snarling cave lion, his son had revealed no such ability.

"He was only a little boy when I led the lions from their caves near the mouth of the Valley," he said. "I took him with me, to see if he had my Power, but he didn't." He winced, remembering. "He cried in fear and held my leg when mother lion walked past me. And if I hadn't been there, I think mother lion would have eaten him."

White Moon's eyes widened. "You never told me that!"

Morning Star patted her shoulder. "I didn't want to worry you. But I had to find out."

Wolf said, "So the boy has shown no special Powers, not even to you, Shaman?"

Gotha wrinkled his eyes. "He learns quickly and well. For his age, he is quite knowledgeable. I have taught him as much as I can—he is only a boy, after all—but he doesn't Dream. Or if he does, he's never told me so."

He sighed. "Our dilemma is simple. We don't know what the One To Come is supposed to do, or even how to know when he's arrived among us. All we know it that he is to come." Gotha rubbed his temples. "The Turtle, it seems, is no more forthcoming than were the Gods. I'm not even certain if the Turtle will play any part in this."

They fell silent. All of them, except for Wolf, had been transported beyond the World when Great Maya had loosed the bounds of the Gods and set Them free of Their creation. All had seen the Turtle, and heard Its words, and felt the World change. But the Turtle was the uncreated creating One, the voice of the Void, and they had even

less idea of Its purpose than they had of the tangled webs
of the Departed Gods.

Gotha said, "Sometimes it's better to do nothing than
to do the wrong thing."

With that, Gotha sat straighter, as if he'd made up his
mind about the matter. "Wolf and I will be spending
much time with the boy over the next two hands of days,
as Rising Sun receives the instruction that will complete
his journey into manhood. And at the end, there is the
Smoke Pit. Perhaps we will discover some hint to guide
us during these days."

Wolf nodded. "Great Maya didn't come fully into her
own until after she was a woman. Perhaps it will be the
same with Rising Sun."

It was unsatisfactory, but they had no choice. Only
time would tell if Rising Sun was the One To Come.

Whatever in the world that meant.

2

In the bright patch of sunlight behind the men's Mystery House Gotha squatted on his haunches in front of the
boy seated cross-legged in the dust.

"Hear now the word the Turtle gave us," he said. His
voice took on a singsong, chanting quality.

> *"this, then, the lineage:*
> *the mammoth and the snake are*
> *the father and the mother of the world*
> *She-Ya and Ga-Ya*
> *are father and mother of the people*
> *and with my power*
> *they made the stone.*
> *then come the Moon and the Star*
> *and from them*
> *the one to come*
> *who inherits the world."*

He beat out the time to this chant with his fist on his
knee. When he finished, he said in more normal cadence,

"Remember this forever, Rising Sun, for it is the heritage not just of our People, but of the World itself. Do you understand what it means?"

Rising Sun, who had never heard the word of the Turtle before, stared up at him in astonishment. "I don't understand, Shaman. Who are the moon and the star? Does it mean the moon overhead, that grows fat and white, then shrinks and disappears? And surely there are more stars than one. But you only speak of one star. Can you explain this to me?"

The young man spoke clearly, with formal gravity. He knew he must understand these teachings in order to be a man.

Gotha nodded, pleased that Rising Sun asked such questions. Most initiates simply memorized the words by rote, with no comprehension of what they meant. He'd expected more of this one, and was happy not to be disappointed.

"The moon and the star are your mother and father, Rising Sun. The Gods themselves gave your father his name." He paused and waited for a response.

The boy looked down at his toes, plainly puzzled. "But, Shaman, how can that be?"

"Never mind, Rising Sun. Just accept that it is true."

Now the boy seemed agitated. "If the Moon and the Star are my parents, then the word of the Turtle says that from them there will be One To Come, who inherits the World. What could that mean?"

The Shaman regarded him carefully. It was, to say the least, a question that had bothered his own mind for many years. Couldn't this young man see the implications in the word? He wasn't stupid. Surely it was obvious that Rising Sun might be the one the Turtle spoke of, the One To Come. "It means that from your parents will come another, who will inherit the World."

He spoke flatly, without emphasis, and with only the faintest lifting of his eyebrows, as if to invite the boy's reply. But Rising Sun appeared to miss the insinuation entirely.

He laughed. "But, Shaman, that's silly. How can somebody inherit the World?" He glanced up at the brisk blue sky, then made a sweeping gesture. "This is the World, all around us. It can't belong to anybody. It belongs to all of us. This is our World."

Gotha's eyes widened. The boy didn't seem to know it, but he spoke blasphemy. The People had always been taught the World belonged to the Gods who made it. It wasn't common knowledge what had transpired beyond the World, in the Void, before his birth.

Worship went on much as before. The rituals stayed the same. The departure of the Gods remained a secret for the Shaman and the other initiates, who feared the People might become terrified at the loss of their ancient Great Spirits, who no longer owned the World, because they were gone.

It had seemed easier to do it that way, especially since they'd agreed among themselves that the One To Come might resolve the situation better than they could. He would, after all, inherit the World, and Gotha rather cynically hoped that his inheritance would include all the problems of the World, as well.

So when Rising Sun said his simple words, he seemed to hint at a truth that only the Shaman and three others knew. And the way he said it! He spoke as if it was so obvious no one could question it, as if the rocks and trees proclaimed the truth. His tone was the same he might use to say, "Look. The sky is blue."

Rising Sun spoke exactly as Gotha imagined the One To Come would speak. Hope suddenly hammered inside his rib cage. For an instant his throat was full of it, and he couldn't answer. But he was a great Shaman. He mastered himself quickly.

"That's a very wise thing to say, Rising Sun. But what of the Gods, the Mother and Father? Don't They rule the World?"

Rising Sun's face cleared, and Gotha almost winced at the innocence that blazed in his features. Rising Sun, indeed! In his dark eyes burned a light that made Gotha want to shield his own face against it.

"The Gods made the World for us, but it is our World forever," Rising Sun said.

He is the One, Gotha thought, as wonder filled his thoughts. *He is the One To Come, but he doesn't know it!*

"Have you spoken about this to anybody else?"

Rising Sun shook his head.

"Why not?"

"Well, it just seems so ... obvious. It would be like telling my friend Jumping Fox that his nose is big."

Yes. Great truths. *Obvious* truths ... Gotha closed his eyes. The Turtle, it seemed, was just as tricky as the Gods had been.

Trickier.

3

"I've seen a sign," Gotha said. "I think Rising Sun is the One To Come."

The other three stared at him. Morning Star said, "What sign, Shaman?"

Gotha told them what the boy had said, and explained the mystery of it. "Somehow, I think he knows the Gods are gone. I'm not sure if he knows it precisely that way, but it's obvious to him that the World belongs to the People. The way he spoke, I got the feeling he'd always understood that. But since only we know what happened in the Void, he must know it in some other way. Unless—"

He looked at White Moon and Morning Star. "Did you tell him, maybe drop a hint accidentally, or something like that?"

They glanced at each other. Then both shook their heads. "No, Shaman," Morning Star said. "If this is what he believes, he didn't learn it from us. We've always been very careful. Remember how unsettled things were after Great Maya freed the Gods? We decided it was better to hide the truth, for fear the People of the Three Tribes would lose all hope at the departure of the Great Spirits and maybe start warring among themselves again."

Gotha sighed. "Well, I didn't think you'd said anything. And the advice still holds true. The clans of the Mammoth, the Bison, and of Fire and Ice had lived in peace for many years. But I wouldn't want to guess what might happen if the truth came out. Old ways are hard ways, and the hardest of all to change. We've been lucky to smooth as much as we have. Great Maya was wise to take the Stone Rejoined when she left us on her last journey. That way it couldn't tempt anybody, the way the Mammoth Stone did."

Wolf looked up at that. "I wonder if my sister still lives in the World somewhere?"

Gotha regarded him with hooded eyes. "I believe your sister was very close to being a Great Spirit herself. If you remember the words of the Turtle, no mention was made of her in the lineage. I think she was beyond the lineage, perhaps a part of the Turtle Itself. And though she never spoke of it, at least not to me, I suspect she knew this. I think the Stone Rejoined is still in the World somewhere, but I believe Great Maya is long departed from it."

Wolf rubbed his wrinkled cheeks. "I think what you say is true, Shaman. I've not dreamed of my sister for many years." He glanced up, his dark eyes soft. "But I believe she is happy now, though I can't explain how I know this."

White Moon broke in, "We can't explain anything about this, Father. The Stone is gone, Maya is gone, and according to the Shaman, my son believes in truths he has no way of knowing. So what does it all mean? A Gift, a Promise, a Test. What role does Rising Sun play in this? For as much as we know, it seems we know almost nothing."

Now Gotha smiled, and the old ironic bitterness touched his face. "God or Turtle, Turtle or God, what difference does it make? The Great Ones were tricksters. Why not the Greatest One, as well?"

But White Moon said, "No. The Turtle plays no tricks. It spoke Its word, and though we don't understand everything, what we do understand is plain enough. From me and my mate will issue the One To Come, and now you say it is Rising Sun. That's clear enough. As for the rest, I'm sure it will come to pass."

Gotha reached over and touched her hand. "Well said. We shouldn't forget the simple things when we try to fathom the more complicated riddles." He leaned back and rubbed his temples slowly.

"In fact, sometimes I wonder if it isn't better to not worry at all, just let everything take its course. My own past tells me it will, anyway."

Morning Star chuckled. "Mine, too. And what a tangled net all *that* was, eh, Shaman? Do you ever miss your boy Speaker, whom you thought spoke for the Father?"

Gotha shrugged. "I did what I had to do, Morning Star who was once Serpent. As did we all, I'm afraid." He sighed. "If everything turned out differently than we planned or hoped, well, the Gods were still with us then."

"But They aren't now," White Moon said.

"No, They aren't. So what comes next, you who were once both Keepers of the Stones?"

"I don't know," she said.

"I don't, either," he replied.

But as they spoke, the answer to their question rode the back of a rat up from the mouth of the Green Valley, along the stream, until the rat arrived at an invitingly large and comfortable pile of refuse heaped man-high at the edge of New Camp. The answer was a small thing, no larger than a flea.

In fact, it *was* a flea.

CHAPTER THREE

1

The flea danced in the warm fur of the rat. The rat had found many brothers and sisters within the damp heat of the refuse pile. Beneath bones, surrounded by rotting scraps of flesh, all of them fed and grew sleek and fat. And as the rats multiplied, so did the fleas, hopping from one small hairy hide to the next, until the refuse dump fairly hummed with their busy, hungry little lives.

Then one fine blue day Humped Wolf, a heavy-bottomed woman of middle age, staggered to the dump with a load of stinking waste. She carried the scraps in a woven basket and sweated in the high sun.

She came to the edge of the pile and halted. She stared up dubiously and wondered how she could possibly heave her cargo to the top of the pile, which was higher than her head.

"So I won't," she muttered firmly. She was given to expressing firm opinions to herself, but only away from any other ears. As the third and least wife of Racing Elk, she had learned to keep her mouth shut.

She tipped out the garbage. It fell at her feet. Desultorily she kicked some of it away. She was in a bad mood. Racing Elk and his first two wives were already in Home Camp, most likely stuffing their faces with rich meat at the feast prepared to celebrate the elevation of several boys into manhood. She had been left behind to watch the three infants of their little family, and she knew neither of the two senior wives would remember to bring her anything from the banquets.

Lost in her ruminations, she didn't see the glossy little beast that crept from the dump and approached her right toe until the rat, fat and fearless, was almost upon her.

"Ahg! Get away!" She stomped at the thing, which dodged nimbly and twitched its whiskers at her. Then, as far as Humped Wolf could see, it vanished without a trace.

But though she didn't notice, it *did* leave a trace behind. Of the many tiny black dots that bounced and tumbled on its shiny back, one jumped too high, and when it came down, it landed on a new kind of flesh.

Human flesh.

It would do. The flea sensed that others of its kind were already in residence on this strange new food. Happily it burrowed in and made itself at home. It was glad the flea God had given it new shelter, for though the rat it formerly occupied had appeared fat and healthy, it was sick. Actually, it was dying.

2

Rising Sun shivered at the touch of chill in the night air. He stood at the edge of the Smoke Pit, naked but for the magic symbols painted on his chest, arms, and face. Beyond the Pit, a large fire snapped in the hearth at the rear of the Mystery House. The sound made him think of small bones crunching in large jaws.

All of Rising Sun's adult uncles and cousins were gathered around him. They patted his shoulder encouragingly or merely smiled at him, and their love and concern helped to ease the tension that locked his spine and made him stand straight as a spear shaft.

After two weeks the circumcision line at the head of his penis had healed into dark scabs. His days of instruction were over. His head was stuffed with the history, legend, and hunt mysteries that all men had to know. Now only one thing remained—perhaps the most important thing of all.

He glanced down into the Pit at his feet. It was square and measured the length of a tall man on each side. It was perhaps half again as deep. Its crumbling rocky walls were braced with rough-finished logs, and its floor was covered with flat stones worn smooth by years of use.

Instead of the frenzied drumming that had accompanied his circumcision ritual, now only a single drum tapped out a soft, mournful beat, like an endless drip of water. Otherwise, the night was silent. Rising Sun had been standing motionless for half an hour, and was prepared to stand until he fell over on his face, if necessary. He was, however, relieved when a stir of movement at the corner of the Mystery House heralded the Shaman's arrival.

The boy kept his eyes on the Pit, and so heard but didn't see Gotha's approach until the Shaman, wearing his pure white caribou robe, his face striped with paint that gleamed like fresh blood in the firelight, stepped in front of him.

Gotha wore a fierce and forbidding expression. The youth who stood so straight and fearless before him was almost a man. Almost, but not quite. One hurdle remained on his path to manhood, and in some ways this final barrier was the most important of all. Though Rising Sun's life was no longer at risk, the kind of life he would lead as a man was very much in question. Moreover, the Shaman had good cause to believe that more than Rising Sun's personal future was involved. If there was to be any revealing of the One To Come, this ultimate ritual must surely show the way.

Gotha raised the wooden rattle he held in his right hand and shook it once. "Tonight you come to the end of your journey, Rising Sun. Great Father Snake has eaten your little-boy penis and left you with a man's opened single eye. You have learned the mysteries of manhood. Only one thing remains for you. The Pit of Smokes at your feet calls you down, that you may come up out of it born at last into a man's estate."

He shook the rattle twice this time.

Rising Sun blinked, but remained otherwise as still as a rock. Gotha almost smiled at him, but that wouldn't do at all.

"Are you ready to go to the land of Dreams beneath the earth, there to hear the words of Great Father Snake?" Gotha said.

Rising Sun licked his lips. His voice was a dry husk. "Yes, Shaman, I am ready to go."

Gotha shook the rattle three times, then turned to the pair of men waiting by the fire and said, "Very well. Prepare the way for this youth's journey beyond the World!"

The two hunters immediately lifted out bundles of green, smoky branches that had been smoldering at the edge of the hearth. They dumped these into the Smoke Pit, being careful to see that the branches fell into one corner only, leaving the rest of the floor open. Then they took a log that had been hacked with steps and let it down into the clear area. When they finished, they bowed first to the Shaman, then to the boy, and spoke in unison: "The way is ready. Let the journey begin!"

"Let the journey begin!" Gotha echoed and began to shake his rattle continuously. The beat of the single drum picked up as well, and the Shaman began to chant as he danced around the boy.

"Weya, weya, weya!"

All the men repeated the chant after the Shaman. Gotha tapped Rising Sun with his rattle, one time on each shoulder. At this signal, the boy stepped forward, walked to the top of the ladder, and began to climb down.

The chanting rose in pitch and grew louder with each step he descended into the earth, until finally it reached a booming crescendo as he vanished from sight.

"Our son and nephew and cousin Rising Sun leaves the World, ayee, ayee!" Gotha sang.

The hunters feigned weeping and wiped imaginary tears from their eyes. "Weya, weya, he goes to Great Father Snake now!"

The two at the hearth lifted up a great square woven of light branches and plaited with straw and leaves. They carried this to the Pit and set it down. It covered the opening completely.

The Shaman dropped his rattle. At this gesture, even the drumming stopped. A wisp of thick gray smoke trickled through the woven cover. Gotha noted its consistency with satisfaction. If the smoke wasn't right, sometimes the Way would not open, but it looked like that would not be a problem here.

"*Weya!*" he called a final time, and then sat down cross-legged in the dirt to wait.

He wondered what Rising Sun might find on his Dream journey. Only he and Wolf, on the other side of the fire, knew that Great Father Snake had departed from the World. If Rising Sun was the One To Come, he would have to learn his life from something other than a God.

3

Rising Sun stood on the stone floor of the Pit and watched as the woven cover blocked off the light from above. It was a relief to move. He'd been standing for a long time, and his muscles felt stiff and clumsy. But when the light disappeared and darkness surrounded him, he almost wished for the discomfort he'd endured rather than face what now awaited him.

He sniffed. Dense clouds of invisible smoke billowed around him. As his eyes adjusted, he could make out the dimly glowing outlines of smoldering branches against the far corner of the Smoke Pit, and feel a bit of heat from the branches. He settled himself carefully in the corner opposite, seating himself cross-legged with his back against the log wall. After a moment he could no longer see the branches, for the smoke grew so thick around him it blotted out all sight.

He coughed. All of a sudden he felt as if some giant had jammed a burning fist down his throat and filled up his chest with fire. He coughed again, a long, racking shudder that left him doubled over, his arms wrapped around his belly.

And now his eyes began to burn. He blinked rapidly, felt tears pour down his cheeks, but to no avail. After a moment he realized there was no reason to keep his eyes open—between the tears and the dark, he couldn't actually see anything—and with relief he screwed his eyelids tight-shut.

But he couldn't relieve the scorching agony in his chest so easily. He could hold his breath, but for how long? He compromised, inhaling in slow, shallow sips. That seemed to help. The fiery sensations lessened, though his nose suddenly tickled and he sneezed twice. Then his head began to spin.

He had no idea what was supposed to happen. He'd asked Gotha during his half moon of instruction, but the Shaman had told him not to worry, that no one could predict what might occur in the Smoke Pit. The only warning the Shaman had offered was that, no matter what *did* occur, Rising Sun must not attempt to leave the Pit before he had his Dream, for he would not be given another chance beneath the earth. And without his Manhood Dream to guide his new life, he could not fully be a man, and the other hunters, while tolerating him, would ever after think him weak.

Now his skin itched fiercely. It was as if a million fire ants crawled over every part of his body. He scratched his arms so ferociously that his fingernails left bloody tracks. Then, as suddenly as it had come, the itching vanished.

That was when he realized he no longer felt dizzy, nor was his chest on fire any longer. In fact, the air he'd sipped so cautiously now tasted sweet and cool. Somehow he understood that this couldn't be, that the Smoke Pit was as full of fumes as before, but now, it seemed, all his discomfort had stopped. He sat up straight and began to take deeper breaths. After several moments he began to feel restless, and so he stood up.

Finally, he began to walk. And though some very dim and distant part of him knew the Pit was only as broad as a tall man, he kept on walking. Walked right through the walls of the Pit, his chest rising and falling smoothly, breathing air as clean as a springtime dawn, and now the dark turned pearly and began to glow.

The Way was open. Rising Sun took his first step onto the shining path of his manhood and kept on going.

4

In utter darkness, Rising Sun teetered on a glowing line that seemed to stretch forever. There was nothing in the dark but him and the golden cord on which he balanced so carefully.

Still, he pressed on. *This is my Dream,* he told himself. *I must follow it to the end.*

The first voice frightened him so much he almost toppled from his tenuous perch.

"Welcome, Rising Sun, to your ancient home!" The voice was low, mournful, and sounded almost lost. His heart thumped once in his chest as he swayed precariously. Then he caught himself, but not before he thought he saw the ghostly outlines of a face. A long face, hollow-eyed, hungry.

He closed his eyes. The distracting glimmers faded, and even the voices fell silent.

The Way beneath his feet felt more solid now. Tentatively he essayed a single step, then another. After a while he opened his eyes again and gasped in surprise at the new vista before him.

The endless dark had vanished. He had pierced the walls of the Void and the guardian ghosts who swarmed there. Now he walked on a narrow dirt path that seemed entirely unremarkable, a path like many that snaked through the woods of the Green Valley.

On every side, rugged forest giants of hickory and oak and maple towered silently above him, their thick leaves heavy and still. He looked about, but did not pause, for this place unnerved him with its silence. There was an air of desolation, of abandonment about the forest, as if whatever had lived here had departed long ago.

Then, astonishingly, he saw a flash of movement ahead. He blinked. Surely it had been a man?

Ah. There it was again, the merest wink of flesh, like the sun glinting off a running heel.

"Wait!" He cupped a hand to his ear, but heard no reply. Unless . . . was it laughter?

"Wait for me!" He began to run along the path.

Branches whipped at his face and chest, but he ignored the painful sharp scratches. The sound was clearer now, remaining just ahead, leading him around another turn, over another low hill, through another green-canopied tunnel.

Something laughing!

But what? There was an eerie cast to the sound, something not quite right, neither the deep tones of a man, nor the higher, sharper trills of a woman.

He didn't realize the path had been steadily climbing until he came to the top of the long rise. For a moment he stood, head forward, sweaty hair dangling in his face, his eyes locked on the vista below.

A gigantic bowl unfolded in the earth beneath his wondering gaze, its sides crowded with trees even taller than those of the forest through which he'd run. The inanimate stillness of that gigantic wood frightened him greatly, for it seemed frozen, as if time had ceased entirely. Or perhaps as if time had never run here at all.

Yes. This place, whatever it was, was *not changed.* It stood as it had been created, for time had never disturbed so much as a single leaf of this immense, eternal grove.

Overhead, the sun hung suspended in the center of a perfect blue bowl of sky. Its light was strange, somehow flat and faded.

Like the air, he thought. *Flat. No echoes.*

On either side, equidistant around the forested rim of that colossal hole in the earth, two rivers spilled straight down in lacy white veils. These twin falls exploded in silent crashing tumult onto the floor of the bowl.

He suddenly understood his eyes sought out these peripheral details because his mind refused to focus on the most extraordinary feature of the stunning vista before him. He could *feel* his heartbeat stutter wildly as his disbelieving gaze followed the gargantuan stone pile that climbed, tier on rocky tier, from the center of the bowl straight up into the sky.

What a Dream this is! he mused to himself, though something whispered inside him that maybe it wasn't a Dream. Maybe in some awful manner this place was as real as the World. More real. *Older . . .*

But empty. This Dream felt like the carcass of a caribou, picked clean, baked to a rack of white sticks in the sun, bereft. Abandoned.

The merest wink of motion tugged at the corner of his eye. He blinked. Nothing. He blinked again.

Ah. There, something moving slowly up the side of the mount. Something small, tiny. Barely visible . . . Then his eye and his mind put the size of that gnatlike figure into sudden perspective against the immense bulk of the mountain, and the sheer, terrible *mass* of the thing slammed him a step backward and spun his thoughts like snowflakes before the storm.

Big. So unimaginably *big*.

When he opened his eyes again, the climbing figure had disappeared. No, a little higher. Still climbing.

He sucked his heart back down his throat, armed sweat from his forehead, and, shaking only a little, stepped over the crest of the bowl and followed the path down at a brisk jog that eventually turned into an arm-pumping, knee-raising, chest-bursting gallop.

When he reached the river at the bottom of the bowl, he raised his head and spotted the figure, now shrunken by distance to near invisibility. Only its movements betrayed its position. But how to get across the water?

He knew how to swim. Sort of. But floundering around in the shallow waters of First Lake was a far cry from making his way across the broad, fast-moving circle that guarded the base of the mountain tower.

So how to cross the water?

He sighed. "I need a way," he said.

Ka-craaack!

The blazing white bolt that erupted from the empty sky took him utterly by surprise, its thunderous roar flattening his eardrums, its dazzling flash leaving sparks floating in his vision.

He watched, dumb with awe, as a huge tree not ten feet away toppled slowly toward the waters. When all the noise and dust and smoke subsided, Rising Sun found himself with an ideal way across. Just as he'd wished for.

Well, it *was* a Dream, after all.

He hesitated only an instant. Once across the water, he

faced the base of the tower, found a likely looking hand-hold, and began to climb.

The rock was warm to the touch, dry and hard. There was a faint inward taper, so that he was able to lean forward slightly, which helped him to keep his balance.

And the mysterious creature he pursued? Perhaps it was a demon. It frightened him. But it was in his Dream.

I've got no choice, he thought slowly. *It's my Dream. I have to see it to the end, if I am to be a man in the World.*

Sweat trickled into his eyes, quivered on the tip of his broad nose. If nothing else, Dreaming was surely hard work.

Then, with dawning understanding, he realized that his Manhood Dream, of all the Dreams he would ever have, was *supposed* to be hard. Smiling faintly, he clambered on.

He'd lost all track of time by the time he crawled, spent and gasping, onto the top of that awesome peak. For a moment he just lay there beneath the flat yellow sun, facedown, belly heaving, right cheek pressing into the gritty dirt.

It was all he could do to lift his head when the laughter sounded again. There was no conceivable way he could have survived this long in the Smoke Pit. Therefore, time in this place was somehow different from time in the real World. He had no answer, except that Dreams were like that sometimes.

The laughter trailed away. He raised his head farther and examined the plateau he'd gained after so much hard work. It was perfectly flat, and covered with a thin layer of shiny black sand. Something about that made him pause. Then he understood. This sand, so fine it was almost powder, would have blown away in any kind of wind. But it was almost as deep as the length of his fingers. How had the sand gotten here? How had it *stayed* here?

The answer was easy enough, though it would have been impossible in the World. No wind had ever brushed this place. The wind Spirits never came here, They who went everywhere in the World, and loved the high places best of all.

He had always been taught that Dreams were the abode of Spirits and ghosts, but this place seemed empty of them.

Brushing the black grit off his front, he climbed to his feet. Evidence of his own arrival was plain enough in the glittering grit—swirls and handprints and footprints. But that was all. There were no other marks in the pristine surface. Whatever had climbed before him had left no evidence of its passage.

Suddenly he felt cold. If the mysterious figure he'd followed *had* preceded him, it was able to walk across powdered stone without leaving a trail. Only a Spirit—or a ghost—could do that.

What to do now? Was this the end of the Dream? He had indeed been tested—the climb was the hardest thing he'd ever done, no matter that it was a Dream. He would return to the World with a mighty tale, one he didn't understand, but perhaps the Shaman could explain it to him.

It's only a Dream, he told himself, but somehow he wasn't comforted. He was directly facing the curious stone shape in the center of the plateau. He shrugged, and began to walk toward it; after a long time he turned to look over his shoulder. The edge of the precipice was far behind him now, though the center of this ebony plain seemed little nearer than it had when he'd begun trekking toward it. He wondered how long he would have to walk before he reached his goal. Maybe forever, he thought.

After what *seemed* like forever, Rising Sun reached the shadow of the great rock structure in the center of the plateau, and stared up at its serrated, receding walls. It made no sense to him, for he'd never seen, or even imagined, anything like it.

But it looked easier to climb than the stone needle he'd already conquered. He shook his head, spat on his palms, and rubbed them together. One more goal to meet.

I'll climb to the top, and then I'll see—what?

He didn't know the answer to that, but he did know one thing. There was only one way to find out, and that way led upward.

He set to it.

When he finally crawled over the top of the final step, the sight that greeted him was as strange as any he'd seen before, but his numbed brain made no more of it than the rest. The pair of thrones that dominated the squared-off space were polished so smoothly they shone with a dark radiance. It made his eyes water when he tried to look at them.

At the foot of the thrones he stopped dead and stared up in simple awe. They faced away from each other, so their empty seats encompassed all possible views. Together, yet separate, each half of some unimaginable whole.

Dead, dead, dead!

The thought pounded as a low, terrible requiem in his mind. This was a dead place. Cold sweat chilled his back, his shoulders, his belly. Something had been here once, but it was gone. Now nothing remained but desolation.

Suddenly he wanted more than anything to climb to those high seats. Fear and longing warred for an instant, and longing won. He licked his lips, dusted his palms against his thighs, and started up. It took only a few moments before he gained the right-hand seat. He settled himself with his legs dangling over the edge, let out a long breath, and looked out.

The Dream fell away, and from the deserted thrones of the World, Rising Sun saw his Vision. It would be with him always. Eventually, it would change his World forever, for in that frozen moment, Rising Sun received his first true sight of the gift and curse of his inheritance. He saw the World that encompassed the world he'd always known, the World that was greater than the world, the World he now irrevocably inhabited. His curse and his power was to know the difference between them. Yet to know that greater World was to weep for it, and for the lesser world within it.

"*Ah!*" he moaned. "*Ah! Ah!*" As for the first time he beheld the Last Mammoth.

CHAPTER FOUR

1

In the camp of the Children of the River, far from the Green Valley, Sleeps With Spirits awoke to find she'd had the Dream again. As always, she had no idea what it meant—except that, like all her Dreams, in some way it portended doom. After she had blinked the sleep from her eyes and straightened her clothes, she went to look for Carries Two Spears, who was her brother, to tell him about it. Sometimes the telling was enough to soothe her worries.

Besides, no one else would listen to her.

Carries Two Spears was nowhere to be found. She searched the entire camp, peeked inside each of the thirty or so rude huts made of hide and shaped branches, but only in the last shelter did she discover what she wanted to know.

"Your brother?" the man named Walks Nose Down said. "He went out with two others before dawn to hunt along the riverbank."

She nodded slowly. Walks Nose Down stared at her. "If you don't want anything else, go away." With that, he rolled himself into his furs, so he wouldn't have to look at her. She stood silently and watched him, until he sensed her still standing there and turned over again. He spat into the dirt. "I said go away, bad luck woman. Go wait for your brother somewhere else."

Still silent, she turned and walked away. The camp was coming awake now. She could hear her mother's raucous voice, berating one of the younger women. Witch Woman was famous for her temper. Sleeps With Spirits understood. She had felt the lash of her tongue more times than she could count.

Slowly, her face pensive, she plodded down to the riverbank. The camp was situated on a knoll overlooking the broad sweep of water toward the west, where the sun disappeared every night. On her left hand, farther south, another river, as great as this one, flowed into it. The sound of that merging filled the air with a thrumming roar. The sound was so pervasive she no longer heard it, but felt it instead as a continual vibration in her bones. Just as the Tribes of the Green Valley clung to their stone-walled haven far away, so did Spirits's People cleave to their mighty river—nor could she know that, though her People had never seen any of the Tribes of the Valley, that was soon to change.

Her People, who called themselves the Children of the River, or, more simply, the Children, had been camped here two seasons now, after a long trek upriver from the South. Her mother proposed they remain two more, through the season of turning and the season of ice, into the season of renewal, before they moved again. Sleeps With Spirits thought her mother would get her way, as usual. Kills Many Buffalo, the Chief, supposedly had the final decision, but his final decisions mirrored Witch Woman's too often for coincidence.

She stared moodily at the fast-moving water and wondered what it would be like to throw herself in. She pictured herself carried away, far into the south, where it was said the sun shone all the time. It seemed tempting. But she knew it wouldn't happen.

Most of the time she wished she didn't know these things, but her dreams were pitiless. Truth, she reflected, was always pitiless. She knew her fate. It had been unfolded for her long before, when she was barely a girl, and had been given her name.

Sleeps With Spirits.

Only she knew just how uncomfortable that bed was, for no one else would believe her tales. No one. Not ever her brother, Carries Two Spears, though he would listen.

She touched one slender, white finger to her pale lips. "Why won't they believe me?" she whispered. But though the Spirits had shown her many things, they'd never revealed the answer to that.

It was frustrating. Maybe when the Faceless One finally came to her, *he* would know the answer. She turned away from the water and faced the camp, which now showed further signs of morning bustle. But the camaraderie of the women wasn't for her, and never would be. She sat down on the grassy bank, hugged her knees, and watched the water.

One thing, at least. Kills Many Buffalo might as well not argue with her mother about leaving this place. When *he* came for her, *he* would find her here—and it would be winter when *he* did.

She could tell the Chief that, but he wouldn't believe her. Two tears leaked slowly from her red-crystal eyes. "Don't come for me," she breathed softly. "Oh, please don't."

But *he* would. Her Dreams were never wrong. They were only never believed.

2

Rising Sun coughed for almost an hour after he crawled up from the Smoke Pit. The Shaman Gotha held the boy in his arms until the hacking shudders lessened, soothing him in low tones, carefully wiping the sweat from his forehead. He was much relieved when he finally laid him down on a soft bed of leaves. In the early going he'd thought Rising Sun might die. The quantity of yellow, frothy spume he'd choked up had frightened the Shaman, but now, as he bent over and placed his ear on the boy's sweat-slick chest, he could hear clean air moving in and out with only a bit of wheezing.

"Good," he said. His knees creaked audibly as he stood. *Getting old,* he thought.

He snorted. Not getting old. *Gotten* old. He'd already lived longer than most men could hope for. The fact that his health was still excellent was a further mystery, proof to all that he was beloved of the Gods.

His lips quirked. Perhaps the Gods—one of Them, at least—had loved him once. But the Gods were gone. Was there a joke in there someplace? In his sourer, more introspective moments he thought there might be, but if so, he didn't want to examine it too closely. The joke might be on him.

"Cover him," he said, and gestured to the boy's uncles who hovered about. Wolf, Rising Sun's grandfather, stood to one side, as befitted the dignity of his position, though Gotha was certain the Chief's stony expression was nothing but a mask.

For he knew Wolf had been worried, too. Gotha smiled at him reassuringly. Wolf inclined his bald head in acknowledgment, but said nothing. Gotha understood. The Chief was reluctant to voice his concern in front of the rest of the hunters.

"Chief, will you join me in the Spirit House?"

Despite his advancing years, Wolf could still move quickly if he wanted to. It seemed he wanted to, for Gotha had barely finished speaking before Wolf reached his side, nodded curtly, and passed on into the darkness beyond the Mystery House. Gotha paused for a final glance over his shoulder at the comatose boy, but everything seemed all right there.

Not boy, he reminded himself. *Not any longer. He's a man now. I wonder what he discovered in his Dream?*

He followed the Chief toward the Spirit House, found him waiting at the door, and pushed his way inside. He held the door flap for Wolf, and noted the Chief's shoulders were as sweaty as Rising Sun's chest had been—though the night air was quite cool, as it had been while they waited above the Smoke Pit.

"I thought the boy was dead for sure," Wolf said, while he waited for the Shaman to seat himself cross-legged at the small fire that burned in the center of the Spirit House.

Gotha pointed at a spot on the other side of the hearth. "Make yourself comfortable, Wolf," he said. When the other man was settled, he said, "I did, too."

"You what? Why didn't you stop it, then?" Wolf spluttered, and his voice rose dangerously. "You're the Shaman—you know how the smoke can kill by accident. You should have pulled him out!"

"I have never seen a boy stay in the Smoke Pit for such a long time. What a Dream he must have had!"

Wolf stared at him. "You *would* have let him die, wouldn't you?"

Gotha shrugged. "A pointless question. He didn't die, did he?"

"But he could have. And you would have let him." A disgusted kind of wonder filled Wolf's voice. "You are a very hard man, Shaman. I don't know if I like you anymore."

The Shaman grinned. "Anymore? Some years back, if I recall, you liked me so much you wanted to cut out my heart."

Wolf grumbled, "That was different. You were the enemy then. Now you are the Shaman, and part of your job is to make sure the boys survive into manhood."

Gotha cupped his chin in one hand and regarded Wolf with brooding eyes. "Most boys, yes. But your grandson is different."

"All the more reason to guard him well!" Wolf exploded. "If he's the—well, what we hope he is, you were foolhardy. No, worse! You risked everything!"

Gotha shook his head. "I risked nothing," he replied calmly. "The boy lives, and now he is a man. Only you and I, and two others, know that the ritual Rising Sun just survived is nothing but a sham. The Gods no longer watch over us, Chief. They are gone. Or had you forgotten?"

Wolf made a grumbling noise deep in his chest. "No, I hadn't forgotten. As I just said, all the more reason—"

"The Test, Chief. A Gift, a Promise, a Test. Had you forgotten the Test?"

"What do you mean?"

"We know so little, Wolf. Only what I saw, and Morning Star and White Moon. The word of the Turtle. What if the Smoke Pit was the Test? What if I *had* pulled the boy out, and somehow ruined what the Turtle prophesied?"

"Oh." Wolf thought a moment. "I see what you mean. I guess . . ." He didn't sound happy about it, though. Gotha understood perfectly.

The times were so dangerous. Once he'd hoped to rule the Green Valley in the name of his departed Lord. Now he sought to help change the World, and that was a task he had never looked for.

"Wolf," he said. "I didn't ask for this. I wish I had more answers, but I don't." He raised one hand to forestall the Chief's reply. "So, since I don't really *know* anything, I have to assume that whatever will happen is beyond my control. Or, if not, that whatever choices I have to make will be the right choices. I chose to leave him in the Smoke Pit. It seems I made the correct choice, for he didn't die."

Wolf couldn't think of anything else, and so he fell silent and stared into the flames. "Strange, isn't it," he said at last.

"What's strange?"

"All of this. I can remember, when I was a young boy, hearing Old Magic and Berry talking about Maya in the same way. And I *know* that Berry and I discussed White Moon's fate just as helplessly. The only difference then was we were trying to decide what the Gods wanted. But now the Gods are gone. So what are we trying to figure out? What the Turtle wants?"

Gotha arched his eyebrows. "I don't think the Turtle wants anything."

"But do you know that?"

"About the Turtle? I don't know *anything* about the Turtle. Except that It is. Somewhere. But I rather suspect the Turtle cares no more about this World than It does any other, and that the path of this World will be determined by things other than the Turtle's wishes."

Gotha leaned forward, took a small stick, and poked

up the fire. A few sparks flew up toward the smoke hole in the ceiling of the Spirit House. "Or that may be the Turtle's wish."

"What?"

"Oh, I don't know. That things just happen. Maybe the Turtle doesn't want to know. Maybe It likes it that way."

Wolf shivered. "That's a terrifying thought, isn't it?"

"It is? You never had to deal with the tricks of the Gods."

"Yes, I did. Every day. But at least we knew there was *something* in charge of things, no matter how treacherous or incomprehensible. There was comfort in that."

"Do you think I don't *know* that? Remember, Chief, I've lived much of my life as a tool of the Gods. And I knew it. In fact, if I hadn't seen Their departure with my own eyes, I wouldn't believe They were gone now."

Wolf raised his head. His eyes were hooded. "Maybe They aren't. Maybe what you think you saw was another of Their tricks."

"No, old friend, I saw. So did your daughter and her mate. And so did your sister, who let Them go, when she opened the Gates of the World with the Stone Rejoined. Don't delude yourself. The Gods are gone." The Shaman rubbed his nose. "Sometimes it scares me to death."

Wolf snorted. "You hide it well. You're just as arrogant and self-assured as you've always been."

Gotha chuckled. "I'm a Shaman. It's in the blood."

Once again, silence descended between the two old men. Finally Wolf sighed heavily and said, "Well? What now?"

"Tomorrow I will speak with Rising Sun, and he will tell me his Dream, and then I will tell him what his Dream means. At least, I hope I will."

"What do you mean by that?"

"I don't know," the Shaman said uneasily. "We'll cross the stream when we come to it."

Wolf eyed him warily. "Be careful, Shaman, that Rising Sun doesn't drown in that stream."

But Gotha didn't look at him, and after a while Wolf got up and left.

3

Morning Star held Rising Sun by his shoulders and looked into his face. "Welcome home, my son. You are a man now, but you are always welcome here," he said formally. Then he grinned widely and pounded his son on the back. "Congratulations, my son! Now you're a man! How does it feel?"

Rising Sun hugged his father and buried his face in Morning Star's shoulder. "Oh, Father," he said. "I'm so glad to see you again."

Morning Star, who had heard about Rising Sun's long sojourn in the Smoke Pit—the ritual did not allow him to be present, and so he'd sat and worried that whole night through—said, "And I'm glad to see you, my son! I heard you did well."

He motioned the boy to a seat. They stood just outside the Chief's house, which was situated in the center of Home Camp, atop the shelf that jutted out beneath the Shield Wall. The Chief's house was old, one of the first houses built in that place. Over the years it had been added to many times. Now hollyhocks rambled up its walls, and red poppies grew in profusion along its foundations. Rising Sun watched a fat bee hum its heavy way from blossom to blossom. For a moment he seemed to forget himself, and stared at the bee as if he'd never seen such a thing before.

"Rising Sun . . .?"

The young man started. What? Oh—yes." He settled himself on one of the time-worn log benches in front of the house, next to his father, who draped one arm over his shoulders.

They sat like this for a time, luxuriating in the high sun of summer, content with each other's presence. From here they looked out over the Jumble, First Lake, and the Meadow into New Camp beyond. At last, Rising Sun said, "So many people. Where did they all come from?"

"The Spirits of the Green Valley have been good to us," Morning Star said. "This has always been a fruitful place. Well, almost always."

Rising Sun glanced at him. "What do you mean?"

"Maya taught me much of the history of this Valley. There was a time of death here, though it passed after a single season." He paused. "She blamed herself for it."

"The Dead of Winter," Rising Sun said.

"Yes. After Maya ran away from the evil Shaman, Ghost, death came here. Many of the People of the Mammoth died in the snows of that season. Maya said it was a punishment from the Mother, because she'd rejected the Mammoth Stone."

Rising Sun nodded. He knew this lore. In fact, he knew most of the lore about Maya, for she was of his family, and his family was the most illustrious in the Valley.

"She was a great woman, wasn't she, Father? Mighty in the World."

"Yes, she was. And her blood flows in your veins, my son. Never forget that."

"I used to wish—" Rising Sun began, but then he trailed off.

"What did you wish?"

The young man sighed. "Once I wanted to be like her, mighty in the World, but now . . ." He shook his head. "Now I don't know anymore."

Morning Star's eyebrows arched, but he didn't speak for a moment, only nodded. "Did you have a Manhood Dream, son?"

"Yes."

"Was it a good one?"

"Yes. No. I don't know." Confusion was evident in his reply, and now he turned and faced his father. "I know I can't speak of my Dream to anybody but the Shaman, but I wish—I wanted to—"

Morning Star tightened his grip on his son's shoulders. "A young man's Dream is often confusing, son. Sometimes it's even scary. Have you talked with Gotha yet?"

Rising Sun shook his head.

"Well, don't think too much about it until you do. He will help you understand it. Sometimes things don't mean what they seem to."

Rising Sun sat silent and thoughtful for a time. "Did your Manhood Dream frighten you, Father?"

A shadow passed across Morning Star's features. "I never had a Manhood Dream."

Rising Sun knew something of his father's past, but only in a general sense. Much about the man who was closest to him remained shrouded in mystery—but the pain in Morning Star's reply was obvious.

"Father?"

"Mm?"

"I know there's a lot about yourself which you've never told me. I always supposed it was because I was a boy, and you were waiting to talk to me as men should speak with each other. Is that true? Can you tell me, now that I am a man?"

He felt the muscles of his father's arm clench, then relax again, though he guessed it took his father some effort to ease himself. "I never thought of it that way, my son. I mean, it's true I haven't told you much about my past, but it wasn't because you weren't a man. It was because . . ." He shook his head and sighed deeply. "I don't know why. Maybe because I was frightened. Maybe because the memories pained me, and I didn't want you to feel that pain. Or maybe it was because I was ashamed."

"Ashamed? What have you to be ashamed of?" Rising Sun couldn't keep the astonishment from his voice. He knew his father had been raised among the People of the Third Tribe of the Green Valley, the People of Fire and Ice, but he'd never been told any details, beyond that his father had been captured by those people at an early age, and that his own great aunt, Maya, had later helped his father to escape from them.

And now, though he sensed his questions were upsetting to the older man, he couldn't help but press on. Perhaps his father might reveal something that would help him with his own fears—which, though he'd felt them only since he awakened from his Dream, also seemed shameful, since they were so very strange and flew at the heart of what he'd been taught before.

"Father, can you tell me now? I promise I will never

speak of what you say to anybody else. Not even to my mother."

Morning Star chuckled softly. "Oh, you needn't worry about White Moon. She knows. She wasn't there, but she knows."

Rising Sun didn't answer, but reached out and squeezed his father's knee in encouragement.

"Ah. Well. You know I was a prisoner for many years, but I've never told you what sort of captivity it was." He paused, marshaling his thoughts. "Here. Feel my chest."

He took Rising Sun's fingers and ran them lightly across the smooth skin. "Feel that?"

The youth nodded. He'd seen the faded web of scar tissue as long as he could remember, though feeling the hard, ropy lumps embedded in his father's flesh for the first time made his stomach tighten queasily. His father released him, and he took his hand away quickly.

"Yes," Morning Star said. "Your aunt Maya healed some of those wounds herself—saved my life, probably."

Rising Sun shook his head. "But what happened? You have those scars all over your body."

Morning Star's eyes stared blankly ahead, as if he looked at something no one else could see. "Torture," he said finally. "I was tortured for those scars."

Something dropped with a sharp thud into the pit of Rising Sun's gut. His mouth fell open. "Torture? But who—what—"

His father shrugged. "Gotha, mostly, but also the Crone. And many others, I guess. I wasn't always ... aware when it happened."

"Gotha? You mean the Shaman?"

"Look at me. Good. Yes, it was the Shaman, the same one who is your friend. And who is still your friend. Don't forget that! What happened to me was long ago, and in another place, and has nothing—*nothing*—to do with today. It's all over. Things change. The World changes, Rising Sun. Do not think badly of Gotha. He had no choice. Nor did I. The Gods—"

He stopped. Rising Sun thought he wanted to say more, but he only shook his head and tightened his lips for a moment. Then he smiled.

"The ways of the Gods were strange in those days," he said.

It was a very curious thing to say—though just how curious Rising Sun didn't realize until he thought about it later. For now, though, he understood his father had spoken all he was going to, at least on the subject of his own past. And though his curiosity was not assuaged, nor had this revelation helped him with his own worries, he felt suddenly closer to the older man than he'd ever felt before.

Impulsively he reached out and wrapped his arms about his father's chest and held him for a long moment. "I love you, Father," he said. "Whatever happens, I love you."

Morning Star blinked several times, as if a bit of sand had gotten into his eye. "I love you, too, son. I always will. Never forget that I do."

Though Rising Sun was much disturbed by what he'd learned, they sat together in the sunlight for a while, content with the comfortable silence of each other's company. Then the sun reached noon high and it was time for Rising Sun to go to the Spirit House, and speak with the man who had tortured his father so many long years before.

4

When Rising Sun came up to the Spirit House, he found Moon Face, the Shaman's apprentice, waiting by the doorway. This man, a few years older than Rising Sun, greeted him cheerfully and said, "Congratulations! Welcome to your manhood, Rising Sun!"

The Spirit House was older than the Chief's house, for Old Magic had been the first to set up his tent on the shelf beneath the Shield Wall, when the Mammoth Clan had first come to the Green Valley. Now, sheltered beneath the black overhang, it, too, had changed and grown from such small beginnings. The Shaman Ghost had added to it, and Muskrat who followed him, and finally Gotha had made his own additions. Over the years it had become part hide

tent, part wicker-woven branches, part mud chinking.
Now it rambled a bit and sagged in places. It was covered
with bright red and yellow flowers and marked with symbols of magical power. Somehow it was both inviting and
forbidding at the same time.

Moon Face lived in a small room off the main enclo-
sure, and did what he could to keep the place orderly and
in good repair. Under ordinary circumstances, the two
young men were as friendly as their respective positions
allowed, for Moon Face had been Gotha's apprentice for
several years, and all during that time Rising Sun had
been as free with the Spirit House as he was with his
own, for Gotha had taken his teaching into his own
hands.

But he understood the teachings of his childhood were
done with now, as he stared into Moon Face's round and
beaming features. "Thank you, my friend," he said
gravely. "Is the Shaman waiting for me?"

Moon Face made a half bow and smiled. "Inside, resting at the fire." Then he stood straighter and said more
formally, "Was your Manhood Dream a good one, Rising
Sun?"

"I don't know. I guess I'll find out now."

Moon Face didn't answer, only pushed the door flap
aside, and showed Rising Sun the way in. As he ducked
through, Rising Sun caught a glimpse of Moon Face's expression, and wondered at the sadness—and something
else?—he saw in it. But before he could think any further,
Gotha said, "Tie the flap shut, please. Then join me at the
hearth."

Rising Sun did as he was told. The door was the only
source of outside light except for the smoke vent in the
roof, and this admitted only a single hazy shaft. He seated
himself across the small hearth from Gotha, finding his
place as much from long habit as from vision, for his eyes
hadn't adjusted to the gloom.

Gotha appeared as a looming shadow across the dimly
glowing coals.

He looks fearsome, Rising Sun thought. Then, recalling his father's tale, he thought: *He is fearsome.* It
was unsettling to think of Gotha that way.

Ever since his earliest days, the tall Shaman had been like an uncle or a foster father to him, letting him play as a baby inside the Spirit House, taking him on long rambles through the Valley, showing him the mysteries of plants and roots and leaves.

In some ways, Gotha had taught him as well as he had his own apprentice. To discover this other, frightening side of the man he thought he knew so well unsettled him greatly, no matter how much his father had protested that it didn't matter anymore.

Of course it mattered! Not so much what Gotha had done, for that *was* past, but why he'd done it, and why he'd kept it secret for so long. And Rising Sun fully intended to unravel the mystery as soon as he could.

But not now, for he had a greater riddle to decipher, and he was by no means certain even Gotha's extraordinary skills could help him with it.

"Greetings, Rising Sun, in the first hours of your manhood," Gotha murmured from across the coals.

Rising Sun could see him more clearly now. The Shaman's hooded eyes seemed to catch red firelight in the cups of his sockets. In that moment he looked dour and terrible. But he also seemed worn and tired, as if he'd carried a great burden for a long time, a burden he had no hope of ever giving up.

He staggers beneath the load of a doom far greater than himself, Rising Sun thought suddenly. And for an instant his eyes opened, much as they had in his Dream, and he saw the netted strands of destiny that held the Shaman fast.

"Thank you, Shaman," Rising Sun replied. "I have come to tell you of my Manhood Dream."

Gotha nodded and spread his hands. "Speak, then, Rising Sun, son of Morning Star, man of the Mammoth Clan."

Rising Sun took a deep breath, and then began the long story of his strange Dream. He told of the pale, red-eyed woman who guided him. He spoke of the great forest bowl, and the night beyond it, and the immense stone spike in its heart. He described the two empty thrones that faced away from each other, and the hole at the back of them. He related how he followed the woman into the earth, and what he found in the fire-shot cave. He revealed everything of his Dream except the moment of Vision when he sat on the deserted throne, for that was his alone, and not for anyone else to know. When he finished, he rocked back and placed his fists on his knees. "That is the tale of my Manhood Dream, Shaman. Is it worthy of a man of the Mammoth Clan?"

Gotha had listened intently to the story, neither his body nor his eyes moving, except for an occasional crimson flicker in his gaze.

Now he sat straight as an arrow shaft and said, "Your Dream is worthy, Rising Sun. The Spirits accept it, and you. Once again, and for the last time, welcome, O man, to the men of the Mammoth Clan."

Rising Sun bowed his head. His breath leaked out in a long sigh of relief. "Thank you, Shaman. I thank you."

When he looked up again, Gotha no longer sat in a formal pose, but now sprawled comfortably on his side, his head propped on one hand. "Good. Now that's done with. Relax, Rising Sun. It's time we got down to the heart of things."

"Among your mother, your father, and myself, we have taught you much of the lore of our Peoples, and of this Valley. But some we've not told you, and of much else we've given you bones without flesh. For instance, you know that I came to the Green Valley as an enemy, and remained as a friend. But do you know why?"

Rising Sun shook his head, his dark eyes rapt. Always he'd known that people weren't telling him everything. Even as a child he'd been aware of the shared glance, the suddenly turned head, the halted sentence. "No, Shaman, I don't. Not really. It is said that my aunt, Great Maya, defeated you in magical battle. But that isn't quite right, is it?"

"We never battled—well, perhaps, for a moment on that day we did, though the battle wasn't hers. I was defeated, if that's the right word, by Powers so great the word 'battle' hardly makes any sense. You, for instance, wouldn't call squashing an ant a battle, would you?"

Gotha shook his head and smiled. "Neither would the ant. No, on that day I faced a God, or rather a God revealed Himself to me, and I understood at last my own helplessness."

He paused, as if remembering, and a bitter wonder suffused his next words. "I saw the net which had held me all my life," he whispered. "And holds me still.

"Your parents and I, and Great Maya, who was far greater than anyone in this Valley understood, were swept beyond the World, into the Void that is the Well of the Gods. And in that place we saw the One Who Was Never Created, Who Creates All. We saw the Turtle."

"Is that the Turtle which is spoken of in the lineage you taught me?" Rising Sun asked. Unbidden, the well-remembered words sprang to his lips:

> "the mammoth and the snake are
> the father and mother of the world
> She-Ya and Ga-Ya
> are the father and mother of the people
> and with my power
> they made the stone.
> then come the Moon and the Star
> and from them
> the one to come
> who inherits the world."

"Yes, those are the words I taught you. Do you recall how you answered me when I questioned you on them?"

Rising Sun's black eyes went soft and dreamy. "You said my parents were the Moon and the Star and I asked you how that could be. And when you asked me how I knew what the Gods had done, that They had made the World for us, and it was ours, I told you it was plain for any to see. But I don't think you believed me."

"Can you answer my questions any plainer now, young man, after the Dream you've had?" With that, Gotha's eyes widened, and sparked with expectancy.

But Rising Sun said, "No, I can't. It still seems obvious to me. The World is for us who live in it. The Gods may have made the World, but They made it for us, and rule it for us."

Gotha chewed his lower lip, deep in thought. "What would you say if I told you the Gods have left the World forever?"

"What?" Rising Sun's features twisted in shock.

"That is part of the meaning of your Dream, my son. Those two empty thrones. You spoke of a feeling of desolation, of emptiness in that place. I have never seen the top of that hidden peak, but I know what it is. It is the seat of the Great Ones, and it is empty now, for They have left, and will not return."

"How can you know this?"

Gotha smiled gently. "I saw Them go, Rising Sun. I saw the Gods depart."

"But that means—the Gods—we are alone, all of us—the World—"

Now it was Gotha's turn to chuckle. "I've had a good amount of time to get used to the idea, but it still scares the shit out of me. How about you?"

Rising Sun had spun many a possibility on those two empty thrones, but Gotha's interpretation of them was so far beyond anything he'd considered that it took him several moments to regain his composure.

"It's very odd, isn't it?" Gotha said at last. "I mean, for a Shaman, at least. We spend our entire lives trying to outwit the Gods, find some way to please Them and stay Their anger, as we constantly search to do what we think is Their bidding. I had a secret thought I used to repeat to myself when times were bad. It was that the Gods cannot be trusted. But now that They are gone, I find I'd much prefer Them to come back, treacherous though They may be."

He snorted softly. "And if *I* feel that way—well, do you understand why neither your parents nor I have ever spoken of what we saw beyond the World that day?"

Gotha thought a moment, then added, "And also why we've waited on the sharp edge of a knife for some sign about you all these turns of the seasons?"

From the tone of Gotha's voice, Rising Sun knew the rude description of the depth of his fear had been meant jokingly—but he found no joke in it, for his bowels felt like they might burst from the terror that filled him as he listened.

He was a smart lad, strong and young, and arrogant as only youth can be. But now his own intelligence was his undoing, for he understood the words Gotha didn't speak, as well as those he did.

He held himself still so his anus would not, in a weak moment, loose a stinking flood in the Spirit House. When he was certain he could control himself, he licked his lips and said in a faint, quavering voice, "It's me, isn't it? That's what you think—what you see in my Dream. I'm the One who inherits, aren't I?"

He stopped then, unwilling to continue with the revelation, for where it led was almost too horrible to contemplate. A tremulous thought passed his lips before he could catch it: "I'm only a boy . . ."

"You are a man!" Gotha said. "You were a boy, but now you are a man. I'm sorry," he continued gently, "but that's how it is. No one can escape their destiny, and yours is to be a man. And then . . . perhaps something else." He spoke this last softly, and the compassion he felt for his one-time student was plainly evident.

But then his voice deepened, for what he spoke was doom as much as destiny, and the doom he named was terrifying for a man who'd only yesterday been a boy.

"You are the One To Come," Gotha said. "I say that is the meaning of your Dream, for in it you saw things you could not have seen otherwise. I don't know who the red-eyed woman is, but I know the thing she led you to, deep in the earth.

"You saw the Stone Rejoined, which Great Maya took with her when she left the World at last. You've never seen the Stone in this World, but you saw it in Dream. And I believe your seeing is the answer to another great riddle.

"The Turtle spoke of a Gift, a Promise, and a Test. I name you the Promise, Rising Sun, and the Stone Rejoined is the Gift. All that remains is the Test, and I think even you know what that Test is." He stopped and glanced at the shivering youth across the smoldering fire.

Rising Sun licked his lips. He couldn't speak, and so only nodded his assent.

"Good!" Then, at last, Gotha sank back again. He'd said what he needed to say, and though he had much else on his mind, his own heart rested easily. For long years he'd struggled with uncertainty and fear, awaiting the coming of the Turtle's prophesy. Now, at last, another could struggle with the fate of the World. Gotha felt a great weight lift from his shoulders and wondered if, somewhere, Maya of the colored eyes smiled her understanding on him.

She'd borne that burden so long, after all.

"Go out and find Moon Face. Have him bring food and water. You will stay here tonight, for we have much to talk about."

Rising Sun felt as if he could stay rooted in his place forever, but he knew that sometime he would have to move, have to stand and walk into his own future. That he rose and made his way out of the Spirit House was as much acceptance of *that* as acknowledgment of any authority the Shaman Gotha might still hold over him.

As he sought the apprentice in his small, rearward room, Rising Sun felt the familiar breezes of dusk touch his face. Even they felt different than they had before.

"Now I am a man," he said wonderingly. He looked up at the lights just beginning to emerge in the sky. Once, he'd thought the Great Ones lived in them, or at least ordered their existence. Now the stars only looked cold. And lonely. And empty.

"Moon Face!" he called. "Where are you? Your master wants you!"

5

Humped Wolf lay in the darkness of the third room of the Spirit House, which the Shaman called his Healing Room. She didn't know it was dark, for her eyes were closed. Nor could she smell the strange herbal odors of leaf and bark, for her nose was clogged with snot. She didn't feel the heat of the small fire burning near her, because fevers wracked her body. In fact, Humped Wolf knew very little of the World any longer, since she'd been delirious for two days and nights.

Great purple swollen things bulged beneath her chin, and in her armpits and groin. She cried out, but the sound was lost immediately in the wet, hacking coughs that shook her like a straw doll.

She would die soon, though she didn't know that. But the fleas that hopped and bounced from her bloated form knew. This meat was bad. They would leave it and find more.

CHAPTER FIVE

1

Running Deer waited until the rest of the girls had moved farther into the woods along Smoke Lake before she eased silently into the concealing greenery. She paused behind a leafy screen until she was certain her absence hadn't been noticed by the two older women who were shepherding this party of root-gatherers. Then, suddenly giddy with the thought of such freedom, she turned and ran as lightly as her namesake into the forest, her feet carrying her toward the place where her secret treasures lay carefully hidden.

The gold-washed leaves of summer barely touched her as she leapt between the trees, moving like a breath of wind with her black hair flowing behind like a flag. Her eyes sparked; her left eye like a flake of obsidian washed by crystal streams, her right eye a flame of sapphire, for she was of the blood of Maya and bore a portion, though not all, of the marks of the Mother.

She only noticed the clearing because it signaled the nearness of her secret place. The tall hickory tree in the center of the patch of green escaped her attention entirely, though she might have paused if she'd known that a girl not much younger than herself had once dangled from its branches like fruit for a ravening mother lion. But the blood that had marked the spot was long vanished beneath waving grass, and Running Deer hurried on.

She came up to the bramble-choked ravine from the back and bounded onto the top of a huge, half-rotted trunk that had fallen across the gap like a bridge. Ancient roots poked up in a thicket at her end of the log. She knelt and thrust her arms into the dusty branches until her fingers found the greasy-slick smoothness of her cache. She drew out a long, hide-wrapped parcel and carried it down from the log, back to the place where she came as often as she could—the falling-down remains of a small chinked house built half into the woods that surrounded the clearing.

The other girls never came here. They whispered that it was haunted by the Spirit of Great Maya, who had lived here with her mate, Caribou, after her last return to the Green Valley. Legend had it that Great Maya's ghost came here often, seeking Caribou, who, it was told, had been slain by the fearless warrior Raging Bison and the evil traitor Sharp Knife. For her part, Running Deer had never noticed any supernatural manifestations, only a blessed silence and solitude that she now thought of as a gift, perhaps from Great Maya herself.

As she slowly unwrapped the unwieldy bundle, she thought about the mighty woman who had vanished before she'd been born. She was of Maya's blood, though her line ran from Bending Tree, the youngest daughter of the old Chief, Wolf, since Maya had birthed no children in the Green Valley. It was rumored that Maya's direct offspring existed elsewhere in the wide World, though nobody could say where they might be, or if they still existed.

In any event, she gave scant thought to those distant relatives. Her reverie turned instead to her great aunt, with whom she shared at least her blue eye and, she hoped, a great deal more.

Her nimble fingers found the secrets of the knots that secured her package soon enough. She sighed as she unfolded the soft, waterproofed hide and lifted up the bow from its bed of arrows, all painstakingly shaped over moons of secret labor.

The men might kill her if they knew she possessed such a thing, but she kept her secrets well. Men were like the pigs that roamed in the forest, she thought, and though dangerous, they were easily outwitted.

She set down the wrappings and the arrows, stood, and bent the bow to string it. The bowstring hummed tautly beneath her fingers, and she nodded with satisfaction. She'd plaited the string from many lengths of mammoth hair and smoothed it with the golden wax she found in a beehive deep in the woods. The hunters used lengths of rawhide instead, but she thought her method the better one—at least her arrows seemed to fly more truly than those of the men who would no doubt slaughter her if they knew how she had stolen their magic.

"Not stolen!" she said aloud. After all, those big strong men wouldn't have their bows at all if Maya had not made the first bow and brought it to them as a gift from the Mother. But Maya was the only woman of the Green Valley who'd ever had a bow, for even though she was the first to make such a thing, she was the last woman to possess it. The men guarded their magic jealously, though the magic came first from a woman.

Running Deer snorted. Men! They were bigger and stronger than women and that counted for a great deal in the World. But they were slower, stupider, and, she thought, not nearly as tough. After all, what did men do?

They hunted, that's what. But only for a few days each moon. The rest of the time they lay about their hearths, or sang songs and pounded drums in their Mystery House, while their women served them in every way.

Women, on the other hand, never rested. Their days were filled with caring for the children, hunting roots and berries that made up most of the People's diet, preparing food, making and repairing the clothing that kept everybody warm—a never-ending round of tasks and duties and labors.

No man could do it, Running Deer thought. And while a woman might not be able to wrestle some hulking hunter to the ground, or keep the snake between his legs out of the hole between her own thighs, she *could* draw a bow as well as any of them.

At least I can, Running Deer thought fiercely as she retrieved her arrows and set off across the clearing. She paused before she reentered the woods and glanced up at the sky. The sun rode about midway up, and she guessed she might have an hour or so before any of the girls became seriously concerned at her absence, if they noted it at all.

The other girls didn't pay her much attention. They didn't like her. She was strange. Or so they said.

Running Deer vanished into the gloom beneath the trees. Strange, indeed. But so had been Great Maya, and Running Deer was of that blood.

They are only girls, but I will be something more. I swear it on her *memory,* Running Deer told herself solemnly. Then the woods swallowed her up, and she was gone.

2

After Moon Face had brought their food and then left the Spirit House, Gotha pushed a well-cooked piece of deer meat toward Rising Sun and said, "There is much I haven't told you. I'm sure you've suspected it before—or at least you do now."

Rising Sun chewed his meat slowly. His stomach had quieted, though his thoughts still churned with the terrible things the Shaman had already revealed to him. Now, from the way Gotha examined him, his black eyes boring into him as if searching for any weakness, Rising Sun thought there was more to come.

"Shaman?" he ventured at last. "Are you sure it's me? Couldn't there be some mistake?"

Gotha wondered how to reply. He knew so much more than the lad who sat across from him. He'd been privy—no, more than that, he'd been a *part*—of doings no mere mortal could ever hope to understand. How to explain the eternal weavings of the Gods who had built the World, and then paved the way for Their own departure? How could a youth who had not witnessed the moment understand it, when Maya had unlocked the Doors of the World, so that the Two might pass beyond, back into the Void where Their own creator dwelled forever?

How could ears that never heard the Turtle speak know the truth of those words, and the doom they laid upon the One To Come?

A Gift, a Promise, a Test. Simple words. So simple they were, in one great sense, misleading, for the destiny they foretold was the destiny of the World, and *that* was not a simple matter.

Yet, if Gotha had read the signs correctly, the instrument of that destiny sat before him in the form of a single, obviously frightened youth. He would have to tread carefully.

"Rising Sun, you received your True Name at birth, given to you by the Keepers of the Two Stones, who are your parents. Most boys don't take up their True Names until after their manhood ceremony, in the following days when their natures become clear to them. Why is that, do you think?"

Rising Sun hadn't thought about it at all. "I thought it would be the same with me, Shaman. Are you telling me it won't be?"

"Yes, Rising Sun, I am. Your name has special meaning. You could almost say that your nature must be shaped by your name, rather than the other way round, as is more usual. For your name has a great meaning! You are the Sun of our People, but greater and more terrible than that, you are the Sun in the morning of the World."

And with that, Gotha raised both his hands palm forward, in a gesture both of shielding and warning, so that Rising Sun saw the many lines in his flesh, which he hadn't truly seen before, and wondered at his great age. Rising Sun lowered his head in submission, though he murmured, "But are you sure I am the One?"

Gotha frowned at him, and at the same question for the second time, but Rising Sun met his fearsome gaze and said yet again, "Tell me, Shaman, are you certain I am the One who is promised To Come?"

So did Rising Sun question his doom three times, but then he fell silent, because he still knew his Vision from the Dreamtime, and many things became clear to him in that moment.

Finally he spoke: "If I am the One To Come, whom the Turtle prophesied, then I am not yet He Who Is Promised, for I haven't passed the Test that was spoken of. You have said that you know my Test, Shaman. Very well, say what it is."

The Shaman Gotha marveled at this, for Rising Sun suddenly seemed to him far beyond his years, and mighty in speech and knowledge, and he was more certain than ever that the One To Come sat cross-legged before him. Then he understood that his own part in the Great Weaving was not yet done with, even though the Gods had left Their looms forever, and a tremor of fear shook him. But he sought his own strength, which was great both in the World and beyond it, for he had journeyed into the Void, and he answered Rising Sun's question.

"Your Test is a task, Rising Sun. None living know where Great Maya went, nor what she did there, except that the Stone Rejoined went with her. Where that Stone now lies, none may say, but you must find it. For over long years the Stones were unbroken until they came together at last, and made the Key which unlocks the Gates of the World. Great Maya used that Key one time only, and her doom was great, indeed.

"Now you must seek that Key, Rising Sun, and though you go onto the empty thrones of the Gods, or into the pits of the World, you must find the Stone Rejoined and bring it back to the World. That is your doom, Sun of the Dawn, mightier even than Great Maya, whose blood runs in your body, and also the Power of the Gods Themselves, who are gone now."

Rising Sun studied the Shaman, who had fallen silent. "If I don't undertake this task . . .?" he whispered.

"Then you are not the One. But I believe you are," Gotha replied.

Rising Sun nodded. "Then I will go, and seek the Stone Rejoined, that is the Key to the World."

With that, both men spoke no more. Each had much to think about, and not much time for it. Even now, they both could hear Humped Wolf through the wall of the Spirit House, hacking her lungs out onto the ground.

3

Running Deer pulled the string of her bow back to her ear and held it until the muscles of her arm quivered. With one black eye and one blue she tracked the squirrel that scampered up the rough barky trunk of a venerable oak tree, holding bow and breath until the small rodent paused and twitched its nose.

She let the arrow fly, then clicked her teeth together triumphantly when the flint arrowhead transfixed the squirrel's neck, pinning it to the tree.

"Let's see one of the mighty hunters do *that*," she muttered as she retrieved the arrow—she only had four and couldn't afford to waste any, not when it took her a moon or more of clandestine labor to make each one.

The limp body of the squirrel felt warm in her hand. She looked down at it, then shrugged and tossed the small carcass into the shrubbery. It would have made a good stew, but she could never explain how she'd come by it, though it pained her to waste food. She watched where it fell, and then frowned as if she'd just thought of something. Nodding to herself, she retrieved the little body, because she'd just remembered one who would eat it, but not betray her secret.

Carefully she cleaned the arrow with a handful of leaves. The shadows were growing now, as the sun slid past noon high. She knew she didn't have much more time, but instead of turning back, she slid down the trunk until she was sitting with her back propped against the sun-warmed wood.

It was all such a waste. She knew she was more skilled with her weapon than any male hunter, but no one else would ever share her achievements. Once again she clicked her white teeth together, this time in frustration. If only she'd been born a man!

She let out a long breath and stared down at her hands, which rested atop the polished bow in her lap. No matter how much she wished differently, they were the hands of a woman, scarred and calloused with a woman's labor. Men's hands were smoother, for they did little work beyond maintaining their weapons and hunting. Otherwise they slept, and danced, and told each other stories of their bravery, and sought women as receptacles for their man-snakes.

None of this marked them much, certainly not with the scrapes and scabs and scars of root digging, wood cutting, fire making, hearth building, trap tending, and all the hundreds of other dull and dreary duties that made the days of women cruel and endlessly hard. Yet it was men who preened and pranced and bragged of their bravery and their glorious hunts—from which, Running Deer knew, came only a finger's worth of the handful of food it took to keep the People from starvation. The rest was woman's work, roots, berries, the working of traps and nets for fish, and grubbing for small white things beneath rocks. Yet women received no honor for their labor, only lifelong drudgery and forgotten death at the end.

Running Deer looked up at the blue sky and said, "I won't do it." In that moment she made her decision, though she hadn't intended to, but had only followed her own thoughts without knowing where they led. But as she decided, a great sense of freedom filled her, and she felt as if the sunlight lifted her up and affirmed her choice.

She stood up, retrieved her bow and arrows, and set off. A fierce joy sang in her veins, and she wondered if men ever felt this thing. But her joy was tempered, for her choice meant her own death, or at least exile forever from the Green Valley—though even with this, she didn't waver, but accepted the doom of her own hand and heart.

"Great Maya be with me," she whispered as she strode along, but only the birds answered, and they didn't speak to her. Then she knew that whatever she did, she must do alone.

4

Rising Sun stared down at the dying woman. Gotha said, "I have used all my magic, but nothing helps. She is dying. The Spirit inside her is burning her up. Feel how hot she is!"

He bent down and touched Humped Wolf's forehead. The woman stirred faintly, but then sank back, too weak to respond further.

Rising Sun nodded. "It must be a terrible Spirit," he said.

The Shaman glanced up at him. "The Gods are gone. But the Spirits remain, and the ghosts, too. All of them, though they were made by the Gods. And many of the Spirits are evil, and kill the People. But the Gods are no longer with us, to restrain Their creations as need be. And the ghosts, which are the Spirits of People, have lost their way and wander alone in the spaces between the World and the Void."

Slowly, Rising Sun began to understand the terrible changes that had occurred in the departure of the Great Spirits. All those lesser Spirits, good and evil, were now free to do as they willed, with no divine hand to restrain them or order them in any way. Nor did the Gods still live in Heaven, where once the Spirits of men might have gone. Those thrones were deserted, and the great bowl barren and empty.

"Do you think my task has anything to do with this?"

Gotha's eyes burned into his. "Everything! You must find the Key, the Stone Rejoined. Only with that Talisman can the Spirits be bound again, and the paths of the ghosts beyond the World opened to them." He paused, looking down, deep in thought.

"I'm not certain, of course. The Turtle spoke nothing of these things, nor have I Dreamed of them. But if the One To Come is to inherit the World, as the Turtle *did* say, then it must be all the World, even the Spirits that are bound to it, and the ghosts which must leave it. These are mighty things, Rising Sun. It is a mighty doom."

"I've said I will go, Shaman," Rising Sun replied,

"though I'm very afraid. I hope you have heard the Turtle's words right, and the other things you say as well. But if I fail, then you are wrong, and all will fall into ruin."

"No!" The Shaman shook his head. "If you aren't the One, the Promise still holds, and that One *will* come. But there is only one way to find out, and you know what it is."

"When should I leave, Shaman? And where should I go?"

"You need not leave right away, Rising Sun. I wish to think awhile. It may seem good to me to send others with you. As for where you go, I don't know that, either. The Way is hidden, and for you to find yourself."

Gotha stood, and led the youth from the Spirit House. They paused in the bright afternoon. Gotha put his hand on Rising Sun's shoulder and said, "Go back to the Chief's house for a while, and think about these things and make ready. When I have decided, I will call for you."

Rising Sun nodded and smiled a bit with relief. He was glad he wouldn't have to set out immediately. He had a lot to think about and farewells to make. But the sound of Humped Wolf's dying was soft in his ears as he turned away. He thought he heard the whisper of many demons gathering about the Green Valley, terrible Spirits no longer bound by any greater Power.

He might wait a while, but not long. Gotha watched him go, and thought, *So young!* but the words of the Turtle gave him hope. Such as it was.

He went back into the Spirit House. After a time, he called for Moon Face and spoke to him for a long while.

5

Running Deer took so much care with wrapping up her bow again as she crouched on the tree trunk that her ears, normally sharp as knives, didn't hear the lumbering approach of the monster. She was deep in thought when she finally stood up, turned, and saw the hulking thing not two steps away.

"*Aarrgh!*" the monster roared.

"Oh!" She leapt back and almost fell off the trunk into the jagged branches in the ravine below, but caught herself just in time. The monster advanced a step and waved his huge arms at her, but she caught one of the great roots of the tree, swung herself around him, and leapt lightly to the ground.

The monster turned slowly, his bloodshot eyes blazing.

"Poor thing!" she said and moved closer to him. "Are you hungry? You frightened me!"

It was a strange tableau; the girl, so small and lithe, and the huge man, his massive shoulders corded with muscle, though his ragged hair and shaggy beard were streaked with gray and white in a tangled mat across his chest and back. He towered over her, but as she came to him, his face crumpled. He cringed back and put his hands across his face and cowered away as if he feared her greatly.

"*Awwroo!*" he howled. Tears leaked from his tightly closed eyes, and he sank to his knees, shivering.

"Oh, dear. I'm sorry," she murmured. Carefully, she began to stroke his back. Then she brought her lips close to his ear and whispered soothingly, until his quivering stopped.

"Poor Frightened Man," she said. "I didn't mean to scare you."

Eventually the crazed giant responded to her soft words and caresses and stood up again. He peered at her dimly, as if she were hard to see. His lips, red as raw meat in the tangled nest of his beard, moved faintly.

"Foood?" he moaned, and then twitched back.

"Oh, that's why you came," she replied. The carcass of the squirrel lay on the ground at the edge of the ravine. She brought it to him and pushed it into his hands. His fingers, long and thick as tent pegs, slowly closed around the morsel. "Food?" he muttered.

"Yes. For you." She patted his shoulder again and smiled encouragingly.

After a moment his broad nostrils began to twitch at the smell of fresh blood, and he lifted the squirrel to his mouth. Yellow fangs snapped, blood ran down into his beard.

"Mmmm," he rumbled and patted his belly. For a moment he stared at her, chaotic thoughts of food and love all mixed up in his shaggy skull. Dimly, he knew he wanted her for his own, but his raddled thoughts were incapable of figuring out how to do *that*, he who could barely feed himself. He shook his head, overwhelmed at the strange emotions she caused in him, and snorted in confusion. Then he turned and shambled away into the dark forest. Running Deer watched him go. He was the Frightened Man, and she had known of him all her life, though she hadn't met him until she'd begun her clandestine excursions. Her first meeting had terrified her; she'd thought him a Spirit or a Demon, until she'd understood why he was called the Frightened Man.

In that first encounter she'd stumbled on him crouched beneath a thorny stand of bushes, and mistaken his terrified efforts to escape her for some kind of attack. She'd drawn her bow on him and almost put an arrow into his eye before she understood he was not attacking, but trying to get away. Later, she discovered that those bushes were his den, where he lived like a wild animal.

Over time, they'd become friends of a sort. She would bring him the small things she killed, if she remembered, and sometimes he would allow her to comb her fingers through his hair and take away the tangles.

He wore no clothing and spoke only a few words. Many times she'd wondered about him, but those who could have told her about him preferred not to speak, and she never thought to ask beyond what everybody knew. The Frightened Man was marked by the Gods, his wits stolen in punishment for some terrible crime against Them.

As he vanished with his booty, she saw the flash of a long white scar on his leg, and wondered how he'd come by it. It looked to her like a spear wound, though nobody in the Green Valley would take a weapon to him, unless somehow they were surprised and struck before they thought.

After he was gone she shrugged and turned back toward the sound of the girls. For once she actually wished to join them and feel a part of them, for now that she'd made up her mind to leave the Green Valley, all things seemed sweeter than they had. Even if one of the women scolded her for wandering off, she promised herself she would only smile and nod. The old women had no power over her, and soon they, too, would be gone from her life.

She knew some of the history of her family, though not all, and so she wondered, *Did Great Maya feel like this, when she first decided to leave the Valley?*

But she was young, and couldn't conceive of the terror of the Shaman Ghost, and the terrible loss that had driven her aunt away. Yet what spurred her was the same blood that had quickened in Maya's veins, and though her destiny was different, it was in many ways no less great.

6

"Have you heard?" Bending Tree said as she and her daughters worked around their hearth preparing the evening meal. "Running Deer! Pay attention! Look, the stew bag is burning. Turn it, quickly!"

Running Deer, who had been gazing dreamily at the hide bag filled with water and roots and chunks of meat that had been dangling over the hot coals, jumped in startlement.

"Oh! What? Oh . . ." Her cheeks flushed as she moved the stick that held the bag, the smell of the charred skin filling her nose. "I'm sorry, Mother," she said.

"Look at you! What are you thinking of, girl? You should pay more attention—what if you burned a hole clean through? There goes our meal, and the bag with it. Your father would be angry." Bending Tree shook her head. "Sometimes I wonder what I'm going to do with you."

Running Deer bowed her head. The back of her neck

was bright red with shame. "I'm sorry, Mother. I'll be careful, I promise."

Running Deer's two sisters, both younger than she, giggled at her discomfiture. Bending Tree snorted. "Not likely. Daughter, why must you daydream so much? Who will mate a silly girl who can't even pay attention to her cooking?" The older woman sighed heavily. Plainly, she foresaw a fate worse than death for her eldest daughter, who seemed to possess none of the virtues a woman needed to make her way in the World.

She watched the girl sharply until she was sure Running Deer was paying her task proper attention. Then she took up where she'd left off. "Anyway," she said, "there is talk that my sister-son is going to leave the Green Valley on a long journey. I heard it has something to do with his Manhood Dream."

Running Deer lifted her head. "Oh?" she said. "Which one?"

"Rising Sun," Bending Tree said. "He's been hiding away in the Spirit House with the Shaman and Moon Face for the last two days. I asked White Moon about it, but she won't tell me anything. It's plain enough that something is going on, though. My father won't talk about it, either."

She paused thoughtfully. "My sister is sewing new clothes for him."

Running Deer's voice was calm, though a faint tic had begun to jump beneath her left eye. "Where is he going?"

Bending Tree shrugged. "I don't know. You know how the men are. Anything to do with their mysteries, they would never speak about *that* to a woman."

Of course they wouldn't, Running Deer thought. If they did, we might find out how silly most of it is. Only a man would think that lying around telling wild tales was important to anybody but the boaster himself. But the news of her cousin interested her far more than she wished to let on.

"Do you know when Rising Sun is supposed to leave?"

Bending Tree glanced at her, then cocked one eyebrow. "And why are you so interested, daughter? He's certainly not going to take *you* along with him."

Running Deer sniffed. "Why would I *want* to go with him? It's just some silly boy playing at being a man."

"Running Deer!" Her mother's voice was shocked. "That's exactly what I mean! Your cousin is a man now, and someday he will probably be the Chief of the Three Tribes. And all you can do is mock him—that's no way for you to find a mate." She rolled her eyes. "Not that any man will have you, as strange as you are."

Running Deer set her jaw. "I wouldn't have any of *them*, you mean."

But her mother only shook her head sadly. "Daughter, daughter. The World belongs to the men. Why can't you see that? And men don't want a woman who laughs at them, who refuses them, who disappears into the woods for hours on end when she should be gathering roots like all the other young women. Yes, I know about that."

Running Deer gave the stew pole a sharp twitch. "Mother, you say it's a man's World. Why, though? We gather most of the food—and even the men come from our bellies, where the Mother plants them. Without us, the men would die."

Bending Tree raised one hand to her chest in horror. "Daughter! You must *never* say that aloud. What if one of the men heard you?"

But Running Deer was considering the news about her cousin and made no reply. So Rising Sun was going on a journey? That was interesting.

7

The summer morning dawned bright overhead, but veils of fog had drifted up the stream from the great river some miles beyond the mouth of the Green Valley. Six figures stood in the swirling mist, speaking quietly.

Rising Sun put his arms around his mother, White Moon, and buried his face in the join of her neck and shoulder. She smelled good to him, clean and fresh, and for a moment he felt like a little boy again.

"You be careful, my son," she whispered into his chest. She sniffed, and he realized she was sobbing quietly.

"Mother, don't cry," he said. "It's just a journey. I'll be fine. I've got Moon Face with me, to make sure I keep to the right path."

But White Moon pushed him back, and though she still wept, she smiled through her tears. "My son ..." she said again, pride touching her words. She wiped her nose. "I love you very much."

He nodded. He hadn't thought it would be this hard.

Then his father stepped up to him and wrapped him in a rib-creaking hug. Neither man spoke aloud, but much was said in that moment.

Finally Rising Sun hoisted his pack to his shoulders. It was half as big as he was, but he bore the weight easily. He turned to the Shaman Gotha, who was also smiling, though his dark eyes were stern.

"Teacher," Rising Sun said.

Gotha raised his arms and displayed the things he had brought. He had sought the blessings of Spirits for these things, though he wondered if such blessings still had any Power. Yet what he handed to Rising Sun now were mighty things in their own right, and he suspected the youth would have great need of them.

"This is the bow of Maya, which she made for Caribou long years ago," he said. Rising Sun took the weapon slowly. It had hung in the Chief's house all his life, and was a mighty trophy of his People. Gotha then passed over a wrapped bundle of arrows. "These are the arrows of Maya, which she also made. It is said that if they are wielded by one of her blood, they will always fly true."

Rising Sun nodded and took those also. He added the bundle to his pack. Then the Chief, Wolf, his grandfather, said, "And this is the spear of Caribou, which was only defeated once. Raging Bison took it as a trophy after he defeated your uncle, and carried it himself until the Gods destroyed him. I have kept it for your coming, daughter-son."

Rising Sun took the long spear, which was an arm's

length taller than he was, and shafted as thick as his wrist
to a great stone point.

"I thank you for these weapons," he said formally. "I
will bear them with honor for myself and for the People."
Then he grinned as he hefted the spear. "It's heavy, isn't
it. Caribou must have been a strong man to wield such a
thing."

"As was Raging Bison, who slew him," Gotha said.
"May you wield it as well as they."

Now the Chief came up and hugged his grandson. Rising Sun marveled at how fragile his grandfather's bones
felt beneath his own muscular arms, and for a fleeting
moment a shadow crossed his face. He wondered if he
would ever see Wolf in this World again.

Finally, Gotha took out a rattle and shook it in Rising
Sun's face. He chanted softly for a moment, then stopped
and said, "I have laid what magic I have on you, Rising
Sun. I hope it will help, but I don't know if it will. In the
end, I fear you will shape your own destiny. But that is
my hope also. Go with my blessings, travel swiftly, return
with speed."

At this, Moon Face shouldered his own pack, which
was somewhat smaller than his companion's and filled
with different things.

Rising Sun stepped a few paces back and said, "A
good morning to you, and my love." His eyes grew distant for a moment, as if he saw some other vista than the
Green Valley before him. "I will return with the Stone
Rejoined, which is mine by right, or I will die."

White Moon sniffed again, but didn't speak, for what
her son had said was his doom, and they all knew it.
Gotha nodded. "Farewell, then. We will await your return. May the Spirits guard and protect you!"

But in the World as it was, no one knew if that was a
blessing or a curse. Without another word, Rising Sun
turned and walked into the mist with his companion. The
others watched until the two figures dwindled and slowly
vanished.

"Now we shall see," Gotha said.

8

Running Deer had heard this clearly from where she crouched not fifty paces away, hidden in the skirts of the woods and the fog. Through some trick of the mist the farewells were easily audible. She shivered when she heard the bow of Maya passed over, and a longing she could barely understand filled her.

But the intent of the farewells was plain enough. Her cousin Rising Sun was indeed undertaking a great journey, and the Stone Rejoined could only be one thing.

She had no future she could bear within the walls of the Valley, and she had made her own decision. "Where he goes, so will I," she whispered softly. "Or I will die."

And so Running Deer spoke her own doom, though she didn't know it.

She shouldered her pack, grasped the great bow she'd made, and crept silently out into the mists. She was so intent on not being discovered that she failed to notice the hulking shadow that followed her into the morning fog, for it crept along as silent as a ghost.

In many ways, of course, that is exactly what it was.

BOOK TWO

DIFFERENT PATHS

"A journey of a thousand miles must begin with a single step."

—Chinese Proverb

CHAPTER SIX

1

Rising Sun and Moon Face stood on top of the last rise before the river, where the stream tumbled over a broad, rocky verge into the larger flood. Rising Sun shrugged. "Well, which way do we go?"

Moon Face shaded his eyes. He turned and scanned upstream, then down. "This is the place Caribou spoke of, where he first touched the Mammoth Stone," he said. "It is a place of Power, I think."

Rising Sun shrugged impatiently. "That was long ago. The Stone isn't here now."

"Are you sure? We don't know where Maya went when she took it away. Perhaps she came here," Moon Face replied.

Rising Sun eyed his companion. Gotha had sent Moon Face along because, aside from himself, his apprentice was the most learned in the lore of the Green Valley, most particularly the legends that surrounded Rising Sun's own family. The Shaman had said, "Moon Face isn't a great warrior or a mighty hunter, but his learning is powerful. You may find it more help than the great bow or the long spear you carry."

"But she left before I was born. You don't think we could find her trail now, do you?" Rising Sun said.

Moon Face shook his head. "No, of course not. Besides, this is a much visited place. Hunting parties often camp here. Unless she hid the Stone carefully, it would have been found by now. I'm only saying that we don't *know* what she did with it. But she was touched by the Great Ones, and I believe that everything she did was for a purpose. She had a reason for leaving the Valley and taking the Twinstone with her. Maybe there is a clue to where she went, even now."

Moon Face rubbed his round chin and stared thoughtfully at the river. "It runs toward the south. We know that's where her People went when she and Caribou led them away at the beginning of her long travels."

Rising Sun chewed his lower lip. He was slowly coming to understand that he knew far less than he'd supposed. Was that part of the Test as well? How could he retrieve the Twinstone when he had no idea where in the wide World it might be?

Moon Face glanced at him. "The Shaman told me all that you revealed to him of your Manhood Dream. Did you leave anything out? Something that might help us?"

Rising Sun's eyes widened. The substance of his Dream was supposed to remain a secret between himself and the Shaman. At least, it had always been that way. But if Gotha had broken that trust by confiding in Moon Face, he must have more faith in his young apprentice than Rising Sun had realized.

"The Shaman told you my Dream?"

"Yes." Moon Face examined him warily. "Gotha told me many things. Perhaps we should talk awhile, my friend. He gave me leave to speak of these things to you. I want no secrets between us, if we can avoid them."

Rising Sun nodded. "I didn't know there were secrets. But since it seems there are, then I do want to know them." He thought a moment and was surprised at how angry Moon Face's words had made him. None of his anger showed on his face, though. He said, "Let's stop here and find out what other things the Shaman hasn't seen fit to tell me."

Moon Face nodded. They clambered over the rocky lip and descended onto the wide rocky bank where once the Shaman Ghost had forsaken the Mammoth Stone, although the small stone pyre he'd built to mark that spot had been scattered long ago.

They settled themselves on a lip of streaky granite warmed by the sun, facing the river and the vast grassy steppe beyond. "Are you hungry?" Rising Sun asked.

Moon Face grinned. "Look at me. I'm always hungry." He pinched a fold of fat at his waist. "If this journey does nothing else, perhaps it will make a thinner man of me."

Rising Sun couldn't help smiling. Poor Moon Face. Swathed in layers of fat, the little man could never endure the rigors of the endless running it took to make a hunter, and sometimes the painful knowledge of the lack made his friend moody. But it was hard to stay angry with Moon Face for long. He'd known him most of his life. He'd learned to appreciate the apprentice's wry, self-deprecating humor. On the other hand, Moon Face's endless stream of jokes, japes, and asides sometimes made it hard to take him seriously. *Maybe he does it on purpose,* Rising Sun thought.

As he fumbled in his pack for some trail meat, Rising Sun began to understand that things weren't always what they seemed. In some obscure way this offended him, just as he'd been upset to discover there were secret paths in his life that others had guessed—or known—without telling him.

Too many secrets!

He offered a portion of meat to Moon Face, who popped a large chunk into his mouth and began chewing immediately. "Good," the apprentice mumbled.

"You'll be sick of it soon enough," Rising Sun told him. "I hope that wherever we go, there will be decent hunting."

As a boy, he'd accompanied his father and his uncles on several hunts and knew how quickly a steady diet of the tough, salty mix of ground-up berries and dried meat could grow tiresome. Moon Face had been apprenticed to Gotha as a young child and had never hunted. He had no trail skills to speak of. Rising Sun wondered if that would become a problem. Then he shrugged to himself. Moon

Face had other skills. Only time would tell if they were necessary.

Moon Face slapped his ample belly. His fingers left a faint imprint in the sheen of sweat on his brown skin. He belched. "That's better," he said.

Rising Sun placed the remaining food in the leaves that had wrapped it and put it back into his pack. His expression turned grave and concentrated. The thought that others had woven webs about him of which he knew nothing frightened him. Had his parents been part of the deception? Abruptly his long relationship with Gotha seemed less benign than he'd imagined. So also his friendship with Moon Face, who evidently possessed depths he'd never suspected.

"You say you want no secrets, my friend. So tell me what you know that I don't—and don't leave anything out!"

The older youth nodded, his features suddenly as serious as Rising Sun's own gaze. He could imagine a little of what his friend must be feeling. Only a few weeks before, Rising Sun had been a boy, ignorant of the meaning of his heritage. His only concern had been to successfully cross the chasm of symbolic death and rebirth that was his bridge to manhood. Now his life was irrevocably changed. He'd been cast out from the Green Valley by his own Dream, charged with a Test by the Turtle Itself. What must he be thinking?

"Gotha said I could tell you what I know, or think," he said at last. "But I can't guarantee it is all that Gotha knows or thinks. Do you understand?"

Rising Sun nodded. More secrets. But he had a secret of his own, didn't he? For a moment, as he stared intently into Moon Face's soft brown eyes, he wondered if he should tell him about the Vision he'd had inside his Dream, when he'd sat on the tall stone throne and seen the Last Mammoth.

Secrets were powerful things. He decided to wait. Also, from Moon Face's tense, unhappy expression, he suddenly understood that the other youth was afraid of him. That revelation shocked him more than anything else, for it hinted that there was something in him to be frightened of. But what could it be? Plainly, much needed to be said.

He reached over and touched Moon Face's knee. "I won't be angry with you, Moon Face," he said quietly. "This journey must be an unlooked-for surprise for you, too."

But Moon Face shook his head. "No," he said somberly. "Gotha had been preparing me for many turns of the seasons. Two hands worth, at least."

Rising Sun raised his eyebrows. "Years, then!"

"Yes. He knew—or at least suspected strongly—that you would undertake a journey of some kind. He went into the Void, you see, and learned much there." Moon Face shrugged. "I don't think he's told me everything about *that,* either."

Rising Sun frowned. "The Void," he said. "The Turtle. The Stone. My family has many secrets—perhaps *too* many. I thought I knew the lore of my own blood, Moon Face. I grew up in the Chief's house, and my parents were White Moon and Morning Star. If any knew of these things, I thought it would be them. But evidently *I* know little. What do you know that I don't, my friend?"

"There is a difference between knowing and understanding," Moon Face replied. "Both of your parents went into the Void as well. But they had their own roles to play in the things that happened there. I've wondered, though—why was Gotha swept into emptiness with them? He is not of your blood, though for a time he told Morning Star that he was his father. It was a lie, though—and the lie was revealed in the Void."

Rising Sun nodded slowly. "My parents have never spoken directly of the Void. At least not to me. What they *did* tell me concerned the role of my mother's mother's sister, who was Great Maya. Though even about that they didn't tell all they knew, it seems. Do you know more about these things?"

Moon Face had been hunched on the natural granite bench almost as unmoving as the rock itself. Now he shifted. His spine made a tiny crackling noise, and he sighed with relief. The river swept past with a low, roaring sound. Wind played in the grass beyond the water.

The World seemed filled with hushed, expectant yearning, a beautiful emptiness waiting to be filled.

"Ahh," Moon Face said. "It's a beautiful day, isn't it?"

"Tell me," Rising Sun said.

Moon Face snorted softly. "Tell you? I wish I could. I've been privy to Gotha's deep thoughts, though not all of them. I know much, but now that I think about it, I wonder if I know anything at all. Things happened. The World changed. Your grandfather's sister was at the heart of most of it. I don't think anybody now living except Gotha understands just how important—how *mighty*— Maya really was. I'm certainly not sure *I* do."

"But you understand more than me," Rising Sun said tartly. "And I need to know. It's my journey and my Test. The time for secrecy is past."

The apprentice shrugged unhappily at the sternness in Rising Sun's voice. "Very well. Gotha taught you the lineage, didn't he?"

Rising Sun nodded his assent.

"Well, think about it. Gotha has, for years. It boils down to this: The Turtle created the Gods, and the Gods created the World. That is the truth, but what does the truth *mean*? The Shaman believed the Gods were bound to the World by that creation, but eventually They grew tired of Their obligation and wished to lay it down. Yet even the Gods were ruled by a greater one, and it would only allow them to leave the World when another had come to take up Their burden. Their creator, who was the Turtle, made the Twin Stones and caused them to be separated, until it was time for the One To Come, who would inherit the World from the Gods."

"So when the Stones came together again," Rising Sun said softly, "they became what they were in the beginning. The Twinstone, which heralded the One To Come."

"More than that! The Twinstone was also the Key that unlocked the chains which bound the Gods to the World. And only Maya could use it. She was the Wielder of the Stones, the Key to the Doors, and many other things. Your parents Kept the Stones, but their role was separate from them. Neither your mother nor your father ever wielded their Stones—only Maya could do that. The doom of your parents was different. It was to bring forth the One To Come—or so Gotha says. The Turtle revealed the lineage—from the Moon and the Star, the One To Come, who will inherit the World."

"Me," Rising Sun said flatly. Once again he felt the shivers of terror that had shaken him so much at Gotha's first explanation of these things.

"Well, it might be you." Moon Face sighed. "Even Gotha wasn't sure. Isn't sure yet, though he hasn't said so. The prophesy said *from* the Moon and Star. It might be one of your brothers or sisters, or it might be your children, or even further into your line. Grandchildren. Great-grandchildren. I don't believe even Gotha *knows*. He only guesses."

Rising Sun rubbed his hands together, to conceal the slight tremor in his fingertips. "He said the Test would reveal the One."

"Yes. But nobody knows what the Test is. The Turtle never said. Gotha believes the Test was revealed in your Manhood Dream, but what if he's wrong?"

Rising Sun stood up. His muscles cried out for movement, anything to distract him from the terrible uncertainty he felt. He paced closer to the river. After a moment Moon Face rose and followed. He came up behind him and put his hand on his shoulder.

"I'm not much help, am I?"

Rising Sun stood silent for a long moment. Then he sighed. "The ways of the Powers—Gods, the Turtle, whatever Spirits there may be—are very strange, aren't they?" He turned. "It's not your fault, though. It's just that . . ." He paused, not quite sure what he wanted to say.

"I thought if I were the One the Turtle prophesied, somehow I would know it. But I don't know anything at all." He looked into Moon Face's sympathetic eyes. "Wouldn't I at least *feel* something? Stronger, or braver, or more knowing? *Something*?"

"I don't know, my friend." He started to speak again, then paused.

"What?" Rising Sun said.

"I'm just glad it's not me," Moon Face said. "It must be terrible."

They both stared at each other. Rising Sun's thoughts
returned to his Manhood Dream, to the cave beneath the
thrones. Something had been nagging at him, but he
couldn't quite think of what it was. His eyes slipped out
of focus as he thought about what he'd seen and heard in
that mystic place.

Seen the bones, the Stone. Her fiery eyes. And heard
the deep bass rumble, which was somehow so familiar . . .

That low vibration was almost like—his eyes cleared.
He glanced at the river, and suddenly knew what the
sound in the cave had been. Water! The vast, rushing passage of water! The cave was near a river, he was certain
of it!

Rising Sun felt his lips twitch. Suddenly he grinned.
"All this gloom! Look at the sun! It's a beautiful day,
Moon Face. Maybe the Gods have gone, but what a wonderful World they left for us! I can't imagine how one
man could inherit it all. It seems impossible! But if it's
true, there's only one way to find out. What's past is
gone. The journey begins with a single step!"

Rising Sun felt a great cheerfulness fill him, and he
burst out laughing. His mirth was full of knowing, as if a
veil had been lifted from his gloom. He slapped Moon
Face on his shoulder, almost knocking the smaller man
down. "She came this way, my friend. I feel it! And she
stopped here, for a time, before she went on downriver."

Moon Face stared at him in wonderment, plainly unconvinced by the sudden change.

"Yes, yes! And when she left here, she followed the
river. Maya went south, my friend. And so will we!"

"Are you sure?"

"Sure? I'm not *sure* of anything. And maybe that's the
way it's supposed to be. But if I'm caught in the Turtle's
weaving, I don't know the strands of it. So I will trust my
own heart, and we will see. Pack up, my friend. We can
make many strides before sunset!"

Moon Face regarded him doubtfully. This abrupt mood
shift made him wonder if some crazed Spirit hadn't taken
hold of his friend. But Maya and Caribou *had* led their
People south when they'd first departed the Valley. Per-

haps Rising Sun was right. Besides, what choice did they have?

Only the choices Rising Sun made. It was, after all, his doom. Moon Face's role was only to be swept along with it and perhaps, if possible, help ride the currents a bit.

"Maybe a little more trail meat before we go?" Moon Face said. "I'm hungry again."

2

Running Deer crept carefully between the dark rocks that rimmed that side of the river like broken teeth. Slowly, trying to keep herself from being silhouetted against the skyline, she raised her head.

The voices she'd heard had fallen silent. Now, squinting against the sun that had tilted over into the west, she saw why. The two young men were loading their packs, checking the thongs that balanced them on their shoulders.

Rising Sun slapped Moon Face on the shoulder and nodded. The apprentice smiled, though Running Deer thought he looked a bit worried. But Rising Sun only grinned cheerfully at him and then, using Caribou's great spear as a walking staff, set out downstream.

She sank back and tiredly armed sweat from her brow. They'd set a fast pace, and for a time she'd been hard put to keep up. It would have been no problem, but she'd had to march crouched over, seeking what protection she could from the shoulder-high grass. Even so, it had been a near thing. At least twice Rising Sun had stopped and scanned the empty steppe, as if he sensed her following. Both times she'd managed to sink to her knees, and she didn't think he'd seen her. For which she breathed a silent prayer of gratitude to the Mother whom she worshiped.

Her plan, as much as she had one, was simple. Follow the two youths until their journey had taken them so far from the Valley they wouldn't want to turn back, even if an unlooked-for companion suddenly joined them. Even if the unexpected arrival was a woman. *Especially* if she was a woman.

She guessed she would have to follow at least three days march before it might be safe to reveal herself. Surely that would be far enough along. She thought her cousin might accept her anyway, but had her doubts about the Shaman's apprentice.

She'd known Rising Sun all his life, and had loved him for much of hers, though from a distance. That was her great secret, greater even than the bow she carried or the skills she'd so quietly taught herself.

Her cousin wouldn't kill her for her sins, but Moon Face might counsel otherwise. She didn't know him well and had mixed feelings about him. The chubby youth seemed friendly enough, what little she'd had to do with him, but his world was full of Spirits. Her life was closer to the earth, to the things that ran and flew and crawled, to things she could *touch,* and she didn't trust him.

In the meantime, though she had no idea what the future held, she luxuriated for the first time in the incredible sense of freedom the steppe kindled in her. Out here, where the grasses blew for endless days, and the river flowed beneath a sky so wide it made her feel like a bug, all her worries and resentments and fears fell away as if they'd never been.

Was this what Maya had felt on her many journeys? The World was so *wide* beyond the Green Valley. No wonder the men loved to hunt so much! It was as if the high walls of the Valley had locked her soul within them, and now, beyond their confines, she was as free to soar as the hawk that floated like a tiny speck in the sky above.

Or maybe it was just that she was no longer surrounded by men, kept prisoner by their traditions that held her to be less than the beasts they hunted. Had Maya broken free of that, too?

"I think so," she whispered to herself. "I *hope* so."

The two figures below dwindled to tiny stick figures beside the gleaming water, which now caught the rays of the sun and cast them back at her in blinding silver shafts.

She blinked to clear her vision. Then, still moving carefully, she began to make her way down to the rocks.

What would they think? What would they *do*? Did it matter? She'd tasted freedom now—even if they killed her, she would never return to the slavery she'd left behind.

She reached the water's edge and stared at the great green flow of it, rushing into the south. Her doom lay that way, where the water ran.

She turned to seek it.

3

Rising Sun raised one hand. "This looks like a good spot," he said.

Dusk lay in thick shadows along the riverbank. The great rock formations were far behind them now. Here the bank sloped from a grassy rise down to dried mud where their footsteps raised faint dusty puffs. Rising Sun pointed to a thin stand of young oak and maple off to the left. "We'll camp there for the night," he said.

Moon Face nodded with relief. A slow, moisture-filled breeze had begun to roll off the river, and his sweaty back felt suddenly clammy and cold. The skin of his shoulders beneath the pack thongs was raw and abraded, and he regretted not having worn his coat during the hot part of the day. Tomorrow, he thought, he would regret it more.

He turned and tramped toward the trees, sliding the pack off as he went. "I'll kindle a fire," he called back to Rising Sun, who was bent over, examining the dusty verge along the water's edge.

"Good," Rising Sun called back. "But don't expect fresh meat tonight! Nothing comes here to drink, and it's too late to hunt rabbits or squirrels."

Moon Face grunted. "I don't care. I'll eat anything I can chew."

There was a good spot beneath the largest of the trees, where they could unroll their sleeping furs facing the water and still be protected from the worst of the wind. Moon Face had just struck a few sparks from his fire flint into a bit of moss when Rising Sun came up.

"Wait a moment," Moon Face said. He puffed out his

cheeks and blew on the sparks until tiny blue flames began to flicker in the dry gray stuff. Then, piece by piece he fed bits of tinder into the moss, until at last a respectable fire burned in the rude stone hearth he'd built. "At least we'll be warm tonight," he said when he finished.

Rising Sun seated himself on his own furs. He had Maya's bow across his knees. Carefully he rubbed the wood with a scrap of hide soaked with fat. The great weapon glistened with every stroke. He felt a calm begin to grow inside him with the soothing regularity of the motion. It felt good to concentrate on something he understood, something he could control.

"Are you hungry?" Moon Face asked.

Rising Sun nodded. "Take it from your pack this time. That way we'll keep the weights evenly balanced."

The apprentice brought out a good-sized hunk and unwrapped its leafy covering. "Here," he grunted, his mouth already full.

Rising Sun set the bow aside. They lay by the fire and watched the sun sink in a silent crimson explosion beyond the river. For one moment the steppe glowed with golden fire, and then the stars began to twinkle.

They spoke little. When they finished their meal, Rising Sun checked their gear, then rolled himself into his furs. Within a few moments he began to snore softly.

Moon Face couldn't drop off so easily. He envied the younger man his hunter's ability to sleep at need. His own skull buzzed with a myriad of thoughts and worries, though there was little he could do about them. Nevertheless, he found sleep difficult, even after he'd wrapped his own furs close around him and closed his eyes.

The sound was so faint that at first he wasn't certain if he was dreaming or still awake. But his ears pricked as the distant howls came again, icy and ominous on the night air.

"Rising Sun!" he whispered.

"Mm? What?"

"What is that?"

Rising Sun pushed himself up on his elbows, his eyes muzzy with sleep. The coals of the dying fire cast glowing shadows on his face.

Again, the long, mournful cries sounded.

Rising Sun looked at Moon Face. "Wolves," he said. "Far away, but wolves."

Then he grinned at Moon Face's apprehension. "Go back to sleep. I said they were far away."

Looking somewhat troubled, Moon Face lay back down. Rising Sun was the hunter. Shaman's apprentices had little experience with the beasts of the World, beyond the calling of their Spirits.

A wolf Spirit would not have frightened him at all. The real beast was a different story. Nevertheless, he pushed his fears away and tried to sleep.

Now Rising Sun lay back and stared at the trillion lights in the sky. The wolves were indeed far away, too distant to bother them tonight. But this was summer. And that was a *pack* of wolves. By the sound, a big pack. Wolves tended to pack like that in winter only. What were they hunting?

The fogs that drifted along the river at night tended to distort noise, but he thought the pack might be gathered at the rocky place where the stream from the Green Valley joined the river. Where the Shaman Ghost had first abandoned the Mammoth Stone, and Caribou had found it. So many animals had been slaughtered there it was sometimes called the Place of Bones.

A good place for wolves. But not in summer.

He dropped off to sleep at last, but even as he did so, he had a final thought: Did those howls sound louder? Closer?

Wolf packs in high summer. Worrisome.

CHAPTER SEVEN

1

Running Deer glanced over her shoulder. The steppe behind her seemed empty—yet she still felt the presence of *something.*

With morning the howling that had made her sleep uneasy finally ended. She'd awakened still tired, feeling as if she'd hardly slept at all. Her muscles ached from the unaccustomed exertions of the previous day. She was a strong woman, toughened by the labors of her daily life, but trekking across the steppe exercised different sinews than she was used to. Now she began to feel the price.

She was hiking just below the top of the rise that led down to the river. She was careful to keep below the summit, so that she wouldn't be silhouetted against the sky in case her quarry looked back and saw her. It was hard going. She tramped along, using her unstrung bow as a walking stick. The wiry steppe grass was waist high. It tugged at her and rustled in sticky protest as she pushed her way through. Her hands and arms were covered with tiny cuts where the saw-edged blades left their marks. Midges buzzed in her ears and hummed across her eyes, an irritating nuisance.

She raised her head and estimated the position of the sun in the empty blue sky. Coming on noon high. It was time to risk another glimpse over the top of the rise.

Maybe Rising Sun and Moon Face had stopped to eat or rest during the hottest part of the day. It was risky, but without occasionally checking on their position, she ran the greater risk of either losing them entirely, or having them turn back onto the steppe and discovering her.

There it was again. That prickly feeling right between her shoulder blades. She whirled, then froze, one hand shading her eyes.

Nothing. The steppe extended out in an unbroken green-gold sea. Distant winds played shadow patterns across the empty land.

She sighed. Just nerves, probably. She'd never felt so lonely before. The land was so *big*. There was freedom in it, but also a kind of fear she'd never experienced before.

She spun round one more time, like a child trying to catch her shadow, but once again was disappointed. Yet the feeling that something was following her, stalking her, remained. The wolves?

She didn't think so. Wolves would be more obvious. She was no hunter, but she'd listened to the men tell their hunting stories, and what she knew of wolves spoke of a different kind of attack. A pack would yip and bark and howl in pursuit, to keep its quarry running in plain sight.

Cave lions crept on their prey in silence, but those great beasts kept close to their rocky lairs. She couldn't imagine that one would stalk her so far out on the steppe. She shook her head, suddenly disgusted with herself.

Stop acting like a frightened woman, she told herself.

She took a firmer grip on her bow stave and moved slowly up the rise. Near the top she dropped to her hands and knees and pushed her way through the grass. The rich smell of hot earth filled her nose. Finally she felt the ground slope away from her and realized she'd reached the crest.

An inch at a time she raised her dark head until she could see the long expanse of riverbank beyond. The sun glared crazily off the silver water. It took her a moment to find them.

"Ah," she breathed in relief.

They were farther ahead than she'd expected. Evidently they were able to make better time along the dried mud that edged the bank than she could through the tall grass. They were almost at the limit of her vision, two tiny black figures against the shining backdrop of the river.

Though she doubted they could pick her out from that distance, she retreated as carefully as she'd come, and didn't stand up until she was sure she wouldn't expose herself.

They were moving too quickly. She would have to hurry to catch up. Her thighs and calves ached. Sweat dripped into her eyes. The midges hummed frantically in her ears.

She would have been miserable, except that she was happier than she'd ever been in her whole miserable life. She grinned at nothing, lifted her bow, and marched forward.

Two more days. Then she would reveal herself.

Those weird feelings of being followed were nothing more than her imagination. She glanced over her shoulder. See? Nothing there at all. Nothing.

Nevertheless, she stopped and took the time to string her bow.

2

"Have you ever heard of wolves hunting in packs during high summer? In the grass?" Moon Face asked. His voice was hesitant. Two worried creases marked the skin above his flat nose.

"Uh. You're really bothered by them, aren't you?"

"Well, aren't you?"

Rising Sun shrugged. "A little. I'd be more worried if I was sure they were hunting us. But those howls were far away upriver. They might have been after something else. In fact, I'd guess they are. Wolves don't hunt men, usually, unless they smell blood or sense a hunter is disabled somehow. Besides, they don't pack up unless it's winter, when hunting is harder for them."

Moon Face eyed him uneasily. "That sounded like a pack to me."

"Well, yes. But it might not have been. It might have been a couple of wolf families on either side of the river howling at each other. Or it might have simply been the corpse of some great beast, a bison or a mammoth, and they all gathered to feed."

"Uh. I hadn't thought of that."

"We haven't heard anything of them today." Rising Sun looked over at the river. "I'm hot," he said. "What do you say we stop and rest awhile? Aren't you hungry?"

Moon Face chuckled. "Are you crazy?"

Rising Sun grinned. "Maybe we should go back and see if it *is* a dead mammoth. As much as you eat, maybe you could drive those wolves away if you thought you could get dinner out of it."

The apprentice chuckled again, but not so heartily. "I think some trail meat will do just fine."

On their right the river had narrowed. It foamed busily over a shoal of slick black rocks that barely showed their shiny crests above the flood. A faint mist rode the air above these rapids, catching the sunlight in a myriad of shifting rainbows.

"It looks shallow there," Rising Sun mused. "I wonder if we should try to cross."

Moon Face's eyes widened. "The water runs very fast. We'd be swept away!"

"Maybe. Maybe not." Rising Sun walked to the river's edge and bent over, examining the way the bank crumbled into the water. He poked the butt of his spear into the river and grunted when only an arm's length of wood came out dark with moisture.

"I doubt if the deepest part even comes up to our waists," he said.

Moon Face shuddered. He knew less about swimming than Rising Sun did, since his childhood had been sheltered from the pleasure of thrashing around in First Lake with the rest of the boys. "Why do you want to cross the river?" he asked.

"If the wolves are on this side, they won't cross the water. We'd be safe."

"And what if they're on the other side? We'd be stepping right into their jaws."

Rising Sun smiled. "That's right. So what do you think we should do?"

"Why are you asking *me*?" Moon Face glanced back upriver. "My opinion is that since we don't know, we might as well stay on this side. Then at least we won't add the chance of drowning to the possibility of being eaten alive."

At this, Rising Sun laughed out loud. "Oh, Moon Face, don't worry so much. Those wolves aren't going to eat us. Remember, they're afraid of fire—so if we just remember to keep a good hearth going, we'll be fine. Besides, even if they come at us during the day, we'll see them and cross the river before they can get at us."

"Yes," Moon Face muttered darkly, "if the river isn't too deep to cross where they find us."

"Well, since you don't want to cross now, we might as well have our meal. What do you say?"

Moon Face brightened. "I say, let's eat!"

When they finished, Moon Face rolled onto his stomach and let the hot sun play on his back. "Feels good." Then, "Rising Sun?"

"Mmm?"

"Where did the Gods go?"

Rising Sun, who lay propped on his elbows, staring dreamily at the sky, raised his eyebrows. "Where? How should I know? That's your problem, yours and the Shaman's. Haven't you two been whispering about it all these years?"

Moon Face mopped sweat off his belly. "Gotha told me what he thought—though whether it's true I don't know. But doesn't it frighten you? I mean, to think that all of this"—Moon Face waved one hand vaguely—"is just rolling along with nothing to guide it?"

Rising Sun pursed his lips. "I don't know. I guess I haven't really thought about it. Remember, the first I knew of the Gods leaving the World was when Gotha told me a moon or so ago. Yes, it scares me, but somehow it's too big to really worry about. You know what I mean?"

"But you *have* to worry about it!" Moon Face said, shocked. "It's all about *you*!"

Rising Sun quirked his lips sourly. "Is it? I don't feel

any different. I certainly don't feel like a God, if that's what you mean. And I still think Gotha's idea that I'm somehow supposed to inherit the World is, well, *wrong*."

Moon Face rolled over on his side and faced his friend. "But, Rising Sun, if that's how you feel, why are we going on this journey? Why the Test?"

Rising Sun stared at him. Finally he moved his shoulders slightly. "Why not? I said I would go. I gave my word as a man, and I have to honor *that*. And who knows? Somehow, the Shaman may be right."

Though I doubt it, he thought.

Moon Face didn't seem at all satisfied with this, but he didn't ask any more questions. It was plain, though, that Rising Sun's disbelief in his own destiny unsettled him. After a moment he said, "Look at the sky."

A gray curdling had begun to rise above the horizon beyond the river. Rising Sun squinted. "Storm," he said at last and sat up. "There's not much cover around here, but I thought I spotted some trees farther along the river."

Moon Face got to his feet and hurriedly began to fasten his pack. He mumbled something about the wind Spirits, but Rising Sun couldn't make out what he said.

He got up and hoisted his own pack to his shoulders. "When the storms come in summer, they come fast," he said. "But they don't come often. This is strange."

Moon Face eyed him glumly. "Like the wolves, you mean."

"Yes," Rising Sun replied. "Let's get going."

They moved off in silence. Rising Sun set a pace that soon had Moon Face puffing, so that what he muttered under his breath was hard to make out.

"What did you say?"

"Too much strangeness," Moon Face replied. "I don't like it."

The wind began to rise.

3

Running Deer watched the thunderheads build over the steppe beyond the river. Though it was still early in the afternoon, the light had faded into somber, dusklike tones. Threads of bright yellow stabbed down beneath the fat bellies of the clouds, partially obscured by drifting veils of silver rain. Low, booming rumbles echoed across the rolling plains, the sound carried on a steadily growing breeze.

She sniffed. The wind was full of water, a thinner, fresher smell than the pervasive damp odor of the river. In the gloom, she could no longer make out the two men she'd been tracking. She supposed they'd already taken shelter—she'd glimpsed a dark patch far ahead that looked like a stand of trees. But there would be no such shelter for her.

She sighed as she looked around. Nothing but grass, and a few smooth boulders down by the riverbank. For fear of discovery, she'd been reluctant to leave the protection afforded by the rise, but now it seemed she had no choice. Those boulders weren't much, but huddling against the lee side of them was better than facing the storm with no shelter at all. Besides, even if the men looked back upriver, in this murk they would see her no more easily than she could them.

Chewing nervously on her lower lip, she mounted the rise and crossed over. A blast of chill, wet wind greeted her as she reached the top. It whipped her dark hair away from her head in two long, black wings. A few spats of rain slapped her cheeks. She lowered her head, hunched her shoulders, and hurried on down to whatever safety the boulders might offer.

Intent on her path, she didn't look either upriver or down, but even if she had, she wouldn't have been able to make out the first muscular shape that trotted alertly to the top of the rise and stood facing the wind. It saw her, though, and its long, pink tongue lolled against sharp fangs as it watched her with red, hungry eyes. Finally, as the others came up to crowd around their leader, the great wolf threw back its head and howled. A moment later the rest joined the chorus, but the wind swallowed their cries.

After a time the dark shapes hunkered down against the wind. They didn't fear storms, only the fires that sometimes came after. They could wait. The scent of their prey filled their nostrils. It was so strong even the rain wouldn't wash it away entirely.

White teeth flashed. Red eyes rolled.

Soon.

4

"Whew!" Rising Sun said. "That was a bad one!"

Moon Face, his black hair pasted against the side of his head by the force of the downpour, peered out from the rude shelter of fallen branches they'd constructed beneath the eaves of the small wood. It had helped some, but not much. They were both soaked to the skin.

The worst of it had swept on past, and now only a few gray sprinkles spattered against the leaves over their heads. The temperature had dropped several degrees with the passage of the storm, and both of them began to shiver. Moon Face's teeth clacked in his jaw like stones in a rattle. For some reason Rising Sun found the combination of that sound, along with the miserable expression on his friend's face, irresistibly funny. First he grinned. Then he chuckled. Then, when he could hold it no longer, he burst into laughter.

"What?" Moon Face moaned. "What's so funny?"

"*You* are. You look like a drowned rat!"

"Well, you don't look so good yourself."

This set Rising Sun off again. He laughed until his sides ached, and only when Moon Face, his expression wounded, stalked away from him and out of the woods entirely, did his mirth finally run down.

"I'm sorry!" he called. "Wait for me!"

He caught up to Moon Face, who stood facing the river. The older youth's back was stiff, and he refused to turn around. Rising Sun put his hand on Moon Face's bare shoulder and said gently, "I'm sorry, my friend. I shouldn't have laughed at you."

Moon Face said, "I didn't ask to be sent on this journey. I'm a Shaman's apprentice, not a hunter." Moon Face's shoulder quivered tensely beneath Rising Sun's hand. Then an odd thing occurred.

Rising Sun's vision shifted crazily. Somehow, it seemed as if he were looking out of two pairs of eyes. He could see his hand on Moon Face's shoulder. But he could also see the river and the steppe beyond, as if he stood in front of himself.

He swayed dizzily. The dual vision was horribly disconcerting, but then something far worse happened. With no warning, he was suddenly seized by a terrible wave of fear. The dark surge of emotion locked up his muscles, turned his belly to ice, and brought stinging tears to his eyes.

i can't do this i don't want to be here he despises me he thinks i'm soft and fat and a spy for Gotha and the wolves the howling the great empty loneliness I CAN'T STAND IT I'LL DIE ON THIS JOURNEY—

Rising Sun swayed before the onslaught of a terror unlike anything he'd ever felt before. He staggered. Without quite understanding why, he ripped his hand away from Moon Face's skin. As soon as he did so, the feeling vanished as if it had never been.

"Gods!" he breathed fervently.

Moon Face turned slowly, a strange expression on his face. "Rising Sun? What's the matter? Why are you staring at me like that?"

Rising Sun didn't know what to say. His lips moved, once, twice, but nothing came out. He felt as if he'd unexpectedly stepped on a poisonous snake. *What had happened?*

He had no idea. The only connection he could make, and it was an extremely dim one, was that those words, those *feelings,* might somehow be connected with Moon Face. With his skin, maybe.

But that idea never really made it to his conscious mind. Not then. Finally something fell out of his mouth.

"Uh," he said.

Moon Face stepped closer, and inadvertently Rising Sun stepped back.

"Are you all right?" Moon Face said. His round face began to wrinkle worriedly, and for one instant Rising Sun thought his friend was about to burst into tears.

"Uh," he tried again. Then—at last!—his mind gave a

funny little hop, and he was able to speak again. "No, nothing. I must have drifted away there. Moon Face, don't look at me like that. I'm fine. Really."

They regarded each other silently for what seemed like a long time. Moon Face's features smoothed out. "Are you sure?"

I'm not sure of anything. Mother, what was that?

"I'm sure," Rising Sun told him. *Maybe it was a demon ...*

His addled thoughts congealed into something that made a bit of sense. "I'm sorry I laughed at you," he said again.

Moon Face shook his head. "It's all right. It's just that sometimes ..." His voice trailed off, as if he couldn't think of any way to continue.

Rising Sun grinned shakily. "I understand," he said. And to his horror, he realized he did. He understood far more than he wished to understand.

No, it wasn't a demon or a Spirit. It was something far worse. It terrified him to the very roots of his bones.

Moon Face? Was it Moon Face's doing? Or was it himself?

5

The storm had been far worse than she'd expected. She'd never endured one of the great maelstroms that flogged the naked steppe before. She hadn't realized how much protection from wind and lightning the safe, tall walls of the Green Valley afforded to those lucky enough to be snug inside them when thunder walked and talked across the World.

The wind-whipped rain had struck her skin like gravel, even with the scrap bit of shelter she'd been able to make for herself huddled against the largest of the riverside boulders. Now, with the wind dying at last, she stood up and stared at her skin, expecting to find bruises, but it was unmarked and she breathed a sigh of relief.

The storm hadn't killed her. It was something.

The guttural sound snapped her head up and she saw

them. They'd come out of the rain and now stood in a wide semicircle that pinned her against the water. Her blood suddenly slowed, then seemed to explode in her ears, cold and hot at the same time. She felt her cheeks flush, though her chest had turned to ice.

At least two hands of wolves, great black-gray beasts, tongues dangling, stood in silence, their hot breath smoking in the after-storm chill. The leader, half again as large as any of the others, took one stiff-legged pace forward, then stopped. His eyes—nuggets of fire ringed with dirty yellow—regarded her almost calmly.

She stared back, imagining she could understand the thoughts that flickered like hot blue flames through that bestial skull. And why shouldn't the leader of the pack be calm? She was dinner, and dinner wasn't going anywhere. Not unless it could swim or fly, and she could do neither.

It seemed as if they stood like this for an eternity, the wolf's eyes boring into her own. Then, although she had no conscious awareness of directing her muscles to move, she began to lean down. Her right arm dropped slowly, slowly, until her fingers touched the rain-slick wood of her bow. Thank the Mother she'd been scared enough earlier to string it.

Still moving with nerve-creaking deliberation, she switched the bow to her left hand and reached for her cache of arrows with her right. She brought one shaft up and nocked it against the bowstring.

The leader twitched. Its jaws fell open in a white, ferocious grin. She drew the bow back until her fingers touched her ear.

Not squirrels. Not rabbits. This isn't a game.

The wolf's hindquarters settled lower, the large muscles along the base of its spine quivering as it began the motion that would end in a leap directly at her throat.

Mother!

She let fly. The arrow made a faint hissing noise as it crossed the distance between them. The pack leader's fang-studded mouth yawned wider. The flinty head of the arrow screamed right down its throat. Its jaws slammed shut. Snap!

The arrow broke off. The wolf's mouth pistoned wide.

A red gout of blood exploded through its teeth. With utmost gravity, almost as if it were acknowledging her, the huge beast sank back down on its haunches. The wet, raspy sound of its lungs stuttered as it began to choke on its own blood. It raised one foreleg and pawed feebly at its muzzle. Then it died.

Its carcass toppled over and fell with a dull, meaty thud. It was only then she realized that time had somehow become slow, elastic, for with the death of their leader, the other members of the pack sprang into motion.

For an instant that hungry circle of flickering ruby eyes shifted away from her toward the fallen chief. A younger wolf snarled, then snapped tentatively at the dead wolf's black nose. It tossed its head. Its glossy black throat worked as it swallowed a tender morsel.

Running Deer nocked another arrow as she clambered to the top of the largest boulder. Now she stood about shoulder high above the plain. The wolves would have to leap to reach her. Two of the beasts, growling low in their throats, sidled toward the boulder. She brought the nearest down. Its partner immediately turned on the fallen brother. She held her breath.

The pack dissolved into a bedlam of flashing teeth and guttural snarling. The smell of fresh blood enraged them. The remaining beasts fell on the two carcasses and began to tear them apart.

She pulled her third arrow to her ear and the rain-weakened bowstring snapped. She stared down at the useless wooden stave she held. The arrow dropped to the ground at the base of the boulder.

The wolves wouldn't feed forever. There was nothing but swift-moving water at her back. She uttered a short prayer, then threw back her head and screamed as loud as she could.

6

Rising Sun turned slowly, his face puzzled. "What was that?"

"What?"

"Didn't you hear it?"

New fear traced itself on Moon Face's features. "Hear what? I don't hear anything."

Rising Sun ignored him. "Back upriver. It's ... it sounds like someone screaming. Shouting ..."

"It's the wind."

"No." Rising Sun's eyes focused abruptly. "It *is* somebody screaming. For help, I think." .

Moon Face glanced at him sullenly. Plainly, he wanted no part of an interruption that would turn their journey toward the wolves. "We can get another three hours march in before dark," he said.

Rising Sun hoisted his pack. "No. We're going back."

"No!" Moon Face's expression turned set and stubborn. His thick lips pooched into a sulky pout. "Our way lies downriver."

Rising Sun stared at him as if he'd just seen him. The weird experience he'd undergone surfaced in his mind again. Moon Face was terrified. He was trying to hide it with his surly recalcitrance, but now, to Rising Sun, the truth was obvious in every taut limb. A strong feeling of pity washed over him. What must it be like to be so terrified all the time?

Automatically, he reached out to touch the apprentice, but once again he pulled back before his fingers actually made contact with Moon Face's skin. "You stay here," he said gently. "Whatever it is, it's not far away. I won't be long."

"I'll be *alone*!" Moon Face wailed.

Rising Sun made up his mind. "You can come with me or you can stay here. But I'm going back." His features were stony with resolution. Moon Face saw it, recognized it for what it was, and understood the nature of his choice.

He shrugged miserably. "I'll come with you."

"Good. Let's get going."

Rising Sun set a hard pace. The distant cries he'd heard had become intermittent. He could imagine whoever it was pausing to draw breath, then starting again.

It had to be the wolves.

Moon Face trailed along behind, stumbling occasionally, but picking himself up and lurching along as fast as he could. Rising Sun didn't look at him, but he thought about him as they pounded onward.

That surge of terror he'd felt *had* to have come from Moon Face. His mind went all skittery when he thought about that, but he couldn't escape the conclusion. It had happened when he'd *touched* the apprentice, and stopped as soon as he removed his hand from Moon Face's shoulder.

What else could it have been? I've never felt that scared of anything before, not even when Gotha told me of the One To Come.

But the questions the experience raised were so utterly frightening it was all he could do to keep from moaning as he jogged. *How could such a thing be?*

He didn't have the experience to grapple with the awful mystery of the thing. His thoughts turned once again to Demons and malevolent Spirits, but even as they did, another part of him knew that such things had nothing to do with this. It was no Spirit filling his thoughts, but truth. He had *tasted* Moon Face somehow, but the *how* of it was completely beyond him.

I told him I didn't feel any different. But that's not the truth now, is it?

No, it wasn't.

Maybe some of that revulsion was what made him so obdurately intent on chasing off upriver. It was a chance to grapple with something he understood, and put off what he didn't understand, didn't even *want* to understand.

Somebody was in trouble. His sharp ears picked out separate sounds now, words. *"Help!"*

It was human, and it was in trouble.

Unless it was a demon, of course.

I don't want to be inside anybody else's thoughts!

But the huge weight that had begun to press down on his own mind seemed to whisper more loudly what he'd first begun to hear in the implacable tones of the Shaman Gotha's unspoken message to him: *You are the One To Come. And you don't have any* choice *about it. Oh, yes I do. That's the essence of it. I do have a choice. And some-how, that's the worst thing of all.*

"Helpppp! Rising Sun, help me!"

"You hear that?" he panted.

Sullenly, from behind, gasping. "I hear it."

"Whoever it is is calling my name."

"Yes."

Rising Sun broke into a full-tilt run, ending the brief conversation. He ignored the questions that bubbled in his skull. He couldn't answer them now, but he would soon enough. That last cry had been close, surely no farther away than around the slow curve of the river.

And now he heard a chorus of frenzied growls. Wolves, beyond a doubt! He almost grinned. He under-stood wolves. Wolves he could deal with. He lowered the spear from his shoulder and cradled it across his chest and raced on.

Moon Face slowly fell back, but Rising Sun didn't no-tice. A fire was beginning to burn in his brain, a fire as thick and hot as fresh blood. The heat put a crimson film across his vision as he rounded the final turn and saw his cousin, Running Deer, swing a long stick at a sleek black beast.

He didn't pause to consider that mystery, either, merely brought the point of Caribou's great weapon around and charged, his battle cry singing wildly in his throat, all mysteries forgotten.

7

"Helppp! Rising Sun, come back, help me!"

Her voice cracked on the last words. She was growing both hoarse and out of breath. The muscles in her arms felt weak and shaky. She'd been swinging her bow stave back and forth for what seemed like hours, slashing and jabbing at the slinking black forms that surged and re-ceded around the base of the rock.

It was a strange dance. Some of the wolves would break off and tear at the flesh of the fallen pair, then re-turn to jump almost halfheartedly at the rock on which

she stood. She sensed their reluctance, but at the same
time felt their hunger. They were torn between which
prey they wished to tear, and so moved back and forth almost casually between the two poles.

She'd wounded another, though not in any major way.
The smallest of the pack, a wolf whose shiny black pelt
was streaked with silver, had held back at first, waiting
for its larger brethren to press the attack. Then, when she
was fully occupied flailing and jabbing at one huge beast,
the smaller one had lunged for the top of the boulder from
her rear. Only the dry, clicking rasp of its claws scrabbling for purchase on the smooth stone had alerted her to
the new attack.

She'd jabbed viciously at the eyes of the wolf in front,
then whirled and stomped down as hard as she could
on the foreleg of the smaller wolf behind. That one had
uttered a high-pitched yelp as it lost its purchase and fell
heavily to the ground, where it now lay hunched around
its wounded leg, licking the broken member frantically
and whining.

Through it all, she screamed for help over and over
again. But as the minutes wore on, she began to lose
hope. Maybe Rising Sun had gotten too far downstream
to hear her shouts. Or if he heard them, he was ignoring
them. Why should he turn back to help a stranger?
Though if he heard her at all, he must wonder who it was
that knew his name. She'd begun to shout *that* after only
a moment's hesitation. Her plans to reveal herself after
two more days had been ruined by the wolves. She
couldn't surprise him if she were dead.

"Help, Rising Sun. Help me!"

But her strength was failing. The long sweeps of the
bow grew slower, the end of it dropped lower. The wolves
sensed her weakness, and more of them gave off ripping
gouts of bloody flesh from the carcasses and turned toward her perch.

At her back, the small wounded one howled softly,
mournfully. Sweat stung her eyes. Her black hair flapped
and flopped across her face, but she couldn't give up her
two-handed grip on the bow to push it away.

And now the largest of the remaining beasts backed

off a bit. Then, massive thighs pistoning, it launched itself
into the air.

"*Aaiieeeee!*"

She met the wolf's leap with the tip of the bow, thrusting it forward in a savage, spearing jab that caught it in
the throat and pushed it backward, twisting as it fell.
Then Rising Sun was among them, his great spear jabbing
and slashing, and without thinking, she leapt down from
the rock into the fray, her numbed muscles galvanized by
some awful, throbbing power she could no more understand than she could deny. It didn't matter. She gave herself up to it.

It was, in its own way, divine.

8

He only glanced at her, not quite comprehending,
before the shock of his first thrust shivered up the spear
shaft and jolted into his shoulders.

The great spear point caught the nearest wolf in the
chest and, rather than slashing a deep wound, simply
crushed skin, bone, and lungs into a bloody mess.

He jerked the point free and wheeled to face two more
slinking, snarling, white-fanged shadows whose muzzles
shone stickily with blood.

Whose? Hers? But she looks all right!

He didn't pause to question why she'd deserted the
relative safety of her perch atop the boulder. Perhaps
some tiny part of him wondered at the strange spectacle
of a woman fighting as if she were a man, but the rest of
him sensed a rightness in her actions that erased all hidden questions.

Call it destiny, or fate, or doom. He would consider all
three, but later. Now there was killing to do. He set to it.

The two wolves in front bracketed him, crouching low
on their hindquarters as they edged forward, searching for
an opportunity to spring at his throat. He felt a wild surge
of elation as he faced them. He had accompanied his father on hunts before, but never had he faced wild animals
on his own in life-and-death battle. Perhaps, like the other

boys, he'd secretly wondered how he would do. Would he be brave enough? Strong enough? Quick enough? There had been no way to tell then, but now, with his first victim dead at his feet, he knew at last he was truly a man.

Leave all the rest aside, the Turtle, the One To Come, the strange experience with Moon Face, now he knew the answer to the question he and all the other men of the Three Tribes were born to struggle with.

I am a MAN!

He lunged for the wolf on his right. His heel slipped on a rain-slick patch of grass and he fell heavily. Caribou's long spear flew from his hands. He crouched on his hands and knees, stunned, shaking his head to clear it, staring dumbly down the red throat of the second charging wolf.

Running Deer was no more than a stride away when he tumbled. She still clutched her bow two-handed, but when his spear flew up she instinctively dropped her weapon and clutched for his. He was still down, hair hanging in his face, when she plunged the spear into the side of the second wolf.

The force of her blow transfixed the beast. The spear head buried itself in the earth, pinning the thrashing animal down. Now Rising Sun scrambled to his feet. For a moment he seemed dazed. Then, to her astonishment, he threw back his head and roared with laughter!

He yanked his weapon free with a single jerk, spun, and killed another wolf. Now, counting the two she'd killed, five of the beasts lay dead, and a sixth lay in huddled agony, out of the fight.

There were only four remaining. Now she saw a third figure approach. Moon Face!

His puffy features were set in a frozen rictus of fear, but he carried a handful of good-sized rocks that he hurled clumsily, one by one, at the remnants of the pack. His aim wasn't good, but a few of his stones struck hide and bone. It was the final straw. The last of the pack, leaderless and missing more than half their number, suddenly turned and loped away.

They stood and watched until the final dark shape

scrambled up the rise and disappeared over the top into the steppe beyond.

A single doleful howl marked their departure. For a long moment only exhausted silence filled the spot. Even the wounded beast by the stone fell quiet.

Moon Face hustled up. The three of them stared at each other. The apprentice dropped his remaining rocks. Rising Sun regarded Running Deer blankly. The expression on his face was unreadable, but his left fist clenched, unclenched, clenched again. He didn't seem to notice the movement. Finally, his voice quavering with disbelief and anger, he spoke.

"What in Mother's name are *you* doing here?"

CHAPTER EIGHT

1

Witch Woman watched her daughter's progress along the edge of the river. The girl moved slowly, her ugly flaxen hair hanging lank in her face beneath the ridiculous floppy hat she wore to protect her pale skin, her ruby eyes downcast and vacant. The Witch shook her head.

By what crime against the Terrible Mother, the Witch wondered, had she been cursed with such a wretched daughter?

It was a question she'd pondered many times before. Today, as she watched Sleeps With Spirits's aimless meanderings, the riddle remained as vexatious as ever. Just look at the worthless girl! Sleeps With Spirits, indeed! More likely she should have been called Sleeps All The Time. She looked asleep now, with her slow, languid steps, her dreamlike expression, her empty eyes.

Of course, the girl was a monster, no doubt cursed by some wandering Demon. Her father hadn't shown any of the marks that burdened the girl, not the colorless hair, the pale, ghostlike skin, or those awful eyes. And her brother, Carries Two Spears, was normal enough.

But though the curse had flowered in Sleeps With Spirits, it was the Witch who felt most encumbered by its effect. She knew what the Children of the River thought; that Sleeps With Spirits was a punishment for her own sins—which, though unspecified, were commonly believed to be considerable.

The heavyset woman turned and spat a chunk of yellowish phlegm into the palm of her hand. Anybody else would have deposited the glistening load on the ground, but she couldn't allow any part of her body—not nails nor flesh, not blood nor juice nor hair, not shit nor piss—to fall into the hands of those who might wish her ill. In those appendages and secretions lay magical power, and there were enemies who would know how to use them against her. That pipsqueak Shaman, Drinks Deep Waters, for instance, who dared suggest his puny abilities were the equal of the Witch's own. The Chief, Kills Many Buffalo, was also one who wouldn't shed tears if the Witch Woman rode the top of a funeral pyre.

She examined the glob, then sighed and wiped it on her robe of mangy rabbit skins, where it glued itself onto an already matted patch. She would have to do something about the Shaman one of these days. And maybe about Sleeps With Spirits, too. The girl's Dreams, which she insisted on telling to anybody who would stand still long enough to listen, were getting even crazier of late. Of course, nobody believed them, but that wasn't the point.

Witch Woman's gaze flicked one more time at her daughter, the action as sharp and furtive as a knife thrust in the back. The real problem wasn't her *Dreams*. It was her presence, her whining, grating, malformed, reproachful *presence*.

Well, something could be done about that, too. Maybe, if she could think of something really clever, she could find a way to kill both bothersome birds with a single stone. Solve the Shaman problem and the crazy daughter problem in one stroke. She rubbed her stubbled chin thoughtfully. Yes, the idea *did* merit some consideration. Not immediately. But soon.

She turned and stumped back toward her house. Sleeps With Spirits wandered on, oblivious.

2

Sleeps With Spirits stared out over the broad brown water with longing in her crimson eyes, as if the turgid flood were some kind of strange, moving meadow on which she might walk and be carried away.

She'd thought of taking that walk many times. She sighed and sank down and sat on folded legs, her hands clasped primly in her lap. It would be so easy, so simple. Just a step or two, until the hidden power of the river had its grip firmly fastened around her. Then, lifting and buoyant, she might float away from all the pain, all the hatred and fear, be carried south into the land of the sun, where everything was soft and warm, and nothing was cruel.

But the Sun was coming from the north, wasn't he? And in the winter, too. The Sun would shine through the snow for her. She'd seen him in her Dreams, and though no one else would believe her, she knew her Dreams were true.

So strange, she thought languidly, as the river soothed her with its low, continuous roaring hiss: *No one believes me. They'll be so* surprised *when he comes to me at last.*

For long moments she savored the thought of that surprise—*when he comes, they'll* have *to believe me*—but then a cloud of darkness seemed to drift across those bright, jewellike musings. She knew that cloud. It had shadowed her from the light all her life. It was a darkness that never entirely dissipated, no matter how hard she tried to vanquish it. And some deep part of her understood: the cloud was as much a part of her as the Dreams. Maybe, she sometimes thought, they were the same thing. Night and prophesy, neither possible without the other.

The bleak darkness of disbelief. She could still remember the first time.

She'd just entered her fifth summer, still too young to understand how her appearance made her an outcast. In those days she hadn't yet realized that other little girls her age had friends, and didn't spend all the time in their parents' houses, hiding from the burning glare of the sun.

Further protected by her mother's dour reputation and abrasive talents, she'd attained her fifth year virtually untouched by any knowledge of her own loneliness. And if someone had cared enough to ask her whether she *was* lonely, she wouldn't have known how to answer. Fish don't notice water, beyond assuming the whole world swims in it.

The Dream had shivered her awake screaming in the early morning, on a day when her father was gone hunting. Her strange ruby eyes bulged with terror. Witch Woman couldn't comfort her. Finally she slapped her across the face. The sudden pain shocked the little girl into silence. Then, with the bruise darkening on her cheek, her eyes rolled back into her head and she began to speak.

"Oh, Father, I see your blood! Rivers of blood! You are killed! Oh, don't leave me!" She paused, threw back her head, and shrieked a final time, *"Blood!"* Then she passed out and didn't wake up the whole day and night. When she came around the following morning, she would not speak of it. And nothing was said, because her mother paid the nightmare no attention.

Witch Woman never really remembered this first prophesy, not even when, two years later, she took her husband's sharpest hunting knife and slashed his throat open while he slept. She dragged the corpse out onto the steppe, where it wasn't discovered until after predators had mauled it beyond recognition.

Her reasons had seemed good at the time, and she was never discovered. But Sleeps With Spirits knew what had happened to her father, for she'd had the Dream several times. But when the prophesy finally came to gory fruition, she knew no one would believe her if she exposed the truth. So she kept silent, and learned to fear her mother, who was as terrible as the Terrible Mother whom Witch Woman worshiped.

Now she stared blankly at the river, her mind filled with the horrors she'd known, and contemplated the terror of the future. She knew the Sun would come. She'd seen him in her Dreams. But she hadn't spoken of him, and wouldn't have even if she'd thought anybody would believe her. The Sun was her secret because for the first time in her life, this Dream concerned her personally. It was a Dream of her own future, and though it was misty and enigmatic—she would lead the Sun on a journey and find a great prize, though she had no idea what it might be—and because it was *hers* she kept it to herself. Nevertheless, the riddle of the Dream troubled her. She had never seen the face of the Sun, because in her Dream it blazed with a terrible light that hid his features. But he bore a great bow and would come with strange companions. Sometimes she wondered about them, for she saw them more clearly than the Sun himself.

A mighty warrior who carried a spear like a thunderbolt, a woman who was a hunter and a fighter, and a wolf. These three would come with the Sun, and she would join them. But she didn't know how or why, or what would come after that joining. Her Dream told her no answer.

She would have to wait. But not much longer, she consoled herself while the waters rushed by. Fall was coming, and then winter, when the Sun would shine through the snow and dark.

"Spirits," the soft voice said. "There you are! I've been looking all over for you!"

Carries Two Spears was as unlike his sister as two siblings could possibly be. He was so unlike her, in fact, that his existence served to fuel much ominous gossip relating to their mother, Witch Woman, for it was well known that the Terrible Mother often made children of the same mates to look like each other. Thus the mutterings spoke either of different mates, or of a curse, as explanation of the hideous dissimilarity of the two. Witch Woman was, of course, painfully aware of the chatter, and added one more blame to her daughter for it.

Startled from her reverie, Sleeps With Spirits looked up wide-eyed. "Oh! Two Spears! Sit and talk with me, won't you?"

She patted a spot in the grass next to her. With an engaging grin, her brother slung a brace of bloody rabbits from his shoulder, set down the two spears that were his namesake—one thin and whippy for small game, the other long and thick, useful against the great beasts—and squatted to join her.

"I heard you were looking for me. I ran into Walks Nose Down when I got back. He was in a bad mood. He doesn't like you."

She sighed. "Nobody likes me, Two Spears. Except for you. You know that."

He grunted as he settled himself. He was a hand taller than she. His features were strong and even, dominated by a pair of wide dark eyes and lashes so long he looked almost girlish. He wore his black hair cropped to just below his ears, a fashion current among the young men at that moment. He took after his mother's physical structure, with a wide, strong body. As he got comfortable, his movements were deliberate, though his sister knew he was capable of great bursts of speed.

He was regarded as an up-and-coming hunter, brave and wily, particularly skilled at slaughtering bison, the big game the River People primarily hunted.

His only flaw that merited any whispering was that he hadn't taken a mate yet. Allowances were made, however, even though he was two years past his manhood, because his sunny personality was well liked by the other men. Most assumed he would make his choice soon, and regarded the delay as merely another evidence of his usual calm, deliberative disposition.

Sleeps With Spirits loved him so desperately she could hardly stand to look at him sometimes. Now she reached over and touched his shoulder gently. "I'm glad you're here," she whispered. "I missed you."

He put his massive left arm around her narrow shoulders and hugged her to him. "I thought of you while I was hunting. It must have been lucky. I got two fat rabbits."

She smiled. Only her brother would think of her as lucky. It was one of the things she loved about him. Another was, of course, that of all the people in the camp of the River Children, he was the only one who loved her in return.

Sometimes she shuddered when she thought of what her life would have been without him. As they'd grown up, he'd shielded her from the worst cruelties of the other children, sometimes even with his fists. And, as best he could, he'd protected her from their mother's uncertain tempers, though not always so successfully.

And now he was the only one who would listen to her Dreams, though she'd spoken less of them as she grew older and it became plain to her that, while he would listen and nod, he didn't believe her either.

Maybe I am cursed, she thought suddenly, but she said nothing. Here, in the bright afternoon, with the sun glinting off the broad back of the river, nestled in the safety of her brother's arm, she didn't want to think about such things. "Maybe I am lucky," she mused. "For you, at least."

"What's the matter, Spirits? You sound sad."

She almost told him about her newest Dream then, but something held her tongue. She realized that she couldn't reveal the coming of the Sun even to Carries Two Spears, because she couldn't bear the disbelief of the one she loved and trusted above all others. *If only someone would believe me!*

But she knew nobody would, and the Sun would come on the River Children unawares, and the doom he brought would follow as inevitably as the Sun rose out of the east.

Sometimes the Dream confused her. The Sun would come to her as a man with a shining face, but this man was also somehow a part of the great light in the sky. And just as she was particularly vulnerable, with her pale skin, to that skyborne fire, she knew that when the man-Sun came, he would bring great danger for her as well.

"I'm not sad, brother. At least, not any more than usual."

She sounded so mournful that he squeezed her tighter, though he didn't know what to say to comfort her. Only he understood the full measure of her pain. It was one of the reasons he'd never taken a mate. He still had a decision to make, and he'd been putting it off. But as he listened to the raw edge of agony hidden in her quiet words, he realized the time was coming soon. He'd put it off long enough.

But hastiness was foreign to his nature. There was still

a little time, he guessed, before the life she lived crushed her forever. He could see that coming, just as surely as the lines etched themselves in her young face, as surely as her shoulders grew more slumped and tired beneath the great burden she tried so hard to bear.

But was the alternative any better? He wasn't sure. He wasn't thinking of himself, though the solution he considered would change his life forever just as much as hers. But before he could decide, he had to assure himself it was the right decision—not for him, but for her.

"I wonder what it would be like to live somewhere else," he murmured.

"We'll be moving on next spring, downriver, Mother says."

He grunted again. He knew of the silent conflict between Witch Woman, the Shaman Drinks Deep Waters, and the Chief, and he guessed his mother would have her way as usual. But that wasn't what he meant. He tried to probe further.

"No, I mean live away from the Children. Someplace else."

She glanced at him, puzzled. "You mean, leave the People? But Mother would never allow it." She thought about it. "Well, me at least. You're a man. You could go where you want."

"What if she didn't have a choice in the matter?"

But Sleeps With Spirits couldn't see what he was edging toward, because the full flower of his intention was so foreign to his conservative inclinations that it was almost unthinkable. So she didn't think it, and the moment passed.

"Well, it's impossible, so there's no point in wondering."

He closed his eyes. "No, I suppose not." He waited several moments, then said, "Have you had any new Dreams?"

She was silent for several beats. "No."

Inwardly he relaxed. He would listen to her Dreams, if only because nobody else would, but they made him feel uncomfortable. He listened because he loved her, but even love wasn't enough to instill belief. Still, he was grateful that this fine day wouldn't be clouded by his pretense of belief. In this moment, at least, they could pretend that nothing was wrong, that theirs was only the unremarkable bond of brother and sister, and that the future was bright.

"Shouldn't you take these fine rabbits I've brought and skin them for evening meal?"

"Oh, goodness. I forgot." She climbed to her feet, shading her tender eyes against the glare off the water. "You carry them."

He shouldered his spears and hoisted the rabbits. "Lead on," he said.

They laughed as they raced toward their house. Witch Woman heard them and frowned. She didn't like the sound of laughter. It had never been lucky for her.

3

"We have to do something about Witch Woman," the Chief, Kills Many Buffalo, complained.

"I know," replied the Shaman.

The two men had left the encampment of the River Children and headed slowly south along the banks of the Muddy River, toward the place where the Great Blue River emptied its dark blue flood into the Joining of the Two. The sound of the confluence was ever present, but neither man remarked on it. That low, hissing roar was as much a part of their lives as the air they breathed.

They spoke in hushed tones, as if they feared that even in the scrub pine through which they trudged, there might be hidden ears.

"The woman is a nuisance. And getting worse every day," the Shaman said.

"She defies me openly," the Chief agreed.

"Hah. I wish that was *my* only worry. I think she's plotting to *kill* me."

The two men paused and stared at each other. "Is that possible?" the Chief said.

The Shaman shrugged, then ran his fingers nervously through his shoulder-length gray hair. He grimaced, and a thousand wrinkles sprang into high relief on his face. "Possible? With her, anything is possible. She knows more about the secrets of roots and berries than I do. And you remember what happened to her mate, Runs With Wolves."

Many Buffalo rubbed his blocky chin thoughtfully. Like many of the River Children, he was short and stocky, heavily muscled through the shoulders and chest. Once he'd been a very strong man, but now age had sagged his belly and made his thighs jiggle when he ran. The one thing that set him off from the rest of the Children was his teeth. They seemed too large for his heavy skull. Wide, yellow, and protruding in front, they gave him the somewhat comical look of a beaver. He wore his silver hair tied in a single long braid, which he decorated with bright feathers.

"Nobody knows how Wolves died. All we found were chewed scraps and cracked bones."

"That's my point," the Shaman said. "Nobody knows."

"Well, what do you *think,* then?"

Again the Shaman's fingers plucked nervously at his hair. "The same as you. She murdered him and dragged his body away. The animals did the rest."

The Shaman's left eye was spotted with white patches, and sometimes, when he was deep in thought, it seemed to break loose from its moorings and float at strange angles inside its socket. He could no longer see out of it, but his right eye, though faded, was still as sharp as the brain hidden behind it. "I *know* who my enemy is, Chief. Do you?"

Many Buffalo didn't reply immediately. The two resumed their stroll in silence. Eventually their path took them out of the shelter of the pine woods and brought them to a place of low, rolling hills covered with a tough carpet of dry, springy grass. The sound of rushing water grew louder as they crested each rise. Finally they topped the last elevation and stared down on the Joining of the Two.

It was an awesome sight. They faced south, with the Great Blue River directly before them. It swept majestically out of the northeast, far wider and stronger than the Muddy River into which it poured. Its clear blue waters clove the slower moving flood of the Muddy like a huge spear, staining the brown water and whirling it into ever-changing patterns. They felt the sound of the Joining in the earth, the air, their own bones. The sight never failed to thrill the Chief, though the Shaman paid it little attention. He had dealt with the Spirits of the Two Rivers many times. His concerns dealt with the unreal to a much greater extent than the real thing displayed in front of him, though even he, at times, was moved by the breathtaking spectacle of the Joining.

But whenever the sight began to seem overpowering, he reminded himself how capricious the Spirits of the Two Rivers could be, and further reminded himself how utterly the lives of the Children depended on placating those changeable deities.

That melancholy thought reminded him of other matters. "The Terrible Mother," he said.

"What?"

"I told you I know who my enemy is, and asked if you did. But you didn't answer, so I will. The Terrible Mother is our enemy, Chief. Don't make the mistake of thinking the Witch Woman is our adversary. She is, but only as the tool of the One she serves. *She* is the One who hates the Thunder God, who is the Father of our Children. Witch Woman must be dealt with, but keep in mind the greater issue."

The Chief closed his eyes. This theological dispute had been an undercurrent of discord running through the history of the Children as long as anybody could remember. Who was the more powerful, the Mother or the Father? Who truly ruled the fates of the Children?

He was a straightforward man. Privately, he doubted there was any solution to the endless war between the two Great Spirits. In any event, he had no desire to be sucked onto that battlefield. He had his own problems with Witch Woman, and they weren't religious. They were problems of power, perhaps less far-reaching than the religious question, but to him more important in the day-to-day life of the Children. As, for instance, the simple question: When to take the Children south?

He wanted to do so now, and avoid the winter's bite. Witch Woman wanted to wait till spring. Whose will would win out? The answer to that question concerned him greatly.

It boiled down to an even more simple issue. One of power. Who led the Children. Him or her?

He understood that kind of riddle. Leave the fine points of religious orthodoxy to those better able to understand them. Like his old friend the Shaman.

"I think the greater issues are yours, Deep Waters. You are the Shaman. I am the Chief, and I have other problems."

The Shaman nodded, his left eye rolling wildly. "Good enough. Have you heard what her daughter is saying lately? She's crazy, of course, you can't believe a word she says, but I think she's upsetting a few people with her ravings."

"You mean that malarkey about the Sun coming to take her away?"

"Yes. Have you ever heard anything so ridiculous?"

"Well, like you say, she's crazy. Why do people pay any attention to her?"

The Shaman lifted one scrawny shoulder, let it fall. "It's not so much what she says. It's more that she says anything at all. I mean, Great Father, *look* at her! She's a monster. Stumbling about, ranting at anybody who will listen, that awful pale skin, like a ghost. She frightens people, Chief. Sometimes I think she even scares her own mother."

"Mmph. To tell the truth, she scares me, too, my friend. I wish Witch Woman had drowned her at birth. I think the only reason she didn't was to spite us—to show that the Thunder God had no power over the mysteries of the women."

"You say a thing as sharp as a knife blade, Chief. You surprise me."

"I'm not a total idiot. I leave the religious problems to you, but that doesn't mean I don't have eyes in my head."

"I never said you didn't. None of which helps with our current problem. What *are* we going to do about that devil woman?"

The Chief clicked his front teeth together. It sounded like a small stick snapping. Often it meant that Kills Many Buffalo had made up his mind about something. "I suppose killing her is out of the question?"

"Yes, unless we can make sure nobody knows we had anything to do with it. If we failed, and she found out about it—" He shuddered, thinking of the Witch's terrible powers, all the more frightening because they were the powers of the Terrible Mother, of *women*.

"Perhaps I could arrange something. Perhaps *you* could arrange something." The Chief arched his eyebrows in question. "Witch Woman may know her herbs and roots better than you, but surely you have some knowledge? Perhaps *sufficient* knowledge?"

Deep Waters said, "Yes, I could brew up something fatal. But you forget the rest of what I said. The Spirits are in these things. What if the Terrible Mother protects her? What if my effort fails, and she somehow learns of my attempt? She *does* know about these things, Chief, and that particular knife is sharp, and definitely can cut both ways. I fear the risk. If I didn't, I would have done something long ago."

He shivered. The Witch was an awful opponent, even for one as skilled as he. The thought of her weaving spells and magic against *him* made his bowels feel loose and weak.

The Chief sighed. "Well, it was worth a thought." He glanced about, as if surprised to find himself standing above the Joining. "Look at the sun! We'd better start back, unless we want to stumble through the woods in the dark. Two old men like us, anything could happen." He chuckled, though his mirth sounded strained and uneasy.

Deep Waters nodded. "Yes, she'd like *that*, wouldn't she."

They eyed each other. Then, as one, they turned and started back. This time, their pace was more brisk than it had been. Dark came swiftly in these parts, and fog off the waters.

They were old. They had learned to fear the night.

4

Witch Woman had watched the two old men leave the camp. She sneered faintly and thought to herself, *They're plotting again. Against me, no doubt.*

She waited until their figures dwindled and disappeared in the shadows of the pine woods. She noticed the Shaman glanced over his shoulder several times. She knew who he was looking for, though his glances never quite reached her standing in the shadow of her tent.

He knows who his enemy is, she thought, not without a tinge of approval. He was a pipsqueak, this Drinker of Deep Waters, but in some ways he could be a worthy adversary. She despised him, but she wasn't so stupid she didn't respect him. After all, he served the Thunder God, and *that* was a foe she found more than worthy.

After they were gone she pushed the door flap aside and ducked into her tent. It was dim inside, the only light a single, dust-filled shaft from the smoke hole overhead. She let the flap fall shut and stood a moment, savoring the silence and solitude. Spirits was outside skinning rabbits. Two Spears had wandered off to find his friends. She was alone. But not lonely. The tent was filled with familiar companions in almost infinite variety.

In that corner over there a pile of thin, dried branches, powdery gray in the golden dimness. Burned, they would make an aromatic smoke that sweetened the air for hours. Ground into dust, a small bit helped an old person breathe. A larger amount would cause bloody vomiting.

Hanging from the bent wooden boughs that supported the tent were bundles of carefully tied herbs, their colors faded but still visible; red, dark green, pink, even lavender. Some could cure. Some could kill. Many could do both. She knew which ones they were.

Near the foot of the pile of furs on which she slept were several shiny brown stalks laden with bright orange berries. They were fresh. They exuded a sharp, acidic scent that she knew would mellow as the berries dried.

And though she couldn't see it, she knew that beneath the head of her bed was an old stone knife, still stained with the blood of her departed mate. It was one of her most prized possessions, a talisman of great power. That stone blade had eaten a life, and the Terrible Mother loved such trinkets.

Many, many memories were stored up in the hide walls of the tent, in the bent branches, in the very air. Witch Woman's face grew soft, its blunt, hard lines relaxing as those memories flickered before her, almost seeming to take shape as tangible forms. In her mind she could still feel them, run her calloused fingertips over their texture. In many ways her memories were more real to her than her everyday life. And she had so many of them, for she never forgot anything. Not a taste or a smell, not a slight or a threat or a favor. She remembered all, and acted accordingly.

This alone would have made her formidable; what made her truly terrible was her patience. She repaid all, no matter how long she had to wait for the repayment, and she never forgot.

"You know who is your enemy," she whispered, thinking of the Shaman's nervous glances. "But I know you."

Witch Woman smiled. All things in their own time. But she thought the time for Drinks Deep Waters to know her wrath was coming soon. Her anger, and the anger of the One she served.

In this, at least, she was half right.

5

Sleeps With Spirits also watched the Chief and the Shaman depart, but from where she squatted at the rear of her mother's tent, she could also see Witch Woman, and the look on her face was frightening. Spirits shivered at the way her mother's expression revealed the slow, cold rage locked beneath her craggy features.

Her slender hands paused in their work. The half-skinned rabbit fell into her lap. Her eyes slipped out of focus. And the *thing* happened.

That was how she thought of it: the *thing*. She had no words to name, even to herself, the sensation that sometimes overcame her when she stared into another's face. Her vision would blur, then darken into a flame-shot haze, while words and sounds hammered into her skull. It had taken her a long time to understand that these sounds weren't real. Just as no one would believe her Dreams, no one could hear these jumbled cacophonies either. No one but her.

She froze, the bloody carcass in her lap forgotten. Blinded, her eyes moved blankly back and forth, a motion like the shifting of vast, empty waters. The *thing* began with the sound of distant thunder.

Boom, boom. Boom, boom, boom.

At least at first it *sounded* like thunder. It grew louder, though, and now she thought of her own heartbeat, but magnified a hundred times.

Boom-ba-boom! Boom-ba-boom!

Then the growling began, a throaty, grinding sound almost too low to make out beneath the pounding overlay. The growling slowly rose in tone, and as it speeded up, it became distinguishable as words.

Sleeps With Spirits turned her face toward her mother as a sunflower seeks the sun. Her mouth gradually fell open. A leak of silver drool slid down her chin. Her eyes were open; they rocked back and forth like waves on a lake.

Inside her skull the words hammered distinctly, each one feeling to her like a single blow, repeated endlessly.

Kill. Kill. Kill. Kill. Kill.

When the seizure passed, her mother was gone. She felt faint, feverish, sweaty. She pawed at her forehead. Her fingers left a smear of bright blood that she neither felt nor noticed.

She looked down into her lap and almost screamed at the gory, half-skinned mess there.

Surely that wasn't Mother? she pleaded with herself. *It couldn't have been her.*

But she knew better. Something hot and sticky rose into her throat, then subsided, leaving behind a bitter, gagging sensation. She hated it when the *thing* occurred. She didn't understand it, but she believed it just as she believed her own Dreams. Of course, she never told anyone, not even Two Spears.

It was her own terrible secret that she was somehow privy to the terrible secrets of others. She didn't want to know these things, to suffer these aural visions, yet somehow she did.

A curse.

Shaking, she scooped up the carcass and tried to work, but the denial remained.

Not Mother?

Yes. Mother.

Kill.

CHAPTER NINE

1

Gotha the Shaman shook his head and wrinkled his nose. The thick, greasy smell of the funeral pyre still clung to his long robe. It would be a long time going. He guessed that before the stench was gone, new, though similar, stinks would take its place.

He was up early. The sky overhead still had a gray-silver cast, the thin twilight between dawn and full sunrise. The breeze that blew softly down from the top of the Shield Wall ruffled his unbound hair. White strands danced gently across his face, tickling his nose. He sneezed suddenly, covered his mouth, looked up.

There were a few women about, but the men still slept. He raised his head as a baby suddenly began to squall. A moment later another joined it. So many babies. The Green Valley was a rich place, and the Three Tribes grew fat here.

Gotha had no way of knowing that others had once mused in a similar vein, before the Goddess had turned the vale into a charnel house with a single puff of Her plague-ridden breath. Perhaps, even if he had known, he wouldn't have drawn the obvious comparison. The Goddess was gone. Her vengeance was no longer to be feared. Or so he believed.

"Shaman."

He turned. "Chief. Good morning."

Wolf came slowly toward him. His bald, liver-spotted skull glowed in the silver light. He limped painfully and rubbed his right thigh as he approached. "Demon blasted joints." He placed one finger on the side of his nose and blew, hard. A glob of snot obligingly flew from his clogged nasal passages.

"Sore this morning?"

"You're the Shaman," Wolf grumped. "You've got eyes, don't you?"

Gotha grinned. He liked the old man. They'd grown old together, and though once mortal enemies, now were closer than most Chiefs and Shamans ever got. Gotha liked to think they understood each other. Perhaps they did.

"I've got better than that. If you'll wait till I brew some tea."

"One of your disgusting potions?"

"It'll soothe your joints. Nothing will soothe your disposition. You've turned into a nasty old man, Wolf."

Now Wolf grinned. "Look who showed me the way, Shaman Smooth Tongue."

"All right, we're both nasty old men. Do you want some tea or not?"

"Make your Demon-ridden bug piss, Shaman. If you say it will help, I'll drink it."

"It'll help. Sit on that bench there, while I get this fire going."

Wolf lowered his aching bones onto the well-worn log slab. He remembered when this wood was fresh and full of splinters, and Old Magic had squatted just about where Gotha now labored to get his fire going. He'd been a boy then, and the World was different. He wasn't at all sure he liked this new World. The passage of the Gods made him uneasy. He hadn't witnessed Their departure, and though he trusted the reports given him by his daughter and sister and Gotha, sometimes, in his heart, he still thought They were in the World. How else to explain that little had changed?

The winds still blew, the snow still fell, and the beasts still roamed across the wide steppe. Men still hunted and women still gathered, and children still came to the People. And if the babies didn't come from the Gods, where *did* they come from?

"Demons take it," the Shaman muttered.

Wolf chuckled. "You miss Moon Face, don't you?"

"Why do you say that?"

"Because evidently you've forgotten how to strike a fire. He did that sort of thing for you, didn't he?"

Gotha threw him an irritated glance. "Chief, I still remember how to use flints." He glanced down doubtfully. "I shouldn't have let this hearth go cold, though."

"Getting forgetful in your old age?"

Gotha ignored him and gritted his teeth. Suddenly he leaned forward. "Ah!" He blew on the tiny spark that had lodged in a handful of moss. A few moments later he had a flame, and then a small fire. He fed twigs to it.

"Yes, I miss Moon Face," he admitted after the water bag was properly positioned over the new blaze. He came back and joined Wolf on the bench. "A good apprentice is hard to find. He would do what I wanted before I even knew I wanted it."

Wolf bent over, plucked a stalk of grass, put it between his lips, and chewed. "I wonder where he is!"

"Who? Moon Face?"

"And Rising Sun."

The Shaman squinted at the rim of sky now turning blue above the Shield Wall. "I don't know."

"No Dreams? No Visions or messages from the Spirits?"

Gotha shook his head.

"Huh. What kind of Shaman are you?"

"Not a very good one, perhaps."

Wolf cut his eyes at him. "You didn't used to be so modest."

"I didn't used to know as much as I do now."

"Is that supposed to make sense?"

Gotha sighed. "I find the more I know, the more I understand how little I *do* know. I used to think I had an answer for everything—or at least the Gods would give me the answer. Now . . ." He shrugged. "I don't know."

Wolf chuckled again, this time from deep in his chest.

"You're getting old, my friend. Younger than me, but still old. You used to believe. Now you doubt. It's a sign of age."

"You, too?"

Wolf nodded. "Maybe because we've seen more than the young ones, and have more time to think about what we've seen. Now I consider questions that have no answers, where before I didn't even know the question existed."

This rambling began to interest Gotha. Sometimes Wolf could still surprise him. But perhaps that was to be expected? The Chief was, after all, of the blood of Maya, and that was always a surprising line.

"What sort of questions concern you now, great Chief, these questions without answers?" His tone was light and mocking.

But Wolf's expression turned somber. "Oh, I don't know. Perhaps you can answer one for me, from the well of your great knowledge and experience. From what you *do* know, as opposed to what you admit you don't."

Gotha nodded. "Ask away."

"Fine. Where do babies come from?"

Without thinking, Gotha said, "From the Gods."

"But the Gods are gone. Yet babies still come. Even more than before, as a matter of fact."

Gotha stared at him. "Well, uh. Babies come from the bellies of women."

"Of course they do. But who *puts* them there? For instance, who put Rising Sun into White Moon's belly?"

The Shaman stared some more. "The Turtle?" he finally ventured, though there wasn't any conviction in his tone.

Wolf snorted. "You've seen the Turtle. My daughter and my sister, even my son-in-law. But I haven't. In fact, I never even heard of the Turtle before you came along."

"You're not suggesting I made It up?"

Wolf shrugged. "No, of course not. You would have had to fool Maya somehow. And, my friend, though I think you're crafty, I don't think you're *that* crafty."

Gotha's lips quirked. "Thanks for the compliment. I think."

"Anyway," Wolf continued, "that's my second question. Who—or what—is the Turtle? And why should I care?"

Gotha recoiled in mock horror. "You almost sound as if you don't believe in anything, Chief. What kind of an example would that set for the young men?"

"Piffle. You're dodging now. Answer the question."

Gotha closed his eyes, opened them. "I don't know," he said simply.

"Ah. That's *two* questions you can't—or won't—answer. And since I'm a nasty old man, just like you, I think 'can't' is the proper explanation. Would you like a third question?"

Gotha shifted on his bench. A slow worm of irritation was starting to work in him. Wolf was an old friend, but the Shaman was a proud man. And even old friends might overstep the bounds.

"Not really," he said. He looked over at the fire, noted that steam was rising from the leather water bag. "Sit still. I've got to make your tea."

He ducked into the Spirit House, conscious of Wolf's eyes on his back. In a way it was an ignominious retreat, but the questions Wolf asked only mirrored the things he asked himself in the depths of his sometimes sleepless nights.

He found the right herbs and returned to brew the medicinal tea in silence. When he had finished, he rejoined Wolf on the bench. "One more question."

"What will happen with my grandson?"

This time Gotha didn't hesitate at all. "He will inherit the World."

"And what does that mean?"

Gotha smiled. "I said, only one more question."

Wolf made a contemptuous sound deep in his throat, then spat into the fire. "Yes, I suppose that sounds better than 'I don't know.' "

"You've become a cynic, I think. Do you believe in anything anymore?"

Wolf laughed out loud. "Of course. I believe the People will continue to be stupid and wayward and loving and crazy and break my heart. I believe the grass will grow and the wind will blow. I believe in the Spirits."

"But not the Gods?"

Wolf shook his head sadly. "No, not the Gods. Not anymore."

The Shaman stood. "I think you should drink your tea. It will make you feel better."

"I'm old," Wolf replied. "Nothing will make me feel better."

To this, the Shaman Gotha chose not to reply. Too often of late, he felt exactly the same way. Besides, he didn't want to further disillusion Wolf about the Spirits. The Gods had made the World and the Spirits in it, but the Mother and Father were gone. Nothing was left to rule Their Children, the Spirits. Perhaps that was why Gotha felt the World itself was spinning slowly out of control. He thought of the stench caught in his robe, and sighed heavily. The oily reek was all that remained of Humped Wolf.

He swung the pole away from the fire and sniffed the steam rising from the bag. "It's ready," he announced.

He brought a pair of wooden bowls from the Spirit House and scooped out tea for both of them. Wolf took his portion and held it cupped between his palms, inhaling the fragrant aroma. "Smells good."

"Drink it."

"It's supposed to help my aching joints?"

"Yes."

"Why are you having some?"

Gotha sighed. "Because my joints ache, too, you old fool."

"Ah," Wolf said. "You hide it better."

"Moon Face knew."

Wolf nodded. He sipped, then smiled. "He'll come back.'

Gotha looked away, his expression troubled. "I hope so."

Torn rags of white cirrus slowly stretched across the sky. Though still in the shadow of the Shield Wall and the high bulwark of the Cliff Walls, Home Camp came slowly alive in the bright morning light. Infants awoke crying for their mothers' tits. Next the youngest children brawled from the tents, shouting and calling to each other as they raced aimlessly along the paths that wound among the many houses. Next came the women, blinking sleep from their eyes, many with babies dangling from their breasts. Finally the men, scratching themselves, sniffing the humid morning air, stumbled out to display their morning erections while they sought a suitable place to piss—usually into the stream or the slick rocks of the Jumble.

Soon many fires sent mingled feathers of white smoke into the sky. The smell of roasting meat and boiling greens made Gotha's nose twitch.

Wolf noticed. "Come eat with us, Shaman," he said. "White Moon is a good cook. And one more mouth to feed certainly won't be noticed in my house."

"Thank you, Chief." Gotha was too proud to admit he hadn't been looking forward to his own cooking for breakfast. Moon Face had taken care of that, too. The Shaman grinned sourly. He'd always thought of his apprentice as a talented, but somewhat bumbling, potential successor. "You don't know how much you'll miss them till they're gone," he remarked.

"Yes. I miss Rising Sun, too."

They both smiled at that, content in their understanding of each other. Wolf knew the Shaman could just as easily be talking about the Gods. Perhaps he was.

Perhaps I am, too, he thought. "Let's go find our breakfast," he said.

2

White Moon was trying to do six things at once. In her arm she cradled her youngest daughter, only recently weaned from the tit, while she turned a haunch of meat that dripped juices into the hearthfire. Laughing Fox, Rising Sun's youngest brother, only six years old, was screaming in red-faced anger at his next older brother, Crawling Lizard. They were fighting over a stick-and-feather toy bird their father, Morning Star, had given them the day before.

"Take that water bag off the fire!" she told her eldest daughter, Glowing Star, who was trying to separate the two brawling boys. The rest of the children, drawn by the smells of breakfast, added to the clamor.

Her mate, Morning Star, stood aloof from it all, grinning.

Men! she thought. It wasn't the first time she'd had that exasperated perception. She loved her mate—and what a struggle that had been!—but at times she almost saw things as her niece, Running Deer, did. Even though she thought Running Deer, barely out of the first flush of girlhood, was too extreme in her views. Not that it mattered much. Life itself would smooth the sharp edges from her sister's daughter, as it always did. Though her niece *was* a strange one, it had to be admitted.

She glanced across the fire and saw Wolf approaching with Gotha, the two old men arm in arm, chuckling at something. Wolf's pink-red gums flashed in the morning light. Only a few snaggles of teeth left there. Her father limped along, though he didn't seem to be in as much pain as usual. Maybe it was a good sign. She'd been worried about him of late. Sometimes she heard him moaning in his sleep.

What a change from the great warrior-leader she remembered from her childhood. She could still see the fire in her father's eyes as he'd faced the traitors Sharp Knife and Raging Bison in battle!

Those had been mighty days, and her father mighty in them. Now he was shrunken and bald. His joints gave him constant agony. When he ate, he gummed his food more than chewed it. But even now, she sometimes saw a flickering ghost of that flame in his eyes, though Sharp Knife was long dead and Raging Bison changed beyond recognition.

"Hello, Shaman," she called. "Will you join us for breakfast?" But before Gotha could reply, she turned her head at an especially loud shriek. "Star! *Do something* about them!"

Chuckling, her mate deigned to take a hand in the battle between his sons, and pried Crawling Lizard and Laughing Fox apart.

White Moon handed the infant to one of the older girls and spread her arms. "Sit anywhere." She grinned. "Anywhere you can find space, that is."

The Shaman put on his fiercest face. "Make way," he growled at the children. "Make way for the Shaman, or I will"—his eyes twinkled—"turn you into *frogs*!"

White Moon laughed at the stricken expressions that appeared on the suddenly silent faces. "Turn them into fish, please. That would be even quieter."

Gotha grinned. "How are you this morning, my dear?"

"Busy," she replied. "And you?"

"Old. Tired."

She glanced at Wolf. "My father woke you this morning? I heard him leave. He was muttering to himself when he left."

"The old," Wolf said with spurious dignity, "often speak to themselves. It's a habit. We speak to the wisest one handy."

"Well, O wise one, breakfast will be ready in a moment."

"Good," Wolf said, and rubbed his hands together. Near toothless he might be, but there was nothing wrong with his appetite.

Morning Star placed Crawling Lizard on the other side of the hearth, gave his naked bottom a hearty thwack, and said, "Now you *sit* there!" The boy, cowed both by the admonition and the fearsome presence of the Shaman, put his thumb into his mouth and stared up with round, silent eyes.

Morning Star came over and sat down next to his father-in-law. "Any news?" he whispered.

Wolf shook his head. "Nothing," he replied. "The Shaman knows no more than we do."

Star glanced at Gotha. "Nothing?"

"No," Gotha replied.

Star let out a long sigh. "I hope they're all right. It's been a week now." He paused, a troubled look on his face. "I Dreamed of wolves last night."

Gotha raised his eyebrows. "Was your son in the Dream?"

"No. Just wolves. A pack of them. They were hunting . . . something. I don't know what. A strange Dream. Wolves don't pack up in summer. Not usually."

Gotha found his interest piqued. He knew well Morning Star's special abilities, and anything he said that dealt with the Spirits of beasts was worthy of attention. "Come sit by me," he said.

Obligingly, Morning Star shifted his place.

"Tell me everything you remember about this Dream," Gotha said. He kept his voice low and glanced meaningfully at White Moon. Morning Star nodded his understanding.

"It was a strange Dream," he said again. He seemed hesitant. Gotha nodded encouragement.

"Well, it seemed I stood on top of a low hill. It was dark, but I sensed flowing water nearby. A river, I think. Then a storm came up, lightning flashing, thunder roaring."

"And then?"

"I stood in the dark and the wind and heard wolves howling. A lot of wolves. Then I saw them. They came up the hill and gathered around me, but they couldn't see me." He shrugged, apologetic. "You know how Dreams are."

"Yes. Go on."

"Yet I could sense them, what was inside them."

Again Morning Star paused. Any discussion of his own special power always seemed to make him uncomfortable.

"What did you sense?"

"They were hunting. Something . . . I tried to understand what it was, but all I could feel was a spark. A spark of light. But wolves don't hunt sparks. They're afraid of fire."

Gotha let his breath out slowly. Morning Star's eyes had gone distant, as if even now he stood upon that hill, surrounded by savage animals.

"What happened next?"

Morning Star shivered. "There was an especially large

bolt of lightning. It lit up the whole sky, turned it bright as day. The wolves howled and ran away. Toward the river, I think."

He turned. "That's all. The Dream faded then, but I woke up frightened."

Gotha rubbed his chin. His snowy hair, still unbound, shimmered around his shoulders. "Nothing else? Just that?"

Morning Star placed his palms on his temples and pushed, as if he could somehow squeeze more recollections from his skull. "Well . . ."

"Yes?"

"I'm not sure about this at all. But I thought I heard something. It sounded like a cry or a scream. But it could have just been the storm, the wind."

"A scream?"

"Yes. A woman. Screaming . . ." He shook his head suddenly. "But I'm not sure."

Gotha glanced at Wolf. The Chief's expression was somber. Anything Morning Star Dreamed about the beasts who were his special province was not to be taken lightly.

"What do you make of it?" Wolf wondered.

"I don't know," Gotha replied, ruefully aware he'd been saying that a lot already this morning. For a moment he felt unbelievably helpless. Once he would have turned to the Gods for help. But who could he turn to now?

Then he brightened. Wolves had Spirits. There was a wolf Spirit, in fact, and he thought such things still lived in the World. The Spirits were his province. Perhaps he could explore Morning Star's Dream more thoroughly.

"Let me think about it," he said.

Wolf nodded. He wasn't reassured. Wolves, a storm, the scream of a woman. It didn't sound like anything that boded well.

"It's ready," White Moon announced.

Relieved at the interruption, the men turned their thoughts to the hearth and breakfast. White Moon was a good cook. Everybody knew that.

3

White Moon directed her daughters as they cleaned up after the breakfast. Gnawed bones from the haunch and half-chewed stalks of greenery littered the earth in front of the hearth. The girls gathered this detritus and carried it to the midden behind the house. She picked up her baby daughter and held her to her breast, which was still swollen with milk. The tiny lips fastened to her nipple and sucked softly. A great warmth flowed through her.

Sometimes, she wondered what had happened to the rebellious girl who had loved the traitor Sharp Knife enough to throw over her family, her People, and her mighty heritage in order to run away with him. Oh, she could remember that younger version of herself well enough, but it seemed as if she recalled another person, one she could scarcely imagine now.

She glanced at Morning Star, who sat with Wolf and the Shaman, their heads together as they conversed. They spoke softly, so that she couldn't make out what they said. Their faces weren't happy, though, and a sudden pang of fear struck her.

"Husband?" she called.

Morning Star looked up. The other two sat straighter, with guilty looks on their faces, as if they'd been caught at something.

"Is anything wrong?" she asked.

"No," her mate said. "We're just talking."

"About what?"

Now Wolf spoke. "Nothing of concern to a woman," he said brusquely, as if that should be answer enough for her.

A waver of resentment swept through her. It was a different kind of rebellion than she'd known as a girl. Then she hadn't known anything. Now she knew too much.

But she bit her lip, and swallowed the first reply she would have spat at him. "Is it about Rising Sun?"

"No," Gotha said and shook his head. The other two nodded in agreement.

"No, nothing about him," Morning Star said.

She stared at her mate. He, at least, was telling the truth. But she thought she'd heard a lie in the Shaman's voice. What was going on here?

She shifted her stare to Gotha, who looked away from it. Proof enough, she thought, and shifted her daughter to her hip. The baby let out a weak squall at being deprived of the tit, but White Moon paid no attention. She was just starting to ask another question when a strident voice interrupted her.

"Morning Star! Oh, there you are."

She turned to see her sister, Bending Tree, bustle up to the hearth. Bending Tree was a year younger, but she'd married earlier than White Moon. It was her eldest daughter, Running Deer, whom White Moon had been thinking about earlier.

Annoyed at being interrupted, White Moon said sharply, "Yes, what is it, sister?" In her time she'd endured many hours of Bending Tree's rambling complaints, for the woman loved to talk of the woes her daughter caused her. White Moon supposed it would be more of the same this morning. Hadn't she just recently heard some fresh rumor about her niece?

Bending Tree, so named in her girlhood because of her slender, supple figure, had turned into a lumbering round lump, her cheeks red as berries. Moreover, she'd grown into something of a shrew, forever complaining about not only her troublesome daughter, but her lazy husband, the rest of her ungrateful children, even the Chief, who was her father. Of course, none of this was voiced outside the circles of the women, but even so, White Moon found the continual complaints wearying.

As if she's the only one with troubles, White Moon thought resentfully.

Oblivious to her chilly reception, Bending Tree waddled around the hearth, panting from her exertions.

"Have you seen Running Deer?" she demanded.

Startled, White Moon drew back from the vehement question. "Why, no. I haven't. Not for days now."

And that was strange, come to think on it. White Moon knew her niece confided in her far more than she did her querulous, whining mother. It *had* been an unusually long time for her not to visit.

"Well," Bending Tree wheezed, "nobody else has, either."

White Moon eyed her sister calmly. "Sit down, catch your breath. You look ready to burst."

She caught Bending Tree's pudgy fingers in her own and led her to the bench on the other side of the hearth, away from the men.

"Sit, sister. Here. Hold Baby Girl." She pried her infant daughter's lips from her tit and handed the squirming bundle over. Bending Tree, with the reflexes of a born mother, gathered the baby immediately to her own abundant bosom and began to make soft, cooing noises. After several moments she looked up. Some of the bright red was fading from her cheeks. "She's so darling!" she breathed. "You haven't named her yet?"

White Moon shrugged. "Not yet. She's too young. All she does is sleep, squall, and suck. But I suppose you could call any baby Sleeping Sucker, or Crying Sleeper, or whatever."

Bending Tree, who possessed no sense of humor whatever, said, "But those are terrible names. Who would name a child something like that?"

"Not me," White Moon said ruefully. "Now. Tell me about Running Deer. What do you mean, nobody's seen her? Has she run away again?"

Bending Tree joggled Baby Girl, then set her on her lap. "I don't *know*," she replied. "You know how she is. So strange. But when she ran away that time, she was only gone overnight. She turned up the next afternoon. Of course, I beat her soundly for scaring us all to death." She smiled grimly.

"But she's been missing seven days now." Suddenly Bending Tree's fat cheeks crumpled. Tears welled in her black eyes. "I'm so *worried*. *Anything* could have happened."

White Moon sat back. This was serious, then. She glanced across the hearth at the men, who were still conversing in low, intent tones.

"Think carefully, sister. Are you sure it's been that

many days? Perhaps you just didn't notice her around? She comes and goes, you know. Perhaps she's staying with one of her friends. Somebody in one of the other camps."

"You ask me if *I* know? I'm her *mother.* I'm the one who has to put up with her outlandish habits. But does anybody pay any attention to me? Of course not. And how is she supposed to find a decent mate, when no man with any sense would ever put up with—"

"Sister."

Bending Tree blinked, startled by the undercurrent of disapproval in her sister's interjection. She'd forgotten that icy streak in her eldest sibling, had even forgotten that White Moon had once been a Keeper of the Stone. The tone of that single word reminded her like a dash of cold water in her face.

"What?" she whispered, a trace of fear in her voice.

"You do run on. Try to get hold of yourself." White Moon narrowed her beautiful green and blue eyes. "Have you looked at her things? Is anything missing?"

"I don't know."

"Well, did you *look*?"

"I don't—I think so—I can't *remember*!" This last came out as a half-suppressed wail, and Baby Girl abruptly began to cry in lusty sympathy. Bending Tree looked down. "Oh, dear. Now look." She bent over and began to coo vigorously in the infant's ear.

White Moon rolled her eyes. Her sister was a dear, sweet woman whose skull seemed stirred by whatever vagrant breeze was in her vicinity. She was good-hearted, but no one would ever accuse her of unwomanly intelligence.

Nevertheless, some sort of intelligence seemed called for here. White Moon made up her mind. She stood. "Come on," she said briskly. "Let's go to your house. I want to see for myself."

They handed Baby Girl over to one of her sisters. She offered no explanation to the men, who equally ignored her departure. *Once,* White Moon thought, *they didn't dare ignore me.*

But that was a long time ago. The World had changed

since then. And White Moon, for one, wasn't convinced all the changes had been for the better.

4

The men watched the women go with varied expressions of relief on their faces. Wolf loved his second eldest daughter, but thought she had the mind of a flea and could hardly abide her constant rambling complaints.

Morning Star well knew the keenness his wife kept hidden, like a knife concealed beneath a bed, and didn't want her to pick up on his worries about their eldest son, and what his Dream might mean in regards to Rising Sun's journey.

Gotha had his own memories of women. Half a lifetime with his mother, the Crone, had left a deep residue of fear and distrust of the other sex that he sometimes found hard to control. White Moon, though he liked and respected her, seemed to trigger that residue more than any other.

Once the two were gone, all three men suddenly sat straighter and began to talk in more normal tones.

"I realize you have to consult the Spirits, Shaman," Wolf said, "but surely you must have *some* thoughts about my son-in-law's strange Dream?"

Gotha spoke slowly. "I don't want to jump to hasty conclusions," he said at last. "It may only be a Dream. But certain things—the spark Morning Star sensed, the screaming woman—" He shook his head. "I just don't know. If it's an omen of some kind, it doesn't seem a good one."

Morning Star nodded his head reluctantly. "But Rising Sun wasn't in my Dream. Surely that must mean something, as well?"

Gotha clicked his teeth in exasperation. It was all very well, in the cynical, half-mocking camaraderie between two old men such as himself and Wolf, to plead ignorance at every turn. But this was different. This was a real problem, not some philosophical ramble.

Gotha well knew that if a Shaman had any value to his

People, at least a great part of that value rested in his
ability to unriddle the secrets of Dreams and Spirits. But
given the fact that he really *didn't* understand the meaning
of Morning Star's Dream, he also knew that an encouraging lie was often better than a disheartening truth.

What that might mean for the truth of religion Gotha
didn't know, nor did he much care. For, over time, all
Shamans became liars, and Gotha no less than any other.

He put on what he thought of as his "Shaman Face,"
an expression he hoped denoted deep wisdom and hidden,
though revealable, truth. "Of course it has a meaning," he
began, "but before I tell you what it is, I must consult
with—" He looked up, startled by the approaching com-
motion.

A single woman, thin as a stick, her eyes wide and
staring, reached the far side of the hearth and burst into
tears.

*"Oh, Shaman, there you are! You must hurry, come
with me! My husband, something's wrong with him—"*

Gotha made it a point to know at least the names of
every male in the Green Valley, but the names of the more
numerous women were beyond him. He relied on Moon
Face's capacious memory for such minor details, but
Moon Face wasn't here.

He stood and waved one hand vaguely, as if brushing
away a fly. "What is it . . . woman? What's wrong with
your husband?"

"I don't know!"

It seemed a morning for distraught women. White
Moon had evidently taken the first such visitor in hand,
but this one would be his to deal with. He sighed heavily,
but in truth he was relieved at the interruption. He had no
more answers to give the Chief or Morning Star, and further talk would only reveal that poverty to them. And
when he had dealt with this, whatever it was, he did intend to consult with the Spirits, if he could.

Particularly the wolf Spirit.

"Very well," he said. "I will come."

He turned and half bowed at the Chief. "We will speak
again."

Wolf nodded.

Gotha aimed his gaze at Morning Star. "If you have any more Dreams, or visions, or *anything*"—he paused, then nodded sharply to himself—"tell me right away."

"I will," Morning Star agreed.

"Shaman!"

"Yes, woman, I'm coming."

He barely noticed the way the stink in his robes seemed to rise into his nostrils as he strode away. His mind was on other things. But not for long.

5

White Moon knelt beside a jumble of hide and fur and poked her fingers into the nest of small bags and sundry items next to it. "Her clothes all seem to be here."

She picked up a shirt made of caribou hide tanned thin and soft as melted fat and nodded approvingly at the stitching. "Running Deer does good work," she said.

But Bending Tree, who had sunk to her knees next to her sister, ignored the compliment and began to sniff loudly. "No, look!" She gestured wildly at an empty space at the back of the bed. "Her winter coat, the thick one. It's gone."

Now the fat woman bent forward and began to scrabble wildly in the piles. "And her best shirt, and the extra pair of boots I made her not a moon ago. Gone!"

She burst into loud sobbing.

White Moon's private opinion—given her perhaps more thorough knowledge of her niece's changeable disposition—was that things weren't yet as disastrous as Bending Tree seemed to think. She put her arm across her sister's broad back and hugged her tightly.

"There, there," she soothed. "It will be all right."

"That *girl*!" Bending Tree wailed.

"I know, I know," White Moon whispered in her ear. *Did I cause my mother this kind of grief?* she wondered to herself. *Probably ...*

She relinquished her sister and squatted back on her haunches, eyeing the disarray of Running Deer's empty bed. "She was in a hurry, it looks like," she mused.

Bending Tree wiped her nose. "It always looks like that."

"Well, at least you know some clothes are missing. She wasn't snatched away in the middle of the night. It looks to me like she planned to go. I guess that's something."

"*Where* could she go?"

White Moon smiled faintly as she recalled her own midnight departure from the Valley with Sharp Knife. But that had been different. That had been love, or so she'd thought at the time. Still, the idea might have some application to this situation.

"Has Running Deer shown any interest in one of the young men?"

Bending Tree's snuffles dried up almost instantly at the impossibility of the suggestion. "Huh. *Her?*"

"I know. But anything's possible. Perhaps she's fallen in love with somebody but kept it secret. My niece likes her secrets."

Bending Tree made a face. "If she had, she certainly didn't let on to me. You know how she is." A flicker of resentment creased her expression. "What about you? She always talked more to you than she did to me."

White Moon shook her head slowly. "I haven't spoken to her in two hands of days or so. I was just thinking about that, in fact."

"What did you talk about? Did she give any sign?"

"No, not that I remember. We talked about Rising Sun, mostly. About his journey."

But Bending Tree had grown up with her sister, and though they weren't as close as they'd once been, the younger woman still knew how to read her sister's voice.

"You're not telling me something. What is it?"

"I don't know . . . Now that I think on it, your daughter showed unusually sharp interest in the doings of my son. She asked a lot of questions." White Moon pushed a lock of black hair away from her face. "I didn't think much of it then, but . . ."

"They've run off together!"

White Moon stared. "Oh, no! Oh, no, sister! Whatever gives you that idea?"

Stubbornly refusing to be crushed, Bending Tree said, "Well, what else, then? Rising Sun leaves, and at the same time my daughter disappears. What could be plainer?"

But White Moon shook her head, obviously trying to keep from laughing in her sister's face. "Dear, they're cousins. They've known each other all their lives. If something were going on between them, don't you think I'd know?" Left unspoken was the observation that White Moon knew both her own child's mind, and that of her niece, better than Bending Tree herself did.

It was true, but it would have been cruel to say so.

Bending Tree evidently sensed the unspoken reproach, however. Her thick lips screwed into a defiant pout. "Well, what *did* happen to her, then?"

White Moon spread her hands. "Who knows? She's strange, that girl, and willful. There are hunting parties, families, and even small clans going in and out of the Valley all the time. It's summer, after all. Perhaps she ran off with one of them. Perhaps she's simply off by herself, somewhere in the Valley. There's still a lot of empty space hereabouts."

"But a whole week or more!"

"I know. It's very worrisome. But until we know more, I don't think we should think the worst."

Another thought grabbed Bending Tree's attention. "She's hurt. She fell off a rock or drowned in one of the lakes! Oh, Mother—"

"Stop it! We don't know. But I think maybe the men should look for her. There might be something to what you say. I'll talk to my father. You tell the other women. They can keep an eye out when they hunt roots."

Bending Tree placed one hand on her huge breast, as if her heart might be about to explode. "I'm so worried," she said.

White Moon patted her hand. "I know, dear. But don't worry. If she's in the Valley, the men will find her. If not, then I'm sure she's run off with one of the hunting families."

"You think so?"

"I'm sure of it."

But she wasn't. Not at all.

Maybe it was Maya's blood. They all shared it, and many of the women in whose veins it flowed had been willful. Her not the least.

And despite her own past, White Moon, once Keeper of the Stone, could not decide whether that blood was a blessing or a curse.

"Come, dear, let's get started."

Bending Tree allowed herself to be led from the house. She paused and glanced forlornly at the empty bed. She feared it would stay empty forever.

In time, she would learn her fear was not unfounded.

CHAPTER TEN

1

For the first time in her life, Running Deer experienced the weird, whippy sensation of utter and complete confusion. *What in Mother's name am I doing here? I have absolutely no idea at all.*

She stared helplessly into Rising Sun's angry, questioning face. Then she gave him the only logical reply she could think of. She took a giant step forward, grabbed his ears in both her hands, and pulled his lips down to hers and pressed them there as hard as she could.

"Wh! Ahg! What—let me go!"

Spluttering and choking, he finally managed to get himself disentangled. Now she saw the same confusion on his face. The effect was so comical it was all she could do not to laugh, but she managed to restrain herself. Somehow, this didn't seem like either the time or the place to let him know just how ludicrous he looked.

He did, however, still look angry.

"You—what! What are you! You! What do you!"

"You're not making any sense, cousin," she said. "Maybe you should try to slow down."

His eyes grew round. Waves of red bloomed, receded, bloomed again on his high cheekbones. He started to speak, stopped. Turned slowly, flapping one arm in a helpless gesture.

"Wolves," he finally said.

"Yes," she agreed. "Dead wolves, thank the Mother. And thank *you*, Rising Sun."

He turned back to stare at her again. Though she still felt the urge to let out the unholy glee bubbling inside her, she understood that right at this moment everything she'd hoped for was teetering in the balance. The next few instants would tell the tale. She took a deep breath.

"I followed you."

His mouth opened, then snapped shut.

"Yes," she continued. "I've been following you ever since you and Moon Face"—she tipped her head toward the little apprentice, who seemed to have been struck dumb—"left the Green Valley."

Rising Sun shook his head sharply, as if something inside was rattling around. Now he took a deep breath. Then another. After the third windy exhalation, he seemed to grow calmer. "But why?" he finally got out.

"Why is another question," she said briskly. "I already answered your first one. What I'm doing here is I followed you here. Now I have a question for you. Where are you going?"

Whatever he was, Rising Sun was also a male of his time and culture. Every word she spoke seemed to increase the expression of disbelief on his face.

Men, she thought. *Amazing how fragile they are.*

"I can't tell you that!" he blurted. "Anyway, it isn't the question. What I want to know is—"

She raised one hand and said calmly, "Oh, but it is the question, cousin. I need to know where you're going. How else can I follow you?"

Rising Sun wiped his forehead with his palm. He was sweating a lot. She didn't think it all came from his recent exertions. *"Are you crazy!"*

"Well," she said reasonably, "I'm not the one acting like it right now. Am I?"

Helplessly, he turned to Moon Face. Moon Face jumped as if somebody had jabbed him in the butt with an arrow. "Don't look at me," he protested. "She's *your* cousin." He paused, his expression growing thoughtful.

"We could drown her, I suppose." And glanced hopefully at the river.

For a moment Running Deer thought her cousin was considering the suggestion seriously, for his own gaze cut from her to the water, then back again. But his initial shock seemed to be lessening. In fact, a tiny smile tugged at his lips.

"Well, yes," he agreed. "But I don't usually kill things I don't want to eat." He looked at Moon Face. "Unless you want to eat her." He eyed the apprentice's round belly appreciatively. "You might, mightn't you?"

"Gods, *no!*"

Things were getting out of hand, and nothing had been decided yet. Running Deer knew she needed to press on, while the cookfire was still hot, as it were.

"Sorry, I don't feel like being dinner today. I've already almost had the experience, and I didn't like it much." Her gaze slid toward the wolf carcasses piled about. Rising Sun's glance followed hers.

He shook his head. He seemed to discover the spear he still held in his hands, and planted it butt first in the soft, wet earth. "You almost got me killed."

"I almost got me killed. Did I say thank you yet?"

"Yes."

Then the ghost of his previous anger returned. His eyes flashed. "You stupid girl! Do you know how much trouble you've caused?"

"I haven't caused any trouble." She looked at the wolves again. "Well, hardly any."

"A lot of trouble," he continued. "Not only this, but now I've got to take you back to the Valley, at least a couple of days march each way, and—"

"No."

"What?"

"No. A simple word. It means no."

"What are you talking about?" He seemed genuinely at a loss.

"No, you're not taking me back to the Green Valley."

Now his tone took on the wheedling sound an adult uses when coaxing a young child. "But you can't go back by yourself. Look what almost happened."

"I have no intention of going back by myself."

"But you just said—"

She stamped her foot. "Rising Sun, you're not *listening* to me. I'm not going back to the Valley, not by myself and not with you. I'm not going back at all."

Once again, his features took on the slow, gasping look of a fish out of water. "But you *have* to go back."

"Why?"

"Well, where *else* could you go?"

"With you," she said firmly.

"With *me*?"

"Cousin, I'm speaking plainly. Why do you keep repeating what I've just said? I'm not going back to the Green Valley, because I'm going with you."

He took a step backward and collided with Moon Face, who was hanging over his shoulder goggle-eyed. "Oof."

"She's crazy," Moon Face said. "I say, drown her."

"Oh, shut up. You're no help."

"I'm cold, and wet, and hungry," Running Deer said. "I suggest we try to build a fire, before some evil Spirit gives us the running snots and the shakes." She looked around her. "Somewhere away from all these bloody carcasses."

Rising Sun pulled his spear free. "Our camp is down that way. Not far. We can rest there before we start back."

Well, at least he wasn't going to take Moon Face's suggestion and drown her. Not yet, at least. She supposed it was an improvement.

"Good idea," she said. She looked around for her pack, saw it lying next to the boulder where she'd stood off the wolves. She went to get it.

Something odd. It took her a moment, then she realized. The small wolf whose foreleg she'd wounded was nowhere to be seen. She glanced around. A twitch of movement in the smaller jumble of boulders beyond the big one caught her gaze. Something glittered. A pair of eyes?

She shrugged. She had more to worry about than one lone wolf.

A lot more.

2

The storm had blown itself away toward the east, leaving the air clean and fresh, by the time they reached the small camp under the trees.

They made the walk in silence. Running Deer trailed along behind the two men, her senses electric with fear and anticipation. She watched Rising Sun's back, and tried to read into the way he walked some clue to his state of mind. It didn't work.

He strode along briskly, his head held high, his back straight. Not once did he turn to see if she still followed, nor did he speak to Moon Face, who clumped beside him, his round shoulders slumped.

Poor Moon Face, she thought suddenly. *This must be awful for him.* She didn't know the apprentice well, but they were of similar ages, and no one in the Green Valley could remain out of contact with the Shaman's helper for long. She tried to recall what she knew of him, and wondered how much influence he had on Rising Sun. They were friends, she knew, for Rising Sun had spent much of his youth in the Spirit House, and she'd seen them together often, walking in the woods or talking quietly beside one of the lakes.

Now that the crisis had passed, Running Deer found her thoughts shifting into high gear. She'd been forced to reveal herself too soon, though the wolves had left her no choice. They were still too close to the Green Valley. A two-day trek was—at least in Rising Sun's mind—still feasible. She wished things could have turned out differently, but she was a plain-headed girl. She had learned not to indulge herself in wishful fantasies. She decided to deal with things as they were. Not that she had any other choice.

Very well. What do I do now?

It was a thorny question. Obviously, neither of the men had counted on her appearance, but now that she was with them, their first reaction would be the simplest: get rid of her. Take her back home.

She grinned to herself. She *hoped* Moon Face's suggestion of drowning her was only a jest.

So the immediate problem was clear enough. Somehow, she had to make them reject their first solution. But how to do that? She wasn't sure. But she was grateful for the hike to the camp. It gave her time to consider her options. Surely there must be a way to convince them to take her along. But what? How?

Slowly, some ideas began to take shape. They were still shaky and ill-formed, but they had possibilities. Much would depend on the nature of the journey the two had undertaken. She was still very hazy about that. There had been rumors, of course, but only the vaguest nuggets of real information. It seemed plain enough that this trek had something to do with Rising Sun's manhood ritual. After all, he'd just completed his initiation.

Whether the journey involved something beyond that remained to be seen. One rumor had intrigued her: something involving Maya, and the Stone Rejoined she'd carried away from the Green Valley. But that was only a rumor. She needed to find out more.

One step at a time, she cautioned herself. *I'm still here, and they haven't started to drag me back to the Valley. Now, how can I make that situation permanent?*

Chewing softly on her lower lip, she marched on, and her thoughts with her. *They think I'm only a stupid girl. But I'm not. I'm of Maya's blood. What would she do in a situation like this?*

And it was that thought that swept some of the cobwebs out of her skull. Slowly she began to smile. Maya would have found a way.

Now, Running Deer thought, *so will I.*

3

"Sit down. Don't talk," Rising Sun said. Obviously the short hike hadn't improved his disposition.

Running Deer did as she was told. She didn't feel like talking, anyway. The reaction to the battle with the wolves was setting in. When it was going on, she'd only reacted. She'd felt no fear, awash in the furious bravery of adrenaline. Now, with the danger behind her, she began to shake.

Sitting down seemed like a good idea. Her knees had gone so weak that falling down seemed the only other option. White-faced, she sank to the wet grass beneath the trees and sat facing the river. She propped herself against her pack and looked down, surprised to find she still held her bow in her lap.

She stared at the broken weapon for several long moments, as if she'd never seen it before. Her mind felt numb. She could see things, but they had no meaning for her. Unconsciously, she began to turn the length of wood in her hands. The broken bowstring tangled itself around her wrists.

It felt very good to sit and think about nothing. Feel nothing. Very good and—*very dangerous!*—something inside her whispered. *Wake up, girl! You don't have much time!*

She blinked. She realized that her senses had gone dim and flat, and that somehow the World around her had faded. But that insistent voice shocked her from the helpless lethargy into which she'd drifted.

Suddenly the low roar of the river rolled loud in her ears. Her nostrils twitched at the rich, wet smell of the grass beneath her and the trees above. She squinted at the colors that blazed around her, emerald-green leaves, deep blue sky, rich brown earth.

She shook her head back and felt wings of wet hair slap her cheeks. She looked down at the bow and said, "Ah."

It took her a moment to disentangle the bowstring. She brought up the two broken ends and examined them. The string had snapped almost exactly in the middle. It would be a job repairing it. Thank the Mother she'd thought to bring a golden lump of beeswax.

Carefully she set to work unwinding the many strands of hair which she'd twisted to make the string. She could use her own hair to make the patch, blending it into the cord, then sealing it with the beeswax. Engrossed in her task, she didn't notice when Rising Sun came over and stood above her.

"What are you doing?"

She looked up, startled. "Huh?"

"What is that?"

Wordlessly, she gestured.

"It doesn't look like any bowstring I've ever seen," he said, squatting. "Here. Let me see."

She watched his face as he fingered the tightly interwoven strands. The anger had gone out of his expression, replaced by concentration, which showed itself in the two deep vertical lines that formed above his nose. He tested one length of the cord by wrapping it in his two fists and pulling.

"Mm. Strong," he said.

"It doesn't stretch when it gets wet, either," she said.

He glanced at her. "No? But it breaks."

"I guess I didn't make it strong enough. I'll fix that when I repair it. Use more hair."

He gave her back the string and rocked back on his heels. "How do you know about things like this?"

She tried a little smile. "You mean because I'm a girl?"

"Uh, yes. I guess."

"Maya knew about bows."

He narrowed his eyes, as if she'd said something she shouldn't have. Her smile disappeared.

"You're not Maya," he told her, frowning.

His words struck to the heart of her fears and hopes. She stared at him, wondering what it was about him that had captured her so completely. Now, still frowning, he waited patiently for her to reply, those lines of concentration still dividing the smooth flesh above his nose. She loved those lines.

"No," she said at last, "but I'm a woman. Like her."

She wondered if she would have to explain, but she hadn't underestimated him.

"Is that it?" he asked. "Is that what this is all about? You think you're another Maya? And you don't have to behave like other women do?"

She didn't want to lie to him, but he'd touched on only a part of her feelings. How to get him to see the rest?

"Cousin, we both bear her blood in our veins. We are of her line. You know how strange that line has been." She paused, marshaling her courage. "Her blood sent you on this journey, didn't it? Perhaps it sent me, as well."

Her shaft turned out better aimed than she had dared to hope. His eyes widened, and he stared at her as if she'd suddenly turned into something else. It was as if he saw her, really *saw* her, for the first time.

"What do you know about my journey?"

She shrugged and tried to look knowing. He reached forward, took her by her shoulders, and shook her gently. "Cousin, we've known each other all our lives. But now it seems I don't know you at all."

She licked her lips and stared into the dark pools of his eyes. A great feeling of joy bloomed in her belly and spread warmly out until her fingers and toes and the roots of her hair tingled with it. The soft pressure of his fingers on her shoulders suddenly made her realize how close he was to her.

"Maybe it's time you knew me," she said.

And for a moment she thought she'd won. He seemed caught in the same warm, dark moment as she was, and she was certain that within their mutual gaze they shared something that both of them understood. Then it was as if some invisible tent flap behind his eyes slipped shut, and he sighed.

"Maybe," he said as he relinquished his grip. "But not now. After I come back, perhaps."

He began to rise, and she said, "I didn't lie to you, Rising Sun. I *couldn't* lie to you. I won't let you take me back to the Green Valley."

He folded his arms across his chest and stared down at her. A hint of the great resolve that fueled him showed on his face, and she shivered inwardly, but pressed on.

"No," she said, her chin outthrust. "You'll have to tie me up and carry me, or I'll run away from you. But then I'll follow again. And if you do get me back to the Valley, I'll escape and come after you. Even if your trail is cold as winter ice, I'll follow."

Now the thunder clouds gathered on his brow. "Oh, you will, will you?"

"I will," she said, and met his gaze with her own, just as stubbornly.

He waved one hand. "Tcha. You're nothing but a crazy girl."

"No, Rising Sun, you're wrong. I'm not a girl. I may be crazy, but I'm a woman."

"Woman, girl, what does it matter? You're still going back."

"No," she said. "I'm not."

It was an impasse, and both knew it. Rising Sun broke it by simply turning his back and stalking away. She let out a long, shuddering breath. This wasn't going well at all.

4

"Well," Moon Face said, "when do we leave?"

"I don't know," Rising Sun replied. "She says she won't go."

The apprentice stared at him disbelievingly. "So what? Who cares what she says? She's a woman. She'll do what she's told."

"I wonder," Rising Sun said.

Moon Face didn't like the distant, thoughtful expression on his friend's face. "You aren't thinking about taking her with us, are you? Because if you are, that makes you as crazy as she is."

"Are you going to start a fire?"

"What?" Moon Face looked around vaguely. "Everything's wet."

"There may be some dry wood deeper in the trees. Why don't you go look?"

"I don't know if I should leave you two alone."

Rising Sun laughed. "Don't worry. I won't let her overpower me."

The apprentice glanced dubiously at Running Deer, who had resumed work on her broken bowstring. "You are, aren't you?"

"I am what?"

"Thinking about her. About bringing her along."

"I don't know," Rising Sun said. "I just don't know."

This equivocation was too much for Moon Face. "You *are* crazy," he blurted. "Why did Gotha send me with you? Two *crazy* people. What am I supposed to *do*?"

Patiently, Rising Sun said, "You're supposed to go look for some dry wood so we can have a fire. I'm cold. And hungry. Aren't you hungry, Moon Face?"

"I'm *always* hungry," Moon Face said as he turned and stomped off. Somehow, it wasn't as funny as it usually was.

Rising Sun squatted and began to rummage through his pack. He could feel Running Deer's gaze on him, but he ignored her as he found trail meat and a dry tunic. He took off his wet shirt and hung it from a tree branch, where it steamed faintly in the bright sunlight.

He started to take off his leg wraps—he only had the one pair—but something stopped him. The thought of being naked in front of his cousin inexplicably bothered him. Inexplicable because she'd seen him naked a thousand times. He stood with his back to her, trying to puzzle it out. They were cousins. They'd grown up together. So why, after all these years, was a huge and painful erection straining at the crotch of his pants?

He stared down in total surprise. Where had *that* come from?

And then he realized it had been there ever since he'd held her shoulders, ever since their eyes had locked in that unspoken embrace.

Now what in the name of all the Spirit Demons was he supposed to do about *this*?

He heard a soft noise behind him and turned. She stood naked before him, her golden skin seeming to glow in the afternoon light. Her full lips were curved in a strange half smile. He remembered how those lips had tasted when she'd pulled him to her.

She looked down. Her smile deepened.

5

What would Maya do?

The question had been drumming in her skull ever since she'd realized the time for decision was upon them both. She'd thought she'd broken through that terrible reserve of his, at least for a moment, but the moment was past. Now he squatted facing away from her, the fine muscles of his back rippling beneath his honey-tinted skin. So smooth . . .

That heat she'd felt beneath his touch suddenly flared into a roaring fire in her belly. *What would Maya do?*

Whatever was necessary. Using whatever weapons she had to hand.

In that moment Running Deer suddenly understood her greatest weapon, which she shared not only with Maya but with all women. She rose to her feet and stripped off her clothing. The breeze touched her skin, hot and cold at the same time. The dark brown aureoles haloing her nipples flushed suddenly pink. The nipples themselves, kissed by the wind, grew hard as acorns.

She felt herself smiling. She stepped forward and met him as he turned. She looked down and saw his man-snake trembling eagerly in the crotch of his pants. Her smile deepened.

Wordlessly she came to him. She placed her head on the smooth, taut expanse of his chest. She wrapped her arms around his slender waist, glorying in the push of his muscled belly against the smooth round of her own flesh.

His man-snake throbbed against her. He breathed a soft, sighing sound. The heat of his exhalation burned in her ear. A shudder ran through him. She let her weight fall against him and slowly pulled him down to the moist, sweet-smelling grass.

His weight settled on her. His scent filled her nostrils. She breathed in deeply, glorying in the sharp, musky aroma that swelled from his armpits.

The pressure of his chest flattened her breasts and rubbed hard against her nipples. Tiny lightning bolts of pain radiated from those tender knots, pain unlike anything she'd ever felt, pain so intense it was pleasure. And still the fire in her belly burned. Overcome, she ground her pelvis against his pulsing snake.

The wiry bush of hair around his member scraped her tender skin. She spread her legs wide, then clamped them around his own, seeking to pull him even more tightly to her. He groaned softly as his lips found hers. She closed her eyes, feeling the soft brush of her long eyelashes against the hard bone of his cheek.

Butterfly kisses, she thought.

She opened her mouth. His tongue—hot, wet, strong— filled her. His arms slid beneath her back, and she locked her own around him. She felt the good strong movement of her hips begin, rhythmic, demanding. Sweat slicked their skin. Their bellies made soft, sucking sounds as they slid against each other.

She lowered her hands and grasped the firm globes of his buttocks. The sinews there clenched, unclenched, clenched again as her strong fingers kneaded the hard flesh.

He moaned into her mouth. His tongue surged into her throat, painful and wonderful. She widened her mouth until her jaws creaked. His chin ground into her cheek as he pressed his face against hers.

"Uh, uh, uh," he panted.

Now she could feel the hard tip of his man-snake poke at the soft flesh of her opening, clumsy, seeking the way in. She reached underneath and took his penis, slick with some unknown fluid, and guided the round head to her vagina. It took her a moment to position it properly. She felt the sheath of skin around his snake slide up and down, covering, then revealing the head with its single eye.

He pushed. The muscles in his rear pistoned once as he entered her.

Ah! The pain!

"Stop!" she shrieked, but he didn't seem to hear her. She could feel his man-snake deep inside her. It felt incredibly large, and she was certain it was splitting her apart. How could it be so big? She'd seen it with her own eyes, but *this—*

"It hurts!"

He withdrew partway, and her stomach collapsed with relief, but just when she thought the agony was over, he thrust again. And again.

She reached around his back and clasped her fingers together in a single fist. He pushed halfway to his knees, the better to drive his member deep into her guts.

She felt all loose down there. Darkness swam in her vision. She spat out his tongue and bit his lip and felt blood flow between her teeth, hot salt on her tongue.

He moaned, and thrust harder.

Then a strange thing occurred. The agony in her bowels began to lessen. The hot rhythm of his strokes caught her up. As the awful pain slowly turned into a pleasure she could never have imagined, she felt her body relax. Her muscles seemed to fill with dark, liquid fire. Every nerve ending tingled. She could feel him against her in a thousand separate sensations: the scrape and rub of his pubic hair as it tangled in her own patch, the pointy knobs of his nipples against her breasts, the sharp bones of his chin grinding into her throat, his teeth abrasive against the strained tendons of her neck.

The flame in her belly had spread. She felt hot and weak and strong at the same time. Her fingernails clawed at the skin on his back. He groaned and pushed harder, his rhythm growing faster, faster.

She felt the same rhythm begin to respond from deep inside her, from that fire, the dark heat rising, rising—

Exploded inside, wave after wave of long honey heat, consuming her.

Dark fire.

She screamed. He bellowed some reply. She felt his flesh inside her expand, pump, then pump again, filling her.

"Oh, God!" she howled.

It was true.

He collapsed on top of her. She took his weight. Drained, he seemed helpless as a baby. Though he was on top of her, she was no longer frightened of him. He rode in the position of victor, but she knew the truth. In the ultimate strength of men lay their greatest weakness.

She knew. She had tested her weapon. It was more potent than she'd ever dreamed. Even Maya, she thought, could have done no better.

6

Moon Face came out of the woods with a small load of dry kindling in his pudgy arms. He stopped dead, transfixed by the spectacle on the ground before him.

"Oh, *no!*" he groaned.

Then he turned and went back into the woods.

CHAPTER ELEVEN

1

"At least ten strides farther," she said, and brushed her hair back from her face.

"Let me see that," he said.

She handed over the bow with its newly repaired string. He took it, hefted it, then twanged the length of cord. "It doesn't stretch as much as mine," he said.

He had those two little lines over his nose again, she saw. It gave him a fierce look that she thought had nothing to do with what was inside him. It made him look older. When he frowned like that, deep in concentration, all the boyishness vanished from his features, and the strength hidden beneath his smooth golden skin came forth.

"It's stronger than your cord," she said. "Even though it broke."

He glanced over at her. "Why did it break, do you think?"

She shrugged. The steppe breeze, fading as dusk approached, lifted the wings of her dark hair. "I didn't weave it properly. There must have been a weak spot. It's harder to make a string like this, but if you do it right, it's stronger. It won't stretch the way your hide cord will."

He nodded slowly. "Yes, I can see that. So you can

pull a stronger bow and send the arrow farther. Harder."
He paused. "I still can't believe you did this."

She smiled. "I'm a woman. I can do lots of things."

Rising Sun was clearly having trouble grappling with
the evidence of his own eyes, and the troubling thoughts
this evidence caused. Women weren't *supposed* to know
about men's things. Hunting secrets. Weapons. But this
woman, whom he'd known all his life—*and not known at
all, it seems,* he reminded himself—was shaking his long-
held prejudices to their very core.

Women were dull, unadventurous creatures. But this
woman had set out alone, armed only with her bow, and
tracked him across the steppe.

Women were fearful creatures. But this woman had
fought off wolves by herself, and perhaps even saved his
life.

Women were lumps suitable only for sex, but this
woman had lit fires inside him he still couldn't fully understand.

Women were inferior to men in every way. But this
woman stood proudly at his side, her raven hair rising to
the wind, and seemed not only to consider herself his
equal, but, in some ways, even his superior.

What was going on here?

He shook his head and handed back the bow. "Do you
think you could make me a string like that?"

"It will take some time. I'll have to do it at night,
when we camp."

He nodded, but said nothing. He knew as well as she
that the question of whether she would accompany him
on his journey had already been settled. She ran her fingers through her hair, as if testing it for the bowstring to
come. The movement lifted her full breasts. The single
motion was enough to ignite the fire in his groin all over
again. With the urge came the reflex common to all men
of his time. He reached for her, but somehow, without
seeming to notice, she moved out of his grasp and wandered a few feet away.

"I'll start tonight," she said, as if she hadn't noticed
his arousal at all.

And when he took a step toward her, she raised her head and said, "Listen. Isn't that Moon Face?"

He stopped. The thin cry was almost lost in the wind, but it was there.

"Come eat ..."

She turned to face him. "Come on. I'm hungry. Race you back!" And then she was off, her heels flashing white in the last of the waning light.

He grinned ruefully. Women were *strange*. At least, this one was. He bounded after, and only caught her right at the top of the ridge above the river.

They rolled into the tiny camp breathless and laughing, and found themselves met by Moon Face's disapproving stare.

He will be a problem, Rising Sun thought. But as he watched Running Deer settle herself gracefully at the edge of the fire, he realized he didn't care.

He still didn't understand the weapon she had used on him. All he knew was that he'd been pierced by it, in a place where the wound would never heal. But it was sweet, just the same.

2

Moon Face said, "Has a Demon stolen your *mind*?"

They were walking downriver from the camp. Overhead, the soft summer stars twinkled like a beach of diamond sand. Half of a fat, golden moon floated over them. To Rising Sun, the moon looked as if it were smiling. But then, everything seemed wonderful—the moon, the stars, the rushing whisper of the river, the stretch and pull of his own muscles as they ambled along.

Why do I feel so good? Maybe a Spirit has stolen my mind, he thought. But those Spirits were evil. Why should an evil Spirit bring such great happiness? He couldn't reconcile the two ideas, and so he simply put them aside.

"No, I feel fine. If there were evil Demons about, wouldn't you know it? I mean, you're the Shaman here."

Moon Face's slumped shoulders straightened a bit at that. In the Green Valley, no one had ever called him Shaman, and no one would, not as long as Gotha still lived. But this wasn't the Green Valley, was it?

"I guess I am," he said, and his shoulders perked up even farther.

"After all, Gotha could have sent anybody—or nobody—with me. But he sent you. And, no offense, my friend, but he didn't send you for your skill at hunting or fighting. It must have been for something like this. You are skilled, aren't you?"

Moon Face stopped, suddenly deep in thought. Indeed he *was* skilled, though not at hunting or fighting. So Rising Sun must be right. Gotha had anticipated a need for the peculiar talents only Moon Face could bring to the journey. The ways of the Spirits, the secrets of the earth and the things that walked and grew upon it.

Yes, Moon Face decided, this sort of situation must be precisely the kind of thing Gotha had intended for his abilities. His features settled into a serious expression as he regarded Rising Sun.

"Maybe I spoke too hastily," he said. "I don't think a Spirit has invaded you, though I don't understand why you are letting that girl tag along with us. I mean, of course you like fucking her, but surely that's no reason to risk your entire quest. Not for nothing more than a hole to stick your snake into."

Moon Face, who was entirely virgin and would remain so until he achieved full Shamanhood, and who, moreover, because of certain hormonal predilections might remain celibate all his life, really had no idea of the welter of feelings that were turning his friend's normally calm and calculating disposition into a steaming porridge. But his own mind was no less calculating, and he understood his weaknesses and made allowances for them.

"I mean, she's only a girl. Well, a woman, I guess. But aside from fucking her, how on earth do you think she can help you achieve your goal?"

"She saved my life. That's helpful, don't you think?"

Patiently, Moon Face said, "Your life wouldn't have been in any danger if not for her. You would have risked nothing if you hadn't gone back to rescue her."

"Are you sure? Do you *know* those wolves were tracking her? Or were they tracking us?"

Moon Face shrugged. "I don't see how it matters."

"Well, neither do I. If Running Deer hadn't been behind us, maybe the wolves would have found us first. Just the two of us. And maybe the outcome would have been different without her help."

Moon Face stood silent. His natural inclination was to dismiss anything a woman might do, but he'd seen Running Deer slay wolves, seen it with his own eyes. And Shamans, more than any other men, learned at their peril not to disregard what they saw. Half the secrets of a Shaman's power lay in simple observation. And so, Moon Face tried to consider the truth within the seeing, though it was hard for him.

Yes, the woman had fought well. He would never have believed such a thing without seeing it for himself, but he had seen it, and now he couldn't deny it. But what did it mean?

"She isn't a warrior," he said at last.

"More of one than you are."

The apprentice only nodded. His own discipline wouldn't let him deny the simple truth. "Yes, but you still haven't answered my question. How can she help us? If Gotha had thought another warrior was needed, he could have sent any number of men far more skilled than she is."

"But Gotha didn't send her. And even you have said that Gotha doesn't claim to know everything about this journey. As far as it goes, I don't believe *anybody* knows. I certainly don't."

"So what are you saying?"

Even Rising Sun wasn't sure, but a satisfying concept was starting to take shape within his own thoughts. "What if this is all something that is *supposed* to happen? It's strange, but then I think this whole *journey* is strange. And since none of us really knows how things are supposed to turn out, maybe it would be better just to accept whatever happens. Maybe there is some meaning in it we won't know until we *do* know it."

Rising Sun paused and shook his head. He knew his

words sounded hopelessly confused. Still, something about what he was trying to say pleased him. It *felt* right, even if he couldn't say it properly.

"Does that make any sense?" he asked plaintively.

"No," Moon Face said. "But then, nothing makes much sense to me right now. I need to think."

"So you won't mind if Running Deer comes with us?"

The apprentice barked out a short laugh. "You're asking me? Well, if you are, yes, I do mind. She still bothers me. But I won't oppose it. Not now, at least." He sighed. "There may be some kernel of truth in that babble you just spouted."

"You think so?" Rising Sun sounded surprised.

"Maybe."

"Well, then."

Moon Face sighed again, but something about the conversation had cheered him a bit. He wasn't sure what it was. Maybe it was the way Rising Sun had called him Shaman.

Still, even Shamans had their responsibilities. Especially Shamans. "Well, let's go back," he said.

"Already?"

"I'm hungry," Moon Face said.

Rising Sun laughed.

3

The small fire had burned down to a low smear of red coals. The fat smiling moon had fallen from the sky. Rising Sun lay with his hands clasped beneath his head, staring blankly at the bright wash of stars overhead. He'd tried to fall asleep, but his whirling thoughts wouldn't give him peace.

He felt utterly alone and adrift. This journey, this *quest*, seemed to make less and less sense all the time. Why was he going? *Where* was he going? What was the *purpose* of it all?

He felt like a child's toy, a stick doll whirled and tossed by forces far beyond his comprehension, forces as distant and impersonal as those blank shining lights in the sky above his head.

And he was horny. Before his experience with Running Deer, unlike many of the boys his own age, he'd still been a virgin—at least with a woman. And that was what mattered, for his encounter with her had been totally unlike the casual masturbatory sex he'd enjoyed with his friends. It had been a fire, and that fire had released another deep inside him, a blaze that roared and crackled and gave off a light so bright it blinded him to almost everything else.

He *wanted* her. And as he lay there, staring at the sky, a faint rime of hot sweat coating his body, he knew he could have her. As much as he wanted to. The thought of her was more than seductive—it was urgent, demanding, overpowering.

It scared him. The fire frightened him because he knew he had to control it somehow—or else give up his quest. The Shaman had told him he would be tested on the journey, but he'd imagined mundane things. Battles with wolves. Well, he'd battled wolves—with *her* help. Was this consuming fire another test?

Rising Sun sighed and rolled over on his side. His erection throbbed painfully. Only a few feet away, as if sensing his need, Running Deer made a soft, cooing sound in her sleep. His nerve endings twitched. Only a few feet—but that space was both a bridge and a barrier. If he couldn't control himself now, if he broke that barrier and irrevocably crossed that bridge, what then?

He groaned to himself and reached down until his fingers found the straining rod of flesh. A few quick strokes brought a handful of hot, sticky stuff, but no real relief.

He rolled over again. The sky looked different, less threatening. In some hidden part of himself he knew he'd managed to survive a great test.

"At least for now," he whispered. His eyelids drooped shut, and finally he fell into a restless, fitful sleep.

4

"Uggh."

"You look terrible," Moon Face told him. "Didn't you sleep last night?" The apprentice's eyes slid knowingly toward Running Deer, who crouched over their small, cold hearth, trying to strike a fire.

"I slept fine," Rising Sun told him as he tried to rub clotted grains of dried mucus from his eyes. His eyelashes felt glued together. "I'll be back," he said, and stalked off toward the river to splash his face.

Moon Face watched him go, then pursed his lips and shook his head. "Not good," he mumbled to himself. "Not good at all."

He turned away and ambled over to the hearth. "Here," he said brusquely, "let me do that."

She glanced up at him. "You don't like me, do you, Moon Face?"

The baldness of her question startled, then angered him. He drew back, his eyebrows rising. "What are you talking about, girl?"

She handed over her flints. "It's not your choice," she said softly. "It's his, and we both know it."

"You be quiet!"

"No. We need to settle this. He's got enough problems, without us making things worse. Don't you understand that?"

The girl's temerity shocked him profoundly. Who did she think she was, to speak to him like that? It was almost as if she considered herself his *equal*. Was she actually *lecturing* him? The enormity of it was more than he could bear. Without conscious thought, he lashed out. His openhanded blow landed squarely on her cheekbone as she knelt before him, and rocked her back.

"I ought to *kill* you!" he hissed.

She placed her long fingers softly on the bright patch of red. Her blue eye flamed. "Don't make threats you can't carry out, apprentice," she whispered.

He stared down at her. Her fearlessness, her defiance, had rendered him utterly speechless. For the first time, he began to wonder if she really *was* a Demon. And if she was, then he must go very carefully. Demon Spirits were cunning creatures, strong and dreadful, and he only an apprentice. Gotha had told him he would face many tests on his journey with Rising Sun. Was this one of them?

He summoned every last dreg of courage and faced her. His lips felt numb, but he forced them to move. "I'm . . . sorry," he managed at last. "I shouldn't have done that."

She seemed as surprised by his apology as he was that he'd been able to speak it.

She stood, and he flinched back. "No, don't," she said. "I'm not going to hit you. He's your friend, Moon Face, but he's more than that. We both have to help him, can't you see?"

He regarded her for a long moment. Something was being offered here, some kind of pact. A trap? Very possibly. But now wasn't the time to try to unravel it.

Demons could be cunning. Well, so could he. He'd learned from the best. "I see," he said. He took a deep breath. "I see a *lot*."

Running Deer smiled at him. The fire in her blue eye softened, became almost tender. Evidently she didn't apprehend the two-edged meaning of his words, for she put out her hand and touched his forearm. "We can be friends, too, Moon Face. For *his* sake."

And though his skin crawled beneath her fingertips, he managed to make a smile of his own, though his face felt as if it were cracking in some great heat. "Yes," he said.

"Ho—what are you talking about so cozily?" Rising Sun called.

They both jumped, then turned.

"Plotting some breakfast, are you? Good. I'm starving!"

Rising Sun's hair fell in damp strands framing his face. His eyes looked bright as new-washed obsidian. Whatever devils had dogged his sleep had disappeared with the morning light, washed away by cold river water.

He strode up to them, rubbing his belly in exaggerated motions. "And you're hungry, too, aren't you, Moon Face? You're *always* hungry."

The old joke was like a door opening inside the apprentice's head. It was a way out of the terrible quandary in which he'd somehow become enmeshed. He let out a belching chuckle. To his own ears the eruption sounded inhuman, but nobody seemed to notice.

"Heh," he belched again. "I'm starving, Rising Sun. You're right, I'm *always* starving." He glanced down, surprised to find he still held Running Deer's flints. To cover his confusion, he knelt quickly and began to work the stones together. Hot, dry sparks seemed to erupt from his clattering fingers. He'd never felt less like eating in his life.

5

It was an odd breaking of the night's fast. One or the other of them would start a conversation with a word or two, but nobody seemed to be able to take the offered threads and weave them into anything whole. It was as if each of them existed only partially in the World, with their larger and deeper parts sunk far into some stunning puzzle that both fascinated and horrified.

Finally Rising Sun could stand it no longer. He was seated cross-legged, as they were, the three of them equidistant around the small hearth. A good fire snapped inside the blackened stones as they chewed thoughtfully on their meal of trail meat and some greens Running Deer had found in the small wood.

"Listen," Rising Sun said. "I guess we'll be going on together. The *three* of us," he added, not aware he'd emphasized the word, though Moon Face cast him a single twitching glance before returning his gaze to his lap.

Running Deer said nothing, but the distance drained out of her mismatched eyes as a faint smile quirked at her lips. Rising Sun felt those hidden fires flare inside him, and resolutely banked them down. Even so, the clear, simple thoughts he'd formulated seemed to shatter into a whirling cloud, and for a moment he paused, until he was able to find the meaning he'd crafted so carefully.

"Now, you, Running Deer, you don't know anything

about what I'm doing, what Moon Face and I set out to do. But now you're a part of it, though I don't understand why. So you ought to know what we do."

"No, wait—" Moon Face's cry was low, hoarse, and anguished. The soft skin around his eyes crumpled as if he were in physical pain. He'd reconciled himself to *her* presence as best he could. But to spill their secrets to her? The idea of it made him want to vomit.

But Rising Sun only shook his head. "No, Moon Face, she has to know. If she is to be a part of our little band, then she *has* to know."

Moon Face shook his head miserably, but said nothing. Running Deer, shifting her attention from one to the other, was struck by an almost palpable sense of fear emanating from the chubby little apprentice. *He's scared to death of me,* she thought with growing wonder. *No, that's not right. He's scared of what I might do.*

Rising Sun turned to face her directly. He appeared to have forgotten Moon Face entirely. "Cousin, perhaps you heard rumors, I don't know. I still don't understand why you followed me. But here is the truth. I—Moon Face and me—are looking for the Mammoth Stone Rejoined. That Stone our great aunt took away long ago, before my birth. The Shaman believes I am the one destined to find it and bring it back to the People of the Valley."

Running Deer felt a slow, pulsating beat begin within her chest. It took her a moment to realize it was her heart. For an instant, all her attention centered on the pounding in her chest. How had she ever been able to ignore that great engine? Had it been hammering away like that all her life? Surely it had. Why hadn't she noticed?

Along with the rhythmic, overpowering cadence came a surge of joy, of vindication. *I knew it,* she thought, though of course she hadn't. Not the details. But it had to do with Maya, and so it had to do with women. All women. It was *right* that she be here, that she become a part of this little band.

The Stone Rejoined! That mysterious Talisman that had, in its many shapes and manifestations, so profoundly affected the lives of all the People, and even—if some of the rumors she'd long been aware of were true—changed the World itself.

Still that feeling of *rightness* flooded through her, as strong and bracing as the river that whispered soft thunder into her ears. *She* shared Maya's blood, as much as the youth who sat across from her, waiting for her reply. All her life she'd felt different, estranged from the common beliefs that all the People seemed to share. But now, one of three lonely travelers, mere dots beneath the vast steppe sky, she felt for the first time what it was to be a part of something greater than she was. In that fleeting moment she understood the riddle, or thought she did, with a clarity so compelling it was all she could do not to weep.

Stone calls blood. Blood calls Stone.

The World was broken, and she would do her part to make it whole again. There had been a great pause, but now the time came to bring the blood and the Stone together again—this time, forever.

She would never after have so compelling a vision of her place in things, of her great role, and even now, within a few moments, the bright burst of it would begin to fade. But it was out of that fire, so like and yet unlike the blaze she'd kindled with Rising Sun, that she said the truest words she would ever speak: *"I love you, Lord. I will be with you always."*

Rising Sun blinked. It wasn't the reply he'd expected. "What?"

But she only smiled at him, and after a time he smiled back. Her answer was odd, but it was enough. In fact, it was the answer he'd needed, to the question he hadn't asked. He just didn't know the question. Not until she gave him her answer.

It was a gift that would shake the World forever.

6

As they finished stowing everything in their packs, a buoyant, almost hysterical sense of glee seemed to overtake them. It was as if they'd all passed through some

great and fearful testing, and somehow emerged un-
scathed from it.

To Rising Sun, it was as if he'd emerged from some
long darkness into a place of peace and light. One part of
him knew that beneath the morning's sunlit glow, other
questions remained unanswered, but that thorn of doubt
was not sharp enough to prick him now. As he finished
tying the thong at the top of his pack, he stole glances at
the faces of the others.

Moon Face, his features now smooth and blank,
worked stolidly, his eyes on the intricate knots he was
fashioning. A Shaman's pack must be protected from
things more complicated and devious than the simple
stress of travel. His dark hair fell across his face, so Rising Sun couldn't see his eyes. Yet, for a moment Rising
Sun thought he saw more than the apprentice's mere eyeballs, and with a tiny shiver he remembered the strange
occurrence of the previous day. But the shiver passed as
quickly as it had come, because now he looked at Running Deer, and a joy quicker and hotter than the sun in the
sky flowed like burning honey through his veins.

I love you, Lord. I will be with you always.

He held the words within him like crystalline emeralds
cupped inside his palm, unutterably precious. He didn't
understand them. What did Lord mean, and why would
she call him that? But, like jewels, he didn't want to examine them too closely, for fear they would be changed
or taken away.

Precious things must be guarded.

He sighed, then crouched and used the thick muscles
of his thighs to help him heave the pack to his shoulders.
The day was already turning hot. The air about them
seemed washed clean of all impurities, limpid and without limits. The river uncoiled itself to their right, a long
snake whose watery scales glittered emerald within emerald banks.

The breeze was at their backs, soft and still touched
with hints of dawn's coolness. "Are we ready?" Rising
Sun asked.

"Lead on," Running Deer said, a cheerful grin transfiguring her lovely features. Moon Face only grunted, but even he seemed about to break into a smile.

Rising Sun planted the butt of his heavy spear into the soft earth and used it to lever himself forward. Almost naturally Running Deer took up station at his right hand, and Moon Face fell into step behind them, already huffing a bit.

The quiet pad of their footsteps masked the sound of a smaller body limping up to poke its curious snout through a screen of shrub. Its bright gaze followed them intently. When they were far enough away, it twitched its wet black nose. Then, tongue lolling, the wolf emerged from the shelter of the wood and took up its own cautious pursuit.

The wolf stayed well back, for now was not yet its time, and somehow it understood that. With its preternaturally sharp senses, it was aware of the other that followed, but that thing was still well out on the steppe. It had been there all along. The wolf didn't know what to make of it. Its emanations were strange.

The wolf's foreleg ached. It felt lonely and frightened without its pack, but the need that drove it forward was overpowering. The light was there, off in front of it, plainly visible to its savage inner eye. The pack had sought that light, but now the pack was gone, and only it remained. It, and the other.

But the other wasn't close. Not yet. The wolf kept an ear cocked and nostrils wide open anyway. In the World of wolves, things changed quickly. In its sharp, wolfish way, the wolf wanted to be ready. Just in case.

CHAPTER TWELVE

1

Sleeps With Spirits could feel him coming to her. She lay on her furs, the hot summer night turning the inside of the small hut into an oven in which she tossed, boiling in her own sweat, her own fever. Hot outside, hot inside. He was like a fire in her chest, her belly, her loins. Coming, yes, coming.

She still couldn't see his face. He was a fiery shadow in her Dreams, a shadow with no features, burning.

"Ahhh!" she moaned, half awake, unsure whether she still Dreamed or not. Sometimes it was hard to tell. The shadows moved around her as she turned her head. The slick surface of her ruby eyes caught a glint of light. The moon poked needles of light through the chinks and slits and cracks of the hut. Their sharp points struck her eyes and she blinked.

Awake.

Now she knew the Dream was gone. She blinked again and the shadows resolved themselves into sharp-edged familiarity; the small stump bench beyond the open door, the passing of swift clouds above the smoke hole, beneath the moon. It seemed very bright inside the hut, as if the stars had dropped out of the sky and now cast their greenish illumination all about.

She thought she saw ghosts in that light—an arm ris-

ing, falling, the glint of bloody stone, but she blinked
again and the ghosts departed as if they'd never been.

"Momma?" she whispered, more to herself than to the
moonlit lump that lay beyond the hearth, swaddled in
ratty fur even in the deadly, wasting heat. She could smell
the Witch's flesh cooking in the dark, a rich, greasy smell
that made her think of hot, furry things caught in her
throat.

Momma snorted suddenly, flung out a heavy arm, let
it fall. Rolled over and flapped her lips together, a moist,
ripping sound.

Spirits had risen to her elbow, her red eyes blank and
questing, but now she sank back. The night was too bright
for her, the Dreams too real. Or the World too dreamlike.
At moments like these, she was sometimes afraid she
would lose the ability to tell the difference, that the World
and her Dreams would mix inextricably together, and she
would never find her way out.

No one would be able to help her, either, for of course
no one would believe her Dreams. Thus if she became
lost in Dream, no one would believe in *her* any longer,
and she would cease to exist.

It was a complicated, extraordinary terror that she
could explain to no one, not even herself. She fell back,
exhausted, and wiped thin fingers across her wet forehead. It felt as if her fingertips left soft indentations in the
skin there, as if her flesh had turned to damp clay. She
closed her eyes.

She waited for him to come back to her, but he didn't.
After a while, she slept.

2

The Witch Woman cast a disapproving glare in the general direction of her still sleeping daughter as she bulled
her way through the opening of her house. The morning
heat struck her with stunning force and she paused, squinting against the glare. Her wise bones told her this was the
hottest day of the season so far. The World along the river,

despite the flowing water, smelled dry and trembling, ready to burst into fire.

The omens of the day, she decided, weren't good. She stood all the way up and shook herself like a huge animal emerging from its burrow, then curled her lip and spat once on the ground. Even her saliva tasted dry, almost solid. It was like spitting out a smooth pebble. She ground the glimmering wad into the dust, so it couldn't be used against her.

She grunted. Almost nobody was about. It was early, but not that early. Most likely, she guessed, people would stay inside. Even the steaming murk of the houses was preferable to the direct blazing blare of the sun.

A few children moved listlessly about, their boundless energies sapped by the heat. She glowered at them, but they didn't notice. This made her angry. The Witch hated to be ignored. Awe was better than fear, but in a pinch, even childish terror would do.

She threw back her head and hissed. The sound, high and harsh, seemed to fly across the camp and impale the children, who froze as one and then, also as one, raised their heads.

She raised her right arm and pointed one blunt, scrag-nailed finger at the nearest boy, who was short and slight and whose almond eyes widened when he understood at whom she pointed. His bottom lip began to quiver, though he stood otherwise motionless, and she knew he was too frightened to move.

She laughed. The sound made his face crumple. She nodded and laughed again, her finger aimed like a rigid spear at his eyes. Twin lines of moisture glittered suddenly on his smooth cheeks.

She hissed. A stream of golden urine braided itself down his slender leg into a dark, sharp-smelling puddle around his foot.

"Go," she whispered, and he ran silently away. When she looked for the rest they were gone, too. She laughed again, this time to herself. The show was over.

Strangely refreshed, near floating with a fizzy, bubbling humor, she walked toward the river through the drowsing camp.

*I'd like to see you make a small boy piss with nothing
but a glance and a finger, Shaman.*

That even if the Shaman could, he wouldn't, never
crossed the Witch's mind. She took her triumphs where
she found them, and savored even the smallest.

She trudged on. The sun roared in the sky over her
head. The World was full of fire.

But the Witch knew that already.

3

Carries Two Spears pulled at his lower lip as he
watched his sister stoop to the water's edge. He was worried, and growing more so with each passing day.

The water moved quickly here, a few hundred paces
upstream from the main camp of the Children. He
watched blankly, sensed the vast, endless pull of the current, hidden just beneath the tawny surface of the great
stream. More thoughtful than many have guessed, Two
Spears often mused on the river and its strength, and how
that strength was only barely kept in check by the banks
that bound the water within. Sometimes even those banks,
made of stone and earth, weren't enough to restrain the
waters. He'd seen the river in spring rise to swallow the
land until it stretched mile upon mile wide across the glittering prairie.

Men were like that, he thought. Placid, controlled, but
always beneath, the strength that threatened to burst the
boundaries of flesh and drown everything within reach.
Even some women—like his mother, for instance.

Which brought his thoughts full circle, back again to
his worries of the moment. The Witch was up to something, he thought. He had few illusions about his mother.
He'd loved his father, and had been old enough at the
time of his father's death to understand the rumors that
had floated about in the wake of that event. At the time
he'd rejected those whispered accusations, but now he
was no longer sure. No, worse than that—he was slowly
becoming sure those rumors *were* true.

His mother might have murdered his father. He knew

he would never know for certain, but the mere possibility frightened him deeply. It meant the Witch would cross any boundary—burst through whatever banks limited her, just as the river rampaged in the spring.

He stared at his sister's lovely back, so graceful as she knelt by the water, trailing her fingers in the treacherous flood. In that moment he loved her more than anything in the World. She couldn't see the danger she was in. Poor thing, her vision was clouded by her Visions, but those sad, fanciful Dreams wouldn't protect her, not from a mother who wouldn't even stop at the murder of her own mate.

No, only he could protect her, because only he understood her danger. He dropped his hands to his sides, clenched his fingers into fists, and stepped forward. The movement was loud enough to startle her, and she looked up, over her shoulder, her eyes widening in surprise.

"Oh, Spears," she said. A faint confusion colored her pale features. "Where did you come from?"

He resisted the urge to grasp her shoulders and shake some sense, some *reality*, into her. But he knew the urge was useless, for his sister was forever barred from the clear-eyed, brutal practicality that was his own burden. He sighed.

"I've been right here. Standing, watching you."

"Oh? I didn't hear you."

No, you were off in your Dream World, sister. I could have walked right up, taken your white, slender neck in my hands, and snapped it like a twig before—

He shook his head. The thought was too vivid, too unsettling. To evocative, perhaps? And how *had* his father died? Had he been a Dreamer, too?

He knelt and put his large hands on Spirits's shoulders. "Sister, you Dream too much. Were you Dreaming just now?"

Her smile was sad. "No . . . not Dreaming. Just thinking."

"Oh? About what?"

He felt her slender shoulders rise, then fall beneath his gentle fingers. "I don't know. Nothing, I guess. You know how I am."

She seemed so sad. He hated that sadness, and hated more his mother for being at the heart of it. In some obscure way he didn't understand, he blamed her for what Sleeps With Spirits was, though in his more reflective moments, he knew that she disliked what her daughter had become even more passionately than he did. Enough, in fact, to take steps. To do something. To ... murder?

That was what frightened him. Not just that Spirits was in danger. But the source of the danger. The idea of a mother killing her own blood unsettled him in his deepest parts, made him wonder even about himself, who had come from her loins, too.

Was all their blood tainted in some awful way?

"You're very quiet today," he said. He loosed her shoulders and settled back in a low squat, a position he could maintain without discomfort for hours on end. He was one of the tribe's best hunters, after all, and much of good hunting was nothing more than patience. That, and a sense of the quarry.

She shrugged again, and in her movement he *felt* that sense of the quarry. He knew her pain and her fear and her hopelessness, and it all sickened him. Yes, the time for decision was upon them, though she would not know it, and he must make the decision. Still, he hesitated.

"How is Mother?" he asked.

"She is ..." Then she shook her head.

"What's the matter? Come on, you can tell me." He reached over and patted her knee. *Her flesh, like a cold fire beneath his fingers.*

Suddenly he was conscious of the river again, of its great power, of its relentlessness, and he shivered.

She felt it. "Spears, what's the matter? Are you cold?"

"It's nothing. Is Mother being mean to you again?"

"No." Just that, nothing more. But he heard a long, drawn-out scream in the single word. He sighed.

"You don't have to stay with her, you know."

"What?" She blinked. Skin sliding over ruby. "Where else could I live? I have no mate. I couldn't live with you. And no one else would have me."

He knew it was true. "We could leave," he said.

"Right now? But we talked about that yesterday. The

People won't be going until Mother and the Chief settle things."

He took a deep breath. "That's not what I meant," he said. He felt like a man taking a long step off the river-bank, as if he was surrendering to deep currents that might sweep him away to completely unknown shores.

"What are you talking about?"

"We could leave together. Just the two of us." He stopped, shaken by the finality of what he'd just said. For a moment time seemed to freeze. He watched the porce-lain smoothness of her pale skin, the crimson of her eyes. In that instant she seemed physically unreal, no more than a creature of her own Dreams, and once again a feeling of undesignated terror crept into his bones.

She smiled. "Oh, no, I won't do that."

Something vital inside his chest popped. He felt it as a distinct sensation, so much so that he looked down to see if a hole had appeared in the center of his breastbone.

"You *won't*?" The curious popping sensation, which had now passed, was replaced by a spreading emptiness, the center of which began to vibrate rapidly. It took him a moment to realize it was his heartbeat.

"You mean," he continued, "you *can't*. That *she* won't let you go. But, sister, she doesn't have to know. She can't stop you if you really want to go."

"No." Sleeps With Spirits shook her head. "You don't understand, brother. I won't go, because it isn't going to happen. Some ... one is coming for me, and he will find me here, where the Two Rivers meet. I've seen it in a Dream."

For a moment he'd felt a flash of the purest rage and wondered who was coming for his sister, but as soon as she spoke the word "Dream," it was as if a soft, gray veil drew itself over his anger. His interest dimmed. He could barely make out her words, her senseless chatter, though she leaned forward and spoke slowly and distinctly. He watched her lips move, listened to the drone of sound that issued from them, and waited for her to finish.

"Yes, yes," he said at last. "But you don't understand, Spirits. I will take you with me. We will leave together, and the Witch, our mother, will never be able to find us."

It seemed so plain to him, so obvious. So easy. Why couldn't she *understand*?

He stood up and dusted his palms on his muscular thighs. If she couldn't understand, it didn't matter. Demons take her ridiculous Dreams. *He* understood. When the time came, he would take her anyway.

4

The Witch Woman stood outside the door of the Chief's house, her eyes narrowed thoughtfully as she stared at the door flap that had been tied shut. She could hear the low murmur of masculine voices within the commodious tent. Her practiced ears easily picked out the voices of the Shaman and the Chief by the tones of authority that suffused their words. It was as she'd guessed; the elders were meeting, and she hadn't been told. Plainly, her two enemies were making a final effort to shut her out of their decisions.

She smiled grimly. It would not be the first time they'd underestimated her power—but it would be one of the most spectacular, at least in the result.

She turned and nodded curtly at the small crowd of women who stood gathered at her rear. "Begin," she said. Her smile grew wider. Malevolent glee sparked in her black eyes.

It was coming up on noon. She knew this meeting would break up shortly, for the men inside would be expecting their noon meal. Her lips tightened as she imagined the scene inside the Chief's tent. The elders, along with the most renowned hunters, would all be squatting or sprawling in a circle around the Chief's hearth. They would be engrossed in the arguments the Shaman and the Chief were presenting in favor of leaving for the southern reaches of the river before the first snows of winter.

She was adamantly opposed to this course of action. At first, it had been merely a minor disagreement. She felt their stores were good enough to last through the winter, and she knew the women were exhausted from almost two years of steady traveling up and down the river. This place was sheltered by water on two sides, and thick forest on the third. It made sense to her to lie up for the snowy season, snug in their tents, with full larders. The People could rest and recuperate from their incessant journeying. Even the gathering here was good—fish fairly leapt into the crude traps the women wove from slender branches, and the woods were full of juicy tubers, even some trees that bore hard, faintly bitter round fruits that nevertheless grew sweet after a time in storage.

She had presented these arguments to the Chief, who had not even bothered to scoff. "We always go south ahead of the snows," he'd said, waving one arthritic hand in her face, as if shooing off a bothersome insect. "We will go south at the end of the summer, as always."

"But the women—the children—so thin, so tired. They need rest!" she'd protested.

He'd regarded her scornfully. What did he care for the women? The women would do as the men decided. As always.

It was this attitude, more than any rational value to his argument, that decided the Witch Woman on her course. The women outnumbered the men four to one. They did the work that kept the Tribe fed and clothed. And she was the leader of the women, if only because she was willing to lead. It was a curious position; hers by default, because none of the others could even imagine defying the men.

Oh, yes, she had her enemies, even among those of her own sex. But no one openly defied her, because, in their secret hearts, all of the women agreed with her. And so the battle had been joined, and she'd begun her protest. At first, her weapons had been few, but as she'd begun to understand the real power that lay in their hands—and between their thighs—she'd taken heart. The Great Mother might not have spoken to her in many long seasons, but the Witch nevertheless felt that She must approve what Her servant had set about to do.

The crowd of her followers held back a moment, despite her command. She raised her head and spoke more sharply. "I said begin!"

When nothing occurred save for some fearful muttering and a few halfhearted shakings of the baskets they carried, Witch Woman lost her patience and stomped over to them.

"Give me that!" she snarled at one of the basket holders, as she scooped both hands deep into the slimy, wriggling cargo within the basket.

"Fish!" she shouted. "Fish for midday meal!" She turned and with a single motion hurled an armload of flopping silver against the closed door flap of the Chief's tent.

Now the rest of the women, emboldened by the Witch's action, stepped up and heaved their own loads against the door and walls of the Chief's house. More fish, a cascade of bright red berries, basketfuls of freshly dug tubers, dark green wads of edible leaves, a few stalks of the mud-swathed cat tails that grew along the river's edge—a rain of food, all of it gathered by women. And none of it ready to eat.

The bounty fell in a rain of moist plops and dull thuds and rasping scratches against the large tent. The Witch's sharp ears noted the sudden silence within, and her smile grew even wider. She opened her mouth and shouted, "Come get your midday meal. It's as ready as it will ever get! Come and eat, wise men of the tribe. Come and eat!"

She folded her arms across her heavy breasts and waited in front of her ragtag army, a glint in her eyes. The rest of the women, suddenly cowed by the enormity of their rebellion, clustered together and rolled their eyes. But they didn't run away, as she'd half expected, and she was proud of them.

The moment of silence seemed to stretch. Even the Witch found herself holding her breath. She forced a soft grunt and began to tap her right foot impatiently.

With a sharp, ripping sound, one of the men inside the Chief's tent flung the door flap open.

It was the Chief himself. "Here, now! What's all the noise? What do you—aieee!"

The last sound, a half-breathy shriek, occurred as the Chief planted one shaky foot on the mound of still flopping fish directly in front of his door. That foot, none too steady to begin with, went out from under him and he collapsed, arms waving, into the piles of fish and roots and berries.

Low gasps sounded from the women at her rear, and one choked-off giggle—the Chief did look hilarious as he scrabbled and clawed about in the heaps that were to have been the midday meal—but the Witch kept her features stern and forbidding.

Now more of the men pushed out of the tent. Warned by the Chief's mishap, they stepped carefully, though their eyes widened in amazement at the sight that greeted them. The Shaman came last, supporting himself on the arm of one young, brawny hunter. The Witch squinted as she noted that the Shaman's prop was her son, Carries Two Spears.

Two of the older men quickly stooped and plucked their Chief from the mushy mélange of fish and vegetables. His once-clean robe was streaked with slime and mud. His rescuers finally got him upright. Sputtering with rage, he pushed them away. Then a curious, *pained* expression came over his face. He slapped at the neck of his robe. A tiny, silvery fish popped forth and fell down his front.

His gaze followed the glittering thing down, paused to watch it flop wildly at the tip of his right foot, and then, slowly, rose again until he had both eyes focused on the Witch.

"You!"

She nodded. Without knowing it, she hunched her muscular shoulders slightly, as if expecting a blow. The Chief saw, though, and her unconscious reaction reinforced his own subconscious intentions. He strode forward, kicking bits of refuse out of his path.

"Have you lost your mind!" He raised his hand to strike her, but before he could bring down the blow—he was flabby, but still strong—she straightened up and glared into his face.

"Don't," she warned, raw intensity in her voice. "You would strike the handmaiden of the Terrible Mother? Look around you, Chief. Look at the ground beneath your feet. Go on, *look* at it!"

Momentarily nonplussed, the Chief paused in midstroke, his initial anger distracted into uncertainty by the Witch's hissing fervor. His gaze wavered, shifted. He looked down at the mess scattered at his feet.

"What? What are you talking about, woman?"

"Your meal, Chief. Why don't you eat it?" She glanced up at the sky. "It's time for midday meal. Aren't you hungry? Don't you want to *eat*?"

Kills Many Buffalo shook his head. "What are you talking about? Eat? What is there to eat? Raw tubers? Flopping fish? What do you mean, eat?"

The hugely vicious grin she'd kept trembling in her throat burped to her lips. The Chief actually quailed in the face of her horrific, triumphant expression. "That's what you get, Chief Kills Many Buffalo. The women are too tired to cook for you anymore. The women have traveled endlessly for many seasons, and now they will rest."

The Witch spread both her arms wide. "Let the men, who hide behind closed door flaps, come out and cook their own food. Let them gather the tubers they will eat. Let them catch their own fish and find their own greens. Let them boil soup! Let them roast roots! Let *them* work, for the women are too tired now!"

There. The rebellion she'd so carefully plotted was out in the open now. The challenge had been issued. The battle was joined.

"The Terrible Mother says wait through the time of falling leaves, wait through the snows, let the women renew themselves!" She paused, and dropped her voice so only the Chief heard her next words: "Otherwise, well . . ."

She glanced at the trampled food. And shrugged.

Kills Many Buffalo opened his mouth. His teeth bulged forward, yellow and pitiful. In that moment he looked old and tired. And defeated.

Witch Woman knew she'd won. The men, stupid, lazy creatures that they were, had no answer to this sort of rebellion. They were good for hunting down animals, but even those trophies were butchered and cooked by the women. Only the Witch had grasped that essential fact, and understood how it might be used to cement her own power. Hers, and that of the Terrible Mother she served.

"What say you, Chief of the River People?" she whispered.

"How dare you!"

The Witch Woman whirled, just in time to receive a pair of stinging slaps across her cheeks. The force of the blows snapped her head sharply one way, then the other. Her mouth fell open as she stared in shock at her assailant.

Drinks Deep Waters seemed to *vibrate* as he stood before her, his eyes spitting black sparks. "The Chief may fear you and your Terrible Goddess, but I speak for the Thunder God!" he roared. "Get your rabble out of here! Go back to your tents, you women!"

Stunned, Witch Woman raised one trembling hand to her cheek, unconsciously stroking the livid finger marks there. She opened her mouth to speak, but the ancient, birdlike man raised his hand to forestall her.

"Don't!" He shook his head and spat on the ground before her. "Don't say anything, just take your poor, deluded followers away, or I will have you all beaten on this very spot!"

"But—but—"

"Go!"

Witch Woman could hear the women behind her, muttering in fright, begin to depart. She *felt* their desertion as a cold wind on her back. She glanced at the men who stood behind their Shaman, now flexing their muscles and clenching their fists eagerly.

It was defeat, utter and complete. Drinks Deep Waters's low, triumphant cackle rang shamefully in her burning ears as she turned and fled.

5

There was much weeping and wailing among the women in the camp of the River People that night, but in the tent of the Witch Woman there was darkness, and silence. The Witch sat at her cold hearth, her hands wrapped around her knees, and stared blankly into the empty ring of stone. Only Sleeps With Spirits, who entered the tent for a moment and then left immediately, understood what was going on there. While another might have interpreted the silence as that of gloom and defeat, the strange Dreaming girl, with her odd powers, immediately sensed the truth. The tent stank of a rage as bleak and voiceless as the storms of winter—and as murderous.

Spirits fled in panic. Carries Two Spears found her at her usual spot by the river, aimlessly sifting water through her pale fingers.

He squatted next to her and said, "I think Mother made a bad mistake today, challenging the Shaman and the Chief like that."

She turned and gazed mutely at him, her ruby eyes shadowed. He thought she looked exhausted, and once again his heart went out to her. He draped one bulky arm gently over her shoulder, and felt her quiver beneath his touch like a frightened bird.

"Have you seen her?" he asked softly.

She nodded.

He sighed. "Listen."

Faint cries of pain wafted through the honeyed darkness at their back. "The Shaman told the men to beat their women." He shook his head. "Not just the ones who went with Mother, but *all* of them. He said they were getting out of hand and needed to be taught a lesson." He paused. "He even told me to beat you and Mother."

She froze, her eyes wide, and he chuckled. "Of course I won't. I would *never* do anything to hurt you, sister. I *promise* that. And as for Mother, well ..."

He didn't need to say anything more. He was no more capable of laying a finger on the Witch Woman than Spirits was. In fact, he still was amazed the Shaman had done so.

"What will she do, do you think?" he whispered.

Spirits finally spoke. "I don't know," she said, and shuddered. "It will be horrible, though."

That mirrored Two Spears's feelings on the matter perfectly. Though not close to his mother, he knew her well enough to fear her. The conflict between the older woman and the Shaman wasn't over, not by a long spear-throw. He only hoped the Tribe, and more specifically himself

and Spirits, would survive whatever terrible vengeance
the Witch and the Terrible Goddess were no doubt planning in the poison dark of the Witch's tent.

"Have you thought anymore about what I said?" he
asked softly.

She shook her head. "I must wait for he who comes,"
she replied.

He clicked his teeth together in frustration. Sometimes
his sister's fancies irritated him almost beyond bearing.
He knew how weak and frightened she was, but didn't
she understand that it needn't always be that way? If only
she could cast off those strange, ridiculous Dreams!

But she couldn't. He would have to accept that, and he
did. As much as he could. He gripped her tighter and
promised himself one thing: whatever happened, he
wouldn't let any harm come to her. If necessary, he would
take her away by force.

For her own good, he told himself. The raw, red throbbing in his groin, he decided, was only further proof of
his own devotion.

"Horrible . . ." Sleeps With Spirits whispered. But her
prophesy, for that is what it was, vanished soundlessly
into the endless rush of the river and, like all of her
Dreams, was swept away unheard.

6

Witch Woman shook herself. Her hide shirt stuck to
her skin as she moved, bathed in the sweat of her own anger. Inside she felt cold, but outside the heat burned her
almost as badly as her own humiliation.

Humiliation! There was no other word for it. The Shaman had disgraced her, confronted and mocked her, *defeated* her. And not only her—for both she and him
represented far greater Powers than their own puny skills.
In some indefinable way the Terrible Mother and the
Thunder God had faced each other before the Chief's
tent, and the result of that confrontation was obvious. Not
only her own humiliation, but the *Mother's* as well.

She could feel her terrible patroness's rage inside her

like a gut full of boiling water, searing her innards, bubbling in her throat, the steam of it blinding her eyes.

"I have failed you, Mother," she whispered as she held herself and rocked before the barren hearth. *"Can you forgive me? Can you help me avenge you?"*

She waited in the dark, hoping for a reply, but nothing came. The Mother had not spoken to her for long years, though she still held the truth of Her inside her heart. *Nothing* could take that truth from her, not time, not defeat, not even death.

Nor did she need the guidance of Dream or Vision to tell her what she must do now. The shame could not be allowed to go unavenged. Nor would she allow it to. But the question was *how*? How to wreak vengeance on the filthy blasphemer, the cursed Shaman who crowed in victory this very night?

She raised her head and listened to the pained cries that echoed softly in the dark beyond her door. She knew what was going on out there. On the morrow, many women would limp and show bruised faces. And the *men*—

That would be the worst of all, how the men would chuckle at her, grin and smirk right to her face, and laugh aloud behind her back. They would walk with a spring in their steps, proud of their strength, their *mastery*. In a single stroke the Shaman had negated much of her power, for the women who were her natural allies would be frightened, and the men strengthened by what had occurred.

Even to the mocking of the Mother Herself!

"Ahhh ..." she moaned, and rocked forward on her haunches, gripping her knees more tightly, as if she could somehow *squeeze* an answer out of her very flesh and bones. Her fingers clenched spasmodically, like the claws of a great bird. Tears rolled silently down her cheeks.

She gasped, and opened her right hand wide. Something had bitten her!

Then she realized what had happened. She raised the small object she'd been holding, and though it was too dark to make out much more than the vaguest outline, she

could see it in her mind's eye clearly; the stone knife that
was her most potent talisman.

One of its edges had cut her palm, and now her blood
mingled on the flaked stone with other, more ancient
gore. As she stared blankly at the almost invisible object,
something began to take more visible shape in her mind.
She froze, lest a stray movement drive the vision from her
before it came to fruition.

"Ahh . . ." she moaned again, but this time, the sound
was one of triumph. Almost—yes, now she had it. Her
fingers, slippery with her own blood, tightened on the
deadly little weapon. Once she'd been directed to use it
on her own mate, and now, once again, that directing
force was speaking to her. Not in words, but in the plan
that now shimmered in the night before her eyes, almost
real enough to touch.

She'd once given thought to killing a pair of birds
with a single stone. Now she knew which birds—and
which stone.

"Thank You," she whispered. "Oh, *thank* You!"

7

The camp was silent and sleeping beneath a bowl of
stars when Sleeps With Spirits finally wandered back
from her tryst by the river. She was half afraid to return
to her tent, but she had nowhere else to go.

She ghosted soundlessly through the shuttered tents,
her feet finding their familiar path without thought. Wisps
of night fog drifted about her. She didn't realize it, but as
she walked, she keened softly. The sound was low and
plaintive and didn't sound at all human.

If only I could think of what to do!

Carries Two Spears's intentions had finally begun to
sink into the pitiful fog of her fear and indecision. She
sensed something amiss, something *wrong* with his feelings toward her, but she knew his love was real enough.
And who else in this whole miserable World loved her
even a little bit?

If only she could explain things to him. If only he

would at least *listen* to the truth of her Dreams. But, like
all the others, he wouldn't. Even his strange, uncomfortably hot love for her wouldn't allow him to believe her.

Why am I so cursed?

The lumpy shape of her tent loomed suddenly before
her. She paused uncertainly, straining to hear any sound
from within. She'd stayed away this long in hopes the
Witch wouldn't be awake to greet her, but with her
mother, one never knew. Maybe, somehow, the Witch
even blamed *her* for the day's debacle.

After a moment, though, she heard a familiar sound; a
low, grunting series of snores. Her mother had gone to
sleep. She let out the breath she'd been holding without
realizing it, and her shoulders slumped with relief. This
night, at least, she'd be safe. The Witch, so sharp and sensitive in most things, once asleep, slept like a log. If she
was careful, she could find her own bed undisturbed.

Moving slowly, she pushed the door flap aside and
crept into the tent. Her nose wrinkled at the thick, ominous odor that greeted her. It was so potent she felt her
eyes begin to sting.

What was it? Herbs of some kind. The stench of the
cold hearth. Sweat. And—blood?

She shivered. Yes, that was it. Blood, cool but still
fresh. What horrid ritual had the Witch played out in her
absence? She couldn't guess—her mother had never
wasted much time trying to train Spirits in the secrets of
her art—but whatever it was, it boded evil for the morrow.

She didn't need any Dream to lay bare the stink of
vengeance that floated like a fog in this stifling interior.
Something terrible had happened here, and it was only a
beginning. She knew that. She wondered what hideous
end her mother envisioned, and shivered again.

Somehow, she was certain, she had her own part to
play in her mother's plots. Maybe Two Spears was right.
Maybe she *should* leave with him. Her Dreams told her
otherwise, but nobody believed her Dreams.

A thrilling thought quivered out to the tips of her
nerves. Why should she believe her own Dreams? Maybe
everybody else was right, and she the one who was

wrong. Mother knew, her Dreams had never brought her any happiness or any safety.

She found her bed and settled down on it. A few twigs crackled beneath her weight. She held her breath for a moment, waiting to see if the noise would disturb her mother, but except for a moist, farting sound, the rhythm of the Witch's snortings remained undisturbed.

She pillowed her palms beneath her head and stared up at the roof of the tent. A single star, glimmering through the smoke hole, caught her eye. It gleamed there like a promise.

Her thoughts slowly turned into a puzzling jumble of impressions, fleeting pictures of a life she could barely imagine. Striding with Two Spears through the endless forests, her mother, her past, the One To Come left far behind. What would such a thing be like?

As she considered all this, a feeling so strange she had no word for it began to grow inside her. Something deep within, stunted and lifeless, began to twist and raise hungry fingers toward a light it could barely see.

The word she sought but couldn't find was freedom. Freedom from her past, from her Dreams, from her destiny. She didn't know what it was, only that it was terrible—and terribly seductive.

It was that unknown word that finally became a boat in her mind and carried her off on the river of sleep. But when her eyes finally closed, and her breathing became soft and regular, her lips formed yet another word, unbeknownst to her waking mind.

Her body spoke a truth her conscious mind had not yet encompassed, for it was a truth yet to come; she saw the future, but knew it not. Though her flesh did, from the truth of Dreams buried deep within it. There was a birth coming, a birth for all the World, and with it, as with all birth—

"Blood," her lips said soundlessly. *"Blood!"*

BOOK THREE

TWO WOMEN

"Life does not give itself to one who tries to keep all its advantages at once. I have often thought morality may perhaps consist solely in the courage of making a choice."

—LEON BLUM

CHAPTER THIRTEEN

1

Rising Sun said, "Something is following us. Do you feel it?"

Running Deer glanced at him and wrinkled her nose. "The only thing I smell is *us*," she said, grinning.

"No, I don't mean that. Can't you *feel* it?" He raised his hands in a puzzled gesture. "I mean, it's like a small cloud or something. I turn around, expecting to see it, but nothing's there. Still . . ." He shrugged, uncomfortable at trying to explain to her what was bothering him. Perhaps because he didn't really understand it himself.

The girl understood enough to know he was serious, and changed her expression accordingly. "No, Rising Sun, I don't feel anything."

He shrugged his frustration and let the matter drop. He was conscious of her gaze on him as they strode along the river. The country hereabouts was rolling and heavily wooded, and from a windblown bald spot on the highest of the low hills, he'd glimpsed an ever-darkening carpet of green in the forward distance. After four hands of days on the trek, the land about them had changed utterly from the steppe that surrounded the Valley in which he'd been raised. Even the trees here were different—darker, thicker, and taller—than those in the sheltered Green Valley, though many of them seemed to be of the same kind.

Another thing he'd noticed was that the sky seemed somehow smaller—lower, more filled with clouds, almost claustrophobic. And this new world teemed with life. The woods were full of game, the branches of the trees heavy with birds. Nevertheless, it was an empty land. In all their days of travel, they'd yet to run across any signs of humanity at all.

He mused on this as he walked along—the contrast between the teeming Tribes of the Green Valley, pressed together between their walls of stone, and this vast emptiness. It was almost as if this new world was empty and waiting. He felt that, as well—that *expectancy*—and wondered what it might portend.

"What?" he said, startled.

"I said we ought to stop for the night. Dusk is coming on, and this place looks as good as any," Moon Face replied.

The chubby little apprentice had ranged several paces ahead, as was his wont. They were three, but somehow the would-be Shaman managed to maintain his separateness from the other two. During the day's marches, he walked either in front or lagged behind, never matching his pace to that of his companions. And at night, when Rising Sun and Running Deer laid their bedrolls as close together as possible, Moon Face always dropped off to sleep on the other side of the fire.

Rising Sun followed Moon Face's sweeping gesture and nodded. "Yes," he replied. "A good idea."

He turned to Running Deer. "Why don't you lay out our packs, while Moon Face makes a fire?"

Their journey had become routine. Without any discussion, each had taken up certain tasks, and now there was no disagreement as each set about their self-appointed chores. Moon Face was far more skilled with fire than either of them. Wordlessly, he ambled down toward the river, seeking smooth stones for their hearth. Smooth stones were important; cracked, rough stones often exploded when subjected to the heat of the fire.

While the apprentice searched, Running Deer opened their packs and set out portions of trail meat. Some of the brown, chewy stuff was almost fresh. They'd paused in their journey two days before and hunted. Rising Sun had speared a small pig deep within the forest near a spring, while Running Deer had brought down a brace of fine rabbits with her bow.

Everything was ready when Moon Face came back, his chubby arms laden with rocks, which he arranged in a circle around the dry wood that Rising Sun had gathered. A moment later a small, cheery blaze crackled cheerfully in the gathering dusk. Running Deer had fashioned a leather pot from scraps of hide and hung it over the hearth. Into the steaming water she dumped handfuls of greens and several chunks of the trail meat. A rich, greasy smell wafted up, accompanied by the sounds of hungry stomachs.

After they had eaten, Rising Sun lay back, his head pillowed on his pack, and picked bits of food from his teeth with a length of sharpened bone. He belched with contentment. For a moment all the thoughts that had disturbed him vanished, and he simply sprawled bonelessly, as comfortable and secure as any other freshly sated animal.

Even Moon Face, normally so tense and jumpy, seemed to catch the relaxed mood, for though he maintained his usual position on the other side of the fire, his round features were slack, almost smiling.

I wish it could be like this all the time, Rising Sun mused. The tensions among the three of them tried him sorely. Moon Face remained sullen and uncommunicative, so unlike the cheerful, joking young man he'd always known. And while his growing closeness with Running Deer—and the passion that night brought them both—was some compensation, even this had its problems. For Running Deer was unlike any woman he'd ever known, or even imagined.

At times, he found her wild independence uplifting, even joyous—but other times, this same rebellious streak frustrated him terribly. She *questioned* him rather than simply acquiescing to his every desire. Moreover, her questions sometimes mirrored the doubts in his own mind, which made him mistrust even his most basic assumptions. Particularly those that pertained to the journey itself.

He sighed. Only for a moment had he been able to forget all this, but now his disquiet returned with crushing force. He glanced over at her and saw the glint of her own eyes reflected in the shifting light of the fire.

It was disconcerting, her way of almost seeming to know the thoughts inside his own skull. He found comfort in the way they could seem to agree with little more than a telling glance, but it made him uneasy, too—was such closeness between a man and a woman entirely natural? It was almost as if they were *equals*.

Yet the fact remained that she was here, and there was nothing now to be done about it. The time for sending her back was long past. Whatever came of this quest, they would face it together.

Ah, yes. The quest. He'd thought of it that way in the beginning—Gotha had even named it so, and at the time it had seemed specific. Even simple. Go on a journey, find the Stone Rejoined, inherit the World. But now, after many days of trekking, nothing seemed simple anymore. In fact, Rising Sun doubted that it had *ever* been simple, and worse—he thought Gotha had known it from the very beginning.

Devious old man!

What would happen, he wondered, if he simply turned around and headed back to the Green Valley? A part of him embraced the idea with a glad ferocity that surprised him. Yes, he could see it—he could return from this wildghost chase with a woman and without the fearful destiny that sometimes seemed to portend nothing but a wandering doom. Relieved of his destiny, he could settle into the day-to-day life of the Valley, raise his children in peace, and let all the rest go hang. Let someone else seek the mysterious Talisman, let someone else thrash in the night from ominous Dreams he could never seem to recall upon awakening.

Yes, a part of him craved such a resolution. It would be the easy way out, an answer of sorts to all questions. It would, in fact, be the perfect solution, except for one thing. He had sat upon the empty seats of the Departed

Ones, and seen the Last Mammoth. He could no more gainsay that than he could doubt his own breathing. And though his understanding of that Dream and the Vision within it was cloudy, the *fact* of it was as real as anything he could touch or taste or feel.

He sighed once again, a mournful sound, and turned toward the solace that only Running Deer could give him. But now, as the fire burned low beneath the carpeted stars above, her eyes had closed. She slept, and though he ached to waken her, he felt a watchful gaze from beyond the hearth.

He rolled back, put his arms beneath his head, and closed his own eyes. He had many aches, it seemed, and the one in his groin was only the least of many. Would surcease ever come?

He didn't know. Of only one thing was he certain: this quest was more than a journey. It would, in time, become a choice. Between or among what, he couldn't begin to guess. Only that choices would come, and he would have to make them. To go or turn back was only one of those choices.

He would have prayed to the Gods for help, but They were gone. Sometimes, that hurt most of all.

2

Terror almost brought him to a halt, but somehow he managed to place one massive foot in front of the other. Sometimes the terror was only fear, and he could cope with it better. Other times, the terror bloomed like some malignant flower inside his skull, becoming red and wet and sucking, and his bowels would collapse, and then his knees, and then he would lie helpless in the slime and stink of his own waste.

It wasn't quite that bad now. Not yet, at least. The smell of the nearby campfire was sharp and acrid in his broad nostrils. The tangled, waist-length thatch of his matted hair scratched softly against his huge shoulders as he moved a step closer, his muscles rigid and quivering with fear.

If only he could clear the clouds from his mind! He was rarely aware of his surroundings, and only the direst obsession had prodded him from the safety of the walls within which he had lived so long. But the obsession wouldn't be denied.

She!

He didn't know her name. He knew nothing at all about her, in fact, except that she fed him, and that the mismatched colors of her eyes kindled longings inside him he couldn't even begin to understand.

Once, he thought vaguely, things had been different. *He* had been different. His world had not always been an all-encompassing well of horror. In fact, in his more lucid moments, he thought it might have been exactly the opposite. He could almost see that man—almost, but not quite. Yet somewhere inside him, trapped by the cage of terror, that man still existed, raging against the mindless bars that bound him.

It was the existence of this prisoner, this nearly forgotten shred of past glory, that allowed him to move yet another step forward. But it was hard.

He felt as if he moved in a darkness more impenetrable than the night that surrounded him, for in his darkness, there were no stars, only nameless, shadowy shapes that drifted close to him, invisible jaws yawning with terrible hunger.

He was only dimly aware of the real World through which he moved, though he moved with surprising grace for his size. Through the long years of his terror, he had learned a stealth far greater than he'd possessed in his previous life. Now he edged closer to the small camp, his flat nostrils twitching at the smoke from the dying fire.

Carefully he pushed aside the last screen of brush and peered out, blinking. For a moment his vision cleared, and he saw the camp as it really was, unencumbered by the cloudiness of his fear.

The fire in the hearth had burned down to softly glowing orange coals. Three lumps lay around the fire, two close together, the third well away from them. He raised his big head, listening, and heard a mingled symphony of soft exhalations.

For some time he was content to remain motionless, his ears straining for the sounds that were both frightening and reassuring to him. *She* was here, and *she* was the reason for his long journey.

He remembered little of that journey. There had been wolves, but he'd stayed well away from their savage howling, and for a time thought he'd lost her trail altogether. Later, he'd come upon the scene of slaughter and poked curiously at the piled carcasses of the pack. He was fairly certain that at least one of the wolves remained. He'd sensed its presence, and several times altered his path to avoid the watchfulness he felt like an itch in the soft flesh of his throat.

Suddenly he stiffened. From one of the indistinct lumps came a series of quiet snorts, then a louder inhalation. The shadow moved!

Quivering with fright, he withdrew behind the screening brush, his muscles almost locked by terror. Here he froze, unable to make any further move. Now he heard the soft pad of footsteps, then the abrupt rattle of leaf against branch. Someone was pushing into the woods, only a few short steps from him!

His reddened eyes rolled wildly in their sockets. Deep inside his broad, grizzled chest, his heart pounded like a mighty drum. Without realizing it, he raised his gnarled hands in a warding motion. He swallowed a moan as the thrashing sounds grew inexorably closer . . .

3

Running Deer was awakened by a griping in her bowels. She rolled over, wincing at the sharp pain, and sighed. It must have been the trail meat. Perhaps she hadn't cured it properly, or maybe the berries she'd ground into the meat and fat hadn't been the right kind.

She got her feet under her and stood, blinking sleepily. The night had turned cool, though the breezes had died away, leaving only the ever-present smells and sounds of the nearby river. Otherwise, all was quiet.

She stepped over Rising Sun's sleeping form and

made her way toward the woods that surrounded the little clearing to make her toilet. Still half asleep, she didn't move as lightly as she was capable, and made a rustling clatter as she shoved her way through the screening brush. In the dim starlight she finally located a likely looking spot, sighed again, and squatted to do her business. It took only a few moments, though in the middle she raised her head, her eyes questioning. An oddly familiar smell, a small sound that didn't quite seem a part of the night—?

She shook her head, reached for a wad of leaves, and completed her toilet. Her disquiet subsided as she began to make her way back to the welcoming warmth of her bedroll. So lulled, she didn't notice the massive, hulking shape until she blundered right into it.

"Uhh—" But her cry was immediately muffled by the huge, callused hand that clamped itself across her lips! She struggled instinctively, biting at the hardened skin, but to no avail! The creature's strength was enormous! Now arms as thick as tree trunks wrapped themselves around her, pinioning her against a mighty chest.

As she twisted and wriggled desperately, her head crushed into a rough thatch of hair, she could hear the pounding of a great heart, as rapid as the frenzied beat of a log drum. Heat welled from the creature, as if a fire burned just beneath his skin.

The hand remained firmly clamped across her mouth, and no sound escaped. Wildly she thought of Rising Sun and Moon Face, so near and yet so distant! If only she could—

But she couldn't. And now, to her horror, she realized she was moving. Lifted as if her weight were no more than that of a bird, helpless in the remorseless grasp of the thing, she was carried backward, away from the camp and the men who were her only hope!

Oh, Mother, help me! she prayed silently as she continued her hopeless struggle. Then something huge and hard slammed into the side of her skull. Sparks fountained white behind her eyes. She toppled into that light, and saw no more.

4

Out of his terror, he had done what he could never have done otherwise; it was a reflex of simple panic that had made him grab the girl when she stumbled into him, and a crescendo of dread that had *forced* him to hold on to her, press his hand across her mouth when she began to scream, and, finally, to back away from the camp with her caught fast in his mighty arms. He'd been trapped by his own instinctive responses, and now there was nothing to do but run!

She fought him, though, and finally, hardly knowing he did so, he clouted her until she hung limply in his ponderous grasp. His mind ceased functioning as such. Flares of alarm roared through his nerves and muscles, their message simple and irresistible—*flee!*

When some semblance of reason finally returned to his thoughts—as much as ever came there nowadays—he set her down and squatted next to her. Sweat dripped from his brow and hung in silver drops from his nose. He glanced around fearfully and saw only the dark boles of forest giants. The dull roar of the river was only a distant whisper in his ears.

He reached out and gently traced the outline of her jaw with one finger. She didn't move or respond in any way. Once again, panic exploded inside him, but then he saw that her chest still rose and fell in even rhythms. So he hadn't killed her!

Thank the Gods—

But They were gone now, weren't They? Somehow he knew that, though he didn't know how. They had ruined him, and then They'd left, discarding him like any cast-off carcass.

He made a soft, hooting sound and hunkered lower. *She* was here before him. But what was he supposed to do *now*?

He couldn't imagine. Still making that deep, chest-wrenching sound, he sank down beside her, hoping to keep her warm with the heat of his own body. It was all too much for him. What few circuits in his smoking brain

still remained began, one by one, to shut down. He
wrapped his arms around her.

He could never have consciously managed to kidnap
her, but his consciousness had not been an issue. Only
panic, and now he found himself struggling with a problem far too great for his tortured mind to handle. Deep inside his huge chest thundered the long booming rush of
his love for her. He could never hurt her, no, never! But
the men would hurt him.

The men with their sharp spears would come. He was
certain of that, and had no idea what he would do. The
overpowering desire to keep her close warred within him
against the uncertainty of releasing her. Would she lead
them to him, those men with the sharp spears? He bashed
his great fists against his forehead once! twice! but the
blows didn't help. *He could not think!* And so, after a
time, even the urge for thought faded. He did what he always did when the terrors of the World grew too great for
him. Snorting softly, painfully though deliciously aware
of *her* closeness, he finally dropped off to sleep—
unaware the strands of his fate had been woven once
again by forces far beyond his comprehension into a
greater weaving, one that would change the World.

5

Rising Sun awoke from a troubled dream to the sense
that something was *wrong*. He blinked awake and stared
blindly at the green treetops waving in the gentle morning
breeze above him. Yes, definitely something *wrong*.

He ran his tongue over his dry lips, uncomfortably
aware of his bladder full to bursting. Even the erection he
always sported upon awakening felt too hard, almost
painful. He stretched, wondering if the *wrong* feeling was
simply a hangover of the unsettling dream he could no
longer remember, and pushed himself upright. Across the
dead hearth, Moon Face was still a shapeless lump rolled
into his bed fur. Rising Sun quirked a grin in that direction, then turned to jostle Running Deer awake.

"Come on, woman—" he began.

Her bedroll was there, but it was empty. He blinked. The feeling of *wrongness* welled up stronger than ever. But at first he did nothing, merely stared at the forlorn pile of fur. Maybe she'd gone into the bushes to do her morning business.

And maybe not. He reared up from his own fur, got his feet under him, and stood. His heart began to thrum inside his suddenly tightened chest. "Running Deer?" he called.

No answer. *"Running Deer!"*

"What? Why are you yelling?" came the muffled, muzzy query from beyond the hearth.

Rising Sun paid no attention. He jumped across Running Deer's bedclothes and rammed his way through the brushy screen into the deeper woods, still calling at the top of his lungs.

"Running Deer! Running Deer! Where are you?"

But in a few seconds his initial panic subsided into an icy focus. He stood stock-still next to a large oak, every muscle tensed and quivering, an expression of absolute concentration on his young features.

He waited, but heard nothing. Slowly he cupped his hands around his mouth and called one more time: *"Running Deer!"*

"What's all the racket?" came the querulous response at his rear. He turned as Moon Face, knuckling sleep from his eyes, blundered up to him. The smaller man was still only half awake.

"You sound like a mammoth shrieking," he muttered. "What's going on?" He paused, scratched himself, then looked around, as the meaning of Rising Sun's cries finally sank in. "Where's the girl?"

"I don't know," Rising Sun replied.

Moon Face shrugged. "She's probably wandered off to take a shit," he ventured. "Don't worry, she'll be back."

Rising Sun was well aware of the low esteem in which the apprentice held Running Deer, whom he viewed as a rival, at best, and possibly something much worse. "Why doesn't she answer, then?" he said.

A petulant expression twisted the would-be Shaman's

lips. "Who knows? She's a woman. Maybe she thinks it's some kind of game."

Rising Sun gave him a disgusted look. "She's not like that. Something's happened."

"Oh? Like what?" Then Moon Face's expression brightened. "Maybe she decided to go home."

Now Rising Sun let the disgust creep into his tone. "Oh, really? Without her pack? Her bedroll? Without her *bow*?" Only Rising Sun truly understood how much that weapon, which she had made with her own hands and strung with her own hair, meant to Running Deer.

Moon Face shrugged again, suddenly seeming to lose interest. "I'm going down to the river," he said shortly. "Maybe she's down there."

"I'll go with you," Rising Sun decided. He looked around again, then said, "Watch where you walk. If she went this way, maybe she left a trail." But as he glanced down, he realized that his own first bungling plunge into the woods might already have obliterated any tracks.

"Go on. I'll catch up in a moment," he told Moon Face's retreating back. The apprentice made no reply. Rising Sun waited until the smaller man had disappeared. Then, slowly, he began to examine every inch of the path he'd taken as he moved toward the campsite.

It was as he'd feared. He botched it right from the start. His own trail was easy enough to read—a plethora of rumpled leaves, broken twigs, heavy footsteps. Only here and there did he find even hints of something else, and those hints were so vague as to be almost useless. A mashed patch of grass, only now springing back up, that was a bit to the right of his own trail. A broken weed, its bright flower bent and bruised. But nothing that might not have been natural, or a result of his own stumbling passage.

"*Demon Spirits!*" he muttered as he reentered the clearing. He walked over to Running Deer's bedroll and squatted down on his haunches, his eyes squinted in thought. There was no sign of a struggle. Her fur had been cast aside, as if she'd merely gotten up in the night. He wrinkled his nose. Something was different here . . .

He couldn't quite figure out what it was. Sighing, he

stood up and headed down to the river. He didn't think he would find her there, and he was right.

He found Moon Face standing at the edge of the water, kicking idly at a clump of sawgrass, and staring blankly at the tree line on the other side of the river.

"Did you find anything?" Rising Sun asked.

Moon Face jumped, then turned, a guilty expression on his face. He shook his head.

"Well," Rising Sun said. "Let's get packed. We'll start as soon as we're ready."

"Start *where*? What are you talking about?"

Rising Sun blinked, startled at the vehemence in his companion's tone. "Running Deer, of course. I found what might be a spoor. Maybe we'll find more."

He turned away, eager to begin the hunt, though afraid of what he might find at the end of it. This was strange, wild country. Only after he'd taken several quick strides back toward their camp did he realize that Moon Face hadn't moved.

"Moon Face. Come on! We have to hurry!"

Moon Face shook his head. There was a stubborn set to his pudgy shoulders. "No. I'm not going."

"What?"

"I said I'm not going. And you shouldn't either."

Rising Sun turned around and came back to the riverside. "Moon Face, what's *wrong* with you? Of *course* I'm going to find her. And I need your help. Now stop this foolishness and let's get going!"

But the apprentice only shook his head more obstinately, his lower lip pushing out in an expression of perfect intransigence. "I'm not going after that . . . *girl*," he spat out finally. His tone changed, became urgent with the effort to convince. He grasped Rising Sun's shoulder. "Don't you *see* it, Rising Sun? Are you so blind you can't *see*?"

Rising Sun shook the smaller man's hand away. Terrible urgency burned in his nerves. A tic had begun to jitter beneath his right eye.

I don't have time for this madness, he thought suddenly.

"Are you coming or not?" he said.

"No."

Without another word, Rising Sun spun on his heel and stalked away.

"Rising Sun, *wait!*"

The plea came out as a long, wailing cry, but Rising Sun paid no attention. He kept on moving and didn't look back.

What's wrong with everybody? Am I the only one whose mind hasn't been stolen by Spirits? Rising Sun thought.

Even so, he suddenly felt more lonely than he ever had before as, carrying a hastily assembled pack, he thrust back into the woods to search for a spoor that might lead him to Running Deer. Though he'd half expected Moon Face to follow him as soon as he got over his strange fit of pique, the apprentice made no appearance.

As he moved carefully through the scrub, surveying the earth beneath his feet and the plants and bushes that grew from it, he remembered Moon Face's fingers on his shoulder. He remembered something else, too, but he would think about that later.

He had more important things on his mind right now.

6

Moon Face watched his friend stride away with a hollow, sinking feeling in the pit of his stomach. His distress was not entirely caused by this latest snub of his wishes, either. For all of his "confessions" to Rising Sun about the thoughts of Gotha the Shaman, and the instructions Gotha had given to him, there was one thing he'd left out. He could remember that final conversation easily. It was burned into his brain. Now, once again, he wrestled with that scene as he trudged back toward the camp, wondering if now was the time Gotha had warned him about.

Gotha leaned forward, his dark eyes intent on his young apprentice's face.

"There is one final thing," he said softly.

Moon Face, sensing the importance of what was to come, nodded slowly. "Yes, teacher?" he whispered.

"The quest Rising Sun is about to attempt is far more important than anything you or I might do. It may involve the survival of all of us, even the World itself. The Gods are gone. This quest may decide what comes after the Gods. Do you understand?"

Moon Face licked his lips. It was hot and smoky in the Spirit House. He could almost imagine that Spirits floated and twined within the fumes that he breathed. "I'm ... not sure," he said at last.

Gotha shook his head. His unbound hair shimmered softly in the gloom, making him look, Moon Face thought, almost like a Spirit himself.

"The quest and its outcome may be even more important than Rising Sun. He may be the One To Come, or he may not be. Only the quest and its ending will determine the truth."

Gotha paused, but when Moon Face made no reply, he shook his head again, his irritation becoming more plain. "What I am saying to you is this, apprentice. If Rising Sun does not complete the quest, or if he strays too far from the path, terrible things may happen. He must follow the road to its finish, and bring the Stone back to the Green Valley. If he doesn't, then I have made a mistake in naming him the One To Come. He would be an impostor, then, and far more dangerous than you can imagine."

Gotha seemed to be dancing around something, but what it might be, Moon Face was unable to guess. He strained for meaning, but nothing came. Finally, he did what he always did when he didn't understand.

"Tell me plainly what you want me to do, Master," he said. "I am only an apprentice. Command me."

Gotha sighed. Sometimes he wished his apprentice showed the quickness and subtlety of mind that Rising Sun so easily managed. But such a creature would not be as dependable as Moon Face, whose stolidity belied strong loyalty and dogged determination. Rising Sun would question what Gotha was about to say, if not openly, at least within his own thoughts. Moon Face would not, and that suited the Shaman perfectly. Never-

theless, what he was about to say so baldy made Gotha feel naked.

"If Rising Sun doesn't follow the path destined for him, if he turns away from the quest for the Stone Rejoined, then he is not the One to Come. And you must end the quest, before the impostor can do any further damage. Because, my apprentice, the hopes of the World ride on the back of the One To Come. If there is any sign that Rising Sun is not that One, then he is something else, something that usurps the path of the true One, whose way leads only to the Stone Rejoined, and the promise it holds for the World. And for Rising Sun to leave that path must not be allowed. Do you understand me now?"

"End the quest? It isn't mine to end. It is Rising Sun's quest."

Gotha nodded. "But if Rising Sun is no more, then it is the same for his impostor's quest."

Finally Moon Face understood. His jaw dropped open. "You mean—?"

"Yes," Gotha said calmly. "If Rising Sun is not the One To Come, the danger lies not just in the wrong path he will take, but in those who would follow him down it. That must not be allowed to happen. If he strays, Moon Face, you must kill him."

Gotha's instructions and warnings filled Moon Face's thoughts now as he walked bleakly into the remains of their camp. A glance told him that Rising Sun was gone. He'd taken one of the packs and his weapons. The rest lay about in dejected heaps, their strewn abandon proclaiming the very dejection and helplessness that stirred Moon Face's mind into a chaotic puddle.

Damn that girl. It was all her fault!

But Gotha had chosen well in his selection of Moon Face. The young apprentice paused only a few moments before he set about straightening up the camp. He checked in his own pack and found the tiny bundle of herbs he had placed there after his final conversation with Gotha. A Shaman knew how to heal. But by the very nature of that knowledge, a Shaman also knew how to do otherwise. Much of Moon Face's secret knowledge was like a knife that cut both ways. He could cure. But he could also kill.

He settled himself next to the ash-filled heart. He would wait a day. If Rising Sun had not returned by then, with the woman or without, then he would follow. He could track somewhat, and doubted that his companion was making any effort to conceal his trail. If he had to, he would find him.

Only then could he decide if there was anything else he had to do.

CHAPTER FOURTEEN

1

As the short northern summer lengthened into a hot golden glow, the slow, terrible carnage inside the walls of the Green Valley grew worse with each passing day. Gotha the Shaman sat on one of the low benches before the Spirit House, felt the morning sun on his slumped shoulders, and realized he was very close to collapsing from sheer exhaustion.

When had he last been able to sleep a whole night through? He couldn't remember. And his days, from earliest dawn until deep into the purple, hazy dusk, were full of sickness and death. More and more he berated himself for sending Moon Face with Rising Sun. He needed his apprentice *here*, and he needed him *now*, but Moon Face was long beyond his desperate, unspoken entreaties.

He blamed himself, of course, but how could he have known? When the One To Come had departed—if he *was* the One To Come, he silently amended—there had been only a single sick woman. Now the Valley reeked of death, of the constant funeral fires, of the greasy smell of burning flesh.

And it was getting worse, if such a thing was possible. He sighed and rubbed his aching temples. The pain in his head hardly ever left him now, despite the bitter herbal teas he brewed for himself. This morning it felt as if unseen hands were driving tiny knife blades into the soft flesh at either side of his reddened eyes.

He didn't know how much longer he could go on like this. He was beginning to see Spirits even when he wasn't trying to summon them. And at night, when he *was* able to sleep, his dreams were horrible—silent, screaming visions full of nameless fire and formless ice. He knew what those dreams were—they were dreams of death, and they were calling to him.

He sighed, rubbed his aching eyes, and forced himself to stand up. Both his knees popped at the same time, two sharp, distinct sounds like dry twigs snapping. He froze, staring downward, the wrinkles at the edges of his eyes like deep black gashes in his leathery skin.

Old, he thought with sudden bitter wonder. *I'm old now.*

For a moment the truth was so hard and so obvious that he was simply stunned. How had this happened? When had he grown old? He'd *never* been old before. He'd seen his contemporaries age and wrinkle, succumb to sickness or injury or some malign Spirit he could not appease, but though he'd watched his own hair grow white, somehow, inside, he felt no older than that day so long ago when he'd first donned a Shaman's robes.

It was a lie. Now, because of two unexpected and brittle sounds, he knew the truth, and it terrified him.

Old.

He shook his head and wondered how much time was left for him. His people were dying around him, and he was old, and his successor was gone into the empty prairies on an errand that no longer seemed important.

Moon Face! he cried in silent anguish. *Come back! I need you!*

But of course there was no answer. Someone came up behind him, a deep, rusty wheezing and abrupt fusillade of moist, wracking coughs telling him all he needed to know. Hopelessly he turned to help, knowing he was as helpless as he was hopeless.

"Wolf," he said. There was no surprise in his voice.

2

"It's just a little snot in my nose," Wolf told him after Gotha had taken the older man into the cooler, dimmer confines of the Spirit House. He left the door flap open to admit some light, though he'd already seen enough to know that a lot more was wrong with the Chief than a snotty summer nose.

He felt a sharp pang of sadness as he helped his old friend to a seat on one of the log stools around the inner hearth. Wolf's ancient bones felt thin, birdlike. The harsh slanting rays of the morning sun made the skin of his bare, mottled skull look soft and rotten, like the rind of a spoiled fruit.

There was a thick, unhealthy odor rising from Wolf. Gotha wrinkled his nose and turned away, breath leaking tiredly between his lips. What could he say?

Wolf watched the Shaman's back as if he could read some message hidden in the play of muscle and tendon there. As Gotha seated himself across the hearth, Wolf abruptly hunched over as a racking series of coughs seized him. Gotha waited until the paroxysm passed, noting glumly the long, glistening ropes of snot that swung from the Chief's nostrils, and the bright smear of crimson that marked the back of his hand where he wiped his mouth.

Wolf sighed and regarded the Shaman with eyes the color of egg yolks. "It's not just the summer snots, is it?"

Gotha winced and closed his eyes.

"You know, I always thought I'd die on the hunt, or in battle, like a man should die," Wolf said slowly.

"You're not going to die!"

Wolf grinned slowly. "For a Shaman, you're a terrible liar," he said. "I hear your words, but the truth is written all over your ugly face, my friend."

Gotha shrugged. In a way it was a relief that Wolf understood. He hadn't wanted to lie to him, though he would have, if he thought that was what Wolf wanted. "You knew anyway," Gotha replied.

Wolf shook his head, that grin still lingering faintly on

his dry, cracking lips. "You know, for some reason I didn't think these evil Spirits would get me." He tried a chuckle, though the sound that came out was strained and rasping and obviously painful. "I don't know why I thought that. These Demons must have got half the People by now. How many have we lost, do you think, Shaman?"

Gotha averted his gaze. He was afraid Wolf would see the shame in his own eyes, see the helplessness. And judge his failure accordingly.

"Do you blame me?" Gotha said.

"Once, I would have."

"Well, I blame myself. I'm the Shaman. I'm supposed to protect the People."

Wolf shook his head. "I said that once. But I've seen too much. The Gods have left us. You saw them go. Now there's nothing, and the People die. Now I die. And though I've lived a long time, I don't want to die. And maybe even you die now, Gotha. Maybe this is the end for all of us. Maybe the evil Spirits will have their triumph, without the Powers to control them."

Gotha stared at him. "I would never say this outside this House, but it may be that you're right, old friend."

Wolf quirked an eyebrow. "A touch of fever? An ache, maybe?"

Gotha shook his head. "No. Just tired." He spread his hands. "I can't *do* anything, Wolf. I've tried everything I know, all the magic, all the prayers—though I don't know what I'm praying to anymore."

"The Turtle . . ." Wolf said. His voice sounded dreamy.

"What?"

Wolf smiled, but made no reply.

"I may have made a mistake with your grandson. With Rising Sun," the Shaman said.

Wolf raised his eyebrows. "Oh?"

"Sending him away. Sending him on that quest. Sending Moon Face with him. I need Moon Face here." Gotha's voice was slurred with exhaustion.

Wolf stared at him for a long moment. Finally, he said,

"Whatever gave you the idea it was *you* who sent Rising Sun on his quest?"

It took Gotha several heartbeats to digest the Chief's question and frame a question of his own.

"You mean you sent him?"

Wolf wiped his lips and stared down without interest at the streak of fresh crimson on his palm. "I don't think he was sent by anything in this World," he said. "At least, I hope not. Otherwise, we will all die, every one of us."

He looked up, his black eyes bright as a sparrow's. "That's what I think," he said.

Gotha regarded him with dull wonder. Even now, Wolf could still surprise him. "You know," he said at last. "You may be right at that."

Wolf nodded. Then he began to cough.

3

"Isn't there anything you can do?" White Moon whispered. She glanced down at her father, who lay on his bed wrapped tightly in thick furs, sweat starting from his forehead though his teeth were chattering.

Gotha took her hand and led her away from the sick-bed. "I've done everything I know to do," he replied, keeping his own voice low, though he doubted Wolf was paying any attention to their conversation.

"He's going to die," she said. "My father."

Gotha sighed. "Yes," he said. "He is. It takes the old ones faster. I've given him ... something. To make him sleep. He won't feel much pain."

She pushed her streaked hair away from her face, a quick, distracted gesture that betrayed her helpless anxiety better than anything she could say. Gotha patted her shoulder. "He's had a good life, White Moon. A long one. It won't be so bad for him, maybe."

White Moon shook her head sharply, mutely, denying it all.

"Where's Star?" Gotha said.

"I don't know. He went out early this morning, just after Father left. He hasn't come back yet."

"Does he know?"

"I think—I don't know. Father's nose filled up with snot yesterday, but he didn't say anything. I'm sure he noticed, though, but—"

The door flap to the Chief's house swung wide, admitting a bright shaft of light and the subject of their conversation. "Oh, Shaman. What are—" Morning Star glanced down, saw Wolf wrapped in his furs. "Oh," he said.

The two men exchanged glances. "It's bad, isn't it?" Gotha nodded.

Morning Star exhaled tiredly. "He got sick yesterday. He looks a lot worse today."

"Where have you been?" White Moon asked.

"I went for a walk. Down the Main Path to Valley's end. I needed to think."

White Moon looked down at her father. He'd begun to make a ragged, snoring sound. Morning Star followed her gaze. "I'm sorry," he said. "I should have stayed here. But I knew he was sick. That's what I wanted to think about."

Gotha said, "Let's go outside. It stinks in here."

They followed him through the door, into the noonday blaze. Nobody mentioned the source of the evil odor. Even outside they could still smell it. It hung in the air, faint but pervasive, and after a moment White Moon realized the origin of the stench was not her own house, but many others as well. She swallowed, feeling suddenly faint.

"Are you all right?" Morning Star said, stepping close to her. "Moon, what's the matter?" His voice was low, urgent.

She rubbed her eyes. "Just tired, that's all."

Star glanced at Gotha. "Shaman?"

Gotha shook his head. A relieved look washed across Morning Star's features. "Dearest, why don't you go inside and lie down? Try to get some rest. I want to talk to the Shaman awhile."

But White Moon glanced at the doorway and grimaced. "Not now. I'm going to go around, see if I can help any of the other women."

"But you're tired."

"We're all *tired*," she flared. "Everybody is *dying*. Of course we're tired . . ." She trailed off. "I'm sorry, husband. But I do want to help. I don't want to go back . . . in there."

"Somebody needs to watch Wolf," Morning Star said.

She swiped blindly at her forehead. "You watch him. I'll be back later." Then, without giving him any chance to reply, she turned and marched away. She didn't look back.

"She's upset," Star observed.

"Wouldn't you be?" Gotha eyed Morning Star quizzically. "For that matter, aren't *you* upset, too?"

"Of course I'm upset. Worse than that. I love that old man. He's become like a father to me." Morning Star looked away from Gotha, suddenly embarrassed. The concept of fatherhood, even after so many years, was not one to be lightly discussed between the two men.

Gotha sensed Morning Star's discomfort, for he shared it himself, and quickly said, "How are *you* feeling?"

Morning Star shrugged. "Like you are, I imagine. Tired, no, exhausted. I'm not sleeping much. Neither is Moon. Neither are you, from what I see."

Gotha nodded impatiently. "That's not what I meant."

"I'm not sick. Not yet," Morning Star said. "Neither is Moon, at least I don't think so."

Gotha swept him with a speculative gaze. "You look all right, I guess," he said finally. "I wonder if you have anything to worry about, anyway." He paused. "I wonder if I do, for that matter." Then he spat, his face bitter. "I mean for myself, of course. Not for the people dying around me while I chant my useless songs and pray to Gods who are no longer there to hear."

"What are you talking about?"

"We went into the Void, don't you remember? We saw the Turtle, we saw the Mother and Father of the People, and we saw the Gods. We are blessed among all those who live in the World. Once, I thought that might mean a greater power to work within the World, but now I wonder if there was no Gift at all, or maybe the Gift was sterile."

Gotha spread his hands helplessly. *"Look around us!"*

He licked his lips. "Death everywhere, and I can do *nothing*, I who went beyond the World and heard the words of They who made the World and all within it. Where is the *Gift*, O Star of the Morning of your People? Where is the *Gift*?"

He shook his head and looked down at the well-trodden earth beneath his feet. "If this is the Gift," he said softly, "it is poisoned."

Morning Star stared at Gotha as if he'd never seen him before—and, in truth, he hadn't. Not like this. Not this shrunken, slump-shouldered, beaten-down wreck of a man. All his life, the Shaman had been a figure larger than life, first as a specter of terror in his youth, later a man full of wisdom, a warrior of healing, a mighty fount of knowledge and lore.

He's old, he thought with sudden wonder, and with a pity he never thought he'd feel toward Gotha the Shaman. *This is destroying him.*

And so, without really understanding why, for the first time in his life, Morning Star who was once Serpent, the Light at the Dawn of the World, stepped forward and wrapped his arms around the older man and hugged him close.

"Yes," he whispered. "The Turtle said, 'A Gift, a Promise, a Test.'" He squeezed the Shaman more tightly, felt the other's heart beating against his own. "Perhaps this is not our Gift, but our Test."

Gotha stared blankly over Morning Star's shoulder, his mouth slowly falling open. "*Our Gift? Our Test?* What are you talking about, Morning Star? The Gift, the Test, are for the One To Come, who is the Promise."

Morning Star released Gotha and pushed him gently back, so that he could look into the Shaman's dark eyes with his own mismatched green and blue gaze—the eyes that marked him as the Turtle's own.

"Are you sure, Shaman? The Turtle never said *who*. The Turtle only said *what*. Perhaps those three are for all of us—for the World itself, and everything within it."

Gotha shook his head. Morning Star could see in that simple motion how much the Shaman had aged—there was confusion in the gesture, and a black weight of dread, and growing despair. "I don't know ..." Gotha began slowly, but before he could finish, they both heard a low moan from inside the Chief's house, followed by a sharp series of hacking coughs.

"I'd better see to him," Gotha said.

Morning Star took a deep breath and said, "Moon Face is gone. But I will help you if I can ... Father."

Gotha's eyes shot wide at that, but he said nothing, only tightened his lips and nodded shortly. But he remembered the feeling of Morning Star's strong arms around him, and as he ducked into the Chief's house, the word he'd never thought to hear on Morning Star's lip's still ringing in his ears, he said, "Thank you, my son."

Gift or Test? He didn't know. He would think about it later.

4

White Moon walked slowly through the camps of Green Valley, her eyes dulled from their normal brilliant colors, her mind a swirl of vacant thoughts. From time to time someone would speak to her, but she ignored these calls as if she were deaf. Once, an ancient woman came up to her and tugged gently at her robe, and the pressure caused her to turn and look down.

"What is happening?" the crone whispered. "What have we done to deserve this?"

Moon stared blankly at the wrinkled claw still clutching her robe. Then, as if she were removing an insect, she gently plucked away those fingers, sighed, and shook her head. The old woman stared at her for a long moment, her rheumy eyes slowly widening. When White Moon turned away from her and plodded on, the old woman began to wail, at first softly, then with greater volume. For all the attention White Moon paid to her, she might as well have been a tree.

Eventually, White Moon's feet took her beyond the camps, along the Main Path toward the mouth of the Valley, past the lakes and the secret places where so much secret history had occurred.

She stumbled past the clearing where Maya had nearly died beneath the claws of mother lion, past the spot where Maya and Caribou had built their last house, now moldered into dust. Here also Morning Star had lived, while White Moon had pursued her terrible flight from her own destiny, even as her destiny awaited her return.

Farther on, though she didn't know it, she passed the spot where Caribou had slain the same mother lion, the place never marked where plague had first come to the Green Valley, and also the juncture that had long before signaled Maya's departure into her own oft-resisted destiny.

When she came to the place she'd sought without knowing she sought it, she stopped. Here, where the Main Path vanished into the unlimited gray-green vista of the high steppe, she found the boulder that marked the limit of the Valley and sat down on it.

A good breeze lifted her hair as it carried away the stink of death that lay about her like a fog. Her nostrils widened. She lifted her head and inhaled the odors on the wind, hints of flowing water from the river beyond, traces of frozen water from the great ice wall to the north.

She folded her hands in her lap. It would be good, she thought, to rise from her seat, turn her face to the horizon, and start walking. Leave it all behind, the death, the fear, the terrible knowledge she carried inside herself like a curse.

The Gods were gone. She had never imagined how awful that could be, she who had struggled against the Gods in her younger days with all her might, only to discover that her struggles were merely part of a greater game, in which her very resistance had drawn her inexorably to the role she'd always been destined to play.

Maya had understood, she thought then, and realized why she'd come to this place. No one had known better than Maya how the strands of fate that bound the World and all within it worked their awful magic. She'd called herself a tool, and in the great climax that had freed the Gods of Their burden forever, she had played out her own role perfectly.

"As did we all," White Moon murmured softly to herself.

Slowly she stood and gazed down at the rock that marked the boundary between the Valley and the World beyond. It was here Maya had stood, the Stone Rejoined gleaming on her breasts, when she'd taken her final leave of the Green Valley. She'd departed with no fanfare. Only Old Berry had witnessed that leave-taking, though the ancient Root Woman had recounted it many times to White Moon, until the younger woman could see the scene in the eye of her mind almost as if she'd been present.

She stood by this rock, her hand resting on its top.

Slowly White Moon rose to her feet, turned, looked down. The top of the boulder was flattened, a dark smooth mound of granite flecked with tiny chips of quartz that sparkled in the sun.

The marks were plain enough, shallow indentations in the surface, their pattern simple and obvious once one understood there *was* a pattern.

A handprint. The last mark of the Great Tool, Maya who was mighty in the World. What did it mean?

White Moon felt her own hand rest lightly on her chest, as if seeking the Mother Stone that had once rested there. *I was once Keeper of the Stone,* she thought. *I was a part of it then. Do I have any role left to play now?*

Then the huge aching voice inside her, as dark and wide as the Void she'd once entered, made itself known to her, expanded around her and blotted out the wind and the sky, the steppe and the Valley, until it filled the World with its awful promise.

But only for a moment, and then it vanished back inside her, leaving her shaken with horror at the emptiness the Gods had left behind.

She shaded her eyes and gazed out across the waving grass and saw nothing. The cry she uttered then came from the void inside, a huge beast of hope and terror.

"Rising Sun! RISING SUN!"

It was a great shout, but the wind snatched up the words and swirled them away, and there was no answer. After a while she gathered her robe more tightly about

her, for the day was turning cooler here, and began to retrace her steps back into the Green Valley.

Once, the walls that enfolded her had seemed like
shelter. Later, the walls of a prison, and finally a stone
cup that held her life.

She raised her head. Her fine chin jutted forward.
Straight-backed and defiant, in that moment she seemed a
Queen, mighty among women, as she strode up the path
with new determination.

There were no walls. The walls were meaningless.
Death came here as easily as anywhere else. The Gods
had gone, but *something* was coming.

She could feel it. This time there would be no resistance. "I can't do everything," she vowed softly. "But I
will do what I can."

5

The Death of Wolf

"I will choose the time and manner of my going. I am
Chief. I have that right," Wolf said.

He spoke softly, slurring the words, the effort it took
him obvious and painful to Morning Star, who had leaned
close to hear him. Now, exhausted, the old man slumped
back into his sweat-soaked furs. Heat baked off him.
Morning Star could feel the glow on his own cheeks, like
that radiance a banked campfire emits.

He waited, in case Wolf had something else to say, but
the dying Chief closed his eyes, clearly drained by the toll
the exertion of speaking had taken.

"What did he say?" White Moon asked softly.

Morning Star rose from his squatting position and
made a motion with his head toward the door. She followed him out into the evening. Stars twinkled overhead,
more visible now that fewer fires burned within the Valley.

He told her what her father had said, and she shuddered. "That's awful," she whispered.

"He has the right. He is Chief."

"I know." She sighed. "Will he take the Fire?"

"He didn't say. He will tell us. Or he won't, if he dies before he can. Then it won't matter."

"I hope he dies first!"

But Morning Star shook his head sadly, for he loved the old man and intended to respect his final wishes. "He won't."

White Moon chewed her lower lip, readying her protest. Then she remembered her journey to the end of the Valley, and knew she wouldn't object. Maybe this, awful as it was, was part of what she'd sensed then. Still, it was horrible.

"How long?" she asked.

Morning Star shrugged. "Who knows? He's old, as Gotha said, and the Demons work faster. I don't think there's much time." He looked up at the sky, at the stars, and for a moment wondered about them. Those lights in the sky, what were they?

"I should see Gotha," he decided. "He will know what needs to be made ready."

White Moon nodded reluctantly. "I suppose so." She half turned. "I'll go back in. I can do that much, keep watch until . . ." Her voice trailed off. There didn't seem much else to say.

"If he says anything, I need to know. I will carry out his wishes," Morning Star told her. His voice was resolute, though it trembled.

"Go find Gotha," she said. "I'll keep watch."

Morning Star stared at her, at the way her carriage remained stiff, proud. Suddenly he came to her, took her in his arms, half lifted her.

"I love you, White Moon," he said fiercely into her ear. "I always have, from the first time I saw you. Do you remember?"

She nodded against his cheek. "I do. But it was fated, husband."

"Does that make it any less?" he asked.

"No. It doesn't. I love you, too, Star of the Morning."

He set her down, watched her disappear inside the Chief's house, and wondered if love was a doom, too.

If so, it was heavy. He turned to go and find the Shaman. There was much to be prepared, if Wolf's last wishes were to be respected.

"*He what?*" Gotha said, when Morning Star finally located him trudging along the Rock Jumble toward the Spirit House.

Morning Star repeated what Wolf had told him. The Shaman shook his head. "I'd hoped he wouldn't do this, but he's a stubborn man. And proud. He's been a great Chief."

Morning Star took the older man's elbow, to guide him over the slippery rocks that bordered the top of the Jumble. "Has he spoken of this before?"

Gotha glanced at him. "Yes," he said finally. "I said nothing, because I'd hoped he would change his mind."

"You talked about it recently?"

"Yes. But before, also. When it was like a game, almost. Before any of this began to happen." Gotha shrugged. "He's an old man, Star. And he's been old for a long time. The thoughts of the old turn to their departure, to how they might leave the World. In some ways, he's lucky. He is allowed to choose, because he is Chief."

"The choice is horrible."

"But it is *his* choice to make, my son."

Morning Star's eyebrows quirked at that final word, but he made no remark. Something had changed in his relationship with Gotha. A healing had occurred, although Star was not entirely certain just when it had happened. Nevertheless, he welcomed the change. Wolf had been like a father to him. Now, too, Gotha seemed willing to take up the role.

For a man who'd had, for much of his childhood, no parents at all, it was a satisfying transformation. Nevertheless, the pleasure he felt was colored by sadness, for one of his foster fathers now lay dying, and that transition must be attended to before considerations of anything else.

"What's involved?" Star asked.

"He may choose to have me help him on his way, or he may choose the Fire."

"The Fire?"

"I can help him with that, as well, if he so chooses. He need not feel much pain. There are herbs . . ."

They arrived at the Spirit House. Gotha's knees made a creaking noise as he ducked through the doorway, and for a moment Morning Star thought the old man would fall. He tightened his grip on the Shaman's arm, but Gotha caught himself and straightened. He smiled bitterly.

"I'm old, too," he observed. "Almost as old as Wolf."

"But you aren't dying."

Gotha shrugged. "My people are. I share that death."

"I suppose so," Morning Star muttered as he came into the Spirit House."

Carefully Gotha lowered himself to his usual seat. "Would you stoke up the fire?" he asked.

Morning Star nodded, rummaged in dark corners until he found dry wood, which he fed to the glowing coals of the Spirit Flame. In a short time, the interior of the House danced with flickering shadows. Morning Star sat cross-legged on the Shaman's left hand. The two men stared at the blaze, each silent within the shroud of his own private thoughts.

Finally Morning Star sighed. "Fire," he observed. "The Lord of Fire. But He is gone."

"Yes," Gotha replied. "The Mother, too. Yet They left much behind."

"Too much, maybe?"

Gotha moved his shoulders. His voice was raspy with tiredness. "We are only men, my son. Even Maya the Great, in the end, was only a woman. We are not Gods. Nor are we . . . greater Powers. The One still remains, remember."

"But the Turtle is not of our World, nor ever was. And the Gods, who were, have gone. What remains?"

"Spirits? Hopes and dreams? The living and the dead? I don't know, Morning Star. Do you?"

Morning Star nodded. "We remain," he said firmly. "We live in the World, and someday One will come who will inherit the World for us. This was Said, and this I believe."

"Yes," Gotha said, "we did see and hear that, didn't

we? Sometimes I wonder why I was there. There must have been a purpose, don't you think?"

"Second thoughts, Shaman?"

"And third, and fourth. Thinking is the lot of Shamans, Morning Star. Once I thought you would know it, too."

"I haven't been a very good Shaman, have I? I know you wanted me to use my Powers, such as they are, but I'm not like you, Gotha."

Gotha cocked his head. "I knew that long ago. I think I knew it even when you were a child. But I wasn't myself then."

"Oh, I think you were. You were in the hands of the Gods—both of Them, as it turns out. A heavy burden for one man to bear. I used to hate you. But I bear you no ill will now."

In the silence that followed, Morning Star could hear Gotha's breath sliding in and out of his lungs. "You don't?"

"No. I don't."

"Why not?"

"I am older. I know more. I have seen more. And now, perhaps, I finally understand more. Especially about tools, Father. Maya taught me that. Tools and the choices of tools. Such choices are limited. You made the ones you could make. The rest was part of something greater than you, and you are not to blame for that."

"Maya taught me that," Gotha said. "It was a lesson that freed me. The Gods told me much the same thing." He paused. "Choice. In the end, perhaps it is all we have."

Morning Star shifted closer and patted Gotha's knee. "Now Wolf is making a choice. What are we to do about that?"

"We will honor it, whatever it is. It is his right. And we owe him. He is, after all, not just Chief. He is of the line of Maya. And that blood has always made choices."

"Yes," Morning Star said. "We have, haven't we?"

Two days later the Great Chief Wolf was carried to the top of the mound of sticks that Gotha had caused to be built, and laid on a pallet made ready there.

His Spirit ascended to the sky on a fountain of fire, accompanied by the wailing of his People. He spoke only one word as the flames consumed him, though the word was strong and loud, and all heard it.

"*Maya!*" he shouted, and some said it was a sound of joy.

But none saw what Wolf saw in that moment, and so none knew what his cry meant.

Thus did the Great Chief Wolf pass from the World of men, and go to whatever place had been prepared for him. Many of his people wept for him, but three did not.

In the moment of his death, his eyes were closed to them. But they suspected they had seen before what he saw now, and their eyes, which had looked Beyond, were dry.

He was a mighty Chief.

CHAPTER FIFTEEN

1

Witch Woman covertly watched Drinks Deep Waters for several days after the incident before the Chief's tent, where the aged Shaman had defeated her so thoroughly. She kept track of him out of the corners of her eyes or screened by other women, for she had no urge to rouse his ire again before she was ready. His forthright blows, and their aftermath, had damaged her standing among the rest of the women even more than she'd feared.

It was because nothing had happened. She knew that much of her stature grew from her relationship with the Terrible Mother, from the aura of protection the worship of that Great Spirit granted to her. But the Shaman had been able to strike her repeatedly and with impunity in front of the rest of the women. Worse, he'd ordered the mass beatings, which had been carried out with speed and vigor, and still the Terrible Mother had done nothing. The Witch understood that this had lessened not only her own influence, but that of the Goddess whom she served, for it seemed to clearly indicate that the Lord of Thunder was far more powerful than the Mother Herself.

She ground her teeth together as she squatted in the scrubby woods, digging at the base of a gnarled tree with her pointed stick. *It was intolerable!*

But she didn't know what to do. The ghost of the plan

she'd almost conceived some days before remained just that—a ghost. She knew it involved her daughter, but she'd not yet been able to decide on the details. She paused in her digging, rocking on her heavy hams, her wide brow creased in thought. A successful plan would have many elements—it would need to rid her of the burden of the crazy girl, destroy the Shaman, and make absolutely clear to everyone that the Mother was the more powerful of the two Greatest Spirits. If, somehow, she could also vanquish that other doddering old fool, Chief Kills Many Buffalo, then so much the better.

She sucked at her yellowed teeth as she considered. Her thoughts most naturally turned to treachery, her own and that of others—or at least what could be made to *appear* as the treachery of others. Take the Shaman, for instance. He was riding high now, flush with victory. But what was his victory based on? Nothing more than his ability to strike the Witch Woman with impunity. It wasn't even the blows that mattered so much, but the lack of retribution for them. Everybody presumed, from this evidence, that the Shaman was more powerful than the Witch Woman. But what if he'd been able to do what he did because of some treachery on his part?

Unconsciously, she began to jam her digging stick harder and harder into the soft earth, as if she were stabbing the soil itself. What kind of treachery would it be? What unholy thing could that ancient man have gotten up to, that would give him the power he'd needed to do what he did?

Just as unconsciously as her stabbing motions, a different view of the whole incident had crept into her feverish mind. Now it seemed to her that what had begun as a plan had become a fact—the Shaman *had* bested her by treacherous means, and all she had to do was discover that treachery and expose it for what it was!

Yes, yes, that was better, she nodded to herself, her teeth grinding, the muscles of her wide shoulders bunching as she jabbed and jabbed.

Stabbing him, yes. For his treachery. *Now what was it, exactly? Something involving Sleeps With Spirits, wasn't it? Some unholy, Goddess-mocking conspiracy between them?*

Witch Woman slipped wholly over the shadowy line into madness without ever noticing that she'd begun to gibber, that drool now traced a shining silvery path down her blocky chin, that her sharpened stick had dug a hole in the earth two feet wide and half as deep.

In her fever trance of revenge, she took yet another step and crossed the boundary between human and divine, so that suddenly she saw herself as the Terrible Mother, filled up and consumed with the essence of that mighty Spirit, bloated with divine rage at the indignities the puny Shaman had dared to heap upon Her inviolate Person.

It was not the first time in human history that the worshiper would confuse herself with the one worshiped, nor would it be the last. The trap would always be seductive, and Witch Woman was ready to be seduced. Mumbling to herself, her eyes wide and white and blind, she tumbled mind first into the swirling divine maelstrom, and lost herself forever.

But out of burning darkness she found something else, and brought it back to the World, and hugged it close. She crooned to it, though it was invisible. An idea only. But the Goddess had put bones into the ghost, and hung flesh on the bones, and Witch Woman saw clearly what she must do.

When she finally stood, absently surprised at the sharp aches that knifed through her knees, thighs, and shoulders—she had no idea how long she'd been squatting in that position—her mind was clear again. She saw what awful treachery had been used against her, against *Her,* and she knew how to expose it. But it would take time, and craft. Well, she had enough of both.

She smiled as she began her walk back to the camp. My. Wouldn't her disgusting daughter and the blasphemous Shaman be surprised when she exposed their hideous treason, and then meted out to them the bloody vengeance they so richly deserved?

She slipped back into camp without encountering anybody and went directly to her tent. There were things to do, much that had to be made ready. One didn't expose such vileness without taking the proper precautions. But she was the Mother, and her knowledge was all-seeing, all-knowing.

She knew what to do. And she could hardly wait to begin doing it.

2

As usual, Sleeps With Spirits awoke from a Dream. She sat bolt upright in her sleeping furs, sodden with sweat, her eyes wide, staring and empty. In the slippery chasm between sleep and waking, she still saw only the Dream World, and His shape rushing through the mists.

"Danger!" she shouted, though her waking body only moved its lips in a soft whisper. She quivered like this for a long instant, then blinked and gazed dumbly about the empty tent as the last wisps of the sending faded away.

She shook her head and exhaled slowly. Then her shoulders slumped as she realized she was back in the World she hated, and He was far away. For it was He, her destiny, whom she'd Dreamed of, and it had been a curious Dream indeed. She wasn't certain whether it was prophesy of something that would occur in the future, or a divine memory of something that had already happened, or even a sort of window on events occurring as she Dreamed them. Not that it mattered, she decided. No one would listen anyway.

She sighed again, a heavy, leaking sound, and slumped back down. What would it be like to sleep without Dreaming? She couldn't imagine a life without the curse she'd borne so long. But it was nice to *try* to imagine it.

What if she did run away with Spears? What would that be like? Would she leave her Dreams behind as well?

It was an interesting speculation, and so for several moments she gave honest consideration to her brother's heatedly whispered proposal. After a time, though, she shook her head slightly and opened her eyes again. There was still something *wrong* about what Carries Two Spears wanted to do. Something hot and dangerous, not only to herself, but to him and to—what?

To Him? To the creature of her Dreams, who was even now coming ever closer to her?

She nodded to herself. Yes, that was it, that was the danger. He would find her *here,* between the Two Rivers, and she would lead Him to the place that had been prepared for Him long before. That was the Dream, the prophesy, and she was never wrong about *that.*

It was all so *complicated!* She couldn't, no matter how much she tried, reconcile the forces tugging at her. Two Spears, her mother, the Dreams, and, most important, He and the culmination of His quest here in the Two Rivers' churning jointure.

It was beyond her, and so, after struggling for several moments, she did as she always did, and pushed it all aside, unresolved, content once again to merely wait. She grunted as she rolled from her bed and looked about the interior of the tent.

Her eyes confirmed what she already knew. Witch Woman was gone, and she was alone. But the angle of the light that slanted through the smoke hole told her the morning was already well advanced. Unusual for her, she'd slept late, and the endless chores that all women shared, even those who Dreamed, awaited her attention. All the more so after the recent fiasco in front of the Chief's tent, for now the men were even more demanding, laughing and strutting as they ordered their subdued chattels about.

Whatever had Mother been thinking of? she wondered suddenly. Openly challenging the Chief and the Shaman had been a recipe for disaster, and now all the women, even those who had not taken part, were reaping the consequences of Witch Woman's rash rebellion. In fact, of all the women only her mother and herself had escaped punishment. Carries Two Spears would not lay a hand on either woman, and the Witch's naturally dour and forbidding mien protected her from any casual attack. It was all well and good for the Shaman to strike her—he acted for his God, after all, and was protected by Him—but certainly no other man, even with the Shaman's example, would dare lay a hand on the Witch.

And so her mother had continued as before, at least to

outward eyes. Sleeps With Spirits knew there had been a change, though. The Witch seemed to burn with a secret fire now, a black and all-consuming flame that only Spirits knew about, for her mother kept that terrible fire well banked inside herself. Even Spirits only noticed the occasional flicker, in the night silence of their tent, when the Witch would sit, eyes focused blindly on her hearth, rocking and hissing to herself.

These scenes terrified Spirits. The atmosphere inside their tent, never good, now seemed poisoned to her, for her mother had begun to ignore her entirely. More than once, bent to her chores, she'd felt the Witch's gaze burning into her shoulder blades, but when she'd turned, the older woman would be gazing somewhere else entirely, as if her daughter no longer existed.

The strange combination of attention and disregard was also frightening. There were times when she felt as if she were being stalked by some dark, bloody animal, something invisible but real snuffling closer and closer to her. Yet even with that spectral knowledge, she was unable to make a connection between it and her mother. Mother was dark and frightening, yes, but Mother was still Mother. In the end, she could mean no real harm for her only daughter.

And so, while Sleeps With Spirits was never wrong in prophesy, in other things she was as human as anybody else. Thus she ignored her greatest peril simply because its source was so close to her.

By the time she pushed through her tent flap to stand blinking in the bright midmorning sun, she'd shaken off the veils of her Dreaming. She dusted her palms on her thighs as she blinked and looked about. She'd been promised for a trip north along the Muddy River with a group of other young women to set traps for fish. Had they already gone?

She sighted the group near the edge of the camp, seven or eight strong, milling about as they hoisted their loads of sticks and plaited vines. She slumped with relief, then hurried toward them. Shortly after, the party trudged out of the camp, Spirits in their midst, ignored but tolerated. It was a fine hot late-summer day, nothing ominous about it. Nothing at all.

Sleeps With Spirits didn't notice the dark eyes that followed her, their gaze narrowed in speculative lust, and even if she had, she wouldn't have thought much about it.

It was only her mother, after all.

3

The two old men moved along briskly enough, their mood mellowed by the hot sun that beat down on their shrunken shoulders. They followed their usual meandering path through the woods, secure in the privacy afforded by the leafy overhangs, their conversation muffled by the constant beat and roar of the converging rivers.

Chief Kills Many Buffalo chuckled softly, the sound surprisingly clear and boyish coming from his ancient vocal chords. "I can still see the look on her face when you marched up and slapped the snot out of her."

Shaman Drinks Deep Waters chuckled as well, though the sound was not as unrestrained as that of his friend. "Yes, I certainly surprised her, didn't I? I think she made her plans carefully, but that was one thing she didn't plan for at all."

The Chief nodded. "What could she have been thinking of? She didn't imagine we would allow such rebellion to go unchallenged, did she?"

Deep Waters pursed his lips. "She's mad, you know. Has been for a long time. And, yes, I believe that's exactly what she thought would happen."

"No."

"Oh, yes. She sits in that noisome tent with the ghost of her murdered husband and that lunatic daughter of hers, almost a ghost herself, and spins her devious webs with no one to gainsay her. After a while, I think she believes her own imaginings to the exclusion of everything else. How else can you explain what she did?"

Many Buffalo shrugged. "Well, you said she's crazy."

"I know. But dangerous crazy, not harmless like her daughter. What an odd family that is. You have Carries

Two Spears, who seems completely normal, and then you have his sister, who, if she wasn't so innocuous, would be nothing more than a monster. And the old woman herself, who is simply frightening."

"Surely *you're* not frightened of her. Not after what happened?"

The Shaman stopped, turned, and faced the other man. "Of course I'm frightened. You don't think she'll just let this all pass, do you? I *know* she's plotting something. It's her nature to plot. And most likely, now that her more peaceable rebellion failed, she's brewing up something really nasty. And guess who her most likely targets are?"

The Chief blanched faintly, raised one hand, and tapped his own chest. His eyebrows arched.

"And me, too, of course," the Shaman sighed. "Me first, most likely. The Witch is many things, but stupid is not one of them. I'm sure she has a special place for me in her thoughts. She's been watching me, you know."

They'd come to a small clearing, a place softened by a thick covering of leaves half rotted into the underlying earth, where the wind-stripped trunk of an ancient fallen tree offered an easy bench for two old men. Buffalo took a seat with a short grunt of relief, settling himself first, then massaging his knees with arthritic fingers. "Getting old," he remarked.

"We both are," the Shaman replied. "And, my friend, we should keep it in mind. It is a weakness, and the Witch loves weakness. She'll try to use it against us somehow, you mark my words."

The Chief glanced about, not really seeing anything, as he chewed his lower lip. "She's really watching you? Are you certain?"

Drinks Deep Waters snorted. "I may be old, but I'm not blind. Not yet. She creeps around, follows me, watches from behind the other women, or lurks at the edge of the camp, in the brush, where she thinks I won't notice her." He leaned back, in a chorus of snapping spinal cartilage, and popped his knuckles one after the other. "It's a weakness of hers. She isn't stupid, but she thinks everybody else is. And so she underestimates people, and makes mistakes because of it. That show in front of your tent was such an error."

"How so?"

"Well, she judged that you and I were both too old and tired to resist her. She thought we'd simply give in if she showed us how powerful her followers had become."

Now it was the Chief's turn to snort. "Powerful? *Them?*" He spat into the humus at his feet. "They were only women, Shaman. How could they be powerful?"

"Don't make the same mistake she does, O Chief!" the Shaman replied sharply.

"What are you talking about?" the Chief said, bristling a bit at the tone of the Shaman's voice.

"Don't underestimate your enemy. And make no mistake, Witch Woman *is* your enemy, just as much as she is mine."

But Kills Many Buffalo only blinked at the Shaman, still not comprehending his warning. Finally, drumming his fingertips on his knee, he said, "What are you trying to say? I thought you vanquished the Witch when you struck her and routed her followers. There was certainly enough wailing in the camp that night."

Deep Waters clicked his teeth in exasperation. "Chief, tell me. If you throw a spear at a cave lion and wound it, and the cave lion runs away, do you then turn your back and ignore the beast simply because it isn't threatening you at the moment?"

The Chief raised his stone-colored eyebrows. "Of course not! Nothing is more dangerous than a wounded lion!"

Drinks Deep Waters shrugged. "Well, then. I wounded Witch Woman. Now she stalks me from the shadows, more dangerous than ever." He exhaled heavily. "Perhaps I should have done more than wound her. Maybe . . ." But his voice trailed off.

"You should have killed her!" the Chief said heartily.

"Oh? Would you hold her while I strike the blow?"

"Well, uh—ah, harrumph."

"I thought so," the Shaman said. He rocked forward, got his knees under him, and climbed to his feet. He turned and offered his hand to the Chief. "Watch yourself, and watch out for me, old friend, and I will do the same for you. This isn't over yet."

"I should drive her and her demon brat from the camp," the Chief said stoutly as Deep Waters hauled him up.

"Maybe," the Shaman replied. "But will you?"

The Chief said nothing to that, and soon enough they found other things to speak of on their ramble. Nevertheless, the Shaman resolved to take certain actions he felt were long overdue. He might not yet see his way clear to the easiest, most lasting solution to the problem of Witch Woman, but now he decided to at least take the first steps down that increasingly necessary path.

"Have you seen Carries Two Spears lately?" he asked, making what seemed no more than idle conversation.

"He's on a hunt," Kills Many Buffalo replied. "Should be back soon, though."

"Let me know when he returns," Drinks Deep Waters said.

4

Carries Two Spears marched triumphantly into the camp on the following day, his wide shoulders bent beneath a load of meat that weighed almost as much as he did.

"Buffalo!" he shouted happily to the laughter and applause of those who witnessed his return. The rest of the small party, similarly laden, trailed along behind, each hunter also grinning as he received his own accolade. They trooped to the great hearth in the center of the camp and dropped their burdens in a bloody heap, barely disturbing the black clouds of flies that buzzed around the meat.

Spears straightened up with an audible sigh of relief and armed sweat from his broad, sun-wrinkled brow. "Good hunting," he remarked to no one in particular. He glanced across the hearth and saw a pair of young women, sisters, gazing at him with open admiration, but their eye-fluttering, hip-switching adoration left him completely unmoved. Once, he might have responded, but a different fire consumed him now.

He sighed again, this time more heavily. During his three days of hunting, he'd been able to push all his other problems to the back of his mind while he gloried in his true talents as a careful, crafty hunter. It was with real regret for that lost sense of aimless freedom that he now surveyed the camp. He watched the hearth area rapidly fill with women intent upon the meat. A few ambling clots of men eyed the catch with mingled approval and envy. Finally, Drinks Deep Waters approached with his slow, hobbling, old-man's gait. Spears nodded as the Shaman caught his eye and motioned him over with a jerk of his head.

"Yes? You want me?" Spears asked.

"Come," the old man said shortly, then turned on his heel and marched briskly toward his tent. Spears shrugged and followed, a puzzled expression on his features.

"Inside," the Shaman said, lifting the door flap and making shooing motions. Carries Two Spears ducked past him into the dimly lit interior, then watched while the Shaman carefully fastened the flap shut before settling himself on the other side of the small inner hearth.

"Sit," the Shaman told him. He did so, alerted finally by the shortness of Deep Water's tone that something was wrong. He thought he knew what it might be.

"I didn't beat my mother. Or my sister. Even though you told me to."

"Tcha." The old man shook his head and spat into the fire. "I know you didn't." He smiled faintly. "I didn't really expect you to. Forget it, that's not what I wanted to talk to you about."

Carries Two Spears relaxed a bit, but the Shaman's smile didn't fully reassure him. Something was up, and if it wasn't his disobedience, then what? There were only two other things, neither of which he wished to discuss with the old man across from him.

"How is your mother?" the Shaman asked.

"My mother?" Spears shrugged. "I don't really know. She doesn't talk to me much."

"Oh, come now. You are her son. Surely you are close to her?"

Two Spears sighed. "Shaman, what do you want from me? There are only a few hands of us here, and we all know how things are. My mother has little to do with me, and I with her, and everybody knows why. So stop running around the rock with me and tell me what's on your mind."

Deep Waters stiffened, then relaxed. Two Spears was a short-worded man, straightforward, and, to the Shaman's mind, neither especially bright nor respectful to his elders. But then, if Witch Woman was his closest elder, how much respect could anybody expect?

"I have made your mother my enemy, I'm afraid."

"She was already your enemy. Nothing has changed."

"No, Carries Two Spears, you are wrong. I know you avoid her as much as you can, but I see you talking with your sister all the time. And Sleeps With Spirits lives with Witch Woman. So you must know something—and if you do, I need your help."

Carries Two Spears spread his hands wide, palms up. "Shaman, what goes on between you and my mother is between the two of *you*. I don't want to be in the middle of it." He leaned forward. "And since I'm a man, now, I don't have to be. You understand?"

He kept his voice low, but there was a vehement quiver in it that startled the Shaman. Perhaps this hadn't been such a good idea, after all.

"Calm down, Two Spears. I'm not asking you to plot against your mother. But you must have noticed the change in her. I think she's going mad—that Demons have stolen her thoughts. I only want to help her. I'm the Shaman, and even Witch Woman—whom I dislike a great deal, I have to admit that—is part of my job. As you say, there are only a few of us, and my duty is to watch over us all."

As you did my father? Two Spears wanted to ask, but that was an old wound well scabbed over, and he knew better than to open it now. With his own plans growing closer to fruition, he wanted nothing to draw the attention of the elders in his direction. So he spoke slowly, for there was an element of truth in the Shaman's words, though he sensed something slippery beneath their smooth surface. "Shaman, shouldn't you deal with my mother about this? I am not the problem, and I have no influence on her at all. And despite what you think, Spirits and I speak little of the Witch. It pains her, too, I think. She isn't the monster you think she is."

But Sleeps With Spirits was far from the Shaman's mind just then, and he waved away Two Spears's words. "I can help your mother, if you are willing to help me."

"What do you want me to do?"

"I want some of her hair, just a finger length."

Two Spears sat up straight, his eyes widening. "A spell? You want me to help you cast a spell on my mother?" He paused, then started to rise.

"Sit down!"

Drinks Deep Waters was old, but his voice had lost none of its ability to command. As if a puppet with its strings suddenly cut, Carries Two Spears dropped back to his seat.

"Now you listen to me, boy. You know nothing of *spells,* nothing of the Spirit World and of the terrible things that can come out of it to steal the souls of our People. When such a thing happens, I *must* do what I can, and you *must* do what I tell you to do. Even if it is your *mother,* it is your *duty* as well. *Do you understand me?*"

Two Spears's lips quavered. He felt as if his head was being squeezed between two flat logs. Sudden lances of pain jabbed behind his eyeballs. How had he gotten himself trapped in the silent war between these two awful old people?

"Shaman, I—"

"Don't say anything yet, Two Spears," the Shaman interrupted him, his tone now soft and persuasive. "Forgive me my anger, too, if you would. This has all been trying to me, as well. I don't like your mother, I freely admit it, but if a Demon has stolen her thoughts, as I fear, then I must try to help her. So must you—especially you, since she *is* your mother. And what I propose won't harm her, I promise you that."

Though he wanted nothing more than to leave this tent,

leave this camp, leave this whole *life* behind (except for his sister, of course), Carries Two Spears understood hunting perfectly well, and knew a trap when he saw it being set. Best to humor the Shaman, lest he arouse the old man's rage—and potentially his closer consideration—all over again.

"Just what *do* you plan? What do you want with her hair? Assuming I can get you some, which is not certain at all."

"Yes, I understand." Drinks Deep Waters raised his right hand, fingers spread, and looked at it. Then he said, "I will cast a spell. But not a spell of harm." He shook his head emphatically. "You are a hunter, Two Spears, and don't understand these things, but I will tell you I would much rather be able to work *with* your mother. Easier, for one thing. But she would never let me do that, not her and her Terrible Mother. So I must use other methods which, I'm afraid, are less certain. But with something of your mother's body—her hair, her fingernails or toenails, her blood, even her spit, perhaps I could drive the Spirit madness from her body and make her well."

Carries Two Spears stared at him speculatively. The old man was persuasive, indeed. That persuasion wasn't hindered by Two Spears having no idea at all whether the Shaman was lying to him. Shamans did whatever it was they did, and a common hunter would have no more idea of the secrets and rituals carried out inside the Spirit Tent than he would of the dark side of the moon. Nevertheless, in order to get out of that tent, Two Spears would have agreed to paint himself with buffalo dung and dance barefoot through the coals of the central hearth.

The hunter raised his own hand, palm out. "All right. I will do what I can, but it will take some time, and I make no guarantees. My mother is crafty, as you well know. And I believe she guards against such things."

Drinks Deep Waters nodded. He knew she did. "Maybe your sister can help."

"Maybe," Two Spears replied. "I will see."

The two men stared at each other for a long, silent moment, each aware of the dangers the other posed. But nei-

ther of them felt they had any choice in what they
planned to do and, in fact, they didn't.

"Come to me anytime," the Shaman said as Carries
Two Spears stood. Deep Waters himself made no effort to
rise. The hunter only nodded, but made no other reply as
he untied the door flap and began to duck out into the
bright light beyond.

"Oh, Spears?"

"What?"

"Ask the Chief to come to me, will you?"

5

Witch Woman watched from a distance. Her two children squatted at the edge of the river, deep in heated conversation. Carries Two Spears gestured, gestured again,
and Sleeps With Spirits shook her head. He leaned closer,
his lips moving. The Witch would have given a deal to
hear what he was saying, but the bank along the river was
far from the leafy screen that sheltered her.

She hadn't missed the Shaman's private signal to
Spears, nor had she overlooked the strained expression on
her son's face when he finally left the Spirit Tent. Something had gone on in there, and she didn't think it had
anything to do with hunting. Her suspicions were more or
less confirmed when Two Spears immediately sought out
his sister and engaged her in what looked to be an argument in which—she knew her daughter well—he was
gradually beating down her objections. But objections to
what?

She watched with narrowed eyes until Sleeps With
Spirits finally, reluctantly, nodded assent to his whispered
demands. The Witch clucked to herself and retreated
deeper into the woods, allowing the two of them to pass
by her not three strides away. Easy earshot, but thy
weren't talking of whatever had been decided. In fact,
they weren't speaking at all. Spears looked nervous but
determined. Spirits merely looked miserable.

Well, girlie, the Witch thought, *let's see if you've*

*learned how to hide anything from me. You never used to
be able, but—well, we'll find out if anything has changed.*

Curiously cheered by this new riddle, the Witch
waited until they were gone, and then stomped back to
her tent, her flat, angry gaze sweeping disdainfully over
several of the women who had let her down earlier. They
weren't worthy of her, and even less worthy of *Her*, but
what else did she have to work with?

More than they think, she told herself.

6

"Drink some of this tea," the Witch said, offering a
hollowed-out wooden cup full of a dark, bitter-smelling
brew. "You look tired."

Sleeps With Spirits stared at her mother, startled by
this sudden bout of solicitousness. It had been years since
the Witch had prepared anything special for her daughter.
"I'm not sick, Mother," she replied.

"Well, drink it anyway. You seem upset, too. It will
calm you and help you to sleep. You haven't been sleeping well lately, either. Maybe that's why you're tired."

Listlessly, for she was never very good at resisting her
mother's wishes, Sleeps With Spirits reached across the
few coals burning in the hearth and took the wooden cup.
She made a face as she sipped the thick, dark liquid, but
got it all down.

Wordlessly she handed the empty vessel back to the
Witch, who inspected it suspiciously to make sure her
daughter had drained the last drop.

"That's a good girl," the Witch said, satisfied. Then
she settled back to wait. She knew it wouldn't take long.
And, indeed, within a hundred breaths Sleeps With Spirits's head began to nod and her eyelids grew heavy over
her ruby-tinted eyes.

"How do you feel, daughter?" she asked softly.

"Sleepy . . ." the girl mumbled.

"Ah, well, you said you were tired. Rest now. The tea
will give you pleasant dreams."

Spirits's lips moved softly, but nothing came out but a

weak, fading sigh. Her head tipped forward. She slumped into her bed. Within moments, her chest began to rise and fall in the regular movement of sleep. The Witch smiled and hiked herself around the hearth until she knelt beside the unconscious girl. She leaned forward until her mouth was close to Spirit's ear and began to whisper.

7

Carries Two Spears awoke with a hunter's sense that something was wrong. He rolled out of his bed, listening to the early morning sounds of the Men's Tent—grunts, farts, deep snores—and wondered what was the cause of the sudden wave of fear that brought a clammy sweat to his forehead.

He stared about blindly, but saw nothing out of the ordinary in the shadowed interior, only the still comatose lumps of the hand or so of his mates with whom he shared the tent.

"Stupid ..." he muttered to himself as he rubbed his nose. "A bad dream." Still, he couldn't fall back to sleep, and after a few minutes of growing anxiety, he got up and silently crept through the door into the gray-blue light of dawn.

He stood up, stretched, and scratched himself. This early only a few of the women were stirring about, stoking up the coals, hauling firewood, beginning the preparations for the morning meal.

He watched them moving like earthbound crows through the aquamarine light, bent beneath their loads, and for a moment felt a wave of pity so strong his knees almost buckled. Shocked at the unexpected feeling, he inhaled sharply, feeling the chill air grate painfully across his teeth.

Something wrong.

He gazed about, knuckled his eyes, gazed some more. The feeling of *wrongness* grew, but he still couldn't connect it with anything concrete. He rubbed his head, idly locating a fat louse, which he picked off and crushed between his fingertips. It made a tiny popping sound.

Must have been a dream, though he couldn't remember it. He turned back to the door and his bed beyond it—maybe a little more sleep would clear this malign residue from his spirit—when he saw her gliding like a ghost along the fringe of the camp.

Sleeps With Spirits!

Suddenly he knew the source of his disquiet. He stared at her with his heart thrumming like the wings of a bird, frightened beyond reason. She moved along, her head turning blindly, as if she were lost. He stretched out his hand and started toward her, her name rising to his lips, but then something so huge and confused seized him in its stony grip that he was suddenly unable to move at all. Instead he stood frozen, a stony creature of eyes, eyes only, and watched her slide along. He had the eerie feeling that there were invisible strings connected to her, moving her arms and legs in smooth harmony, and that behind her eyes there was nothing, nothing at all.

Her Dreams! he thought frantically. *She's in one of her Dreams!* Yet still he was unable to move, planted in the earth by a swirling force that severed him from the use of his own body, until something else plucked at his gaze.

He watched the Witch, whose path traced her daughter's, though a good piece behind, and suddenly he understood their mutual destination. His eyes moved in the prison of his skull. Yes!

Sleeps With Spirits, still moving with the grace of an antelope, reached the Shaman's house and ducked inside. The Witch followed but didn't enter. Instead, her shoulders bunched—she cradled something Spears couldn't see in her blunt, capable fingers—she crept to the back of the tent and out of sight.

And in the horror of that congealing instant, Carries Two Spears understood something so poignant it almost tore him apart. The paralysis that bound him was his own helplessness. All his plans, all his hot, swampy dreams, were nothing in the face of things that had been ordained. Sleeps With Spirits *did* Dream, and the Witch *had* murdered his own father, and he couldn't do anything about that. Just as he couldn't alter, by the tiniest fragment, what was about to happen.

His impotence was the impotence of all men in the face of destiny, when the unseen tides begin to turn, and the World reveals its essential hostility to the things that live in it.

A shriek rent the air, and the invisible chains that bound him disappeared as if they'd never been. But too late, *too late*!

He began to run.

CHAPTER SIXTEEN

1

Rising Sun finally came to a halt deep within the forest, the sound of the river only a faint whisper in his ears. He leaned against the bole of a tall, green maple and stared blankly about, his thoughts puddled in confusion.

The trail, such as it was, had petered out sometime back. He'd found the spot where they'd lain up, the two of them. That had been easy.

Her tracks were there, and the depressions where they'd slept. The trail led away into the woods. He followed it to find a small bubbling spring. Then back to the clearing, where he squatted, examining the rumpled grass, noting that the second set of tracks was much larger than hers. Almost too large and heavy to be human . . .

That line of thought sent chills up his spine. He was prepared for wild beasts, even a raiding party of some sort—but not Demons. Now, leaning against the tree and remembering, he suddenly missed Moon Face terribly. Moon Face knew about Demons. But Moon Face was far behind, nursing his wounded sensibilities.

For a bleak moment, Rising Sun contemplated returning to the camp and dragging the apprentice along by main force, if necessary, but then he shook his head.

The . . . man-thing (Demon?) had risen from its resting spot and set off again. His spoor quickly vanished, but not before Rising Sun determined there was only a single set of tracks. He knew what that meant. The kidnapper had carried Running Deer away.

The fine hairs on his forearms stood up as he considered *that* bit of news. Carried, not walking. What did it mean? Was she dead? Injured?

And then the trail utterly disappeared. Even the wild beasts left *something,* at least for a trained stalker, but he saw nothing at all. Perhaps one of the skilled trackers from the Valley could have found a trail, but he was no amateur, and that meant the abductor wasn't either.

Not wild beasts. Perhaps not even a man. But whatever it was, it had Running Deer, and he knew he wouldn't rest until he found her. *Found her body?*

Resolutely he pushed *that* thought away, though not out, for he couldn't banish it entirely. In frustration, he threw back his head. *"Running Deer! Running Deer!"*

His throat-wrenching yells vanished into the deep woods as if they'd never been. In silence, he listened, but heard only the bright calls of birds, the distant hushed whisper of the river.

Suddenly the silence seemed to press in on him. It was as if the eye of his mind took leave of his body and soared up, rising over the bowl of the World, the vast, green, empty World, and with no warning he was catapulted back into his Manhood Dream.

He felt himself wracked by spasms, a clonic seizure that nailed him like a post into that spot, riveted by the terror of his revelation.

The Dream World and this World were the same!

And now he felt the full force of the yawning hunger of the World, the *need* with which it ached, the eternal lust for completion that could only be achieved by a joining almost beyond his imagination.

Almost, but not quite. He knew whom the World awaited.

He sank down on his knees and vomited the few remaining scraps in his stomach. That was how Moon Face found him, kneeling in his own puke, tears streaming down his face.

2

The scene shocked Moon Face profoundly. For a moment, after he pushed into the little clearing and realized what he was looking at, he felt inexplicably ashamed, as if what he saw was something not meant for another man to witness. Moreover, the sight of Rising Sun seemingly crushed to the earth, weeping in the stink of his own juices, frightened him. Whatever he thought of Rising Sun's craziness with the girl, Moon Face's belief in the prophesy as Gotha related it to him had never wavered.

Rising Sun was the One To Come. But could this battered figure, sobbing in his own filth like a helpless child, be the same who would inherit the World? And so he dithered a moment, his pudgy hands wringing together, his forehead creased and his fat lips turned down in revulsion, before his natural good-heartedness came to his rescue and propelled him forward.

"Rising Sun," he whispered as he took the other by the shoulders and gently pulled him up. "What's the matter? What happened?"

Rising Sun stared at him as if he'd never seen him before, and for a moment Moon Face's fright returned with even greater power. There was such an emptiness in that stare that the chubby little apprentice wondered if his worst nightmare had come true, and a Demon had stolen his friend's soul.

He faced Rising Sun, reached up and put his hands on his shoulders. Nothing. A thread of stinking drool ran down the other's chin. His eyes wandered emptily. For a moment Moon Face wondered if Rising Sun had been struck blind.

Panic surged in him again. He shook Rising Sun harshly, appalled at how bonelessly the other man flopped in his grip. Finally, near tears himself, he slapped Rising Sun hard across the cheeks, once, twice.

The blows snapped Rising Sun's head back and forth, but as Moon Face drew back to strike again, he felt limp muscles stiffen in his one-handed grip and Rising Sun said, "Don't."

"Ah, thank the Gods."

Rising Sun, his dark eyes now focused, stepped away and rubbed his chin gingerly. "Quite a wallop you pack there, Moon Face. Is that part of your Shaman's training?"

"I'm sorry. I didn't know what else to do. You scared me."

Rising Sun shook his head, then twitched his nose. "What's that stink?"

Moon Face didn't say anything, but his eyes were expressive. Rising Sun looked down his front, then at the noisome puddle at his feet. "Ugh. I did that?"

Moon Face nodded.

"I don't remember."

Moon Face took a deep breath. Gotha's admonitions rattled hollowly in his skull. All he could think of was that he had to *know*!"

"Rising Sun, what was the matter with you? You were crying, and you'd puked, and you didn't know me when I found you. Were you fighting with some Demon Spirit?"

For just an instant Rising Sun's eyes went unfocused again, but only for one flash. Then he shook his head. "No," he said shortly. "I was remembering something."

"What?"

"My Manhood Dream."

Surprisingly, it was the only answer he could have given that would have mollified the apprentice. Dreams, particularly Manhood Dreams, were ticklish things— ordinarily, they were the most powerful Dreams men would ever know. So it wasn't entirely inexplicable that the effects of such a thing might be long-lasting. Moon Face had seen other instances, though none as pronounced as what he'd just witnessed. Nevertheless, he was inclined to accept Rising Sun's explanation—the Dream of the One To Come might be more powerful than anybody could imagine.

"Just that? Your Manhood Dream?"

Rising Sun nodded. For the space of several breaths, the two young men stared at each other. Finally, Moon

Face shrugged. "You're right," he said. "You stink." Then, "I'm sorry I hit you."

But instead of a simple acknowledgment of the apology, Rising Sun wrapped the chubby apprentice in a reeking hug that, despite the stench, was the most welcome thing Moon Face could have imagined. In the warmth of that embrace, the chill that had grown between them melted entirely.

Finally, Rising Sun released him and said, "You came after me."

"Yes."

Rising Sun cocked his head. "Why?"

Moon Face himself didn't know the answer until it sprang to his lips. "Because I love you."

The morning wind sighed through the leaves, making a soft sound much like the exhalation that leaked slowly from Rising Sun's chest. Moon Face thought he'd never seen a man look so tired, and in the drawn planes of that other face he saw what Rising Sun would look like when he was old.

"I love you, too," Rising Sun replied slowly. For some reason Moon Face heard it more as a promise than a statement, though the words warmed him even more greatly than the embrace.

Moon Face kicked shyly at a swirl of moss near his feet. "Well. What do we do now? Did you find any sign of her?"

As Rising Sun used a wad of leaves to clean himself, he explained what he'd discovered. He threw the stinking leaves away and said, "So what do you think, Shaman? Is it a Demon or not?"

"I'm not a Shaman," Moon Face said absently, his forehead wrinkled in thought. "Can you find those tracks again?"

"Sure. Right this way."

They squatted over the marks while Moon Face rubbed his chin and hummed to himself. "It's not a Demon," he said at last. He looked up. "It's a man. What's more, I know which man it is."

3

Running Deer awoke to find him looming over her. She felt hot and feverish and her head ached abominably. The sun thrust its sharp light into her eyes like bright bone needles. She raised her fists to ward him off, and tried to summon a scream through her wooziness, but when she opened her mouth, he wrapped his massive paw around her jaw and squeezed off the sound as easily as he would crush a grape. She felt his weight settle across her waist, pinioning her into the dewy grass. She struggled, but had no more success than an ant trying to shift a boulder. Finally she subsided and lay still, trying to blink the sun's glare out of her vision. He leaned over her, covering her face with his shadow, and for the first time she got a good look at her abductor.

"Mmpph. Et me *oh*!"

She snapped at his palm, but it was like trying to get her teeth into sun-cured leather. His huge, bearded face came lower, and for a moment—as his yellowed fangs came out from behind his thick lips—she thought he was going to bite her. Instead, he squeezed her jaws gently. He repeated this twice before she understood it was a question—will you not try to scream?

She forced herself to stop wiggling, opened her eyes wide, and nodded assent. His eyebrows lifted. She nodded again. Slowly he lifted his hand an inch or so, and when she remained quiet, finally took it away.

"Frightened Man," she said softly, for it was him, the strange, shambling creature she'd often fed after her secret hunts, "let me up."

She fought to keep her voice calm and steady, for now she realized he was trembling, obviously more terrified of her than she was of him. He made a rumbling sound deep in his throat, and she pushed at his belly. It felt like pushing a skin bag full of fire logs.

"Umm?" he said.

"Get *off* me," she replied. "You're *heavy*. You're *hurting* me."

"Hurt?"

"Yes. Let me up." She pushed again.

His fat red lips squirmed in the nest of his beard as he considered her words. His thoughts were so slow, and so obvious, that for a moment she felt sorry for him. He was still trembling.

Then he did something that scared the spit right out of her mouth. He leaned down again, his dark eyes suddenly clear and calculating.

"I will let you up," he said. "But if you try to scream or run away, I will knock you unconscious. Do you understand?"

Amazed at the transformation, she could only bob her head weakly.

"Good. I have to protect *him*," the Frightened Man said. And with that, the light went out of his eyes and he looked away vaguely, before whoofing out a forlorn grunt and climbing off her.

For the length of several breaths she lay still, afraid of disturbing him, but finally, after he'd turned away from her and wandered off a few steps, she gingerly got herself to her feet. The movement sent a new wave of dizziness washing through her aching skull, and she spread her arms to steady herself. Nausea curdled her stomach and thrust a wad of bile into the back of her throat. For a moment she thought she'd puke, but then the feeling passed, and she felt a little better.

Thirsty.

A thousand questions fluttered like moths behind her eyes, but the thirst, at least for the moment, overrode everything else.

"Water?" she asked softly. "Is there water around here?"

At the sound of her voice the Frightened Man jumped as if someone had stuck a spear into his buttocks. He whirled, astonishingly light on his feet, his eyes wild with terror. Once again, she felt that jerk of pity, but right then she was more afraid he might lash out at her in his panic, and so she stepped back and said nothing more. She tried to imagine herself as the least frightening thing she could think of, a baby rabbit, a smiling toothless infant. He watched her tensely, and then, finally, began to relax.

"Water?" she asked again, even more softly. "Drink? I'm ... thirsty."

This time, her plea seemed to penetrate whatever fogs wrapped his thoughts, and he half-smiled. "Water," he agreed.

"Yes, water. Where is it?"

He raised his head and sniffed, then turned halfway around and pointed vaguely off into the woods. "Water," he said again. Then he lumbered off.

Wild hope exploded in her brain, banishing the headache for a moment. He was several paces away, his back to her, moving farther away by the instant. If she turned and ran now, could he catch her?

Her breath hitched in her chest as her muscles contracted for flight when she remembered the way he'd changed, the way the Frightened Man she'd always known had vanished, and something much darker and stronger had seemed to take his place.

"*If you try to scream or run away, I will knock you unconscious ... I have to protect* him."

Him? Who was the Frightened Man protecting? Why had he changed like that?

The sudden questions short-circuited her flight reflexes. The Frightened Man seemed to sense her indecision, for he paused and looked over his shoulder. She could see, even from the distance, the sharp light had come back into his black eyes.

"Don't," the thing that *wasn't* the Frightened Man warned, and there was no fright in his steady voice at all.

"I'm coming," she replied, feeling her knees go weak and watery. "Wait for me."

The Frightened Man licked absently at the trail of drool that leaked into his beard while he waited for her. She followed him into the woods, wishing her headache would end. It made it so hard to *think*.

4

"See this print here?" Moon Face said. "Look at the little toe."

Rising Sun, his head close to Moon Face's, both of them hunkered over a scrabble of footprints, nodded slowly. "Much shorter than the other one. Like it was cut off or something."

"Yes. Well, I've seen that print before."

"You have? *Where*?"

Moon Face sighed. "Calm down. It's very strange. I can't imagine what it means . . ." His voice trailed off.

"Moon Face, if you know who this print belongs to, tell me *now*!"

"Um. It's the Frightened Man."

Rising Sun blinked. "The *who*?"

Moon Face shrugged. "Oh, you know," he said absently. "He's been in the Valley forever. Demons stole his thoughts. He lives like an animal in the deep woods. Gotha knows about him, why he's like the way he is, but he's never told me. I think your parents know him, too. Haven't they ever talked about him?"

Rising Sun wrinkled his forehead. "I remember something . . . but I thought it was just a tale to scare children with. I've never seen him. You mean to tell me the Frightened Man is real?"

"As real as these footprints." Moon Face clambered up. "Anyway, *I've* seen him, so I know he's no Spirit tale. He's as real as you or me, but a whole lot stranger."

Rising Sun glanced up, his teeth unconsciously gnawing at his lower lip. "All I remember is childhood stories. Uh . . . something about a punishment?" He shook his head. "Cursed by the Gods, was that it? And something about Great Maya." He wrestled with it a moment, but couldn't think of anything more.

"You say he's real?"

Moon Face nodded.

"But he hides in the deep woods? I've ranged the whole Valley, many times, but I've never seen him. It's because he hides, right?"

"Yes. It's why he's called the Frightened Man. He's even scared of his own shadow."

Rising Sun stood up. "Well, if he's so frightened of everything, *what is he doing following us*?" Then, more calmly, "And if he's so scared of everything, how could he drag Running Deer away? She's strong, she would have fought—and sometimes she even scares *me*."

"Rising Sun, I haven't the faintest idea." Moon Face sounded wounded, as if he thought his friend blamed him for this latest turn of events.

Rising Sun exhaled harshly, slapped his thighs in exasperation. "Are you *sure* these tracks are his?"

Moon Face gestured. "Well, he's the biggest man I've ever seen. Huge, like a bear. And the missing toe is correct. What odds of another man like that?"

Rising Sun looked down, thought a moment, then shook his head. "Okay. Say it *is* the Frightened Man. You say you've seen him?"

"Yes."

"Talked with him?"

"Well, not exactly. He doesn't talk the way you or I would. But Gotha can communicate with him. I think Gotha has known him for a long time, and doesn't scare him as much as somebody else would." He paused. "Actually, I've never seen him unless Gotha was with me— although sometimes I've thought he was around somewhere, watching while I searched for herbs."

Rising Sun scraped his fingers through his hair, making it stick out in places. "Okay. I'll take your word." He squinted at the surrounding greenery, as if perhaps the Frightened Man was hiding near at hand.

"So this Frightened Man has somehow followed us all the way from the Green Valley, and then in the middle of the night managed to steal Running Deer away without making any noise at all."

"He's very crafty in the woods. I said he's like an animal."

"I'll kill him like an animal when I find him," Rising Sun said grimly.

"First you have to find him."

"No," Rising Sun said, "first *we* have to find him. I know how you feel about Running Deer, Moon Face. But she's as important to me as you are. Will you help me?"

Moon Face had already decided to do what he could— Rising Sun's embrace and the magical words after it had

melted all his reservations, at least for the time being—
but he couldn't resist the question.

"I will help, yes, of course," he replied. "But I wish
you would tell me, because I really don't understand, and
it's important to me that I do. *Why* is the girl so valuable?"

Rising Sun began to chew his lip again as he regarded
the smaller man. "Because I love her," he said. "And because she's a part of it."

"Part of what?"

"Of me. Of the quest. Of the One to Come."

Chills shivered across Moon Face's shoulder blades.
He knew the truth when he heard it. Rising Sun's expression had gone distant and hard as he'd spoken, as if he
saw something far beyond the ken of mere mortals, something too sad and at the same time too glorious to ever explain. And Moon Face also sensed that this inability to
explain had made Rising Sun more lonely than any human had ever been in all the seasons of the World. Invol-
untarily he flinched at the pain he saw in his friend's face.

"Well." He sighed. "If she means so much to you, then
that's enough. I don't understand, but I'm not here to understand. Only to help." He didn't blush at the lie, because right then he believed it. He squatted again,
examining the footprints with narrowed eyes. "We'd better get to it."

Rising Sun slapped him on the back. They set off.

5

In a way, Running Deer thought, it would have been
sort of enjoyable, if it hadn't been so strange and scary at
the same time.

After she found the tiny spring and drank her fill, her
headache lessened a bit, and she discovered she was able
to think coherently again. Obediently she followed the
Frightened Man back to the clearing, saying nothing,
though her mind worked at a furious pace.

Escape seemed impossible, at least for the moment. As
she followed, she noted how lightly the huge man

stepped, how surely—almost instinctively—he avoided brushing leaves or crumpling the dew-laden grass. His broad feet—the little toe missing on the right, how strange—seemed to find the hard places without conscious effort, so even as big as he was, he left no trace in the earth of his passage.

Like a great bear, she thought. A bear would move like that. And a bear could catch her in an instant if she ran. It was that knowledge, along with her sudden realization that even if she *did* successfully elude him for a time, she had no idea in which direction to go. This part of the World was totally alien—she could lose herself in the woods forever. At least if she stayed with the Frightened Man, there was a chance Rising Sun would be able to track them down.

Rising Sun!

She realized with a start that she hadn't thought of him at all since she'd awakened. Of course he would try to find her! Thus she conceived her sketchy plan. Remain with the Frightened Man, try to keep him calm, but slow him down. Find a way to leave spoor that Rising Sun could find. A broken branch here, crushed grasses there. The Frightened Man might move like a ghost through the landscape, but she—if she was careful—could leave a trail as plain as a broad path for any experienced tracker following her. And Rising Sun was known as a good tracker. She suspected Moon Face also had skills in that area. Most Shamans did.

Thus buoyed by what seemed a workable plan, she was almost smiling when she reentered the clearing a pace or so behind the Frightened Man and he turned and scooped her up.

"What! Put me down, you big—" She balled her fists, but he squeezed her once, almost gently, and shook his head. Suddenly she was conscious of just how *strong* he was. He'd lifted her as easily as she would lift a bird, and now he cradled her in the hammock of his arms as if she weighed nothing. She saw the muscles in his biceps bulge slightly, looking as smooth and hard as the large rocks lying water-rounded in the Rock Jumble of the Green Valley.

Then they were off. She rocked gently in his grasp, lulled by the graceful rhythm of his march. But his arms were a prison, for she wasn't able to move except to shift her weight every now and then. So much for her clever plan to lay a trail. It was almost as if the Frightened Man had anticipated her, though she couldn't figure out how. Certainly nothing in the way he ambled along, snorting occasionally, eyes vague and filmy, hinted at any such devious intelligence.

She had plenty of time to think. They were still moving through woods, heading in a generally southwesterly direction, from what she could see of the sun when it managed to penetrate the deep forest canopy. His footsteps made no sound, so that if she closed her eyes, she could almost imagine she was floating silently through the World, listening to the sharp cries of the birds overhead, the saw and wheeze and hum of busy insects, the soft rustling of wind through the trees.

It lulled her. Amazingly, she dropped off to sleep, only to start awake later, the memory of the Frightened Man's eyes terrifyingly bright and clear. The answer was so plain, right in front of her face! Why hadn't she seen it?

Maybe, she thought, *because I didn't want to.*

A Demon. A Demon had taken possession of the Frightened Man's Spirit. *That* was what peeked out when the Frightened Man changed. It wasn't the Frightened Man at all, but the *Demon.*

Her breath caught in her throat. It explained so much. It unraveled the puzzle of how the Frightened Man could have left the safety of the Green Valley and followed them all the way south. It answered the question of how the Frightened Man could imprison her like this, despite his obvious terror. And most important, it made those changes in his eyes and voice and manner frightfully clear. Not him, but the Demon. She was in the power of a *Demon.*

How in the World could she possibly escape that?

For an instant the peril of her situation—of her *Spirit*—overpowered her. Her thoughts whirled wildly, and she had to fight the urge to begin screaming. No, no, she couldn't do *that*! What would the Demon do? Knock her out, as it had promised? Or worse?

Worse. That was the real problem, wasn't it? What would a Demon want with her? Forcing herself to take deep breaths—the Frightened Man glanced down at her, shook his head faintly, then looked away just as her heart seemed to stop beating—she fought down her panic by main force of will.

When the spasm subsided, she closed her eyes again, but not to sleep. Only to blot out the face of the specter above her. She couldn't think, with that broad, blank face that hid so much staring down at her. But with her eyes closed it was better.

Caught by a Demon! She tried to remember what little she knew about those malign Spirits. What she knew was depressingly little—women weren't knowledgeable about such things, because they didn't need to be. That's what Shamans were for. Only Shamans had the art, the craft, the will to deal with Demons.

As she thought about this, she regretted that she and Moon Face hadn't been able to get along better. Even Rising Sun wouldn't know how to handle a Demon—hunters occasionally encountered such things, she believed, but when they did, they turned to the Shaman as well—but Moon Face, after all his years of apprenticeship a Shaman in all but name, doubtless had the ability to vanquish the creature. If he desired to do so.

Then another horrifying thought struck her. Moon Face hated her, and Moon Face *knew about Demons*. She knew the apprentice envied her closeness to Rising Sun, and hated that she'd managed to insinuate herself into their party in the first place. What if this Demon was his summoning, to carry her away from them and fulfill his desire to get rid of her?

She moaned softly. If that was the case, then there was no hope at all!

6

"I answered your question," Rising Sun said. "Now you answer one for me. Why do you dislike Running Deer so much?"

They were moving deeper into the woods. Moon Face had discovered a few traces leading southwest from the clearing that might have been the spoor of the Frightened Man. But for the past few hours, they'd found nothing to confirm this, and Rising Sun was feeling increasingly helpless. The Frightened Man seemed almost supernaturally adept at concealing his trail.

To take his mind off his worries as best he could—he knew a distracted stalker might miss some tiny, vital sign—he began to chat with his companion. Somehow, the conversation helped to focus his thoughts—and his tracker's vision.

Moon Face remained silent for several moments. Rising Sun understood that the apprentice had heard him, but suspected he was taking his time formulating a reply.

I wish I could read his thoughts! Rising Sun thought, and then realized that he *could*. Or at least one time, he *had* done so. But it had only been the one time. Just a while ago he'd hugged Moon Face and felt nothing.

He was chewing on this when Moon Face said, "I don't really hate *her*, you know. It's what she *is* that bothers me."

"A woman, you mean?" He had already sensed Moon Face's general dislike—and disdain for—women in general. Nor did he find the apprentice's feelings all that odd. Many men felt that way.

But Moon Face shook his head. "No. A distraction."

"What do you mean?"

Moon Face sighed in exasperation. "Have you forgotten why we left the Green Valley, Rising Sun? It had nothing to do with Running Deer. But here we are, wandering around in the woods, trying to find her instead of doing what we set out to do. The *quest*, my friend. You say she is a part of it, but is it true? Or is it just your penis talking to you—and to me?"

Rising Sun ruminated a moment. "But you hated her from the beginning. Before any of this happened. Why?"

"Maybe," Moon Face said slowly, "because I feared something like this would happen."

Rising Sun stared at him. "Is there something you aren't telling me?"

Moon face shook his head.

If I could only know his real thoughts, Rising Sun wished a second time. *Perhaps, if I took his shoulders and looked into his eyes and* wished *hard enough . . .*

But even as he turned, considering, Moon Face raised his head and said, "What's that?"

Rising Sun paused. "What?"

Wordlessly the apprentice pointed off to their left. "Something there . . . a shadow, maybe. Or an animal of some kind. But close—I just got a glimpse. Blackish-gray, I think."

"Don't move," Rising Sun whispered. Carefully he took his bow and strung it, then nocked an arrow to the string. "Right over there?" he whispered.

Moon Face nodded.

They stood in frozen tableau for several seconds, Rising Sun with his bow fully drawn, Moon Face staring through squinted eyes, waiting.

Nothing. "I don't see anything now," Moon Face said.

Rising Sun lowered his bow. "Maybe it *was* a shadow."

Stepping delicately, the young wolf limped out of the brush several yards away and stood, eyeing them brightly, his bloodred tongue lolling between teeth as white as sun-bleached bone.

7

No longer lulled by the ease of her method of travel, instead wound tense as a baited game-trap by the knowledge that she rode in the unbreakable clutch of a Demon, Running Deer tried to think.

It was very hard. The Frightened Man had glanced

down at her again when she'd loosed her inadvertent moan, but soon lost interest.

In between bouts of pure terror, she found moments of lucidity that, over time, grew longer. Her heart would still throb frantically and then subside, but she was learning to ignore these tangible evidences of her fear, to think through them.

The problem, she decided, had not changed, though her initial analysis of it had. Now, she longed for Moon Face, rather than Rising Sun. Her mate could have dealt with the Frightened Man easily enough, if he could find him. Perhaps Moon Face could do likewise with the Demon that had possessed the shambling brute.

She'd decided she must proceed as if this was true. If her first terrified suspicion that the Demon was the apprentice's work *was* true, then everything was lost. Nothing she could do would make any difference. So she must assume that it *wasn't* the case, and build her plot accordingly. The first order of business still seemed to be to find a way to leave a trail so that her pursuers could find her. But how?

She certainly wasn't going to be breaking any branches or leaving any strategic footprints. The Frightened Man showed no inclination to allow her feet to touch the earth at all. She supposed they would stop sometime, if only to sleep—did Demons sleep?—but no doubt her abductor would pick his spot carefully and make sure he left no more traces than his already ghostly passage had done.

No, what she needed was something he couldn't prevent, something that would also leave a spoor he couldn't erase. And, if possible, something that would look like an accident. She didn't look forward to being clouted unconscious for her pains—although she had no idea whether anything she might do would deceive a Demon.

She closed her eyes and tried to think, though her head ached and her belly seemed to have shrunk into a tight, hard knot of hunger. A surge of nausea swept her, but she ignored it. There wasn't anything in her stomach to puke up.

Puke up?

Ah.

She opened her eyes. Her lips felt dry and chapped, her tongue faintly swollen, but the words came out clear enough. "Hungry," she said. "I'm hungry."

His broad, vacant face looked down at her. She thought she saw that harder glint in his eyes for just a moment, but she wasn't certain. She made a fist and tapped his broad chest. "I want something to eat! I've fed you before, many times. Now you find something for *me*!"

She held her breath. His pace slowed. Finally, that great head moved. "Hungry ..." It almost seemed as if the Frightened Man were recalling all those times she'd given him the game she'd brought down with her bow.

He nodded. "Food. I will feed ... you."

And with that, his path changed abruptly, and he set off in an entirely new direction.

8

"Wolf!" Moon Face hissed. "Kill it."

Rising Sun's fingers itched on the bowstring. A simple flick would send the deadly arrow winging on its way. And while he wasn't as good with a bow as Running Deer, he had no doubt of his ability to hit a stationary target as close as that strange animal who stood stiff-legged and frozen, eyeing him brightly.

Something familiar about it ...

A picture suddenly bloomed in the eye of his mind. The wolf who limped away from the slaughter that seemed half a lifetime ago. That wolf had looked a lot like this one. A *lot* like it. But why would a wolf follow the man who had killed its pack?

Sighing, he lowered his bow.

"What's wrong with you? *Kill it!*"

The wolf twitched, but remained otherwise motionless.

"No. There's something strange here."

"Are you crazy?"

Rising Sun shook his head. "That's one of the wolves that got away after the attack on Running Deer."

"So? They tried to kill us then. Maybe there's more of them about." Moon Face glanced around uneasily.

Slowly Rising Sun stooped and laid his bow on the ground. Then, remaining crouched over, he faced the young wolf and began to inch his way forward, never turning his eyes from the black gaze of the beast.

"Rising Sun! What are you *doing*?"

"I don't know. Don't move."

Moon Face opened his mouth to speak, then clicked it shut and shook his head.

Rising Sun eased across the several paces of ground between himself and the wolf. As he approached, he could see the animal was quivering. He extended his right hand, palm down, fingers dangling limply. He began to hum softly, deep in his throat, a soothing sound.

The wolf's ears pricked up. He swallowed his red tongue, snorted, then opened his mouth again. Now Rising Sun was less than an arm's length away. He could see the flashing white canines of the beast. This close, the wolf looked much larger than it had from a distance. A single snap of those jaws would take his fingers off at the lower knuckles.

Rising Sun held his breath. Slowly, slowly . . .

His fingers dangled right in front of the animal's muzzle. This close, he could see the tiny yellow centers of the wolf's black eyes, watch as the orbs focused on his fingertips. The wolf blinked.

Rising Sun could feel the sweat rolling down his brow, filling his eyes with hot, astringent salt. But he didn't move. And finally, with a long, curious snuffle, the wolf stretched forward and placed the wet black ball of its nose on Rising Sun's fingers.

It felt cold.

The most curious sensation overcame him. As the wolf snuffled and sniffed at his hand, then flicked out its rough, hot tongue and licked his fingertips, Rising Sun felt the World begin to fade. His vision grew dark around the edges until all he could see were the eyes of the wolf, great black rings with small golden circles in their centers.

In the stretching of the moment he felt himself begin

to fall, toppling forward into those glowing orbs, like a rock dropped into a bottomless pool.

Plink.

The pictures—no, they weren't really pictures, but something *else*—wavered through his skull like water flowing over smooth rocks. He was immersed, drowning in them, all the sights, smells, tastes, sounds, sensations.

Rough, rough stone beneath claws, the *click-click* sound, heat, the burning light overhead. Fear! Yes yes the smell of hot red blood, *yes*! Thirst, long red tongue dangling, dry in the hot breeze, the hunger. Day night day night day endlessly. Cool green. Yes yes yes.

Blood the howling bones snapping teeth snapping the bite of whistling sticks the manthings the womanthing blood. Rocks and pain no no no yes!

Limping . . .

Run hide run walk pace hide night day the cool woods the taste of flowing water scent in nose. Smell hot hard bright the man things salt and sweat and shit and piss so many . . . the light.

The light ahead yes yes always ahead. Follow the light.

Follow the light! Yes yes *yes* . . .

"Rising Sun, get back!"

The separation was so sudden, so painful, that Rising Sun gasped away from the sound. He looked up, blinking and confused, to see Moon Face's contorted features, see the long spear the apprentice held over his head in a two-handed, stabbing grip.

"No!"

He flung out one arm, barely deflecting the great stone point as he flung himself over the wolf's body with a heavy thump.

The spear head buried itself in the earth not a hand's breadth away from his ribs. The wolf squirmed beneath him, whining. Its wiry fur scratched against the soft skin of his belly.

"Moon Face, stop that. Let go of the spear, do it NOW!"

Something of his panic and anger penetrated the red killing flush that disfigured the would-be Shaman's features. He gave off wrenching at the spear shaft and stepped away, staring in wonderment at his hands, as if he'd never seen them before.

Rising Sun couldn't imagine where the chubby little apprentice had found the courage to wield the great spear, and for an instant his heart went out to him. "Get back, get away from me," he said, more softly but with iron firmness.

Utterly confused, shaking from adrenaline rush, Moon Face backed off. "I was only trying . . ." He looked as if he might burst into tears.

"I know," Rising Sun soothed him. "But it's all right. Leave me alone."

"Awroo?"

The low, muffled howl turned his attention back to the wolf, who was trying to lift Rising Sun's full weight off its back by main force. He rolled off the beast, who scrabbled up but made no effort to run away. Instead, that long red tongue lapped out and scraped across Rising Sun's cheek. Rising Sun smelled a sour billow of rotting meat in the animal's hot breath.

Wondering, he reached out and scratched behind the wolf's ears. Somehow he knew the animal would enjoy it.

The wolf grinned at him, waiting.

Rising Sun stared into those black and golden eyes, trying to understand what had just happened. The pictures—no, they were much more than that, it was almost as if he'd somehow become a wolf himself, experiencing all that the animal before him experienced— Was this what his father knew, in the mystery of his power to control the savage beasts?

Those things he'd felt weren't human. He knew that. But how? Then it hit him. He knew, because he'd had a similar experience with Moon Face. Somehow gotten inside his thoughts. It had been like this, but different.

The realization rocked him so heavily that he didn't make the obvious connection, would not make it for long miles of travel, and then it would be almost too late.

Suddenly he remembered that long-ago time when Morning Star had taken his small hand in his own and led him down the Main Path to the caves set into the walls just inside the mouth of the Green Valley.

He'd been tiny then, toddling along, trusting in the dry warm comfort of his father's grasp. The sun had been a blinding hole in the blue summer sky. Their feet had made soft, whooshing sounds in the path, raising small clouds of brown dust that hung in the still air after they had passed.

Eventually they turned off the Main Path, his father thrusting through the thick green brush, Rising Sun trailing along behind, until the land rose sharply into barren rock. Here they stopped. Morning Star seated himself on the top of a flat boulder and gathered the little boy into his lap.

"See up there?" he said, pointing.

Obediently Rising Sun tilted his baby face up and stared at the cliff face above him. It was scarred with many ledges and outcroppings and fissures. He didn't know what he was supposed to see, and so he nodded doubtfully.

"Do you see the caves? Those dark holes in the cliff?"

Now he did see them, several shadowy openings in the stone, halfway up the side of the Valley wall.

"I see," he replied, still not understanding.

"That is where the lions live," his father said.

Rising Sun squirmed against Morning Star's chest. For as long as he could remember, he'd been warned against the great tawny-black beasts, told of how they loved boy-meat, of how dangerous it was to stray from the watchful safety of the adults.

"It's all right," Morning Star soothed him. "I'm with you. Would you like to see the lions?"

Rising Sun shook his head, then tried to bury his face in Morning Star's armpit. Morning Star laughed. "You have nothing to be afraid of, my son. And after today, you will never have to fear the lions again."

Rising Sun stared up at his father's face, not understanding. In fact, he wouldn't fully understand for many long years, but it was his father and he trusted him absolutely.

Then, still holding the boy's hand, Morning Star stood

up on the flat rock and began to call softly. "Come out, Mother. Come out, mighty Father. Bring all your children, for now you must leave your home of endless seasons and find another place. Come out, come out, for I, the Star of the Morning, command you!"

Rising Sun looked up and saw that his father's features had gone still and slack, though his green and blue eyes seemed even wider than usual, and they flashed in the high sunlight like jewels.

A stone clicked and tumbled down the wall. The sound snapped his head up, and Rising Sun saw a strange and terrible sight. The caves were no longer vague black holes. Great tawny shapes emerged, slowly, reluctantly. Shivering, he wrapped his little-boy arms around his father's leg and watched as the huge beasts, whining and coughing, made their way down the cliffside.

The lions seemed to move slowly, their muscles flowing beneath soft hides, but it was an illusion. In less than two hands of heartbeats, a river of gold and ebony fur gathered around the flat stone, restlessly moving, circling, running like a river.

Their acrid stench made Rising Sun's eyes water.

His father ruffled his hair and said, "Do you have my Power, son? I wonder . . ." Then, with a single motion, he unwrapped him from his leg and pushed him forward, right to the edge of the stone.

"Reach out to them, Rising Sun. To the mother, there, see her? Tell her what to do, command her . . . if you can," he finished, in a rough, low whisper.

Rising Sun squealed in terror. The gigantic beast directly below him paused in her pacing, squatted down, stared up at him. He looked into her green-yellow gaze and felt his heart stop in his chest. She yawned, exposing tarnished fangs as long as his forearm.

He felt his bladder go.

She smelled his urine. It seemed to agitate her. She heaved herself up on her hindquarters, which brought her great head almost to the level of his knees. Coughed. Moaned deep in her throat. Then, preternaturally quick, she lunged forward.

Her great jaws snapped shut on empty air, only be-

cause Morning Star swung him up and away. His voice
boomed out.

"Back. Down, Mother, he isn't for you!"

Mewing, she fell away, her broad shoulders hunched
as if she'd been whipped. Morning Star sighed. "If you
have it, I see no sign," he said. Disappointment colored
his tone. He shook his head. "Well, maybe you will have
other things."

Then, briskly, he shoved the boy behind him and
raised his arms. "I command you, leave the Valley. Leave
your caves and come no more here. This place is not
yours any longer!"

Rising Sun blinked. The wolf blinked back at him and
licked his palm again. His father had possessed the Power
to command the beasts of the World. Did he, only now after so many years, also have such Power? He looked at
the Wolf, looked into its eyes, remembered that hot, panting place he'd just experienced, and tried to reenter it
again, this time consciously, willingly.

"Lie down," he whispered.

Nothing.

He looked deeper into those savage eyes, tried to
imagine himself falling as before. Nothing.

"Lie down," he said again.

The wolf whined uneasily.

He wrapped his fingers in the dry rough fur, felt the
hard ridge of skull bone beneath his fingers. Felt something tingle.

"Lie down!"

The wolf flopped over and lay on its side, panting.

"Rising Sun!" Moon Face whispered, awe in his
voice.

Rising Sun ignored him. "Up."

Obediently the wolf clambered up. Rising Sun stood,
careful to keep his hand on the wolf's head. But some . . .
connection had been established. He looked down into the
wolf's eyes and imagined them as caves, as a place he
could enter. Slowly he removed his hand.

"Down . . ." he said.

Once again the wolf slumped over. Its brushy tail beat against the ground.

"Up."

The wolf came up again. Rising Sun sighed. He turned and looked at Moon Face. "Well?"

"You have the Power. You have your father's rule over the beasts."

Rising Sun nodded. "Yes," he said. "It seems that I do."

They stared at each other. "What does it mean?" Moon Face said finally.

Rising Sun smiled. "This." He squatted, took the wolf's head between his hands, stared into its eyes, summoned the picture in his own mind, held it steady until he felt the click of recognition.

"Yes." He nodded. "Find the woman. Find Running Deer. *Find her!*"

CHAPTER SEVENTEEN

1

Carries Two Spears crashed into the Spirit Tent so wildly that his charge carried him all the way to the other side, scattering the hearth in his passage. A cloud of sparks exploded behind him as he turned to see the horrid work that had been done in the darkness of the tent.

Sleeps With Spirits screamed again. She stood rigidly next to the door, illumined in the morning light, one hand fluttering in front of her lips. Her red eyes were fixed and wild.

Midway between the two of them, the Witch crouched like a carrion bird over the body of her prey. Her eyes, full of a dark, brutal joy, peered brightly up at him. "I caught them," she croaked. "They were fucking. It was part of their plot."

She looked down, almost without interest, then spat into Drinks Deep Waters's bulging eyes. *"It was him!"* She looked up again. "But he won't do any more plotting, will he?"

Carries Two Spears stared down in horror at the scene before him. Drinks Deep Waters's pitiful, wattled neck was a red ruin. The hilt of a stone knife protruded from the spot where his Adam's apple had been. Blood spread in a dark, sticky pool around his head. His bulging gaze was fixed on the roof of the tent in a frozen spasm of ultimate surprise.

The Witch raised her clawed hands. The same gluey red stain disfigured her curved fingers. The coppery smell of bloody death filled the still air.

Spirits screamed a third time. Spears turned and looked at her, saw that she was naked. Blood was spattered on her face, her neck, her pale white breasts. Her hands dripped with it. The color was shocking against her skin.

He moved toward her.

"Don't touch her!" the Witch growled. *"She is tainted, unclean!"*

Somebody shouted outside the tent. The Witch glanced up at the sound, her face calm, calculating. She raised her head and cried out. "He is dead! Come in, catch her. She is a Demon!"

The shouting outside grew louder. Spears heard the thump of running feet. Sleeps With Spirits inhaled deeply, beginning another scream. It seemed to be all she could do. Freeze, breathe, scream. Then freeze again.

Spears thought he couldn't bear to hear her scream again. The sound was empty, cold, loud. It hurt his ears. It hurt his heart. He reached down, scrabbled, hooked up a blanket made of tanned hide, soft as butter, and threw it over her. It blotted out her face, her eyes, and that was better. It muffled her terrible screams, and that was better still.

The blanket draped below her waist, like a sack. He scooped her up, hoisted her over his shoulder. Behind him, the Witch gabbled something, but he paid her no attention.

He plunged through the door into the crowd that had gathered outside, scattering them. He ran blindly for several paces, then made a sharp turn. He galloped to the Men's Tent, conscious that the cries behind him had redoubled. He ducked inside, found his pack and his spears. It was awkward, carrying everything. When he emerged, two hunters were almost on him. He thrust with both spears and they stopped.

He turned and ran. Four bounding strides took him

into the woods. Spirits bounced on his shoulder as limply as the carcass of some animal. A deer, maybe. The weight was about right. He had carried deer many times. He knew he could go a long way, carrying her.

He ran north, deeper into the woods. The morning light grew dim and the trees grew taller. After a time he paused and turned, but saw nothing. Faint, tumultuous cries ghosted on the breeze from the direction he'd come, but far away. Nobody seemed to be following.

"Spirits?" he whispered.

Nothing. He swung her down, pulled the robe off her blood-spattered face. Her eyes were closed. Panic curdled his gut. He put his ear close to her lips, was rewarded with a weak breath of warmth. He shuddered with relief, wrapped her more carefully, and lifted her again.

He arranged his pack and his spears and turned again to the north. He began to jog. He didn't look back. There was no reason. There was nothing for either of them in that direction.

He remembered the Witch's face. There was nothing but death for them in the camp between the Two Rivers.

2

They roared and stamped into the tent, the men first, the women crowding after, the children milling in confusion outside. The Witch looked up at them and hissed. The small sharp sound cut through the clamor like a knife. They fell silent as they slowly made out the tableau before them. The Witch waited until the time was right. When it was, she nodded.

"Drinks Deep Waters is dead," she intoned. "My daughter, the cursed one, the Demon, killed him. I was ... too late."

Breaths whistled sharply in. The small crowd stirred then, making way for Kills Many Buffalo. The Chief limped to the front, stopped, gazed down at the scene. His old face was crumpled with shock. Slowly his expression changed to one of cold loathing. His slumped shoulders straightened a bit. His buck teeth protruded as he spoke.

"This is your doing?"

She shook her head, and seemed to realize her disadvantage, squatting below him. Slowly she stood up. One of her knees creaked in the silence. "No. My daughter."

They stared at each other. His glance flickered down. "His blood is on your hands, Witch."

She knew that everything hung in the balance of this moment. She clenched her teeth. "I was too late," she answered. "I tried to stanch the flow of his blood with my own hands, but his life leaked out between my fingers." She raised her hands and showed him. "I tried, though."

The old man spat. "Tell me," he said.

She stared into his tired, broken face and knew she had won. They had faced each other over the body of the Shaman, and in the end he asked for an explanation. It was the same as a surrender. She felt a great warm clot of relief fill her lungs. The tension went out of her heavy shoulders for the first time that morning.

"I knew my daughter and the Shaman were plotting against me," she began. She continued, her voice soft, hypnotic. The same tones she'd whispered into Spirits's ear the night before. She spoke quietly, plausibly, though she knew it didn't matter. The Chief had asked for an explanation. It didn't matter what it was, because he could no longer resist her. Not with the slaughtered corpse of his friend and ally at his feet.

She understood, and gave him what he wanted. What he needed. Eventually it was over, and they went out into the bright morning sunlight. Into the new day.

She felt tight, fierce, joyful. He had turned away from her, his face slack, and she caught up to him. She patted him on the shoulder. Her tale had terrified everyone. She knew they believed it because they *wanted* to believe it. It was easier to believe than to fight her anymore. She touched him on his shoulder, felt the old, birdlike bones there.

"There are things we must do, to remove the curse," she said.

He didn't turn. "Then do them," he said.

She dropped her hand, releasing him. She watched

him trudge away. She would let him live, she decided. He was broken. He might be useful in the future.

"Mother," a reedy voice at her side whispered. She turned. The Shaman's apprentice, a thin, bitter man of middle age, stared at her thoughtfully. His name was Looks Into Dreams, and he had not figured in her plans at all. He had been the shadow of the Shaman for so long that nobody paid him any more attention than a real shadow. But now, she realized with a start, he *was* the Shaman.

She experienced a sudden strange sinking feeling. She stared at him, wondering if she'd made some kind of unfixable mistake by not figuring him into her plans—and the idea of that made her feel even queasier. For she was of the Goddess, was she not? And the Goddess could not be guilty of error.

"What is it . . . Shaman?" she said.

Looks Into Dreams licked his lips. He wrung his fingers together. "You will have to help me, Mother," he whispered. "To be a good Shaman."

His terror was so evident she wondered how she could have missed it. She watched him a moment longer, to make sure, and he began to fidget beneath her flat, appraising gaze. "Please," he whimpered.

No, the Goddess had not made a mistake. "I will help you," the Witch said.

He nodded eagerly. "Shall I prepare Drinks Deep Waters for his final journey?"

"Yes. That would be good." He turned. "Wait."

"What?" So terribly *willing*.

"Bring me the knife. From his throat. I will need it to undo the damage he has done. The curse."

He nodded quickly, his head flopping atop his skinny neck. "Yes, of course."

She smiled. Of course.

She watched him half bow, turn, scramble back to the Spirit Tent, and duck inside. The watchfulness left her with shocking suddenness. She felt herself begin to slump in a boneless wave of relief, and forced herself to straighten. No show of weakness for her. The next few days would be critical.

Carries Two Spears. She hadn't counted on *that*. It put an unexpected kink in her plans. Unexpected, but not entirely unwelcome. No doubt the stupid fool had carried his sister away.

For a moment she wanted to grapple with the why of it, and how she'd missed what must have begun between the two of them. But the urge subsided. It didn't matter. Whatever it was, it had happened, and they were gone.

She had prepared a certain role for Sleeps With Spirits, but now that would no longer work. The girl would live. For a short time, at least.

The Witch thought about that. It was all she could do to keep from laughing out loud. He thought he'd rescued her. She'd seen it plain in his stunned eyes as he looked down on her with utter and complete loathing, before he whirled to scoop up the girl.

That look had been familiar. Her husband had looked at her like that, just before—

She shook her head. Make sure that stupid Shaman brought her the knife. The knife had proved its worth many times. She could trust the knife.

Idly, as she turned to retrace her steps, she wondered how long it would take. Three turns of the sun was about right, she guessed, and it would be painful. At first he would be puzzled. Then, as he understood, he would become terrified. He wouldn't be back.

Looks Into Dreams floundered from the tent, holding the bloody, dripping thing in his hand as gingerly as if it were a poisonous snake. Wordlessly he extended it to her.

She took it, making no effort to avoid the blood. What was a little blood to her?

3

When he was certain there was no close pursuit, Carries Two Spears stopped and set her down next to a fallen tree. She had still not awakened. He sat down heavily on the trunk, his shoulders quivering from exhaustion, and shrugged off his pack. Carefully he leaned his two spears against the wood, points up. He stared down at her.

Her nakedness seemed pitiful to him. She looked somehow shrunken, and so pale that if he hadn't been able to make out the rise and fall of her chest, he would have thought she was dead. He had no idea at all what to do next.

The forest was deep here, dark and cool, the leafy canopy so thick that little sunlight penetrated to the woody floor. This lack of light stunted the smaller growth, so that the space between the great trees was almost clear of underbrush. Tufts of bright green coated the tops of rolling swales of rich brown humus. Except for the birds and the distant thunderous river, it was silent. His own harsh breathing seemed unbearably loud, and he looked around uneasily. He couldn't shake the feeling that something—somebody—was watching him.

Well, this was what he'd wanted, wasn't it? Him and her, free of the Witch at last, free of the Tribe and the curse that had weighed her down all her life. He looked at her face, so still, so innocent. In sleep, all the pain in it went away, and he could see the outlines of the child she'd once been. But that was a long time ago, and this was now, and things had changed for both of them.

He sighed and kicked absently at his pack. Then he bent over, opened it, and spread its contents on the ground. There wasn't much. He'd just returned from hunting, had made no preparations for a new trek, and so many of the things that might have been in his pack were not. No trail meat, for instance. No extra stone heads for his two spears. No spare knife. No knife, in fact, at all. There were a pair of fire flints, though, and he breathed a relieved sigh at that. At least they would be able to kindle a fire.

But there were real problems. He was no flint-knapper. Any knife he would make would be a poor approximation of the real thing. If his spear heads shattered—and they would, they always did—his replacements would be crude and less effective.

For a moment he considered trying to sneak back into the camp and steal some proper provisions, but he quickly discarded the idea. *She* was in the camp, and as long as that was true, he would not risk coming within the reach of her power again. He had looked into her eyes as she'd crouched over the Shaman's mutilated carcass, and seen the Demon lurking within. The hungry Demon, the same one that had killed his father. He shuddered. Had he lived with that Demon all these years unknowing? It seemed that he had, though he was certain that on some deep level he'd known it was there all along. And maybe that knowing had saved his life, because he'd left her as soon as he could, and that had protected him. It was the ones close to her, and her enemies, who seemed to die. He had managed to become neither, and so he had survived to come to—what?

This is what, he thought, looking at Sleeps With Spirits's unconscious form. Outcasts, non-People, tribesmen without a Tribe. Lonely and vulnerable. Too vulnerable, perhaps?

He grunted. Enough of this. He had his hands, he had the breath in his lungs, he had two spears. He could make fire and he could hunt. Somehow they would survive.

On the other side of the river, though. That was first. Get away from her for all time, so far that she would never think of following.

Maybe they could find another Tribe. He knew there were others out there, though he'd never seen them for himself. But he'd seen traces in his hunts. Particularly along the Great Blue River's eastern bank. That might be the way to go. Cross the Big Blue and head south. Warmer country, maybe easier hunting. He would think about it soon, but first things first.

Gently he nudged Spirits's shoulder with his toe. "Sister, wake up."

She moaned softly, and he nudged again. "Wake up!"

The old fire was a dull heat burning in his groin. He wondered what he would say to her. How to explain how much he loved her. How much he needed her.

"Wake up."

Her eyelids flickered. He bent down, trying to fashion the words, but they wouldn't come. And when he lifted her, he almost dropped her, shocked at how limp she was. Almost as if she were dead.

4

The Witch busied herself with details. Her mind seemed to have become a cold thing filled with twisted shapes, hard and impermeable, yet nevertheless comforting in their precision. She spoke softly with other women, explaining how she'd found the hank of her own hair grasped tightly in the Shaman's fist. She didn't clearly explain how she'd found them, rolling on his furs, locked together in a final embrace before the knife had come out, and down—but she made certain she conveyed enough, through sighs and shrugs and mumbled, fragmentary sentences, that the message got through. The rumors ran all through the camp, as she knew they would, and that suited her. Rumors were always more believable than truth. And Sleeps With Spirits would not be returning to tell a different story.

Now the women, their faith in her renewed, clustered around her. The plot had been exposed. The Shaman had made common cause with the Demon daughter to overthrow the mother. She had stolen bits of the Witch—hair, spit, other things—and brought them to the Shaman, who had then cast his spells. It was such a spell that had led to the abortive uprising. The Shaman could not have triumphed as he had without his black magic.

The story was loose, full of holes, but that was all right. No one wanted to inquire too closely. The doings of Spirits and Demons, the working of evil spells, the clash of Gods, were not the concern of ordinary mortals. Most people preferred to keep their heads down, their mouths shut, their eyes blank and empty, lest the attention of malign forces be drawn to them.

The men avoided her as much as they could, and when they spoke to her, they spoke softly and averted their eyes. She didn't mind. She'd always understood fear much better than love.

The children simply ran away, and that jollied her more than anything else. When those children grew up, they would worship her. She had staked everything on a single gamble, and it had turned out. Now she cemented her triumph for all time. The new Shaman, pitiful thing, deferred to her in every way. The old Chief only nodded his assent to everything she asked, and sighed in relief when she left him.

The women approached her with awe. All thought of her recent defeat vanished as the smoke from the Drinks Deep Waters's funeral pyre disappeared into the sharp blue sky.

On the third day she wondered if it was finally over. It had been enough time. Surely Sleeps With Spirits was dead by now—she knew of only one antidote to the slow-working poison she'd administered, and that was not something an untrained hunter could discover. Even another Shaman might have trouble figuring it out, and Carries Two Spears was no Shaman.

No, she thought as she sat before her tent, savoring the silence at her back, basking in the fearful, shifting glances from the front, it was over. She had won.

As if to confirm this, she looked up to see Kills Many Buffalo approach with the new Shaman in tow. The mere fact that *they* were coming to *her* sent a thrill of joy shivering through her stolid body. It was a final proof of the new arrangements, a further cementing of the edifice of power she had managed to construct. She had no intention of trying to assume either of their offices. The men would never accept a female Chief, nor would a woman Shaman suit her purposes, either. It was enough that she would control both of them, and their successors. That the Goddess would rule, no matter who sat in the Worldly seats of power.

The two men clumped up to her. They didn't quite bow. She eyed them, noting the Chief's sagging shoulders, the way his jowls sagged over his protruding teeth, his empty, uncaring eyes. He was, she thought, a dead man walking. The Shaman was simply afraid. He betrayed it with every nervous twitch, with the way he armed snot from a nose that wouldn't stop leaking, and the way he refused to look at her directly. He would slide his glances toward her from the corner of his eyes, and just when it seemed he was looking at her directly, his eyeballs would jerk back.

Altogether satisfying that. She would have to decide on his apprentice soon.

"Hello, Mother," the Chief said. That was another thing. Nobody called her Witch any longer.

"Hello, mighty Chief," she replied. She could afford to be magnanimous with such titles of respect. They both understood how little such things meant.

The Chief sighed, as if he could read her thoughts. He glanced up at the sky, chewed his pendulous lower lip, sighed again. "The summer wears on," he said. "Soon we must decide where our People will go for the winter."

We must decide. We. How wonderful that word rang in her ears. And this question was what had started the whole thing. Now it no longer seemed so important. The battle over it had been fought and won. She could afford to be generous.

"I know you wish to go south, Chief. And if you still wish to do so, I won't object."

He blinked. It wasn't what he'd expected. It brought a certain wariness into his faded old eyes. "You won't?"

She shook her head. After all, it had only been a ploy. The women hadn't wanted to leave, but what did she care about that now? "No, although I would like to leave a little later than usual, to give the women more time for rest." There. Throw them a sop. Keep everybody happy.

He nodded. "Very well, that seems reasonable." The wariness slowly subsided and he merely looked ancient and beaten again.

She reflected a moment on the fact that men were far more easy to manipulate than women. They paraded their masculine strength, pretended that all the power was theirs by virtue of their bulging muscles, but if you whipped one of them, you whipped them all. She was still mildly astonished at how easy it had been. One knife into one throat, and her whole life had changed.

She looked up to find the Chief staring about vaguely, as if he could no longer remember why he had come. She looked at the Shaman, who immediately looked away. "Kills Many Buffalo seems tired this morning," she said. "Perhaps you should brew him an elixir."

Looks Into Dreams nodded and, unconsciously,

reached out to take the Chief's elbow and steady him.
Kills Many Buffalo seemed to be shrinking before her
eyes, becoming older, more frail with every heartbeat.
She looked at him and decided he wouldn't last through
the winter. All the strength had gone out of him. She
would have to give some thought to *his* successor, as
well. And soon.

The burdens of power.

Suddenly she wanted to leap up, raise her brawny
arms over her head, fists clenched like stones, and loose
such a shriek of triumph that the leaves would fall from
the trees and little children would run away weeping. But
she couldn't do that. It would be too strange, too terrible,
too frightening. And it was best not to scare them with
the truth, that a Goddess walked among them. She
slumped back and knew she would pass this test, keep her
triumph safely hidden. But the shriek would nurture her
because it would always be rising in her ears and quivering in her teeth.

"Shaman?"

He had turned the old man and begun to lead him
away. "Yes, Mother?"

"Come back to me. I have things to tell you."

He nodded. "Let me take him back to the Chief's
tent."

She flapped her fingers in a shooing motion of assent
and dismissal. They walked away, two men, fragile as all
men were, beneath the finery of their frightened pride.

It was true. Women *were* stronger.

5

"Spirits, darling, *please* wake up."

But she wouldn't.

Carries Two Spears looked around frantically, as if he
might find some help in the empty trees that overlooked
their meager camp. Nothing answered him. The silence
sat on him like a load of stones, pressed him down. His
shoulders slumped beneath the invisible weight of it.

He had been carrying a lot of weight lately. The

weight of memory. And *her* weight, he'd carried that clear across the arrow-shaped land between the rivers, and then, struggling mightily, across the Big Blue itself into the vast empty forest on the far side. He'd felt a little better when he clambered off the big log and stood, dripping, on the bank. Now there was water between him and the Witch.

It had been a hard crossing, because Spirits couldn't help. She'd never awakened, not once, and he'd taken one of the tough rawhide thongs he'd found in his pack and tied her wrist to his, in case she slipped off the floating log. It had almost happened twice, but he'd caught her limp form both times, and now they were safe.

So why didn't he feel safe? He'd lugged her across the open space between the riverbank and the edge of the forest, because the thought of making camp underneath all that open sky had made him nervous. He'd pushed deep into the trees, noting that they were smaller and more wind-gnarled on this side, and the scrub was thicker.

The place he'd found was next to a tiny spring that leaked up through its graveled source without a sound into a small round pool. The pool emptied, equally soundlessly, into a twisting crystalline trickle that soon lost itself beneath a thick mulch of fallen leaves.

He'd made her a soft bed of that mulch and wrapped her as well as he could in the blanket he'd snatched from the Shaman's house, and he'd built a small fire. It was all he could do. At first he thought it was the shock she'd endured. He'd seen such things before. Then, later, he realized it was more than that.

She was on fire now. Her cheeks were pale, except for two hot, bright spots that burned just over her cheekbones. She would cry out in her sleep sometimes, but the words made no sense. Something about the sun. But the sun barely penetrated the thick shelf of leaves overhead, certainly not enough to cause her any discomfort.

Besides, now she shivered constantly, as if she were freezing to death. Even though she still felt hot to his touch. He crouched over her and knew that she was going to die, and that knowledge punched all the strength out of him and left him feeling as if his knees wouldn't hold him up.

He had done all he knew how to do, all he *could* do—except for one thing—and he knew it wasn't going to be enough. Gently he stroked her cheek, marveling at the smoothness of it, and the ghost of that old hot feeling squirmed in his balls for an instant before subsiding.

It made him feel ashamed, though he couldn't define the source of the shame. Like he'd sometimes felt as a boy, when one of the hunters would whack him for a mistake he didn't know he'd made. There was no one to whack him now and explain his error.

He'd never felt so alone in his life. The trees stretched out around him, their branches whispering and scraping together, bearing their loads of invisible birds and their clouds of invisible humming insects. Always before he'd felt comfortable in the woods, part of them, at peace with their Spirits. Now he felt alien, some kind of intruder, unwelcome. He had somehow dislocated himself from his time and place, and that dislocation frightened him because it made him feel helpless.

He sat down cross-legged and knuckled his eyes until sharp pains lanced out from the pressure, deep into his skull. The pain seemed to clear a lot of the fog from his thoughts, and he opened his eyes and stared at her. What to do now?

The only thing that seemed to offer even the ghost of a chance was to take her back. Maybe the Witch would know what was wrong and how to fix it. But he had seen the Witch squatting like a huge black vulture over the bloody Shaman, and the memory made him shudder. Would Sleeps With Spirits want to return to *that,* even to save her own life?

What had happened to them? What had happened to that hot, bright dream he'd cherished for so long?

In the gray clarity of utter desolation, he saw that he knew the answer. His mother had happened, just as she had always happened, to him, to his sister, to his father. He'd seen what had peeped so gleefully out of her eyes in the Spirit Tent. That burning lustful *thing* that, he knew, had been there as long as he'd known her. He thought that it had always been there, hiding itself carefully, only allowing the tiniest flicker of its presence to show. And then only when it felt absolutely safe.

Was that thing his mother? Or had there once been something else there, a real woman and not a Demon from the most fearsome part of the World?

Could the Demon see him now? He hunched uneasily in the silence. He didn't know. But there was a watchfulness about this place, something that made the skin on the back of his neck itch, so that he would find himself spinning about and staring at—nothing.

"Uhhh."

She'd been quiet for so long that the sound startled him, galvanized him. He was kneeling at her head, bent down, touching her cheek without knowing how he got there.

"Spirits? *Spirits?*"

As if responding to the sound of his hoarse whisper, her eyes popped open. A wave of relief swept through him, sweeping away all the dark ruminations, the nameless fears he hadn't quite been able to acknowledge. It would be all right! But, of course, it wouldn't be. As he knelt over her, willing her to be awake, to be lucid and speak to him, he realized that there was a thin film over her eyeballs, barely visible, but it made her red eyes look flat and empty.

"The sun . . ." she whispered through cracked lips. "The sun, so bright . . ."

"Spirits?"

Her eyes snapped shut and she moaned again, and he could feel the fever blistering off her. He knew she hadn't seen him, and that her words, whatever they meant, weren't for him.

Trembling, he settled back. He rearranged the blanket around her, moving it here, patting it there, knowing the action was as meaningless to her as it was to him.

She was dying and there wasn't anything he could do about it. Well, one thing.

His time had run out. It was time to decide.

He touched her shoulder. "Don't worry," he told her. "Everything will be all right."

CHAPTER EIGHTEEN

1

He came back to her with some indistinguishable small animal. He'd twisted and crushed it beyond recognition in the vise of his huge hands. She couldn't imagine how, as large as he was, he could catch such a small, nimble thing. But he'd managed to survive in the Green Valley. Maybe that was how.

He leaned over and dropped it in front of her. She'd watched him go. He'd simply walked off, faded into the brush in that eerie silent way he had of moving, and then, later, he'd come back.

"Food," he grunted. When she looked up at him he looked quickly away, as if even her gaze frightened him. He wandered off, making small whuffling sounds, and once again she thought of a great shaggy bear.

She picked up the ragged corpse. The smooth brown fur was split in places. He'd twisted off its head, and from the wound spilled pink flesh, bits of white gristle, a sharp stick of bone.

Her stomach heaved. She really *was* hungry, but could she eat this? Yes, she could. She had before, when the hunting was bad, when the snows piled up around the valley, when the winds were too strong for the cook fires and they dwindled and were whipped away.

She sank her teeth into it and yanked and chewed

slowly. The salty juices tasted good. She spat out a hank of fur, then used her teeth to peel back the skin from the meat beneath. She ate until there was nothing left but fur and bones. Then she sighed and patted her belly. Her hunger had receded until there was only a tiny knot of it left, a small hard reminder in her gut that would grow again, but for now was quiescent.

She didn't know if she would be able to do it. The Frightened Man came back and lifted her up, and then they were off. She was glad she hadn't tried to leave any trail while he hunted. He'd set her on a rock and there she'd stayed. While she ate, he shuffled around, seemingly aimlessly, but she saw how his red, piggy eyes gazed sharply at the ground, at the shrubs, at any place she might have left a mark.

He hadn't found anything, because there was nothing to find. Even so, she'd held her breath, fearing the return of that Demon that lurked behind his eyes and spoke from his mouth.

She settled herself into the familiar rolling cadence of his gait, and thought about maggots. At first it was hard, and she had to reach into her memory for something suitable. All maggots weren't bad. The heavy white grubs she found in the rotting leaves at the base of trees made good additions to the stew bag, as did similar crawling things that lived beneath rocks.

She closed her eyes, and finally she had it. When she was a little girl, she had gone out with one of the older women to hunt for duck eggs. A stench had attracted their attention, led them to the body of a squirrel. The old woman poked at the decomposed corpse with her stick, and the head fell right off.

Sort of like the small headless thing the Frightened Man had brought her to eat.

For a moment the two images superimposed in her thoughts and she knew she was making progress. Deliberately she brought the old memory further into the light. After a time she was able to recall the awful stench of the little thing, and the way a puff of foul air had seemed to rise from the hole where the head had been.

The movement disturbed the feeding things inside, and

they poured forth, a tiny writhing tide. On that day, her
nostrils full of the reek of rotting flesh, the strange shiny
green color of decomposition, and, worst of all, the crawling blind surge of shiny things that fed on dead meat had
been too much. Her belly cramped, cramped again, and
she vomited up her morning meal while the older woman
laughed at her for her childishness.

Now, feeling the warm chunk of flesh riding in her
belly, she worked her imagination again. Imagined that
instead of the small fresh clean thing she'd just eaten, she
had bit down into that ancient squirrel, into the soft flesh,
and felt her mouth suddenly fill with squirming slimy
maggots . . .

It came up in a single convulsive spraying heave. It
spattered across the Frightened Man's chest, dripped
down his legs, sprayed the ground and the bushes alongside the path.

He dropped her, made grunting sounds as he tried to
wipe himself off. Her convulsion passed almost as soon
as it had come, leaving her empty. It really hadn't been all
that much of a meal. But enough, she thought, as he
hoisted her quickly up, his flat nose wrinkled against
the stink, and trotted quickly away. She wasn't sure, but
just for an instant she thought she saw something in his
eyes . . .

The way he carried her left her looking over his shoulder, and she could see his hasty prints, at least three of
them, in the softer earth beside the stony trail he'd been
traveling.

Would Rising Sun be able to figure it out? Would he
even be able to find it in the first place?

She didn't know. But she had done what she could.
Only time would tell if it would be enough.

2

It was hard to keep the wolf in sight. The animal
bounded ahead, its silvery-black fur blending into the
shadows, until they could no longer see it at all. They
blundered on in the direction it indicated, and eventually

they found it again, waiting, panting, its eyes alight with the glow of the chase.

It was rough thrusting through the brush. Something about the land hereabouts seemed to attract bugs—Rising Sun thought it might be the small bogs they stumbled across—and the midges whined and screamed in their ears. Within a short time both of them were covered with sweat. The wolf, protected by its thick coat, had no such problems. And because of its small size, it was able to slip between the scrub they had to bull their way through. Small scratches crisscrossed their chests and arms, and the sweat stung in them.

A little after noon Rising Sun glanced over his shoulder and saw that Moon Face had vanished. He stopped, turned, called.

The reply came from a distance, and sounded faint and constricted.

"Wait ... wait for me."

Rising Sun shook his head. He knew what had happened. He was young, in perfect shape, strong as the most hardened hunter. He was sweating, but his muscles felt loose and oily, and the breath in his chest slid easily in and out. He knew a man could run down a deer or an elk, if he kept at it long enough. But Moon Face was soft, a Shaman's apprentice, untrained in the long hunt. Burdened by flab. No doubt the air was a fire in his lungs by now, and his stomach twisting with the nausea of exhaustion.

And so it was. He found his companion doubled over, sitting on a log with his arms wrapped around his belly. He looked pale, and his skin felt hot and dry to the touch.

"I'm sorry, Moon Face," he said softly as he knelt by him. "I should have thought."

The chubby little apprentice looked bad. His breathing was rapid and labored, and the reply he gasped out was unintelligible. Rising Sun knew the signs, and knew he would have to fight the terrible urgency that demanded him to run, run forward, follow the wolf, leave Moon Face behind.

He couldn't do it. Occasionally a hunter, in the frenzy of the chase, loping beneath the burning sun, would forget. Would go too far, too fast, and forget to drink from his water gourd. Then the sun Spirit would strike him down, turn his lungs into pits of fire, make his skin feel dry, then wet and clammy. And sometimes, the hunter would die from the sun Spirit's heat.

He stood, his head cocked, and listened. Sniffed the air. Moon Face made a soft, moaning sound, then toppled sideways off the log. Rising Sun moved off into the woods and found the small stream a hundred strides away. He went back and scooped up Moon Face, surprised at how little the other man weighed. He carried him over his shoulder to the stream and gently set him down in it. He took off his shirt and soaked it in the cool water and draped it over Moon Face's head. He put one edge into his mouth and let him suck on it. Then he waited.

The tension built in him as he squatted at the edge of the stream, holding Moon Face steady in the gentle flow. After what seemed a much longer time than it was, Moon Face came back. He snorted beneath the wet shirt, reached up, pushed it away. His color looked much better, and his dark eyes had lost that glazed, filmy look.

"What happened?" he asked.

"The sun struck you down. Don't worry. You look all right now."

Moon Face looked down. "Why am I sitting in a stream?"

Rising Sun grinned at him. "To cool you off. The water Spirits soothe the sun Spirit."

"Oh."

Rising Sun reached out, took his hand, and hoisted him out of the water. "We'll have to go slower, I guess. How do you feel?"

"Weak."

Rising Sun nodded. "It will pass. But for now, you'll have to rest awhile."

Moon Face looked relieved, then apprehensive. "But what about Running Deer? The wolf?"

"I can't leave you, my friend. We'll go at your speed. The wolf will come back."

"Are you sure?"

"Yes." Rising Sun realized, to his surprise, that he *was*

sure. The wolf ranged far ahead, but it always came back. He could feel the Spirit of the wolf in his thoughts, like a faint, glowing spark.

"Come on," he said. "I want you to lie down over here, in the shade for a while. I'll bring you water. Drink it slowly, or you'll puke."

Moon Face nodded. "I know what's wrong with me. I've seen it before. I just never imagined it would happen to *me*."

The thought made Rising Sun chuckle. "A lot of things we never imagined are happening."

Moon Face only looked at him and nodded.

The wolf came back in the middle of the afternoon and sat down with a dusty thump, eyeing the two of them and grinning merrily. Twice it got up, leapt into the brush, and disappeared, but returned shortly after, as if to say, *Come! Why aren't you following? Yes yes yes!*

Rising Sun felt the spark of its Spirit as a small burning fire. It warmed him. He felt, deep inside himself, the pounding urgency to be off, to take up the hunt again, but he fought against it. He was learning something, but he wasn't sure what. Patience, perhaps. The limits of a man. The exigencies of destiny, though he didn't think of it in exactly those terms.

Finally the wolf trotted to within a couple of paces of them and flopped over on its side, placed its muzzle between its front paws, and appeared to drop off to sleep.

Moon Face watched. "It's strange to see a beast do that," he said.

"I once saw a bear lick my father's hand."

"But he had the Power over the Spirits of animals."

"So do I, it seems."

Dusk had begun to creep in purple shadows through the trees. Rising Sun made a small hearth and kindled a fire. The snapping of the flames woke the wolf, who whined deep in its throat and backed away from the little blaze.

"It's all right," Rising Sun told it. "It won't hurt you."

The wolf didn't seem entirely convinced, though it settled back down, this time farther away. He could see its eyes reflecting miniature hearths redly in the gloom.

He sighed to himself and glanced over at Moon Face. The little apprentice had dropped off to sleep, snoring softly. Rising Sun still felt that terrible urgency, but now he realized that something else was mixed in with it. A strange certainty that it would turn out, not necessarily that he would find Running Deer, but that things would turn out.

That idea seemed so inexplicable that he thought he should be troubled even considering it, but still, it offered comfort. He couldn't find any reason that it should, but it did. And so, because it was all he had, he cradled that comfort and let it warm him into sleep.

"Moon Face, look at this."

The chubby youth looked much recovered from the rigors of the previous day. His slow grin seemed almost chipper as he knelt next to Rising Sun, bent forward, and inhaled deeply.

"It's human," he said. "Somebody vomited here."

Rising Sun nodded thoughtfully as he counted the footprints—three of them, each one the mark of a giant.

"He's been carrying her. He dropped her right here. Probably because she puked on him."

Moon Face scratched his chin. "Still heading south. I wonder if he's making for the river again."

A scrabble of claws on soft leaves brought Rising Sun's head up. The wolf pranced in place a few strides away, its expression plainly saying *yes yes yes*!

"All right," Rising Sun grunted as he stood, "we're coming."

He paused. "How long, do you think?"

Moon Face shrugged. "A day? Not much more."

"That's my guess, too." He adjusted his pack, checked his bow and his spears. "When I find him, I'm going to kill him."

Moon Face sucked his teeth, alarmed. "He's very big."

"If he's as scared of everything as you say he is, he'll run. He'll show me his back, and it will be easy."

Moon Face sucked some more. "There's only one thing wrong with that. If he's still as scared as he used to be, he could never have dragged her away."

"I've thought that all along. I'll kill him anyway."

"Be careful."

"I will."

They set off again.

3

They had slept in a rocky bower next to a stream, he next to her, one meaty hand clasped around her wrist even in sleep. Though she hated to admit it even to herself, she welcomed his closeness for the warmth it gave her. The night had been cool, almost cold, with the beginnings of a fall bite to it. She'd started awake several times, confused, her heart pounding, wondering why she felt half frozen. Then it would come back. Finally the sky had grayed into blue and he'd whuffed and snorted, his hairy back twitching. He sat up and stared at her as if he'd never seen her before, then uttered a low moan, bounded to his feet, and ran into the scrubby brush around their lair.

Now what? she wondered, idly rubbing the red mark around her wrist where he'd gripped it. She looked around, measuring the distances, wondering if there was any possibility of escape. But the thought was only fleeting. And it wasn't just the grogginess of bad sleep and early rising and fear. It was as if in the trick she'd played on him the day before, she had placed a bet. Everything she had, her life, in fact, on Rising Sun.

She shook her head slightly. Was that right? He was barely more than a boy. She didn't understand why he was making this trek downriver with Moon Face. He was looking for the Maya Stone, the Stone Rejoined, but he was still a boy. Younger than she was. So why did she feel this inexplicable trust, this certainty that everything would turn out?

She was still poking mentally at that thought when the Frightened Man returned, ghosting up to her with that eerie silent way of his, scaring her half out of her wits.

"Oh!"

He hunkered down in front of her and showed her

what he'd brought. Another rodent, again headless, but enough of the tail remained for her to know it was a squirrel. She wondered what the thing yesterday had been. A rabbit, maybe. Or a rat.

She took it from him greedily, nodding and gnawing, half turning away from him as the red juice ran down her chin. The more she ate, the more she realized how hungry she was. She tossed the carcass away and said, "More. Hungry."

He eyed her warily as he retrieved the bones of the squirrel, then took them into the brush, scooped out a hole, and buried them. He arranged a layer of leaves over the small mound, and when he was done, she couldn't see where he'd masked the grave, even though she'd watched him do it.

So crafty.

After she had eaten again, she felt his eyes on her as she drank from the little stream. He continued to watch her as he scooped her up, and suddenly she realized that it wasn't the Frightened Man who observed her so steadily, so coldly, but the *other.*

"Sick?" he asked.

She shook her head, suddenly rigid with fear. Those fearsome, red-rimmed black eyes seemed to peer into her soul! He smiled, a rubbery stretching of lips that had no friendliness in it whatsoever, and then the sharpness leaked away from his gaze. She could *see* it depart, watch his eyes go filmy and unfocused. Almost as if he were blind. He shrugged her higher against his chest and set off.

She knew that not a single trace of their presence remained in the tiny bower by the stream. Not one. If Rising Sun was going to track down the Demon, he would need magic. And though a few shreds of that curious feeling of confidence still remained with her, they were growing fainter with each careful step the Frightened Man took.

Magic, yes. But would Moon Face use his magic for her? Or was he already using it *against* her?

Somewhere in the distance, a wolf howled. She felt

the Frightened Man's arms tense against her. His pace picked up.

4

They'd been smelling water for hours, and now they could hear it as well. The deep hissing roar of the river filled their ears, almost drowning out the intermittent cries of the wolf.

"We've circled clear around," Rising Sun said as he jogged along. "We're almost back to the river, but farther south."

Moon Face, streaming sweat, nodded his assent. The midafternoon sound pounded on them both, made worse by the thinning of the forest as they came closer to the river, but Moon Face was taking the worst of it. Rising Sun watched him with concern. With the help of the wolf baying out ahead, they'd made good time. It was plain the beast had found a trail—whether it was the *right* trail remained to be seen.

The feeling had been growing in Rising Sun all day that it *was* the right trail, and furthermore, they were quickly coming to its end. Dread mingled with a fierce, murderous anticipation as he jogged along, the heavy spear grasped firmly in his right fist, the bow, strung, hanging from his shoulder where he could grab it quickly.

He wondered if Moon Face was going to faint on him again.

"Are you—" he began, but a howl that broke into a cascade of barking yips interrupted him. It was startlingly close.

He looked at Moon Face and made a quick decision. "You wait here," he said, "and follow when you've got your wind back. I think it's got something."

Moon Face stopped, bent over, put his palms on his knees, and gasped for breath. "I'll . . . come . . . as quick . . . as I can . . ."

But he was speaking to thin air. Rising Sun had spun around, leapt over a blood-crimson thorn bush, and was gone. Moon Face held his aching belly for several moments, his face like a red balloon, but after that he straightened himself up and stumbled forward, only the force of his own determination holding him up. He'd let Rising Sun down too often lately with his weakness. He wouldn't this time, not if he could help it.

He heard Rising Sun let out a mighty shout. When he shoved through the last screen of leafy scrub he found himself at the top of a low rise, looking down across a broad grassy drop toward the bank of the river. He faltered, his jaw dropping wide. For the life of him, he couldn't figure out the scene unfolding below.

5

Something was very wrong. Running Deer heard a staccato volley of snarls off to her left, at the same time that the Frightened Man broke into a full, lumbering run.

Her head flopped back and forth. She was vaguely aware of bushes whipping by as he squeezed her tighter. Then, without warning, they burst into the open, his bellows breathing filling her ears. She could feel his heart pounding against her cheek.

Something wet splattered against her face. She looked up and realized the huge man was weeping as he bulled along. He was running blind, eyes screwed shut and leaking tears of terror.

Suddenly she was terrified for herself. Galloping aimlessly like that, he might drop her or trip over something and fall on her. The change in the air, and the subconscious awareness of a deep thrumming, made her think they were very close to the river again.

"Stop! Put me down!" She squirmed in his grip. She might as well have been yelling at a rock, for all the notice he paid her.

Again that cascade of barking growls sounded, so close she knew the source must be nipping at their heels. The sound of a wolf in full battle cry. She twisted against his massive arms, trying to see. She got herself almost turned sideways when he dropped her.

She landed hard, rolled over twice, and saw a gray-black form launch itself above her in a swirl of scrabbling claws and snapping white jaws. She raised her arms to fend it off, then realized she wasn't the prey. Not this time.

She propped herself up on one abraded elbow, wincing at the pain, feeling dazed and unreal. They were close to the river, wolf and man. Somehow the man had fended off the first charge. Now he crouched, a smooth rock held in his right fist, turning as he faced the circling animal. His eyes were wide open, and the dimness in them had disappeared. They flashed with knowing darkness, a savage glee, and she knew the Demon had returned.

Panting, she began to drag herself away, knowing that the fall had stunned her too badly, that she couldn't simply leap to her feet and run while the Demon fought the wolf. Still, she could feel a little bit of strength returning, and hope for more.

"Running Deer!"

She gasped at the sound she'd thought she might never hear again. He was fifty paces away, running down the slight incline, his great spear balanced in both hands at his waist, at the killing position. She'd seen the hunters do it that way. Backed by the force of his charge, he could thrust the stony point clear through anything smaller than a mammoth. From the look on his face, she knew he had every intention of doing exactly that to the Frightened Man. And she felt a pang.

It was the outcome she'd dreamed of and savored almost constantly since she'd blundered through the night into a nightmare. She had imagined that great spear impaling the huge man, spilling his guts on the ground, cherished the bloody image in the savage parts of the night. The heat of it had kept her warm when everything else was cold.

"No! Don't!" she cried. Then she stopped, because of course it was too late, and because she had no idea how those words had burst from her mouth, or where they'd come from. Momentarily shocked into stillness, she got herself to her knees, which was as far as she could go before a wave of dizziness threatened to slap her back

down. And so she knelt, hands waving weakly for balance, and watched the strange tableau create itself.

Rising Sun's first charge would have been enough, but for the incredible quickness of the larger man. He'd spun like a child's top at the first cry, ignoring the wolf, tensing his huge thighs as he hefted the stone. The wolf snapped at his hamstring and he lashed out with one foot, catching the animal in the ribs with a clubbing blow. The wolf rolled away, whining, then limped to its feet warily.

Rising Sun had made a mistake. His charge was too headlong. He couldn't turn his path in time, and this was not an elk or bison he faced. The Frightened Man dipped, reached out, and with an absolute elegance of motion as perfect as anything Running Deer had ever seen, deflected the spear shaft when the point was only fingers from his belly, brushed it aside, and brought the rock down overhead on Rising Sun's shoulder.

It was a glancing blow, but the crunching sound of it was clearly audible. Had it been a hand's length to the right, the egg-breaking sound would have come from Rising Sun's skull, and the battle would have been over right there.

But Rising Sun's reflexes were as quick, and he was younger, and he was already dodging down and away from the blow when the stone split the flesh of his shoulder in a dripping line of red.

He managed to keep his grip on the spear, spinning and falling backward, rolling once before he came to his feet. He seemed unaware that he'd been wounded. And the battle settled into a strange symmetry.

They were arranged in a loose circle, the four of them. The wolf, smelling blood, snarled in confusion. Rising Sun spared it a single glance. "Down!" he barked and, to Running Deer's amazement, the wolf sank back on its haunches, though it continued to growl with white ferocity at the Frightened Man.

Rising Sun faced the Frightened Man, who still crouched, dark eyes blazing, the rock with its streak of bright red clutched ready in his fist. "Are you all right?" he whispered tensely from the side of his mouth.

"Yes ... Rising Sun, be careful! He's a Demon, I think!"

Rising Sun nodded, as if she'd told him something interesting but irrelevant to the situation at hand.

"Demon or man, now I'm going to kill you," he told the Frightened Man. He began a shuffling, stabbing dance toward the larger man that Running Deer knew was far deadlier than it looked. Stung once, Rising Sun would be careful now, and he had the double advantage of youth and the spear on his side.

She watched, wide-eyed, knowing it would be over in a matter of moments, when the Frightened Man did the strangest thing. She'd seen it before, but never as an uninvolved observer. The fear took him and blotted the dark light from his eyes, shook him and flung him whimpering to the ground.

"Noooo!" he howled. A horrid stink arose when he shat and pissed himself at the same time. Rising Sun paused, his face slackening with surprise.

"What's wrong with him?" he asked.

Wearily she climbed to her feet, dusted her hands against her hips, feeling as if her whole body was one large bruise. "It's the Frightened Man," she said. "He's come back."

Rising Sun looked at the groveling, stinking, moaning mess before him and shook his head, looking embarrassed. "I was going to kill him. But I can't, not like that." Slowly he raised his spear.

"No, wait, you don't understand—" she began, just as the Frightened Man exploded from the ground in a full, wide-armed charge. The most frightening thing about it was that he made no sound, and kept his burning, fearsome eyes focused on Rising Sun's throat as he came on.

But Rising Sun had not raised his spear very far. His young, tough body was still overcharged with adrenaline, and long before the Frightened Man could reach him, Running Deer saw the charge would fail.

The wolf loosed a short howl and bounced brightly to its feet and trotted forward. Rising Sun dropped the spear head down and planted his feet to take the rush.

The Frightened Man collapsed as if somebody had cut

his legs off at the knees. Once again, he moaned and cried. Rising Sun stepped back, waiting.

The Frightened Man flipped up with rubbery quickness, lurched forward with deadly eyes, said, "The *spear!*"

And fell again, and spasmed sickeningly. Began a horrid, frozen-spine howling—and rose again. Up, down. Faster and faster.

"The spear! My spear!"

6

Moon Face had most of his wind back. He shook his head in wonderment as he trotted down the decline. There didn't seem to be much need for hurry.

He could see them in the distance, but he couldn't figure out what was wrong with the big one, whom he now recognized for certain as the Frightened Man. That he was here at all was a mystery in itself. What he was doing was an even greater one.

At first he thought Rising Sun had speared him, but as he jogged up to them, taking a wide and wary path around the Frightened Man's thrashing convulsions, he saw that Rising Sun was as puzzled as he was.

"What's wrong with him?" he asked nervously.

"I don't know. She says he's a Demon."

Running Deer, holding her scraped elbow, limped over to them. "There's a Demon *in* him," she whispered.

"Moon Face, hold her. I need to—" He kept his eyes on the Frightened Man.

Dazed, she turned toward the little Shaman, who lifted his head, then stepped up resolutely and wrapped his arms around her. She collapsed limply against him, but he held her up until he could settle her gently on the ground.

"I was so frightened," she murmured.

"There. You'll be all right."

Suddenly he felt a tremendous sense of responsibility for her. She felt fragile, delicate in his arms. Silent tears made bright tracks down her cheeks. He couldn't explain what he felt. Maybe it was something about being a Shaman he hadn't learned yet.

"Hawroooo!"

"Will you be all right?"

She nodded.

"I'd better go help him. If it's a Demon, he'll need my help." He got up and walked back to Rising Sun, who still guarded the thrashing, raving giant.

"What should I do?" Rising Sun said. "I was going to kill him." He glanced down and shivered. "What's *wrong* with him?"

"Running Deer says a Demon. And now that I see him, I say so, too."

"Can you do anything?"

"I don't know. It might be better to kill him. Safer, anyway."

"But if it's a Demon . . ."

Moon Face sighed. "I just don't understand *what*—" He stopped. "Spear," he said mildly. "The spear."

"What are you talking about?"

"That's what he keeps screaming. It's kind of hard to understand, but it's the same word over and over again. Spear."

"So?"

Moon Face turned slowly, stared at the great weapon Rising Sun held in his fists.

"You don't know who the Frightened Man really is, do you?"

Rising Sun shook his head.

Moon Face smiled thinly. "That crazy *thing* in front of us was once the greatest warrior ever to enter the Green Valley. He defeated the mighty Caribou, mate of Maya herself, in fair combat. His name was Raging Bison, and the spear you hold was once his."

Rising Sun shook his head. The Frightened Man had curled in on himself. He made small choking noises deep in his throat. Now he began to gnaw at his own wrist.

"Awful . . ." Rising Sun whispered. "What *happened* to him?"

"You know the stories, don't you? He was touched by the Gods. They destroyed him somehow, as They were leaving the World forever. They made him frightened of everything." Moon Face shook his head. "The Gods must have a terrible sense of humor. He was once the bravest of all. Now look at him."

He turned away. "Now that I see him, I don't think he is a Demon. It's the curse of the Great Ones." He glanced up at Rising Sun. "But it might be a mercy to kill him, just the same."

The feeling that had been growing in Rising Sun ever since his first deadly thrust had been parried so easily, almost as if in warning, suddenly bloomed like a vast silent white flower in the center of his confusion. There was certainty in that blossom, the sure knowledge that whatever he did now would be the *right* thing to do.

"This was his spear?"

"After he took it from Caribou."

Rising Sun inhaled. "Then he should have it," he said, and flipped it in his hands, butt downward. He stepped forward.

"No!" Running Deer gasped.

But Moon Face raised his hand and shook his head. He watched what happened next with fixed intensity.

Rising Sun planted the butt of the great weapon in the grass a hand's length away from the Frightened Man's head. At first there seemed to be no reaction. Then, like scrabbling, hairy insects, his hands scuttled out and wrapped themselves around the ancient wood.

At once, all movement ceased.

"Spear," the Frightened Man said, clear and calm as a pool beneath winter ice. And the first great connection from what *had been* to what *would be* was made at last.

7

Rising Sun saw his own hands at one end of the spear, and the Frightened Man's at the other, and then the World fell away with a silent sliding twist, and the spear between them came alive. It writhed slowly, like a snake, and energies flowed along it, rippling licks of fire.

They floated in darkness, connected, and then the

darkness split wide. From that hideous wound bulged forth the Void, which squirmed and crawled and festered with manic energies. And written upon the Void in suppurating lines of force was a face. The face was far older than the World, seamed and wrinkled and leaking unnameable fluids, crawling with the pustulence of aeons, oozing with the wounds of Time itself. And from sockets of utter darkness within that cosmic horror burned two eyes.

Rising Sun looked into those eyes, and saw they were abomination, and so he looked down at the spear that had turned into a snake. The eyes of the snake were rubies, and the tongue of the snake was Fire.

"Look up, for I bring you the Gift you thought to have earned in My service."

Somehow, Rising Sun understood that this message was not for him, but for the pitiful wreck before him, and that the words were echoes from a past long dead. Then Rising Sun looked up and saw the face of Him Whose Face Was Fear, and knew he looked upon One who had sat upon the empty thrones.

"You forgot your way, and served a false Spirit, who lived inside your breast and ate your guts," the terrible visage said. Dimly Rising Sun heard the Frightened Man begin to howl again, and thought that this horrid vision was coming *from* the Frightened Man, and was something he'd long carried within himself. Pity stabbed at him—it was a doom far more horrible than any he could have imagined. It was a doom of God-like dimensions.

"You," the God roared, *"you, in all your fearlessness, served Death, and I am not Death, O worthless servant!"*

The Frightened Man shrieked and tried to lift the spear, but it squirmed and twitched in his hands. He sobbed as he fought the weapon. The Voice ground on like an avalanche falling from the sky above.

"Just as I took fear from you, now I return it full measure," the Snake said. Then it struck at his eyes, and blinded him, and in the dark, the Frightened Man spun once again into the pit that had been prepared for him. And the madness took him.

With that, the Vision ended, and Rising Sun staggered

back, breaking the connection. He looked down and saw the Frightened Man shaking and weeping on the ground, and he understood what had been done to him. The revelation was shattering in its power and intensity. The wrath of the Great Ones had indeed been terrible.

But what tore at him even more strongly was the kinship he'd felt with that awesome ancient face, the current of dark knowledge that had surged between the two of them. Rising Sun knew that such a resonance was not possible, unless they had both sat upon a throne and looked upon the World naked through the endless eye of Time.

That face, Rising Sun knew, had also seen the Last Mammoth.

"Are you all right?" Moon Face asked softly, but Rising Sun waved him away.

"Look at him," he told them. "He's blind. At least a part of him is. The part you call the Frightened Man."

They stared at him, uncomprehending, shaken by things they hadn't seen, but had felt on some deep level, far beneath that of the flesh.

"It is a curse of the Gods," he murmured as he knelt. "But I can heal it."

He took the Frightened Man's great head and lifted it up and stared into the blank red pools of his eyes, and let himself sink beneath the crimson surface, into the darkness beneath. And then he broke the walls of terror that had bound Raging Bison, and healed the terrible wounds so casually inflicted, and smoothed away all that had gone before. Finally he rose again.

The giant stood with him.

"Who are you?" Rising Sun said.

"I am Raging Bison, who was lost, but has been found again," he replied, soft wonder in his voice.

Rising Sun thrust the great spear forward. "Take this, for it is yours, earned in fair combat. Take it as token of what I have done this day, and never forget."

Raging Bison, who had once been the greatest warrior of all the Three Tribes, sank to his knees. He wrapped his huge arms around Rising Sun's waist, and sobbed softly.

Rising Sun bore him up again, and wiped the tears from his cheeks, and gave him the spear.

"Master," Raging Bison said.

"Yes," Rising Son acknowledged, feeling the bonds of his destiny grip him ever more tightly, knowing that he acknowledged a mastery far greater than any of them could understand. He sighed. "But never forget that I am also a man."

They stared at him, wondering, not understanding. His slow smile was tinged with sadness, perhaps mourning what once might have been, when he still had choices to make. Now, no choices remained, only the destiny.

"Though not entirely," he said, shaking his head gently. "Not anymore." He knew they wouldn't understand *that*, either. But they would.

8

And so they walked through the golden autumn of that year, down the winding blue trail of the river: the warrior and the Shaman, the woman and the man who was no longer entirely a man. And the wolf, yes yes yes, the wolf.

They journeyed through the fall, and in the drifting whiteness of the first snows, they reached the place where the rivers meet to sing the songs of past, present, and future, and speak in watery whispers of the endless fate of the World.

Here they paused, for a time.

BOOK FOUR

THE COMING OF THE SUN

"God is but a word invented to explain the world."

—LAMARTINE

CHAPTER NINETEEN

1

Carries Two Spears woke from his fitful sleep in the silvery-gray sheen just before dawn, and knew that she was going to die. The small fire had burned down to a few coals, and his breath smoked in the air. Fall was coming down hard, burning the colors of the forest into spurious gaudy brightness, the final fling of dying summer before winter claimed its inevitable victory.

He had thought too much, hoped too strongly, and waited too long. Now even the slim chance of returning to the River Camp had slipped away, just as he knew she was slipping away from him.

The Witch had done something to her. Something deadly and irreversible, something that leached her skin and slowed her breath and burned her up.

He crawled around the dregs of the fire and straightened the robe around her wasted frame. Already she looked like a ghost, more dead than alive. She'd never been colorful or vibrant, but now her paleness had become the color of ashes and her eyes, open but unseeing, were swirls of milky blood.

It was the morning of the third day, and he guessed tiredly he would remember it henceforth as their last day together. There was a shrunken look to her, and he had seen that kind of look before. It meant her life could be measured in hours, maybe only minutes.

Suddenly he felt very lonely and very cold. He stoked the coals until he had a few small blue flames, then piled on scraps of deadwood until he had a sizable blaze. The sun came up and made the tall streams of fire invisible, but the heat felt good. It got his blood moving. He realized he was hungry, but he fought the pangs, because he didn't want to leave her. Somehow, he thought she knew he was there, and he didn't want her to die alone. Her Spirit would remember his desertion.

And so he sat, his thick, workmanlike fingers clasped together between his knees, and watched her slowly drift away from him. Those long morning moments, as the sun warmed the woods to wakefulness, became the longest of his life; wistful and dreamy, with none of the heat he'd felt before. *That* fire had left him, and he became her brother again, remembering the things that only brothers will. Toward noon, she gave a great shudder and sat straight up. Her eyes seemed to fix on him as if she actually saw him, but only for an instant. Then, trembling, they fell closed, and she sank back.

She dropped the last few inches with no more animation than a stone, and he knew it was over. A host of half-remembered images filled his skull, a flood of recollection so sudden and sharp-edged it made him gasp. When that seizure released his soul, for it had struck that deep, he realized he was weeping, for her, for what had been and what might have been, and for himself.

He cried out for the World and all that lived within it, knowing but unable to articulate the terrible dilemma that all men faced; how to live knowing that death will come. When he finished, he got up and kicked dirt over the fire, then wrapped her more securely in her blanket and began the trek back to the river.

He had already decided. Sleeps With Spirits was not for burning or for the cold earth. He had a gentler end in mind for her.

2

The Witch who was called Mother, who thought she was a Goddess, had noticed the thin trail of white smoke rising to the south, on the far bank of the Big Blue River, several times over the past few days. She knew who warmed himself at that fire, and suspected that perhaps the flames might yet comfort her daughter, as well. And when, on the third day, the smoke guttered out, she thought she knew the reason for that, too, and she smiled to herself.

Things had settled out nicely. She still felt the undivided attention of all eyes upon her when she left the dark safety of her tent, but since these appraisals weren't that different from what she'd known before, they didn't bother her any more than the previous wary speculation had.

They feared her. Since they would never love her, fear would have to be enough. She understood fear.

The other changes were more heartening. No more fish-eyed watchfulness from the Shaman. Drinks Deep Waters had gone to the Spirit World in a greasy cloud of foul-smelling smoke that had whispered like the finest flowers in her nostrils. She had performed certain rites in the seclusion of her tent to ensure that her old enemy *remained* in the Land of Spirits. Her dreams had been untroubled, always a good sign.

Further harbingers of the extent of her triumph abounded. Aside from the satisfying amount of fear she now inspired, she began to note affirmations of her new-found power. They came to her, the frightened ones, the sick ones, even the ones who normally would have nothing to do with her at all, and they brought her gifts. Tokens. An armload of fruit. A fresh-trapped rabbit. Fish from the river. Herbs and roots. Some handed their offerings to her personally, with murmured consolations for her great loss. Others simply left them at the door like sacrifices, and she found that even more fitting.

Kills Many Buffalo had shrunk, in an astonishingly short time, into a wizened husk of himself, helped about by the new Shaman, who shivered when she looked at him.

But the best part of all was the things that were missing. No hideously marked daughter, moping about the camp, wailing her ridiculous prophesies as a living reproach to her mother. No sharp-tongued Shaman, no wary, antagonistic Chief. No loafing, lazy son, either, whom she was surprised to discover had bothered her more than she had realized. She thought she had erased Carries Two Spears from her thoughts long ago, but evidently he had hovered in the hazy background of her mind, more plain to her in his absence than he'd ever been in his presence.

It was as if her life had been washed clean of all threats, and it was immensely satisfying that she had accomplished the cleansing by herself. It was a secret affirmation of her private strength, of the power she could summon from her own center, where something greater than she was had taken up residence.

Let them bring their pitiful, hopeful gifts. She had her own mighty tokens, gifts from the Goddess Herself.

So why wouldn't the Goddess speak to her? It was a puzzle that gnawed at her. Now she sat at the front of her tent, watching the bustle and hustle of the camp with stony eyes, acknowledging with a grunt or a shrug the glances of those who passed fearfully by.

In a way, that lapse was frightening. Oh, she had no doubt of the Presence inside her, but why wouldn't She manifest Herself to Her most faithful servant? It was almost as if the Goddess disapproved of her in some way—but how had she *failed*?

The question sat like a lump in her heavy gut as she noted that the line of smoke had disappeared, and smiled her hard little smile to herself in the morning of what should have been a perfect day.

It was pleasant, despite her unease about the Goddess, to sit there drowsing, imagining Carries Two Spears and his lifeless burden. What would he do? Scoop out some shallow hole and tumble her in, she guessed. She grinned faintly at the tawdriness of Sleeps With Spirits's final end, her imagination giving her yet another pleasurable little morsel to savor.

Then her lizardlike eyelids popped wide with an audible click. And when her son was finished with his dolorous task? What would he do then? Come back? Come back *here*?"

Suddenly every iota of her concentration centered on him. *Now* she understood why the Goddess had withheld Her ultimate blessing—it was a *warning*.

She had been careless, oh, my yes. But it wasn't too late. She still had time. That smoke had been gone for less than a tenth of the day. She would have to hurry, though, to be certain.

She heaved herself up and shaded her eyes. Now where was that wretched Shaman? Nowhere in sight, of course. It was such a typical masculine trait, never to be around when you needed them.

She grunted. It was a small camp. It wouldn't take her long to find him.

3

"Kill them?" the Shaman said.

"The Goddess Spoke to me," she said, feeling a little twinge at the lie. "She revealed much to me, and told me what must be done. Do you understand, Shaman? It was a mighty curse, and it must be cleansed from the World entirely."

The force of her words shook him. She eyed him with utter contempt, but she was willing to wait as long as it took. As long as it didn't take too long.

"Looks Into Dreams, are you *listening* to me?"

"Um, ah. I'm sorry. It just seemed—are you *sure*?"

"Do you doubt the Goddess?"

"Oh, uh, no, of course not." His dark eyes jittered away from her. His meatless jaw reminded her of a skull baking in the sun.

"I hadn't suspected, but Carries Two Spears must have been part of the Shaman's plot, as well. He and the Demon. He carried her away, helped her to escape. He was *there,* Shaman. How could that have been if he hadn't *known*?"

She had the gift of observation. She could see her relentless words were hammering him down. He was no harder than fat melting in the fire, anyway. It wouldn't take much.

"I know you've seen their smoke. They aren't far away. Send out the men, Shaman. Hunt them down and kill them. It is the only way—as long as the Demon lives, the curse remains. This the Goddess has told me. *Will you defy the Goddess?*"

The challenge snapped the fragile stick of his will as easily as a lion would snap the neck of a helpless doe.

"Oh, no, I would never—" He stopped, perhaps recalling that he worshiped another, but it was too late, and he was too weak. He sighed and spread his shaking hands.

"Of course I understand. The curse must be removed. I will send out the hunters." He glared at her, and she allowed him his gesture of hollow defiance. Men were so weak, so conscious of their pitiful pride.

But she was already losing interest. "Do it now," she said absently as she got to her feet and stumped to the doorway of the Spirit Tent.

She was aware of him rising behind her, puffing himself up, as she stepped into the harsh noon light. She glanced up and made a quick calculation. Enough time left. They might even catch him before dusk.

She wasn't worried about the girl. She already knew how *that* had turned out.

4

He carried her down to the water, wrapped in what had once been a blanket and was now a shroud. His thoughts still seemed dreamlike to him. He felt no pain, though he could sense it lurking just beyond the hazy edge of whatever was keeping him so unnaturally calm.

"Poor Spirits," he murmured, over and over again. She felt so light, and he felt so sad, carrying her like that. He laid her gently down on a grassy hummock where fat bees hummed amid the last of the flowers. He examined the head of his largest spear, and decided the edge was sharp enough to do what he wanted to do. Then he set out, searching for drifted logs of a suitable size.

Finally, ranging up and down the bank, he found three dark, wet logs that seemed to float well enough to suit him. He used the edge of his spear head to cut down a thin sapling and strip it, and used this pole to guide the logs together. When he was certain they wouldn't float away, he walked back to the edge of the woods and began to hack down supple lengths of vine. Bright purple berries glistened on them, and he ate them as he worked. The berries were very sweet. They made him think of Sleeps With Spirits, for some reason.

He took the vines back to the riverside and used them to lash the three logs together. The muddy bottom dropped off quickly here. He had to be careful not to go too far out. When he finished, he half hoisted himself up on the makeshift raft and grunted his satisfaction at the way it held his weight. She was far lighter and would ride high above the glittering water.

He glanced over and saw that she lay undisturbed. Even the bees flew above her, but never lighted *on* her. Somehow it seemed a fitting tribute. She had always loved all wild things.

It took him a while to gather the prettiest wildflowers, the dark blue ones, and the nodding yellow ones, and the ones small and white as stars. When he had a sufficient armload, he laid them on the bank, and then, unconscious tears shining on his cheeks, he went back for her. He would send her on the waters, wrapped in the soft skin, covered with flowers. Send her into the south, away from the harsh darkness of the winter.

He sighed, bent down, and gently lifted her. He was spending a final moment, holding her at the edge of the river, when he saw them. Five or six, too far north to make out their features, but he could hear their cries easily enough.

Hunting cries. It was no problem at all to imagine who

they were hunting. He hadn't got far enough away from the Witch, after all.

Stifling a sob, he found his pack and his spears and adjusted everything so he could carry her. Then he headed south, a shadowy figure bearing a burden through the dusk.

He wouldn't let them have her. He wouldn't.

5

Floating . . .

It was an odd sensation. She walked through a space with nothing to set her feet on, yet she walked. Very strange. It was silent. Tiny lights burned in the unimaginable distance—there was nothing to measure the distance by, but she knew it was great. The lights reminded her of stars, though they didn't twinkle.

She had no idea how long she'd been floating, walking. Time didn't seem to mean anything in this place. She wondered what had happened to her, how she'd gotten here. She thought about it for a long time, but couldn't remember. The last image she saw clearly was of the Witch, crouching and hacking and cackling.

But here, even that terrible memory had no power. It was as if it had happened to another woman, in another place. Nothing to do with her any longer.

Floating . . .

She wondered if she were Dreaming, but this wasn't like any of her other visions. Those had been dark things, full of fire and motion and rushing winds. This was so peaceful.

Time passed. Or, perhaps, no time passed.

One of the distant lights began to grow brighter. She watched it because it was something to watch. It had no other meaning, and was of interest only because all the other lights remained still and unchanged.

As it strengthened, the light began to change colors. Red, blue, green, white. It resolved itself from a point into a dot into a tiny round spot, whirling, flickering, glittering faster and faster through its panoply of colors.

Then, with heart-grabbing suddenness, her perceptions changed. Suddenly the space through which she floated assumed dimension. There was an up and a down to it. She didn't float *through,* she floated *above.*

Above the spot. And falling toward it, through the vast silence, faster and faster. Now there was motion. Now there was speed. Now she *fell!*

The spot flashed through its changes, a dot, a circle, a blinding hole in the fabric of the dark. She tried to put out her arms to slow her descent, but she had no arms. She opened her mouth to scream, but she had no mouth, nor lungs to swell with breath.

Then the hole was a chasm, an ocean of light, a World of color, and she plummeted into it, silent as a stone, and was swallowed up.

Noise.

A vast roaring waste of Light, and endless burning vista, a screeching cacophony like the sound of a billion voices screaming, gabbling, pleading, laughing—"

And she was through. She had entered a Place, but the Place was not for her, not yet, and so she bulleted *through* it, and came out the other side in less time than the blink of an eye.

The greensward stretched around her. She looked down dumbly, saw grass, tiny white flowers, her hands.

I have hands, she thought, wondering.

She looked up, and out. Mountains hulked above the hazy horizon, far away. In the middle distance stood a grove of trees, maples and oaks and a sprinkling of pines, their greenery so bright she had to squint. The sky was blue and empty, though Light filled this place, and she wondered what had happened to the sun.

And so she sat, her legs tucked beneath her, smelling perfumes she couldn't name, content that she was here, that she was safe, that she *was.*

I am, she thought softly, the two words chanting themselves within her, a secret mantra of existence whose strength and endurance seemed so obvious, once she knew it was there.

"Welcome, daughter."

She blinked, startled. The woman must have come

from the trees, though she hadn't seen her. She walked
alone across the grass, and for a moment Sleeps With
Spirits had the idea that the woman's bare feet didn't
quite *touch* the ground, that she floated just the smallest
bit above the earth.

Then she saw she must have been mistaken, because
the woman stood only a stride or so in front of her,
looking down at her and smiling the most wonderful,
comforting smile Spirits had ever seen.

"I will sit with you," the woman said. She sank gracefully down—*floated* down, almost—and arranged her
white robe around herself. She patted the grass next to her
and said, "This is nice, isn't it? So soft. I'm very glad you
have finally come to me, daughter."

"Why do you call me daughter? You aren't my
mother. My mother is—" But Sleeps With Spirits couldn't
remember who her mother was. She shook her head, puzzled, but not terribly so. It seemed an unimportant thing
to try to recall.

The woman leaned forward and took Spirits's hand.
"Don't worry, dear. My name is Maya. It is a Secret
Word, and it means mother."

Her touch was as light, as gentle and reassuring as the
first kiss of the sun on a summer's morning. "Are you my
mother?" Spirits asked.

"Yes, dear. In a way. You carry my blood within you,
also in a way."

"I don't understand."

"No, of course not. That's why I am here. I will teach
you, so you can understand."

Sleeps With Spirits stared at her. She'd never seen a
woman so strange, nor so beautiful. Maya-Mother wore a
robe that fell to her knees, made of the purest white skin,
from some beast Spirits couldn't identify. She thought
that maybe the animal from which it had come had never
walked in the World. It seemed to shed a soft, white light,
which illumined Maya's eyes.

Ancient eyes, yet young as spring, twinkling with
laughter. One green eye, one blue, both like gems beneath
clear flowing water.

There were seams and wrinkles in the soft flesh of her

face. But through those marks of age glowed a youthful vitality so strong it was almost frightening. Spirits could feel that power surrounding her, filling her up with unnamed joy. She basked in Maya's radiance for what seemed like a long time, though once again she had the sense that time meant little here.

"What are the Secret Words?" Spirits murmured. Her lips had moved without volition, and she had no idea where the question had come from.

Maya squeezed her fingers gently. "There are many Secret Words, my dear. I will teach them to you."

"You will?"

Maya nodded. "Yes. That is why *you* are here, so that I can teach you what you need to know. You will stay here with me for a time. Would you like that?"

Wordlessly Sleeps With Spirits nodded. She felt dimly sad, because what Maya-Mother said hinted that she couldn't stay here always, and she wanted that more than anything else. But with that same deep knowing, she understood that this place was not for her, just as the bellowing whiteness through which she'd come was also not for her.

Not yet, at least.

Maya lifted her up then and said, "Come, my dear."

She led Spirits across the grass toward the woods. Between them a stream of crystal gurgled gently across a bed of white stone. But when they came to the stream, Sleeps With Spirits saw there was a small cave in the earth at its edge. She looked in and saw the strangest thing of all. Laid out, as if merely resting, was a perfect skeleton, but that bony frame shone with a flat, hard light, as if an invisible fire burned within it. And on the breasts lay something hard to see, though it was golden.

"What is that?" Sleeps With Spirits said.

"It is mine," Maya said, "though I will give it away soon."

So much light! It fell from the empty sky, it radiated from the bones, from the golden thing within the bones, from Maya herself. Sleeps With Spirits had the idea that if she wasn't in some way protected from that light, it would burn her into ashes, quicker than she could take a single breath.

"What is it?" Sleeps With Spirits asked again.

"It is a Gift," Maya said. "I will give it when the sun rises in the sky."

"Who will you give it to?"

But Maya-Mother only smiled, and drew her away, deeper into the place where the World could not come, to keep her safe until it was time.

6

He didn't go far in the night, because he knew they wouldn't. He kept far enough ahead of them so they wouldn't spot him, and when they camped for the night, he laid her down and arranged himself next to her. He couldn't light a fire, because they were too close. If the wind shifted, they would smell the smoke.

He'd seen them splashing up from the river, the logs on which they'd floated across bobbing high in the water. There were at least five of them. He could probably guess who they were, but he didn't care. No doubt they'd once been friends, fellow hunters, compatriots. Now they hunted him. He could imagine what the Witch had told them.

Fall in this part of the World came quick, hard, and short, only a handful of days between the summer heat and the white cold of winter. He lay next to her, his thoughts a swirl of pain. The simplest thing would be to abandon her, let them find her and carry her body back for whatever horrid rituals the Witch had in mind.

He couldn't do it. He lay on his back, watching the hard twinkle of the stars overhead, and swore by whatever he felt for her, he wouldn't allow them to take her. Even if it cost him his life.

How had it come to this? How could his mother, who had borne him in her belly, and filled his veins with her own blood, become such a monster? Had she always been this way?

But that was a tangle with no unraveling. He sighed heavily, watched the white cloud of his breath float away, then closed his eyes. It was very cold. In his haste to escape, he hadn't brought a heavy robe for himself, though his shirt and bound leggings provided some protection. If he managed to elude the party chasing him, he would have to hunt something large enough to make a warm hide cloak.

Automatically he snuggled closer to his sister, seeking warmth. After a time, he drifted off to sleep.

When he woke in the chill silvery gloom of false dawn, at first he couldn't remember where he was. Half of him felt frozen solid. The muscles of that half screamed silently when he tried to flex the chill out of them. The other half wasn't so bad. The half closest to Sleeps With Spirits.

Sitting up, he slowly turned at the waist and stared down. Not so cold—as if her heat had warmed him. But of course that wasn't possible. Dead meat offered no warmth of its own.

Slowly his eyes began to bulge. He reached out a trembling hand and laid it on her cheek.

Warm!

Gabbling nonsense sounds deep in his throat, he crouched over her, touching, feeling. Yet, heat, the heat of life! His fingers shot to her throat, seeking the pulse of hot blood—

And found nothing. He put his ear on her breast, but heard only silence. Finally he lowered the cold flesh of his cheek to her lips, and waited. And waited. And just when he thought there was nothing, he felt it.

The faintest exhalation, discernible only because that fleeting breath was warm enough against his cold skin to—barely—be perceived.

She lived!

He rocked back on his haunches, staring at her in joyous disbelief. How could it be possible? He couldn't detect any pulse or heartbeat, nor could he see any motion to her chest, yet somehow she was warm, and somehow she breathed!

Dead, and yet—

Not dead.

He shook her and pleaded into her ear and lifted her,

and let her fall again, feeling the limpness of death in her heavy limbs. Yet she wasn't dead!

Then what?

"Ah, Witch-Mother," he moaned aloud. "You put a *spell* on her!"

And with that thought, it all suddenly seemed so terribly clear. He almost gagged at the horror, the cruelty of it, but it was the only answer. His mother had turned her daughter into a zombie, most likely by stealing her Spirit somehow. He had no doubt the Witch was capable of such a thing. The one who had slaughtered her own mate, his father, was capable of *anything*.

But what to do? He stared at Sleeps With Spirits, who lay like a corpse, so near and yet so far away, and tried to think of what to *do*. Finally, as the light of true dawn gilded the woods and turned the water of the Big Blue to silver, he decided.

It offered only the slenderest thread of hope, but that was better than nothing. If the Witch had stolen his sister's Spirit, perhaps, at some later time when she'd achieved whatever horrible end she had in mind, she would release that Spirit from its prison. And then, maybe, the Spirit would return to its true home, and Sleeps With Spirits would come back to him.

It wasn't much—but it was all he had. *Provided* he could keep her away from the hunters.

Ignoring the aches and pains in his protesting muscles, he gathered her up and smoothed the robe around her. Speed was essential now—*they* would awaken soon, and soon after they would resume the chase.

He brushed out whatever traces of their camp he could find, turned toward the south, and lumbered off. He could make better time in the open grass along the river rather than trying to bull through the woods burdened by her weight. Perhaps, if he got far enough south, they would give up the hunt.

Perhaps. He couldn't guess how much fear the Witch had put into them, or what awful instructions she might have given. So maybe time and distance would be enough. He didn't know. But he had to try.

Run!

7

By midafternoon, Carries Two Spears knew he would fail. His lungs were bellows scorched by fire, his arms numb with carrying her, his squat, muscular thighs numb with exhaustion. The sun wrung sweat out of him until his tongue swelled up and nearly choked him on its dry, hot meat.

A terrible hysteria seized him. He knew he was staggering, but he didn't know how to stop. Only one single message still drummed inside his skull—*run!* And so he did, though his strides dwindled to steps, and his course wavered drunkenly back and forth, from the edge of the forest to the verge of the water.

For a long time the only sound he'd heard was the sound of his raspy breathing, but now he began to hear—to feel—a greater sound. Slowly he stumbled to a halt and looked up, dazed.

Off to his right the spectacle unfolded beneath the windblown, sandy bluff on which he stood. He'd seen it before, many times, but as always it caught his breath in his throat and made him blink. The Big Blue met its end here, swallowed by the Great Muddy River, in a joining so vast it numbed the mind.

Transfixed, he watched the blue waters mingle with the brown, swirling and boiling beneath drifting clouds of mist that sparkled with all the colors of the rainbow. The sound was more than physical—he felt it as a low vibration rising from the earth, electrifying his bones, tightening his muscles.

It made him feel infinitely tiny, smaller than the bugs beneath his feet. With the suddenness of all revelation, it snared him. He might have stood there for hours, his mouth open, but the faint cries finally penetrated, and he turned and stared dumbly up his back trail.

The sight filled him with horror and broke the stasis of the rivers. Five of them, screeching and shouting, so filled with triumph they leapt up and down as they ran, waving their spears. He spun in a circle and saw that he was trapped. He could reach the woods, but they could follow more quickly with their unburdened speed.

The way south was wide and clear. Too clear. They'd seen him now, and if he continued that way, they would simply run him down.

Only one path offered the faintest hope. If he could get to the rivers themselves, he might find a log large enough to hold them both. South of the Joining, the Great Muddy picked up speed. It would sweep him away faster than they could run. To follow, they would have to find their own logs—if they were crazy enough to dare the river.

He made up his mind in an instant, and began to pick his way down the river side of the bluff. Lower toward the bank of the Big Blue, the ground turned rocky. The waters had churned away the soil and exposed jumbled fields of boulders.

He descended, slipping and sliding and holding frantically to Spirits as he stumbled to the gardens of stone. He glanced back up the ridge and saw nothing, though he could still her their cries. They seemed to be growing stronger.

Gasping, he made his way through the rocky maze. Here the granite and limestone was always slick. He didn't worry about leaving a trail. Spirits bumped limply in his arms, a flopping doll. But she still felt warm.

Finally, winded and shaking, he came to the edge of the water and realized his hopes had been in vain. He stood a few feet above the river and looked down to see how its enormous power had scoured the stones into smoothness, leaving nothing to catch a floating log.

He choked back an involuntary sob, but knew he had reached the end. He could hear them, yipping and screaming through the rocks, hunting him. And he had no place left to hide, no way open to escape.

He looked down. "Ah, Spirits," he whispered. "I won't let them have you. I will give you to the rivers first, even if you still live. Will you forgive me?"

But she didn't answer. The gleeful shouts grew louder, and he stepped forward, raising his sister in his arms to lift her over the edge.

Something fluttered at the edge of his eye. He stopped,

trying to see. Some river animal, an otter or a rat of some kind. Gone now.

But the dark hole from which it had lunged was still there, a stride or two away. A dark hole large enough for a man to enter. Large enough even for two.

Without hesitation, he carried her over. Looked down into the mouth of the small cave and saw that while it wasn't very deep, it might be deep enough. Something white glinted inside.

He stooped and thrust Sleeps With Spirits inside, then got down on his knees and crawled after her. The little cave was surprisingly dry and snug for being so close to the river. He pulled her as far back as he could, and then placed himself before her. He could see out the entrance, and knew that anybody who looked inside would also see him. But first they would have to notice the cave, and that might not be an easy thing.

Something crunched dryly beneath his right leg as he reached for loose stones to arm himself with. He looked down and gave a start. Bones!

He shifted himself away. Another chill crawled the ladder of his spine as he realized the bones weren't animal, but human. And something glittered in the caged ribs. He looked more closely, but he couldn't see anything. A shaft of sunlight glinting off a bit of quartz, perhaps. He chuckled hollowly.

Nothing to fear. The bones were long dead and couldn't harm him. Quickly he gathered a good pile of smooth rocks, handy for throwing, large enough to do some damage if it came down to hand-to-hand fighting.

A tight smile stretched across his features. First they would have to find him. And if they did, they would find it wouldn't be as easy as they imagined.

No, he thought as he hefted a goodly sized shard, *I won't let it be easy at all.*

8

For a time he thought his luck had turned. He heard no sound, saw no hunters. Maybe the maze of rock had protected him. He began to hope they wouldn't find him at all.

His thick hams ached as he crouched near the mouth of the cave, adrenaline spurting into tense muscles at every tiny change in the texture of sounds.

Finally, his thighs simply wouldn't hold him anymore. His toes felt numb. He sank back into a cross-legged sitting position, crunching more bones as he settled himself.

Click.

Came up again, quivering at the distinctive rattle of a falling pebble. Peered out and saw a broken leg appear from the top of a black pile of stones across from him. He watched breathlessly as Stone The Crow carefully lowered himself down the slimy granite, then paused at the bottom while somebody tossed his spear down to him.

Stone The Crow looked tired and bedraggled. Mud streaked his cheeks. His dark eyes were still sharp, though, as he slowly turned, lowering his spear into a short-gripped defensive position. Carries Two Spears held his breath, but nobody else clambered down. He understood. The others were atop the boulders. Crow was scouting. If he found something, the rest would come whooping down.

Slowly Spears sucked in air, readying himself. Discovery must only be a few moments away. He tried to imagine his chances. Crow was smaller than he was, and slower as well. If he could bull his way out, club Crow with a rock and stun him, he might have just enough time to gather up Spirits and consign her to the river. The others would get him, but he didn't care about that anymore.

Slowly, moving in a cautious crouch, Crow edged forward. A step, two, and then his roving gaze fastened on Spears's own eyes—

And slid away.

The yell that had bubbled in Spears's throat died away. *I know he saw me. How could he not? He looked right at me.*

But Crow gave no sign. He edged forward, sharp eyes missing nothing, stepped carefully across smooth, slick stones, keeping his balance. He came right up to the mouth of the cave, looked down into Carries Two

Spears's face, and did nothing. His watchful expression didn't change. Finally he turned away.

"Nothing down here," he called. A moment later he began to climb back up the rocks, after tossing his spear over the top.

What happened? Somehow he didn't see me. He wasn't pretending. He was never a great friend of mine. There was no reason for him to protect me.

The thoughts ran uselessly through his brain. Then he realized it didn't matter. He might never know or understand the reason for his escape, but he had escaped. He decided to hide here for a while—there was a small chance that Stone The Crow was a better actor than he could imagine, and that for some reason they were waiting for him to come out, but he didn't think so.

Somehow, this hole in the ground was a place of safety, for Spirits and for him. He brightened further as he heard shouts, this time receding in the distance. Headed on downriver.

For the first time in hours he relaxed. The snugness of the cave seemed to enfold him, welcome him. There was protection here, from the elements and, evidently, from the Witch and her minions as well.

He looked down and grinned weakly. Who cared about a few dusty old bones? He could share this place with them happily, at least until he could figure out what to do next.

The reaction set in, and he began to shudder.

CHAPTER TWENTY

1

Walking and walking they came down the long miles of the river. Once again the group had realigned itself. The two newest members developed a strangely close relationship and walked the point together, the wolf skipping and skittering out ahead of Raging Bison, who had once been the Frightened Man.

Running Deer and Rising Sun followed, always together, and Moon Face, as was his habit, either roamed ahead or fell behind as the mood seized him.

They made good time. They watched summer burn itself to a red-golden husk around them, and huddled beneath falling leaves to escape the harsh, chill rains. Finally, one bright blue morning, when black branches scribbled skeletal pictures against the sky, they woke to find a dusting of white on the world.

Rising Sun pried one eye open and grunted. "It snowed."

A rattling snore answered him from his left, where Raging Bison had made his bedroll. The huge man, restored to his former faculties, had made quick use of the spear that had been returned to him. Between them, Moon Face and Running Deer had made a long cloak, breeks and leggings, and a shirt for him. Every once in a while, Rising Sun would notice the mighty warrior fingering the buttery skins, a look of wonder in his eyes. The soft expression was childlike, impossibly youthful against the streaked gray hair and beard, and when he saw it, Rising Sun smiled to himself.

They had spoken of the events only once. "I feel reborn," Raging Bison said to him one day as they marched along. It was a rare moment of privacy, with the rest of their fellows ranging farther afield. "Everything looks new . . ." he continued, then stopped, at a loss for words.

"You were in a far place," Rising Sun told him gently, "but now you are back."

Raging Bison turned and stared at him with an intensity that the Shaman Gotha would have well remembered, as would have Rising Sun's parents, the Moon and the Star.

"*You* brought me back, Master!"

"Call me Rising Sun," he replied. "I am no one's master."

Raging Bison nodded once, the heavy spear jouncing on his shoulder as they strode along. "Whatever you wish, Mast—Rising Sun." They walked in silence for a few moments. Raging Bison made a fist and looked down at it. "So many seasons," he sighed. "I am old now. I wish I knew what happened. The last thing I remember—" He shook his head.

Rising Sun, who had shared that awful memory with him, reached up and patted one massive shoulder. "The One who did that to you is gone forever, Bison. You have nothing to fear from Him again."

Bison snorted. "Fear? Yes, I suppose I know it now. But once I had no idea. I used to worry that I could never be a hero unless I could be afraid, and conquer my own fear. I had already conquered everything else. Even Gotha would not oppose me openly."

Rising Sun stared up at the bigger man, wondering what he could say to him to set his thoughts at rest. Plainly, Raging Bison still didn't understand what had happened to him. "My friend," he said at last, "what would you think of a hunter who, through no fault of his own, walked beneath a cliff at the exact time a boulder fell from it and crushed him?"

"Mm? Bad luck, bad Spirits, whatever. It happens. What has that to do with me?"

"Well, something very like that happened to you. Only the cliff was the World, and the boulder was a God. It was a cruel joke, played on you for reasons that had nothing to do with you. You didn't bring it on yourself. You were merely part of something much greater than you—greater and more indifferent than you can imagine."

It was a hard concept for Raging Bison to get his mind around. He shook his shaggy head in puzzlement. "Indifferent?"

"The Gods didn't care, not really," Rising Sun told him. "Not for one man, not even for all men. The World was Theirs, and They cared for *that*, at least until the very end, when They wanted only to leave the World and return from whence They came. So what They did to you was less than if you brushed a mosquito away from your ear. Do you care anything for the mosquito?"

Raging Bison screwed up his forehead. "No, I guess I don't. I mean, whether I hurt it, or kill it, or whatever."

"Do you even think about mosquitoes?"

Bison chuckled. It was becoming plainer to him. And more bitter. "No. Is that how the Gods thought about us?"

"As many fingers on as many hands of all the people you've known in your whole life, that much greater and more is Their indifference to us."

At that, Raging Bison stopped and stared at him in astonishment. "But *you* are a God, Rising Sun. Aren't you? How else could you defeat the God and rescue me from His trap?"

Rising Sun laughed out loud. "A God? Me? The Gods are gone, Raging Bison. I'm not a God. I'm a man. I battled nobody. I only found your Spirit, and brought it back to you . . ."

Raging Bison shook his head again, plainly unconvinced—but equally plainly, not willing to argue with the young man at his side.

Rising Sun sighed. He couldn't tell Raging Bison what he knew, what he'd seen in the apocalyptic horror Bison had buried within himself. He couldn't even make the warrior understand *how* he'd learned these things, for he wasn't certain himself. "Anyway, my friend, I'm glad you've come back to the World."

Raging Bison smiled down at him. The simple love in that smile was so pure, so searing, that Rising Sun could hardly bear to look at it. And what he didn't know was that his own answering smile burned as bright as the sun that was his namesake.

Perhaps only one whose soul had been blinded by the Gods Themselves could have endured that smile, or felt even a glimmer of the mighty doom of which it was only the faintest reflection.

2

"Ga. Cold!"

Rising Sun rolled over and rubbed sleep from his eyes. "You're awake? I guess that's everybody."

Running Deer disentangled herself from him. "Where's Moon Face?"

Raging Bison, hunched over the small fire he'd built, looked up. "He went off into the woods. Mumbling something about roots. I didn't understand him."

Deer and Sun grinned at each other. Moon Face had become more preoccupied of late, pensive and given to muttering under his breath. Rising Sun had tried to draw him out, with meager results. He finally decided it was better to let the little apprentice work things out for himself. He would, anyway.

Quite the fatalist, aren't I? Rising Sun thought. For one who had seen the Last Mammoth, there was a sour humor to the conceit.

He pushed himself up. The cold seemed to have sunk into his bones. He rubbed his arms and clapped his hands and jumped in place until his blood felt like it might start flowing again. Then he joined Deer and Bison at the fire, squatted, and put out his hands in hopes of thawing his fingers. His breath made pale plumes in front of his face.

"Not much longer, I think," he said.

Running Deer understood, and Raging Bison didn't care. Each had their own reasons for knowing their path would follow his, and so Deer merely arched one eyebrow and said, "Can you feel it, or something?"

He paused, at the same loss for words that always came over him when he tried to explain anything about what had happened to him as the quest unfolded, what was *still* happening to him. "The Stone, you mean? Yes, I guess I do. It's like an itch, sometimes stronger, sometimes weaker, but now it's more like a burn. It hurts."

"Oh, Sun."

"It must be very near. The place where it is. And I've had the Dream again."

He had told her much, but not all, of the Manhood Dream that had been the beginning of his quest. If such a thing could *have* a beginning—he was beginning to doubt he would ever know or understand the roots of his predicament.

Running Deer nodded slowly. "Are you hungry?"

Sun slapped his gut. "Does that sound as hollow to you as it does to me?"

She laughed. "Let me get my bow."

"Your bow? But there are hunters here. Me and Bison." He twinkled at her.

She twinkled right back. "Yes, dear. And when either of you two big, strong men can put an arrow into the eye of a rabbit at ten paces, then you may call yourselves whatever you like. Until then, I'll go hunt us up some breakfast."

He watched her go, this time with a smile entirely earthy. Bison poked him in the ribs with a finger like a small club. "That's one fine woman, your mate," he said. "One fine woman."

Mate? But yes, of course. That's what she was. Why hadn't he figured it out? "Yes," he said, grinning. "She sure is, isn't she?"

Raging Bison hoorawed and clapped him on the shoulder briskly enough to knock him sprawling beyond the hearth. The wolf pranced and sniggered at him a few paces away as he propped himself on his elbows, still grinning. For one moment he forgot all about the high purpose of the quest, about the destiny whose threads were becoming clearer to him every day, and about the things he'd seen in his Manhood Dream. He even forgot about the Last Mammoth and became, if only in that instant, a boy again. A boy in love.

"Ah, Bison. Did you ever love anybody?"

The big man hunkered down. "No," he said seriously. "If you mean a woman. I loved a God for a long time, but that didn't turn out well—and it didn't make me very happy, either." He scratched his beard, his forehead wrinkling. "I think I'm happier now than I've ever been."

The simple statement made Rising Sun feel like weeping, though he couldn't understand why. Somehow, encapsulated in the few words, was a searing indictment of the way the World had been when the Gods ruled it, balanced by the possibility that, with luck, man *could* find happiness on his own, without the ceaseless stirring and plotting of the Gods. That happiness could be found both within a man, and within his relationship to the World and all the things of the World.

Hope, he thought slowly, that's what it is. Only hope. And there is nothing more powerful.

It was the kind of revelation that doesn't shake the spine or roil the mind. It was more a peaceful kind of *growing*, as if the light in the mind's eye becomes both brighter and more clear, and so illumines everything.

He stared at Raging Bison. "Does it bother you that the Gods are gone?"

Bison scratched some more. "I think that somehow I knew it all along. When the God struck me down, I sensed it then. It was like a blow in passing, in parting. The way you might leave your tent and smack one of your kids on the way out." He rocked back. "Yes, it bothers me. There is nothing now for the World to rest on. The Gods may have been terrible, but They were all we had. Now we have nothing."

Once again, Rising Sun felt the faint sting of tears lurking just behind his eyes, for once again, Raging Bison had touched on the core of things with awful simplicity. He could feel it, too, that yearning for a center, for something to *stand* on, and it came not only from a World bereft of support, but from all the things that were in the World, from the smallest stone to the mightiest beast to the tallest tree. The mountains groaned for it, the earth shifted uneasily, the winds moaned.

Everything waited. He knew for whom. But could he make that sacrifice, greater than any ever demanded before by the World? Especially when acceptance meant taking the path that led to the Last Mammoth?

"Oh, Bison," he said softly.

The big man reached out and patted his shoulder. "It will be all right."

"I'm so frightened."

"When the time comes, you will know what to do."

"I will?"

Bison smiled. "I trust you, Master."

And that was the greatest weight of all.

"Hey!"

Both men looked up. Running Deer loped across the fast-melting snow dust, a pair of bloody somethings in her raised right hand. "Breakfast!"

Feeling more than a bit odd, Rising Sun climbed to his feet. "Ho, mighty hunter!" he shouted back. "What have you brought us?"

Her cheeks were flushed with a good rosy glow as she trotted up. "Rabbits. Big ones. Come on, Bison, get that fire going. I caught 'em. You can cook 'em."

In the ensuing clatter and chatter, the moment slowly faded away. But Rising Sun would remember it always. And much later, he would know it for what it was; the last time in his life when he was fully human, fully connected to the World in the way all people are connected. In a very real sense, it was the last time he *was* human, and, eventually, the memory of it would become one of his greatest treasures. But that was later.

Hot fat dripped into the flames, sending up rich, lip-smacking aromas. They settled around the hearth to eat, though the wolf refused the cooked food and sat, red-tongued, white-fanged, and grinning, several paces away.

"I wonder how come Moon Face isn't back yet?" Running Deer said.

Bison shrugged, but Rising Sun looked up, feeling the itching on his chest flare up into burning heat again. "I don't know. It isn't like him to miss a meal. *Any* meal."

He tried a grin, but it didn't feel right, so he let it slip away. "Bison? How long has he been gone?"

The big man shrugged. "Dawn was just breaking. He woke me up, rummaging around in his pack."

"He was going to hunt roots?"

"That's what he said." With thick fingers, Bison combed grease from his beard, then took another huge bite of his piece of rabbit.

"Mm. He's been gone a long time."

The wolf hopped stiff-legged into the air and let out a series of sharp little yips. It capered in place, its wet black snout pointing eagerly toward the south.

"Now what—?"

It was very faint, hard to hear because of the dull hiss of the river.

"Helllpppp!"

"That's him," Rising Sun said, rising. Bison was already on his feet and reaching for his great spear.

"You stay here," Rising Sun told Running Deer.

"No." She strung her bow.

He started to say something, then shrugged. "Be careful. Let us go first."

"Yes."

They loped off, the wolf in the lead, laughing.

3

Carries Two Spears heard the sliding crack of gravel against stone before he saw the fat little man clambering among the rocks. He ducked back into the small cave, groping for his shorter spear, hoping he wouldn't have to use it.

He'd been here almost a moon, and nothing had changed. He'd spent a great deal of time listening to his own heartbeat. He had no choice. No matter how many times he bent over her and listened, he couldn't hear her heart make the slightest sound.

After he was sure the hunters from the River Camp were gone, he'd gone out, climbed the low rocky cliff, and brought back great loads of leaves to make a bed for

her. He arranged her on it and there she lay, unmoving.
He'd lifted her hand once, and it had stayed, until he'd
gently pressed it down again.

He would soak the corner of her blanket with water
and place it between her lips. He had no way of telling if
any of the moisture was actually absorbed, but she didn't
waste away. She merely lay unmoving, pale, like a living
ghost.

Which, he was certain, was exactly what she was.

At first he'd guarded her constantly, afraid to leave her
side even to take a piss, but after many days he'd begun
to believe she might never change. And so, driven by his
own hunger, he'd gone out to hunt what he needed. Over
time, he made a good robe for himself, chipped a crude
knife, built a hearth just inside the mouth of the cave. The
fire kept it warm in there. Once these necessities were accomplished, he simply waited, though he didn't know
what he waited for. Dimly he understood that he would
eventually have to make a decision of some kind, but he
wasn't ready, and so he slipped into a kind of fog, in
which the days passed almost without him noticing.

Now, tensely crouched, white knuckles firm on the
spear shaft, he realized he was fully awake for the first
time in days. But he hadn't wanted this kind of awakening. Who was this stranger? What did he want? What was
he doing? *Were there more of them?*

That was the crucial question. Carries Two Spears
didn't doubt he could put his spear right through that fat
little gut if he had to. And certainly no feeling of goodwill for a stranger would stay his hand if that became
necessary. After all, what he was protecting meant far
more to him than some wandering *other.* If he was ready
to kill those of his own People, he wouldn't stick at con-
signing this one's bloody corpse to the river. But if he had
friends, and they were nearby, and this one managed to
cry out, then . . .

What was he *doing?*

He squinted, trying to make sense of the little stranger's actions. He would clamber down, stop, bring his
face close to a piece of rock, sniff, then either shake his
head and make a face, or use the knife he held to scrape

something from the stone and put it in the pouch tied at his waist.

Very strange. A puzzlement, but Spears was perfectly willing to stay puzzled, if only the mysterious stranger would take his odd doings somewhere else. Yet it looked as if that wasn't going to happen.

Spears carefully scuttled as far back in the cave as he could, while he watched the chubby man move closer and closer to him. Now he was so close the only thing that would prevent discovery was if the same protection, the blinding of sight, that had worked before was still guarding them.

The stranger looked up, startled. "What?" he said as he looked into the cave mouth. Then, *"Oh!"* as Carries Two Spears lunged out, his weapon seeking soft flesh.

The little man was far quicker than Spears had expected. Though the sudden discovery that he wasn't alone must have stunned him, he somehow managed, in a twisting fall, to avoid Spears's first thrust. And by the time Spears got out of the cave, the little man was halfway up the slippery cliff, screaming his lungs out.

"Help! Hellpppp!"

Wondering if his luck would *ever* turn, Carries Two Spears scrambled after him. Obviously, the stranger had friends. The only question now was how close they were. The way things had been going, no doubt they were probably waiting—a great armed band of them—right at the top of the rocky rise. But he had to try. What other choice did he have?

"Help! Help!"

He skinned elbows and knees clambering to the top, and when he reached it, the little man had disappeared. Spears grinned tightly. The man was no hunter, that was obvious. He was still yelling his stupid head off. If he'd kept quiet, scurried away like a rabbit, he could have escaped easily into the maze along the riverbank. At least nobody else was in sight. Not yet.

His skin felt tight on him as he bounded in the direction of the cries. *Keep yelling, little man,* he prayed silently. *Just keep yelling.*

4

It was a long, shallow scrape along his right forearm, acquired when he went straight up the rocky wall, and it bled a lot more than it ought to. Or so Moon Face thought as, heart thumping, he lunged breathlessly through the looming boulders and jagged outcroppings along the riverbank.

He'd given up shouting for two reasons. First, it finally sank in that he was probably advertising his position to the man who was trying to kill him, and, second, he didn't have any extra breath to spare.

Why did I decide this was a perfect morning to go hunting that special moss that only grows on river rocks?

They'd discussed it the previous evening around the fire. He, Rising Sun, and most especially Raging Bison, whose skills in tracking were the sharpest Moon Face had ever seen, had all noticed the signs. There were People about. Strange People. Even the wolf acted nervous, yipping for no reason, pausing at certain spots to snuffle and snort at the new man scents it found.

Rising Sun hadn't seemed worried, though, and that had reassured Moon Face. His companion had changed so much since they'd begun the quest, demonstrating unlooked-for powers and abilities with each new day, it seemed. Moon Face had discovered that Rising Sun could not only control the wolf, he could somehow *become* the wolf, see out of its eyes, smell through its nose. He would send the wolf ranging out far ahead, a dreamy look on his face, and then announce they would reach a good camping spot by evening.

There was also a strange relationship growing between Rising Sun and Raging Bison. Moon Face couldn't decide if the big man was more terrifying as the Frightened Man he'd known before or as the calm-eyed warrior who handled Caribou's spear as if it were a twig. But Raging Bison seemed to be able to know Rising Sun's thoughts before he spoke them. And more than once, Moon Face had seen the two of them walking silently, Bison's brawny arm draped over Sun's shoulder, and he could have *sworn* they were deep in conversation, though they spoke no words aloud.

It was eerie. He didn't know what to make of it. He wondered if even the Shaman Gotha, with all his knowledge and experience, would understand what was happening. Sometimes he wondered if that wasn't the true reason Gotha had sent him—that the old fox had expected things to get very strange, and decided that he'd had enough strangeness already in his life, so why not let his apprentice get his toes singed?

Like now. Like running for his life through slick and slimy rocks, the sound of the man who wanted to kill him clattering along a few paces behind.

He lurched around a particularly large pile of rock and flattened himself against the far side, scanning frantically for some crack or hole large enough to hide in. His blood buzzed in his ears as he tried to muffle the hoarse gasps of his breathing.

The sun had risen far enough to put a hard shell of heat on his shoulders, despite the chill in the air and the dusting of frosty snow on the tops of the rocks. Sweat streamed from his pores, slicked his skin, burned at the edge of his eyes. He kept trying to blink his vision clear, and the sweat kept pouring in. And the blood kept pouring out of his wounded arm. He stared down at it dumbly. He was Shaman enough to know the wound was only a scratch, but something about it bothered him. Something he'd forgotten but shouldn't have. Something dangerous.

Look how it bled. It was beginning to dry up, but his arm and hand were streaked with red where blood had dripped from his fingertips, making bright spatters on the dark rock . . .

Making a perfect trail. *That* was what he'd forgotten.

"Oh," said Moon Face as the short, heavyset man stepped around the rock pile and pointed a light but lethal-looking spear at his chest.

Some part of Moon Face's mind—the Shaman part, he supposed—sat calmly off to the side, describing in a tiny, monotonous voice the details of the scene in which he was about to die.

The heavyset man looked tired. His face was bony,

though a squashed nose right in the middle of his features
offset the harsh planes a bit. He wore crude clothing, a
robe badly cured and stiff over better-quality leggings and
shirt. His shoulders were very broad, thick with muscle.
His eyes were dark and rimmed with red, as if he wasn't
sleeping well. Deep lines of worry had carved themselves
from his nose to his mouth, and between his eyes at the
bridge of his nose.

There was a damp, sour odor to him, a combination of
sweat and mold and still, mossy water. His teeth, when he
cracked his lips and said something unintelligible, were
strong and yellow.

Holding his spear with both hands, he drew back for
the fatal plunge. Moon Face raised his own hands instinctively, as if he could ward off the sharp point with bare
flesh.

A shadow fell between them, growing. Somehow,
magically, the shadow became Raging Bison, dropping
from the rocks above them with a silent grace that seemed
so ghostly that Moon Face wondered if he was dreaming
it.

"No," Raging Bison said, but the stranger, his face
crumpling, tried anyway. It all happened very quickly. To
Moon Face it was almost a blur, but he made out details.

The shorter man lunged, his speed as blinding as a
striking snake. Moon Face thought sure Raging Bison
was a dead man, particularly since Bison hardly seemed
to move. But somehow Caribou's great spear spun in his
hands, and the lower shaft knocked the driving point
aside. Then, with no discernible motion on Bison's part,
there was a resounding crack and the other man staggered
back, his eyes crossed beneath a blue lump on his forehead.

Bison took one step forward, rammed the butt of his
spear precisely into a spot where chest and belly met,
then stepped back as the stranger gave out a mighty
whoosh! and dropped as if he'd been turned to stone.

Rising Sun dropped down, light as a bird, looked at
Moon Face, and said, "There you are. We wondered
where you'd gotten to."

5

They stared at their prisoner. He sat before them, shoulders hunched, head down in obvious misery. Raging Bison squatted nearby, no more expression on his face than when he'd defeated the man with what had looked like no more than a shrug or two. Moon Face had never really believed Gotha's tale that the Frightened Man had once been the greatest warrior ever known to the Three Tribes, but if he could do this after so many years, he must have been an absolute terror in his prime. Even now, his easy watchfulness was in a way frightening; the way he lazed back on his heels reminded Moon Face of a great lion he'd once seen, all power and grace and explosive motion, leashed for the moment but waiting. Watching Raging Bison made Moon Face want to shiver.

The stranger wasn't watching anybody. His shoulders moved in little jerks, and Moon Face realized the man was sobbing. He wanted to look away then, but he couldn't. Watching a grown man cry, even a stranger, was like watching a snake eat a bird. Horrible, but sickly fascinating.

Rising Sun hunkered down in front of him. Gently he placed both his hands on the man's shoulders. Then he waited. After a time the man looked up. He said something, again in a tongue Moon Face had never heard before. And Rising Sun replied in the same tongue.

The stranger's eyes grew almost as wide as Moon Face's own. Only Raging Bison seemed unperturbed. He cocked one eyebrow when Running Deer came around the rock and joined them, but that was all.

Their captive paid her no attention. He stared up into Rising Sun's face, his jaw dropping slackly. Then a torrent of words erupted. Rising Sun listened, nodding, interjecting a word or two. And finally the man smiled, a watery, relieved expression that changed his face entirely. Moon Face realized the stranger was younger than he'd first guessed. Fear or despair had aged him, but somehow Rising Sun had wiped that away.

"Well," Rising Sun said. He stood up and dusted his hands against his thighs. "What a strange story."

Running Deer glanced at him, then at Moon Face. "Are you all right? That's a nasty cut on your arm."

Moon Face waved her off. "Rising Sun, how—who is—what did he say? How can you understand him?"

Rising Sun shrugged. "I don't know. I just do. His name is Carries Two Spears. I already told him who you are."

Moon Face looked over. The stranger bobbed his head, a shy smile on his lips. "He tried to kill me!" Moon face said.

"Yes, he did. But not out of any ill will toward you. He was protecting something. Somebody."

"What? Who?"

Rising Sun smiled slowly. To Moon Face, the smile looked faintly sad. "Come with us. You'll see."

And with that, he helped their captive to his feet, and the two of them walked slowly off into the rocks.

Rising Sun walked to the small cave as if he'd known all along where it was. Moon Face gave a little start as he realized Sun had led the way, not the stranger, who'd been just a step behind. They stopped a pace or two outside. Rising Sun glanced at Carries Two Spears, whose expression was worried but not afraid.

Moon Face felt a curious itching sensation in his shoulder blades, and a heaviness in his ears that muffled the sound of the river. He didn't recognize the sensation until they stopped, but then knew why it was familiar. Sometimes, just before the big storms of spring came blowing and wailing over the Valley, prickly with lightning, he would feel the same thing. A knowing expectancy, a pregnant waiting, portending the imminent unleashing of great forces. A premonition of mighty Spirits, come to walk and talk upon the World.

He'd never felt the sensation as strongly. The hair at the nape of his neck stood up, and something crawled from chunk to chunk along his spine.

But there was no storm, only the two men standing before the cave. Feeling faintly foolish, he glanced at the others and saw that Running Deer seemed wary and preoccupied, and even Raging Bison, so imperturbable, now stood straight and held his spear in a stiff, rigid grip.

Carries Two Spears said something. Rising Sun nodded and then—reluctantly, Moon Face thought—stepped forward, ducked down, and entered the cave.

He didn't come out for a long time, and when he did, the World was changed, and once again was new.

6

Rising Sun had recognized the place instantly, of course. He'd Dreamed of it intermittently since he'd first experienced it, beyond the World, beneath the thrones, in his Manhood Dream. So his knees felt loose and shaky, and there was a queasy heaving in his gut and a pressure between his ears as he ducked inside. He could feel them watching him, and he repressed a burp of nervous laughter.

He saw her in the light, the thin and watery gray light (*the deadlight,* he thought—for it was the light of the Departed Gods, drear and deadly), and for the first time fully understood that it was *true,* that it was all going to *happen.* Then, with a little curl of terror, he knew that it had been inevitable, inevitable long before he was born, and was still as inevitable as the stones at the root of the World.

For all men, every moment of before leads inexorably to the moment of now. He stood in his moment, swaying slightly, looking down at her. He could smell the bitter tang of the poison in her flesh.

The Power had been growing in him. It had been expressing itself in what seemed like a lot of little Powers, but it was really only one. Raging Bison had sensed it, when he began to call him Master.

With each step south, the Power unfolded itself inside him, like a leaf growing on a tree. One perfectly formed spine of the leaf gave him the knowledge of beasts, of the quick, bright instincts that flowed inside their skulls. And another unlocked the secrets of the human soul, spilling a torrent of words, images, memories. And yet another revealed itself in the songs of the green things, the long slow groan of trees, the bright chatter of flowers, the sigh of grasses broad across the prairies.

Now the World and all the things within it spoke to him, so that the sum of the speech was like a mighty wave, filling each of his senses.

He regarded her thoughtfully, knowing what poison had been used and how to negate it. But that wasn't the challenge here. The poison should have, *would have,* killed her long ago. It hadn't, because something else had entered through the way the poison had made. Now it crouched within her, slow, scaly eyes aglitter, watching and waiting. It had kept her alive because it needed a place to wait. To wait for him. To wait for the coming of the Sun.

He sighed. Her name was Sleeps With Spirits. No one believed her prophesies, yet they were true. Even her *name* was a prophesy. She slept with a Spirit now, a force both dread and terrible, almost as ancient as the World itself. Something only the Gods had ever leashed, but freed once again in the wake of Their passing.

Cruel, he thought. *They were so cruel.*

Then he realized it wasn't exactly true. The Gods could not be judged by human standards. The Gods informed the World. At the touch of Their fingers the waters rolled, the stones creaked, the trees sprouted up. What was cruelty to one was beneficence to another. The Gods concerned Themselves with balance, and in the awful weight of Their scales, cruelty, love, hope, hate, kindness, all were merely bits added to one side or the other.

No, the Gods had not been cruel. They had not unleashed this Spirit, so dark and strong. But Their departure had freed it, for without the Gods, nothing remained in the World strong enough to bind it. And so the World was out of balance, waiting for the One To Come.

Each thing had its own Spirit, but this Spirit possessed no thing. It was an idea, an action, an existence complete unto itself. Sly, crafty, immortal, a vast Power in its own right. It lived in the dark. It hated the Light, because the Light was stronger. And it loved men, for in the souls of men it found sustenance. It could be defeated for a time, but it always sprang back, renewed, for men created it. It was of the World. It was the other side of the Balance.

It was Evil. And now it waited, a Test no man could have imagined.

But I am not a man, Rising Sun thought. *Not anymore.*

He sank to his knees and put his hands on either side of her head, and entered into the Place of which she was the Gate, to face what awaited him there, on the hinge of the Balance of the World.

7

It was not what he expected. He didn't find himself at the place of the thrones, where he'd first seen Sleeps With Spirits as a small, retreating Dream-shape. Instead, he floated far above the World, seeing as a hawk might. The earth below seemed deserted, until a flicker of movement caught his attention and he descended.

Two figures, one prone, the other crouching over him. The boy lay flat, the woman hovered, moving her hands. As he came closer, a mist began to rise, until all that remained were the two figures.

What was the woman *doing*? He drifted closer still, seeming to move about with only the force of his will. He couldn't see anything of his body. It was like a Dream— but not the way he remembered his Manhood Dream. In that, he'd been aware of his body, of the effort of motion, of sweat and pain and exhaustion. Here he simply floated, a viewpoint, a watcher. It had felt *real. Perhaps,* he thought calmly, *it isn't my Dream. Maybe I'm in someone else's Dream.*

The explanation seemed sufficient. Something about it struck him as right, even fitting. But whose Dream was it? He didn't recognize either of the two below. The boy was slender, scarred and wounded. He was unconscious. One leg was terribly swollen. The thigh looked twice as big as the other leg. A putrescent hole oozed vile yellow fluid. The woman, whose back was to him, her gray-streaked hair falling forward to shield her face, knelt next to the boy. Her fingers pressed the gash gently, with the sureness of one who had seen many such wounds.

With Gotha, Rising Sun had also seen such things. Almost never could even the most powerful Shaman exorcise the evil Spirits from such injuries and make the victim whole again. He wondered why he was seeing this. The boy would die, no doubt. Was it a warning? Now that he looked, there *was* something hauntingly familiar about the broken child.

He willed himself lower, until he could make out fine details. The webbing of pale pink scar tissue that disfigured much of the boy's body. Once again, the sharp pang of familiarity knifed deep—where had he seen such a thing? Then, for only a flicker of time, the boy's eyes popped open, and Rising Sun felt something in his soul leap.

Blue and green! The colors brought the memory of other scars to him, a net of faded pain that his father had shown and explained to him. But they weren't *other* other scars. They were *these* scars.

Somehow he Dreamed of Morning Star, his own father, as a child! But if that was true, then the woman must be—

She absently pushed her hair away from her face as she examined the wound, her gaze strong and intent as she worked. She noticed the delirious boy staring at her and stroked his sweating brow until he closed his eyes again.

And her mismatched eyes were like emerald and sapphire! But it *wasn't* his mother, White Moon, the only woman he'd ever seen with those twin marks. And Running Deer had the blue only.

Maya. Somehow, passing through the winds of Time, he had entered a Dream of Great Maya herself! Then this must be the time she'd saved his father with her Power, a time Gotha had once told him about.

He felt itchy, nervous. This had already happened. Maya was long dead. Yet he sensed this thing was *still* occurring, that he had a role to play here, that this moment had *waited* for him.

He had absolutely no idea what he was supposed to do. And so he waited, a presence only.

If I am the One To Come, he thought, *then I will come to many places. This is one of them.*

Suddenly Rising Sun realized that just as Moon Face's thoughts had filled his skull in babbling cascades, he had become connected to Maya's own thoughts. But the joining was stronger, so complete that in some way he *became* her. Only a tiny bit of himself remained aside, barely there, watching. With that realization, something new began to happen. But he experienced it as *her,* not as himself.

It began as a wisp of smoke rising lazily from the glowing wound on the boy's thigh. The smoke was strange, glimmering, full of iridescent color, not really dark at all. It was transparent, but somehow it possessed a weird kind of solidity. Rising Sun knew it was quite real, at least in this place.

It ascended from the wound with sinuous grace, making him think of snakes, though he knew it wasn't a snake. No, this was a malevolent Spirit but not the Great Power Maya had known of old. Those Powers had ruled it, but with difficulty, for the dark half of the World's soul was immensely strong, and would bow to no lesser Power than a God.

The glittering fume spread slowly into a fanlike hood that hovered over the boy, and in it, glaring out at her, two red eyes. Furious eyes, bubbling pits of rage.

He watched it from inside her, knowing that his own time was upon him. *I have come,* he thought silently. *I am here.*

8

You don't like it, do you? she thought.

Almost as if in reply, a spot of darkness yawned beneath those eyes, and from it issued a howl of such savagery Maya thought her ears would break. Then came the breath of the thing—a thick, hot cloud whose stench sharply reminded her of a childhood memory of a rotting duck on a nest of spoiled eggs.

The stench that had arisen then was the awful memory this monstrous whiff of Demon breath brought back to Maya now. She wanted to turn away, but that would be fatal, for the boy, perhaps even for her. In this half world where Shamans and Spirits could meet, you never turned your back on a Demon.

Especially not one with great yellow dripping fangs, a tongue like a lump of swollen, sickly red meat lolling between those fangs, and spurlike claws as long as her fingers.

It towered over the boy, seemed to crouch on him as if she'd interrupted its feeding. Which was exactly what she had done.

If it's anything, it's a wolf, she thought as she stared at it with awe. She'd never seen a Demon Spirit so huge, so full of rage and hunger. *How did the boy survive this long?*

The coat of the beast was torn and matted, clumps of twisted, metallike hair springing out, bulging in unlikely places over misshapen clots of muscle and bone. The thing exuded an overwhelming aura of power, a black, exploding rage, an inexhaustible hunger, and now it turned its insane boiling eyes on her, as if it saw her for the first time.

Be careful now, that still, remote voice whispered in her ear, sounding thin and drawn, as if it had been stretched over some unimaginable distance.

Oh, yes, she thought. She willed herself toward the towering thing, and now it reared up, its grotesque paws clicking bunches of claws in and out, in and out, with a sound like bones being shaken in a bag. Smoke dribbled from its distended nostrils, and a rue of bloody fire began to leak out the sides of its jaws and trace a smoldering path through the rusty thatch of its muzzle.

Another wave of gruesome stenches smote her full in the face as she approached it. The boy at her feet seemed shrunken and far away, a tiny doll caught like a discarded plaything between the two of them. She spared him a single glance and saw that he still slept, pale and waxy as a corpse, two unhealthy bright spots burning on his cheeks.

Now she could hear the bellows thunder of the beast's lungs, and the gale of its reeking breath tugged at her hair, scorched the lashes around her eyes. Its claws, sharp as new-broken bones, clicked and clacked at each other.

Let him go! she shrieked suddenly. *He is mine now, not yours. Leave him! Get out of him!*

The awful howling that ensued nearly shattered her ears, and then, with preternatural suddenness, the beast sprang upon her, its mighty thighs pistoning as the talons there sought the soft meat of her belly while its snapping jaws bore down toward her throat.

She grasped it just behind its forepaws and pushed it back while it screamed in fury. Fire bloomed suddenly in its gullet, a new red tongue that blistered the skin on her face, but Maya wrestled on, pitting the strength of her years, of the Power she'd gathered over those years, against the Power she despised.

Down, beast! DOWN, *I say!*

But it fought her, even as her voice tore at it and wounded it terribly. The sound blasted one eye clean out of its skull, and ripped great chunks of smoking flesh from its heaving chest, yet it fought on, its frenzy unabated. If anything, its wounds galvanized it to greater strength, and it twisted against her grip while it barked and growled and rumbled its hate.

Yet Maya felt she was winning, felt the strength of the beast begin to ebb, and for a moment she allowed herself a small feeling of triumph.

You know your mistress, beast! she screamed at it as she forced it backward, away from the boy. The rope of smoke that connected it to the wound on the boy's leg stretched, thinned, and she knew it was close to snapping, and she thought, *One more good shove,* and—

The walls of the Dream World cracked apart.

Power roared in from everywhere, fantastic jagged bolts of light that struck the beast again and again and filled it from snout to tail with a strength so terrible that Maya felt her own bones breaking beneath the weight of it.

Fangs like bloody spears closed around her, shook her as a bear shakes a rat, and flung her away. It was that quick, a single toss, and she felt herself falling, falling out of the Dream World.

Nooooo!

But it was over and she had lost, she *knew* it with terrible clarity, and a great sadness filled her. Too old, too tired. She had failed. The boy would die now.

Papa?

The tiny cry cut through the raging well of Power with a force so absolute, so complete, that for an instant everything stopped.

And into the utter silence—

Papa, where are you? I'm so tired ...

That plea, so lost, so lonely, tore at her heart. Somehow she gathered the rags of her strength and righted herself. The beast, oddly diminished, loomed over the tiny form, which had not moved at all as far as she could tell. Nevertheless, she had no doubt it was the boy himself who had spoken.

My son! she thought, and threw herself forward once again, heedless of the churning Power that enveloped the beast as it rose to meet her new attack.

This time their clash shook the very foundations of the Dream, and for an instant she saw the real World, saw two figures stretched out next to each other as the dead would lie upon the ground, and then the vision vanished and she fought in the heart of the beast while it ravened all about her, continually renewed by the surging waves of force that battered in from every corner of the Dream World.

She vised her hands around its neck, and though it roared at her touch, it seemed unable to escape. Tighter and tighter she drew the noose of her fingers while its molten eyes bulged like bubbles filled with fire.

And then she felt it come, a very tornado of Power. Her hair stood out from her skull, spitting and snapping with tiny lightnings. The beast was renewed once again. Its mighty neck expanded with a single jerk and broke her hold.

Maya prayed, *Ah, Mother, He comes, Your ancient Enemy is upon me now. Come to me, Mother! Come now!*

But as a terrible, claw-studded paw raked across her belly, and she felt the awful warm-cold-empty sensation of her own bowels spilling out, she knew her prayer had not been answered.

I will die in this place ...

It was a forlorn thought, but she knew it was true. It was the great danger of these things, and all Shamans feared it. Anything was possible in the World of Dreams, even the death of the Dreamer herself.

She fell heavily against the boy's body, draped across it, her guts spilling out and soiling his alabaster skin. One hand flopped across his pelvis, thumped on something hard, rolled away.

It was all she could do to think, but somehow she managed it. *What?* His pouch. Even in the Dream he wore his pouch, and something hard was inside it. Her fingers scrabbled, reached inside, touched the bony little figurine—

No, the vast calm voice tolled, *it is mine.*

And Rising Sun realized the voice was *his own,* though he wouldn't have recognized it. The sound of it brought him back to himself, wrenched him away from the incredible union he'd experienced with Great Maya. It was the sight of the Stone that had once been called the Fatherstone, one half of the Great Talisman, that called to him.

The light was dying from Maya's eyes as she rolled off the boy and stared up into the slavering jaws of the beast. But even that dread creature must have heard *something,* for its vast muzzle withdrew. It cocked its head as if trying to hear something perhaps too high for any other ears, but then as suddenly as it had withdrawn it snapped forward again.

And stopped.

For the boy stood between them, the boy and ... *something else.*

Only Rising Sun knew what that *something else* was. It was him, the One To Come.

Gasping, he cried out: *"Now I Come, to take what is mine!"*

He felt the Power of the World in all its myriad shapes and forms and manifestations surge through him, felt it join and mingle with the boy's Power, felt it flow like a great river into Maya's uncanny might, which had been from One greater even than the Gods Themselves. All this came to him in that moment, came to him as he came to It.

He knew Maya couldn't make out anything but the boy's slim form, nor had she heard his words. He thought she might know the boy did not stand alone. *He* stood, too, and in one hand was the Fatherstone, and in the other all the Power that was in the World, and he burned with the light of a thousand stars.

He paid her no attention, did not so much as glance at her. His attention was for the beast. But he didn't wrestle with it. He merely stared at it for a long moment, and then, with a tiny shake of his head, said, "I have Come. You may go now."

And with that he reached down and, gently, took the cord of smoke that bound the beast to him and snapped it with a single motion.

"You are free," he told it sadly, knowing the two of them would meet again, endlessly.

The beast dwindled, acknowledging a new Master. Rising Sun thought there was almost a look of relief in those hideously flaming eyes. Then a mist rose around him, blotting out the boy and the woman, and he knew this moment was now fading forever. It had waited for him to Come, and he had. Now Maya was truly beyond the World. He had mastered the beast, and in so doing, freed this tiny remnant of her to return from whence she came.

In the end, he was alone. As he would always be, for he was the One To Come.

The mist of destiny surrounded him, but did not blind him, for he would always see. It was the doom of the Master. It was his doom. As he fell back into the World, he laughed bitterly. Even knowing he would take it up, and bear it forever, he had not imagined the weight of that doom.

Rising Sun opened his eyes. The mist was gone. He squatted in a shadowed cave, memory still ringing a great bell in the halls of his mind, the Power he'd absorbed in defeating the Great World Demon still tingling in his fingertips, the vanished weight of the Fatherstone still curving his palm.

He looked down into her wide ruby eyes, marveled at the beauty of her pale, pale face. Her lips moved.

"Master, you have come," she whispered.

"Yes, I have," he told her, for it was true.

Beneath her, in its nest of ancient bones, a great Light began to glow. Gently he lifted her from her leafy bed, her weight no more than a handful of feathers. He set her aside and brushed away the leaves and exposed the bones beneath. In the heart of them it lay burning with secret golden fire. The twin mammoths regarded each other with timeless eyes. The primordial ivory from which they'd been carved still bore faint scratch marks from Ga-Ya's tools, when she'd fashioned them in the deeps of Time.

The light from the Stone Rejoined, the Talisman, the Key of Maya, and all the other Names it had borne over the years, illumined the tiny cave with a Light from beyond the World. It bathed his face as he bent over it. It made the bones of his fingers visible through amber flesh when he picked it up. It soothed the burning in his chest when he placed it there, suspended by the same thong that had once enclosed the neck of Maya herself. And it shone unquenchably from his eyes as he took Sleeps With Spirits's waxen fingers, helped her to her feet, and led her from the cave into pale winter daylight.

He looked at them standing there, their faces slack with wonder, and said, "This is Sleeps With Spirits. And this"—he touched the Talisman on his chest—"is what I was doomed to find."

Then Sleeps With Spirits threw back her head and cried out in a ringing voice, "This is the One prophesied. He is the One To Come, and he will inherit the World."

And each of them believed her utterly, for she proph-

esied in the name of the One, and spoke only truth. So did
Rising Sun take up the Talisman that was his, having begun his quest as a boy, become a man, and in the end become more than a man.

The first part of the Test was done. Only he knew of
the second, for only he had seen it, though Sleeps With
Spirits prophesied it now. No other Power could oppose
him in the World, for he had vanquished the most terrible
of the World's Powers.

His fingers sought the golden Talisman that had been
made from the tusks of a great mammoth Mother when
the World was new. No other Power but himself. The Talisman was his. No one could take it from him. No one but
himself.

He shivered, thinking of it. Thinking of the Last Mammoth. Thinking of the Choice that was hard upon him.

I have the Power, but do I have the strength? Do I?

He knew he would discover the answer soon enough,
for his Test was not yet done. The World had tested him.
Now he must test himself.

CHAPTER TWENTY-ONE

1

Running Deer was the first to understand what had happened. She saw it in his glowing face, in the way his dark eyes seemed like coals, black and hot, just before they exploded. She saw his hand guiding the wraith-woman, the Ghost Woman, and she knew immediately that this was the woman he'd met in his Manhood Dream. Never in her wildest imaginings had she thought that woman would be real, though. Then the woman threw back her head and made her prophesy, each word falling into Running Deer's heart with the stonelike thudding of truth, and she knew she'd lost him. But she didn't understand *what* she'd lost him to. She thought it was Sleeps With Spirits, who was beautiful. The pain she felt then was like nothing she'd ever known before.

Raging Bison, who had not known of the Dream, watched the woman guardedly. He knew *something* had happened—and he recognized the Talisman at once. He'd been present at the Joining of the Two Stones. So Rising Sun, the Master, had achieved the goal of his quest. Now he wore the Twinstone. Bison wondered what it portended—but he was content to wait. Just as once he'd worshiped a God with all his soul, now he followed another. The Master would decide.

Moon Face gasped at the fulfillment of the Dream. He,

too, recognized the woman from the description both Gotha and Rising Sun had given him. And he was less surprised than Deer that the woman of the Dream had turned out to be real. Dreams were real things, after all, and sometimes things lived in both Dream and World. The woman was the gatekeeper to the Talisman, the guide for the One to Come. Her presence, and the small, shining Talisman on Rising Sun's chest, told him all he needed to know. The quest was done. Rising Sun was the One To Come.

Sleeps With Spirits's prophesy flamed with truth, but Moon Face didn't need her to know truth when he saw it. All he felt was a vast relief, that he would not have to betray Rising Sun in the name of a false quest. Rising Sun, in finding the Talisman, had proved himself. He would inherit the World. Now they could all go home.

The wolf said nothing. In its small, silver-red cup of darting thoughts, it saw the Light it had followed so long now burn like the sun overhead. It sat down and grinned.

Carries Two Spears, squat and sturdy, crouched off at the side like a snide comment. *I'm here, too. Don't forget me.*

Yes yes yes! panted the wolf.

For one instant they were a tableau that would shake down the ages: Rising Sun in the center, his face afire; on his right, Running Deer, her bow in her hands; on his left, Sleeps With Spirits, her ruby eyes alight with truth, burning with prophesy; Moon Face and Raging Bison before him, Bison's head bowed, Moon Face adoring; and the wolf, grinning, at his feet. In that suspended moment lay mighty tales of the past, and even mightier songs for the future.

But only one of them understood it all, understood the *weight* of what it portended. Rising Sun wondered who would betray him when the time came. One of them would. But which one?

He pushed the thought away. Carefully he helped Spirits to a low rock and settled her down. "Bison, Running Deer. She needs food."

They both nodded, then turned and raced away through the rocks. Rising Sun watched them disappear over the top. Then he turned to Moon Face. "Stoke up that fire, my friend. And get out your potions. She is very weak. I will tell you later what happened to her, but you can help, I think."

Moon Face set to work. He brushed bones out of his way inside the cave, never stopping to wonder whose bones they might be. If he'd known, he would have recoiled in horror at his disrespect.

"Carries Two Spears," Rising Sun said in the alien tongue, "now for your story. I want to know everything."

Obligingly the river man squatted and began to talk.

2

The next day they moved up from the river to their old camp, where it was dryer and warmer. Sleeps With Spirits was very weak. Moon Face dosed her with his potions, paying particular attention to brewing the antidote to the poison Rising Sun told him about. At first, Carries Two Spears was nervous about leaving his hiding place, but Rising Sun reassured him.

"You saw what Raging Bison did to you?"

Spears nodded.

"He could, by himself, slay all the hunters of your People just as easily. Do you believe it?" Rising Sun asked.

Spears remembered the awful ease with which Bison had disarmed him. It had been fast and tricky and, in retrospect, inevitable. It was far easier to slay than to disarm. And Carries Two Spears had judged himself as one of the best of his own People.

"I believe," he said finally. Raging Bison winked at him. "And if my People came for me and my sister again, I would help him."

"Then don't worry."

"All right," Spears said.

The two hunters had brought back much food—three fat rabbits, their fur turned from brown to white by the winter's snowy kiss, a squirrel for soup, and an unwary doe that Bison carted back on his broad shoulders.

Moon Face and Running Deer managed to find a few sturdy greens and even a cache of mushrooms protected in the cavity of a fallen tree. Now, the morning of the second day, the One To Come sat next to the fire, his nose twitching at the rich, fatty odors of breakfast.

Moon Face squatted next to him. "The sky is gray. I fear a storm. Will we head north today, or wait it out before we start for home?"

Rising Sun looked up at him. "Neither, my friend. We go across the river."

Moon Face rocked back. "But why?"

Rising Sun regarded him calmly. "Because that is where the camp of the River People is, and we are going there."

Moon Face stared at him. In the thin light of morning, Rising Sun looked as he always had. Moon Face could no longer see the unearthly glow that had illumined his face. Once again he looked at his companion, and almost forgot that he also looked at the One To Come.

"Why on earth do you want to go there? We have what we came for." He gestured at the Twinstone that rested on Rising Sun's chest. "You have fulfilled the prophesy. The quest is over. Why aren't we going back to the Green Valley?"

A faint, quizzical smile played on Rising Sun's lips. "Do you recall the rest of the prophesy, my friend? That the One To Come will inherit the World?"

Moon Face grimaced. "Of course I do. That's why I don't understand. We should go back now, so you can take up your inheritance."

Rising Sun shook his head. "Oh, Moon Face, is that what you think? That the Green Valley is the World?"

Moon Face stared at him, nonplussed. "Well, of course. Isn't it?"

"The World is the World, my friend." Rising Sun made a sweeping gesture with his right hand. "All of this. The Green Valley, the rivers, the high steppe, and the forests. All we have seen, and all we haven't seen."

"But—" Moon Face fell silent. His brain was good, but he couldn't encompass the *idea* of so much. The concept of the World was suddenly too much for him. The

World was the Green Valley, wasn't it? How could Rising
Sun talk of the *World*? How could one man inherit the
World?

And so, for a moment only, Moon Face tasted the awful terror and exultation of the prophesy, which Rising
Sun had been struggling with ever since the Shaman
Gotha had explained it to him. Then, because it was simply too *large* for him to get his thoughts around, he banished it. It was ridiculous. They must get back, bearing
the precious Stone, before winter snows blocked their
path. He had a formless premonition about the Green Valley. Nothing specific, just a general feeling of dread. The
One To Come was needed in his rightful place, and that
place wasn't here.

Moon Face clamped his lips shut, then said stubbornly,
"We should go back to the Green Valley. Right now.
What about the rest of us?"

Rising Sun grinned serenely. "The rest? Why don't
you ask them what they want to do, Moon Face?"

Moon Face sighed. Rising Sun had him there. The rest
of them, right down to the wolf, would do whatever Rising Sun wanted to do. Even the two newcomers, that
Carries Two Spears and his weird, ghostly sister, listened
with open mouths and shining eyes to anything Rising
Sun had to say, nodding their agreement to everything.

"Well," he said uncomfortably, "maybe I'm the only
one left who can see things clearly."

"Oh? And what do you see so clearly, my Shaman?"
Rising Sun spoke in a bantering tone, but there was an
edge beneath it that made Moon Face realize that if he
had any sense at all, he should tread carefully. But, for
reasons he couldn't define even to himself, he was still
frightened. He'd felt that way ever since they'd begun the
quest, during all the long days when nothing had gone as
he'd expected, when he'd slept fitfully or not at all while
he worried about how to keep the quest on its rightful
path.

The quest was over. So why did he still feel that
queasy churning in his gut? He didn't know, but it was
from that dank swamp of fear that his next words grew.

"Rising Sun, you *have* to lead us back. They *need* you

in the Green Valley. You belong to us—or the quest was a false one."

Rising Sun stared at his face for several moments, his own features somber. His dark eyes looked sad and resigned at the same time.

"The quest false? How do you mean?" Gently he stroked the Talisman on his chest. "I bear the Stone. Isn't that what we came for?"

"No!"

"Ah. I see. Then, what *did* we come for, Moon Face?"

A fire was burning inside Moon Face's skull. Why couldn't Rising Sun *see*? "For you to find the Stone, and bring it back to the Green Valley, and then . . . then—"

"Then what?"

Moon Face didn't know what he would say until he blurted out the words. *"Then be our God!"*

"Oh." To Moon Face's amazement, Rising Sun didn't seem upset at all. He merely stroked the Mammoth Stone lightly, his black eyes more sad than ever. "What would you say if I told you that I may return to the Valley, but *this* won't? Would I still be your God if I didn't have the Stone?"

Moon Face's mouth dropped slowly open. "Without the *Stone*? Rising Sun, what are you talking about?"

Suddenly Rising Sun seemed to lose interest in their conversation. His eyelids slowly dropped to hood his eyes. He said, "I don't know, Moon Face. It doesn't matter." He sighed and began to stand up. "No, don't say anything else. We are going to the camp by the river. After that, we'll see." And with that, he turned and walked away from the little apprentice without a backward glance.

"What are you, Rising Sun?" Moon Face whispered under his breath. "What have you become?" And silently, inside his skull, a voice only dimly recognizable as his own shrieked over and over, *"What am I going to do now?"*

3

The Witch didn't see them across the river to the south, floating and shivering atop the logs they'd shaped into crude rafts. She was preoccupied with planning the journey that would soon begin. The River People would have left already, but for the mysterious illness that had struck down their Chief, Kills Many Buffalo. The new Shaman had tried all his tricks, but to no avail. Finally he had called on the Witch, but by then it was too late. Despite her best efforts, the old man died. The smell of his burning still lingered like perfume in her nostrils. When the smoke was still rising, she had turned to the Shaman and said, "I told you evil things would come, if the curse wasn't cleared completely."

She had questioned the hunting party herself when they'd returned empty-handed. "What do you mean, you couldn't find them?"

But they'd shrugged, and muttered, and grinned at her in sheepish embarrassment, and finally she'd let it go. No doubt her son had wandered away after his sister died. The World was wide. If he didn't wish to be found, he wouldn't be. Over time, her fear that he would return and somehow threaten her subsided. With both the old Shaman and the Chief gone, there was no one left to oppose her. The men would select a new Chief. The most likely candidate, a certain Runs Like Antelopes, had been a part of the hunting party she'd sent out. He was thin and wiry and terrified of her. When the rituals and ceremonies were finally done, the new Chief would be as cowed by her as the new Shaman already was.

A boy came to her as she sat before her tent, pulling careful stitches into a new cloak she was making for herself.

"Mm—Mother," he stammered, refusing to meet her eyes. She recognized him. He was the one who'd pissed himself when she'd put her eyes on him, once upon a time.

"Well," she said shortly, "speak up. What is it?"

"The Shaman, he sent me. He said to tell you they've come back."

Her hands quit moving. She looked up. There was shouting at the far southern end of the camp. "What? *Who* has come back, you little fool? What are you talking about?"

The tone of her voice brought quick tears to his eyes. Quivering, he managed to blurt out the names. Carries Two Spears. And Sleeps With Spirits! Then, his duty done, he turned and ran from her glowering face as fast as he could.

"You! Come back here!" But he was gone.

Dumbly she looked down at the work she'd been doing. She spat on the ground, but didn't bother to erase the mark of her spit. She needn't fear *that* any longer.

She tossed the cape into the tent, turned, and stumped toward the noise. If they *had* been stupid enough to return, she was ready. The fire was always ready, and its hunger could never be assuaged.

4

Rising Sun followed behind Carries Two Spears and Sleeps With Spirits, who led the way. He was flanked on either side by Raging Bison and Running Deer, both holding their weapons ready. Running Deer had an arrow nocked against her bowstring. She turned her head slowly from side to side, watching everything. Moon Face followed behind, and the wolf behind him.

They came upon the River Camp from the south. Nobody saw them until they came within a hundred paces of the southernmost tent, where an old hunter lounging on a split log glanced up, then sprang to his feet, his eyes wide with surprise. He stared a moment more, as if he couldn't believe what he saw, then turned and ran deeper into the camp, hallooing at the top of his lungs.

"Stop here," Rising Sun said.

They waited and watched while the camp emptied into a small crowd of chattering onlookers who stood and gabbled just inside the edge of the first tent.

Not very many, Rising Sun thought. *Less than three hands of hunters. Raging Bison could kill them all himself.*

"Is your mother, the Witch, among them?" he whispered to Spears, who stood tensely, clutching his sister's hand. His fear was obvious—but Sleeps With Spirits waited calmly, her pale head tilted high, her white hair streaming in the harsh breeze. There was no fear in her. Her prophesy was truth, and it would go as she knew it would. There was nothing to fear.

Carries Two Spears shook his head. "No. Not yet—but she will come."

Rising Sun felt her coming before he actually saw her. It was like the approach of a shadow, a small dark cold spot, like a cloud passing beneath the sun. She cut through the crowd like a knife through hot fat, scattering them like rabbits. She stumped to the front and stared across the distance, her face set like a stone, her eyes black and cold. Rising Sun felt the chill of that gaze, so similar to the frigid heart of the beast he'd just vanquished, and knew that he hadn't defeated the beast at all. Knew that he never would. The battle was endless, for it was the Balance of the World.

But he understood who faced him across the barren ground. Not the woman who had slain her husband, and tried to destroy her children, not merely a woman with blood on her hands, but something else. A shell for the beast that lived in her heart, a treacherous beast that pretended it was a God.

"Hello again, beast," he whispered, then smiled at Running Deer's curious glance.

The Witch's voice was rough, gravellike, too deep for a woman. "What do you want?" she called. "Why have you come back, treacherous ones?"

Carries Two Spears opened his mouth to reply, but Rising Sun said, "No, let me." He walked to the front of the party and stood and looked at her. For an instant, beneath his steady examination, she seemed uncomfortable, but she recovered quickly.

"Who are you, strangers? Why do you bring the bearers of a curse back to the scene of their crimes?"

"We are just wanderers. We come for shelter, for a time. A storm is brewing. When it passes, we will leave."

He could see the lines chiseled into her face grow deeper as she considered. He knew she was in a quandary. She had thought Sleeps With Spirits dead, and Carries Two Spears long departed. But now they returned, part of a new band. Allies? Enemies? Why had they come back? How did Spirits survive the poison? Who *were* they?

Her first instinct would be to slay them all, but that would tell her nothing. If she was at all curious, her sense of self-preservation would demand she find out what had happened, how Spirits had managed to survive. And *why* her children had returned.

He banked on the hope that her curiosity would overrule her instinctively murderous reactions, and so was unsurprised when she called back, "You may camp where you are. But you have two cursed ones with you, so none of you may enter the camp of the River Children. And when the storm is over, you must leave. Otherwise, we will kill you all."

Emboldened by her words, the men around her raised their spears and shouted dire threats. Raging Bison eyed them with a faint, sardonic smile, but made no gesture in return.

The beast welcomed them to enter a trap. Rising Sun saw it clearly, for he was Master. But the trap was preordained, though its outcome was not. It was the second part of the Test.

"Thank you!" he called back. "We accept what you say."

With that, some of the tension drained out of the confrontation, to be replaced with curiosity as the hunters lowered their spears.

"I will come to you later, for I am the Witch, and I fear no curses!"

Rising Sun only nodded and replied, "We will welcome you."

The Talisman was heavy on his chest, but if he survived the second Test, he would bear its weight no longer. Thinking of this, he turned away, to help prepare their small camp and make ready for the visit of the Witch, and the beast inside her.

5

The Witch watched him turn away, but as soon as he did, she turned her eyes to her children. Sleeps With Spirits, looking as much like a monster as ever, stood slightly in the van, as if protecting her older brother. But that was ridiculous—surely the girl couldn't protect anything. But there *was* something different about her. It took the Witch a couple of breaths to figure it out. Fear. Sleeps With Spirits didn't look frightened anymore. She stood straight, with her shoulders back and her chin up, and she gazed unblinkingly across the distance between them. If it had been anybody else, the Witch would have called it a challenge, but she couldn't imagine Spirits ever being able to defy her. It just wasn't possible.

Her brother was another story, but when the Witch stared at him, he could only hold her eyes a scant moment before he looked away.

How had the girl survived?

That was the first, though not the most important, question. The real riddle was, knowing what she must know, why had Spirits returned? Revenge, because the Witch certainly understood *that,* seemed to be the most obvious answer.

But the *way* she came back made no sense at all. If she sought vengeance on her mother, to simply walk up to the camp and announce her presence was crazy. Even though she'd somewhere found others, strangers, who took her in, they were a small band. It would be easy for the hunters of the River Children to overpower them all—and if Spirits didn't understand that, surely Carries Two Spears did.

Yet they both had returned. It made her wary, made her wonder what she was missing. She didn't know enough, not yet. So that was the first order of business. Find out what the missing parts were. And if she couldn't, well—the hunters would do what she told them to.

She turned away, wondering why her heart was still beating so quickly. Then she realized. It was the stranger who had spoken. Something about him frightened her. But she couldn't figure out what it was.

"Go on, leave them to me," she snarled as she stomped through the crowd. She paused. "Nobody goes to their camp without my leave. Do you understand?"

Sullen matters of agreement. "Good. Remember, they are cursed, and they bear a curse. I can guard you from it, but only if you do exactly what I say."

More mutters, but the clot of hunters began slowly to disperse. She watched them go, then turned to the Shaman who stood subserviently at her side. He looked worried, but then, he always looked worried. She grinned up at him. "What's wrong, Looks Into Dreams?"

"You said they were cursed—"

"And they are. But I am stronger than the curse. Don't worry yourself, Shaman. I will handle it."

"Of course," he replied dubiously.

"Do you doubt me? Doubt the Mother?"

"Oh, no," he said, his tone horrified.

"Good. See that you don't." She paused. "I will go to their camp at sundown." Then she left him, to go and make herself ready. After a few steps, another idea struck her. She looked over her shoulder at the Shaman. Her glance made his eyes roll. "Build a great hearth," she said shortly. "And kindle a great fire inside it."

After all, some answers were more satisfying—and more permanent—than others. She would pick the one that suited her best.

And thank the Mother she'd managed to destroy the old Shaman and the Chief before the girl came back. But what could she do now, her and her raggle-taggle band?

Nothing. The Witch smiled. The little children saw it, and ran away crying.

6

"What did you mean, about not bringing the Talisman back to the Green Valley?" Moon Face asked.

The sky to the west, beyond the Big Muddy River, was banded with pink and gold. A single star glittered cold as an emerald in the purple dusk. Rising Sun sat cross-legged before their small hearth, the flames making shadows on his face. Moon Face looked at him; in those shadows he suddenly saw how Rising Sun would appear when he was old. He would be gaunt and lined and terrible. The revelation frightened him even more.

"I didn't mean anything," Rising Sun said.

"But you must have. Why won't you tell me what you're thinking?"

Rising Sun shrugged. "We all have secrets, my friend. Even *you* have secrets, don't you? Have you told me everything?"

The question twisted a screw of guilt deeper into Moon Face's soul. Every time he thought about what Gotha had told him, he squirmed inwardly. But Gotha was old and his thoughts were powerful. Who was an apprentice Shaman to gainsay him?

Yet how could he bring himself to harm Rising Sun? He was the One To Come. Even Gotha, were he here, wouldn't deny *that*. But, of course, Gotha wasn't here. Just his apprentice, charged with duties far beyond any he was capable of.

"I have told you everything," Moon Face whispered. "Why won't you do the same for me?"

Rising Sun reached out and touched Moon Face's shoulder. For a moment he tensed, as if expecting something, but then he relaxed and squeezed gently. "Don't worry, old friend. Everything will work out for the best. I promise."

"When you say that, you sound so sad," Moon Face said miserably.

"There is much sadness in the World," Rising Sun told him. Then, brightening, he said, "But there's no need for sadness now, Moon Face. Relax. We won't be here long. And then we can go back to the Green Valley."

Maybe. But that word he didn't say out loud. Moon Face stared at him a moment longer, then sighed, shrugged, and hitched himself to his feet.

"You promise?" Moon Face said.

"Yes. I promise."

Moon Face turned and, slump-shouldered, shuffled away. Rising Sun raised his head, sensing a cold approach. *Now it begins,* he thought.

He stood and turned to face the darkness beyond the hearth.

7

The Witch thought long and hard before deciding to come alone. On the one hand, a little protection might have been handy—that big warrior, the stranger, had bothered her a bit with his calm, flat stare. But an escort meant witnesses, and she wasn't yet sure what might be said. If the wrong things were spoken of, she didn't want the wrong ears to hear them. She felt reasonably secure in her control of the River Children, but there was no reason to take unnecessary chances, either. In the end, she compromised.

"You stay here, at the edge of the camp," she told Walks Nose Down, who led the small band of hunters gathered around her. "Don't go out of the camp unless I call for you." She looked up at him, her black eyes gleaming. "But if I *do* call, you come running. You understand?"

Walks Nose Down nodded.

"Good. Wait for me." She turned, squared her shoulders, and marched into the dark. The strangers' campfire gleamed softly, a tiny yellow star caught in the earth.

As she walked along the familiar ground, beneath the scudding clouds and the stars, she suddenly felt intensely alive, full of power. It was a great, clean feeling, and it surprised her with its strength. Somehow all the years fell away, and she felt young again, the weight of all the things she'd done—*had to do*—since her childhood magically lifted up and washed away as if the rivers themselves flowed through her veins.

She stopped, her face turned up toward the sky. The Mother was with her, she knew then, filling her up with Her strength, so that nothing in the night could harm her.

She need fear no curses, no weapons, no strangers, not with the limitless Power of the Mother burning in her flesh.

"Ah, yes," she whispered. *"Yes."*

She began to walk again, her steps light and sure. She could make them out, shadows gathered around the small hearth, and a fierce joy came over her. Nothing could stop her, not her awful daughter nor her dull son, nor any wandering pack of strangers. This was *her* place, here where the Two Rivers joined.

So she thought as she stepped into the circle of firelight and stood, arms folded across her chest, her features stern and forbidding. She looked down on them, nodded once, and said, "Now, strangers, tell me why you are here. And if you value your lives at all, speak only the truth to me, for I am the Witch, and this is my place of Power, and I hold you helpless in the palm of my hand." With that, she stretched out of her right hand, and squeezed her fingers together as if crushing something.

She noticed that Carries Two Spears winced as she mimed her little threat, but Sleeps With Spirits said nothing, only looked up at her with calm red eyes.

The Witch locked her gaze with her daughter. "And you, O cursed one. What have you to say for yourself? Speak quickly, now, before I lose my temper!"

But before Sleeps With Spirits could reply, the youth, who had been watching her with a quizzical expression on his face, stood up and faced her. "Hold a moment, Mother," he said softly. "I am the one you have business with, I think."

She stared at him across the bulwark of her breasts, her expression haughty. "And who might you be, young man?"

"I am Rising Sun. I am the One To Come."

"Oh? And what are you to me?" She turned her head, made to spit, then stopped. "These two with you, they are mine, and I will have them back."

But he shook his head and said, "No, you won't. They are mine now, and I will protect them."

Sleeps With Spirits closed her eyes, opened her mouth,

and spoke sonorously, "He is the One To Come. He is the One prophesied. He will inherit the World."

The Witch staggered. She had never once in her life paid the slightest attention to her daughter's ravings. But now each word slammed into her with inexorable force, sharp as a spear, heavy as stones. There was no gainsaying Spirits's words, for she spoke the truth, and the beast's curse had been lifted from her by the One To Come. Yet though the force of her daughter's truth-speaking shocked her profoundly, the Witch managed to bear up. Yes, the youth was the One To Come, whatever that was. And he was the One prophesied, though by whom the Witch didn't know. And he would no doubt inherit the World. But what world? Which? What did it all mean?

These were the questions she clung to, to survive the maelstrom of Sleeps With Spirits's truth-saying. So she staggered but did not fall, and when her daughter lapsed into silence, she curled her lip at her and sniggered.

"Oho, so now you are a mighty prophet. You have changed, my girl. Have you come to seek vengeance on your poor wicked mother?"

But Spirits only shook her head, and would say no more.

The Witch glared at her, then looked back at Rising Sun. "She tells me who you are, but that tells me nothing. She tells me what you will do, but I don't understand it, though I believe it. My heart tells me you are evil. I don't know why you came here, or why you brought them with you. But I have changed my mind. You must leave, or I will have you killed."

The threat seemed to make no impression on any of them, except perhaps for the short, chubby one who crouched near the fire, staring thoughtfully up at her. *That* one, she thought, has something on his mind. As she watched, he scooted back from the hearth, stood, and walked away.

Rising Sun, however, only smiled at her again and said, "We will leave with the dawn light, if that suits you."

She clamped her lips shut. Was he *laughing* at her?

"Yes," she said tightly, "that will do." Then, without another word, she turned and stalked from the camp. Once
beyond the circle of their firelight, though, she slowed her
pace, waiting.

"Mother . . ." the soft voice called.

"Yes?"

"My name is Moon Face. I wish to speak to you."

8

She took him away from the camp, walking carefully
through the darkness. She could see occasional glints of
starlight reflected from his wide, dark eyes. When she
judged they'd gone far enough, she raised her hand and
said, "Stop. Now, what do you want of me?"

The star-glow was just bright enough to illumine his
shadow-shape, though she couldn't read his expression
very well. But she sensed nervousness and fear—his odor
was sharp and acrid, a stink she was familiar with.

She'd been badly shaken by her experience with Rising Sun and Sleeps With Spirits. More than anybody else,
she understood what her daughter's new Power meant. As
brutally ignored as she had been, she would be that much
more listened to now. Listened to, and obeyed. The threat
was intolerable, far worse than if Sleeps With Spirits had
returned only with knowledge of the Witch's plottings.

"You lead?" Moon Face asked.

She debated how to reply. She understood his question
well enough, but was wary of revealing the true extent of
her power. But this one wanted something. Her hunters
were within easy shouting distance. Best to find out what
he wanted. The smell of treachery was in the air, and for
her, the stench was like the aroma of wildflowers.

"Yes. I lead the Children of the River. They will do
what I tell them."

"Ah."

"So what do you want of me, stranger called Moon
Face?"

He hesitated for a moment. "Rising Sun is—you must

kill him, Mother. He is your enemy, and he will kill you if he can. You serve the Mother, don't you?"

"Of course," she snapped.

"Rising Sun says the Great Mother is gone. That She has deserted the World forever. And that he will take Her Place."

"*Blasphemy,*" she hissed. "I will summon my hunters—"

"*No!*"

The cry died in her throat. "Why not?"

"Mother, I am a Shaman. I tell you Rising Sun has great Powers. You cannot kill him, not as he is. A mighty Talisman protects him. You see what he did to your daughter, how he changed her, turned her against you."

From the way his voice quavered, the Witch thought this young Shaman might not be as certain of things as he professed to be. Nevertheless, the sounds he made were music to her ears, for they were a song of treachery. And who knew? There might be truth in his words.

"Well, Shaman Moon Face, if what you say is true, how can I help you? How can anybody help you?"

"I will help myself, and you as well, Mother. It is the Talisman that protects him, that gives him his mighty Powers. He wears it around his neck, resting on his chest. You saw it—the two mammoths?"

Yes, she thought, *I did. A trinket. Could it be true?*

"I saw it," she admitted.

"It is a Talisman that belongs to my People, far to the north of here. He promised to bring it back to them, but I don't think he will. I think a Demon has stolen his soul. But without the Talisman, his Powers will be weak, I think, and you can destroy him. For his, uh, blasphemy."

She knew he lied. Everything he said stank of falsehood. It was plain he had some plan of his own. He was treacherous—but she understood treachery, and how to twist it to her own uses.

She reached out and wrapped one claw around his upper arm and pulled him close. He whimpered softly. "Tell me more," she croaked.

He did.

9

He crept back into their small camp as quietly as he could. The fire was low. Coals popped softly, the sound nearly lost in the rising wind. He shivered. It would snow tonight, or his name wasn't Moon Face.

"Where have you been?" Running Deer asked.

He looked across the hearth and saw her watching him. She lay next to Rising Sun, whose eyes were closed. "I went out to ... relieve myself," he said.

She made no reply, but her blue eye seemed to glow in the dim light. He felt as if that eye could see into his soul, though he knew it couldn't. Already he was regretting what he'd agreed to with the Witch. But it was too late. He had no choice now.

"I'm going to sleep. Good night," he said and wrapped his blanket tightly around him. After a time he heard a soft rustle of movement as she settled down. Later still, he heard her breathing change, become deep and regular. He could tell the difference between the sounds of wakefulness and sleep. Now, he guessed he was the only one still awake, but he continued to wait. Best to be absolutely certain. But in the waiting, he had to cope with his own terrors, and that was nearly his undoing.

In his own way, Moon Face felt he was doing the right thing, the only thing. He had watched Rising Sun change before his eyes, change in ways Gotha had never anticipated. But always the *idea* of the quest had remained uppermost in his own mind—the quest Gotha had described. Go out, find the Talisman, bring it back. Inherit the World? What did that mean? What could it mean but inherit the Green Valley?

Familiarity had bred a curious kind of contempt. He had seen Rising Sun's weaknesses, his youthfulness, his pliancy in the grip of passion. This was no God, nor could he be. His talk of inheriting the entire World was no more than the crazy babbling of a child. He was not fit to bear the Talisman. Moon Face knew it. He had seen the truth.

But still, the Talisman must be returned to its rightful place in the Valley. Gotha had given him permission to do what was necessary to ensure that outcome. Had even given him orders, if it came to that. And he did not allow himself to think that whoever *did* bring back the Talisman must, by the nature of the prophesy, be the One To Come. To think about that would make him feel greasy and selfish. A traitor. But he wasn't a traitor. He was only doing his *duty*.

And so he cuddled that rationalization to his heart, not understanding that it would be used an infinite number of times by an infinite number of good men contemplating selfish evil. Rising Sun might be the first God betrayed by such twistings, but he would not be the last.

He lay in a miserable, huddled lump, trying to pretend sleep, until the stars disappeared and the sky turned black and it began to snow. The drifting flakes hissed when they struck the fading coals. Other than that, only the wind moaned in the empty night.

When he judged the time was right, Moon Face slowly opened his bedroll and crept out. His hand shook uncontrollably as he found the small sharp knife in his pouch and drew it out. Then, as silently as he knew how, he began to make his way around the sleeping ring, until he reached the doubled hump of two bodies. Rising Sun slept on the outside of her, his arm around her waist, spooned close for warmth.

Inch by shaking inch, Moon Face moved closer, until finally he knelt by Rising Sun's head. His own breath mingled with their frosty plumes as he brought the knife to Rising Sun's neck. Carefully he lifted the thong just enough to slip the razored edge beneath. Then he nerved himself for the stroke, just one more moment, until—

"Shaman!"

The bull roar came from across the hearth, from the vast shadow of Raging Bull rising from his sleeping fur, Caribou's great spear clutched in one gnarled fist.

But for one time in his life, Moon Face didn't panic. As Rising Sun twitched in response to the noise, Moon Face jerked the knife through and up, severing the tough leather thong as if it were a blade of grass. Then he was up and running, the swirling snow masking his escape, the Talisman clutched in his hand.

As he ran, he shouted, "Now! I have it! Now is the time!"

Chuckling to herself, the Witch waved the hunters of the River Children forward.

10

They rushed out of the swirling snow like white ghosts, shouting and waving their spears, but within moments their cries of triumph turned to squeals of panic as the hunters in the van charged headlong into the spear of Caribou, wielded by the greatest warrior ever to walk the World. Raging Bison, his eyes pits of fire, sent Walks Nose Down into the Spirit World with a single stroke. His next thrust slashed a throat into bloody ruin, stopping forever a half-shouted battle cry.

But Moon Face's treachery had been thorough. Raging Bison sensed too late the three hunters armed with heavy stones who circled behind him, screened by the wind-whipped white. As he turned to face the new threat, a rock half the size of his head crashed into his temple and he fell.

More hunters poured out of the dark. Without Raging Bison, the battle was hideously one-sided. Carries Two Spears fell beneath a wave of thrashing bodies. Running Deer had barely reached her bow before it was snatched away, and a crushing blow sent stars spinning through her skull.

Rising Sun struggled to his feet and shouted, "Enough. We surrender!"

But they felled him, too, and trussed him like a deer carried home on a pole. Only Sleeps With Spirits remained untouched, because they were afraid to approach her. She bore the curse. She was for the Witch only.

And so at last the Witch came, and looked upon the battlefield, and found it good. "Bring them," she snarled. "Tie them well. Any who lets one escape forfeits his life in the same manner as they will."

Since all the hunters had seen the great fire made ready in the hearth, they shivered at her threat and made doubly certain the bindings were as tight as they could be. But they treated Raging Bison with respect, for he was a mighty warrior—though the same respect made them use extra rawhide thongs knotted twice around his legs and arms.

They bound Rising Sun's arms behind his back, but let him walk as they prodded him with their spear tips. The same for Carries Two Spears, for he had once been their brother. But the Witch took charge of her daughter, seeing to her restraints herself. And before anything else, she tied a sturdy gag across Sleeps With Spirits's lips, so that nothing she said could be understood.

Then they took the prisoners to the hearth and lit the fire. By morning there would be a suitable pile of white-crusted coals. The prisoners sat or lay close, grateful for the heat. Then the Witch gave further orders. Moon Face made no protest at his binding. It was almost as if he expected it. The Witch showed no interest in his trinket, whose cord he knotted so he could wear it around his neck.

They placed him with the others to await the morning, and when that was done, the circle of treachery was complete.

"I'm sorry," he whispered.

Rising Sun looked at him. "I forgive you," he said.

11

The storm was a bad one. Morning showed itself as a gradual brightening in the blinding white sheets of snow. Only the hearth, where the snow couldn't stay, was sharp and clear, though swirls of steam rose from the coal bed, and the coals themselves hissed and snapped.

Rising Sun tried to stretch the kinks out of his shoulders, but his arms were bound too tightly. Moon Face watched him from where the hunters had dumped him, a few paces away.

"Rising Sun?"

"Yes, my friend?"

"I'm sorry. I ruined everything."

"The way of the quest is strange, indeed," Rising Sun told him softly.

Moon Face made a short, sobbing sound. "Gotha charged me with seeing the quest to its end, to making sure you were the One, and bringing the Stone back to the Valley. I didn't know what to do. You seem so odd, so . . . changed. It frightened me."

Rising Sun nodded. "Poor Gotha."

"You forgive him, too?"

"Of course. I knew this would happen. I just didn't know who or how."

Moon Face fell silent, digesting this. "But if you knew, why didn't you stop me?"

Rising Sun smiled faintly. "All things may be chosen now, old friend. That is the meaning of the Gods' departure. We, who are the children of the Gods, are free to choose."

Moon Face thought about it. "Choice is a terrible thing, isn't it?"

"It is the curse and the gift of all men. We are free now." Rising Sun said this, though he knew it wasn't quite true. Not yet. He had his own choice to make.

Shadowy figures began to drift through the snow. They heard muffled voices, and fell silent.

The Witch appeared, pushing Sleeps With Spirits in front of her. The girl seemed unbowed. Her head, with the crude gag still fastened about her jaws, rode her graceful neck proudly. The Witch gave her a vicious shove. She tried to catch her balance, but failed and fell heavily to the ground. The Witch spat.

She looked at them, her black eyes bright with scorn. "When the snow stops," she said ominously. She glanced up, measuring the clouds. "Soon, I think. Make yourselves ready. The Great Mother lusts for your souls. So I will send them to Her."

"The Great Mother is gone from the World," Rising Sun said softly. "So is the Father. We are alone now."

The Witch glared at him. She seemed about to speak, but then shook her head, turned, and stomped away. Carries Two Spears edged himself over to Spirits and whispered, "Are you all right?"

Spirits nodded. They both ignored the tiny cuts that disfigured her cheeks and hands. Evidently the Witch had enjoyed some sport during the dark hours.

People came and went. Children came to gawk, women to shout insults. Every now and then a hunter came to look at Raging Bison. The snow began to lessen, and the wind died down. By noon the air was clear. The clouds overhead began to break up.

When the Witch returned, wearing her finest robe, pale yellow shafts of light illuminated the hearth and the people who began to gather there.

Rising Sun noticed there was no formality to it. The people might have easily been gathering to watch the roasting of a deer. It was not a ritual hallowed by tradition, even murderous tradition. It was only a slaughter, and the Witch the head butcher.

The Witch waited, her arms folded across her chest, until all the Children of the River were gathered around. There was no chanting or praying, no drums, nothing to signify the moment as anything other than ordinary.

Rising Sun tried to sort out what he felt. Mostly, he felt tired. It had been a long journey to reach this squalid end, and the very squalidness increased his exhaustion. Once, he had thought that merely attaining the Talisman would be enough, but now he knew it was only the beginning. He wondered if he would find the strength to do what was necessary. He felt weak and unworthy. He also felt a certain anger that the Gods, those eternal meddlers, had played a final trick even as they departed the World They had made.

And a fine joke it was.

He signed and climbed awkwardly to his feet. The Witch glanced at him. Then, without moving, she spat out her commands.

"Throw them into the fire," she said. "Sleeps With Spirits first—she bears the curse."

"No," Rising Sun said. He walked to the edge of the pit. "I will go first."

The Witch shrugged. "As you like. Throw *him* in, then."

But before the hunters could reach him, Rising Sun smiled, stepped up, and walked to the center of the coals.

"My love!" Running Deer shrieked.

"Master!" Raging Bison boomed.

"Ah, forgive me!" Moon Face moaned.

And the wolf darted through the crowd like a streak of black lightning. Things happened very quickly then.

12

Rising Sun looked down and saw the skin on his feet was blackening and curling. Where it ruptured, a pustulent redness oozed out. The pain was excruciating, but it seemed apart from him, as if it were happening to someone else's body.

I'm burning up, he thought with something akin to wonder.

The smoke that rose around him was rich with the smell of scorching flesh. His own. It made him feel nauseous. But he stood, because he was the One To Come, and he was waiting.

While he waited, he looked beyond the hearth into the horrified eyes of his companions. Running Deer was weeping frantically, and Raging Bison heaving titanically at his bonds. Moon Face crouched on his knees, head down, the Mammoth Stone dangling from his neck. Carries Two Spears had closed his eyes, but Sleeps With Spirits regarded him calmly, even expectantly.

Of course she knew. She had guided him here, hadn't she? She even smiled when the wolf skittered through the mob, scattering them as it arrowed toward Moon Face. Those grinning white jaws snapped once, severing the cord, and the wolf caught the Talisman neatly in its teeth before it could hit the ground. One more bound took it halfway across the coals. The wolf dropped the Stone at Rising Sun's feet and was gone, howling triumphantly.

Rising Sun squatted and thrust his bound wrists deep into the coals. The heat seared flesh and cord alike, so that when he stood again, his binding cords burned through, he held the Talisman in ragged claws disfigured by tatters of charred flesh. Running Deer began to shriek, over and over, at the sight of what had been his hands. Even Sleeps With Spirits, gagged as she was, managed to loose a low, terrible moaning sound.

But the Witch stood implacably, watching him burn, a thin, grim smile playing on her heavy lips. He met her dark gaze with his own. "You think you are a Goddess?" he said. "Very well. Let me show you your domain."

And with that, he let the Stone take him, as it took her, into the Dream that was real, the Dream of the World.

13

"What have you done to me, Demon?" she demanded. She held her hands in front of her face, twisting her fingers into various magical warding signs. He felt the aching familiarity of the place where it had all begun—or ended, depending on the viewpoint, he supposed.

He stood near the edge of the throne space, his back to the empty air, the flat dead sky, the timeless bowl of trees. She faced him, and so couldn't see the two thrones behind her, but he could. They were still empty. Something burned on his chest and he looked down.

The Mammoth Stone, the Twinstone, rested just above his heart. It glowed with an unearthly golden light. She lowered her hands. Her eyes twitched nervously. "Where is this place? What have you done to me?"

He laughed softly. "It is what you wanted, isn't it? To be a Goddess? Well, look"—he pointed—"and see what a Goddess has left behind."

She turned slowly. He watched her freeze, her head tilting back, back as she looked up at the mighty seats.

"I told you They were gone," he murmured. "Those were Their thrones, from which They ordered the World. Would you like to climb up?"

She turned to face him. "This is some trick . . ." She sounded as if somebody had just kicked her in the belly.

He smiled. "I wish it were. But it isn't. Come." He held out his hand.

Her lips moved as if she were working up a glob of spit, but instead she let him take her hand.

"This way," he said, and led her to the left-hand steps. As they climbed, he looked down at her. "This one was Hers," he said.

She glanced up at him, her face set, but said nothing. At the top, he led her over to the seat, helped her to climb up, and then seated himself beside her. The Stone on his chest pulsed and flamed.

He brushed his hand gently across her eyes and felt her stiffen. "Before, you were blind, but now you can see. *Behold the World!*"

Then he waited. After a time, the first seizure took her. It began at the base of her spine and worked its way up, exquisitely cracking each bony knot as it passed, finally shaking her neck until her teeth rattled in her skull. The second spasm was more generalized, ripping tendon from bone in a dozen different places. The third, and final convulsion exploded her heart in her chest, popped tiny arteries in her brain, and broke blood vessels in her eyes, so that the whites turned instantly bloodred.

She slumped bonelessly off the edge of the great seat, then toppled and bumped and rolled down the stairs. What ended up as a crumpled heap at the bottom resembled nothing even remotely human.

Rising Sun sighed. In the end, she'd been lucky. The Truth of the World had only killed her. It could have done much worse. And now, it was time for him to face it.

He stood up on the seat and lifted the Twinstone from his breast. He held it out, and watched its golden flare, while uncountable visions ebbed and flowed within his skull.

Choice.

The throne had destroyed the Witch because she couldn't choose. She could only serve. And the Truth of the throne was simple—there were no Gods left to serve, and so she must choose. But she couldn't, and so she destroyed herself. There was a dreadful, God-like humor in her fate. She had found her support outside herself, and when it was taken away, nothing was left but a flaccid

bag, unable to stand on its own. Her own emptiness had
brought her down.

Choice.

He blinked, and regarded the Stone thoughtfully. The
Stone of many Powers, of many Names. One of those
Names was the Key That Unlocks All Doors.

Through Raging Bison, he had seen the face of a God.
But the God was gone, departed through a door this Key
unlocked. Yet the Key remained in the World, and a part
of the Gods remained in the Key. The Turtle had made
it, and into it he had put something from each of the Powers. Maya was in it, with her Powers of loosing and locking. The Gods were in it, with their Powers both of the
World and the Void. The Turtle Itself, the Uncreated Creating One, was in it also. And Ga-Ya the Mother, and all
the other Mothers, the beasts and the birds, the trees and
the grasses, the mountains and the waters below. The
World was in it.

Choice.

The Key, the Stone, was his, if he wished it. He could
take it and become wholly a God, no different from the
Gods who had gone before. Or he could refuse, and
become—something else.

Sighing, he settled himself on the cold black stone and
looked out on the place of the Gods, here in the stopped
heart of the World.

Time made no move here, yet from here all Time was
visible. He closed his eyes, and once again saw the Last
Mammoth, and the same sadness overtook him now that
had overcome him the first time.

Choice.

Become a God, or choose the way that led inexorably
to the Last Mammoth? If he chose the first, the thrones
would become one throne, and he would sit upon it.
There were no thrones in the second choice, only the endless battle to find the Balance of the World.

With heart-stopping suddenness, the moment came
upon him. Time itself trembled, and the Balance swung
wildly back and forth. *This* was the Test, undreamed of by
Gotha or Moon Face or any other—except the red-eyed
girl who spoke only truth.

In that terrible moment he saw it all, with a clarity so bright and awful he could hardly bear it. He had tried to explain to Raging Bison about the Old Gods and their indifference to human fate. Just as he had tried to show Moon Face the terrible weight of the gift of freedom that the Gods had bestowed in their departure.

On the one hand, the temptation of the thrones, and the endless Power that came with them. On the other, the Power of a different kind that came with choice. It was in his hands to make the World free and dangerous, or enslaved and safe forever.

"Ahh!" he groaned. *"Why me?"*

But even on the thrones of the Gods there was no answer to that, and so, with the Vision of the Last Mammoth burning in his soul, Rising Sun let out a mighty shout and threw the Key into the dead, waiting sky.

As he stood and watched it rise, higher and higher, he whispered to himself, "I pass the Test. I will not be a God, nor will this Stone tempt the World any longer. I am the One To Come, and I have come here!"

With those words, the Twinstone burst into mighty golden flames, rising, ever rising, until its light illuminated the place where once the light of the Gods had blazed.

He felt a shifting and rumbling beneath him, and looked down to see the throne on which he stood begin to crack and shatter.

Choice.

I have chosen the Last Mammoth. And there are no Gods left in the World to forgive me.

He wept as he came down from the steps, the rock behind him dissolving into dust. At the bottom, she waited for him, her crimson eyes burning with love, she whom he'd first seen, and somehow known, as a tiny, fleeting figure in this place.

"Behold the One To Come, who is mighty in the World forever more!"

It was a true prophesy, but he only smiled tiredly, took her hand, and said, "Bring me home, my dear. Take me back to the World, for I will never return here again."

And so she did, while overhead, the new-risen sun, the

Stone at the heart of the World, burned a great beacon in the eternal sky. He heard the faraway sound of birds, singing in the great bowl of the forest below.

Nothing had ever lived here before. Nor had anything ever died here. But now the Balance had come even to this place.

He had made his Choice.

The Gift of the Stone had been offered—and refused. Thus ended the Test of the One To Come, who had been promised in the Dawn of the World.

CHAPTER TWENTY-TWO

1

Running Deer watched it all with a frozen heart. She knew everything had changed. Maybe too much. She screamed when he plunged his hands into the smoking coals. She uttered a short, barking cry when the Witch suddenly threw her hands up and collapsed backward. From the way the older woman fell—straight down, boneless—Running Deer knew she was dead. So did the Children of the River, for a long, low sighing sound echoed through their ranks. For one small moment she thought she saw something smoky and beastlike and terrible crouching over the fallen woman, but she blinked and it vanished.

She watched Rising Sun raise the Mammoth Stone up. It was so bright she had to squint to make him out in the glare it cast. Then he let out a great shout. The sound was so loud she thought the earth had begun to shake. It startled her into closing her eyes entirely. When she opened them again, something intolerably brilliant was rising rapidly into the sky. Up and up it went, until finally the blaze of it mingled with the sun, and disappeared into it.

"Sunrise," she said to no one in particular.

When she looked back at Rising Sun, he was walking across the coals, his hands held in front of him. There was nothing wrong with his hands now. They were entirely healed, as if the terrible wounds she'd seen before had never happened at all. That was when she realized the coals had turned into harmless dry ash. He strode through them. His steps raised tiny puffs of gray dust. He came out of the dead fire and paused next to the Witch's broken corpse. He shook his head and sighed.

She wanted only to run to him, take him in her arms, comfort him. His face looked drawn and raddled, and at the same time somehow radiant. It did not look like the face she remembered. It was old and young at the same time, and terribly sad. But she couldn't move. So she stood, and waited, and wondered who he would go to first. Her, or the red-eyed woman?

He did neither. Instead, he squatted down to greet the wolf who came bounding up to him. He patted the animal on the head and said clearly, "I name you Friend of the People. You and all yours that come after shall walk beside men, and love them."

Then he stood, turned, and nodded at Sleeps With Spirits. She stood tall and straight, the rubies of her eyes smoldering with truth.

"This is the One To Come, who was promised," she cried out. "The Test is done. The World and all within it have been given into his keeping. Now he gives the World to you, for the Gods are gone forever!"

And the power of her Speaking was so great that all over the World, in places both far and near, those who could hear her in their souls raised their heads and knew the World had changed.

When she finished her Speaking, Sleeps With Spirits knelt by the body of her mother and soothed shut those staring eyes. "I will take care of her now," she said, "for she has suffered enough."

Rising Sun touched her shoulder gently and nodded. "That is good," he said. Then, finally, he turned to the place where Running Deer stood. He smiled, walked over, and took her in his arms.

Her paralysis fell away. He looked down at her and said, "I passed the Test, Running Deer. Some part of me is yet a man. Can you love that part?"

And she could.

2

They walked through the storms of winter, but none of the white winds touched them. At night, Rising Sun slept next to Running Deer. His passions seemed unchanged to her, though at times, after they were done, he would hold her tightly and whisper over and over, *"Help me, Running Deer. You must help me."*

When that happened, she would press close to him and say, "I will help you, my love. Anything I can do, just tell me."

But he would fall silent, and sometimes she would feel his tears hot and wet on her cheek.

When they finally came up from the river to begin the last passage across the frozen steppe to the Green Valley, he called Moon Face to him. The little apprentice Shaman, who had been strangely silent, came and stood before him.

"Yes, Master?" he said.

"I am not Master," Rising Sun told him. "I am the Keeper. The Balance is in my hands, but I'm not Master. I renounced that when I refused the Gift."

Moon Face was unsure what Rising Sun was talking about, but he was sure about one thing. He had betrayed him, whether he called himself Master or Keeper, and there would have to be a reckoning.

Rising Sun seemed to sense these thoughts. He took his companion by the arm and led him several paces away from the rest of the band.

"We will come back to the Green Valley soon. And I don't bear the Talisman. What do you say to that?"

Moon Face shifted uncomfortably. "You threw it away. It burned up. I saw it."

"Then, am I the One To Come or not?" Rising Sun asked softly.

"I betrayed you," Moon Face said.

"That's no answer."

Moon Face looked up at him, his features twisted in agony. "It's all the answer I *have!*"

Rising Sun put one hand on each of Moon Face's shoulders. "Then I will give you another, my apprentice."

With that, the door between them opened, and all of Moon Face's thoughts and memories mingled with Rising Sun's thoughts and memories. For what seemed an eternity Moon Face experienced all that had shaped the One To Come, and in the end, he too saw the Last Mammoth.

Rising Sun dropped his hands. "Well?" he said.

Moon Face sank to his knees. "I didn't know," he said. "Can you ever forgive me?"

Rising Sun lifted him up. "I did long ago, Moon Face. And I name you Shaman, apprentice no longer, for you are my Shaman now. Can you forgive *me*?"

Slowly Moon Face nodded. "Yes," he whispered. "I can. I do."

"Thank you, my old friend."

Then the strange band trekked across the steppe until they stood at the mouth of the Green Valley, where many things had begun, and many things had ended. Rising Sun paused there for a time. "Wait here," he told them.

He found the place where she had said her final farewells to the Valley, knelt down, and brushed away the snow from the spot. In the eye of his mind he could see her there still, tall and straight and proud, her multicolored eyes glinting with eternal Light.

"Thank you, O Great One," he said, "for showing me the Way."

It seemed to him that her Spirit heard this, and smiled. Then it was gone, and he knew that the last part of Maya had also left the World forever.

He came back and led them up the path.

3

The seasons had not been kind to the Shaman Gotha. Moon Face gasped inwardly when he saw his old mentor so terribly changed. Always slender, now Gotha looked starved, the rack of his jawbone sharp and hungry, his cheeks sunken. His bloodshot eyes were muddy with exhaustion, and his once-white hair, now dirty and yellow, had thinned to reveal a brown-spotted pate.

He met them alone, near the end of Second Lake, before they reached the New Camp. The day was gray and cold. He stood wrapped in thick black furs and raised his hand in greeting.

"Ho, travelers, I bid you a welcome return." His voice was thick and rusty, and even those few words seemed to snatch his breath.

Rising Sun walked up to him, took him in his arms, and said, "Mighty Shaman, greetings. I have come back to you, as I promised."

Gotha stepped back and looked at him. "Perhaps too late, Rising Sun. While you were gone, the Dead of Winter returned."

"I know," Rising Sun said. "It is why I have come."

"Ah! You brought the Talisman, then?"

Rising Sun shook his head slowly. "You know I haven't."

Gotha seemed unsurprised by this. "Yes, I had Dreamed ... but I had hoped my Dreams weren't true." He glanced at Moon Face. "So you aren't the One To Come?"

Sleeps With Spirits, who was near, said softly, "He is the One to Come. He is the Sun rising over the World, and he is the Balance of the World."

But Gotha, alone of all men, was proof against her Speaking. He looked at Rising Sun and said, "Are you?"

Rising Sun spread his cloak for a moment and showed Gotha his bare chest. There, above his heart, a ghostly light gleamed beneath his flesh: the soul of the Twinstone, the faintest memory of what had been transformed in the making of a new World. Then Gotha believed, and smiled, and opened his arms to Rising Sun. "Will you save us?"

Rising Sun nodded gravely. "What is left, I will save." He paused. "My parents, the Moon and the Star?"

Gotha looked away. "Dead," he said.

Rising Sun stared at him a moment, then sighed. "I knew it, Shaman. But I wanted to hear. The old things are vanishing as the new things come into the World."

Gotha shrugged. "I am very old."

Rising Sun understood what he meant, and embraced him again. "Do not fear, Shaman. Choice is its own reward, and you made your choices. Be glad." And under the touch of Rising Sun's hands, the Shaman felt himself grow strong again, and when he led them into the heart of the Valley, his back was straight and his eyes were clear.

Then Rising Sun went among the People of the Three Tribes and healed those who were sick, and blessed those who had died, and freed their Spirits to leave the World. And wherever he found the beast, he vanquished it.

When spring came at last, only two fingers' worth of two hands of each Tribe remained alive, but those who had survived were all well and strong. Then, with the pale green shoots of grass beginning to mark the rolling steppe once again, Rising Sun called all the People together and divided them into groups.

"You, Raging Bison, will lead one. And you, Moon Face, another. And I will lead yet a third. For the time has come at last for the People to go out into the World. The Green Valley sheltered us for a time, but that time has passed. The World calls to us, and we must answer."

So great was Rising Sun's Power that no one questioned this, but instead gathered up their belongings and made ready for the endless journeys to come.

One by one, each band departed, until finally only the few that Rising Sun had selected remained. He led them to the mouth of the Valley, and watched as they marched out, leaving only silence behind. Then he stood between the two women, for he had a final choice to make.

He closed his eyes and once again the Vision took him. He stood in a high place beyond the World, looking out, and saw the strings of Time arrayed before him, and saw that each string depended on a choice. This eternal weaving stretched back into the single strand of the Void, and forward into a time he could barely understand, into a World filled with houses large as mountains, and more people than grains of sand, and frantic, rushing change. But that was far away. Closer was something else, the threads of Time that extended from his own choice.

The World hung suspended, dark and silent. Across

the great lands marched long lines of light, each line made up of glowing dots. He knew each dot was human, each glow a soul capable of choice.

Those thin lines moved down the World, and where they passed, nothing remained of the greatest beasts, the mammoths. This march took only a short time, as the World numbered such things. Less than a thousand full turns of the seasons to complete the great slaughter. And at the end of it, far away to the south, the Last Mammoth trumpeted her despair as she died beneath human spears. So short a time, so great a tragedy. As a God, he could have prevented it. But had he so chosen, then man would never know his greatest gift, his most poignant curse.

For the Balance of the World was in the choosing, and the weights of the Balance made their own harsh judgments. To him was given the first True Choice, free of all the Gods. And in his own choice, he'd given to men the right to choose.

But he bore the blood of those noble and mighty beasts, and all the others who might so succumb, now and forevermore.

Once again he watched the great beast fall, and once again he whispered to himself, "Can you forgive me, Mother?"

But the beast still died, and he knew he would never hear Her answer. He opened his eyes and looked at the two women. "You wish me to choose between you," he said softly. "But there is no need."

He pulled Running Deer close. "I am a man," he told her. "Love the man."

She nodded, and chose, and put her arms around him.

He turned to Sleeps With Spirits, whose eyes shone like fresh blood. "And I am more than a man. I am the Balance. Worship the Balance."

She knelt, and chose, and bowed to him, and worshiped. So did the One To Come resolve the dilemma of his love, and the love of the World for him; for in this matter of Choice, his very existence affirmed that each of his children was forever free to Choose, even—and especially—unto the shape and vision of he himself.

4

Thus ends the long tale of the Two Stones, their Keepers and the Talisman Rejoined, the Departure of the Gods from the World, the Last Mammoth, the Rising of the Sun and with him the Balance of the World. The tale after is a human one. It is still being written; for the gift of Choice is with us yet, even to this day.

San Francisco
1991–93

THE PEOPLE OF THE MAMMOTH

have wandered the world for thousands of years,
surviving starvation, plague, and predators,
fleeing the ever encroaching ice, following
the mammoth herds for life and sustenance.
Finally they come to a place of prophecy where twin
children are born to the People of the Mammoth:
Wolf, who would grow to be a mighty warrior,
and Maya, whom some call an Evil Spirit
because she has the mark of the Great Mother—
one eye of blue and one of green. This is
the sign of She who is born to wield the Mammoth
Stone, an ancient and mystical talisman
bearing both a promise and a curse. And thus great
events and remarkable people are
set in motion as Maya, the once outcast child,
learns the Stone's powers and secrets . . . as she
chooses a brave and passionate mate and
goes with him into the endless plains . . . and
as she embarks on a great adventure of
terrible beauty, leading her people through
the timeless wonders and perils of
the thrilling new world.

THE GREAT MAGIC

Maya was born to be keeper of the Mammoth
Stone, the age-old talisman believed to protect the
People of the Mammoth in their struggle for survival
in the vastness of the prehistoric American West.
But now another woman had taken her place, and
Maya was in exile with the mighty hunter who
loved her, Black Caribou.

Then her most fearful dreams of prophecy came to
pass. Two brutal warriors with an injured youth as
captive took her prisoner as well, to use for their
pleasure and to torture. But they did not suspect
what Maya learned about the captive boy and
his secret possession. He, like Maya, had one
blue eye and one green. He, like Maya, was keeper
of a stone—a stone that was the match and mate
of the Mammoth Stone.

Now Maya was sure that they had to come
together—no matter what odds she had to
overcome. And she trembled to imagine what might
happen when the mightiest magic of all burst like a
flaming dawn across the land. . . .

KEEPER OF THE STONE

GREEN KNIGHT, RED MOURNING

by RICHARD E. OGDEN

ZEBRA BOOKS
KENSINGTON PUBLISHING CORP.

ZEBRA BOOKS

are published by

Kensington Publishing Corp.
475 Park Avenue South
New York, NY 10016

First printing: July 1985

Printed in the United States of America

Dedicated to the 2.8 million Americans who served in Vietnam.

Be proud; it wasn't your mistake. With the social consciousness concerning humanity that was prevalent in the sixties and seventies, any war for any reason, justifiable or not, would have been unconscionable . . . Our country was not proud of itself; therefore it was unwilling, if not crippled, in showing us any pride or compassion . . . Be proud you served and grateful you survived. You know more about life than anyone else around you.

A special thank you to Beth, who pushed and insisted that I read; to Patricia Chapman, who insisted that I write; to Maureen Wilkinson, Greg Hill, Jane Stewart and Martin George; and to my parents, Dell and Jack, who gave me the courage and will to survive in a "rough" world; to J.A.S., and to the great John D. McDonald.

R.E.O.

CHAPTER ONE

The company commander was a tall, lean Naval Academy graduate from Austin, Texas, who spoke with a soft twang influenced most of the time by a wad of chewing tobacco.

"I regret I can't wish you boys a good morning. Your squad leaders informed you earlier this morning that our listening post was hit last night, and as a result we have two dead Marines; two KIAs. As I see it, one of them killed the other."

Confusion and anxiety rushed up and down the ranks. A small Marine at the end of the first rank raised his hand and was called on.

"Sir, how was it possible? They were buddies, the best of friends."

"We all know that, don't we?" the captain answered. "One of them killed the other just as though he pulled a K-Bar and sliced his throat where he slept."

His voice and temperament changed back and forth

radically with each sentence like an evangelist at the pulpit. His young tanned skin stretched over high cheekbones and a wide jaw. He had piercing brown eyes accented by a dark, thin brush of eyebrows that revealed perhaps a drop or two of Indian blood. He scanned every member of the congregation and looked each of them right in the eye—the juvenile delinquents, the honor students, the junior high school dropouts, the choirboys, the muggers, the cowards, the Blacks, the Chicanos, the Orientals, the Marxists, the Catholics, the Jews, the leaders, and the shitbirds. The cross section of his company was a cross section of every Marine outfit.

"Either Edwards or Holmes was supposed to be awake on watch but went to sleep, allowing the Vietcong to get to them. Their remains were found at the listening post. The enemy was not only giving us an object lesson on what happens to the man who goes to sleep on watch, but something far more reaching. Something that can destroy everything we've learned in training: courage and morale. If we allow them to tamper with our brains and souls, we will be ineffective in our role here. I am going to use this incident as an object lesson of my own, since we've already paid a heavy price for it. We are new here in Vietnam, and things are much different than we expected. I know most of you are barely out of Algebra One and Two, figuratively speaking. We've made mistakes, but we'll learn. Your job is to engage and destroy the enemy, and my job is to keep you alive. It's also my job to write your mother and tell her you won't be coming home. My primary purpose right now is to impress upon you that we are in the middle of a real war. The enemy means business, and so do we. Thanks to the Vietcong last night, I think I've found the ultimate solution. I guarantee no one will fall asleep on watch or take their duties lightly after what you experience this morning."

Each squad filed off from the formation and followed the captain around to the rear of the CP tent. No one spoke. The seriousness of the situation began to penetrate and register on their faces.

Two corpsmen (medics) stood solemnly, adjacent to a large mound lying on a canvas covered with a shelter half. The perimeter of the exposed canvas was saturated with blood. Tiny drops of blood slowly dripped off onto the ground, refusing to be absorbed by the fine dust, and formed tiny wine-colored beads of perfect symmetry that rolled across the powder into the giant crater of a nearby footprint.

The sight and the metallic, pungent odor of human blood was already changing the color and the stomachs of the onlooking troops. The corpsmen pulled back the bloody shroud and dropped it in the dust. A synchronized gasp of horror and a spontaneous rush of nausea swept the paralyzed, captive audience. Some immediately turned away, pushing through the crowd to hide their weakness and embarrassment, while others in the rear pushed forward to see what was creating the fervor. Most held their ground and stared, immobilized, in shock.

Somehow the bodies of the two Marines had been meshed together, integrated into one single mound of horrifying flesh and bone as if they had been quartered and dropped into a blender with the setting on "coarse chop." It was first thought by the corpsmen that the heads had been severed and were missing; but after closer examination, they discovered the presence of broken teeth and fragments of jawbone. The skulls had been smashed and pulverized. The eyes had been extracted intact and were scattered on top of the mound. They stared out in all directions, one set blue and the other brown, giving the hideous mass a lifelike appearance, as if it could slide off the canvas in any direction, either to escape or to attack. The large bones of the bodies—the femures, tibias, and pelvises—were completely filleted of flesh, cracked and pulled apart, revealing the bone marrow. The hearts, livers, and genitals were left intact and were on display.

"What madness compels a human to such diabolical butchery? What is its disguise—survival, politics, religion?" the captain reflected.

The sick and shocked did not hear him, lost momentarily in the horror and the confusion of the incident. There was the irony surrounding the two casualties, even in contemporary times of diminished social unrest. They were unique only for the reason that they had been very good friends and they had inadvertently killed one another. They would be buried together, but in separate places; one box in New Mexico and the other in Michigan; one black and the other white.

A small white-faced Marine sagged on an ammo box against a tree. He hung his head and wiped the slime of an erupted breakfast off his lapel with a handful of grass.

The corpsman kneeled down. "You all right, pardner?"

"No, I'm not all right. I'm not going to be sick any more, but I don't think I can handle it. I mean this war, this place . . ."

"You'll be all right. We all will. I think the captain was right in showing us the bodies. I'm sure it was a hard decision. He wanted to impress upon all of us the fact that this isn't another training maneuver or war game. It didn't seem like a war was going on here in this lush, beautiful community. Last night proved there is."

"Doc, you're older and you know a lot. What kind of a human or animal stalks around here and can do something like this?"

"I know it's hard to believe. They're men like you and me, with families and dreams."

The little one stood up in a rage. "You're out of your goddamn mind. You're crazy!" He stomped away.

Doc sat down on the ammo box, rested his elbows on his knees, chin in hand, and looked after the pathetic little Marine. He mumbled into his folded hands: "The Vietnam War welcomes you to Algebra One and Two."

The early rise of the demon sun had not yet sucked the much-relished residual moisture from the air or devoured the pleasantness of the morning. The silence of mourning replaced the symphony of crickets, frogs, and beautiful, nocturnal feathered spirits that haunt the night.

Defensive positions are the same in every war. Through the centuries the materials change; sandbags replace logs and stones, the strains of concertina wire replace thorn bushes. But the trench lines are the same, the men are the same, and the reasons are the same.

CHAPTER TWO

On November 10, 1945, in the tiny seacoast town of Bellingham in northwest Washington, another unimportant statistic was recorded.

I always envied the few kids I knew who were born on Halloween. It was a special, if not classic, date. I missed it by eleven days. I had mixed emotions regarding the irony surrounding my own shred of uniqueness. Due to my introversion—which is a kinder word for just plain backwardness—and the Marine Corps' intense passion for celebration, I was ready to keep my secret under wraps forever. I was born on the 170th birthday of the Marine Corps.

We were a divorced family living in North Seattle when I was four years old. A combination of prolonged months of commercial fishing in Alaskan waters and other phantom jobs, plus the peculiarities of temperament between the older city-wise man and the younger backwoods woman frayed the fabric of family unity beyond repair. My mother remarried, and a desperate plan was put into motion. We decided to load up the Model A Ford with kin and courage and flee to the country, away from the ghetto of auto courts, rats, bedbugs, and unscrupulous landlords.

The change of worlds was exciting. Our tiny parcel of land at the end of a very long gravel road left us in the middle of nowhere. The land was lush, clean, and green. It was thickly carpeted with fern and well-guarded with thick, heavy alders. There were so many things for a four-year-old to explore, uproot, chew on, and get lost in, it was mind-boggling. We lived in a tent until our poor excuse of a house was built. It was a two-room, tar-paper shack constructed of used lumber collected from a construction job where my stepdad worked; someone's old barn was transformed into our little house at the end of the road. Laura Ingalls Wilder would have been delighted. The rats and bedbugs we left behind in Seattle would pass in review and weep for us.

My mother was seven months pregnant but insisted on climbing up to the roof to help finish laying it down before the winter weather came. We planted an enormous garden filled with anything that could be grown and consumed. Nearly everything grown, foraged, or hunted was canned in preparation for the long cold winter. There were plenty of deer, pheasants, and grouse in the surrounding woods. The population of our modest farm seemed to grow daily with chickens, ducks, turkeys, and rabbits. Pens, hutches, and coops sprang like a zoological ghetto to keep them from the garden. The work load increased when frost began to lay on the hardiest of garden vegetables, the pumpkin. My chores included anything I could be trained to do at such a young age. I carried wood to the house or fetched water from the nearby creek under close supervision. I never fell in or got wet . . . much.

The first year, the little house was without lights, water, or a sewer. Before sundown, coal-oil lanterns were lit. When the winter of 1950 finally came, it was the worst in years. The tar-paper mansion held up remarkably well against the driving blizzards. It offered very little resistance; the wind whipped through the knotholes and cracks. The tar paper was expensive; we substituted cardboard for insulation. My brother and I slept in cardboard boxes lined with newspapers. Below us, under the floorboards, huddled the hounds and other livestock. Baby turkeys and newborn chicks were brought into the house and put in a makeshift brooder next to the wood stove. Turkeys were very hard to raise in their early stages; they died easily in the slightest draft, but when they were grown, they could sit in the trees in the wintertime during a blizzard without a problem. For years to come, in the winter months there was always someone in the intensive-care ward next to the stove.

Our most insufferable, uncelebrated convenience was the very little house at the end of the road without its folklore mail-order catalog. My most unsavory memory of it was when I accidentally dropped a flashlight down the hole and was ordered to retrieve it. Never underestimate the genius of a six-year-old.

When my brother and I were older, we converted the chicken coop into a bunkhouse. We were delighted with it. We had our own place, and the chickens didn't seem to mind; they weren't giving up much. We didn't realize until we started school that we were going to be subjected to a different kind of burden. Not everyone seemed wealthy, but we were below the poverty-line poor. We went barefoot all summer so there would be money for boots in the winter. We were treated like we had some kind of scourge, or leprosy. We did not understand.

I was an educational contradiction. I was a poor student, but never missed a day of school. I excelled in the classes that consumed my interest, like music and art, and failed at those I found boring, which I later regretted. I needed school for its social life. It was still limited, but it was a diversion from the hard, never-ending chores on the farm. I had grown to hate the chores, the poor excuse for a home, and everything else. I had little reward other than something to eat and a place to sleep.

I enjoyed sports, even though I was too small to be very competitive. I was overjoyed to suit up, sit on the bench, and be a part of the fraternity. The little things pleased me, but the chores and the family's lack of understanding intervened.

By the time I was sixteen, the confrontations with my mother had become more frequent and more intense, almost to the point of violence; she was tiny, endurably strong, and very stubborn, and I was getting more and more frustrated. My stepdad understood my problems;

I guess he understood all our problems. He tried to keep the peace and to mediate the best he could. One day at the highest point of my restlessness and frustration, I was surprised when my mother agreed I should enlist. I chose the Marine Corps because I liked their song.

CHAPTER THREE

At 10:00 A.M., April 10, 1965, with a command from the bridge, Second Battalion, Third Marine Division, climbed over the side of the four-story-high assault ship. We headed down the debarkation nets that went taut and slack with each roll of the great ship. The nets stretched to the waiting landing craft hugged against the ship like debris, bouncing and straining against the tide and the breeze.

It was a bright sunny morning. The sea was more black than blue, accented with wind-lashed whitecaps. We hung three abreast in mid-air in the net. We looked down at the tiny buffeted target on the surface and waited for the net to go taut with the next roll of the ship. We scrambled down like spiders clinging to a communal web under siege, refusing to be popped off by the increased gusts of wind or washed off by the sea now beginning to dash up between the hull of the ship and the LCPs. We were carrying about forty pounds of gear each. Men had fallen off in training and had been crushed under milder circumstances.

Grinning Charlie, to my right, was still grinning, and Red, to my left, was expressionless. He licked the salt from his cheeks, waiting for another wave. One of the secrets to getting down safely was staying abreast to balance out the net and not letting anyone get ahead of the others. At the right time, I gave the signal. We scrambled down the rest of the way. When the landing craft was considered full we were jammed in tight, life jacket to life jacket. It was like any other training maneuver we had endured hundreds of times before, but the three bold letters of WAR stood out in a gray haze on the bulletin board of my mind, which was already cluttered with diesel exhaust fumes and the oncoming twinges of seasickness. One of the reasons I joined the Corps was to stay out of the Navy, because I was chronically seasick every time we went fishing as a kid. I did not know the Marine Corps was part of the Navy—the worst part!

Before we made the long haul from San Diego to Yokohama, I had been a reasonably respected and trusted leader. I was the smallest and the youngest at seventeen. I was doing well until seasickness dropped me to my knees and I became almost totally delirious for the entire trip. I was incapable of taking care of myself, let alone commanding a fire team. Members of the fire team had to carry me back and forth from cot to chow. Left under a ladder or stairwell during the day, I sometimes lay in my own puke, unable to get to the rail. I couldn't go below and lie in the cots during the day. I was in a minor running conflict with two of the squad leaders of the platoon. Now that I was incapacitated, they were unforgiving. I was relieved of my fire team.

At one point, it seemed I had recovered; I had developed stronger, though still less than adequate, sea legs. On a fire watch down in one of the compartments in violent seas, I had a relapse and passed out where a seabag and some valuable equipment, including a rifle, were stolen. I nearly got into a fight with one of the squad leaders when he kept calling me a shitbird during the investigation. I told him what he could do with himself in very explicit language. It even startled me, the believer, who carried a small New Testament tucked away in the web of my helmet. My whole world was falling apart. I was found guilty of dereliction of duty at an Office Hours proceeding. I wasn't busted since I had an unblemished service record, but I spent a week in the hot filthy bilges stripping paint. It was a less-than-adequate remedial exercise for seasickness.

Everything I had worked for in the last couple of years was shot away. I'd always felt that the self-confidence I painstakingly laminated together was like tiny shreds of courage the thickness of veneer. No matter how small the triumphs were, I was building something . . . somebody I wanted to be . . . someone I could have more pride in. But from then on, the troops reacted a little differently around me—not cold, but cool. My own fire team was less than warm, and when snide remarks surfaced from others behind my back like platoon pussy, a dissident, and a shitbird, I didn't blame the team. My reputation was at its lowest ebb. Grinning Charlie was the exception. He patted me on the back reassuringly.

"Don't let them kid you. Those assholes are just as fucking scared as anybody!" He was one of the older privates in the platoon, and elected to remain a private.

We continued to circle in a wide berth around the mother ship, waiting for the entire battalion to debark, join up, organize, and assault the beach in waves. I doubt if anyone got any sleep the night before. Most of the troops lay around in their racks, quiet and sullen, thinking and wondering. Others, not thinking or contemplating any less, showed more exuberance by burning up nervous tension sharpening and re-sharpening bayonets and shaving each other in tests of their ability. They stripped down weapons, reassembled them time and time again, polished rounds of ammo, counted hand grenades, and many tried to get more than the regular allotment of ammunition and hand grenades. No one seemed to be afraid of what could happen tomorrow. They were high on anxiety and excitement, like Olympians eager to be tested after years of bone-crushing agony in training, sacrifice, and discipline.

We had been living literally on top of each other in the hold of the ship for nearly a month. Racks or bunks were stacked eight high. Heavy seas, undue harassment by Naval Personnel, bad food, endless drills, endless inspections, rough seas, seasickness, and more rough seas caused nerves and tempers to fray to their last thread. Everyone was more than ready, and God help anyone who opposed us on the beach. Even after lights-out the locker-room antics continued, with self-confirmed cowards listening to self-confirmed heroes brag about how psychotic and volatile they were going to be tomorrow. I lay in my rack with two darning needles in my wooly brain busily working on all the tangled fabric, trying to construct some kind of an emotional pattern. But when some of the more arduous knots and confused snarls were worked free, a chilling thought would tug on the strands, seizing them up again. The thought of killing someone terrified the hell out of me.

The lip of the monster popped. Its great jaw slammed down to the white, hot Vietnamese beach and spewed out hundreds of green, screaming and yelling moronic organisms programmed and primed for trouble. With the race of diesel engines, the traditional primal cry of an attack battalion, the momentary confusion of finding one's prospective unit and getting into proper order on line, to advance on a single command was nearly impossible. A mile-long line of men at five-yard intervals can advance inland in a matter of seconds if unopposed. Unless someone fell, there was no way to tell if we were drawing hostile fire.

We came ashore several miles north of Danang in the area technically known as Red Beach, characterized by white sand dunes and scrub pine trees, and intense heat. The surrounding area was referred to as the I Corps; Elephant Valley to the indigents, and Phu

Young Province to the map makers of old. All this information we were painstakingly supplied with didn't mean a damn thing. We, the subordinates, were lost any time we left the ship in any country.

We lay in our firing positions at the crest of the searing hot sand dunes competing for lungs full of almost-useless hot air. From time to time we caught our breath. The awesome gripping sound of absolutely nothing grabbed one's head as though it were trapped in the clutches of a fist. We were told we could expect a "hot" beach in the military sense of the word (bullets). Sweat dripped into the mechanisms of our immaculate, freshly oiled weapons, safeties off and fingers laid heavy on the triggers, while blood pounded back and forth from one ear to the other. Salt-irritated eyes scanned the lower sand dunes; shrubbery danced like a fantasy in the intenseness of the heat waves—and after long agonizing minutes of nothing but silence, the slow, withdrawing relief from the intense pressure was frustrating and demoralizing. It was like being the victim of an unfunny hoax. Would we have been elated had there been machine guns waiting for us? Fear is healthy and stimulating, but risking your life looking for trouble is not.

Silence was broken somewhere down the line like a rock shattering a window pane.

"I see something."

The needles in the built-in human survival mechanism jumped back to red again; pivoting eyeballs locked up; the entire respiratory system froze. Without the slightest warning the wind began to blow, carrying sand and creating a foglike mist over the ground. Nothing could be trusted, animate or inanimate, with the combination of blowing sand and heat waves. Everything danced. Without taking my eyes from the front, I popped open the breech of the M-79 and felt for the butt end of the shell, like I had done so many times before, to make sure I hadn't forgotten to put in a shell. I had inherited the M-79 grenade launcher from Morales, who had taken over my fire team. I was almost totally unfamiliar with it. It resembled the twenty-millimeter sawed-off shotgun, and looked similar to a tear-gas gun. It throws out a shell three hundred meters with the explosiveness of a hand grenade. It gives a man one hell of a throwing arm.

A small, dark, squiggling mass appeared on the crest of a sand dune about three hundred yards away. It grew to be the unstable outline of a man, then another, and another. The enemy was advancing down the barrels of the entire battalion. A battalion-sized ambush in broad daylight in open terrain was hard to believe. Speculations and explanations began to filter up and down the line. "It must be a Bonsai attack!" More figures appeared over the horizon. They were growing into a small mob heading in a straight line toward Hotel Company and our platoon. They opened up with machine guns! . . . No! It was the turbo engine on a chopper gunship flying in the background. The mob kept growing bigger and getting closer. The word was passed down the line to hold our fire. Every rifleman and machine-gun crew had a single individual as a target. I kept re-estimating the range and re-adjusting the rear sights. Again, the word came down to hold our fire. They were about two hundred yards away. There were three dozen in a very loose group about platoon size. They didn't seem to be very disciplined, and didn't practice the five-yard interval between each man. A good-sized mortar neatly placed would nearly wipe them out. Once more the word was passed. The tiny nerves under my left eye began to twitch. My hands began to shake. I looked around to see if anyone was watching me. Grinning Charlie had no grin for the first time since I'd known him. Trudeau, the squad leader, was breathing heavy with clenched teeth and open mouth. Red blinked hard and frequently to keep salt-filled perspiration from burning his eyes.

"It's the press corps!"

Immediately the machine guns they carried on their shoulders began to look more like cameras, and the mortar baseplates and ammo boxes began to look more like sound equipment. There wasn't a weapon among the whole group. We remained rigid in our firing positions, exhausted and dumbfounded. It was literally an invasion of the press. They greeted us with smiles and hellos. The logos on the cameras read ABC, CBS, and NBC. The assault on Red Beach had turned into a television special!

"Where's the war, for crissakes?" a Marine yelled.

"Walter Crankcase here?"

"I thought I saw Huntley and Brinkley over there somewhere, and Mike Wallace, too!"

"It's not Wallace, but it looks like Roger Mudd!"

"I prefer Eric Sevareid, myself!"

"Shut up, you guys," Trudeau yelled. "Stay in your positions and watch your front!"

A reporter with a very dark tan, clad in a Hawaiian shirt, shorts, and sandals, came over and stuck a mike up to my mouth. A cameraman went down on his knees and moved in close, racked and focused.

"How do you like the Vietnam war so far, son?"

I stammered and stuttered.

"Look into the camera now and say hello to Mom. She may catch the six o'clock news."

I looked into the lens that kept moving in and out. I could see myself reflected in the glass. I gave a weak sheepish hello and a terrified grin.

Charlie was up grinning for the still photographers. Red had attracted another network. Nellis, on the other end of the squad, was busy scribbling something in a reporter's notebook, probably something to his dad in Chicago.

When the camera was turned off, I asked a reporter where the fighting was going on.

"There's fighting going on everywhere, but it's at night. The farmers till the rice fields during the day and pick up weapons at night. Nothing ever happens during the day around here." That was all too obvious.

I didn't understand, but I thanked him. The word was passed not to talk to reporters.

"Don't tell them anything!" Charlie yelled up the line.

"Tell the colonel to relax. His secret mission has been uncovered. It's six o'clock news now."

We had somehow survived our first beachhead and

human-wave assault. The press party had been hastily terminated by the irate colonel and his staff. He suffered the humiliation, while we thought it was hilarious.

When we calmed down from our precombat jitters, we weren't anticipating the hot trek across Elephant Valley to the mountains. The one-hundred-degree heat and gusting furnacelike air was a little more tolerable when we learned that a six-bi, "troop truck" convoy was going to pick us up. No one complained about the bone-crushing nontorsion air ride, the bronchial-clogging iron-rich dust, or the teenage drivers cursed with "Indie" phobia. The only fear I had of trucks were antitank mines capable of throwing a Volkswagon three stories into the air.

The mountains, saddlebacks, and gullies surrounding Elephant Valley were remarkably familiar; not unlike Camp Pendleton, only much greener. The convoy had moved more than a mile across the valley; and still the sugar-white sand dunes, although diminished in size and sprinkled sparsely with green, dominated the terrain. Farther on, patches of grass and low-lying shrubs began to appear along the tiny elevated road. We noticed some mounds in the area. They were sculptured and looked like large blisters of sand. They were meticulously manicured and preserved from the hot breezes that blew across the valley. We learned later that they were individual peasant graves maintained for generations without the benefit of granite.

We continued. Foliage of a more practical vein

appeared, vast colored carpets of rice paddies, each with its own perimeter of dikes. To the north of the sea of rice lay a large green island of banana trees, coconut palms, and an occasional grass hut. A life of another kind began to appear. Farmers looked up, unconcerned, then went back to their backbreaking work of planting rice seedlings in the decaying mud. I wondered if what the reporter had said was true about night and day.

The convoy arrived at the end of the road at the base of what no longer looked like low-lying foothills, but very steep mountains. Somehow, they'd quadrupled in size since we left the beach. The trucks formed a defensive circle, like a wagon train waiting for Indians, so we could dismount safely. Parts of the convoy veered off. The other companies had their own areas of responsibility, and eventually we would all be tied together along the top of the ridge, forming a battalion defensive line.

The heat was even more than we had endured before. In the beginning, the rugged, rock-strewn trail was wide enough for a column of twos, and the company angled up and along the slithering trail like a great menacing worm invading virgin territory. During the first hour, the first heat exhaustion casualties began to appear. This most harassing casualty occurs when all the salt is pumped out of the body and the built-in cooling system goes haywire. A deathlike weakness comes. And in the midst of one hundred degrees plus, a chill comes that cripples like a heavy strain of flu virus. The skin becomes pale and clammy, and the man is unable to perspire.

The heat and the terrain could be measured in the faces of the men whose guts were beginning to fray. The seasickness had left me a few pounds lighter, but not as weak as I thought I might be. I was doing very well. In boot camp, my size and frailty had been used against me. The drill instructors were determined to wash me out; but not being very bright, I pledged myself to the task of making myself physically perfect. I would never give up and consider myself physically inferior, because I had some control over it, unlike the weakness between the ears. To our amazement, months of undaunted, personal harassment, along with the overall boot camp program, shaped me into one of the strongest men in the platoon. After extensive testing I was surpassed by only one man who was huge, all hair and teeth. I wished there was something they could have done to prepare me better socially and emotionally.

More agonizing bodies began to give up and sit down on the trail. Some pushed further until their legs and minds gave out. They fell on their faces without even trying to break their fall. I grinned inside like a Cheshire cat, eardrum to eardrum. What's the matter, Momma's boys? Die, you helpless, unmerciful bastards!

Usually, I helped as many as I could to make the rest of the march—but not this time. The innocent were going to pay along with the guilty. Their labels—"shitbird," "misfit," "pussy"—did not sit very well. I found myself enjoying the climb after a surge of mental vengeance, almost as though I had some kind of telekinetic powers that heightened their agony. I felt a lot better.

The worm and the trail disappeared into heavy brush in the near-vertical side of the mountain. We grabbed at rocks, roots, and brush that many times gave way from too much use. I was summoned to the front of the column because I carried a machete. We slashed through the jungle. We rested and peered up at a great, towering, forbidden mountain. Up until now, it had protected religious myths and the secrets of the ancient high priests. It was glutted with treasures protected by prehistoric monsters, King Kong, and a tribe of beautiful people: women with beautiful hair, perfectly plucked eyebrows, and theatrical rouge. We were going to conquer this mountain today without John Hall and his native guide.

Using our final reserves of blood, sweat, and spit, we finally caught up with the late-afternoon sun. We had left the jungle behind littered with casualties and jumping corpsmen. We covered the last few yards on hands and knees. Those who were first to stand on the summit did not rejoice or congratulate each other, but I'm sure there was a touch of Sir Hillary in all of us. Our faces and clothes were starched dry with white crystals of salt. Body fluid and energy never existed. I felt sorry for the troops who were still climbing to the top at dusk. We had survived our second encounter of the day, the terrain.

CHAPTER FOUR

We survived and recouped from the ordeal up the side of the forbidden mountain, but we found no prehistoric monsters or treasure. Our only reward . . . it was over. The price was exhaustion, dehydration, and sunburn.

Tiny pieces of real estate were assigned in two-man lots along the irregular ridge-line that doglegged in and out, up and down. The summit seemed to have a grade to it, as though an ancient road had been carved all along the top. On one side of the ridge our defensive positions would face the sea and Elephant Valley. The sun set on rugged mountainous jungle bordering Laos to the west. On the south tip of our peninsula in the sky, a huge ravine lay. It was a natural pass through the mountains, and both companies set up machine-gun positions lacing together each other's field of fire. We were able to cover every square foot of the terrain without firing in each other's direction. Once on the ridge, it was easy to see why we were here. A few miles to the southeast lay Danang Field, where Skyhawks and Phantoms lifted off and landed night and day. The division was systematically populating the high ground throughout the Danang area in an attempt to curb the traffic of guerillas and equipment crossing Elephant Valley and entering the suburbs of Danang.

The clank of the entrenching tools attempting to penetrate the chastity of the sacred mountain sounded more like a Water and Power crew trying to penetrate Second Avenue downtown. No one was surprised when our tools bounced off the mountain like rubber mallets, or when we were told to move our positions several yards to the north, to spread out to cover more territory and start over again by Caswell, the platoon sergeant. He was a big, heavy, ex-drill instructor whose mind still wandered around the recruiting depot in San Diego. He had little or no consciousness of today's contemporary corps.

The grenadier is the odd man in the squad, and tactically shares a firing position with the squad leader behind the squad and the forward defensive positions. I would be living in a four-by-five hole in the ground with "Chicken Foot" Trudeau. He was vicariously named by the comedic underground within the platoon because of his skinny legs and a disturbing birdlike walk. Living in the same hole with him was going to be an interesting domestic experience. We had been at odds the moment he arrived in the division, ousted from a lush guard-duty assignment in Spain and thrown into a dirty, despicable infantry outfit training to go overseas. He was designated squad leader because of his time in grade and rank.

The squad was a mockery in the field and training. He was incapable of taking advice. I was not the most competent leader, but at least I had knowledge of the fundamentals. His egomania and insensitivity got him into hot water. The troops refused to listen to him but would listen to me, which put me in hot water. The pressure was on him, and he attempted to conceal his insecurities by yelling and screaming all the time. My own insecurities were covered over and hidden with more insecurity, which just barely worked for me. I did not give in to his micropolitics. He probed the chain of men for its weak links and pitted one against the other. He promoted the ambitious into allied positions and demoted anyone who threatened his security and conscience.

I was too young and naive to roll with the punches. I went from second in command to last in command. The rat pack, as they so mercifully called themselves, were not intimidated. Grinning Charlie, Red, Nellis (sometimes labeled "Richard III"), and Campbell (sometimes justly called "The Horn") had nothing approaching undaunted loyalty to me, but they were my friends. They were considered by the NCOs as a rare species of shitbird, and incorrigible. They were more like an adaptation of the Bowery Boys: too bright to get into real trouble, and too ambitionless to be intimidated with promotions. There was a single, silver thread of solidarity that bound us together. I had once loaned them bail money to get out of the Tijuana jail. During the days of my seasickness and disciplinary problems aboard ship, Trudeau managed to slip a wedge between us. I did not blame them for not wanting to chip paint in the hot bilge. It would have taken the grin out of anyone's fun. Temperatures had been cool ever since.

I sheltered our newly acquired parcel of land with a poncho and some sticks. Now, in the luxury of shade, I sat and tried to figure out how to extract nearly a hundred cubic feet of earth hard enough to dull a jack hammer. I thought of the virtues of no longer being a team leader. I didn't have to baby-sit anyone else twenty-four hours a day, and with the pressure off, I could relax. Relax, be cool, do my job, stay out of trouble—and perhaps Chicken Foot would get off my back. There was a good chance we would all be in a tough spot one of these days. There must be a war going on somewhere around here.

I etched out the perimeter of the hole with a stick right down to the centimeter. I was not about to make a hole any larger than regulation specified. I had joined the symphony of picking, scraping, and clanking when The Foot arrived. He threw himself down in the shade in my makeshift cabana, sweaty and tired from his motherly squad-leader duties. "Ogden, this whole mountain is nothing but a fucking rock. There isn't anything resembling dirt in any one of these positions."

"I just can't believe it. You mean this rock is nothing but a dirtless mountain? I'm glad to hear no one else has any dirt either. It wouldn't be fair if you and I were the only ones without dirt. Without dirt, the Marine Corps isn't the Marine Corps. There can't be a war without dirt. Maybe we can requisition some dirt. We can have it flown in by dirt-carrying helicopters and dropped right here." I purposely rattled on mindlessly to see if I could break the tension between us.

"Ogden, shut up and keep digging!"

"Yes, Corporal. Corporal, if you want your own room with a private bath, you'll have to give me about six months."

"Don't worry, I'll do my share. The lieutenant wants one man to dig, the other to stand watch, then trade off."

I went back to work. For the moment, we seemed to be getting along. He wasn't bitchy. He was still an NCO. But I was curious to know what went on behind those little brown eyes showcased in a lean, small-boned, almost feminine-looking face accented with a little bird nose and a less-than-predominant chin and jaw. He was frail in stature and didn't fit the description of a fighter, but probably could be dangerous; his eyes took on an occasional psychotic glare when enraged. He had learned English in high school and spoke without a trace of a French accent. He had a particularly fine-tuned ear for phonetics and had picked up Vietnamese in language school quickly. When he stuttered slightly it was another tip-off he was on the warpath. He was a classic example of a French Canadian from Quebec.

A heavy work day ended without a whistle. The dinner hour was announced without a bell. Before too long, the ridge line was permeated with the aroma of an all-too-familiar but welcome cuisine of beans and meatballs, beans and franks, ham and lima beans, instant coffee, or whatever else luck had bestowed. C-ration mealtime was always an interesting and creative phenomenon. An amusing array of unissued spices, sauces, and other exotic condiments awakened and titillated a dormant palate.

After the meal, I was about to take a pull on a canteen and wash down the grease when the second squad leader showed up passing the word again to conserve water. I took two pulls instead of the required half-dozen or more. J. P. Jason was a Texan in the classical sense. He thought everything was bigger and better in the Lone Star State, of course. They all bragged about it like it was a democratic capitalistic entity all by itself, a sovereignty within the United States, equal to the rest of the world on every front.

The only thing impressive about Tex was his big gut hanging from an average-to-lean frame. He seemed physically old for a man in his mid-twenties. The muscle seemed to have lost its elasticity, and everything hung. He had receding sandy hair; two little smoke-blue marbles pasted in deep, narrow slits; a pointed, almost abstract, impression of a nose; and a mouth larger than normal and fitted with so many perfect teeth it resembled the grill of an old Buick.

"Well, how are you and shitbird getting along here, Trudeau?"

I could have gone all week without that remark. He had to keep pushing, and Trudeau wasn't about to do me any favors. Jason and I had locked horns aboard ship. In the old days, he would have been the one to tie a rope around one leg and throw me overboard to be dragged behind the ship until I washed innocent or drowned. I fantasized grabbing him by his skinny, Texas-turkey neck, throwing him on his back on the ground, squeezing until his eyes popped, and making him promise to leave me alone. My fantasy ended, and I was still glaring into the tiny, smoke-blue marbles. I would never understand myself. Why was I so hollow and inept? Make-believe men have make-believe guts, and the thought of jail scared the hell out of me.

I grabbed my helmet and walked away to the edge of the ridge to be alone. I threw the helmet to the ground and sat on it. I drew up my knees, wrapped my arms around them, resting my chin on my knees, and looked out across Elephant Valley to the sea. I wondered where the elephants were. In the first moments of peace and quiet I had had all day, it was difficult to turn my mind off and indulge in the beauty before me.

The land we had invaded and trekked across was more beautiful and exotic than any place I had ever seen before. The meticulously cultivated floor of the valley began at the lower foothills and stretched to the sea. Toward the sea the floor was broken up by vast, sugary sand lakes and dunes. The valley floor was a spectacle of colored tapestry: vast sectors of tiny, irregularly shaped rice paddies fitting perfectly against their neighbors. They were divided neatly and manicured by small canals, hedgerows, or small mud dikes. Each paddy had its own hue of brown or yellow or any shade in between. A breeze gusted in off the water and circled the half-moon shape of the valley while each

tiny rice stalk waved in one direction and then in the
other in unison, giving an inadvertent but practical art
form a gentle sense of motion.

The mountains and foothills grew larger as they
stretched north, extending to the northern tip of the
valley and then dropping straight down to the beach.

At its most northern point, the valley appeared as
though it might have been a giant cove the land had
reclaimed over millions of years. To the other side the
valley was open, devoid of hills and mountains, lushly
covered with a carpet of jungle and elephant grass. I
assumed that many villages and hamlets thrived
beneath its green canopy.

Several ships listed peacefully in the harbor, including the one besieged by the scourge of my own
dread personal disease, seasickness and insolence.
Danang, the most fortified air base in the history of
modern warfare lay to the southwest, rarely seen but
often heard. Often the ancient peacefulness of the
valley would be disrupted by the clap of thunder from
the Skyhawks and Phantoms igniting their booster
rockets and accelerating like a missile to a near-vertical
flight pattern, then leveling off toward North Vietnam
with a payload of volatile mail, paid for by the good
citizens of Tacoma, Toledo, and Tallahassee. They
barely cleared the mountains to the north. The residue
of the afterburners in a space-age war trickled down
onto the valley floor, settling upon a medieval
castlelike fortress that stood at the north end of the
valley. It was a monument to the other wars, a symbol
of defeat, and its presence was awesome—like an

unexplained time warp with strange silver ships flying overhead.

The standard of native human existence in the valley had risen modestly and painstakingly above Neanderthal stages within the last ten thousand years. A cobblestone road led from the castle, inching across the valley, giving the appearance and accenting the centuries of European influence. At any moment, a troop of mounted armored knights would appear, horses' hooves clattering on the cobblestones and echoing through the valley in search of ancient adventure.

The long nights were dull and uneventful except for an occasional barrage of illumination flares from artillery batteries up the valley. Illumination flares drifted slowly on the warm night air currents suspended from tiny linen parachutes. If enough were dropped simultaneously, the entire valley would experience a premature sunrise. Sunburned eyes and necks strained then to see a sign of life or any movement at all. Each man fantasized hordes of enemy guerillas coming across the rice paddies.

We had scratched and hammered at our fighting holes for nearly a week, and C-rations were cut back to two meals a day. The water rations had been cut in half without an explanation. Sunburn turned to deep, dark brown; layers of fatty tissue were replaced by hard muscle; and blisters matured into hard protective callouses. Conditions were worse than on an Alabama chain gang.

The water rations were cut again. Lips began to

crack, along with tempers. Work was finally cut back to early morning and early evening to conserve body fluids. We sat all day watching choppers flying out of the air base. Why couldn't they fly over and kick out a few cans of water? More military bungling and red tape was going to cost us more misery than we already had. No one ever dreamed it was going to take weeks of hard labor to construct fighting positions on the ridge line.

CHAPTER FIVE

The dry blistering days passed like decades. A patrol was sent out into the mountains to find a small stream or some source of water, but found nothing. Dehydration started to set in, and all work was curtailed. The savers and the hoarders began sharing with the careless. The Foot and I had half a canteen between us. We sat around in the hot shade watching the clock, and every thirty minutes we took a canteen capful of water. Several times a day a chopper was sighted heading in our direction. All eyes would lock onto it. Hearts stopped, and leathery tongues began to moisten. The engines ground out a dull moan and the blades chopped the hot air as it continued toward the ridge, turning away at the last moment to another heading as though we were the subject of a great tease. The great and honorable warring knights of the West were being defeated by peasantry because someone forgot the drinking water. There must be a great proverb or limerick there, somewhere.

A squad leader's meeting was called and the world's greatest drill instructor never got up from the shade in his lean-to. He gave whatever instructions he had to pass on like a great sultan; only the peeled grapes and a young black servant with a large fan were missing. We wondered what his highness was going to do for a fighting hole if the need should arise—probably wait for the lieutenant to dig one for him.

While The Foot was away absorbing motherly knowledge, I entertained myself by playing with a large black beetle that had carelessly fallen into the hole, inadvertently caught up in an unexpected adventure on its long odyssey of exploration. It had a large horn on its head, so it was safe to assume it was a rhinocerous beetle. I made it perform impossible feats of mountain climbing. Up the sheer rock face of El Capitan, then on to the Devil's Tower. It was free-climbing without the benefit of rigging or pitons, climbing on sheer nerve, looking for hand- and foot-holds. I marveled at its endurance. I wondered if it was bad tempered and nearsighted, and if it lowered its horn and charged other creatures in the bush. Kids in the Philippines strung them and sold them in the streets like candy. I've seen the ad before: Hard and crunchy on the outside, creamy, rich and smooth on the inside. Melts in your mouth, not in your hand.

The Foot jumped into the hole, causing an earth tremor, and my hero fell off the south slope of Mt. Everest, landed on his back on a glacier, and slid to the bottom. I put him back on his trail of adventure into the bushes, disgruntled and indignant.

"What's the earth-shattering news, Corporal?"

He quickly began tearing through his pack. "Rifle inspection!"

"You're kidding! We're slowly dying of thirst like a lost brigade of Legionnaires, and he wants a rifle inspection?"

"That's right. He figures because the work has stopped, we should be able to do other things; and a rifle inspection seems to be his first plan. We are going up one at a time. You're first!"

"Me? The platoon shitbird? I get it. You send me up there and find out how bad he's gonna grind me up—and you know he will. And you can warn everyone. Right?"

He didn't answer. He started breaking down his M-14.

"Give me your forty-five. I'll clean it. That's the least I can do. I like the idea of using it to check the lines instead of this thing."

This would be interesting. Everyone knew these rifle inspections were always rigged. Somebody has to burn, no matter how clean the weapons are. I just happened to be popping out all over the popularity charts these days.

"Here, I'm trusting you with this." He threw me his barrel assembly. "Clean it!"

"Now, Corporal, that's not fair."

"Who said anything has to be fair?"

I grinned. "But Corporal, I'm not to be trusted."

"Do you think I'm gonna sit here and clean all these

weapons while you play around with bugs? You're crazy. Get busy!"

I walked across the perimeter with an immaculate forty-five on my hip and felt like I was headed for the OK Corral. We had even taken apart the magazine and dusted out the holster. I scanned the other positions as I walked by. Every weapon was now reduced to little pieces while tiny brushes, cloths, swabs, toothbrushes, and any other imaginable tools of the trade were being reluctantly applied.

There was a time in my military career when any kind of an inspection was a piece of cake—I was spit and polish right down to the last screw on a butt plate, and my service record book was proof perfect in proficiency and conduct. This didn't sit very well with new NCOs coming into the company. It was cause for contempt. They didn't care for perfect subordinates when they themselves were untrained, inept; and only rank, not merit, gave them positions of leadership.

Corporal Sheldon, the third squad leader, and I had been two of thirteen men picked out of the company to perform in the Marine Corps' squad competition. We were a perfectly tuned thirteen-man squad competing with other squads throughout the Marine Corp. It was a grueling thirty days of training and competition in every phase of combat tactics and proficiency. We outclassed all the other companies. We swept the battalion with no problem at all. We missed representing the First Marine Division and traveling to Virginia for the final challenge for the top squad in the Marine Corps, but lost by only a few points. We were honored by the battalion with thirty days leave. When the battalion began to reform to go overseas, Sheldon was promoted to corporal and the squad leader. He kept his mouth shut and stayed cool. But not me. I was the bright boy, and challenged injustice and incompetence at every turn. They plucked the feathers out of the primal bird one by one. I was now the principal jester in a court of clowns and fools.

I didn't know how Caswell was going to conduct this mockery of readiness and efficiency. I decided to go formal all the way, and stood in front of the lean-to at attention.

"Private First Class Ogden reporting as ordered." I pulled out the forty-five, pulled back the slide, ejected the magazine into my left hand, and waited. He continued to lay on his back in the shade and watched me in silence.

I was unnerved by him. He had punched troops while they stood at attention in formation, especially the smaller ones, but he hadn't hit or gone after me yet. I wondered how I had avoided his wrath so far. I was overdue. I wasn't sure why the lieutenant had let him get away with so much. Either he didn't know or he didn't care.

Caswell should have been a movie star. He had one of those faces too perfect to be born with, painstakingly built by Beverly Hills plastic surgeons. Perfect dark hair, perfect dark eyes, perfect nose, perfect square jaw, perfect teeth, perfect nails, perfect clothes, and perfect gear to clean, just like the psycho who knows he's perfectly sane but must wash his hands vigorously every two minutes of the day. Even "Rock" would be envious. He was tall, lean, fit, and well over six feet, with a stride familiarized by "The Duke." He would have been great bullying young actors and actresses around, intimidating new insecure directors, and making outrageous demands to producers and networks.

He sat up and reached. I placed the weapon in his hand and held my breath. He kept it much too long and went over it like a baboon mother looking for a flea. He barked loud and clear. "This thing looks like shit!" He handed it back. I holstered it. "Go back to your position, crud, and clean it. Then I want to see it again."

I turned and headed back to the position, thoroughly convinced he was mad in the clinical sense. I was totally fed up. The games crazies play were becoming a bore. Jail didn't seem so frightening. At least, they didn't send you back to the same outfit when you were released.

Trudeau had put himself in a precarious position when he cleaned the forty-five. No matter how immaculate he made it, we both had known I was going to get burned. I was stuck in the middle, the loser. Maybe Trudeau would sweat and have a little sympathy.

I handed the forty-five back to its adopted caretaker. I couldn't resist the temptation. "You're a crud, Corporal. This thing's a piece of shit!"

He looked at me, shook his head slowly, and

suppressed dialogue unbecoming a motherly NCO.

I grinned with anticipation. "I told him you cleaned it for me."

He jumped to his feet, feathers ruffled. "Stop fucking around. You know what could happen if he finds out what we're doing."

"I have a fair idea, Corporal. I'm already in the middle of it with no way out. I've been there a lot lately. Maybe I should tell him. You and your friend Tex over there have dealt me some pretty crummy cards."

He felt the mental armhole pressure and squirmed a little. His fingers fumbled trying to get the barrel assembly out of the pistol.

"I'll tell you, Corporal; I'm going to give it to you up front. I'm going to play my final role in this Mickey Mouse Club right to the hilt. But things better change around here. If we don't start playing together, we're going to get screwed, every last one of us. Imagine taking orders in combat from that idiot."

He looked at me. It was the first time since I'd known him that he didn't have anything to say. He just fumbled with the pieces of the pistol. He wiped the sweat from his brow. He blew for the last time into the barrel and handed it to me. "I've got to see how the rest of the squad's doing."

He started to climb out of the hole and I stopped him. "Relax, Corporal. Maybe he'll get bored with me."

He smiled. "I hope so. The Mickey Mouse Club is starting to bore me to tears."

*　　*　　*

Caswell's nostrils and eyebrows flared. He growled through clenched teeth. "You fucking shitbird. Go back to your squad leader and tell him I want you back here with an entrenching tool. You're going to dig me a four-by-four, and I don't care how long it takes you."

Well, that answered a few questions. I was sentenced to weeks of hard labor for nothing. The fear of jail nearly dissipated entirely. I wanted to put my foot in his perfectly miserable face and break it. It was still a fantasy. No guts! I walked back to the position. I was getting catcalls from the platoon. They must have overheard Caswell's profane diatribe.

"Hey Ogden, you can borrow my entrenching tool!"

"Tell me, how does it feel to be the biggest shitbird in the crotch, you gutless wonder?"

"Why don't you get seasick?"

The sound of a chopper diverted their attention. It changed course.

I stood alone on the patch of ground where my punitive inquisition was to take place. There was no breeze, no shade; only a swarm of flies. My head throbbed; my lungs and stomach ached with rage. My eyes were fixed on the spot, but I saw nothing but a blur. My entrenching tool hung from a limp arm. I was on the edge. The burn of a breaker circuit had been forthcoming. I had endured my emotional incarceration for so long that the iron bars began to bulge and give way under the stress. The rivets began to pop. I raised the entrenching tool slowly over my head. Gristle and cartilage snapped and popped in the shoulders. I came crashing down on all my enemies like a ceremonial samurai. I was smashing and whacking the unwilling soil. Muscle and gut tightened with each burst of energy. I was swinging faster and faster, out of control. A psychotic, epileptic animal in full frenzy, head pounding and eyes nearly swollen shut with sweat. The more it hurt, the more I accelerated. I was consumed with vicarious anguish, physical for mental. Through a fog of froth and fit in a delirious state almost below the level of consciousness, I felt an acidlike pain in my hands. My knees were numb from falling down and getting up. I began to wind down like a ridiculous dime-store toy. I collapsed in the dust and lay there. No appreciable depth had materialized from the precision craftsmanship, only dust.

I looked around me through one partially unimpaired eye to see if anyone had caught my overzealous contribution to the safety of our platoon sergeant. I was on a gentle slope from the main perimeter. No one had. Had anyone seen me, they would have hastily summoned the corpsman, who would have sprung a net and carried me off to the nearest infirmary. I sat up. I felt embarrassed and foolish, but I was calm. The trauma had passed. Pain in heart was transferred to pain in hand. Large blisters had developed under the tough, calloused skin and had burst. They were grim-looking meat hooks. It was time to see the corpsman and add malingering to a long list of transgressions.

I headed to the lean-to, shaky but in better spirits. I could hardly wait to tell him the sad news. I was no longer a healthy indentured servant. In a bemused, clear voice, I startled him out of a little catnap.

"Sergeant Caswell, I've got a problem. I'm going to see the corpsman." I held my hands up. One was bleeding.

He came on with a fiendish growl and the usual facial contortions and gnashing of teeth. This time there was a new ingredient in the kabuki act: he slobbered on himself.

"Get back to work! You're not going to see any goddamn corpsman. I'm going to work you until the meat comes off your goddamn bones."

Now was the time for all young men to come to their own aid. I yelled so loud the entire Elephant Valley could hear me. "You're not doing anything to me, asshole!"

I wasn't scared of anything. I loved the sound of the word as it rolled off my lips. Especially the phonetics and the accent on "ol." I loved the expression on his face; as though I had kicked him in the groin and the pain hadn't caught up to the brain yet. I loved the whole world. It was a wonderful place to be! I was back in it and among the living again, if for just one triumphant moment.

He sprang to his feet, too quick and agile for a man of his size. The huge paw missed me, and I stumbled back. It slashed through the air with the size and heft of a tree trunk. The uneven, sloping ground was against me. Its unevenness made him seem more massive than he was and made the difference between us an absurdity, as though I were on my knees before him. I was never in proper balance. I took one impressive swing, but it only managed to throw me the rest of the way off balance and down into the gravel and dust.

You asked for it, stupid. The least you can do is participate. He'll only send your head into the next Vietnamese county. Maybe I should be groveling around in the gravel looking for a perfectly round, smooth stone. Meanwhile, the Philistine with the finesse of a dinosaur mentally measured the distance between me and a size thirteen, triple-E boot. The enormous kick was close enough to knock the dust off my utility jacket, and missed my rib cage by the thickness of the fabric.

I rolled again and got up onto my feet before he could regain his balance for another strike. Without giving it the slightest thought, and with lightning precision as though I had been doing it all my life, I drew my forty-five and pulled back the slide, let it go home, and aimed it between two perfect eyes. Nothing I could have done physically would have frozen his action so quickly. It was like using a high-speed shutter, freezing the freight train in frame. The immaculate forty-five glistening in the sun rendered me a moment of freedom from a world gone mad.

I rose to my feet. "You miserable son of a bitch, if you ever touch me or anybody else in this platoon, I'll blow your fucking head off!"

Fear and uncertainty began to surge again. My gun hand shook, and I supported it with the other.

He had no expression. His hands rose slowly over his head. He knew I could flip at any second and empty a seven-round magazine in five seconds. Irony had also made a fool of him. I was so preoccupied with him that

I hadn't remembered to reload the magazine. I would go to jail knowing I had brought the house down with a broken straight, the ultimate bluff.

He slowed backed up the hill to give me room. His head turned, eyeing the perimeter. I followed. Every man in the outfit was watching this incredible drama unfold. It was right out of the pages of a bad novel, but could we tag it with a cheap happy ending?

The body's built-in anesthesia, "numbness," began to lift, and salty sweat poured into the open contusions. My arms holding the weapon so purposefully and rigidly began to ache. My mind began to whirl like a carousel. I was having second thoughts about the stupid stunt I had pulled. My whole future life turned before me. Jail, court-martial, jail, court-martial, and maybe even a firing squad.

Jason stepped in like Marshall Dillon. "Okay, Ogden, put it away!"

Gee, Marshall, you just got here in the nick of time, or I would have blown him away for sure. You probably saved me from hanging!

I holstered the weapon. I looked both Caswell and Jason in the eye and scanned the perimeter myself. "I'm gonna see the corpsman now." I took off toward the CP tent.

Caswell began yelling and screaming. "You goddamn son of a bitch, I'm gonna have you court-martialed. You son of a bitch!" He took his forty-five out and shook it at me. He looked at it and realized the mistake, and put it away. He continued to yell and rave as his spellbound platoon looked on.

52

The iodine brought tears to my eyes as he bandaged my hands. I told the corpsman my bizarre, impossible story.

"It sounds like a clear-cut case of maltreatment to me."

"Are you sure, Doc?"

"Of course, you understand there will probably be some kind of a hearing to unravel some of the legal ramifications, witnesses, and evidence. It looks like a stand-off. It would be easier to settle out of court, so to speak."

"I'll settle out of court. Loan me a forty-five shell. I left mine back at the ranch."

He grinned. "Now don't be rash, my friend. You've already had an eventful afternoon. I'l snip this off. There you go. Come back tomorrow and let me check it."

"Thanks, Doc. You certainly know how to turn a bad day into a good one. With your know-it-all, see-it-all bedside manner, you'd make one hell of a witch doctor."

He gave me a puzzled smile.

When I got to the hatchway of the tent, Caswell was stomping by. I'd give anything to hear his side of the story. What irony: one homicidal maniac tattling on another. The words of the doc had given me some emotional footing. In fact, I felt rather good. I looked at the sterile white cheesecloth. I had handled some very hot potatoes today.

I headed back slowly to the OK Corral and wondered how the rest of the hands would react to a natural-born gun slinger.

"Freeze, Ogden!" I recognized the sharp, nasal resonance of the company executive officer, First Lieutenant Bailey. He was short, thick, and as amusing as a fifty-gallon barrel of crude oil. He also had a funny walk that led the underground comedy writers to nickname him "Baby Hughie." He overreacted to everything. He probably had his forty-five aimed between my shoulder blades, or perhaps the whole squad on line. When Caswell told him the whole horrifying story, he had probably had to sit down to keep from fainting. I was confused about where to put my hands. Caswell had looked rather stupid with them over his head. With my hands bandaged, hitting the ground, rolling, and getting the drop on him was definitely out; but Steve McQueen could probably have pulled it off.

Where's Marshall Dillon when I need him? What strange, childlike reveries pass through our almost-grownup minds in the presence of adversity.

He stepped up behind me. "Drop your pistol belt and turn around." I was almost disappointed; he had no gun and he was alone. "Private Ogden, you threatened the life of a fellow Marine in a combat situation."

"Sir, our fellow Marine was trying to kick my sides in."

"Shut up! I'm going to see they throw the book at you." Not very original material for a college man. "Go to your squad leader and tell him I want all of your weapons; knife, every grenade, and all your ammo. I want them left at my tent right away!"

If I were so dangerous, why didn't he arrest me, tie me up, and gag me so I wouldn't froth at the mouth? After all, I could be working up some heinous plot to knock over Caswell in the still of the night. If I had such a plan, I'm sure someone would see that I had an entire truckload of weapons at my disposal if I needed them.

I headed across the perimeter toward the position, mouth so dry there was no room for the growth of a large, useless tongue. As I walked into the area, heads popped up everywhere from their holes like little prairie dogs. Someone began to clap, then another. Cheers went up. I was being applauded and not jeered. I didn't know what to do. I grinned like a fool and waved like a politician. The squad leaders were frantic. They yelled for everyone to shut up.

Trudeau and Jason were at the position. I sat down in the shade and grabbed the canteen.

"What in the fuck are you trying to pull, Ogden, a mutiny? You'll wind up in Portsmouth for the rest of your life."

"Just trying to survive, Corporal Jason, just trying to survive," I said smugly. I turned to The Foot. "Tell him the story, Corporal."

"I didn't know you were going to pull a dumb-ass stunt like that."

"To tell you the truth, neither did I. I kinda got pushed into it."

All hell broke loose within the perimeter. Jason yelled. "Ogden, you have started a goddamn mutiny!"

I grinned at both of them and we stood up. I must admit the idea was very appealing.

A much more important moment was happening. Somehow, a chopper had got in close to the ridge without anyone seeing it, and from its belly swung a net full of very precious cargo. Water cans!

When they were dispersed, we had all the water we could possibly drink. I was cordially invited to a house party at Charlie's, and all the "good old boys" were there. I was the toast of the town. The first anti-hero of the war for First Platoon, Hotel Company. We drank until our bellies were bloated while each one of them congratulated me and recreated his own version of what had happened.

With the day's soap opera and the critical arrival of water, morale was so high that the squad leaders did everything they could to keep the lid on. Everyone was jubilant. For all of us, a very important and unexplained crisis had passed.

I still had a personal crisis to face, though—at least a general court-martial. The more I thought about it, the less credence I gave to the doc's comments. Eddie Slovik had never thought for a moment he would be shot for desertion in World War Two.

CHAPTER SIX

"Saddle up! We're moving out!" the squad leaders yelled.

I had just finished breakfast and stepped out on the patio to stretch. The Foot had made it back from the squad leaders' meeting in a hurry.

"What's up, Corporal? Where are all the king's men headed now? Did they call off the war for lack of participation?" I asked as the rest of the squad gathered around.

"The battalion CP is moving and setting up on the other side of the hill. We're gonna provide a perimeter for them. Golf Company is gonna fill in here. The battalion's geared for hot chow! Get your asses in gear and be ready to move out!" Everyone cheered and moved back to their positions.

"Is there any word about yesterday?" I asked as we started to tear the roof off our summer home and packed up.

"The lieutenant said you would report directly to the captain when we get to the battalion area. Caswell didn't say a thing during the briefing. I don't know what to tell you."

I continued to pack the few pieces of gear I had left. The scourge of my uncertain fate settled on top of a hastily prepared cold breakfast like a rock. I wondered what poor fool at company headquarters would be carrying my material burden down the mountain. I wondered why the lieutenant hadn't jumped down my throat before this. Maybe he thought Caswell was a lunatic also. The captain must be going to handle it. I decided to keep my mouth shut and not discuss it with anyone. I would do exactly what I was told. I would be a good clown in this traveling circus.

We slid and stumbled down the mountainside we had so painstakingly clawed our way up. I felt foolish and naked without my weapons. I had to be the only combat soldier in the whole of South Asia armed with only a fork and spoon.

By the time we were halfway down the mountain, the sun had burned off the morning dampness and chill. It began to cook us in a boundless laser oven. A few troops again felt the effects of heat exhaustion, but not as badly as when we'd climbed up. Following the trail of footholds, I kept from careening down the slope by holding onto branches and bushes. Some men never adapt to rough terrain no matter how hard they train. Red had given up. He was sitting down in the middle of the trail, close to passing out. His round, fat, freckled face was nearly as red as the tuft of curly hair that hung down under the lip of his helmet. When I got to him, he was puffing too hard and his skin was dry.

"How are you feeling, Red?"

He snorted through a rubbery, flat, no-cartilage nose pulverized by too many left jabs in the amateur light-heavyweight division. "Fuck this motherfucking corps, and fuck Vietnam!"

"We've still got ten rounds to go, and you told me you always go the distance. I'll get the doc to give you a couple of salt tablets and you'll be all right. In the meantime, give me your pack. I'm traveling pretty damn light."

I helped him wiggle out of it. Charlie and Nellis slid to a stop, and threw the pack on top of mine and tied it down. Charlie stood by with a grin.

"At least you're good for something: a damn pack mule. Here, let me put my rifle up there, too. It's getting too heavy for me." He laid it up there for a moment. "Nellis, why don't you give him our pack, too?" He laughed and took off down the trail.

Ten minutes later, I realized I had bitten off more than I could chew. I was having trouble shifting the weight back and forth on two numb shoulders with two useless paws. The weight was riding high and the pack straps were digging deep. The pain and pinching became unbearable. I stopped alongside the trail to figure out what to do besides quit. A moment later, Caswell was behind me.

"Move out, Ogden!" I had been wondering when and how he would start something. "Move out, Ogden!" I ignored him. He leaned over close to the back of my

59

neck and hissed through locked jaws. "You son of a bitch, I'm gonna put you out on point on a combat patrol without any weapons."

It was this idiotic statement, so uncreative and childish, that clued me in solidly that there was a gross lack of any appreciable intelligence. He sounded like something out of the mouth of a cartoon character in a twenty-five-year-old combat comic book.

"Move out, shitbird!" He gave me a good shove from behind.

I staggered forward with forty pounds of extra weight tied around my neck. My center of gravity was lost. In seconds I was careening helplessly down the mountainside. I landed on my back on a pile of rocks, racking a knee. I hoped it was broken in a dozen places. The only thing that saved me was the fact that I landed belly-up on the rocks, and the packs absorbed the impact. I tried to get up, but the packs were wedged in the rocks and I was totally helpless.

Caswell started down the bank as Lieutenant Bailey rushed up. "Knock it off, Caswell. Get back to your platoon!" Maybe Bailey thought Caswell was coming down to finish me off. Maybe he was. The lieutenant climbed down the bank. "Are you all right, Ogden?" Bailey turned and yelled to the troops congregating on the trail above. "Keep it moving. Get a corpsman here. We've got a man down!" I tried to get up. "Don't move until the doc gets here. You may have broken something!"

The doc lost his footing and slid on his butt down the bank. "What are you doing here, boy, trying to take a shortcut? Where does it hurt?"

"I banged up my left knee, Doc."

He grabbed the ankle and moved the knee back and forth gently. "How does that feel? Is there any sharp pain? Let's get you up. See if you can walk on it. You're in one hell of a tangled mess here! What in the hell are you doing carrying two packs? What do you think you are—a damn billy goat?"

I put some weight on it, and leaned on his shoulder and whispered. "I think our case is looking a little better, Doc. The plaintiff just attempted to kill the defendant in the presence of a key witness. If I keep hanging around you, I'll be talking like a lawyer."

"If you keep getting into trouble like this you're going to need it, too. How does it feel?"

"Just awful, Doc," I whispered and grinned. "Do you think you can get me a stretcher to make it look good?"

Lieutenant O'Connor stood at the top of the bank. "What happened, Ogden?"

"I tripped and lost my balance, sir."

"Are you gonna be able to make it?"

"Yes, sir, I think so."

O'Connor turned to Trudeau. "Get a couple of men and make sure that gear gets down to the battalion area."

I favored the knee as much as possible, especially when Bailey was near. With a boost from the doc, I was put on the trail heading down toward some hot chow. I felt pretty good with forty pounds of weight off my back and the smell of reprieve in the air. Two acts of maltreatment. One witnessed by the XO, who probably would have hanged me just on hearsay yesterday, but was now on my side.

The battalion command post was nestled in a canyon at the foot of the mountains. It was about a half-mile to the south from where our defensive positions were. From a distance, it took on the appearance of a traveling circus. The column moved past tanks deployed outside the mouth of the canyon. Once we were inside the hastily erected canvas housing project, we made good use of the city's public water supply, which consisted of a water buffalo, a strange animal that looked like a giant oil drum on two wheels. The company was deployed in a huge semicircle at the mouth of the canyon. Each platoon was tied in with a tank. Company headquarters set up mid-ground between the perimeter and the battalion area. To our amazement, we spent the rest of the afternoon digging into soft ground. We were all thinking of fresh food, instead of something that had been packed away in cans for ten or twelve years. No one was greatly surprised when the hot meals and showers turned out to be a rumor, a mistake, or a hoax.

Captain Martin was on the radio to the battalion when I approached. I waited for him to sign off, then reported. He returned the salute. "At ease, Ogden."

He seemed very young and a little on the frail side to be running a Marine company. But he was an impressive leader. He exuded an air of confidence and spoke well when addressing troops.

I remembered Lieutenant O'Connor's first introduction to the platoon. He was so terrified, he could hardly speak. He stuttered, stammered, hemmed, and hawed. He was a tall, gangly Irishman with red hair. Somebody immediately tagged him "Muldoon." During training he overcame his insecurities and became a good, confident platoon leader, but the name "Muldoon" was too cute to drop. They started calling Red "Little Muldoon," but he was quick to put a stop to it. We all agreed that the leadership of the other platoon leaders was rather questionable.

I liked and respected Captain Martin. I was embarrassed to be coming up again in front of him for yet another disciplinary problem. I also felt like a live chicken looking into a hot frying pan.

He took off his helmet. He sat down on a pile of C-ration cases, folded his hands, looked down at the ground, and took in a deep breath. He looked up at me rather strangely while still holding his breath. I took in my own breath and held it.

"Were you blowing off steam up there?"

"Yes, sir, I was."

"How are your hands?"

"They're fine, sir."

"Go back to your platoon and keep your nose clean."

I was stunned! It was obvious something else was on his mind. He had changed it at the last moment. I was speechless and didn't move. He put on his helmet and turned around. "Move it, Marine!" I saluted smartly. I did an about-face, forgetting all about a return salute. I started back toward the squad position as fast as I could.

"Ogden," he yelled.

I put on the brakes, slid, and nearly fell down. He was pointing to the ground next to him.

"You forgot your gear."

I rushed back and flung the M-79 on my shoulder. I threw the bandoliers of rounds around my neck, gathered up the K-Bar killing knife, and put the hand grenades on my belt. I lumbered away like a new recruit who had been issued his first set of toys and couldn't wait to play with them.

We spent two days in the battalion area, then were relieved by another company and climbed back to our summer homes on the ridge line. We sent out squad-sized recognizance patrols throughout the valley. We were briefed that the farmers were indeed farmers during the day and were playing games at night. The weeks of intense patrol were tedious and exhausting. The excitement of our very first combat patrol had given way to a dull, hot, tiring routine. Our morale seemed to decline in direct proportion to the increase in physical fitness, stamina, and adaptability to climate and terrain. Through miles of deep rice paddies, shifting sands, and vertical hills and mountains, we found no evidence of any weapons and no acts of overt aggression or open hostility. But we still looked upon the indigenous population with contempt and suspicion. The farmers continued on with their daily lives as though we didn't exist. We had specific orders not to enter the village under any circumstances. In our speculations and fantasies, we knew the village hosted several battalions of Vietcong and hundreds of

Vietcong sympathizers. The war machine was laboring under a stagnant and poignant silence. The climb from the valley floor to the top of the ridge line after each patrol had become nothing but a mere inconvenience.

Only the sound of sand shifting underfoot, the squeak of shifting gear, or the occasional clank of a canteen broke the ominous stillness of the valley floor. Salt and saliva had formed around the corners of our mouths and hardened. The sun had scorched our bodies for what seemed like thousands of hours and had turned our exposed skins a deep, rich brown. The only relief from a robotlike motor reflex was to move forward and take a pull from a canteen to keep the sides of the throat from collapsing in the middle and adhering together. The water was at least eighty-five degrees cool, a lot cooler than the ambient air surrounding us. Not even the tiniest leaf or spider's web clinging to a bush moved in the stillness of the stagnant hot air.

Jason broke in on our numbed senses. "Pass the word up to the point to veer to the right toward that grass hut; we'll take a break."

Corporal Jason looked back at me. "Goddamn it, Ogden, it's hot! This has to be the hottest fucking day since we landed."

I didn't want to waste any energy replying. Tex, The Foot, and I seemed to be getting along a little better. I was assigned to Tex's squad for a patrol because his own grenadier had suffered a sprained ankle. Lucky guy!

The squad was spread out over a lot of territory

because of the openness of the terrain and the lack of cover. I looked back over my shoulder. The last man was just coming over a small sandy knoll. His image was distorted like a mirage drifting in and out of the heat waves, like a ghost. To be able to sit down in the shade for a few minutes would be as welcome as tumbling into a Cascade mountain stream.

The next instant, I froze in stride and breath. My eardrums snapped with the crack of automatic weapons fire. All ten of the highly conditioned and programmed computers hit the deck simultaneously with muscles flexed to their capacity. Blood and adrenalin accelerated, triggering the most primitive of survival mechanisms. Eyeballs focused and refocused on the periphery of the jungle that surrounded Le Mai Village approximately five hundred yards from the left flank. The volume and intensity of automatic weapons fire was unimaginable. The valley had been so extremely quiet since our occupation; I'm certain everyone imagined hordes of armed enemy would come rushing out of the jungle toward our position any second.

Jason began yelling orders up and down the line. "Keep down!" "Keep your positions!" "Lock and load!" He didn't realize it, but everyone had been shoving magazines into their rifles, and bolts were already going home.

Jason and I were laying belly down behind a low sandy knoll. The squad was stretched out on either side of us on line. I flipped over on my back and broke open my pop gun. I fumbled for a round, shoved it in the breech, and slammed it closed. I rolled over and began to work with the front sight blade. We were edgy as hell. Our minds worked flawlessly from subconscious reflex. There was no evidence of any incoming rounds, but it would have been hard to confirm because of the soft sand. The firing was loud enough to cover the sound of any rounds breaking the air over our heads. Only a hit would let us know for sure.

Jason reached the company commander on the radio. "We are under fire, sir. It's coming from the village. I have no casualties." The radio cracked and buzzed, but was audible.

"Get your squad back here as soon as possible, Jason. Hotel Actual, out."

"Roger, sir."

"Ogden, pass the word we are going home. The rear guard is now the point."

We were literally frying where we lay, but the thought of just staying alive banished all thoughts of discomfort of the day. We got up and moved out in a quick crouch. No one took his eyes off the tree line until we were well out of range.

When we got back to the company, we learned that our anxiety and near heatstroke was due to a Golf Company patrol that had broken the rules and jumped a Vietcong inside the village. They'd blown away a sixteen-year-old kid carrying a Thompson submachine gun after he gunned down their squad leader.

One tended to forget that every member of a squad carrying an M-14 had commandeered an illegal selector switch that made the M-14 optional, semiautomatic or fully automatic. Extreme overkill was flagrant with this much fire power in the hands of the overzealous. Only three members of the squad were issued this automatic switch. Each squad had virtually nine or ten machine guns, a fully automatic weapon resting on every trigger finger. We had never experienced that kind of fire power in training. Who could stand up to that much fire superiority? Ever since the battalion had hit the beach in March, there'd been feverish bragging and betting on what company, platoon, or individual would score the first kill. Golf Company cancelled all bets when one of their own went down. The young Vietcong was torn to shreds.

It was ten o'clock in the evening when Red scrambled over to our position. He was excited. "Hey Oggie, we've finally got a station speaking American!"

He rushed back to his position and I followed quickly. Nellis had tried for weeks to tune in the armed forces station overseas on a tiny radio, the size of a pack of cigarettes. This evening, he had inadvertently laid the radio down on the comp wire that stretched from the battalion to each company, and the huge network of wire, thousands of yards long, acted as an aerial. But it was not an armed forces station. It was the eeriest and most bizarre broadcast we had ever heard.

A soothing, provocative voice said, "I want to give a special hello this evening to the Marines in Hotel Company on top of Hill 853."

Everyone immediately moved in closer to hear. "That's us! She's talking about us!"

Nellis began to laugh. "I know who it is now. It's

Peking Polly. Yeah, my cousin's in the Navy, and he told me about her. She's like Tokyo Rose!"

"She sounds so sexy, I could go down on her in a minute."

"Shut up, Red, and listen!"

She said we were sitting in dark, cold foxholes when we could be at home with our friends and loved ones. We agreed with that. She said members of the National Liberation Front, whoever they were, crawled up the side of the mountain, stole our boots and equipment, scared us to death, and we could be heard crying in the night.

Such ridiculous commentary broke us all up with jeers and laughter. The whole broadcast was saturated with farcical, ludicrous statements. Originating from Peking meant it was traveling around the globe. We were in the midst of international intrigue. We were where the action was, and it made us feel important.

We adopted the show as regular late-night entertainment for awhile. Before long, though, we walked away, either bored or amused by the same silly rhetoric. We fantasized about the mystic Oriental beauty with the mouth of an angel. We had lewd thoughts about an enemy who was specializing in outrageous propaganda and who attacked our masculinity. Maybe she was a defected exchange student from Cincinnati or Seattle. She spoke impeccable English.

CHAPTER SEVEN

I was not surprised when word came down we were going to assault the village in the morning. It would be a company-sized predawn assault sweeping the entire length of the village. Trudeau delivered a skimpy combat order taken at a hastily gathered squad leaders' meeting.

"We'll leave at 0400. We'll be in position on line along the trail on the west side of the village. We'll sweep toward the sea. We'll take prisoners if possible. They'll be herded back to the rear to a designated staging area until after the operation. We'll carry packs with one meal. A green star cluster will signal attack. A med-evac L.Z. will be designated by yellow smoke. The lieutenant wants every man to break down his magazines, pull out the old rounds, and clean them to cut down on the chance of malfunctions. Are there any questions?"

No one spoke.

"This is going to be a surprise attack. Like it or not, I want socks around the canteens so they don't rattle, and dog tags taped if they aren't already. No talking or bullshitting around. Oh, another thing. This is a search-by-fire operation. We will open fire on the green star cluster. Ogden, the lieutenant designated you to stay with him to spot M-79 rounds. Okay, everybody back to your positions and turn to while we still have daylight left."

That doesn't make sense, I thought. I'm the least qualified of the three men in the platoon at firing the M-79. I had fired it once in training just to get the feel of it. I thought about the search-by-fire routine. It would be like turning loose a massive lawn mower on a hamlet built of bamboo and grass.

I rested on my knees in the predawn darkness. We were drenched, and shivered from the dew that hung heavy in the towering elephant grass around us. It was a long, tedious battle to get into our final positions.

My body began to shake more from the chill and excitement. I remembered my first duck-hunting expedition, sitting in a blind in the darkness, waiting for daylight and a flock of mallards. It felt much the same, but I couldn't remember the knot in my stomach.

The minutes dragged on. A cock crowed. Then another. The darkness began to give way to shadows that formed recognizable objects. The terrain began to appear ever so slightly like a very slow developer solution breaking down the chemical and allowing the hidden image to be exposed on a print. The silence of the moment was heightened by the pungent sweet and sour scent of the primitive existence. It was different from the scent of stagnant, fermenting rice paddies. I began to pray for comfort. I hoped nothing would happen today that I would regret.

Lieutenant O'Connor and Trudeau were on each side of me as the hand signals for everyone to get up on their feet were given. The flare popped over the village, piercing the senses and signaling the dawning of the war we had so painstakingly anticipated. A wave of men in green stepped through the concealing hedgerows and moved cautiously across the fields toward the village. The order to commence firing was given. Automatic weapons began to chatter up and down the lines, spewing out hot glowing chaser rounds that disappeared into the shadows.

I stayed behind the advancing platoon with Lieutenant O'Connor as he barked orders to keep the interval, stay on line, and keep firing. He yelled at the members of the weapons platoon attached to our squad that rocket teams were only to fire on solid structures. An M-60 crew was in front of us barely keeping up the pace. The gunner had the M-60 slung from his shoulder and was firing from the hip. The assistant gunner fed a belt of ammo into the breech. The gunner was slightly bigger than me, but each burst of the gun sent him back two or three steps. At the end of each burst, the crew would run forward to catch up with the line.

The M-60 is a heavy weapon designed to be mounted on a tripod or on a vehicle. The gun crew enjoyed what they called "John Wayning it." It gave them more mobility and more power to the platoon during an assault. The rocket teams on the line waited patiently for an appropriate target and a command. The gunner carried the stove-pipelike apparatus on his shoulders. His assistant, heavily laden with a pack board carrying the rocket rounds, guided the tail section of the rocket launcher that held the rocket.

I could see many bamboo huts shrouded and camouflaged by banana palms as I looked through the blue haze of burning powder and hot gun oil. There were many trails worn smooth by decades of bare feet. They led from the village down to the rice-paddy dikes holding in the water that submerged the cultivated land and surrounded the village.

The second platoon rocket team cut loose with a screaming round. It went deep into the village and detonated, sending tiny streaming particles of white phosphorus in all directions. We were now just a few yards short of entering the village, and there was a lull in the firing. The troops extracted empty magazines and replaced them with full ones.

I scanned up and down the line intensely, trying to take in everything. The awesome, unforgettable sight and sound of our first combat assignment was exhilarating almost to the point of hysterical excitement. Frustration and anxiety were exuded like sweat from the pores. In the frenzy of the moment, we had forgotten what damage, death, and agony we could incur or had incurred. We only knew we were getting paid to do a job.

After the company entered the village, the pace and

firing slowed down considerably. Then an unexpected horror stopped the entire line of troops cold. Pungee sticks! Thousands of them. Some were partially camouflaged, while others were in the open. They were needle-sharp bamboo stakes tempered hard as iron by heat and sometimes dipped in dung. Their presence triggered another terrifying thought: booby traps! Yells of caution and discovery ran up and down the lines like a panic. Orders to watch for trip wires were called out. Sheldon's squad found a pungee trap. It was a neat little hole about the size of a shoe box, with pungee stakes in the bottom and a well-camouflaged layer over the top. If hit right, the stake would jab all the way through the sole of the boot and into the bone of the foot. The lieutenant and squad leader continued to bark orders to keep the interval and the line moving.

"Ogden! See the temple, the thing with the red tiles on the roof? Hit it!"

"Yes, sir!" I estimated the range to be about three hundred yards. I lifted the rear sight, locked it into place, and slid the yardage marker all the way to the top. I lined up the rear blade and front sight blade with the target. I took in a deep breath. My forearm shook. I was afraid of missing! I needed to do something right for a change. With the barrel stretched almost straight up in the air, I pulled the trigger. The round leaving the barrel sounded like a plug being extracted from a thermos bottle. I waited for what seemed like forever to see where it would hit. To my astonishment, it blew several large tiles from the corner of the roof.

"Good hit, Ogden," the lieutenant said with mild

amusement. "That weapon is not heavy enough to do any damage on that heavy a structure. We'll concentrate on the huts."

I couldn't believe it. I just couldn't miss. The secret was not only aiming the weapon, but also calculating the yards to the target.

I moved up the line with the rest of the troops. The lieutenant ran over to the rocket teams to give them instructions. We moved deeper into the village. The going was getting tough. We stayed off the trails to avoid the booby traps. We fought and clawed through the heavy hedgerows that dissected the village. I wondered why we weren't receiving any incoming fire.

Trudeau yelled from the right side of the line. "Lieutenant, we've got bunkers over here!"

"Clean them out," came the reply.

The assault wave broke up slightly and took on the appearance of a search-and-destroy mission. Corporal Jason came crashing through a hedgerow from the left flank. "Spread it out, you guys! Mortars will get you all. Move it out!"

At that moment, a dog raced from a hut that smoldered with white phosphorus. The dog, a German shepherd, headed in my direction at top speed. It immediately disappeared into a hole a few yards in front of me. It was a strange sight to see—a domestic animal acting like a wild cornered beast in the presence of humans. It was the first sign of life all morning.

"Throw a hand grenade in that hole!" Jason yelled. "Pop one in and let's get out of here!"

The first sign of life, I thought again. I stopped in my

tracks. My mind raced. We hadn't seen or heard a soul all morning. It could mean they had fled during the night or early morning. Or had they? I took a closer look around me. Spread out everywhere in the sun to dry was food: peanuts, potatoes, beans, and rice. There was laundry hanging near the huts. Some were children's pants and shirts. My imagination was racing again. There wasn't any hostile fire this morning. Pets were staying behind instead of running away with their owners. It didn't make sense. Then it hit me: they were underground! Grown men with weapons did not hide in holes waiting for the enemy to poke a rifle or a grenade into it, but defenseless noncombatants might. I let out a yell. "They're underground, all of them!"

"You're goddamn right, they're underground," Jason yelled back. "Throw a hand grenade in there, goddamn it, and let's go!"

"I can't! They're underground!" I yelled irrationally. "Where there's a dog, there's kids! Don't you see?" I pleaded. "We're blowing them up and burying them at the same time, without giving them a chance. Women, kids, babies, for crissake!"

Jason tore a hand grenade off his belt, pulled the pin, and threw it in. He gave me a sickening cliché: "Ogden, war is hell! I'm going to run you up for disobeying an order and for cowardice in the face of the enemy. What are you standing around for? Move it!"

The grenade blew with a dull thud that shook the ground underfoot. My mind was dazed and confused. My stomach was sick. I ran over to the hut and snatched a tiny pair of trousers from the clothesline. I ran back and threw them in his face. He caught them and looked at them with a total lack of concern. He still didn't understand.

"There's your goddamn enemy. You kill 'em all!"

He grit his teeth. "I'm warning you, Ogden!" He looked down at the muzzle of his rifle, then back to me.

I looked at the muzzle also, then we locked eyeballs. "If you're thinking what I think you're thinking," I said, "you'd better pull the trigger." I was ashamed for the lack of a better cliché.

He quickly relaxed. "You're under stress. You've had a bad time of it lately."

He still hadn't figured it out. Maybe he had, and didn't care. I propped open my grenade launcher, extracted the shell, and walked away. I didn't know who or what was around me. I was embroiled in an undercurrent of outrage and despair. I didn't fire the weapon again that day.

There were tears of rage, fear, and confusion for the next few minutes. Maybe I'm wrong, maybe I'm just overreacting. I knew for sure a perfectly harmless pet had been wasted. The morning's feelings of excitement and exhilaration seemed distant and unreal. I knew unequivocally that I didn't want to be there. We didn't belong there; and if we did, there had to be another alternative. We didn't know what we were doing. The fun was over!

The operation had taken on an even more fragmented posture; more search and probe by sight instead of mow-them-down tactics. The word was passed down to conserve ammo with no looting or unnecessary destruction. I'm sure that looting never crossed anyone's mind. Perhaps they had a few dollers in piasters. We could possibly go for a chicken or a duck, feathers and all.

I was still moving on line adjacent to the machine gun crew when the ground gave way—or what I thought was the ground crumbled beneath my feet. I was seized with panic. I flailed my arms like a goose, and with quick, spasmodic twists of the body, I attempted to become lighter than air. I fell, but the angle of the pungee stake was slightly off. In the midst of my wild gyrations, I had managed to do something right. It gouged through the soft leather of the arch of my boot but managed to miss the fleshy part of my instep. I pulled my foot from the trap and pried the nasty little stake from the canvas of my boot. There were several other stakes in the pit. I pulled all the sod away and broke the sticks with the butt of my weapon. The incident served a good purpose: it woke me sharply out of a morose stupor of guilt and confusion. It made me recognize the continuing hazardous situation and focused my senses on walking around fifty to sixty pounds lighter.

The machine gun crew opened up on another bamboo hut about thirty yards in front of us. The gunner never let up until his finger became cramped. The wall of the structure quivered and vibrated during the tempest of hot lead and splintered bamboo. I watched the wall of the hut partially disintegrate. For some reason, my entire concentration was on the hut. It was just another hut like all the rest behind us, but I sensed a strange feeling. My entire body felt like it had taken a low-voltage charge. It gave my body a tingling, buzzing sensation, especially the scalp. I was experiencing some kind of a deep, low-level extrasensory perception I had never experienced before. My pulse raced and kept time with the machine gun. My wide, unblinking eyes still focused on the smoldering hut. There was something about it. I had no meaningful thought.

I yelled, "Cease fire! Cease fire!" I ran back and forth up and down the firing line. No one seemed to believe or hear the command until I started shrieking, "Cease fire! Cease fire!" I had literally taken over control of the troops in my immediate vicinity, those who were within hearing distance.

I hadn't become disoriented. My eyes were still glued on the hut. My commands finally registered. I had no business taking over Lieutenant O'Connor's command. He stood there locked in amazement. The men turned and observed my wild antics as though I had flipped out.

I quickly shoved my grenade launcher at the assistant machine gunner, turned, and moved out at a dead run toward the hut. I was running on instinct and fear at top speed. I took my forty-five from my holster, and by the time I had pulled back the slide, I had covered the distance. In full stride, I hurled my body to the ground, landing heavily on my belly and chest. I wiggled and slithered quickly on knees and elbows toward the open doorway. I quickly pushed the forty-five around the corner of the doorsill. Even though I was functioning with mindless instinct or insanity, I still had the presence of mind to be careful. The rest of the men were confused at the present situation but acted instinctively. They dropped to their bellies and took up firing positions.

With my face shoved tightly up against the pole that reinforced the door, I inched around to see what was inside. I could feel the blood bang on the sides of my head with each pulsebeat. I stopped breathing; it had become a nuisance that impaired my hearing. I let one eye adjust to the darkness. I scanned the room, trying to penetrate the shadows. Nothing moved, nothing happened. I inched in closer. My eyes began to dilate and adjust. I crawled in slowly, like an unwanted reptile.

The body of a woman or a girl lay on the floor in the middle of the hut. Her back was to me. Her head was tucked down and her knees drawn up in the fetal position. My eyes adjusted with the help of the tiny, thin rays of sunlight filtering through the thatched walls.

Continued discoveries were more startling. Another girl lay on the smooth, almost polished, earthen floor. She was facing the other woman with her knees drawn up, also. Together, the two bodies formed a near circle. To my astonishment, within the circle were a number of babies. They were no older than eighteen months. They were also huddled together on their sides with their knees drawn up like little unborn fetuses. I knew they were all dead. One, two, three, four. There were five. Their mothers or guardians had tried to protect them with their own bodies. In a corner on the opposite side of the hut lay a little red mongrel dog. He was stretched out on his belly with his head resting on his paws. He was alive! He watched me and growled deep in his throat.

"How did you survive this, fellow?" I asked.

Out of the corner of my eye, I caught a movement and jumped. The body closest and with its back to me had turned around and looked me right in the eye. She straightened out her legs, rolled over, and sat up with no sign of pain. A little baby stirred and looked around. The girl sat up. I was crazy with excitement. I couldn't believe my eyes. The entire nursery began to stir. I realized I was still pointing my forty-five, and quickly holstered it. I moved in closer, and knelt down and looked them over for wounds. There wasn't a scratch on any of them. What kind of miracle kept babies motionless without a whimper, spared them from the onslaught of machine-gun fire, and had compelled me to act in such a bizarre, irrational manner? I'd seen nothing. I'd heard nothing consciously—or had I?

I turned and ran out of the hut. I was overcome with joy to near embarrassment at the discovery, and was pleased to know that I wasn't a candidate for a net. I yelled and waved for the men to move in. I ran back into the hut, and within moments the whole squad was crowding around the door.

"Look at this." I picked up one of the babies. "Now one of them has a scratch. A whole damn nursery!"

"You musta heard them, huh, Oggie?" Nellis asked.

"I must have," I lied.

Trudeau pushed everyone back outside. "Okay, back out. We've still got a job to do!"

Each woman picked up a baby. Trudeau, Nellis, and I filed out, each carrying a baby. They started crying and fussing. We sat the family down, if that's what it was, under the shade of a breadfruit tree just outside the hut. The females were all young girls of child-bearing age, but it was inconceivable that they were the mothers of all these babies. Perhaps it was a day-care center. They sat together on the ground in a little huddle. The little red dog stood guard.

Through the yards and little plots of vegetables the troops were still advancing, slowly but deadly. An occasional rocket zipped through the trees and detonated. At this point, we didn't know what to do. Trudeau gave an order for the first squad to quit bunching up and spread out. Nellis asked if it was okay to give our tiny prisoners some water. Canteen cups and candy bars appeared.

Trudeau slapped me lightly on the back. "Ogden, go get the lieutenant. Nellis, go get the doc."

The lieutenant and radio operator were already on their way to the scene. When the lieutenant arrived, the doc had one of the little ones on his lap. The lieutenant crouched down and scanned our catch of tiny prisoners of war already covered with chocolate. He winced and shook his head. "How are they, Doc?"

"They're just fine, Lieutenant. They're not even scared anymore."

The lieutenant gave Jason some orders to spread out the squad and stay put. He summoned Morales, the radio operator. The lieutenant spoke to the captain and explained the situation. It took about five minutes of passing the word up and down the line to get the rest of the company to cease fire.

A bluish-white fog of sulfur and smoke lay undisturbed over the silent village. The search-and-destroy mission had been reduced to search only. The spot where the babies were found was designated a refugee area. The third squad remained behind and the rest of the platoon continued to sweep through the area. The remainder of the morning was tedious, and the air hummed with millions of flies. We no longer felt the village was a threat, but we proceeded with caution. Most of our attention and concern had shifted from the huts and structures to the tunnels and holes. Trudeau used both his French and Vietnamese to coax the hideaways to the surface. Hunting for people burrowed under the ground was a strange treasure hunt, but now and then our patience was rewarded.

We lay on our bellies near the hole, listening for signs of life. Trudeau spoke gently into the hole while we held our breaths and listened. The silence was broken by a tiny, muffled voice deep within.

"Somebody's in there, Corporal," I said with excitement.

We both grinned. It was like fishing; some bit and some didn't. I'm sure everyone was grateful there was an alternative to our earlier tactics.

I'm sure we all entertained the thought of the silence

at the bottom of a black pit, terrified, surrounded by snakes, bugs, and rodents. Your babies cling to you as machine guns and rockets devastate everything you've loved and owned above the ground. The sound of strange voices and boots above your head, then the mysterious appearance of a tiny, white-hot flame that sputters and rolls closer, giving off a sulphur vapor that completely chokes off the air.

"She's coming out," Trudeau said, and we moved back.

The head of a woman appeared. She was a little older than the others, and she was covered from head to foot with dirt. She shaded her eyes from the pain of the sun. Clutching her breast like a tiny monkey was a six-month-old baby. It didn't seem to inconvenience the little one in the least when her mother left the dark cool hole and crawled into the bright hot sunshine. Her breakfast continued right on without a hitch.

Lieutenant O'Connor designated Red to escort the women and children back to Corporal Jason at the staging area. The third squad was now up to its elbows in women, young kids, and babies. The sight of Jason bouncing a three-month-old baby on his knee made me want to confront him and paraphrase his earlier statement, but I thought better of it. I thought all of us had learned a painful lesson. For us, war was not cut and dried as it was for our predecessors. We had one hell of a responsibility.

We found that cutting some bamboo sticks and probing the least-worn paths for unwanted little surprises enabled us to move through the village with greater ease.

Someone had given the word to hold up. We stopped and listened. There was a low moaning sound coming from the other side of a high, thick hedgerow. We approached cautiously. It was a very old woman rocking an old man in her arms, and both were in a near-skeletal state. As she moaned, tears rolled down her wrinkled face past a mouth full of black betel-nut stained lips and teeth. They wore black pajamalike clothing. The old man's pant legs were rolled up above his knees to keep them from getting wet when he worked in the rice paddies. On his right leg was a makeshift bandage or tourniquet. He must have been hurt by a stray round or piece of shrapnel while trying to save their hut. It lay in ruins. Lieutenant O'Connor removed the makeshift bandage. A round had gone through the calf and out the other side. The old man was unconscious, either from shock or perhaps a stroke.

I couldn't get over how ancient and pathetic they appeared. Anyone their age back home would have been in their nineties. The average lifespan in Vietnam is only thirty years. How could these people survive for so long in such a primitive life style?

They were both ravaged with arthritis and other bone-related diseases. Their knuckles and joints were swollen and deformed. Even without the wound, their suffering must have been intolerable. Betel nut, a mild narcotic, offered little comfort.

Lieutenant O'Connor took the old man's arm and felt for a pulse. The woman resisted and pushed his arm away, but finally gave in.

"Trudeau, send a man back for the doc, quick. The old man still has a pulse!"

I picked up a conical straw hat and began to fan them. I felt helpless, and derived very little pleasure from the knowledge that they were miserable before we came. We had sent in a 3.5-inch white phosphorus rocket that had burned and blown everything they owned to dust.

"How can these gooks live like this?" the assistant gunner asked. "I thought Asia had a rather sophisticated culture, but the people are more primitive than those we came across in Malaysia or in the jungles of the Philippines. I thought the niggers in Africa were the only ones in this squalor."

I knew that I was not a student of this planet's cultural theme; but if I had had an answer for him, I would have chosen not to discuss the subject on his level. The labels "gooks" and "niggers" didn't roll off my tongue very well.

Around mid-afternoon, the village was considered secured. We had rounded up and accounted for about four hundred people. A few were still hidden, and some were hidden forever. The exact count of the missing would take some time, preferably after we were gone.

The assault on Le Mai was a gross error. It was the first actual assault by Americans in Vietnam, an order that came directly from President Johnson. The day's event set a precedent for most American combatants.

There are millions of innocent people caught in the middle of war, and it is our responsibility to protect them and gain their confidence in order to deal with the Vietcong effectively. It was a good theory, and sometimes it worked. In the case of Le Mai, it worked. The division helped rebuild it, immediately setting up a hospital and a school and delivering much-needed supplies, making life as tolerable for the people as it could be after being squeezed by the Vietcong.

It is unfortunate that we could not have helped all of the villages. To my knowledge, never again was a village arbitrarily stepped on unless its people insisted on harboring Vietcong.

CHAPTER EIGHT

The Ca De River runs peacefully down out of the mountain and flows past Le Mai Village and onto the South China Sea. It was more like a creek, and not navigable in many places. It was a main Vietcong arterial from the mountains to Elephant Valley.

Le Mai Village had been considered a major Vietcong supply center before it was stomped on by the Third Battalion. To the east, in the mountainous jungle, another tiny village lay nestled on the river. Recon teams learned the village was under Vietcong control. With Le Mai Village under marine control, the Vietcong could no longer move freely in the area to supply themselves. They recruited inhabitants of the village to make the hazardous trek down the mountain past the patrols and ambushes to get supplies. The pressure and the danger became too great, and the people began to refuse. The Vietcong applied more pressure with torture and extortion. The request was granted to relocate the villagers to a safe area. The new location would serve two purposes: it would protect the villagers, forcing the Vietcong back into the mountains to look for another source of supply; and it would cut their mobility and freedom to forage and recruit.

It was 0430, and another chilly morning was coming to life. We were standing outside a column of amtracks near Le Mai receiving our final orders. We were baffled, and mumbled among ourselves. A combat patrol going up a mountain pass in a column of amtracks was a novel, if not crazy, idea. But when it was explained, it appeared to make sense and seemed to fit the operation—at least in theory. We were not to engage the enemy. We would attempt to get the villagers out of their grasp. Tracked, armored breadboxes big enough to carry nearly two squads gave us protection from snipers and ambushers.

The mouths of the great monsters dropped open in unison and we walked up the ramp and down into the belly. We packed in our benches and found something sturdy to hang onto. We knew it was going to be a rough ride.

We were used to driving out of the mouth of a ship and plunging off the ramp into the open sea. In a rough sea, they sometimes completely submerged for a moment or two then came bobbing back to the surface, venting out their exhaust system like a young great whale. The tracks turned, continuously treading water, and kept the craft from sinking while we headed toward the nearest beach. Each time one of these unlikely sea creatures grabbed hold of the bottom and dragged itself up on the beach, it seemed like a miracle.

The engines began to whine and the cables went taut as the huge gate swung upward like the power gate of a commercial truck. The crew chief sealed the door and switched on a tiny red lamp. Only the coxswain and crew chief could actually see where we were going. Their seats and controls were up forward, on stanchions, and their heads stuck out of hatches in the overhead when the craft was not totally buttoned up. They wore helmets, with communication systems in them similar to a pilot's. The crew chief manned a thirty-caliber machine gun mounted topside. The engines whined under greater strain, and the coxswain slammed the machine into gear. It jolted forward like it had no transmission, only "go" and "stop," and no in-between. We jiggled and bounced inside the belly of this manmade dinosaur. We could barely see each other in the dim red shadows. The steel-footed monster bucked, pivoted, and swayed, crunching over rock and clawing through marsh as the strange, steel wormlike column angled its way up the gorge. Trudeau and Charlie sat on either side of me, and Lieutenant O'Connor, Morales, and Campbell straddled the bench running down the center.

I could barely hear myself over the roar of the engines. "Lieutenant, sir, whose idea was it to use amtracks to evacuate the village?"

"Mine."

The rest of us looked at each other quickly as though our own leader, Muldoon, didn't have the quality to dream up such a hare-brained idea, much less sell it to the battalion commander. His voice held an edge of reluctance, as though he didn't care to discuss such an urgent plan with peons—or maybe it was plain modesty.

He explained: "The steep mountain jungle terrain makes it impossible to evacuate people by helicopter, and to bring the whole village down the trail would invite every sniper and ambush artist in the country down on us. Can you imagine running into an ambush with a bunch of women and children? Their lives would be in jeopardy, as well as the lives of every man here. We'll load all the inhabitants in tractors and send them down the gorge. We'll take to the trail on foot. An evacuation like this in broad daylight will probably draw some enemy—"

Blam!!!

It sounded like someone had hit the outside of the tractor with a brick. The crew chief opened up with a machine gun. It was incoming enemy small-arms fire bouncing off the skin of the craft. The skin was not thick enough to withstand an armor-piercing bullet. Lieutenant O'Connor jumped up and braced himself, holding onto the overhead. He got to the phone near the coxswain and found out the others were also drawing small-arms fire. The word was to keep on moving. We looked around at each other and hung on. Our machine gun kept blazing. The almost-useless air-conditioning was working overtime, but we could hardly notice it. The tension wrung the sweat from our bodies, and it flowed freely.

Another round slammed into the side. Each time we

were hit, the head snapped, the lungs froze, the bowels turned to ice water. We knew that if one of these rounds found its way through the skin of the craft, more than one of us would get hurt.

I turned to Trudeau. "If they have any mortars or rockets, even little ones, we're screwed."

He didn't say anything. He gritted his teeth, sweat, and hung on.

The crew chief yelled down for some more ammo. Charlie bent down under the bench and dragged out an ammo can. He popped it open and handed it to him. He helped him feed the belt into the gun. It continued to cook. I had visions of running out of ammo and fuel while hundreds of Vietcong swarmed over us and dropped hand grenades down the hatches. In each man's face there was a contortion of tension and anticipation of a hit that might rip through the side, shatter into tiny fragments, and volley around the inside of the compartment.

Someone up forward yelled out, "Let's stop and get the hell out of here!" I agreed in my mind immediately. O'Connor told him to shut up and sit down. I closed my eyes, hung on, and continued to sweat.

Charlie turned from the machine gun and yelled at me. "Give me more ammo. He doesn't see anything out there; we're just spraying the area."

I reached down, popped open the metal box, dragged out a dangling belt of ammo, and handed it to him. The platoon clown with big, bushy eyebrows and an infectious grin was doing a good job. I was proud of him. He fed the ammo into the breech. He waved for another belt. I dropped it over his shoulder and around his neck. It was our first time in a combat situation, and our fate was in the hands of a coxswain and a crew chief. We were as helpless as blind rats at the bottom of a well. I knew that popping open the ammo cans was only a small contribution, but it kept me from feeling helpless.

The heat in the rolling sauna was no longer taken for granted. My eyes began to burn and swell from the briny perspiration trickling down from under my helmet, and the river continued to flow down the middle of my back into my shorts.

A volley of rounds slammed into the outside. A violent shiver momentarily raced up and down my back as I flexed to pop open another ammo can. We continued to pitch, roll, and bang our way to our destination. The tension and pensiveness gave way to a more wide-eyed, elusive expression on the faces of the men. I knew none of us would be able to handle a hell of a lot more of this.

The coxswain reached down and tapped O'Connor on the shoulder. O'Connor quickly put his head up near the hatch, hoping for some information. He patted the coxswain on the back and turned around.

"All right, men, listen up! Make sure you have all your gear. The minute the gate drops, we'll get out of here and tie in with the rest of the platoon."

At that moment the craft hit something and nosed up, nearly knocking the lieutenant down on us. It slammed down again hard on its belly. The engines raced and screamed, but we were no longer moving.

The coxswain frantically slammed the vehicle in and out of gear and quickly moved the jockey stick that controlled the vehicle's every movement. The engines screamed in and out of gear. His inaudible lips worked feverishly at the mike in front of his mouth. We had bottomed out on some rock. The engine of the tractor couldn't get any traction forward or in reverse. The noise was still at a tremendous level, but we were motionless. Another round bounced off the overhead. Panic set in. We were trapped!

Some of the men got out of their seats, screaming and yelling. "We're sitting ducks. Let's get the fuck out of here!" The rest of us were probably too scared to move or yell. Breathing had become more difficult.

O'Connor yelled and shoved the men back down to their seats to maintain order. "Goddamn it, listen up! We're all right. Sit down and shut up! Keep your heads!"

At that instant, something slammed into the rear of the vehicle like an explosion. It knocked O'Connor back against the bulkhead and everyone else back into their seats. He quickly recovered and found something to hang onto. We were hit from behind again by another amtrack in the convoy and knocked free. We were rocking and pitching forward on our own again. A round of cheers went up. It was the longest thirty-minute ride any of us would ever experience.

The gate popped and had hardly begun to drop when we scrambled out. The cool, damp morning hit us like a welcome icy blizzard. The intake into the lungs was like the first breath at birth.

We tramped around in the jungle in typical confusion. We finally got on line and swept to within one hundred yards of the village, anticipating snipers every inch of the way.

A Vietnamese interpreter was assigned to first squad. His name was Nugent Cao Tai. He was above-average height for a Vietnamese and was dressed in perfectly tailored and starched tiger-striped utilities with a black beret. He seemed too young for the job, but spoke better English than anyone else in the squad—or in the company, for that matter. He was a startling contrast to the Vietnamese villagers and the Vietnamese army we had come across.

The first squad was assigned to get into the village and inform the people. Our own interpreter, "The Foot," had proven a success, but even a Vietnamese organizing and mobilizing an entire village was going to have a difficult job.

We entered the village cautiously. The village was considerably smaller than Le Mai. It nestled on the bank of the tiny river and was protected by towering, exotic, floral-covered hillsides. It was a beautiful lost Shangri-La.

Portions of the jungle high on the hillside gave way to neatly cultivated terraces. It was peaceful and quiet. The intense tranquility gave way to nervousness. The sound of one's own heavy, labored breathing did not fit in with this scheme of beauty.

We assumed that the villagers would be desperately trying to evade the jaws of the Vietcong terrorism. We anticipated a pushing, shoving, unruly mob trying to evacuate—but the village appeared to be already cleared. There wasn't a sign of life anywhere.

We spotted the probable cause. In the center of a tiny courtyard, we discovered the body of a man about forty years old, clad only in a pair of shorts. The body lay chest-down in an enormous pool of blood. The bloodless face with liquid, staring eyes gazed up into the morning sunrise. The eyes were still clear, and seemed to be staring in wonder. The head had been severed cleanly above the collarbone, leaving the entire neck with the head. To see your first death was shocking, but to see a human head totally separated was horrifying.

For a moment we were speechless, unable to move, strangely entranced by the horror that lay at our feet. Blood has a strange metallic smell like tarnished brass when exposed to air; it jells, contracts, and turns black. There were tiny, diminishing furls of steam rising out of the severed esophagus and trachea of the torso.

Trudeau began to unstrap his poncho that was folded and tied to his cartridge belt. His eyes squinted and his forehead wrinkled as though in deep pain. "Jesus Christ!" There was a strong undertone of "why?" in his words. We covered the body with the poncho.

The interpreter spoke in perfect English. "This is a Vietcong execution. By the signs, it happened a few moments ago. He was probably a village leader or chief. To defy the Vietcong means a sure death. The alternatives to the people are traumatic. To leave their homes and ancestors behind and break with ancient binds to the land would be sacrilege. They would suffer the loss of dignity and hope."

We began to search the village for more casualties or for anyone at all. Trudeau and the interpreter began to speak in Vietnamese, asking the people to come out from hiding and telling them we were there to take them to a safe place. Their voices echoed strongly from mountain to mountain. We stood motionless, listening and watching for any sign of life. The strange Vietnamese dialogue echoed off the hillsides for about ten minutes.

Charlie and I stood in the shade of a hut. He fumbled for a pack of cigarettes, put one in his mouth, and was about to light it. The cigarette got away from him as he pointed and yelled. "There they come! Across the river!"

We looked through the grove of banana palms that grew on the river bank. On the opposite bank, a slow progression of people entered the water, coming in our direction out of the jungle. There were men, women, and children of all ages. They walked with heads down as if in mourning. The water was about knee high, and the mothers lifted the little ones and carried them across.

Leading the forlorn procession was a very old man carrying a young boy of nine or ten. The child was very limp in his arms, either sick or dead. They drew near the courtyard, and I could see tears streaming down the face of the old man. The woman directly behind was being helped by two young girls. Probably the mother, she was also crying.

The old man stopped in front of Trudeau and the interpreter. The rest of the group gathered around. Charlie and I approached the sad procession. The old man was speaking rapidly. The little boy's chest was a mass of meat and blood. Someone had cut the skin and then peeled it away in long strips, literally skinning him alive.

The interpreter relayed to us what had happened. The old man was the father of the dead man and the grandfather of the little boy. The villagers had been forced to watch the torture of the child and the anguish of the father, who was held and made to observe closely and listen to the screams of the boy. Then they cut off the father's head in the presence of the mother and forced her to hold it.

"Tell them to get their belongings. We are getting out of here," Trudeau said. He turned to Campbell, who was on the radio. "Tell the lieutenant we are almost ready to roll."

He quizzed the old man, who told him that the Vietcong had left about fifteen minutes ago, headed east back into the higher mountains.

The interpreter told the people to get their belongings and anything they could carry. The villagers dispersed in all directions, except for the old man and woman. He continued to speak. He said he wanted to remain behind to bury his son and grandson. He would never leave the village, no matter what happened. Someone had to stay behind to take care of the village.

"They'll come back and kill him for sure," I said.

He said he would rather die with his family and

ancestors than in a strange place.

I could hear the amtrack engines start to hum and grind further down the canyon. The exodus had commenced. The remainder of their broken lives began to pile up in the courtyard: material things with little intrinsic value; things that could easily be replaced but that had much-needed sentimental and esthetic value to these people who were being torn from mental and spiritual sustenance. There was an endless array of baskets of all sizes filled with everything imaginable. Crude pack boards, poles, grass mats, chickens, ducks, calves, goats, and piglets.

The amtracks pulled up behind the village and dropped their gates like huge hungry beasts. We helped carry their gear, but they were reluctant to enter the jaws of the beast. We coaxed them, then showed them by example that there was no danger. The old were more reluctant to leave than the young. It registered sharply in the faces of the old women who chattered feverishly, probably cursing the Vietcong—and us, for that matter. Some just went along with the excitement of boarding the vehicle, nursing naked babies and cradling lambs and piglets. One old lady in her conical straw hat clutched a great white goose as though it were the last of her family.

We loaded as much gear topside as we could possibly tie down. We packed the inside of the vehicle with as many humans and creatures as it could hold.

Trudeau walked over to me as I heaved another basket of rice up to Charlie. He handed me a puppy about eight weeks old.

"This has got to be the strangest Marine Corps combat assignment of all time—juggling ducklings, puppies and babies. What am I going to do with this?" I asked.

"I don't know. Find its mother, or it's gonna be left behind."

The puppy was cute and alert, his big brown eyes and needle-sharp teeth that found a finger to chew on.

"It's sure a fuzzy little thing," I said. I looked around for a place to put it.

Charlie, arms spread out as if to envelope the whole mourning scene, said, "Gentlemen, how does it feel to be contemporary Noahs with your little steel arks?"

"Why don't you jump down here and take a whiff inside of one of these little arks? Then tell me what you think, Noah."

"Where's your spirit, Oggie?"

I paused. "I've got a handful of it," I said. "This dog just pissed all over me!"

He laughed and nearly fell off the amtrack.

Our experience this morning would never be forgotten. Helping and protecting these people who were caught between two hard spots had enlightened our spirits.

The captain gave the word to move out. The amtracks looked like huge piles of mechanized rubbish, pivoting and bucking down the trail, grinding up over tree stumps and fresh earth that they had gouged out coming up from the river banks.

CHAPTER NINE

Military buildup around Danang was evident day by day. We watched Uncle Sam's warships sail in and out of the harbor. The early rumors of going home within weeks gave way to new rumors of an extension for as much as one year. Total control of the Elephant Valley was crucial to the protection of Danang Air Base. The taking of Le Mai Village, the control of the Ca De River, and the use of the French castle to the north end of the valley as a tactical observatory was further restricting the Vietcong's mobility and easy access to the supplies. In retaliation they blew bridges along the main supply route from Danang that led to the castle.

The vast, complex irrigation system of the valley was facilitated by numerous bridges which were crucial to the local population and the resupply of the Third Marine Regiment. The road was cluttered daily with supply trucks, civilian bases, bicycles, scooters, and numbers of pedestrians coming and going from the marketplace.

With so many Americans present, tiny vendors and shops sprang up along the roadway. They were always on the move with their little baskets and carts. Some of the more industrious sellers even climbed to the top of the ridge line to sell to the troops in the foxholes, right under the noses of the unsuspecting—or lenient— leadership.

It seemed like everyone was selling Coca Cola, and even the tiny kids who could only carry one or two bottles were out trying to make a buck. Tiger Beer, crudely brewed in the village, and loaves of French bread, were the next biggest sellers. They were a delectable relief from C-rations. It sometimes became a nuisance when overzealous little kids attempted to follow us on patrols. The rear guard had to continuously shoo them away.

It seemed as though we had established a good rapport with the people of this sector. And why not? Commerce and trade was indeed a universal language. The Americans had become captured victims of consumerism, supply and demand, the root of capitalism, the sinister, cultural, polluting system these Vietnamese were supposedly fighting against. Who cares about all that while sucking on a popsicle on a combat patrol in one-hundred-ten-degree heat in enemy and bug-infested Southeast Asia?

Our next assignment was to ensure that the main arterial between town and village, supply ship and troop concentration, was kept from being interrupted. Iron Bridge Ridge was probably named by some classroom lieutenant carrying a map case three times practical size—but at least it had more of a creative ring than Monkey Mountain, or some of the others. I preferred native names for things and places. A name like Iron Bridge Ridge could have been anywhere in the world—even along the banks of the Snohomish River in Snohomish County, where hardy, overdressed, overenthusiastic anglers braving the sleet-filled Northwesterly, possessed less intelligence than the highly prized steelhead that lurked in the dark, swirling pools.

The ridge was a tiny island populated by palm trees and low, impossible brush. It rose from the ebb and flow of a golden sea of rice that covered thousands of acres in all directions. The tiny microdot of uncultivated land was divided by a deep, stagnant slough on which sat a bridge built by a nineteenth-century French genius with an oversized erector set. It was strong and wide enough for a tank and a hundred more years of bare feet, if the Vietcong didn't blow it first. The rusty angle-iron, worn beams, and rivets had already survived several of their attempts. All traffic, vehicle and pedestrian, would have to check through Hotel Company for the time being.

The captain assigned platoon areas, long stretches of real estate around the island that seemed like a beach front. Palm trees and a never-ending stream of vendors and pretty girls to admire made the area seem like an envious place to be.

Speculation on luxurious Iron Bridge Ridge was quickly laid to rest when a complex network of trench lines had to be dug with bunkers every twenty yards.

The whole island would become a series of rat paths and burrows with weeks of gophering and filling sandbags. Sandbags were issued to each platoon in one-hundred-pound lots, along with axes, picks, and long-handled shovels. The shovels were reverently referred to as "Ethiopian back-hoes."

The trench lines were three-feet wide and about waist deep. Three layers of sandbags were stacked up on the outsides of the parapet, which would give a rifleman a good firing position. I would need a box to stand on just to look over it. The bunkers were six by six, and shoulder-deep with edges also lined with sandbags laid overlapping each other like bricks and spaced to allow portholes on three sides.

The biggest and most beautiful palm trees came crashing down in all directions, falling prey to hordes of self-ordained lumberjacks, most of whom did not know or care to know how to fell a tree properly as long as it tumbled from the sky into their clutches. I guess the enthusiasm could be attributed to the first-time syndrome. Knocking your first huge tree out of the sky can be paralleled with knocking your first mallard down or catching your first rainbow trout. I never quite understood the fervor and zealousness that surrounded the building of bunkers and diggings of trench lines. It was very mundane and unexciting work except for the tiny ceremonial celebration when two squads would meet, and only six inches of earth remained to link the two projects. Larger commemorations were celebrated when platoon projects came together. If such nonsense were allowed to get out of hand, I could see the ultimate trench-tying ceremony: a command chopper landing, with Secretary of Defense McNamara and General Walt stepping out, carrying bottles of champagne and wielding golden Ethiopian back-hoes.

It took the entire weapons platoon to carry and lift each log they put on top of their bunkers. Each log was twelve feet long and eighteen inches thick, which made more than formidable roof. They squabbled among themselves like they were in competition or they knew something that we didn't, like the Vietcong had B-52 bombers or they had taken over the Seventh Fleet and were wielding twelve-inch naval guns.

We watched them build their pyramids in the sun. They relished their achievements with the same idiotic pride that motivated their smallest men to carry the biggest, heaviest, and most cumbersome weapons. We were all glad we were not part of their idiotic circus. We would be considered underachievers.

I was glad our platoon was a little lazy and didn't see the need or compulsion to show how strong or brainless we could be. Our projects met practical minimum requirements. Whether they were suffering from lack of leadership or some other peculiarity, weapons platoons were still a necessary evil. If they had had Caswell, they would have pushed him into a well-needed straight jacket a long time ago.

Concertina wire circled the entire ridge, two sections high, looking like huge tunnels of hair coming off a hot curler before brushing. In front of each squad's field of fire on the other side of the defense line, small anti-personnel mines called claymores were set strategically, one per squad. These remained above the surface, and when detonated electrically, blew thousands of tiny, diced steel fragments in a one-hundred-sixty degree front. Their firing patterns overlapped the entire perimeter. They were un-booby-trapped each morning and brought in, and were set out each evening; they were also booby-trapped to blow if not disarmed in proper sequence. Empty C-ration cans with a pebble inside were tied to the concertina wire. They swung freely in the breeze and sometimes sounded off with the least amount of disturbance.

Sheldon, the third squad leader, wasn't quite satisfied with our defensive setup. He scrounged a fifty-five-gallon oil drum and some plastic explosives from engineers who were studying the bridge. He decided to devise an anti-personnel mine of his own creation. Taking two pounds of plastics which had the consistency of modeling clay, he fastened it to the bottom of the barrel on the inside. We dig the barrel into the side of the ridge below the concertina wire. When completely dug in, the mouth of the barrel pointed out across the paddies like a giant cannon. He crawled in the mouth of the cannon and placed electrical blasting caps with two lead wires. He strung the wires back up the hill to his position and tied them off, then we commenced to scrounge for Coke bottles. We roamed the entire island scavenging empty throwaways from the rest of the company. Coke bottles are ideal: extremely thick, with a heavy base; and when broken, they can be very effective in a blast. We were enthusiastic as sadistic fiends breaking up bottles and filling our cannon to the brim. Crude but ingenious. When detonated, it could conceivably cover the entire platoon area.

Sheldon grinned with a set of teeth big enough to pearl-handle a forty-five. "If them motha fuckas come after me, they gonna get glass in they ass."

"Amen, brother," a Richard Pryor fan yelled.

Later, I began to wonder and worry about all the fortifications and precautions. Next to the castle, this was the most perfectly fortified and strategic spot in the entire valley. I just couldn't imagine the enemy getting close enough to need anti-personnel mines. We were slightly elevated, and there were thousands of yards of open space with just rice stalks for cover. Even at night, eighty-ones and artillery could send up illuminations. It would be suicidal even to get close to this place; they would have to come by the thousands. The more I thought about it, the more ridiculous it sounded. We'd probably never see anyone.

After the construction on the island had been completed, the furor of activity during the day dwindled to playing cards and throwing the football around. There were numerous farmers peacefully attending their rice crops every day. I was amazed how they worked from sunup to sundown in extreme heat without taking a break. Unlike Mexico, there didn't seem to be a siesta. If they were resting or taking shifts, we were unaware of it. We were preoccupied with looking for little antidotes to escape the boredom of hot, tropical afternoons.

Ed and I shared the responsibility of one of the

bunkers. Fifty-fifty watch night and day; we could break it up any way we liked. Ed was from my old fire team, one of the original members of the squad back at Pendleton. He was tall, but very frail, and timid. He had huge brown eyes like those of a lemur, and little chipmunk teeth, and tiny wiry hands. His helmet and uniform were always too big for him, and he looked like a squirrel monkey in green. He managed to do everything wrong and jumped nervously when anyone called his name. In training, the NCOs gave up on him and considered him just another shitbird. We got along well. He was unintentionally funny. It was like having Don Knotts around.

When I became fire-team leader, my quest for perfection was relentless. The night before inspections we would stay up until the wee hours of the morning trying to get him ready. I had to do practically everything for him, but somehow we always managed to make it; he would pass.

One day he told me that he appreciated my helping him a lot, and asked me if I could care to go on liberty with him. He lived in San Diego, which was only a couple of hours away. He said he could probably fix me up with a girlfriend for the weekend. I thought it was a good idea. If nothing came of it, we could scoot across to Tijuana.

It was during liberty that I discovered I was dealing with two different human beings. He was a fine dresser with above-average taste. He drove his mother's Chevy Malibu as though it were a formula car. But the most astonishing trait of this dual character was that, despite his inadequacies, he had an inexhaustible, voracious appetite for women. This was why the underground nicknamed him "The Horn."

He was not just another mouth, but a man of action. During the course of a better weekend, he introduced me to two or three different girls. He didn't have great taste, but his string of sun bunnies were tanned, soft, and giggly. We frolicked in the sun and surf of San Diego's Mission Bay. At last, the endless nights of midnight classes in the fine art of spit shines were paying off.

I asked him why he'd joined the Marine Corps. I thought he should have joined another branch of the service, since he was born right in the middle of the naval community. He said it was a drunken dare. His buddies said he wouldn't last a week. They were almost correct.

I admired his guts in carrying it through. But, like some other people, he just couldn't adjust to the Marine Corps way of doing things. Most people end up with severe disciplinary problems; but with his mild temperament and my patience, he just barely climbed the hurdles.

When he was off on liberty, though, there were no holes barred, and the sky was the limit. He did not need help from anyone. The tables were turned. I needed help with the women.

CHAPTER TEN

To break the monotony, I decided to take a tour of the area. I hadn't been away from my position for a number of days. I walked over a grassy knoll toward the CP area. The ground leveled off and was bare. It was the center of the island, and to my right was an old French blockhouse. It was green and black from generations of moss. The west wall was knocked down and part of the roof was caved in. It was obviously constructed for the same reason: to protect the bridge from the same type of political factions. Only the names had changed.

Toward the west end of the island they had managed to move in a four-deuce artillery piece. I started down the other side of the knoll. The CP bunker jumped up at me like a brand new supermarket that had been constructed across the street when you go away on vacation, and you wonder how they could have built it so quickly. It was quite an awesome structure for this tiny island. It was about five times longer than any other bunkers, with walls three- to four-feet thick. There must have been literally tons of sandbags used, and there was comm wire leading from it in all directions. It had a corrugated tin roof. We on the front lines had not thought of having to keep these things dry during an occasional monsoon. The bunkers would fill up like septic tanks.

The island was crescent shaped from east to west, the eastern end being more open and free of brush. The tiny trench lines with their high sandbag walls resembled the great wall of China at a long distance; a ribbonlike mass arching over each knoll, then broken and hidden in the valley, to appear and disappear again.

I waded through the normal CP activity: men standing around drinking water from a lister bag that stood in the middle of the area, swinging freely on three poles fashioned in teepee style. The canvas bag of water was always saturated, which created evaporation and dropped the temperature of the water a little. I decided to try some.

The eighty-one mortar team was going through mock drills. Other than that, it was a siesta lull. I heard little bits of chatter and laughter coming from the bridge and decided to investigate. A little coke on ice, and maybe a glance at a pretty girl.

I started down the trail past the CP. It was already a well-used path down into a gully and up the other side to the road. The gully was full of brush, cool and hidden from the sun, and on the opposite bank hidden back in the shadows was another bunker.

There were two marines sitting on the roof, relaxing in the shade, one reading and the other wiping down his rifle. I recognized the one with the rifle as Cable, and realized that this was the third platoon area. Cable and I had gone surfing together at San Onofre Beach—or at least he had tried to teach me. I was a hopeless case. I could not keep from slipping off the board, even with tons of wax. Then I got a brainstorm. I put on some tennis shoes and paddled out. I caught a couple of good ones coming in and actually looked like I knew what I was doing. I wasn't hanging five, but it felt good after all the frustration. I got a lot of laughs for lack of class and being square, but it had worked.

"Hey, Oggie, what are you doing?" He chuckled to his bookworm friend, "I love that name."

"Just out roaming the neighborhood. It's changed a lot since I moved in. I think the value of the property has gone down considerably."

"I bet you are. I bet you heard about the fine little chickies, and you're sniffing around. There's been some fine-looking stuff coming across that bridge. Asshole here," he nudged the bookworm with his foot, "could have had one a couple of days ago, if he had been cool. Some of these gook broads are looking so fine."

"Can't hurt to look," I said. "See you later."

I started up the bank, got up on the road, and headed toward the bridge. The bridge itself had become a regular carnival. Giggling, screaming, naked kids were jumping off the bridge into the slough. Every now and then a Marine would grab a skinny brown little swimmer and hurl him out into space. He'd scream, fold up, and do a cannonball on his friends below. The little one would surface again, yell, and shake his fist in mock protest.

There were dozens of vendors just off the east end of the bridge. I enjoyed the mayhem on the bridge for a while and then decided to do some shopping. Everyone mobbed the potential buyer. The ages of the competitive hard-selling group seemed like eight to eighty. The ladies were clad in their pajamalike satin traditionals, baggy pants, and a long-sleeved, no-frill blouse. Their blouses and shirts were of neutral colors. It was plain, hard-working, practical attire, loose-fitting and cool, and served no other purpose than to cover the body. There was nothing garish about these people.

Betel-nut blackened teeth glistened like slate from under conical grass hats. It was said that black teeth was a sign of beauty. I'll leave that up to personal taste. The grossly deformed lips, and mud-and-cow-dung hairdos of Africa are also considered beautiful.

Age was very difficult to determine. Some were wrinkled and some were not. There seemed to be no in-between. The young girls stood about and smiled. They had not yet been blessed with the black-beauty syndrome, much to my satisfaction and approval of pearly whites and unstained lips. I determined their ages to be from fourteen to sixteen, or even more, because of the nicely shaped breasts. Their long, lovely, perfectly straight hair would have fallen somewhere to the midpoint of their backs had it not been tied up in a bun. Their eyes were big, brown, and bright, like soft velour. On their faces were tiny beads of perspiration that left a subtle sheen, soft and golden as the purest honey.

One girl, slightly smaller and more beautiful than the others, turned away, embarrassed at my prolonged staring, obviously more sensitive than the others. She aroused my curiosity and maleness so strongly that I was embarrassed myself, and hoped that my suntan hid my blushing. She was so small and beautiful. Tiny, silklike hairs waved with the breeze from the nape of her neck and all along her hairline in the back. They were yet too fine and immature to be restricted within the confines of the mature hair that made up her bun. Curves—youthful and not completely mature—did not give way; or were they restricted by the baggy shabbiness of her clothing? Even her small, dirty bare feet that protruded out from pant legs that were too long and dragged in the dirt, could be forgiven. I knew she could be no more than fourteen.

I was brought abruptly out of my enjoyable trance by a little boy about five years old tugging on my utility coat. "You number one, you number one, okay?"

He was dressed only in shorts and was very brown. He pointed to an unlit cigarette he had stuck in a cavity where two front baby teeth were missing. He kept pointing to the cigarette as though he wanted me to light it. I reached into the deep baggy pockets of my utility pants, pulled out a candy bar, and took off the wrapper. I took the cigarette from its neat little toothless holder and replaced it with the candy bar before he had time to protest. He immediately bit down on it, nodded with approval at the transaction and beamed in delight. I threw the cigarette down on the ground and stepped on it. I shook my head. "Bad, bad, number ten, number ten."

One of the mamas handed me a nice, cold Coca Cola and I gave her more than enough piasters to cover the transaction. I didn't feel like bartering. I tipped it back and opened my throat, letting it fall unrestricted into a deprived and deserving cavity until the nerves, activated by the cold, collided with each other somehwere in the back of my head and throat, causing a painful signal that my lungs and pipes were about to collapse from the carbonation. It was absolutely exhilarating! Thank God Coke can be purchased anywhere in the world. I bought some more Cokes, some of Fred's favorite green stuff, and a couple of loaves of French bread for later. It would be nice to empty their little bamboo carryalls, but I was short on piasters. I had a few greenbacks, but it was illegal for Americans to have them in their possession, let alone spend them. They were of great black market value to the communists, and I didn't want to finance someone's AK-47 and end up on the wrong end of it. I waved to the mamasans and kids, winked at the beauties. We exchanged smiles, and I started back across the bridge.

By now, the slough was even more alive with action. Troops were now jumping off the bridge and having as much fun as the kids. My short excursion was a pleasant and much-needed diversion. Under different circumstances, this could indeed be a paradise.

I headed back to my position. It was the hottest part of the day. Ed was sitting in the shade of the lean-to that extended down from the top of the bunker. He seemed to be in deep thought, gazing out across the rice fields. I sat myself down in the shade.

"What's happening, Oggie?" he asked, with a smile that quickly faded away. "How did you like those foxy chicks at the bridge?"

"I tell you what, I was sure surprised. The women here are better looking than in Okinawa, Japan, or the Philippines."

"Look, I'm gonna find me the right one, marry her, and take her home."

I couldn't believe what I had heard, and laughed. I guess it was the depressed, melancholy way he said it. I almost thought he meant it.

"You attempt a numbskull act like that and they'll have you in the brig or in a straight jacket for sure. We're not here to marry the country and take it home with us, we're here to save it and leave it here. What's the matter with you, anyway? You're acting kind of wierd. You're not thinking of bailing out, are you?"

"No," he said as he abruptly threw away the twig he had been sucking on. He looked back over the sandbags and pushed his cap back on his forehead. "You remember the tall redhead I introduced you to at Mission Beach?"

"Yeah, I think her name was Sharon, wasn't it? She had great legs and good chocolate cake."

"Yeah, that's the one, the bitch. I got a letter from her. She's going with somebody else."

"I didn't realize you were so hung up on her."

"I'm not hung up."

"Then what's your problem?"

"They can't write me off like this."

"They?" I asked. "You mean you have letters from others?"

"Yeah."

"Well, buddy, what do you expect them to do? Stand in platoon formation down at the docks in San Diego when the ship comes in? I can see them all now. Sitting around at a Tupperware party biting their nails and waiting for The Horn to come home. The Horn's gonna show up in San Diego with a little nasan bride and a couple of little babysans! That oughta fix them!"

He smiled. "Shut up!" He swung at me playfully. I ducked.

"Here, Casanova." I handed him a not-so-cold soda pop and a loaf of French bread. "This ought to take care of a broken heart for a while."

He popped the top off with his belt buckle and proceeded to examine the contents of the bottle, especially the sediment on the bottom. He cracked open the loaf of French bread to examine any impurities, and picked it apart like a hungry raccoon. Occasionally there would be grass, twigs, or a tiny stone, but nothing we couldn't get around. After all, the bread was baked in the village; and, in fact, sometimes it looked as though they had rolled the dough on the ground. Other than a few pickings here and there, the bread was great, and it smelled too good not to eat. It was made out in the open in a not-too-sanitary bakery, but as long as half a bug didn't show up. I was not going to worry."

I was always entertained and totally amazed by Ed's sterile, antiseptic fetish. It was not quite to the point of mental imbalance, but very comical. He checked all the food and drink of native origin like a mad pathologist. After all the films and lectures we had in training about V.D., Ed took it much more seriously than most of us. Although we were aware of the problem and took it seriously, Ed was totally consumed with the idea. On his first liberty in Okinawa, after a cute but commercial date, he raced back to the barracks and scrubbed himself vigorously for hours. The whole platoon had become aware of his feverish sterilizing process and gathered around to watch. Two days later, it was confirmed, he had contracted something. He was the first, and one of the very few, who contracted anything. The platoon screamed and howled for days. I felt a little sorry for him, but it was indeed classical. He was the butt of every V.D. joke for months.

"Oh, I almost forgot." He pulled a letter out of his breast pocket. "They had mail call while you were gone. This is for you."

The thickness of the letter was unusual. Mom didn't usually write long letters. My heart stopped when I recognized the flawless, beautiful handwriting on the envelope. No one will ever write my name so beautifully in longhand.

The postmark was a month ago. I hesitated, almost too afraid to open the letter. I let the faint perfume do its provocative work inside my head. Why now, after all these months? I took out my pocketknife and slid it under the flap so as not to destroy the envelope. The small pages of stationery were robin-egg blue, with a tiny forget-me-not monogrammed on the upper left-hand corner. It's a strange sensation to hold something clean and fragrant, with words beautifully written and passed secretly and silently from one mind to another, like the private communion of two people who have only eye contact across a crowded room.

My mother hated the nickname "Dick," but I liked it. Only my grandfather and one other person used it. The letter was from her:

Dear Dick:

I'm sorry for not continuing to write to you after I became a mother, but things became terribly hectic. I'm sure you can understand, though, being from a large family yourself. You were like a brother to me, always kind and understanding, and quite mature for your age. Although you were younger and shy, you were unique, and you were my friend.

I remember when you came and told me you had joined the Marine Corps. I laughed at you and you got angry. I'm sorry for that. It was only a reflex. I thought we were both too young to accept something so worldly, within our idealistic and immature world. Silly girls grow up too, and I was proud of you. I was especially proud when you came home on leave and stopped by Dad's in your uniform and met Bob.

I don't want to burden you with my problems. I'm sure you have all you can handle right now in the war, but we were close, and I know you'll understand. We had been married almost two years, and he's gone now. He was killed a month ago, when his truck overturned on the way to work. I can't believe it has happened to me. I still cry at night. Sometimes, when I'm in the kitchen in the late afternoon, I hear him coming through the front door and I run to the front room, and there's no one there.

He left something behind, so precious and dear, that enables me to carry on. A part of himself, a part of us, a part of what life is all about. Bethany is ten months old now, and just as beautifiul as her daddy. The same hair and nose, and when I look into her eyes I feel a mixture of great joy and heartache.

I've been wondering how you were and where you were. Writing a letter to you has always been special to me and has always lifted my spirits. I hope you'll take care of yourself and come home soon. We've both come a long way from the strawberry fields.

I don't know if you've heard or not, but I got so excited when I read about it in the *Herald*. It seems that you and your family are becoming celebrities in town. There was a half-page article about your little brothers John and Mike, and the Cedarcrest School. You are the only one in town who is in the Vietnam War, and the kids at school wanted to do something for the cause. It was in the Sunday supplement. There they were in living color, Mike and John and the other kids, holding a large care package with cake and cookies. I thought it was marvelous . . .

She continued on about her plans and the security that Bob had left her. She said that no one need worry about her, as she was in good financial shape. She also included a little typical small-town gossip. Diana had invited her to a dinner party, but she said she couldn't handle the seaweed hors d'ourvres. I was already aware of Japanese customs, food, and beauty.

Our families had known each other for many years, and Diana and I practically grew up together. I remember once when I was home on leave, and Diana called to ask me if I wanted to go horseback riding. I told her I would be delighted. She was fifteen at the time, and I was seventeen. I was somewhat puzzled when she showed up with only one horse, since they had a full stable. But Diana was no longer a skinny-kneed silly little girl, and I learned that a horse was very comfortable carrying two people.

The letter was signed, "Love, Elizabeth. P.S. Do you still have the St. Christopher medal I gave you?"

I got up and stepped out from under the lean-to. I noticed Fred peering at the last ounce of green stuff in the bottle and eyeballing it clinically, looking for impurities. The bread looked as though an unhungry but inquisitive raccoon had gone through it.

"You don't look so good. Did you get a Dear John letter too?"

I didn't want to go into it with him just then.

"See, I told you them broads have no heart." He went back to picking at the bread and putting little pieces in his mouth.

A gust of hot, moist wind blew directly into my face as I walked along the barbed wire barrier and squinted out across the rice fields. The smooth bronze embossed figure felt comfortable between my thumb and index finger. I remembered meeting Bob before they were married, the only time we ever met. He was tall and good looking, with dark hair and eyes and fair skin. Elizabeth seemed electrified, with a sparkle in her eye I'd never seen before. I sensed a slight uneasiness in her when she introduced us, and thought that perhaps Bob didn't understand our relationship. Somehow her uneasiness made me feel more important to her and seemed to add substance to our unique relationship. I did not want her to feel uncomfortable in any way, though.

Our love, as I interpreted it, was a mere fantasy— and I flagrantly indulged myself. Much like a sister, she would introduce me to some of her dates and then ask me what I thought of them.

I gave earnest congratulations to Elizabeth and Bob and did not prolong my stay with them. I left with a feeling of consolation: I had known her and loved her first. In a fantasy, you can get bruised a little; but in reality, you can get hurt.

Looking back on it now, I thought I needed love

then. But when all in my life seemed lost, she was my first real friend. She took a genuine interest in me as a person, and she made me feel unique. She added an entirely different dimension to a dull, insecure life. She was the most beautiful girl I had ever seen, but I never looked at her as if she were a girl. I always looked at her as a woman. I was totally captivated and mesmerized by her at age fifteen.

From the day I met her, the changes that came over me were humorous and immediate. One day she asked me if I would like to read a book she had enjoyed, *The Jungle,* by Upton Sinclair. I was a poor student, and hated books and reading, but I wasn't about to let her know that she had a dumbbell friend. I took the book and read it frantically. I read through each class in school, and at night in the bunkhouse by candlelight, until it was completed. I was amazed at what I had done, since she had only casually asked me if I wanted to. It was the first time I had ever read a complete novel. I was so proud when we got together and discussed our enjoyment of certain facets of the book. It was strange and exciting to listen to myself discussing an important literary work. (I later learned that my objectionable attitude toward reading was due to headaches related to a minor eye disorder.) I did a book report on *The Jungle* and got the first *B* in English I ever received. She also introduced me to Steinbeck's *Of Mice and Men.* It was fascinating.

My entire outlook on education changed, and all of my grades improved. My whole attitude toward myself changed, as well.

What a strange relationship we had. I felt bad because I thought I was not repaying her for what she was doing for me. I did not have a car, and did not even have any money for dates. Sometimes we just went for walks and I would buy her an ice cream at the general store. For the first time in my life, I was in love. I was proud and happy, and it made the rest of my life bearable. I didn't care if it was half fantasy and half reality.

She would call on the phone and invite me over to her house, where she lived with her father and younger brother. Her mother had died. We spent endless hours talking about everything and nothing, laughing and having fun like two friends will. I adored her, and at that time in my life, I needed her.

Now was my chance to repay her for saving me. But I was so far away. I let the medal slip through my fingers and fall back on my chest. The sun was going down. I turned and walked back toward the bunker. I took the first watch of the evening and let Ed sleep until early morning.

I knew that my head would be full of the letter for some time. I tried to picture Elizabeth's little Sherry as she had described her, but I couldn't. My mind didn't register dark hair and eyes, but rather large pools of deep liquid blue, rich auburn hair, a full round face with high cheekbones and dimples, a short, perky nose, and a small upturned mouth showing extraordinary pearly teeth.

CHAPTER ELEVEN

The days at Iron Bridge Ridge had become long, hot, and uneventful. Our bunker was no longer a cool quiet refuge from the heat of the day. At no time could we risk using a light during hours of darkness. Toads, salamanders, and other nuisances were inadvertently crushed underfoot in the darkness. Even after a daily policing of casualties, the air in the basement was still somewhat less than fresh.

The evenings were becoming increasingly more active. 81mm mortars were called on to illuminate the area. We hoped to catch the enemy with their pants down out in the open, but the pop out of the tube and the crack in the air before the flair hit left ample time for them to hit the ground and hide among the rice stalks, if, in fact, they were there.

Weapons platoon, on our right, seemed to be more active (or skittish) than anyone else. Periodically, someone would hear something, or think they heard something, and lay on the trigger, sending tracer rounds skimming out over the tops of the rice for hundreds of yards into the darkness. It became so frequent that other platoons started joining in. Some fool along the line would open up arbitrarily to create some excitement in order to break up the boredom. It was fine for those who were on watch, but it was hell when you were trying to sleep. Weapons platoon said they had heard voices out in the fields, and other strange sounds. But we never took seriously anything those idiots said. I figured it was just the sound of the sand shifting between their ears.

The fire watch games at night had also gotten out of hand. It looked as though Iron Bridge Ridge was under siege all the time. I enjoyed popping a few rounds of H.E. (high explosive) myself, to see them flare.

During one of the fun-and-game periods, Fred and I decided to throw our first hand grenades at the enemy to see who could outthrow the other. Ed claimed that he won by default because I threw a dud. It bothered both of us. The first time I had thrown a grenade in Vietnam, and it malfunctioned. It wasn't very good odds. It left me with the burden of wondering whether I had received all of mine from the same crate. Maybe they were all defective. Without blowing, they are heavy enough to crush a man's skull. Of course, the Vietcong may grin and kill you for trying to take him out with a rock. Grenade throwing was finally wisely curtailed by the command post, or they would have had to call San Diego and request another freighter of ammo.

The next morning, third platoon reported that someone had tampered with the booby traps on the claymore mine. A Ho Chi Minh sandal print was discovered. These sandals are popular native footwear. The soles are punched out of old automobile tires, and when you walk around they leave tracks like an old Chevy.

It took a lot of guts to crawl in there with all of the trigger-happy thrill seekers. To get close enough to fool with a booby trap in total darkness either takes someone brainless or someone with a frightening amount of talent. In any event, the fun was over and the heat was on. Everyone felt a degree of believability in the rumors, which made us very alert.

The short-scan method was the most effective way to get optimum vision at night. It did not allow one to see in total darkness, but it was an effective method that allowed one to see things otherwise obscured or overlooked by tension in the eyes. Straining, by trying too hard and moving the eyes from side to side, created undue stress; but locking the eyes within the sockets and moving the head only from side to side in short scanning movements was more effective. For terrain directly in front, we started in close and used the same method, moving the eyes and head in short increments outward to infinity. It was like looking at squares on a checkerboard one at a time, but never allowing the eye to become fixed on one square for too long. Focusing too hard and allowing the eyes to become fixed on one object or area for more than a moment aroused the imagination. We began to see things that did not exist.

Obscure, inanimate objects began to move almost invariably during periods of mental or physical fatigue, or excitement. The secret was to relax the eyes and keep them moving.

Listening had the same peculiarity, even in total darkness. I would cover my eyes and my ears seemed to be more effective. A blind man can hear more than a sighted man could ever think possible because the energy is channeled in one direction instead of two. The eyes, although they may be looking into total darkness, are still drawing energy from the brain.

I squirted some thick, greasy bug repellent and rubbed it on my face and neck. It burned the skin a little and was too strong for the sinuses. But it was a minor nuisance compared to feasting mosquitos. Somehow, Supply had screwed up and had filled all the little containers they issued with repellent designed to saturate tents and to spray in billetting areas. No one had yet discovered whether it was toxic or lethal. You could hear the hungry hum all night, but no way would they try to penetrate the invisible iron curtain.

An eighty-one mortar popped out of its tube with a hollow, airless sound. Several seconds later, at about six hundred feet, it cracked and illuminated, swaying back and forth gently in its tiny silk parachute, giving all the scanning eyes on the ground a well-needed break. The shadows around me created by the flare also swayed in gentle unison. I eyeballed as much territory as many times as I possibly could before the flare went out. I hoped to have the first crack at some sorry soul with no place to hide.

The flare began to sputter and go dim. To the left, I spotted something out of the corner of my eye that didn't feel right. About twenty yards out between the wire and the slough was a bush about three-feet tall. I concentrated and tried to visualize the area during the day, but I couldn't remember if it was there or not. My imagination must be working overtime; still, I wondered why I wasn't drawn to it the night before. Perhaps it was the height and angle of the flare that illuminated it differently and made it more predominant. My God, what was I worrying about a damn tree for? I knew what kind of an answer I would get if I had to bring it to anyone's attention. Maybe bushes grew fast around here.

Ed and I were enjoying a quiet breakfast. By the luck of the draw, we had drawn too decent meals for breakfast instead of his ham and lima beans and my beans and franks like the morning before. We decided to pool our groceries. We took his canned ham and mixed it with my chopped ham and eggs in a canteen cup. We heated it over a couple of heat tabs. It smelled and resembled a Denver omelet that was grossly overloaded with ham. I added a little sugar to cut the salt. Fred sliced little pieces of French bread and toasted them on a twig, then spread them with peanut butter and marmalade. I brewed a canteen cup of hot chocolate. Everything was going fine at the breakfast table until tasteful Fred pulled out a warm bottle of his favorite green elixir, followed by a chocolate-covered coconut candy bar.

"How in the hell can you drink that warm nasty crap so early in the morning and ruin a good breakfast?"

"No problem. I just pretend it's orange juice."

"I'll bet from green oranges. That crap is so dark green, it's probably artificially colored."

"What's wrong with that? There's nothing wrong with artificial colors." He paused. "What's wrong with artificial colors?"

"Well, in the village they probably use algae to color things green."

"What's algae?"

"They're tiny microscopic green bugs that live in water," I lied.

His eyes bugged; he choked a little and blew out the remainder of the soda pop. He poured some of the contents of the bottle into his palm, eyeballed it closely, and sniffed it like an inquisitive chimpanzee.

I looked at him with a stern, sober face. "Fred, you're sick." I cracked up and fell over backward in a screaming howl. I was rolling around in the dirt, totally out of control.

The seriousness of his expression began to fade. "Why, you little bastard!"

He lunged for me and I rolled out of the way and stumbled out of the canopy into the sunshine. Still hysterical, I nearly ran headlong into Trudeau. Fred was close behind me.

"What are you guys up to? Cut out the grab ass."

"The Horn here gets a little frisky after breakfast."

Trudeau, as usual, was not interested in our fooling

around. "Well, he can get frisky on a work party at the CP this morning. First, I've got to talk to the squad."

Fred raised his eyebrows and smiled. I couldn't figure his angle. Nobody's happy to go on a work party. Then I remembered the girls on the bridge.

Trudeau yelled for squad leaders up, and in a few minutes we had a small huddle eager to hear the day's news.

"We've got trouble. The Vietcong are moving in and probing at night. The corpsmen carried away Chavez, from weapons platoon, practically in a bag. The Lieutenant says he'll probably get discharged with a Section Eight."

"I guess he really took a jolt last night. He went out to bring in his claymore and found that somebody had deactivated both of the mousetrap devices and disconnected the lead wire. They turned the whole damn thing around and re-imbedded it in the ground facing the squad area. For some reason, they didn't re-booby trap it, but reconnected the lead wire. They could have gotten him for sure, and took a hell of a lot of other people, too. The strange part is that he was awake all night listening."

"Get this: rearming it was not an oversight. They left a piece of paper attached to the claymore with his name on it. He was considered the best booby-trap man that weapons platoon had. Now he is a basket case."

This information was more than a little unnerving. In the raw sense of the word, it was frightening. Behind young faces, minds labored quicker than high-speed computers, racing through years of index input, searching for answers, ideas, and rationalizations. For the moment, the imagination applied small amounts of pressure on the circuits and resisters of the mind.

The enemy was no longer warm flesh and blood; they were now an intangible, evil, macabre force. They were a commando raid of microscopic saboteurs entering the mind undetected to sever and splice intricate circuits of communication, causing havoc within the integral part of the computer, altering circuits, changing impulses, then escaping to safety to watch the huge, magnificent war machine self-destruct.

Neither tanks, machine guns, mines, barbed wire, nor indestructable bunkers—no amount of physical arsenal or defense—can deter such a haunting and effective invasion. Only an informed and alert mind is invulnerable.

I stared out into the darkness, sometimes forgetting my night-vision techniques. A dull, unhelpful moon was obscured by a thin cloud layer which broke up the monotony of the invisible black ceiling. It glistened like a sullen ghost squirming on the surface of the slough. I sat erect, legs folded Indian style. I had the forty-five in my lap, a round in the chamber on half-cock. Fred's oily M-14 lay at my left knee; and on my right, within finger's reach, lay my six hand grenades, all in a row.

I turned my head to the right sharply as someone came scurrying along the trail. I picked up the forty-five, pulled back the hammer, and challenged.

"It's Sheldon." His voice was low, almost a whisper, and out of breath.

I recognized the voice and didn't bother to ask for

the password. I released the hammer back to half-cock and laid the gun back on my lap. I told him to come in. He dropped down beside me, out of breath, and I could see the dull moonlight reflect off the sheen of his sweaty cheekbones and forehead. The whites of fearful eyes scanned the darkness too erratically and too intensely. His voice was shaky and unnatural. It scared the hell out of me.

"Oggie, they know my name, man. They know I'm here."

"How do you know they do?"

"I heard them, man, in plain English. Morales heard them, too." There was more stress in his voice. "How in the hell do they know me?"

Sheldon was a natural leader who probably dominated all of the basketball courts in the east side of Detroit. He was built like a thoroughbred racehorse, and was intelligent.

The Marine Corps could care less who you are or what race you are. Early in training, if they sense any leadership capabilities, they will give you every opportunity to develop them. I had blown it miserably. I was just too young and insecure. I could have probably succeeded in a limited degree if I'd let myself become an unconscionable tyrant, pushing around guys who were more intelligent, and older and bigger than I in order to compensate for my inadequacies— but that was not my style.

Sheldon didn't appear to have any insecurities. He kept up his courage even under the pressure of Jason and Trudeau. He never had any of the problems I did.

His bag was security. He was a better leader than either Jason or Trudeau, who were older and supposedly more experienced.

"Listen." He grabbed my arm. "Listen."

He was on his knees. He sat back on his heels, facing me, swaying back and forth gently, trying to ease the tension. We both held our breaths and concentrated with everything we could muster.

Then I heard it. My whole body shuddered with disbelief. It was impossible to locate the range. The low-key perfect English floated in from the darkness, riding on the warm breeze.

"Corporal Sheldon, we want you."

If they had used my name, I probably would have cracked. It was frightening enough to listen to them use someone else's. How could we be so inept, unprepared, and vulnerable? We didn't even know what they looked like or anything about them. They seemed to have us all figured out, and they were applying effective pressure. The microscopic commando teams were here.

Ed woke up, rolled over on his sleeping bag, and sat up. "What's going on?"

"Shut up and listen."

The voice spoke again. He heard it, but didn't believe it.

"Sheldon, somebody's bullshitting around with you out there. It must be a joke."

"Just listen and shut up, Ed, goddamn it."

Ed realized what direction it was coming from. He scrambled after his M-14, took the safety off, and let the bolt go home. Sheldon did the same.

"Come on, you guys, cool it. Sheldon, you're playing right into their hands. You can't see a thing out there. If we start to pop off, they're going to know they've already got to us."

Before we could take another breath, an M-14 opened up in weapons platoon area. Sheldon sat down. Whoever they were shooting at was right on top of their position. The tracer rounds bounced off the ground at such a sharp angle, it was as though someone had crawled into their position. Tracer rounds bounced off the ground and streaked out into the darkness like tiny comets. We asked each other what in hell could be going on over there. Maybe someone got through the wire and into a foxhole.

Sheldon stood up. "I think I had better go on down the line and make sure no one panics, before these motha fuckas start name-dropping again."

"Just think, Sheldon, you're a celebrity to them creeps out there. They must think you're awfully bad."

"Them sneaking, little motha fuckas are gonna know I'm bad, and I ain't gonna do no talking about it. You all take it easy, now."

He disappeared into the darkness. He was immediately challenged by the next position. He seemed to be less nervous and a little more confident after realizing that he was being used by the Vietcong as a football in a game designed to bend us all.

Ed challenged someone else scurrying down the trail, and we both concurred that it certainly wasn't a boring night. The new arrival was Jason. He was more out of breath and more excited than Sheldon had been. I wondered if he, too, was receiving little love calls through the night, or whether they even cared enough about him to bother.

Jason squatted native style and leaned in our direction. He whispered, "You know that kid, Smith, the quiet one in weapons platoon? He just blew up Osborne, his team leader, with twenty rounds. Osborne was sound asleep outside their bunker. He just blew half his head right off at point-blank. That's what all the tracers in the sky were."

"Yeah, we know, we saw them."

"The captain's calling it murder. They want me to take him back to the division tomorrow because of my M.P. experience. The company is on one hundred percent alert for the rest of the night. That means every swinging dick stays awake all night."

He disappeared into the darkness.

Both Ed and I agreed that Smith was kind of weird and that Osborne was a complete asshole, but that he didn't deserve to die for it. We wondered how he'd made team leader. There was definitely something wrong with that pack of hyenas. It was probably the reason they suffered more casualties than the other platoons.

Another mortar left the tube and cracked over our heads and blossomed out. I grabbed my pop gun and stood up. My peek-a-boo tree had moved a good ten feet. I pulled down on my gun and blew it into a fine mulch.

"What in the hell did you do that for?"

"I'm getting tired of it creeping around on me all

the time."

He looked at me strangely. "What?"

"I'll explain to you in the morning."

We sat down.

"Since we're going to be up for the night, do you have anything to eat?"

"There's some crackers and peanut butter around here somewhere."

"That sounds good to me."

We started looking, taking advantage of the light.

"Oh, I could probably be persuaded to try some of that green slime you call orange juice, too."

The only other event of the night was a med-evac chopper sent to haul out the murder victim. It could have waited until morning. That would have been less risky.

How do you explain to a mother that her son was murdered in combat by a foxhole buddy? The incident seemed to jolt the company back to a rational consciousness. We agreed that the enemy was here and they were actively attempting to destroy us. We discovered that their effectiveness was not due to genius or superhuman powers, but to their audacity, guts, and ability to play effectively on our naivete and carelessness. We discovered that the docile farmers planting rice around the Iron Bridge Ridge were Vietcong! All eyes, all ears!

CHAPTER TWELVE

I scrubbed my greasy, salt-encrusted utilities, under-wear and socks with a ball of crude, scented Viet-namese hand soap, and spread everything out on the bank to dry. I scrubbed off the dead hide accumulated by weeks of neglect. After the much-overdue chores were completed, and the childlike frolicking (disguised as swimming) in the dark, still, unstagnant slough was over, I rolled over on my back. The air and water were very near body temperature. I lay motionless, senses almost in a state of meditation, trying with reasonable success to purge my mind of thoughts. I closed my eyes and felt no physical sensation at all. I experienced a combination of euphoria, vertigo, and ecstasy. The nerves slowly and reluctantly gave up their desperate hold on muscles, allowing them to give up the strain on tendons. The body floated listlessly, as though it were a wooden puppet with members and joints fastened together with a single thread. To relax any more would give the heart an unexpected, premature rest. The controllable revolving carousel of a free-wheeling mind slows down to a near standstill and strains to keep from becoming motionless, allowing the various steeds of emotion to catch their wind and continue to endure. To stop this endless revolution is to withdraw and deteriorate. A nebulous group of complex entities drifting through time and space, the mind is suspended like the universe, confined only by the word "infinity."

The bump of tiny, fingerlike minnows subtly disturbed the total experience. A frog in the cool green shadows stirred and watched the forlorn, dubious monster climb up the bank and out of sight, carrying an odd-looking bundle.

Our first monsoon pounded us throughout the night. It kept us busy trying to sleep and keep dry. The bunker provided some protection from the relentless downpour for the lucky men off duty. It was like sleeping in a leaky cavern with six inches of water on the floor and the constant siege of dripping from above. We fashioned a cot of sandbags to keep out the muck and hoped the water wouldn't rise much further. We wrapped the neoprene poncho around the sleeping bags, but little snakes of water still somehow found their way inside.

The canopy outside had become a nuisance. It caught the rain like a funnel and poured it directly into the bunker. We pulled it in and wrapped it around the body, as it was first intended.

The rain was heavy enough to tear up the ground and carry it away. There was virtually no watching or effective listening while on watch. The only pastime of the evening was to stare at a perfectly good luminous wristwatch that you knew beyond a doubt was malfunctioning when it took the second hand a full hour to make a sweep; the hour hand seemed to be rusted in place forever. Even when counting off the seconds in the mind, a minute still took an hour. *(We humbly repented our transgressions of cursing the inferno that besieged us by day. May we not curse the flood of night, for fear of releasing the wrath of holocaust which would surely destroy the earth.)*

The rising sun revealed that the world had been washed away and a new one had taken its place. The loose earth and our positions had been washed into the bunkers and trench lines like a sewer system.

The spirit of the morning was like that of spring, purged and cleansed. The breeze carried the sweet fragrance of rice flowers. Shy and simple flowers seemed to be coaxed from their hiding places, and indistinguishable birds sang enthusiastically of the welcome change. The overall landscape seemed to be more green and lush than the day before. Even the sky seemed to be a deeper, richer blue, with a handful of tiny white fluffs racing toward the east to catch up with the storm that had left them behind. To my amazement, the dark slough had vanished. It had climbed its banks and flooded the surrounding rice paddies, creating a sizeable lake no longer segmented by a variety of dikes.

Steam rolled off everything and everyone as we prepared for a long-range patrol, a search-and-destroy mission across the valley and up into the foothills. First squad moved out led by Lieutenant O'Connor. There was a bunch-up at the small opening in the barbed wire in front of my position. It was just large enough for a man to squeeze through if he was lucky enough not to get hung up on it. With my size, I had no difficulty; but I had to hold the PRC 6, usually called by its more fashionable acronym "Prick," over my head and inch sideways through the opening in the wire.

The radio was not too heavy, but was bulky and cumbersome. Having the responsibility of the radio meant that I didn't have to participate in the flank security or point. They could have stuck me with the big brother PRC 10, which required a packboard.

The squad had finally spread itself out to normal intervals, and our first heading was south toward a small crude footbridge across the slough. We sloshed along in knee-deep water, giving the hidden slough a wide berth in fear of the deep. The sun began to burn and the perspiration began to pour. At least there were no flies or mosquitoes to clutter up the air. The water was drawn in with each step and squirted out again through the portholes in our canvas boots. It was warm, and massaged our feet.

Nellis was well out in front of point man, and by the time he had reached the end of the small bridge, he was up to his waist in water. He was six feet tall. I began to worry. Unlike going off the end of a landing craft and going over my five-foot-five limit, there wasn't anyone near enough now to grab me by the nape of my neck and drag me to the surface. I began to walk more carefully and in a direct line with Lieutenant O'Connor in front. I wished I had a walking stick. The amount of water that had accumulated overnight in these fields was unbelievable.

Lieutenant O'Connor put a hand up to his mouth. "Nellis, take it nice and easy, and watch your step. We are in no big hurry today."

Nellis stepped up onto the footbridge. There was a single log running down the middle for walking on. On each side, at about shoulder height, there were railings. He slung his weapon and hung onto the railings. He was now in knee-deep water. He felt along the submerged log one foot at a time. The submerged log was suspended in a cradle of bamboo strips laced to the two rails on the surface.

Nellis turned around and grinned. "Don't worry, sir, frogman school was my second choice."

Before he could turn his head back, his foot had slipped and he had crashed into the water up to his neck. He hung onto the right rail with one hand. The bamboo strips had helped break his fall, and one leg was still hanging over the submerged log. He slowly pulled himself back until he was on his feet again.

I continued to worry. In boot camp, I had drunk, breathed, and puked a lot of chlorine water. They had physically thrown me into the deep end time after time, poking me with long rods as I wildly thrashed the water to get to the side of the pool. Undisturbed, I could float on my back. But to this day, I have never experienced swimming strokes without terror.

With the radio and grenade launcher hanging around my neck, jaw locked, and knuckles white from holding on, I started across the bridge with the caution of a blind man exploring the Grand Canyon.

After Nellis got off the bridge, some yards further on, he took a second unexpected plunge. I froze on the bridge. Morales waded frantically in his direction, feeling the bottom so he wouldn't take the same plunge. The long seconds and the stillness of the water where Nellis had gone down were terrifying. It was as if a great shark had grabbed him from below and pulled him to the deep. Finally, a convulsing hand broke the surface. Morales laid a rifle stock right into the clutching fingers. You could see the power generated in the quivering fingers almost as though they were strong enough to squeeze the linseed oil from the hardwood of the stock. Morales closed his eyes, gritted his teeth, and strained. Nellis's helmet broke the surface like a hard-hat driver. He blinked a half-dozen times and sputtered.

Morales grinned and spoke to Nellis, almost falling in himself. "How did you like it down there, frogman? See any Victor Charlies?"

Nellis clawed his way back up to the shallow water. Despite the gravity of the moment, I could not help but wonder whether Nellis was carrying his volumes of *Hamlet* and *The Taming of the Shrew* in his pack, and whether they had gotten wet. He was a tall, skinny Jeff

Chandler type with a flat top. He was from Chicago, and Charlie called him "Richard III." Nellis seemed to have an innate passion for Shakespeare. On several occasions I would find him reading feverishly, then breaking up in heavy laughter. He would ask me to read a paragraph. I would oblige. He would ask me what I thought. I would lie and give him a bemused smile. I didn't want to appear totally illiterate and foolish, which I was. I didn't understand a word of it. There were words I had never seen before, and I couldn't quite get hysterical about them.

I did feel that I was missing out on something. I had served two terms in the fourth grade and had walked away from school in the ninth grade, still reading on a fifth-grade level. Any more than plain English and I was out of business. I guess that was the reason I enjoyed Steinbeck; I had something in common with his characters.

I hadn't really wanted to leave the classroom. The mysteries of education still fascinate me, and I plan to do some heavy digging at my first opportunity. Friends who attempt to placate my embarrassment often remind me of numerous millionaires who never made it through grade school. I appreciate their kindness, but doubt that there will be very many dropouts in the seventies and eighties. I'll start somewhere, but it won't be with *The Taming of the Shrew*.

I hoped that the fruits of Bill Shakespeare's labor hadn't gone to ruin at the hands of a frogman. Nellis's rifle was lost forever somewhere off the Great Barrier Reef. I knew how he felt. Get yourself a fork and spoon, boy!

The patrol moved on, fighting a slow, tedious, unsuspecting battle, sloshing and sliding and being sucked in and out of the toothless jaws of the greasy, plasterlike mud. It could easily suck off a boot and leave it several feet under the surface. An entrenching tool would be needed to rescue an important part of oneself, like a foot.

Nellis finally pulled the patrol up out of the quagmire to high ground toward some high elephant grass growing along the base of the foothills. We had already burned up too much energy in this morning's water and mud fest, and we vowed to find an alternate route back. The tiny bleeding cuts from the savage, towering elephant grass added to the discomfort from the ten o'clock ball of sulphurous hell. With each movement the dry mud dropped away, leaving dust on the surface or mixed with perspiration and saturated along with the salt that crusted on the fabric.

My dog tags were heating up and burning my chest, so I slipped them around to the back. I was glad I had risked the opportunity to take an unwarranted, unofficial, against orders, court-martial offense, firing-squad level, refreshing dip in the slough yesterday.

I noticed while on long patrols that if the inside of my thighs were unclean, they became easily chafed when rubbed with the utility trousers. The buildup of salt and filth contributed to a raw, bone-crushing agony. I seemed to sweat more and expend valuable energy. It takes a little of the fun and glamor away from a combat patrol. Something so minor and simple could be crippling. I hope some brasshead dies of terminal jungle rot.

I lay face down in a clear, fresh creek and drank as much as I could hold, then popped in a couple of salt tablets and washed them down. I filled up both canteens and faked putting the brackish, iodine-tasting halazone tablets into each canteen as we were ordered to do. If we had to resort to drinking out of rice paddies or out of village wells, I could see it; but a mountain stream is the purest of water.

It was nice to know there would be an abundance of water to drink at will instead of sipping and conserving as much as possible, as we did when we were out on the flat ground in the direct heat. But drinking all we wanted, with the heat and exhaustion, would be dangerous if the priceless, life-giving salt tablets weren't used.

The cliffside was green, lush, and dangerous. We were poking around in Victor Charlie's backyard, and the odds were in his favor. He had more control of the situation and more mobility, knowing the gorge we were entering, the high ground, and our lack of experience at jungle fighting. They wouldn't be able to wipe us out unless there were a lot of them, but they could pick at us and make it rough if we weren't careful.

Nellis was relieved at point and Ed took his place. The point man is in the most dangerous, vulnerable position on a patrol in dense jungle. The enemy lies in ambush waiting for the point man to come into very close range, then they hit him and run like hell. I knew Ed was nervous enough to stay alert all the time; and with those big, lemur-like eyes, nothing would escape him.

The creek had a good swiftness after the running off, but it was the only way we were going to penetrate the mountains. The years of erosion had left steep banks on both sides thick with brush and vines. We tried putting out flankers, but it was impossible for them to move effectively.

We penetrated deeper into the mountains. The walls began to jut up on each side like skyscrapers, and gigantic boulders that had been carved loose lay in midstream. We waded through the deep, dark, but still-moving water with equipment and weapons held high over our heads. We crossed the sand bars and entered the current again.

Every so often Ed would raise his hands. We would freeze and listen. We waited for him to check out possible ambush sites such as blind bends in the creek. His job was to stick his neck out to keep us safe. This whole gorge was filled with ambush sites.

They could probably see us frolicking across the muddy valley floor, coming haphazardly in their direction, from the trees that towered high on the hillsides. It would give them plenty of time to set up for us. Or maybe they thought they were really dealing with kids who cried in the night and had their boots and equipment stolen.

We moved deeper into the bowels of the massive green sauna. The surrounding mountains blocked out any hope of a light breeze. When not fighting the current, we were still drowning in our own sweat. The surrounding jungle steamed as though it was reaching its kindling point and would burst into flames at any moment.

Lieutenant O'Connor halted the column for a ten-minute break. When we had relaxed and gotten our wind back, the complainers complained and the smokers smoked. I sat down on a rock. I was starving. I popped open a can of sticky fruitcake. It was sweet and nourishing, and it only took a half-quart of water to get it down.

I stared down into the crystal-clear pool at my feet. Minnows darted in and out of the shadows. I was homesick for fishing, picnicking, crawdadding, bull-frogging, dam building, the old swimming hole, the beatings I got for catching a cold, the nearly drowning and dragging in mud.

The sound of anxious, predestined water flowing licked at my ears. I was far away. "Goddamn it! Goddamn it!" Morales began to yell and jump forward.

We thought at first that he had been hit. He flung his butt down on a sand bar and hastily began to untie his boot. He quickly pulled it off and tipped it up. A mixture of blood and water poured out. We knew he was hit. He pulled off his socks and pulled his pant legs up. He was covered with leeches!

I shuddered, afraid to examine myself. My next thought was of Ed. If he found anything like that, he would die of a coronary.

Everyone began pawing and examining themselves. The smokers began puffing on several cigarettes and handing them to the nonsmokers. A touch on the back from a hot cigarette, and the ferocious little vampires would unleash their jaws and could be easily flicked away. A series of good and bad blood jokes broke the tension of working loose from these tiny sucking invertebrates.

I was amazed at my luck; I fit under the "bad blood" category. I found one under my jacket sleeve that was rolled above the elbow. Like pigs, they had aggressive, voracious little appetites, and wasted a lot of what they craved. There was blood running from almost everyone afflicted. Just as I should have imagined, Ed found one clinging to his testicles. For a moment I thought he was going to be in desperate need of a sedative—but we all managed to survive, and we saddled up and continued on.

The terrain became rougher and steeper, and the current swifter. We slipped, slid, and crawled over wet slimy boulders. We clung to roots and vines hanging from the canyon wall, trying to stay out of the white, cascading water. We helped each other with a hand or an occasional extended rifle butt while keeping an alert, wary eye over our shoulders and the high horizon.

The front of the patrol seemed to have reached a summit, and some disappeared over the top. Past the boulders at the summit there was a wide, still pool. It was nearly motionless until it spilled over the rim of the rocks and down the canyon. The left side of the gorge gave way to a small canyon that ran perpendicular to the gorge. Thick colonies of green moss clung to the bare face of the rock that towered above. Outcroppings of short, indestructible brush grew between the cracks and crevices. Below, there was a thicket of bamboo surrounding a small clearing.

Trudeau dispatched a man to keep a watch down the canyon, and another to watch the area ahead of us while the rest of the patrol went in to poke around the clearing. Somehow we had caught them by surprise— but not quickly enough to overtake them at their rice and fish-sauce lunch, which was thrown around on the ground. The campfire was steaming. There was a large lean-to at the far end of the clearing and about four or five smaller ones scattered throughout the area. There was a lot of debris strewn around, old tennis shoes and trash. We were surprised to find out that they were eating as well as we were. There were C-rations and garbage strewn everywhere. A slovenly lot, these Victor Charlies.

Trudeau, along with Morales's fire team, was probing through the trash behind the large lean-to with their rifle barrels when they called for the lieutenant. We hurried over, hoping they had found something important. Trudeau handed the lieutenant the remnants of a small, white, heavy cardboard box. In his other hand he held some gauze and used syringes.

"Look, sir. It's some kind of a medical kit. Look where it's from, sir."

He looked at the other side of the sopping-wet cardboard. In big, black, bold letters it read: "The University of California, Berkeley."

"Where in hell are they getting this stuff, Lieutenant,

sir?" Red asked.

"Probably the same place they're getting the C-rations. Captured from the ARVN."

Charlie spoke as he took off his helmet and scratched the back of his head. "Berkeley is too liberal to openly oppose a nice Marxist like Uncle Ho Chi. Something smells."

The lieutenant gave him a funny look that I did not understand. No one else paid any attention to either of them.

The lieutenant scanned the periphery of the rocks high above us with squinted eyes. The rest of us followed suit. We all agreed without a word that they were probably watching us right now.

"Trudeau, round up your men and let's get out of here fast. We've found out what we want to know. This place is suicidal. Make sure your front and rear guard keep their little eyeballs open. We're like fish in a barrel all the way down until we reach the valley floor."

We kept a good interval and moved out quickly through the waist-deep water.

CHAPTER THIRTEEN

Like a thousand leather whips cracking in the air, M-2 carbines blasted down on us like a shower of hail. We were all out in the open, and there was a moment of confusion over which way to duck for cover. The squad split right down the middle, and the front half thrashed and clawed to the other side of the pool at the base of the wall. The fire was coming from over their heads, and they made it safely. The rest of us had to backtrack. Four of us, still in the line of fire, slammed into the water and slithered in between some rocks on the opposite side.

Charlie emptied a magazine into the brush along the top of the canyon wall so at least they wouldn't be able to breathe, squeeze, and pick us off.

Red, still scrambling from the pool, let out a yell and went down. He was fighting to keep his head above water. "I'm hit bad!"

Nellis jumped out from behind a rock with my forty-

Villagers graciously sharing food and favors with Marine Patrol.

French fort remains—monument of the last futile war—overlooking Elephant Valley.

Marine Lieutenant O'Connor getting acquainted with children of Le Mai Village.

The human tragedy after the assault on Le Mai Village (Note: mother nursing her child).

Marines checking on indigenous males for proper identification—looking for Vietcong.

Marines checking river traffic for Vietcong suspects and contraband.

Marine Patrol in Elephant Valley in I Corp. near Danang.

Watching for Vietcong ground fire from Marine helicopter UH34.

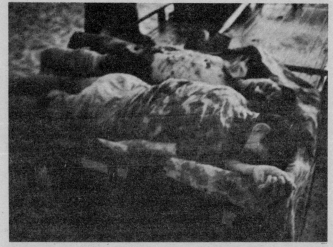
Vietcong dead after Hotel Company, 3rd. Marines assault on Le Mai Village.

Third Battalion's outlying perimeter protecting Danang airbase.

Marines having first Christmas dinner in Vietnam 1965.

Hotel Company, 3rd. Marines relocating entire village from the terror and exploitation of the Vietcong.

A puzzling dilemma of the war, what do we do with the innocent people caught in the middle?

It was nearly impossible not to attract a horde of curious children.

An honorary Battalion Commander.

Marines on patrol near Danang.

Vietcong captured after assault on Le Mai Village.

Sergeant Jackson, Hotel Company, reminiscing what it was like to hold his own child.

Rebuilding the village. Women and babies miraculously survived a machine gun and rocket attack on their home in Le Mai Village. Because of this incident and others like it, indiscriminate assaults and search by fire unless fired upon were abandoned to protect innocent lives.

Disembarking of Third Battalion, Third Marines, March 10, 1965 at Danang Red Beach.

The author.

As early as 1965, the army of South Vietnam was a ragged, undisciplined group posing as a fighting force. The Marines would have absolutely nothing to do with them.

Hotel Company Marines bring back proof of their success on a combat patrol. Body count was the measure of success.

five still barking in his hand. He dove out into the water and grabbed Red by his jacket collar and dragged him back to safety. Red screamed in agony but never let loose of his rifle. I helped Nellis drag him to cover.

By the size of the hole, it looked like a thirty caliber round had smashed through the thigh bone.

The troops on the other side of the pool were safe from enemy fire for the moment. They searched in vain for a firing position to get a shot at the enemy, far away up the embankment. When a lull in the firing came, I yelled across to them and shook my M-79 over my head. They quickly got the message and moved downstream away from the impact area. Looking over their heads, they clung tightly to the side of the gorge.

We still couldn't pinpoint precisely where the firing was coming from. There was no flash and no smoke. I aimed the pop gun high into the trees that hung over the gorge. With an air burst, maybe I could rain shrapnel down on the angry lunch crowd. I pulled the trigger, and the explosion severed a four-inch-diameter bamboo trunk. It came crashing straight down into the water.

The three of us were on our knees in water up to our waists behind a huge boulder. Nellis and Charlie had a rhythm going; one flared while the other one loaded a full magazine, which kept the automatic weapons fire constant on the ridge line. I fired as fast as I could open the breech and pop in another shell. The others helplessly cheered us on.

Red was still conscious but in agony behind us. He had taken off his helmet, filled it with his own magazines, and with his upper leg blown all to hell, he managed to crawl over next to Nellis and sit up with his back against the boulder. He cradled the helmet full of magazines in his lap while he lay his head back until he was facing the sky. His eyes were closed and his teeth were clenched. Tears of pain rolled down his face and dripped off his chin into the helmet.

Nellis looked down on him, and smiled and patted him on his wet bristly head like a mother would a little boy. "It's okay, champ. You're still cooking. We'll get you home."

Red opened his eyes, registered a faint smile, and handed Nellis a magazine. It was the first time I had experienced something they call "guts," and it was moving.

I saw Ed waving frantically from the other side and hesitated on the trigger. I guess someone from the other side was bound to try something out of sheer helplessness and desperation, but I didn't think it would be Ed. But why not Ed? He always managed to be amusing, if not crazy.

He quickly stumbled out into the water, armed with only a hand grenade. As soon as he was beyond the overhang of the embankment and waist deep in the water, he let the spoon fly on the grenade. It popped and fizzled. He threw it up over his head and waded frantically back to safety. The grenade hit the top of the cliff, fell back into the pool, and blew harmlessly in the same spot he had thrown it from. Another foot and he would have made it. Another display of guts.

We continued to chip the jungle with a barrage of fire

until we heard a hideous scream only a human could make. A body crashed through the brush on the cliff. I could see the grotesque, twisted face as the body seemed to fly through the air in slow motion. It hit the water face and belly first with a stinging, hollow slap. It spasmed and flopped in the water like a downed goose for a time, then it was still. When it stopped bubbling, a slick of blood began to appear on the surface around the body. Again it was silent. In this forbidden land, the only sound was water on the rocks echoing down the canyon.

When we were certain the enemy had disengaged, at least for the moment, the rest of the squad moved over to what Charlie jokingly called the business side of the canyon and set up a perimeter. Red was fading in and out of consciousness as we carefully carried him back to the clearing to prepare him for the long, hard journey home. There was no chance of a med-evac until we got further down the gorge.

We hoped there would be a break in the jungle canopy. No one could remember when he had last seen blue sky or sunlight on the way up. The radio still hung around my neck, useless in these mountains. I chopped some small but sturdy bamboo stalks and lashed them to Red's leg as tightly as I could with several rifle slings. Morales and Trudeau were fashioning a litter with a couple of poles and a poncho.

We headed down the canyon as quickly as we could go. Going down was more difficult than going up, not only because of the litter but also the ominous threat of another, and perhaps more successful, ambush. All eyes and ears were turned to the ridge as we listened and tried to keep our hand- and foot-holds at the same time. Knuckles and knees were barked, swollen, and numb.

We switched carrying the litter often. Nellis was reluctant to give up his turn and rest. He barked orders to whoever was carrying the other end to be more careful.

Because of our hasty withdrawal, I did not seem to recognize any of the terrain. We hadn't given too much thought to the terrain on the way in, but the canopy was now beginning to thin and sunshine illuminated the gorge below. Without luck, I kept trying to raise the company on the radio.

After checking the overhead thoroughly, Lieutenant O'Connor held up the squad. Red was unconscious, with a quick heartbeat but normal breathing. I unslung the radio, turned down the squelch, and turned up the gain. Nothing. Trudeau, the lieutenant, and I were sitting on our heels around Red.

"Anything at all?" the lieutenant asked.

"No, sir, not even a break on the other end."

"Okay, Ogden," he pointed over his shoulder. "See that knoll up there over the ridge? I think if you get your butt up there, you can probably get some reception."

"Yes sir."

I gave Nellis my M-79 and took the forty-five back. I took off through the water and up the bank. I leaped, scratching and clawing at the bank, and managed to get hold of a securely anchored bush and pull myself up.

The bank was going to be the hardest point of the climb. The rest of it was steep but not impossible. I had toed, kneed, and knuckled it as fast as I could go all the way up the side of the slope. The urgency of the situation warranted no less.

The breezeless heat, the fatigue of the patrol, and the under-four-minute scaling of the "Matterhorn" left me strangling for air and almost nauseous as I crawled over the summit and lay on my back. I waited for a moment to see if I was going to come back to life and stop breathing like a carp out of water. I stood up, faced Iron Bridge Ridge, and pushed the button.

"Hotel One, this is Hotel One Bravo, over."

I took my finger off the button and listened intently to the relentless hissing sound of the open channel, waiting for it to break. Waiting for a voice.

I did everything I could think of for the next ten minutes, playing with the switches and jockeying the antenna around. Everything but throw it away, like the sole surviving legionnaire who never believed or appreciated such frivolous technology and knew the only hope of survival would be to march five hundred miles across the scorching sand dunes to be saved.

Then I thought of the extra battery. I started back down the slope. I followed the trail I had unknowingly gouged out like a heavy land turtle. I jumped in awkward leaps and bounds. I lost my footing and slid for what seemed like ten or twenty yards at a time. At one time I curled up in a ball and got off the trail and crashed through the brush like a lifeless rock. In the last roll, the radio slammed into my jaw and left me senseless. I lay on my back, with lungs and mouth full of dust and anything else I had stirred up. I was like a maniac running aimlessly and dangerously out of control. I laid on my back looking up at the sky from under a small shrub. I began to laugh out loud. I finally got a hold of myself and continued the rest of the way down in a more sure and constructive fashion.

When I reached the bottom, I filled my helmet with water and poured it over me. I told eager ears that I had had no luck. I quickly changed the battery.

Nellis kept wetting a handkerchief and applying it to Red's forehead. He lay motionless, and it was pointless to ask how he was.

I immediately took to the slope again, trying to muster as much strength and exuberance as the first time. But the legs began quickly to give out, and then the arms. The healthful flood of perspiration began to dry up, the solar plexus began to ache, and the whole stomach cavity began to send out its own subtle warnings that the body had very little left to give. Someone else could have just as easily made the second trip, but the lieutenant had entrusted me with the responsibility of getting a chopper in here and getting a man out. I took it on as a personal test, and I was going to see it through to the end with gratifying results.

By the time I flopped down on the summit again, I had a mild case of the shakes. I was out of salt tablets and nearly gagged myself on half a canteen of water. I stood up a little unsteadily and faced toward Iron Bridge Ridge.

"Hotel One Alpha, this is Hotel One Bravo, over.

Hotel One Alpha, this is Hotel Two Bravo, over."

The radio ignored me and continued on its dead, unconcerned hissing sound. Then it broke, and my heart stopped!

"Hotel One Bravo, this is Hotel One Alpha, go ahead."

I squeezed the button and opened my mouth; then it dawned on me that I didn't know what to say. I knew what I had to say, but I was not competent with radio procedures, I was like a child learning to talk on the telephone.

A carbine cracked, sounding like the snap of a large branch. They were above me in the tree line. I flattened my body like a large halibut at the bottom of a bay, pretending to be invisible. I was right out in the open without even a blade of grass to hide behind. I drew the forty-five and pulled the trigger fast, not even knowing which direction the Vietcong were firing from. When I had run out of rounds the hammer was still hitting an empty chamber as I flung a rubbery, scared body down the slope again. I slid a couple of yards to cover, hoping I could once again make radio contact. I waited till I had caught my breath.

I stuttered a little at first, but then began. "Hotel One Alpha, we have been ambushed and have one severe casualty."

"Hold on, Hotel One Bravo."

I waited for an endless three or four minutes. Finally, crazy with impatience, I began to shout into the mouthpiece.

"Hotel One Alpha, what's going on?"

I waited for about another minute, then the silence broke. "Hotel One Bravo, this is Hotel One Actual, do you read me?"

I recognized Captain Martin's voice.

"Captain, sir, this is Ogden. We ran into an ambush at an enemy encampment. We have one man severely wounded in the leg, and he is being carried in a litter. We have one confirmed enemy KIA."

I was surprised to hear myself speak in a calm, confident manner, remembering the important details and explaining them clearly. I fumbled in my breast pocket for a piece of paper that Lieutenant O'Connor had given me with our coordinate numbers.

"There was no paper or weapons confiscated. We made it back down the gorge to where we think is the most accessible med-evac area. We will use yellow smoke. Over."

"Hotel One Bravo, hold your position. Repeat, hold your position and wait for further transmissions. Hotel One Actual, out."

I headed back down my favorite ski slope with rubbery legs. I hoped that I had thought of everything, because I wouldn't be making another trip back up. I relayed the final instructions to the lieutenant. He thanked me for a good job and asked if I was all right.

"I'm okay," I lied.

I felt weak and shaky, as though I had contracted some kind of exotic bug. But an "I don't feel well" comment didn't seem appropriate with a man in shock who had a leg nearly blown off.

Part of the patrol was assigned to fan out around and

make a perimeter while the rest of us began tearing out the jungle with our entrenching tools and the only machete we had to clear out a reasonable landing zone. I began to move about as though I was programmed, a mindless machine with the batteries nearly gone. I kept looking up, wondering if the hole in the canopy would be large enough. We only had a few minutes to chop out the brush so the heavy bird could settle down. If it punctured the underside, damaged the oil lines, or started whacking at the jungle with its rotors, it would self-destruct. With enemy in the area, the pilot had only a few seconds to drop into the hole, pick up our man and be out of here.

"I can hear it!" We stopped for a moment of silence as we listened to the welcome, unmistakable sound of heavy metal wings chopping through the hot, dense tropical air.

With no breeze, the bright yellow smoke feathered itself and lay for a time on our hastily prepared LZ. Then it slowly began to ascend from the depths of the jungle, guided by a thick, heavy green chimney big enough to land a dinosaur.

The heavy piece of machinery hovered over us, blacking out the sun like a magnificent prehistoric insect. Its invisible wings created a hurricane as it descended upon us. Flying debris made it almost impossible to see or maneuver. The front landing gear that projected heavy rubber tires telescoped back into itself as the tires slowly accepted the weight of the heavy bird, allowing it to settle gently on the ground.

I held up one of the corners of the litter as we

crowded the hatch. We lifted Red safely inside. The last surge of energy was too much. My legs gave out as though they weren't there any more. For a moment, I hung onto the bottom of the hatch with one hand and tried desperately to keep from dropping my corner of the litter, until someone from behind rescued me from the weight. I fell to the ground and my mind spun out of control with dizziness and delirium, like a little kid jumping off a playground merry-go-round.

I hadn't completely passed out, but I felt as though I were on the opposite end of a long tunnel. I could see a light and hear voices.

"Ogden passed out cold, sir. He's white as a sheet!"

"Load him up. Keep the M-79 and the ammo. Climbing that hill in the heat would have killed anyone. He deserves the ride home."

With all due respect and very little reverence, they lifted me to the hatch. The corpsman grabbed me by the limp arms, dragged me in, and laid me down on the deck face down. Still semiconscious, I seemed to know what was going on. I began to crawl away from the hatch with great effort, dragging a dead body.

"It looks like heat exhaustion. Take her away," the lieutenant yelled.

The chopper began to shake as it developed power to take off. As we lifted off, the corpsman quickly rolled me over, unbuttoned my jacket, belt, and fly, and sloshed me down with water from a five-gallon can. Then he immediately went to work on Red. The water was warm, but quickly evaporated with the cool air whipping through the hatch. I felt a chill, and it quickly brought me around. A little dizzy but coming back to reality, with a body still like putty, I managed to sit up in the corner against the bulkhead.

The corpsman was on his knees working feverishly over Red. He clawed through a medical kit, and brought out a syringe and gave him an injection. With the engines screaming, there could be no conversation. He looked over in my direction and gave me a thumbs up. I returned the gesture. He pointed to Red and gave another one to indicate that he was going to be all right.

After making sure that his patients were stable, he quickly went back to his secondary job. He sat back in the gunner's chair by the hatch to search and traverse with the M-60 machine gun, anticipating enemy ground fire.

Red began to stir back to life. I envied him. He might end up with a bad leg, or it could heal perfectly, but one thing was certain: he was going home. He would be in Fenway Park rooting for the Sox in no time.

My head was clear, but I had mixed emotions. I was very glad to be sitting here in a nice cool breeze, heading back to the rear, but guilt kept creeping in over leaving the others behind. I felt like I had somehow managed to get out of something. Too bad they all couldn't have piled in and flown back. It was such a long, arduous, and dangerous journey back for them.

The doc quickly glanced at his patient, then went back to the business of the machine gun. There wasn't much to tell about him except that he was tall, lean, and blond. I wondered if while going through Navy boot camp he'd ever dreamed of ending up as a crew chief and corpsman aboard a marine Med-evac. Most of the corpsmen I knew had no idea that after training they were destined for a marine grunt outfit. Most of them didn't care, but they were excellent at the job. When we'd sat in the classrooms in boot camp, no one dreamed for a moment that any of us would be out running through the rice paddies in combat.

The chopper sat down in its torrent of wind, dust, and debris. Four men came running from the cluster of squad-size tents that made up the division medical unit. I tried to assist with the litter, but realized I'd be doing well if I could get off the chopper under my own steam.

After jumping down and grabbing my pack, helmet, and cartridge belt off the deck, I smiled and waved to the flying doc and mimed a thanks. They rose and banked into the breezeless late-afternoon sun.

I turned in the dust and followed the entourage of medical people fussing over their new patient. Once inside the tent, one of the corpsmen noticed that I looked a little ragged around the edges. I told him that with a few salt tablets and six months sleep, I would be fine.

I sat outside the tent on a bench under a sign that said "Sick Call" to wait for the word of Red's true condition. I scanned the surrounding terrain and wondered where I was in relation to the battalion area. I wondered how the patrol was doing and how Nellis was handling my M-79, radio, and his old buddy Shakespeare. I sat on the bench, fighting to stay conscious. I felt a faint sadness, as though I were the only survivor of a tragedy.

I was brought back to my senses by the unsympathetic slam of a spring-loaded screen door, which hung on the wood-frame tent and kept the flies in. A young corpsman stepped around the corner.

"Ogden, your friend's going to be okay. He's going to need surgery to get the bullet. It's going to take pins and a lot of mending, but he's going to be all right."

"Thanks, Doc. Can I see him?"

"I'm afraid not. He's completely under anesthetic already."

"How can I get to Second Battalion CP?"

"Wait and I'll check for you."

CHAPTER FOURTEEN

I jumped out of the jeep, thanked the driver, and went into the CP tent. I was assigned a cot, but I didn't need one. I could have dropped and died anywhere.

The last squad tent in the row was sagging miserably as though it were an afterthought and no one cared if it stayed up or not. It was crowded with empty cots that seemed to cling desperately to the ghastly, uneven ground that ran steeply downhill and to the right. I found the only level cot in a dark corner. I dropped my gear and kicked it underneath, and died while falling onto the cot.

I must have gone into a deep coma. When I opened my eyes, I was startled by the strange surroundings. Then it all came back: the patrol, the ambush, and the evacuation. The computer, clogged with fuzz, was slowly starting to warm up.

I sat up to test the mechanical parts. Everything seemed functional. Up on my feet I was still a little weak, and I noticed an enormous cavity where my stomach used to be. The sun had gone down and it was cool and peaceful. I felt like an invalid who had been locked away for a considerable length of time and suddenly turned loose to go out and check the new world. Everything looked strangely different and non-routine. There was not a soul in sight.

I decided I had better start begging and scrounging around for something to eat, for I knew that chow call was over. I decided to begin at the CP tent.

The company sergeant major sat behind a green desk with green utilities and shuffled through a green folder. The only things amiss were the green goat eyes of Lucifer himself. He had a heavy, hairless, glowing head like the Wizard of Oz, and a grotesque, carniverous beak.

The sergeant major and I had less-than-warm affection for each other. He had unsuccessfully run me up for battalion office hours, a lesser facsimile of a court-martial. The incident stemmed from the seasickness and missing sea bag and the subsequent disrespect to Jason. He had had to settle for company office hours. I spent five days at hard labor in the bilge of the ship—an obviously sensitive antidote to a helpless, chronic seasick victim.

The sergeant major had not seen me standing in the doorway. I wasn't hungry enough to dicker with him about why I had missed the chow call. I went immediately to the radio shack to see what the disposition was on the patrol.

Kruger, the weight lifter, was on radio watch. He sat

at a small table with two PRC 10 radios propped up on an ammo can. They were connected to a high aerial outside and made up a crude, makeshift field radio communication system.

Back in the States, Kruger had convinced me to explore the rewards and benefits of weight lifting. I was curious and had tried it for a few weeks, but quickly came to the conclusion that I would remain a ninety-pound weakling. It was just too much work.

Some of the typical nuisances snickered behind his back—way, way behind his back—because of his size and bulk. They thought he was a little slow and dull upstairs, and maybe on the gay side; but I knew different. He wasn't the brightest guy I knew, but he was pleasant. On the weekends, we hung around the cantinas in Tijuana, daring each other with the fattest and ugliest señoritas.

"Oggie, what are you doing here? The patrol isn't supposed to be back yet, and I heard you talking to Captain Martin this afternoon."

"I decided to ride back in style with the med-evac. I hailed a taxi and rode her home."

I could tell he wasn't in the least amused by my attitude.

"Two more are coming home, but they're not coming home in style."

I knew something was wrong before he completed the sentence. There was no sparkle in the voice, no comedy.

"What happened?"

"They were hit again. There're two dead."

He hesitated and turned away. Kruger had been part of the first platoon and had gotten to know everyone before he had become the company radio operator.

"Who, goddamn it, who?"

"Charlie and Nellis."

"No!" I yelled as I threw a tightly clenched fist through space, trying to crush the invisible source of my anguish. I began to rant and rave like an actor, giving wild gyrations in all directions of the stage. Kruger sat quietly as I kept yelling, as though there was something he could have done to prevent it or something he could do now to change it.

"They should have been pulled out of there with Red and me! The whole damn gorge was a death trap and the whole patrol was ill-fated from the start! Nellis damn near drowned before we got to the foothills, then he risked his ass to save Red's. All for what? Just to take a fatal bullet later on in the afternoon!"

I began to laugh. It was a frivolous attempt to try and cover it up, to black it out.

"We all laughed at the idea of stuffing each other in plastic bags when we first got here, didn't we?"

The scene was over. The actor was exhausted and in tears.

I stepped outside and was brushed by a young second lieutenant I had never seen before. He didn't even have a tan. I felt numb and mindless, like a cloud of lethargy had just descended and was choking off the air. I heard music and voices coming from a tent down in the wash. It was a makeshift bar, better known as a "slopshoot."

169

I handed a dime to a corporal I had seen before but didn't know. He fished out a can of Schlitz from a washtub of ice. There were about twelve men sitting at picnic tables, some talking about going home and some idiot talking about being extended for about a year to grab the combat pay. I tuned them out and guzzled my beer, which I had already begun to feel. The mood was bad and the decor of the bar was rotten, but the price was right.

I was sitting close enough to the washtub bartender that I didn't have to get up. I am sure he had his orders not to serve anyone he considered drunk. I had four, then put number five in my pocket. For a nondrinker, that would be enough.

I stood up, and only then did I realize I was totally paralyzed from the eyebrows down. I managed to make it to the doorway. Only drunks have a talent for finding hidden things to trip on. I ended up sprawled out in the road face down. The deep powdered dust was like falling into a vat of dry flour. I rolled over and sat up slowly. The open can of beer I had shoved into one of my lower utility pockets trickled down my leg. I retrieved it and took a long drink to wash the dirt out of my mouth. I was disoriented and felt no pain—like a forlorn clown who had gotten into the wrong-colored makeup. I sat in the roadway with thick dust clinging to my skin, eyebrows, and eyelashes. Only the wetness of unclear eyes gave the lifeless face of the sad mannequin away. When I had tipped the can of beer too far, a huge muddy frown appeared, extending from my lips to the corners of my mouth and down to the base of my jaw. I sat with the world whirring around me and wondered if I should get up or just sit there and finish the beer.

Four men came walking down the road and stopped where I was sitting. I couldn't see too well for the dirt and the booze.

One spoke in a mock Irish brogue. "Well, lookee here. A wee little drunken leprechaun."

They surrounded me and began to taunt and sneer. One took the remainder of the beer and poured it over my head. I didn't care. I was a clown, and they were the laughing audience. I got to my feet unsteadily, and they realized I was totally helpless. They started shoving me around playfully, curious about the drunk. One would shove me and the other would catch me.

"What's the matter, drunk, can't you handle your booze? Or maybe you can't handle the war? Maybe you're drowning your sorrows and you want to go back home to momma? Maybe you're just a scared little chickenshit, afraid they're going to send you to the front lines."

Even through the fog and the catch-push game, I knew the dialogue couldn't be coming from anyone who had been here for any length of time. No one ever talked to anyone like that—not even his enemy. They had to be replacements; very young, green, and stupid.

As far as I was concerned, the fun was over. But they got caught up in the fervor of their own game and began to get rough. The ground under my feet was listing and rolling like the deck of a ship. The four hyenas weren't big—they were just bigger than me.

I took a hard shot from the back and went careening

toward another grinning punk ready to catch me. I came in way off balance and fast; and to his surprise and mine, I managed to smash him in the face with as much of an off-balance fist as I could muster. In a cloud of dust, he went down on his back. I fell on top, knocking all the wind and pride out of him.

I rolled off him slowly, got halfway up on my feet, took a direct shot right in the face, and went back down again. Someone got a firm hold on me from behind and dragged me to my feet. I couldn't shake loose. Another one threw a fist into my midsection. It was hard enough for me to give up a little Schlitz, gag, and nearly pass out. I still felt I was good for one more shot—one of theirs or one of mine. The drunken leprechaun coiled, still being held by the goon from behind. With proper timing and the spring of a grasshopper, I scored a direct hit with both feet to the chest, sending a no-longer-grinning idiot about ten or fifteen feet into the tent. He nearly tore it down, bounded off, and finally landed on the ground.

The force of the kick brought us all down. Somehow I had managed to bring down three of the four pimply faced juvenile delinquents to the leprechaun's level.

The next thing I remember was being smacked lightly on my crusty, muddy cheeks. I came to. It was the young second lieutenant with no suntan.

"Are you all right? What happened?"

Still in a drunken stupor, I grinned. "Playing volleyball, sir."

"Volleyball? You look like you went through a shredder before you went through the brewery. On

172

your feet. Let's go to the CP."

Next morning, I stood before the battalion commander like a ruffian grade-school kid standing before the principal. My head and body ached so bad inside and out that being reduced in rank from pfc to private didn't faze me in the least. At least not for the moment.

I was marched over to the company CP, where the great wizard informed me I was being transferred into a new green outfit, Third Battalion, Third Marines. He assured me that my office hours had no bearing on this. Many men from this battalion would be transferred into that battalion to give them combat-experienced men. I grinned. Sure, Wiz, I believe you.

I found an unattended jeep parked alongside a tent. I lucked out; the keys were still in the ignition. I only had an hour before I would have to board a C-130 heading for Chu Lai, wherever that was.

The sides of the tents were rolled up and secured, allowing plenty of sunlight and fresh air in. Red was lying on his back staring up at the ceiling. He heard me clomping across the wooden floor.

He smiled. "Well, look here, if it isn't the fucking midget." He got up on an elbow.

I could tell by the tone of his voice that he was feeling pretty good. I sat down on a locker box.

"How are you doing, champ? I hear they're going to put you aboard one of these big, fancy, sterile hospital ships today."

He clenched my fist and shook it and beamed with a big smile. "I'm going home, too. Hey, where are the rest of them assholes? How come they aren't here to see me off? What in the hell happened to your face?"

"Playing volleyball," I answered.

"You must have had a pretty rough game by the looks of that eye. Where's the rest of them, huh?"

I swallowed, emotion beginning to build. Even though he was being transferred away I knew I had to tell him, as he was a letter writer and would find out anyway.

I finally forced it out. "Charlie and Nellis didn't make it!"

Without a word, he quickly flopped down on his back and stared up at the ceiling. There was a long silence.

"I'm getting out of this neck of the woods myself. I'm being transferred to 3-3."

He continued to stare at the ceiling. His eyes began to glisten and a small tear developed out of the corner of his eye. It quivered but didn't break off. He turned to me without a word and stretched out his hand. We squeezed hard together.

"Good-bye, champ. It was good to know you."

He smiled but didn't say a word. I replaced the steel pot on my head, clomped across the wooden floor, and got back into my grand-theft auto.

CHAPTER FIFTEEN

My mind wandered back and forth, in and out, like a
C-130 dodging turbulence, drifting, correcting course
and heading for a new outfit, new terrain, and new
circumstances. It couldn't possibly be as much fun as
the one I had just left. I had to reach hard for a tiny
shred of optimism. I felt like a child bride after the
wedding: misused, abuse, annulled, broken in spirit,
abruptly packaged up and sent parcel post, stamped
"last priority," and given no consideration. I was a
goodwill package consisting of old, discarded necessities with some use left in them on route to another
needy, unappreciative group of morons. Yes, the
honeymoon was over—and so was the marriage.

The fog of frivolousness had dissipated and the path
forward seemed sharp and clear. There is a strange
feeling of uniqueness that comes with being on the very
bottom of the social order; like an ex con, feared,
misunderstood but romanticized, a threat and an

enigma within a dubious social order, and no longer a slave in the realm of mediocrity. I believe in rules, laws, and order much like Hammurabi. My rules, my laws, and my order, all of which will be implemented toward my survival. There is nothing further they can do to me. If necessary, I will fight on two fronts: against them and the enemy.

I walked down the ramp and out of the belly of the huge cargo plane. I could have been stepping onto an eight thousand-foot prefabricated aluminum runway somewhere in the west section of the Gobi Desert. A green nylon, overweight, weather-faced crew chief checked our manifest cards like a good little stewardess. I slung my seabag and followed a line of men toward a group of tents a couple of hundred yards from the aircraft. The temperature was well over one hundred degrees.

The view in any direction was obscured by hot, forceful gusts of wind laced heavily with sand, dirt, and dust as though there were far less gravity here on this newly charted, uninhabitable planet. It was nearly impossible to look beyond the air base to see what kind of terrain lay out there. The heat waves reflected off the griddle-hot runway, reflecting like a glossy, mirrored lake. The heat rays played havoc with the light rays, everything partially visible waving and dancing.

For a moment, the gust of wind subsided, releasing its grip on the sand. And without warning, the thunder of an aircraft vibrated the aluminum sections of runway underfoot. An A4D Skyhawk rocketed into view, heavily laden with bombs. It screamed down the runway. The pilot flipped the switch, igniting the jato rockets strapped to the belly. They exploded like a truckload of TNT, catapulting man, machine, and tons of death into the sky.

After a lot of names were called, we boarded trucks headed for our designated companies. There are approximately sixty miles of sandy coastline between Danang and Chu Lai. The rapidly growing air facility takes up only a tiny portion of the many square miles of the white, sandy, almost totally arid territory stretching from the sea inland ten or fifteen miles to the low-lying mountains that run all the way into Elephant Valley.

At the end of the not-completed four-thousand-foot runway is jungle. It hides a network of small villages.

A comfortable grove of pine trees between the runway and the beach protects hundreds of the Marine Air Group, Third Battalion, and Third Marine headquarters from the sometimes one-hundred-thirty-degree heat.

I waited for hours outside the company CP tent with the others. We were interrogated and given a pep talk by a tall, skinny, bald, middle-aged captain who looked more like a retired major general. I felt more uneasy than I had expected, coming into a new outfit with the left side of my face still purple and puffed. I looked and felt like I'd been KOed by Jake Lamotta.

With all the questions he fired at me about my conduct and recent office hours, plus the addition of his own personal L Company discipline dissertation, I felt like either a prisoner of war or a slave that has just been traded from one tribe to another. At any moment, one of the NCOs standing there would step up and rip off my shirt, open my mouth, and check my teeth. With my five-foot-five frame and unruly, spirited disposition, the bidding would have to start low.

After a few more minutes of waiting, a young corporal came out of the CP tent with several service-record books under his arm. He called out three names, and we climbed aboard a jeep. He introduced himself as Corporal Daniels. He was average sized, with sandy hair, brown eyes, and cheeks that had been ravaged by years of acne that had since healed, leaving a relief map of the moon on either side of his face. The jeep sped off through the pine trees and down a back road. The Third Platoon was down at the north end of the runway, he said.

He turned around. "Which one of you is Ogden?"

I tipped the helmet back off my face.

"Oh, I didn't recognize you from your picture here in your record book with your helmet on and your new face."

"I feel a little different too, Corporal. Like a new man," I said sincerely.

"What happened, anyways?"

"Playing volleyball," I answered.

"It looks as though they were using you for the ball."

I didn't need to invite any further humiliation by letting him know how right he was.

The driver of the jeep, who looked only twelve years old, almost had control. He was driving much too fast and was trying to hit every chuckhole and loose rock on the newly graded roadway. The road ran straight and narrow down the backside of the airstrip.

Between the road and the open air hangers that housed individual Skyhawks by the dozens, a number of gigantic rubber bladders filled with jet fuel lay exposed on the surface of the sand. Each of them stretched over an area the size of an Olympic-sized swimming pool, and when completely filled they were about four feet thick. In such heat, I wondered how they kept the gas from evaporating, expanding, and exploding the tanks.

The airfield was now obscured by sand dunes as we came to a Y in the road and the driver kept to the left. The road divided a large sand dune, and we drove out toward the end of the runway and cut back along the edge. The Third Platoon CP tent sat on top of the dune that ran parallel to the runway and was about twenty yards away.

The jeep whined and slipped in the sand as it labored up the incline. The twelve-year-old stepped on the brakes, nearly throwing us all over the windshield or through it. I grabbed my gear, readjusted my helmet and jumped down.

"This guy's terrific, Corporal," I said. "You ought to get him full time. I think he thinks he's A. J. Foyt."

The twelve-year-old going on eighteen gave me a dirty look; and when everyone had bailed out he ground the gears, floored it, tried to twist the wheels right off the axles, and headed out of the pit area.

I followed the others to the platoon CP tent. Starting

from this end of the platoon area, there were sandbag positions protected from the sun by shelter halfs, and ponchos stretching south along the runway as far as I could see. They appeared to be facing the runway. To the rear lay the fuel bladders, and one hundred yards south to the rear was an extension of the maintenance and refueling area. It was like a long dock or peninsula extending out into the sand to the fuel bladders where the planes would taxi to refuel.

It looked like the Third Platoon Lima Company was right in the middle of things. But why in the middle and not on the perimeter? It could only be the very last defense. There must be perimeter after perimeter out there, and this is just the last hope. If they get this far with all this fuel and equipment lying around, somebody's going to play hell.

It took a while for the eyes to adjust from the white sand and sun to the gloom of the inside of the tent. The tent smelled of coal oil and musty close-quarter living. The platoon sergeant stood behind a cluttered table in the middle of the tent. There were several lanterns, half-burned candles, C-rations, map boxes, binoculars, and a chess set with captured pieces lying helter skelter as though it were the last game that would ever be played and they would never be needed again.

The sergeant was about five-foot-ten inches, small-to-average build with too much gut, an olive-brown complexion stretched over fine features. His eyes were like cigar burns in a terry-cloth hand towel. His head was literally shaved from the tops of his ears down all the way around the back. A small dark island of stubble remained on top of the head.

This polished dome syndrome, radical beyond the regulations haircut, seemed to exemplify an acute fanaticism among lifers. FOR OURS IS NOT TO REASON WHY, BUT OURS IS TO DO OR DIE. The unbending, unyielding android that prayed to no God but to its true creator and savior, the Marine Corps, had a name that had too many *l*'s and too many *p*'s, and not enough vowels, and stretched endlessly across his left breast pocket.

Sergeant Nickopoppollopales (I couldn't spell it or pronounce it) began to speak louder and more authoritatively than was necessary.

"Lance Corporal Rudy, you go with Corporal Anderson of second squad. PFC Sims, you go with Corporal Burnett here of third squad. Now get out of here. Ogden, you stay put."

To one side of the tent was a sergeant sitting on a cot. He looked like a very young Glen Ford with a close, light-brown flattop. He fondled and rubbed with an oilcloth what appeared to be a British Sten as though it were a delicate animal. He probably bought it from someone but would brag of its capture.

The cigar-hole eyes began to assess the purple and puff.

"So we have ourselves a real live shitbird here, just busted this morning. You've got two choices. You can do things my way and do your job, or you can go to the brig. I'm not about to put up with some scum from another outfit."

He turned to Corporal Daniels and started to yell as

though Daniels was responsible for my past.

"If this shitbird fucks up just once, I want to know about it. And if you don't straighten him out, your ass is in a sling."

He pointed back at me with his finger, still ranting. "Go ahead and screw up, and I'll clobber the other side of your face."

I began to boil. You'd better bring your volleyball team, sergeant. That's what it took and that's what it's gonna take from now on, I thought.

The diatribe continued. Yelling at an NCO in the presence of junior rank is irresponsible and shows weakness and insecurity. It's like Dad yelling at Mom, or vice versa, in the presence of the children. It promotes confusion and erodes the virtues of respect and discipline. Whether it was Nickopoppollopales . . . or Napoleon, I was in deep trouble again. I hoped I was not dealing with another personality with a hairline fracture lying dormant, just waiting for the right pressure in the right place at the right time.

I hoped it would not be me again. How could I be so lucky? I felt like I had a clandestine role in an intelligence-type high command investigation seeking out character aberrations in staff NCOs. Okay, General Walt, you keep transferring me from unit to unit and I'll come up with a psychotic every time. I will apply the thumbscrews and the electrodes to the head and flush them out into the open so special troops can bag them, take them to a lab, dismantle them, discard the old, defective parts, replace them with new ones, and send them to the Marine Corps Recruit Depot to train "boots."

Daniels and I were dismissed. The sergeant on the cot continued to fondle his over-the-counter war trophy. He must be the platoon guide. I wondered where the platoon commander was.

Once outside, we headed to the nearest position next to the CP tent. I stopped for a moment.

"Tell me, Corporal Daniels, is our leader always that nervous?"

He didn't stop or speak. The reluctance to discuss it was either out of loyalty, out of respect for the rank, or a belief that you do not talk to shitbirds about such matters.

I caught up with him outside the sandbag hootch. "What's the platoon commander like?"

"Sergeant Nick is the platoon commander."

So that's what it was all about. That explained the nervousness and the tantrumlike attack. A staff sergeant playing first lieutenant and platoon commander and not quite sure he could handle the job.

"Johnson, get your black ass out here." He began to grin as Black Johnson stuck his head out of the hatch.

"Yessuh, Boss, is that you, Mr. Benny?"

Black Johnson was grinning also. He was on his knees with just his head sticking out of the hootch.

"I brought a new foxhole buddy for you. This is Private Ogden. This is Lance Corporal Johnson."

"If he's a bigot, I'll frag and eat him for sure." He scanned me up and down. "On second thought, he's too

183

damn little and skinny. Now, Corporal Daniels, why can't you get me somebody big and mean and ugly I can fight with?"

"I think he'll work out all right. Ogden here likes to play contact volleyball. He looks almost like a brother with half his face black and blue."

Daniels unslung his M-14 and reslung it on the opposite shoulder. "You remember what Sergeant Nick told you, Ogden, and maybe both of us will stay out of trouble. Just maybe!"

Rochester disappeared back inside his sandbag hootch. I was not sure, but I felt as though the welcome mat had not been dusted in quite a while.

With an armload of gear, I ducked into the shade of the hootch. I dumped my gear in the corner of a patio arrangement attached to the pup tent like a front porch. I sat on a sandbag in the corner. The roll of sandbags that encircled the patio were about shoulder high, and I could see in all directions.

Johnson was sitting inside the two-man tent on one of two cots that were dug down into the sand so they would fit but still remain about three inches off the sand. A great idea; I knew some people who would dig and pick their hearts out for a cot in a foxhole.

Fighting holes were obviously impossible in this sandy country. Each position was just a ring of sandbags around a two-man tent.

My new residence sat on the end of a large fingerlike sand dune. It was cut through abruptly by the access road that led to the runway, and the dune continued on toward the jungle. There was a position on the other side and I assumed there were positions all the way to the edge of the jungle, some two hundred to two hundred and fifty yards distant. At the very end of the runway stood air traffic guide-markers, lights on stanchions of various elevations. They were visible signs for pilots that said, That's all there is. And if you don't make it over us you'll tear out a chunk of jungle big enough to build a supermarket, parking lot and all. On the opposite side of the runway lay a massive junkyard, piles of empty oil barrels, heaps and miles of broken aluminum runway.

As a kid I was always fascinated by junkyards, dumps, or vacant houses. At home there was no such thing as trash. Sometimes, in desperate need of something to do, I would paddle my bike some four miles further into the country to an illegal dump site. I rummaged through it as though it were a staging area for Santa Claus. I would claw feverishly through fragmented treasure. On one rewarding day, to my astonishment, I found a J. C. Higgins bold-action twelve-gauge shotgun in perfect condition with only a minimum amount of rust.

My mother sharply curtailed my bountiful treasure hunting when I arrived home on another day after several healthy spills off my bike on the mountain road coming from the dump with a shirt pocket full of dynamite blasting caps. I had positively no idea what they were. I had found them all nicely packed in a small cardboard box, bright and brassy. There was enough explosive to slip me into a plastic bag, size small. "One man's trash is another man's treasure" was still the most eloquent phrase I had ever heard. In the case of this junkyard, one man's trash could be another man's warning. I thought I saw a blackened wing tip from a Skyhawk, the eyesore maybe just enough to take the edge off an overzealous pilot.

CHAPTER SIXTEEN

My reluctant host continued to ignore me as I went on with the visual orientation of the hot, lifeless, disgusting terrain. What irony! How could I already miss the slop and stink of rick paddies, the humidity and leeches of the mountainous jungle?

I decided to break all the rules I had hastily formulated for my new environment about keeping my mouth shut and staying on the defensive. An excellent way to keep from drowning is to stay out of the water—but what happens one day when you inadvertently fall off a bridge?

My interpretation of the Monroe Doctrine would not work. Sometimes standing off and keeping to one's self is misconstrued as arrogance and conceit. The world is too small, the hootch too cramped. The smell of defensiveness hung in the air like a gas to warn me that I was in the wrong league. Notwithstanding, I took the initiative to break the ice.

"Johnson, what happened to your partner?"

He continued cleaning his M-14, running a small patch through the grooves of the fire suppressor.

At this point, I did not want to be proven right about my frivolous, philosophical rhetoric. As the seconds ticked by, and as the cleaning patch passed through another groove, insecurity began to grab me. Insecurity, paranoia, and needless defensiveness; garbage packed into the mind like bundles of old useless newspapers packed tightly in the attic. There is no room left for fresh air.

I wanted to jump up and tell him to get fucked in big red letters. Talk to me, anything! But then with the timing of a brilliant comic who waits until every tear has been wrung dry and the fatigue of laughter has subsided, he let me off the hook. He began to speak. And to my astonishment, he spoke in flawless, elegant diction unhindered by colloquial dialect. It was as though he were miming a Sidney Portier soundtrack. There was an air of "Let's make everything perfectly clear."

"He contacted an acute case of dysentery from field mess. Sergeant Nick accused him of malingering." His eyes never seemed to blink, and they never once left me. "He was a very sick man. I knew for a fact that he was bleeding. He was my friend, and yes, he was black."

He went back to rubbing his M-14. If the ice was melting, I did not want to inhibit it. Now at least we had conversation, even though it was tainted a bit with a wisp of anger and discord.

"I'm sorry for your friend." I decided to jump in with

both feet, foolish and naive but in earnest. "Is there a racial problem in this platoon?"

"There is racial tension throughout this entire planet. Have you ever been to L.A.?"

"Once, coming through on the way to boot camp."

"There's a section of Los Angeles called Watts, and right this very moment black people are burning, rioting, and looting that part of the city."

I sat and listened like man's best friend, alert, cocking head and ear to the master's voice, ready to spring to any decipherable command. But nothing came—just words I did not understand. Flashes of Seattle burning, people running through the streets in horror, came to my mind. Seattle, Los Angeles, and San Diego were the only large American cities I had ever seen.

"You've got to be kidding. Burning and rioting doesn't happen in the United States. Here, maybe, but not at home."

"It's true! It's my neighborhood! My momma has been keeping me posted. It's been coming for a long time."

"But why?"

"Do you know what the word bigotry means?"

"No."

"Do you know what ghetto means?"

"No."

"Mr. Ogden, where pray tell have you existed your whole life? Another plant, perhaps? Maybe a white, upper class, sterile capsule?"

Neither one of us knew what kind of an animal we

were up against, but the common denominator obviously became curiosity. When the heat of animosity becomes dampened, healthy little specks of perspiration begin to appear on the ice that forms on and cripples the vital communication systems. Curiosity has done more than just kill the cat—it has evolved society from frolicking in the trees to landing on the moon.

"I'm from Washington, the state of. I was raised in the woods on a tiny ranch."

I no longer found myself reluctant to tell what I always considered a rather grim story. Instead, a feeling of exuberance and pride seemed to have taken over. He listened intently as I babbled on and on. From time to time, I would patch into the system and listen to myself. I was good.

As I listened to myself I realized that I may have traveled eighteen years of rough and crazy terrain—but now, in a strange and subtle way, I began to be less sensitive. For the first time in my life, I was appreciative of my background; but I did not understand why.

"When my mom and dad separated, we would go live with my grandmother. She owned and operated a restaurant on the Yakima Indian Reservation. I was six or seven years old. I still remember so many different kinds and colors of kids that lived around the neighborhood on the reservation. There weren't too many white kids, but there were Indian kids, Mexican kids and Negro kids. We had a lot of fun.

"Grandma treated us all the same. In the mornings

and evenings the family would eat together, but at lunchtime every kid in the neighborhood would end up out back of the restaurant. We would all eat sandwiches made from the leftover bread. Grandma was a hard woman and sometimes difficult to understand, but she loved kids. She treated us all alike, even though I was the grandchild."

I was so caught up in my own storytelling I didn't realize Johnson had put down his rifle and leaned back on his cot to listen.

"Grandma had a very good friend whom I remember well. He used to drive by after working in the woods logging to help with the few heavy chores around the restaurant. After the work was done he would bounce me on his knee and sing crazy songs like 'La Cucaracha' and 'Open the Door, Richard.' He was always singing and smiling. He had a gold front tooth that was fascinating to me. He would let me fondle through his pockets like a raccoon, and I always found the one full of candy corn.

"Sometimes on the weekends he would drive us out to his little ranch not far away in an old, rickety pickup truck. His little, old dilapidated farmhouse looked worse than ours on the coast, but for some reason it seemed a lot nicer. It smelled like disinfectant and chili peppers. Sometimes we would stay for lunch, and he would put too many peppers in the peas. I would cry and my nose would run into my mouth, but I wouldn't give up. He really got a charge out of it because I would come back for more. He had a pack of hounds that I liked to play with. We had hounds of our own at home, and when I got bigger the old man would take me out coon hunting on the weekends."

"What kind of coons?" There was a faint curl of his lip that could have been misconstrued as a wisp of a smile.

"I don't know what you mean."

"Forget it. Continue on."

"Yeah, old Tom Jackson was just like one of the family. He was like one of my uncles. They all worked in the logging camps. In fact, he became one of the family. My grandmother married him. I guess you could say he was kind of a grandfather."

I didn't purposely intend my story to come off as a setup or to have a punch line, but that was exactly where it was heading. I was almost reluctant to finish. I did not know how he was going to take it. He allowed me to talk at great length, and that in itself was encouraging. I knew I was into things I had been exposed to from time to time, but I was still naive about racial problems. If I knew or felt anything from childhood, it was very minimal. The only thing now was to be honest and take the consequences as they came.

"You see, Tom Jackson had skin darker than yours. He was a negro, and I liked him a hell of a lot. If there was any hatred in the family or the community, and I'm sure there was, they kept it from me. I thank them for that. It may have left me confused all these years, but they didn't pass on their own hatred to a dumb little kid to carry around for the rest of his life."

There was a painfully long silence. Then Johnson

sprang up from the cot. He slapped both knees, looked me right in the eye with a straight face bearing a serious, inquisitive expression. I knew I had pulled the trigger on everything.

"Mr. Ogden, that's the most contrived crock of honky bullshit I have ever heard in my entire life."

There was another long, painful pause. Then the corner of his mouth went slightly taut, a tooth was revealed, and then another, until there was an actual full-blown smile.

In a calm breath, he said, "I believe you! Like the Irish say, I don't think you've been blessed with the virtue of blarney; you're too naive. Your grandfather Tom sounds like an 'Uncle Tom' to me."

"What do you mean by that?"

"Far be it from me to puncture your low class, poverty stricken, country-bumpkin capsule."

He began to chuckle. I smiled out of relief. Most of what he had said had gone over my head, but I knew from the tone of his voice it was not malicious.

"What became of this Unc—I mean, Grandfather Tom Jackson of yours?"

"I was told somebody murdered him. He was shot over some kind of gambling thing, and my grandmother closed the restaurant."

"That doesn't surprise me at all. Just another hustling nigger!"

That statement really shocked and confused me.

A gust of hot wind rattled the hootch. The hot sand that traveled with it stung momentarily like ground glass. Johnson rummaged around in a haversack, a large pouch that hangs independently from the bottom of the pack. It is designed to make a twelve-pound pack twelve pounds heavier if necessary. He dug out a couple of cans of rations and threw one in my direction.

In this climate and these circumstances, canned fruit was valued far more than gold. Peaches were the most coveted of all and it was unthinkable to give them away, even to your best friend. In an amazed state, I thanked him and we both ate. Even at ninety degrees plus, the fruit slid down the throat with the tantalizing excitement of melting ice cream.

Between bits, slurps, and licks, I listened while Johnson showed his hand at storytelling. I interrupted him from time to time to get a clarification on what a ghetto or a bigot was. A dormant, frozen mind was beginning to thaw. I thought poverty and degradation were only indigenous to rural areas. I thought all city dwellers had nice houses and fancy apartments, ice cream parlors, movie shows, bicycles and paved roads, no fields to hoe, no wood to chop, and no water to carry. What I was hearing about ghetto life was scaring the hell out of me.

I sensed a subtle mood change, a sense of pride and enthusiasm, perhaps much like I felt when I told my own cluttered epic. He had an extraordinarily large family who clawed and scraped together. He told me of his success in high school, a basketball scholarship to college, the dream of becoming a teacher, and the idealism of perhaps going back to teach at the same junior high school or high school.

"With all that going for you, why did you join the

'crotch' like the rest of us meatheads?"

"I'm a meathead, as you call it, just like everyone else. I wanted to get away for a while, affirm my convictions, and make sure beyond a reasonable doubt that that's what I wanted to do. I wanted to get my head straight. And besides, my friends were getting drafted. I wanted to have some choice in the matter. On the other hand, just like all the other meatheads, I wanted to find out if I could hack it."

"Well, I knew I could hack it. I've been going through pre-boot camp all my life. What's liberty like here?"

"Liberty? You've got to be out of your mind, boy. There aren't even any towns around here."

"Shit! I knew it didn't look so good from the air, but I didn't think it was this bad. What's the scoop on Daniels and Nick? I want to know what kind of a circus I've been sold to."

"Daniels is cool. We get along fine. Nick leans on him hard and runs the jesus out of him. He has to pass Nick's bullshit along. He gets frustrated, but he's fair. Anderson's leadership is silly and simple, but okay. He's trying to do a good job, but he has too much fun at it. The tall skinny redhead is Burnett. He thinks he's gunnery sergeant already. As far as Nick is concerned, my first preliminary prognosis was paranoia. I've come to the conclusion, however, that it's an acute case of schizophrenia brought on by the insecurity and inability to accept the responsibility of leadership. Some days he's amiable as your best friend, and some days something will set him off and he's into a tirade and everyone catches hell."

"I'll let you explain the scientific jazz later, but it sure doesn't sound good."

"We're just one big happy family."

All the time that Johnson was talking, something was buzzing around in the back of my mind. It finally landed on the wall, like a listless fly. I had never before in my life sat down and had a lengthy discussion about myself and then listened to someone else. The storytelling had been a lot of common ground, and I took for granted that the feeling was mutual.

Several uneventful days passed. We rotated the watch, staring out into the empty white hot desert by day and the emptier blackness by night. We entertained each other with more storytelling. Can you top this one? As we grew short of material, another fly buzzed the darkness of the inner cavern that housed a small but imaginative mind.

"Know something, professor? Seeing as how we're stuck in this big happy family of yours, I've got one brilliant idea to help pass the time. We can make it worthwhile. You want to be a teacher, right? I don't know anything, right? I'm as dumb as a post about a lot of things. I never went to high school. You could teach me. I could be your first student."

He laughed and shook his head. "No way. That would be kind of counterproductive, wouldn't it? Me teaching a dumb honky everything I know."

"I think I read somewhere that the key to the peace and goodwill among all mankind is education."

He raised an eyebrow and began to smirk. "Don't

patronize me." He paused, looking at me for a long time. "Well, you may not be as dumb as you look. But if you're as dumb as you are small, we may have to ship over for four more years to get you educated."

We chuckled. It felt good. I was long overdue for a good laugh.

CHAPTER SEVENTEEN

After sundown, I got a chance to meet some of the "family" hanging around the platoon CP next door. The professor's quick summary was very close to the mark.

Roy Anderson was not very tall, but had thick arms and legs and massive shoulders. His size twenty-two neck and twelve-inch grin made him look like he had swallowed all of an accordian but the keys.

Burnett was tall and gangly with bushy red hair. He could have passed for Red's older brother. I sensed him watching me without emotion. His features reminded me of a petulant, dry redbone hound puppy. They are forever grinning and slobbering.

A blond lance corporal came out of the CP tent and announced there would be a squad leader's meeting in ten minutes. I recognized him as a replacement from the old outfit. He had a medium build, blond hair, gigantic ears, and no lips. He had just a slit where a ticket came out when you pushed a button, and you had to read what he said if you were not from Alabama. He was in Burnett's squad, and apparently Sergeant Mick had taken a liking to him and made him a house mouse, or the gofer. Go for this, go for that.

Sergeant Mick noticed me outside and called me in. I entered the dragon's smoky den. He was sitting behind his makeshift desk with a dead cigar butt in his mouth. He had his shirt off and his dog tags dripped with perspiration. In his surroundings, as he shuffled the papers on his desk, he looked like a porno theater manager skimming off the profits of skin money.

"Ogden, I'm screening a few people. What was your job in your old outfit?"

"Grenadier."

He looked surprised. "You were? How come it's not in your service record book? How come it doesn't show you qualified with either the forty-five or M-79?"

"It was a last-minute change before we left the ship."

"Are you good with the M-79? I'm looking for someone who's really good."

"I'm the best there is in combat."

"What makes you so sure?"

"Sure has nothing to do with it. I just know."

He stopped chewing his cigar and looked at me. No one was more surprised at my candor than I was. He waved me out.

"Get out of here. You've got the job. Have Corporal Daniels take you down to supply after the squad leader's meeting. We are going on an operation tomorrow."

I had surfaced back into the fresh air with a smile. I had just bluffed my way back into my favorite job. I gave myself a mental pat on the back. You've got your shit together, boy!

I went back to the hootch. The professor was still wiping down his rifle. I sat down in my favorite spot in the corner.

"You know, you're gonna rub the blueing right off that thing. Then you'll really be in trouble with rust."

"Cleanliness is next to godliness. May my blueing never come off, praise the Lord." Before I could say another word, he began firing questions. "What do you know about the United States government?"

I stuttered. "I don't know very much."

"What are the three branches of government?"

I was delighted, but my mind began to whirl. "The executive, the ah . . . I've got it, I've got it, the legislative. Oh, damn it, I used to know it. I can't think of it."

"Two out of three isn't bad. It's the judicial system. Do you know what each of them are?"

"Yes. The executive branch is the presidency, the legislative branch is the Senate and the House of Representatives, and the judicial branch is the Supreme Court."

"That's good, Mr. Ogden. Now you may sit back down and contain yourself, please. I appreciate optimum enthusiasm from my students, but please keep your seat."

I sat down. I was exhilarated that I had remembered a few things.

"Do you know what the first amendment to the Constitution is?"

"No."

"The first amendment is the freedom of speech, which is essentially one of the cornerstones and the key to a democratic society. Do you know anything in particular about the Constitution?"

"Ah, let me see. 'We hold these truths to be self evident, that all men are created equal and they are endowed by their creator with certain inalienable rights. Among these rights are life, liberty and the pursuit of happiness. To secure these rights, governments are instituted among men, deriving their powers from the consent of the governed. When any form of government becomes destructive of these ends, it becomes the right of the people to alter or abolish it.'"

"Not bad, Mr. Ogden. That's from the Declaration of Independence, not the Constitution, but your memorizing of it shows that your learning ability is notably unimpaired. At least with a retentive mind, we have something to start with."

"Professor, could you do me a favor? I feel kind of funny when you always call me Mr. Ogden."

"We must maintain a student-teacher rapport to keep discipline and respect in their right perspective."

He was having fun.

"Look, all I want is a tutor—not Sidney Poitier."

"Ah, that's very good." He drew an imaginary score on the air with his finger. "There's one for good old what's-his-name."

"By the way, what is your first name?" I asked.

He stood up at attention and put his hand over his heart. "Elgin Walter Johnson the second."

"Wow, I'm sorry I asked."

"What's yours?"

"Richard Edwin Ogden the first. I never heard the name Elgin before."

"You mean you've never heard of Elgin Baylor?"

"Oh sure, I remember. It's just that Elgin sounds different all by itself. I'll just call you Professor, okay?"

"Let's see . . . what shall I all you? Richard seems a bit Victorian. Aha, I've got it! Has anyone called you Oggie Doggie before? You know that cartoon that used to come on on Saturday morning?"

I said no a little too abruptly.

"Ah, just as I thought. They did, and you loved it."

"I can't stand it."

"I christen you Oggie Doggie, in the name of the Father, the Son, and Victor Hugo. May you never grow a hump on your back. Amen!"

"What the hell are you talking about?"

"Never mine." We both laughed. "Back to school, Master Oggie."

"Yes sir, Sidney."

"What kind of exposure have you had, if any, to the fine arts?"

"Drawing was my favorite subject."

"That's not what I mean. I'm talking about the family of arts."

"Oh, I got straight *A*'s in art and music, and an occasional *A* in writing, but only if I got to write about what I wanted to write about."

"Who was Matisse?"

"I remember him really good. He drew funny, naked, fat women."

"That's not all, but that's good. You remember who I'm talking about. I think we will have you in UCLA or Harvard in no time. But seriously, I think we can get you ready for the GED test to get your high school diploma."

School was out, and I promised an apple a day—or at least half a peach.

An unexpected but welcome thunderstorm blew in off the South China Sea. I brushed heavy gun oil on my new forty-five and twenty millimeter. There seems to be something personal and intimately comforting about having a forty-five on your hip or tucked in your belt. This issue to certain special weapons carriers was a last-chance resort. It is only reasonably accurate at twenty-five yards, depending on the talent of the trigger finger. A forty-five caliber round traveling at nine hundred feet per second is like a shot put compared to the high velocity 7.62 rifle round, but it is still capable of stopping anything made of flesh and bones with one hell of a wallop. I put the toys to bed within reach inside the hootch. I did not bother to cover up.

I tilted my head back to the falling sky, stuck out my tongue, and let the warm refreshing rain rinse the salt away along with a great many of my cares. Every now and then I would probe the upper extremities of my mouth with my tongue and feel the tenderness of the hemorrhaged, nearly broken cheekbone. It was a harsh reminder of bad times. I am getting a fresh, clean start, I recited to myself. I am going to make the very best of it. I am stuck in another psycho circus; but I think I have a friend, and that will make a difference.

The chopper flew us westward over the short mountain range bordering the desert around Chu Lai. From the hatch door, I could see two other choppers flying to our right flank in formation. Their windshield wipers flapped in sync. We flew through a clear but wet corridor of air hemmed in on all four sides by the dark mountainous jungle below. The ominous, dark ceiling of storm clouds was above, and to the sides was an infinity of invisible mist.

Once again the exhilaration of the hunt; with the cold dampness of the morning altitude, the body jittered and chattered along with the vibration of machinery.

I remember back to other mornings, when I was ten or eleven years old, when I'd lay in the hay in the back of my stepdad's 1946 Chevrolet pickup with a couple of hounds on each side. They kept me warm on our way to a hunt in bear country. We would rendezvous with a dozen other people who had their own packs of hounds. These hunters were friends of my stepdad. He called them Tarheels because they lived far deeper into the wilderness than we did. They also lived more off the land. We were urbanites compared to these modern-day mountain people.

Early in the morning, with that many people and hounds, there was always mass confusion. An exuberant hound would get a whiff of a trail and the whole menagerie would be set into fierce motion, like a British foxhunt without the horses. My stepdad would make sure I survived the ordeal and did not get lost by literally tethering one of the hound's leashes onto my arm and putting a large piece of rat cheese in one of my pockets and a pint of loganberry wine in another to keep me warm. The dog lashed to me, in its excitement with the scent of the trail, would literally drag me up the most rugged, mountainous terrain in the state. All I had to do was hang on.

Black bear meat is good eating. I felt sorry for the bear only when the meat was discovered to be unpalatable because the bear had been fishing for salmon in the rivers and creeks rather than foraging in the orchards. a fishing bear will take on the smell and taste of fish.

I was taught to hunt anything to keep from going hungry; but now, in retrospect, I realized it was basically sport disguised as survival.

We second-checked equipment, buckled chin straps, and braced for a landing. Daniels crouched by the hatch. He kept us at even intervals as we bailed out into the cold, wet, turbulent elephant grass. The snake eyes of the gunner crew chief scanned the LZ over the top of the M-60 machine gun as it traversed back and forth, hoping to see or hear something in time to strike (or, hopefully, not see anything to strike at). As the empty choppers lifted off, the rotors seemed to slap the wet air more than chop it.

The ceiling finally cracked open all the way and the downpour restricted visibility to near zero. In a half-crouch position, we ran around in the confusion of the LZ until we got our bearings in conjunction with the rest of the platoon. When we finally got on line in proper interval with everyone facing the same direction, the sweep began.

This was the best weather the Vietcong could hope for. We wouldn't be able to hear snipers over the downpour. We prayed for relief, and when it came it was so abrupt that it startled us. It was as if a big hand had reached over and turned off the spigot, bringing back the squeak of wet gear and the clinking of canteens.

Lakes and channels of waist-high elephant grass lay before us, broken up by peninsulas of dense jungle. At times, the vast body of grass doglegged out of sight, about a par five. It was like a massive Pebble Beach that had been unkempt for centuries.

We began to draw sniper fire from the right flank, and we hit the deck. The right flank of the company broke off and started an assault in the direction of the firing. The word came down for each platoon to take cover in the jungle a squad at a time while the rest laid back to cover them. First squad held ground until it was our turn. At any other time, running thirty or so yards fully laden with gear in waist-high jungle would have been nearly impossible; but under the circumstances, it was almost effortless.

Someone to my right rear yelled that he was hit. I looked back. It was the assistant machine gunner who was, surprisingly, still burning up real estate with the rest of us. He finally went down. The professor and I were closest, and we went back to get him. I put his machine-gun tripods around my neck, and we both grabbed an arm and began to run like hell. We were able to drag him over the slick, wet elephant grass with ease, but we were seriously lagging behind. I was taking three steps to the professor's one. I tripped and brought us all down. We gathered up our patient and took off again. The troops already in cover cheered as we stretched to make the final yards. Everyone was smiling and happy, and congratulated us as though we had just won a sack race at a picnic. Even the patient was grinning.

"What in hell are you grinning about?" I asked. "Where are you hit?"

"In the leg."

He pulled up his trouser leg. There was a small hole in the calf, clotted with blood but not bleeding to any degree, and another clean exit hole where the round had penetrated the entire calf without striking bone. He had gone as hard and as far as he could until the muscle had seized up.

"Someone call for the doc," I yelled. "You know, this looks like a million-dollar wound to me. You'll be home by Christmas."

The adrenalin began to subside and the pain started to catch up. He winced but continued to grin, like a defensive lineman who had intercepted on the fifty-yard line and gotten racked up in the end zone scoring his first and last career touchdown.

CHAPTER EIGHTEEN

The assault on the snipers was fruitless. It only drew them out of the area to come back and hit from another direction, at another time. Their spooklike hit-and-run tactics left gaping holes in our morale. The frustration of not being able to react in time creates a condition of tired, angry blood. It is a common withdrawal symptom like the aching of a junkie in need of a main vein surge of adrenalin that sends the whole body system into a high and renders thought effortless and almost euphoric. Sometimes it is a good feeling, and sometimes bad. Perhaps it is the very last sensation before death, when the pilot light flickers and goes out.

The Vietcong knew exactly what they were doing, and they were effective. Their continual harassment and evasion kept our anger, frustration, and jagged nerves at an optimum peak. Sniping inflicts minimum casualties; but its ominous danger can keep a well-trained alert mind from thinking of the ambush that may lie ahead.

A single casualty can preoccupy an entire crew of men—a crew designed to handle many men, but that must go into action for just one. It brings into play the med-evac chopper, a slow, easy, lush target. It is a slow but constant attrition of manpower, logistics, and morale. The enemy risks everything in the process as they have no immediate resupply, no adequate medical treatment, or hospitalization. He is restricted to lightweight, small-arms weapons, mortars, and rockets, for mobility. And if there is any hint of concentration in numbers, an air strike is called for—something he cannot outrun.

The smell of yellow smoke subsided as the med-evac chopper flew steadily out of earshot carrying our grinning wounded. The company continued its sweep through a sector of very dense, difficult jungle laced with footpaths that had to be meticulously searched for booby traps. We had to push, pull back, and fake out the plant life that seemed to be alive in order to get through.

The man-versus-plant contest stopped immediately as the sound of heavy volumes of automatic weapons fire bounced off the wet jungle. The volumes seemed to increase to enormous proportion. The left flank of first and second squads had stumbled into an ambush for sure. The volume of firing increased as though the outcome of the entire war would be determined here and now. The rest of us lay on the jungle floor, maybe fifteen or twenty yards to the right of the invisible ambush, waiting for orders.

The word came down for the grenadier up. I nearly passed the word myself, then remembered it was for me. I took off, following the line of prone bodies laying in the jungle. I tripped over Daniels and nearly landed on the professor.

"Keep your head down, Oggie. It sounds kind of interesting down there."

"Don't worry, Professor. I won't be missing any class."

Everyone continued to call for the grenadier. I pressed forward as fast as I could. I fell at the base of a hedgerow, out of breath. This time I wanted to take a look before I took a leap.

We had been ambushed at the edge of a river. It was slow moving and more than a hundred yards wide. There was fire coming from the opposite bank. It crashed through the trees just above my head. On our side of the river was a tiny ornate temple with a tile roof, oriental carvings, and paintings on the exterior walls. It faced the river squarely and the machine gun teams had set up on each corner. It looked like the entire platoon had taken cover behind the structure.

Both gunners were firing at a tremendous rate, neither releasing their trigger until the entire belt of ammo was gone. Some fools were leaving cover and firing from the hip, then stumbling back behind the structure.

Ten yards to the right of the temple there was a man down. He was lying on his back. He was a big man with a huge chest and gut. For some reason, he had managed to get his shirt off. I could tell he was alive; his arms moved and he tried to sit up, then lay back down. Why in the hell hadn't they gotten him out of there? He was drawing fire. Incoming rounds were leaving tiny divots in the packed barren soil around him. He took off his helmet. The fool must have been delirious and in shock.

I crawled over the hedgerow, hooked the canteen on a vine, and fell hard on the other side. I slid across the ground on my belly as fast as I could go; but like a baby alligator, I was not quite confident with my technique. When I got to him, I realized that with his size it would be a good idea to keep him between me and the river.

I looked up at a sweaty face. He was grinning. I swore if I ever saw another wounded Marine grinning, I would kill myself! What was wrong with these people?

He tried to sit up. "I'm going home. I'm going home."

I shoved him back down and put his helmet back on. "Sure you are, partner. In your own plastic sleeping bag if you don't stay down."

Lead bumblebees were passing by my ears at over a thousand feet per second. There was a huge earthen jar that must have held thirty gallons within reach. I rolled it over in front of him to give us a little protection. He continued to babble about going home.

Just below his navel there was a hole about the size of a quarter. A very big gut with a very big hole in it. I wondered how he was still alive. His mind was probably on a first-class champagne flight back to the States instead of the burning deep in his guts. For some reason, it was not bleeding like other stomach wounds I had seen. A geyser of blood should spurt out with every inhalation, but it was not occurring in this case.

The machine guns still chugged away. Reeves, the corpsman, flopped down beside me.

"Hello, Doc. Nice to see a friendly face. We've got a very sick boy here."

The friendly face was full of terror. "What am I gonna do? I've got Thompson back there with half his groin shot away."

"Pull yourself together, man. There's not a hell of a lot of you can for either one of them. Give me your B-1 unit."

I reached in the doctor's little black bag and pulled out the biggest bandage I could find. I tore open the wrapper with my teeth and unraveled the ties. I held it against the wound until I figured out how I was going to tie the ties around this huge gut. I began to realize just how green this outfit was; the corpsman had never seen a gunshot wound before, and he had panicked.

I shoved his B-1 back to him. "Go back and take care of the other patient, Doc. And don't tell anybody I'm practicing without a license."

A round hit the large earthen jar and rung it like a bell. I noticed on my patient's lower forearm what looked like a self-inflicted tattoo. It was a large heart that said "Jim and Sue."

"Okay, Jimbo, see if you can help me. I'm gonna

have to get this strap around you so I can tie it down and you won't bleed to death."

"I'm starting to go numb all over."

"Relax, then."

I finally worked my arm underneath him. I grabbed the tie on the other side and dragged it through. There was a slight lull in the machine gun fire, and I heard Sergeant Nick yell.

"Ogden, put some rounds out there!"

I yelled back to get some help out here and get this man back to cover.

Another round hit the bell. Big Jim was no longer grinning or mumbling about going home. He was beginning to bleed badly. I wondered where the other grenadier was. I hadn't heard one all day. The ties on the bandage were too short to tie in a knot, so I held it in one hand and reached for my cannon that lay across big Jim's huge thigh. I felt like a buffalo hunter hiding behind his downed quarry while being attacked by angry red men.

I was in a very curious firing position, in refuge behind the hulk of a body. My right hand pulled the ties under his body, applying pressure to the bandage, while with the other hand I put the cannon to my shoulder and let a round fly. It fell miserably short and blew in the water. Loading with one hand was slow and tiring. I was only guessing where the target was. The tracer rounds from the machine guns were only a partial clue. They were traversing the whole wide front of the jungle, so I concentrated on the center of the field of fire.

As I was loading, the cavalry came. Before I could pick myself up out of the mud, they carried Jim back to safety behind the temple. I crawled behind the Liberty Bell, hoping it would not crack with another direct hit. I launched a couple more rounds, but they did not seem to be effective.

I alligatored my way through the mud to the back of the temple, which was overcrowded with heroes and casualties. Sergeant Nick was screaming at his machine gun crews like a madman. He turned to me.

"Goddamn it, Ogden, when I call for the grenadier up, you'd better hustle, damn it. We've got corpsmen to take care of casualties."

I knew at that moment that I disliked the man intensely; but this was no time to let him know it.

The temple was good cover, but it rendered us ineffective as a complete team offensively. There was only room for a machine gun team on each corner. The rest of us were huddled behind. Anderson's grenadier was the other casualty. Anderson had taken over the weapon himself, but there was no firing position from behind the temple for either of us. We were totally useless back there.

Then an idea came to mind. From where the Liberty Bell was, I noticed there was a front door on the temple facing the river. There was also a side entrance. I explained to Sergeant Nick my idea to turn the temple into a bunker to be more effective. All Nick said was "go."

I beckoned for Anderson, who fell right in behind me. I got next to the machine gunner and tapped him on the helmet, and told him what I was going to do. He nodded and kept firing. I held my breath and thought ahead to exactly what I was going to do in the next thirty seconds.

I slung my cannon and lunged forward. I put my head down and slithered along to the side entrance. It seemed further than it was. I flung myself in and rolled. Two idiots were already inside playing John Wayne. They were taking turns firing from the hip in full profile of the door.

"Get your goddamn asses down!" I didn't need any more grinning idiots today.

They looked at me funny but did not argue. Anderson flew through the doorway in midair like a running back on fourth down at the goal line, and landed in a heap in the corner. We lay flat on the floor. Rounds were coming through the doorway and bouncing off the hard adobe walls. The John Wayne brothers began to realize how foolish they had been.

I began to have reservations about my brilliant plan. Outside the hive, we had only had to worry about bees going in one direction. Now that we had so intelligently crawled inside the hive, we were vulnerable from every direction.

I yelled to Anderson. "Do you know how to use that thing?"

He held up his finger, indicating he had fired it once.

"Corporal, that's all you need. That's all the training

I had when I started out."

We took prone firing positions on each side of the door. Chinks of plaster kept popping off the walls in our little bunker, creating a dust we could taste and smell. To expose one eye to get a fix on the target was unnerving.

I told Anderson I would fire a couple of rounds to get the distance and true elevation. Most of my rounds were falling short. I gave the barrel a lot of elevation and pulled the trigger. The round blew just outside the temple. I was so conscious of getting dinged in the head that I had failed to look up. I had blown off a large tree branch, and it had come crashing down. Anderson just grinned. Now we had a clear field of fire.

I reloaded and took aim again. The enemy did not seem to be rousting very easily. They must be dug in. The bamboo grove on the other side was about thirty feet tall. If I could land a shell midway up I would get a good air burst showering down on them. I pulled the trigger and watched the round travel in a high arc against the backdrop of gray sky. As it plunged toward the jungle I lost track of it. Like magic, it seemed to land just where I wanted it to. A patch of large, sturdy bamboo splintered and tumbled to the ground.

"Got it! Just keep your barrel at the same angle and let it fly!"

We fired together, both right on target. Both rounds detonated about ten feet apart, bringing down a curtain of jungle. We fired as fast as we could load. I thought I heard cheering out back above the machine-gun roar. Each time I reloaded, I had to flip over on my back. I noticed the dust was settling. There were no more bees buzzing around inside.

Someone right outside began to yell. "They're running! They're running! They're on the run!"

Machine guns began to slacken up, and only sporadic fire was mixed with the cheers from outside. Neither one of us had even seen the enemy. No one cared. We had rousted them and put them on the run. Morale was back! Everyone got their badly needed dose of adrenalin. Two unlucky ones got a dose of morphine.

The depression of a long dreary day was forgotten. Everyone seemed to be in a jubilant mood, like tarheels after a wild bear hunt. I watched a pack of less experienced kids pat each other on the back for a job well done. They were high from their very first taste of combat.

Thunder clapped around us. The hand reached once again and turned on a warm, steady downpour. It was a refreshing shower which washed the tainted battle area clean.

It was not known what casualties lay on the other bank. The river was too risky to ford. Whatever there were, we had paid for them. The company formed up and headed to the LZ with casualties in tow.

Jim and Sue were very lucky people. A thirty-caliber round had tipped his belt buckle, spun out, and dug out a chunk of flesh, instead of going through and blowing out his spine. It had penetrated into his massive gut but did not pierce the stomach cavity. I learned that Jim's last name was Tweedy. With a name like that, it was no wonder he survived. He had to be damn tough.

The grenadier was not so lucky. And after I saw him, I kept visualizing myself lying on a stretcher, delirious with morphine, with only half or nothing left of what I was born with.

CHAPTER NINETEEN

We sat for days and watched the rain come down from inside the comfort of our hootches. The lack of visibility kept the aircraft grounded, and the total activity around the airstrip was minimal. The ever-drifting, white powdered sand was now a dingy gray. In contrast, all objects throughout the landscape were dark with wetness. It was like a vast countryside winterland, where the rains had come and washed away the crispness and cleanliness of the snow.

To break the monotony, there were occasional work parties. No one seemed to mind because the effort expended in storing water was in direct relation to our comfort. In the vast junkyard on the other side of the runway, we salvaged fifty-five-gallon drums. We chiseled out the ends and cleaned them out the best we could, then sunk them into the ground to catch water for bathing and other utilities. We saved the drinking water that had to be transported in. It was a good idea because we remembered how scarce water could be when the sun was high. The weather of late seemed like a freak of nature, as there is rarely any water in the desert. But I had to keep telling myself that this was not a desert; it was only extended beach.

One morning as I was chiseling out the top of a drum, Simms walked up. I had worked up a sweat and had already cracked a portion of my thumb, a good one, between two pieces of cold steel. I had never spoken to the man, and I was surprised at the contempt in his voice. It went beyond contempt; it was the most vile form of hatred.

"I heard you and the nigger have become good old buddies. Why, I heard he gave you that stupid nickname. If a nigger ever did that to me, I would skin him alive."

My ears started to singe, but I kept chipping the steel. Others in the work party had heard the dialogue and began gathering around.

"Why don't you leave him alone, Simms? He's not doing anything to you."

Now that Simms had an audience, I knew he was really going to let me have it.

"This here is a nigger lover, boys. You know what we do with people who fraternize with niggers? We hang them, that's what we do. We don't mess around back home." He turned back to me. "I heered you think you're a bad ass. I heered you took on three boys in your old outfit and really gave them a roust. I think you're a little sweet-ass cunt."

Sweat began to roll off the end of my nose almost in a

steady drip. My muscles became taut from holding in the reins of emotion. I had promised myself I would stay out of trouble. I was hoping to keep that promise. But this degenerate throwback from fourteenth century Alabama had become tight with the platoon sergeant in just the short period of time he had been here.

"Leave him alone, Simms."

I did not look up to see who was making sense. Instead, I tried to continue working; but my hands were sweating and shaking too badly. The hammer and chisel began to slip through my sweaty palms. I was still down on one knee, and Simms began to crowd me from the rear.

"You know what I think, boys? I think Miss Oggie here is sucking the nigger's cock. That's got to be the reason you're so tight."

I took in a deep breath, dropped the tools, and shifted my weight. I shoved one leg nearly three inches into the sand for support and spring, then twisted my body and let out a massive grunt. I caught him with my left shoulder below the rib cage and sent him sprawling.

He was so unprepared that his helmet came off and slammed into mine. The impact knocked him a couple of yards. Still on my knees, I dug and clawed at the ground to get momentum to rush him. He had tumbled over several times and had ended up facing me. He got to his hands and knees. I clipped him under the chin with a twenty-yard onside kick. His jaw slamming shut sounded like the tailgate of a dump truck as he went up over backward. A fifty-yard field goal attempt would have killed him. Why I held back, I will never know.

I jumped on him, coming down as fast and heavy as one hundred-forty pounds could fall. I grabbed a handful of yellow thatch and scalp, and cracked his face on my knee several times to make sure he was out of commission. An interesting, if not funny, thought occurred to me: He has no lips; but when I get done with him, he will.

His mouth was agape and gasping like a freshly caught red snapper on the deck of a boat. I grabbed up a handful of wet sand and packed it into his mouth tightly. His eyes bulged nearly out of their sockets. I pulled my K-Bar out and placed the blade under his jaw. I put the flat part of the tip against the underside of his jawbone—not to draw blood, but to apply pressure on the mouthful. In a whisper of controlled rage, I spoke.

"You little, filthy mouthed, bigot motherfucker. If you ever open that slime trap around me, or even come near me again, I'm going to give you lesson number two. Do you hear me?"

I applied more pressure to the jawbone. He went completely white. He nodded furiously as he choked and gagged. I got up and grabbed him by the lapels, pulled him partway up with me, and threw him back down. I got to my feet and looked around. Everything had happened so fast that the group gathered around us also looked like they had just been popped out of deep water. I turned and walked away. I could hear Simms cough and puke as I walked the entire distance to my hootch. It was music to my ears.

I decided to bypass the hootch and instead walked out to the end of the sand dune, where I could sit and relax alone to take the edge off the moment. I knew that all hell would break loose soon. These moments of peace were earned. I set my mind on low frequency and sent it home.

It had been so long that I got a foggy picture in return. Things about home that were particularly unsavory at the time now seemed to have lost their significance. Let's face it: I missed everything about home—even the smell of the barnyard. Homesickness had reached its highest ebb. I thought of what I would do when I got home and out of the Corps. Maybe I would work construction or get work in the woods logging for a while, at least until I could get enough money to go to school. Maybe there was still a chance for Elizabeth and me. Maybe I would become a family man, work days and go to school at night. I wanted to accomplish something, be somebody.

I must have sat in the sand, totally consumed in my problems and my future, for nearly an hour. Then I sensed someone standing behind me. It was the professor.

"I heard you had quite a row with Simms."

My arms remained folded around my legs and my chin rested on my knees. "He's got an ugly way about him and a filthy mouth."

"I know. That's what I want to talk to you about. I know what it was about. I don't need you or anybody to fight my battles."

I looked up at him. "What are you talking about?"

"You bashed Simms because of me, didn't you?" The voice began to change, and he pointed down at me. "I don't need you or anybody else to fight my battles! I'm an intelligent, rational human being, and I can take care of myself! Mind your own business!"

The stress in his voice was real, but the confidence in what he said was not convincing. This tiny shred of weakness and insecurity left me confused. My easiest and most predictable attitude was to get angry. I jumped to my feet.

"Let's get something straight, brother. That sick son of a bitch was headhunting for me. I busted him for what he said about me, and nobody else. I mind my own business! I fight my own battles and look out for number one! I don't fight for anybody except me! I don't know about the rest of the world, but I'm gonna survive assholes like that! I'm here to stay. The world's full of sick degenerates running loose. They come down on people like me to show their manhood, and they come down on people like you to show how ignorant they are. I don't want to hear any shit about fighting your battle. I fight for me!"

There was a long silence. He looked down at the ground before he spoke. "Sergeant Nick wants to see you." He turned and walked away.

Once again, the tattered green knight in rusted tomato-can armor was summoned to the high court. What else could happen today?

"Ogden, you're a walking contradiction far beyond

anything I've ever experienced before in the Marine Corp. You transfer into this outfit busted and beaten. Your service record book is, in part, one of the best I've ever seen. But the last twelve months of it reads like a toilet novel. Now this."

Nick was referring to a piece of paper in his hand.

"According to this, First Lieutenant O'Connor has recommended you for a Bronze Star. How does one go about getting office hours, getting into a brawl, being transferred to another outfit, and getting a medal on top of it? It's insane!"

"I agree, Sergeant. It's insane!"

"Don't get smug with me. What's Lieutenant O'Connor recommending you for?"

"I don't know, Sergeant. He didn't say anything to me. We were pretty busy up there."

"You must have done something to have your platoon commander bestow such a high honor on you."

At the blink of an eye, his mood changed. He paced back and forth behind his desk, arms behind his back with fingers laced. He walked around behind me and placed his hand on my shoulder.

"Look, you don't have to be modest. You can tell me. I'm your platoon commander, remember? Listen, how would you like to be the platoon runner? You could have that cot right over there. Simms has been screwing up lately, and he has a big mouth."

That's not all he's got, Sergeant, I thought.

"I don't think I would be very good at that sort of

thing." I was confused again, but I decided not to get mad. Instead, I would go along with what was happening for a while.

He walked around behind his table. "Now, tell me all about your getting a Bronze Star."

I began to get impatient. "Sergeant, I don't have a Bronze Star. It's only a recommendation."

"It's as good as in the bag. I know about these things. Before I head stateside, I'm gonna have me one. Maybe even two."

He was no longer looking at me. His stare went right on by. His grin was disturbing. He was no longer in the tent or in the present; he was out winning handfuls of medals on the battlefield.

"Sergeant Nick, may I be excused?"

His trance broke. "What? Oh, not until you tell me how you got your medal."

"Like I told you, I don't know. I don't even care about the medal if it's gonna create a fuss."

His mood changed again. "What do you mean? You don't care! You . . . don't care? The country is bestowing an honor on you for a job well done, and you don't care? Boy, there's something wrong with you!"

He started to lose control and shook his finger at me. "You know what I think? I think you're a smartass! I think you're smug and arrogant! You shitbird, you disgust me! Get out of my sight!"

By the time I got outside again, I was really confused. I didn't know whether to get mad at a psycho sergeant or rejoice at the fact that Lieutenant O'Connor had remembered me. It was the only time I had the opportunity to display an individual effort. Pride, and the idea of a medal, did enlighten my spirits. It is gratifying to know that someone has confidence in you; it fortifies your own. I think I know how it feels to be nominated for an Academy Award. "For best supporting actor in a foreign campaign, the nominees are . . ."

The professor was wearing off some more blueing with an oily rag. I flopped down on my cot.

"What did Sergeant Nick want?"

"Oh, he just wanted me to become his new house mouse or runner. I figured he'd run me up for shaking up his number-one boy. I guess he wants me to tell him how he can be a hero."

"What?"

"I think he's more schizophredic than you thought he was."

"It's schizophrenic."

"Well, whatever! He's giving me the creeps. A letter came from my old outfit recommending me for a medal, and Nick started to act kind of funny about it."

"Well, what did you get it for?"

"Come on, not you, too."

"I'm sorry about coming down on you today."

"Forget it."

"How about a peace offering?" He uncovered two cans of Budweiser and I sat up.

"Sounds good to me, but you don't have to." I nearly dropped it because of the shock of the unexpected pleasure. "It's cold! Really cold!"

We'd been getting a warm beer ration every day since

I had been here, and a can of cold Budweiser made peaches look like a can of ham and lima beans. The professor did the honors of opening.

"Give a toast, Professor!"

"Why not. Here's to all the bigots and schizophrenics in this fucking war!"

We clicked cans and tipped them up.

CHAPTER TWENTY

The resonance of my name came slashing through the night, like electricity through a conduit to a brain partially deadened by sleep and an accumulated ration of Bud, Schlitz, or Ole. The professor's hideous scream penetrated the inner cosmos of my mind, reaching beyond my soul. It would never be penetrated again—not even by a host of psychiatrists.

I sat up on the cot. Dreaming!? Having a nightmare!? The area outside the hootch was lit up and the shadows were doing the dance of fire. I tried to assess what was real and what was not. I remembered the professor taking the first watch after our little party. I had gotten tired and crashed . . . or was I drunk?

An explosion outside set off another charge of electricity, this time to the heart. We're being attacked! We're being overrun! I rushed outside. The platoon CP tent was in flames. An exploding Skyhawk sent a huge bolt of fire into the sky like a nuclear bomb. There were people running and yelling. But I saw no enemy. I thought I would wake up in a cold sweat and it would be over. How could they have penetrated so many perimeters of defense? The sight was so awesome and unbelievable that my mind had not begun to function properly.

My total attention was diverted to the left where the action was, but out of the corner of my right eye I saw something that froze my warm blood to a sludge and jammed my nervous system with an overload of confusing signals. My entire system nearly shut down, causing near-total paralysis.

Not more than ten feet to my direct front, halfway down the side of the sand dune, it stood, partially lit by the dancing flames of the burning tent. It was barefooted, with black shorts that seemed too large. The sleeves of its black shirt were rolled up past the elbow and protected the skin from bandoliers of hand grenades that hung across the chest. A bandanna across the forehead hung down the side, like an Apache warrior. Highlights frozen motionless on highly polished steel eyes reminded me of a humanoid built to pass as the real thing. Its engineer had been unable to duplicate the spirit of life, as can our true Creator. It smiled, showing black polished teeth.

A physical tremor began to develop in my gut. I started to shake all over. Bud, Schlitz, and Ole soaked my trousers and ran down the inside of my knees. I had never had a weak bladder before.

He held a hand grenade, while I had no weapon. One thing was for sure; whether it was human or not, it was the enemy. I was caught cold, suspended in my own terror, entrapped by a lifeless creature from some science fiction novel. He broke off his hypnotic stare that flowed like electrons and began to work the pin loose on a hand grenade. I wanted to cry. I wanted to get on my hands and knees, to ask forgiveness and make amends.

My body hurled through the air. Whether it is true, imagination, or just a contrived cliché, odd lengths of footage of my entire life did race across my mental screen. I landed on him hard, like a terrorized house cat, grabbing and clawing and holding onto anything that would fit my paws. We hit the sand and rolled around endlessly out into the darkness.

He was more powerful than I could have imagined for his size. He must be on drugs; that would account for the dazed, lifeless expression. His muscles were hard, lean, and taut like knots, from years of toiling in the fields. My own strength seemed nonexistent . . . just enough to hang on. The greasy, rotten clothing and the putrid stench of body odor, mixed with my fear of not finding the necessary energy reserves, made my stomach begin to retch. I also had a fear of one of his comrades coming up and blowing the back of my head out.

Each time we rolled over and over, locked in a death embrace, more sand got into my eyes, nose, and mouth. We each had an arm around the other's neck. I held his wrist that clawed at my face, keeping it from extracting my eyes. I managed to turn my face away, and his clawing was ineffective. He was arching his back; and just by brute strength alone, I was losing my hold on him. He tried to roll one more time to take advantage, but I flattened my body and stiffened. I began to ride higher on his body. He bucked and kicked in all directions.

It was perhaps a lifesaving thought that entered my mind: One of us was going to die at the hand of the other. Another thought dripped from the roof of the dark, icy cavern of my mind: If one of these grenades blows we will both go, and they will find a pile of bloody arms and legs they will not be able to explain.

I took a chance, freed one of my hands from its hold, and slammed a clenched fist into his groin. He began to yell and spit. I knew I had just taken the advantage. The more he yelled, the more I hammered. Then I went for the kill. I reached up under the baggy leg of his shorts and grabbed a handful of testicles. He began to scream. I took one massive yank, using all the muscles in my body clear down to my thighs. The flesh gave and tore in a silent, fluid, surprisingly easy motion. Once it gave way it was like stripping the excess fat from a chicken before broiling.

At that moment, I knew I was going to live. I was running on the last of the adrenalin. The barrel was dry. His relentless, high-pitched scream pierced both sides of my head like a sharp probe. I let go of what he did not have left and shifted my body. I slammed my fist into his vibrating throat, crushing the tiny frail bones of the larynx and the trachea. His screams were diminished to the sound of a toy doll whose whine is generated by a tiny bellows inside. His body convulsed and twitched. Blood bubbled from his nose and mouth as the air continued to escape slowly, vibrating tiny broken bones in his throat like the reed in a clarinet.

I staggered back up the hill, fell down, and crawled the rest of the way to the hootch. The CP tent was still burning. The ammo stored inside was going off. I found my pop gun and forty-five belt, slung a bandolier of twenty millimeters around my neck, and crawled out the back. Flares from eighty-ones began to pop overhead, lighting up the area. I scrambled down the other side of the sand dune and took up a firing position facing the edge in the direction from which I had come. My mind was still teetering on the edge. I knew the Vietcong would storm over the top by the thousands to get revenge for their comrade.

The professor was attending to someone on the ground. Sergeant Nick was walking around in a daze. He walked over in my direction. He was dressed only in a pair of trousers rolled up the knees, with no shirt, boots, or weapon. He was disoriented and nearly in tears.

"I lost my equipment, weapons, and everything. What am I going to do?"

I tossed him my forty-five, but could not resist a smart remark. "I want it back after this is over."

The fear of the unknown lurked everywhere. We did not know how many there were or what they were doing. The most frightening thought that came to mind was that they had probably already wiped out the entire squad closest to the jungle.

We started to yell for them. I was afraid that the

Vietcong might have found somebody asleep and cut throats along the line to get to the CP tent. But the return yells of a live and kicking squad gave us new confidence, and we organized a counteroffensive. Rounds continued to pop intermittently in the smoking rubble of the CP tent, and we crawled to the crest of the sand dune as more eighty-one flares ignited over the area and illuminated the junkyard.

The Vietcong left the temporary cover of the junkyard and ran for their lives out across the open sand. They ran one behind the other, entrants from the same country, one running for the gold medal and one for the silver in the one hundred meters. They were coming into the last stretch and heading for the tape, two men running for their lives. They could have made a new world's record. A strange remorsefulness came over me as I watched their final seconds. Even with all that effort, there was no way in hell they were going to make it. M-60s cut loose a thousand yards away, and the first burst was miraculously on target. The tracer rounds burned through them and streaked off into the darkness. The impact of the bodies in full stride seemed like slow motion. The bodies flew end over end, seven or eight feet in the air. They plunged to the ground and plowed through the sand like wiped-out downhill racers through the snow, and then came to rest.

The ten- or eleven-man suicide squad had been reasonably successful. They had completely totalled one Skyhawk, and a chain reaction had set off some highly volatile liquid oxygen that damaged two more planes. Sergeant James (the Sten-carrying platoon guide whom I had not met because of his time-consuming duties as platoon supply sergeant and scrounger) had taken shrapnel in the leg.

The professor had initially spotted four or five Vietcong running across the runway toward the CP tent in the dark, but he was unable to get the tape off his magazine or his hand grenades. Because of a bureaucratic safety precaution after some fool had shot his foot off in the rear and another had accidentally blown up a truckload of troops playing with a grenade, an insane safety program had been initiated. So the professor hadn't been able to stop them.

The Vietcong had thrown incendiary grenades into the CP tent. The professor returned the fire with a barrage of hand grenades with the spoons still taped. He actually hit one and knocked him down. He would have been just as effective with a bucket of rocks, like a caveman. He had screamed my name as he ran toward the flaming tent, and his scream saved my life. They would have blown me away in my sleep and I would have never known a thing.

The occupants of the CP tent were nearly overcome by the heat and the smoke. They were confused and disoriented. The professor rushed in and dragged each one of them out, then threw them into the sand to safety.

There was a one-hundred-percent alert for the rest of the night. We watched and waited for another attack, but it never came. I tried in vain to keep my mind occupied with something other than the dead body that lay somewhere out there in the darkness. There were reoccurring memories of terror laced with the sadness of destroying another human being, especially hand to hand.

Dawn came like a repealed death sentence, and a warm comfort of joy began to grow inside as the light in the sky widened and brightened. The dismal, bleak, but absolutely beautiful countryside that I would have missed began to unfold. I told myself that never again would I feel remorse or sadness for killing, because I was alive and it felt wonderful.

I searched the sand; the body was gone. I was glad. It was probably dragged off by a comrade and buried in the sand nearby without a trace. It relieved me of explaining the details of the savagery and the method I had used to initiate the kill. I knew, though, that if necessary I would do it again and again.

It was still dark inside the hootch when I felt around for a canteen. Everything was in disarray because of the attack. There were full C-ration cans strewn around the sand. I picked them up and threw them into a pile underneath the foot of the cot. The last one I picked up I thought was probably a can of ham and lima beans, but it seemed heavier. I shook it. It rattled. I turned around on my knees to find the light coming from the hatchway.

I froze and stopped breathing. The can of ham and lima beans had a bamboo cork and a braided trigger release that had already been pulled, and it sounded like it was full of black powder. I inched out cautiously on my knees through the hatchway. I yelled loudly but in fear that the vibration of my voice alone would set it off.

"I've got a live Vietcong grenade!"

The activity around the rubble of the CP tent stopped. Everyone froze. They grabbed their helmets. Still on my knees in a praying position, I cradled the bomb with both hands in front of me.

"Take it easy, Ogden. What are you going to do?" Sergeant Mick asked.

"I'm going to throw it. The pin's pulled. I can't tell right now, but if it's the type without a primer it's live as hell, and it might blow at any time. I don't know how far I can throw it underhand and in this position. Would somebody put my helmet on?"

The professor scrambled over and placed the helmet gingerly on my head as though it were a crown in a holy ceremony.

He smiled at me. "Take it easy, Plato. The republic will miss you."

I smiled back. "Don't worry, teach."

I was sweating and beginning to chill in the cool of the morning.

"I'll count to three and throw it. One . . . two . . . three . . . *fire in the hole!*"

I threw my whole back into it to get as high an arc and distance as possible. We flattened our bodies into the sand. It blew on impact. I lay in the sand, exhausted. I did not ever want to get up again. They rallied around me, cheering, banging me on the helmet and patting me on the back as though I had something to do with their salvation.

The grenade must have come with the first volley through the hatch, landing under my cot just three inches from my body. All of a sudden the war seemed more personal, as though they were after me and me alone. They had missed twice. What were the odds?

The professor went with the patrol that was sent out to find bodies and weapons. To their astonishment and discontent, they found no bodies. The professor did find a Thompson submachine gun that was overlooked in the dark. Third platoon had two enemy kills and the bodies to prove it. One of their "kills" was found at dawn wandering around close to the perimeter. He was shot in the gut, and he held what he could inside with his hands while he dragged the escaped intestines behind him in the sand. As the Vietcong soldier shuffled his feet forward through the sand, the second platoon commander stepped behind him and drew his forty-five. He placed it at the back of the head and pulled the trigger. It was a mistake he was never likely to forget. He did the man a kindness, but in the process he blew flecks of flesh, blood, and brain all over himself.

The body count and kill ratio were considered by the experts in the Pentagon the most important factors in determining the progress of the war, at least in combat. Each unit leader's efficiency was unofficially judged by the number of enemy KIAs to his credit. Each kill was treated as though it were a trophy. The Vietcong picked up their dead and weapons at any cost in order to refute any compiled statistics against them. It was demoralizing to find just specks of blood and rarely ever find a body. It made them seem elusive and impossible to kill.

Evening came. The professor offered to take the first watch, and I did not argue. I lay down, exhausted. I had nearly dozed off when the familiar scream rocked me wide awake again. I sat straight up in the cot, just as I had done before. The professor was sitting out in the patio on an ammo can, wiping down his new-found trophy. I realized that I was getting a videotape rerun of the night before. I got up and went outside.

"Why don't you hit the sack if you want to? I can't sleep at all."

"I can sleep any time. Are you all right?"

"My mind's still going around and around about last night and this morning. I just thought of something: did anybody thank you for bailing them out last night?"

"I don't know. I can't remember. I think you had a lot on your mind."

"You can say that again. But goddamn it, I'm thanking you right now. I owe you a lot."

"It's okay. I hope I don't have to collect."

He got up and handed me the Thompson, and I sat down.

"Go back to bed. You need your beauty sleep."

"Who, me? The pride of Watts? Beauty sleep?"

"Good night, pretty boy."

As the quietness of the dark, warm evening lingered on, I became uneasy and unable to relax. Instant replays kept cropping up. I tried to think of more pleasant things, but the override was too much. As a diversion, I began rubbing down the Thompson. In the moonlight, I noticed there was dried blood on the cloth; and when I looked closer, I found small flecks of dried flesh and skin in the crevices of the weapon. I was repulsed, and leaned the weapon against the sandbags.

Something flicked out of the corner of my eye. I gasped and froze, then relaxed. It was just a mouse scampering along in the sand outside the patio. I was not intimidated by mice; but for some reason, every tiny movement caught my attention and my heart stopped. Hair has the uncanny ability to stand up by itself, and mine seemed forever on the ready. My goose bumps also seemed to be out in force on this warm evening. Why was I so uptight?

The warm wind changed direction and blew in from across the sand. It brought the stench of blood and remains that had baked all day in the sun. It was the smell of death, strong and revolting.

The Thompson kept drawing my attention like a magnet. How could an intelligent, educated, sensitive person like the professor relish this thing so much when it was covered with blood and guts from its previous owner? I could smell it. He must be sick. That's it, sick like the others, and I didn't even sense it. I was the only one left who was sane and rational. The only one.

I heard the professor scream again. Then the Vietcong hand grenade exploded the hootch with me in it. I smelled the rancid, greasy body odor, and a hand yanked unmercifully at my testicles. I began to shake, sweat, and my mind whirled. I picked up the Thompson and slammed a round into the chamber. They were coming back! They would do anything to get their Thompson back and avenge their comrades!

I stood up. I could hear them yelling and screaming. There must have been a thousand of them! I could hear equipment banging and metal scraping. I could see flashes of swords and machetes in the moonlight.

I sensed someone directly behind me. Without turning, I saw a piece of shadow cast on the sand. I dropped the Thompson, whirled, and grabbed the figure by its clothing. I pulled him around and threw him down on the sandbag parapet. I got ahold of his throat. I cut off most of his wind. Then he managed to say my name, and I snapped out of it.

"Doc? What are you doing here?"

I let him up and pulled him to his feet. He spoke as he assessed his neck.

"I didn't sleep, so I got up. But I didn't expect to be mugged by one of my own troops. What are you so jumpy about? You're shaking apart."

"Doc, I was having a nightmare, but I was awake! I was hearing things and seeing things. Stay here and talk to me for awhile, will you? Are you all right? I'm sorry about grabbing you. I think I completely flipped out until you came along. I mean, damn near totally crazy!"

"The stress just finally caught up to you, Oggie. You had a pretty hairy twenty-four hours. I'll send you back to the rear for some rest."

"Come on, Doc, I haven't completely jumped out of

my tree. Stay here and talk to me. Now that I know what's happening, I'll be all right. You don't know how glad I am that you're sitting there and you don't hear or see anything. From what I've heard about nut houses, I think I'd rather go home in a rubber bag than in a straight jacket."

CHAPTER TWENTY-ONE

The war had the earmark of going on for another hundred years. There were rumors of massive escalation, rumors of being extended as much as a year after we had served the first year, rumors of only spot bombing in the north instead of total destruction, rumors of Russian supply ships still entering Haiphong Harbor in the north, rumors of corruption and military coups within the Vietnamese government (the government we supported and were fighting for), and rumors of drug experimentation among troops in other outfits. That was impossible. Marines didn't take drugs—just more than a crippling share of booze when it was available. Captive and isolated in the jungles and paddies, there was no way to refute any of the rumors. They were depressing, demoralizing, and probably true.

The unexpected rumor of "R & R," rest and relaxation—or "rape and ruin" in Bangkok or Tokyo, as it was more accurately referred to by some—lightened my spirits until I was told I would be on the bottom of the roster with the rest of the troops that came from Second Battalion. We were expected to rotate home before all the troops in this outfit. This was a marvelous rationalization. We had been in the bush fighting three months longer than Third Battalion, but we were going to be the last to enjoy any relief. We were still the bastards of the regiment.

One rumor—that we were moving out to become part of a large operation somewhere to the south—lasted for only a few days. No one was impressed. We had all been there before, or to a place just like it. No one seemed to care.

We were transported from Chu Lai beach through choppy seas in an LCU, the big brother of the landing craft family designed to carry a medium-sized tank to the beaches and back. We climbed up the debarkation nets of the LST and got a surprisingly warm welcome from the navy. They pulled us aboard, showered us with kindness, and overwhelmed us with questions about the fighting. It was like a big, noisy press conference held for the dead who had just returned from hell, and curiosity was killing the living.

Most of them expressed a willingness to take our places just to get away from the boredom of the ship and find out what combat was all about. But we knew that a couple of days in the jungle and they would be crying for clean sheets, real mattresses, the ship's store, showers, air-conditioning, fresh vegetables, red meat, bread, milk, apple pie, ice cream, nightly movies, and all of the other "boredom." We would be staying with this glorified floating day-care center for only a day and a night, then make our beach assault at dawn.

We took full advantage of the entire ship, everything but the bridge and the engine room. The galley was the most celebrated area. We nearly bathed in gallons of reconstituted milk, and ate until we were sick. The months of C-rations and bad field chow were forgotten for awhile. Sailors catered to our every whim, and the mess hall became a madhouse. We indulged like looting conquerors or death-defying prisoners from a concentration camp. We were trying to press a whole week of liberty or R & R into a few hours.

After the Roman feast, I took an endless, scalding shower. I wasted enough water to make the Indian farmers in Arizona weep. I put on clean underwear and crawled into a cot. It was difficult to remember when I had last had a full night's sleep. I grinned inside from ear to ear, jubilant over a few hours of peace and rest. I did not care to think about tomorrow. Today was wonderful! I closed my eyes and saw Elizabeth waving at me from the strawberry fields . . .

School was out, and for the four of us it was going to be a long, hot, wonderful summer. We were going to fish, camp, play baseball, and take long bicycle hikes. Somehow, I would have to work at a part-time job so I would have new clothes for school next fall.

We were fourteen and fifteen. We ran around together in a small pack, forever thwarting the pangs of boredom. I was considered the runt. We were not really mischievous, but the sisters who were a few years older thought we were obnoxious and unruly. Each of them had a sister. I liked the sisters and got along with them, but I was still condemned for associating with an entourage of brat brothers.

This summer we found ourselves hard-pressed for cash for important necessities like a new baseball, a Coke, candy bars, and other life-support items. We decided that for a couple of weeks we would lower ourselves and join the annual migration to the berry fields with all the boring and practical kids in the neighborhood.

Getting up at five o'clock in the morning was not as tough for me as it was for the others because of the crack-of-dawn chores I had. We were a pretty loyal group; if one could make it, even the slowest and most reluctant seemed to close up ranks. The bus picked us up at the general store, and it was a forty-minute ride into the Snohomish Valley to the fields. We quickly captured the rear of the bus and took it over, far from the authority of a reasonable but still adult lady bus driver.

Picking strawberries was hard work and boring. We all vowed we would not come back the next day. But at the end of the day, we added up the money we had made collectively. We were amazed at how well we had done, in spite of eating and throwing away so many strawberries. We had thought we would be thrown out by the straw bosses.

By the next afternoon we had become more restless

and bored than usual. We were loud and obnoxious, much to the dismay of some boring, practical girls who sat in front of us on the way home. The more they turned around, raised their eyebrows, and stuck up their noses, the more we showed off.

During these free-for-alls, the runt always seemed to be the brunt of the practical jokes or the teases. This time it was "keep away the baseball cap." I was proud of the cap. My uncle had given me his gold wings from World War Two to wear on it. I hated to admit it to myself, but I didn't mind being teased some of the time. It was a small price to pay for acceptance.

During the free-for-all, my hat went sailing up to the front of the bus. I went up to see where it had landed. A voice from behind me asked, "Is this yours?" I turned and reached for it, but she seemed reluctant to hand it over. When she spoke again, I detected a light wisp of delightful perfume. She asked me why I let them pick on me.

Her presence and attitude left me overwhelmed, speechless, and confused. She looked up at me with beautiful sky-blue eyes and a lovely smile. Her hair was gone in a French roll and held with an attractive pin, which added to an air of sedateness about her. She wore a red, short-sleeved print blouse and blue jeans cut off at mid-thigh but neatly rolled up and creased. Her beautiful, short, tanned legs and bare feet with red-painted nails rested on dirty, strawberry-stained sneakers.

Still partially tongue-tied, I explained to her that they were my friends and I didn't mind them. She moved an eyebrow as though she didn't quite under-stand. I asked her if I might have my hat back. I thanked her and walked back to the rear of the bus.

I sat by myself, no longer interested in the gang and their stupid games. Something had happened! Even my prized hat no longer seemed significant. I did not eat or sleep that night. I tossed and turned and thought about her. Why did I feel so strange, as though she had some sort of power over me? I was totally consumed with the thought of her.

I popped out of bed the next day, more enthused about the berry fields than ever. I rummaged through the dresser and found a white shirt that my mother had just bought for a dime at our most frequented department store, the Salvation Army. I left the baseball cap with the gold wings hanging on a nail. I applied Wildroot Cream Oil and attempted to find a long-lost part in my hair. I rolled my shirt sleeves up to my elbows and did my chores. The white shirt was not the most intelligent choice for picking strawberries, but I didn't care. I wanted to look nice. It would detract from my dirty Levis and sneakers.

After breakfast and a nice, cold sponge bath from the livestock spigot, I headed down the narrow gravel road to the general store. The sun was coming up. Hundreds of frogs croaked along the way, and a robin sang. It seemed as though I had never heard such delightful sounds before. What was happening to me? I had to run most of the way to make sure I did not miss the bus, because my bicycle had a broken chain.

The others noticed that something had come over

me. I did not ignore them completely, but sat quietly alone. My heart stopped when the bus pulled up to her stop and she got on and sat with her girlfriend. I noticed how nicely the top of her brown paper lunch bag was folded, just like her jeans. Mine was always crunched and wadded at the top. I tried to straighten it out a bit. I had made my own lunch. Since I was tired of peanut butter and rhubarb jam, I had decided on cheese and mayonnaise. I was tired of that, too, but the other options were even less appealing.

The gang was carrying on as usual, but I rode the whole forty miles without an incident, except for an occasional hair rearrangement from one of them. My hair was hard to keep combed because it was very curly, and when it dried out the Wildroot made it wilder.

I wondered how it had come to her attention that my friends were always picking on me, when she sat so far forward on the bus. I did not mind them, but I wondered why she cared. I sensed in her tone of voice the day before that she did not approve. No one would pick on me again if I could help it.

The bus reached the fields and the straw bosses waited outside, like Georgia prison guards, to assign each person to what seemed to be a ten-mile-long row. One person on each end picked toward the middle, and they might meet each other around noon. Everyone was assigned as soon as they got off the bus.

An idea came to me. When I got up to file off the bus, I stepped in behind her girlfriend. They stepped off the bus together and both were assigned to the same row, to their dismay. I was assigned to the row adjacent. My scheme had worked.

We got our flats off the stack and began picking; to my astonishment, she picked so fast that my whole gimmick to be close to her was crumbling before my eyes. I panicked and began ravishing the plants, making sure I left no berries behind, because the straw bosses would come and spot-check the row. I managed to keep slightly behind her, but I could not believe the amount of strawberries I was picking. This girl had come here to make money.

I looked around. We were pulling well ahead of the others around us. The wild bunch were about fifteen rows over and well behind us, so I decided to relax. I began whistling along in good spirits when she stopped to stretch.

"What are you whistling? It sounds nice."

I smiled and told her I really did not know, and kept on picking. She asked me what my name was. I tripped over my tongue, but managed to answer. I concentrated on picking to cover my shyness. She told me I should take a breather, so I stood up and stretched, too. We talked for awhile, and I could hardly believe it when she told me her father was the barber at the general store. They were planning to move into the neighborhood across from the store. Her father cut my hair every other week, a daring attempt to rectify a hopeless ball of fuzz.

My shyness began to dissipate as we went back to work. I was glowing inside. We had something in common. I learned she was a year older and was going to be a junior in high school. I did not have the guts to tell her my age or where I would be in the fall. Her name was Elizabeth. It fit my image of her; it sounded sophisticated. She asked me if anyone called me Dick instead of Richard, and I told her only my grandfather. She told me she liked the name Dick very much.

Something whizzed by my head. I stopped to look around. I thought I was seeing or hearing things, and went back to work until a soft strawberry hit me on the back of the head. The wild bunch had jumped their rows and had the two of us surrounded. I was steaming. I did not need these clowns fooling around in the presence of a lady.

They moved in and introduced themselves in a silly, pretentious manner for my benefit, keeping one eye on me to see my reaction. Each handed her a full box of strawberries. She gave me a brief, inquisitive look, shrugged her shoulders, and gave them a nice thank you. They continued to pick for her. I was furious, and went back to ravaging the plants. They were older and bigger, and all was lost. My jealousy was running wild.

The noon whistle blew, and to my absolute shock she asked me if we could have lunch together. She placed two boxes of strawberries into my flat to give us both half a flat so we could have our tickets punched together and go to lunch. What an incredible triumph! The berries they had picked for her she gave to me. I picked up both flats, and we headed for lunch. Cheese and mayonnaise never tasted so great.

On the way home I sat with her and her girlfriend, and never heard a whisper from the rear of the bus.

Something was brewing. As soon as we got off the bus they grabbed me, wrestled me to the ground, and pulled off my jeans. It was the current fad. The bus drove on, and I hoped she did not see me in my most undignified hour.

From that moment on, none of us was ever the same. They congratulated me for having such a fantastic girlfriend. I was never again the subject of their jokes or pranks. We had all grown up a little, and I was in love. The whole world took on a slight rosy tint. Nothing else mattered.

CHAPTER TWENTY-TWO

A massive charge detonated, splitting the air like an axe. It knocked us to the sand, blowing others in the platoon back into the amtrack. L and M Companies found themselves right in the middle of a fortified beach assault. A barrage of rockets, mortars, and machine-gun fire pinned us to the sand. Ironically, it was beautiful sand, and over the jungle towered lush coconut palms. The only ingredient missing was Sergeant Striker, the "Duke."

The clash and roar of all-out combat to get inland off the naked dangerous beach was so deafening that it numbed the senses, leaving the strange silence of animation only. Slightly bulging eyes reacted and overreacted to take in such an awesome, incredible scene. A cross wind carrying the black smoke of burning diesel fuel temporarily blinded us, and the stench of detonated sulphur was sickening.

Over the roar I heard men screaming. A barrage of

B-40 rockets hissed out of the jungle, and one slammed into an amtrack partially loaded with troops. A tank rolled off an LCU and took a direct hit, blowing off one of its tracks and rendering it immobile but not ineffective. Its big gun traversed the tree line spitting out shells as fast as the loader could load, exploding large chunks of jungle to dust and vapor. A constant rain of machine-gun fire kept the sand around us boiling. Our mission was to put a cork on a bottle that surrounded a regiment of over two thousand crack North Vietnamese troops.

We had landed on the southernmost coast of the Van Tounge Peninsula. The peninsula itself was discovered by reconnaissance to be a staging area, or jumping-off point, for attacks on the air base just a few miles away. It had only taken a handful of suicidal junkies a few weeks ago to give us something to think about. The airfield was not impregnable.

The campaign was officially called Operation Starlight. Companies from the Fourth and Seventh Marine Regiment were heli-lifted deep into the jungle to set up a blocking force, using six-inch naval guns, Skyhawks, and Phantoms. They were pounding the center of the arena with cannon fire, bombs, and napalm. The idea of getting off the beach and buying some real estate with cover was our only thought the first few seconds on the beach.

A flame thrower team crawled within striking distance of a grass hut on the edge of the tree line. Their objective was to silence the machine gun. A blast of liquid, volatile napalm burned the thatch from the structure, revealing a concrete bunker. The occupants inside were baked quicker than microwave.

Two Phantoms with speed up to sixteen hundred miles per hour just barely topped the trees as they screamed along parallel to the beach. They veered off into the jungle, lifting their noses and kicking loose two five-hundred-pound napalm pods less than a hundred yards from our four-hundred-man assault team. On impact, the entire landing team (minus a few) got up and charged the tree line. We screamed and yelled as we swept across the sand into the jungle. The air strike had given us the necessary split seconds to get off the beach. Our yells were met by screams from several flaming Vietcong running our way. Machine guns relieved their pain. The bodies dropped, to burn for days.

It was difficult to keep our interval in the dense jungle with a cross wind carrying heavy black smoke. M Company had to penetrate the heaviest part of the Vietcong beach defense, and paid for it heavily with many wounded and the loss of their company commander. L Company was lucky, with only a few casualties. No one in Third Platoon was hit. We passed smoldering concrete bunkers and jumped over trench lines, their bottoms and parapets littered with expended brass.

Daniels remained behind the squad, working hard at keeping the interval and making sure no one got lost. We rounded up a few prisoners, some badly injured. Angry troops were restrained by Daniels and myself from an occasional butt stroke or kicking of prisoners. I could not tolerate the abuse of helpless or injured prisoners. All of them were bound with comm wire and gagged, then sent to the rear. From the rumors we had heard, they were as good as dead already. ARVN interrogators employed ingenious methods to get them to talk. They would take several of them aloft in a chopper, arbitrarily toss one out of the hatch, and then start the interrogation with the rest of them. Or they would fasten hot wires or heat tabs to the prisoners' testicles.

The sun disappeared as though nightfall were coming. There was occasional sniper fire up and down the line, and the return of machine-gun fire. The professor and I were trying to decide how to break through a solid wall of vines when an AK-47 opened up. I flew through the air and landed behind some rocks. I looked back in confusion. The professor had not taken cover.

"Professor, get down!"

He went down to his knees. His eyes were fixed ahead. He momentarily braced himself with his rifle butt. His head slowly tilted back and he looked up into the tree tops where a tiny ray of sunlight shone down. He said "Oggie" almost under his breath and fell over frontward.

Another burst of rounds slammed into the rock. One exploded, sending a piece of shrapnel into my left forearm. I crawled over to the professor, turned him over, and laid his head in my lap as I checked the jugular for a pulse. I checked the wrists and then the breathing. I checked the chest for a heartbeat and found a hole. Just a tiny hole; the bleeding could have been stopped with a band-aid. I took off his helmet. His hair felt soft, warm, and strange.

There would be no more fighting over who had to eat the ham and lima beans, no more sharing peaches, no more late-night multiplication drills. He would not get to know how well his student would do on the GED Test. There would not be any college basketball star or proud junior high school teacher. The fires of Watts would burn out and be replaced by just a single candle.

Now was the time to cry, but there weren't any tears. With forefinger and thumb, I gently closed the shades of an empty dwelling. Elgin Walter Johnson the Second did not live in there anymore.

"Goddamn it!" I yelled as loud as I could with every muscle of my body. I replaced his helmet and laid him back gently on the ground. I headed into the jungle screaming, *"You sons of bitches! You bastards!"*

When I came to my senses, I found myself tangled in vines, exhausted and lost. In my childish frenzy, I had placed myself in the hands of the enemy. My breathing and the blood pounding in my ears sounded like they were coming over a public address system amplified a hundred times.

In its dreadful silence, the jungle harbors death just as darkness plays host to evil. The thought of dying had been entertained a great deal the last few months, but the thought of dying alone added a new dimension, a congenital frailty never to be overcome from womb to tomb. Why are we preoccupied with our physical fate after death? If I dropped on the jungle floor and it grew over me, I would vanish without a trace, to rot for thousands of years on a loosely charted part of the planet. It would be excavated by an urban renewal project, creating a wrinkle in future paleontology. This species is not indigenous to this area.

While fighting a losing battle with the jungle, I stopped breathing from time to time to try to detect sounds from other living things. I wasn't aware of which direction I had begun in, since in my carelessness I had probably stopped and headed in several different directions. The sun was nowhere to be seen. I slung my cannon, which would be useless in such close quarters, and drew my forty-five. By brilliant deduction, a course of action was set: follow my nose. Again, the dreadful silence made me feel and sound like a massive, exasperated prehistoric animal trying to sneak across the ground covered with dry autumn leaves.

With five thousand Marines and probably an equal number of Vietcong in the area, I was bound to run into someone. On the other hand, I could stumble around out here for a month. As I trampled along as silently as a baby rhino, I eased but did not preoccupy my mind by switching back and forth from the Twenty-Third Psalm to my multiplication tables. I was all the way up to my eights. The professor would have been proud. Eight times nine equals . . .

Automatic M-2 carbines opened up from different directions in front of me, and I got my answer. The high-pitched crack of the rounds sounded like they were point-blank. The concentration of rounds coming in was so heavy that it seemed like volley after volley of buckshot. The ground around me began to come apart in a blur of dust, while vines, branches, and leaves splintered and disintegrated into a flying mulch before my eyes. I had just been sucked into a wheat combine, and the blades had not yet reduced me to ground round, medium lean. It took forever to get to the ground.

I sprang toward an impression in the jungle floor at the base of a large banana palm. I tried to flatten out and become invisible like a chameleon that hadn't learned what buttons to push to get the right color. I could not believe that I was not hit.

I was more concerned with my head than the rest of my body. I began to curse my helmet, and nearly took it off because it restricted me from pushing my head further down into the soft soil. Ostriches are my kind of people. My face was butted tightly against the base of the banana palm that was more like a house plant than a tree. More false security. Rounds passed through its soft, wet cortex like a sponge. Rounds blew through the opposite side of the stalk just inches from my face, blinding me with spattering juice. At this point, I would have traded a hundred acres of banana palms for just one douglas fir. Dust and debris continued to fly around me. I did not have the courage to lift my head and look around me to see where they were.

I finally got up a thread of courage (or stupidity) and spotted a puff of smoke coming from the top of a large Japanese-style ambush. They had tied themselves in trees and waited for prey to come along. There was another one up there somewhere, but I could not spot him. Easy prey came along, so why didn't they hit it?

This was no time for multiplication tables; the Twenty-Third Psalm might be in order.

They should have had me with the first volley, but any second their luck was going to change. If I got up and ran, even a chimpanzee couldn't miss. If I lay there, I would be dead for sure. I caught myself giving up and wanting to go to sleep just so the fear would go away and I would wake up in a nicer place.

"Yea, though I walk through the valley of the shadow of death, I will fear no evil."

I started to get angry with their incompetence. "You stupid bastards, I've changed my mind. You can't have me!"

In what seemed like one single movement, I was up and in full stride out of my grave. I lowered my head and galloped ahead in a straight line through the greenery like a flatfooted ostrich in full charge. I had once seen an ill-fated event much like this before from the grandstands. The object of the event is to get out of the starting blocks and get to the tape before the starter shoots you in the back. No gold, no silver, and hopefully no lead.

I was so busy and noisy crashing through the brush that I didn't know if they were still firing or not. I was still moving and wasn't leaking anywhere unnaturally; but with luck and preseverance, I would probably stumble right into their main base camp, and they would have me for lunch.

After falling down a dozen or more times I stayed down, exhausted and unable to breathe. I lay on my back and gagged for air. Another machine gun opened up, strafing the jungle overhead, then another and another. So much fire power erupted that the entire jungle overhead began to break off and fall on me. I was right! My luck had led me to the entire Vietcong regiment. How could I be so stupid? If I got out of this one, I'd better turn myself over to the doc.

Wait a minute! The lull in the firing came at familiar time intervals. Those were M-14s with only twenty rounds to each magazine. I had single-handedly found the lost brigade!

I screamed and yelled. "Cease fire! Cease fire! This is PFC Ogden from L Company! Cease fire!"

I got the answer I had anticipated. "What in the fuck are you doing out there?"

I didn't have a short, concise explanation, so I said nothing. I decided to stay put and let them come to me. There's always a trigger-happy hunter who never gets the word. I sat in the brush and waited, like a small runaway child just barely walking age. I tried to assess the events of the day.

Who is this silly, errant, twentieth-century Cervantes character who stumbles blindly but nobly from one intense ambush to another, unharmed, unblemished, in and out of the jaws of the dragon, to avenge the death of a friend named Socrates? He becomes more weary, the sword becomes heavier; the armor of his spirit has tarnished and nearly rusted away. The impossible dreams and ideals have faded. There will be no more restraining combat-crazed school kids from stomping and battering prisoners. There will be no more prisoners, if I can help it!

CHAPTER TWENTY-THREE

Our specific objective was to push the trapped enemy toward a river on the south while another company crossed the river and delta to form a blocking force from the north. At the same time, three other companies were landed by helicopter in the paddies at the backside of the peninsula to the west.

The skirmish line had slowed down because of huge hedgerows and light jungle. At calculated intervals, an invisible freight train would pass overhead and blow in the jungle a good distance ahead of us. Sometimes the six-inch artillery shells fell short, sending back stray chunks of twisted steel weighing as much as two or three pounds, able to sever a good-sized tree like a meat cleaver through a spongy house plant. We hit the deck when the Northern Pacific came in, just in case.

It's impossible to imagine being in a war with an enemy that had naval gun power or jet fighters and bombers hounding you every second, and you had no place to go. Thank God they didn't.

Reports came in that the enemy had attempted to scale a ridge line en masse and were observed by our forward artillery observer. They were right out in the open when our big guns had wiped them out—a sure sign of panic. Just when we thought the North Vietnamese regulars were going to be a piece of cake, they opened up on us from a good-sized hill that lay in front of us. We again hit the deck as machine-gun fire walloped the ground around us.

We waited for Sergeant Nick's command to assault. When it came, we charged up the hill, our fingers going numb on the trigger. The only way for men to survive out in the open in a frontal assault is to gain firing superiority, throwing up a wall of lead so intense that the enemy does not have the opportunity to aim, squeeze, and plink us off from their cover. Keep their heads down and they're ineffective.

The squad leaders remained behind their squads, barking orders to keep the interval and keep moving out, making sure each man, fire team, and squad was abreast of the other. We attacked the objective running and yelling. Balls of smoke blew from every weapon at an incredible rate, the only way we could survive the most dangerous of offensive tactics, facing a concealed enemy while traveling over open ground uphill.

I could see the enemy when they changed positions or got up to run. They had tied brush to themselves for concealment. The frontal attack was working perfectly, in fact, until a hairline fracture in the personality cracked like the sharp, crisp snap of a deadly carbine—

Sergeant Nick began yelling and screaming, ordering us to cease fire, the most moronic and abominable mistake he had ever made in his life. There is only one other thing he could have done that would have been equally mindless: he could have opened up and shot us all in the back.

He continued to yell. All three squad leaders yelled in defiance, afraid for the lives of the men and themselves. He continued to scream till his voice cracked.

"Cease fire and conserve ammo!"

The platoon was loaded with ammo—enough for weeks. But it was too late; erratic orders were penetrating regimented minds. The firing drifted off and the pace slowed down.

As expected, fire from the hilltop picked up. For an instant we stood around like confused offensive linemen in the midst of a broken play. Two men from Anderson's squad dropped like sacks of wheat. They hit the ground almost simultaneously, stone dead. I, and several men around me, hit the ground equally as hard, but alive and without a scratch.

The Swede was several yards to my left. He dropped his canteen and bent over to pick it up. A round entered his shoulder inside his collar bone and blew up the small of his back. I crawled toward him. He was white. His eyes bulged, crossed, and tried to focus. He shook, and then died.

He had been a nice guy. Although I was openly reluctant, he had tried to take me under his wing. To pass some of the long hot days on the runway, he had taken on the tedious, arduous task of teaching me chess. We both had an innate aching and longing for music of any kind. He enjoyed my miserable rendition of Pat Boone, and asked me to sing him to sleep every night. If I would have allowed another friend, he would have been it.

There were three dead. The rest of us were pinned down midway to the objective. But there was no organized effort to continue our assault, though walking brush continued to aim, breathe, and squeeze, keeping a vexed hold on our mobility and effectiveness. We kept firing—but more discriminately, and not in such heavy volume—concentrating on where we had last seen movement.

Burnett and his squad had found cover in the low brush on the right flank. He and two of his men were standing up behind a large clump of green. I felt like yelling over to them just to hear myself yell. But I didn't have the energy. Besides, I was sure that they didn't want to be bothered with the dumb cliché "one round will get you all!" They appeared to be lounging in the shade, seemingly unconcerned, with enemy only a hundred yards away. I blinked, and the three of them disappeared in a puff of blue and red smoke. The clap of the explosion sounded like a massive hand grenade. The bodies flew through the air in slow motion, like Hollywood dummies, in three different directions. One body opened up and came apart with a splash of blood and flesh that turned partially into a vapor. As the sun reflected through the volatile scene, it took on a ghostly hue of pale rose. As the bodies reached the apex of their flight they crashed to the ground, smoldering.

Someone began to yell: *"Incoming! Incoming!"*

Heavy firing came from Second Platoon, which was tied in on the left flank. They had advanced further than we had, and had wrapped around the left side of the objective. It sounded like they were assaulting from the other side. Our part of the deal had gone sour. I wondered why no on had cracked and shot our psychotic leader right where he stood.

When the objective was secured, we took up the grim task of wrapping bodies in ponchos. I found a helmet in the grass with a head still in it. The body was ten feet away. I didn't know his name. I was intrigued, if not entranced, with the fact that there was no blood on the unmarred face. Big blue eyes continued to blink with a lost gaze of confusion about what had just happened. The forehead continued to perspire, framed in damp, matted blond hair. The bottom lip quivered. I knew that it was dead, but I turned away before it spoke . . . before it started asking stupid questions, or for help. I pointed to it for the corpsman to find.

Second Platoon had taken the hill, putting the Vietcong on the run, brush and all. We learned that it was a 60mm mortar that had landed on Burnett and his men. It was one of our own from Second Platoon. They said they had thought they were Vietcong. It was a likely story. Burnett and his friends were only about twenty yards from my position, and we were out in the open. No wonder. It was the same leader who had stepped up behind a gutshot Vietcong on the runway, laying his pistol to the back of the head and blowing it all over himself.

We set up a perimeter around our self-inflicted

carnage and waited for the crosstown bus to cart them to the morgue. For the first time since I'd landed on Red Beach in Danang, I was experiencing a new fear: not the gut-grabbing, heart-stopping terror; it was an all-consuming fear that lay at the base of the brain like a termite. A subtle, bleak depression of hopelessness. We all felt the morale get chewed up along with the spirit, digested and laid to waste, because of so much needless death within a few minutes time. We were faced for the first time, I think, with the stark reality of how dispensable we were and how vulnerable we were by entrusting our lives into the hands of idiots. Gosh, sir, I'm sure sorry. That was a terrible mistake. I'll get it right the next time. Besides, boot camp is cranking them out as fast as we can kill them. We sure ain't gonna run short, are we, sir?

In the meantime, choppers were flying continuously, laden with wounded and dead. Bodies were stacked in the back of trucks five or six deep. There is a lab in Danang that works around the clock, placing bodies in large plastic bags and keeping them refrigerated, as though they were being shipped to Safeway instead of mom.

As we watched them stack the unfortunates aboard the chopper, a thin curtain of darkness and mourning covered the day like a great hand had turned down the rheostat in the sun several clicks.

It was nearly dark when we dropped in our tracks, scraping out a nesting place in the soft jungle earth and crawling in. We washed our C-rations down cold.

I shared the radio watch with Daniels. I took the first watch. I was so exhausted that if I had gone to sleep and then awakened, it would have been impossible to stay awake. As I listened to the lifeless, empty hiss of the radio, I thought of the Vietcong slithering through the jungle, grinning like lizards, like Geronimo's band in the movies. Never getting thirsty or hungry or tired, having no horses and running great distances, no guns, able to creep up behind a wide-awake cowboy and cut his throat. Good communications, and the advantage of fighting in their own backyard . . . Geronimo, considered the greatest military tactician the world has ever known. And still he lost every battle on the screen. Incredible.

My eyelids were so heavy that it took every muscle in my body to keep them from slamming shut. My head began to nod. I found a short stick and tapped myself on the skull to stay alive. It had been a very rough day in too many ways. I tried to peel away the scabs from a dull brain and think of something more pleasant.

Days, weeks, or months no longer held any significance. Life was reduced to intense intervals of minutes and seconds. A five-minute rest; a three-second pull on the canteen; a ten-minute meal; a thirty-second flashback to something homey and pleasant; a shorter flashback to death; a brief, cool breeze; a piece of shade and one could almost forget the anguish of the preceding hours. Even a bowel movement was deemed as a moment of peacefulness, momentarily cutting out the ambient, chaotic world, a moment becoming less frequent because of a lack of fresh food.

The enemy had pulled back so rapidly that we could

not keep up with them. Through more dense jungle, then down into the open sandy hills, sparsely covered with low brush and densely populated with pungee sticks that glistened in the sun and pointed in our direction like porcupine quills.

I seemed to be more exhausted than the troops around me. I must have burned up a lot of energy running through the jungle alone like a mindless idiot. No signs of heat exhaustion that had knocked me down before, but I was hurting bad.

For a moment I fantasized a dirty, sharply jagged pungee stick penetrating deep into a meaty calf, or a sniper's round finding a clean exit after entering a shoulder instead of merely nicking me in the arm. It was only my left arm. I wished they had blown it off; then they couldn't make me participate any longer in this maddening game. The big bird could come and rescue me. I would live to go home and die of cancer, old age, or on the freeway, like it should be.

This boyish man recently turned nineteen had never had a checking account, never learned to drive a car, never held a part-time job that paid more than seventy-five cents an hour, had never felt sex with someone loved or someone liked, or just some nice girl who lived in the neighborhood.

I would gladly give an arm to stand in my mother's kitchen sipping a tall glass of pure, cold Northwest water while watching her fuss over a steaming batch of rhubarb jelly while we happily chatted with enthusiasm, planning my future.

CHAPTER TWENTY-FOUR

As we continued the pursuit there was more and more incredible evidence of a one-sided battle. There were craters in the area big enough to park a truck in, left by the ten-inch naval gunfire or five-hundred-pound bombs dropped by Phantoms. Chunks of dense jungle had literally disappeared, leaving smoldering earth from yesterday's concentrated bombing.

Third Platoon sent a message they had found a lot of bodies. The message stiffened the alert, since partially alive enemy are still dangerous due to booby traps or possum. Why not? They had used every other desperate jungle tactic.

The company slowed down to a creep. Everyone was on edge, waiting to jump some half-charred soul who had survived the bombing.

Part of my concentration and tension was diverted to Sergeant Nick. I wondered if he had any guilt, and how many of us he would get killed today. I was not certain about the others, but my morale was so low that he would never again blunder and jeopardize a single life. He had earned my respect and fear, just as the enemy had. I would never let him out of my sight.

As we continued forward, more bodies and more evidence of bombing was found.

"I think we're headed to where the main event took place," Corporal Daniels commented.

The rest of us silently agreed. The air was filled with the familiar scent of burning napalm and sulphur. It was also laced with the sweet acidic scent of burnt protein. The scent itself was not repugnant, only the thought.

The sun had found its favorite perch and rested on the backs of our necks and shoulders. There was an inordinate amount of flies and other insects hosting this garbage dump of dead trees and bodies.

Even in the face of the great victory, counting the bodies became boring. Viewing death was a curious and intriguing thing at first, but no more. As a kid I had felt terrible during slaughtering season, and ran and hid; but now I felt almost smug and arrogant: better these little pathetic bastards than me.

The company came to a halt at the edge of a huge clearing.

"Jesus Christ!" someone exclaimed slowly.

A chunk of jungle the size of two football fields was missing. It looked like a logging company had moved in, taken the choice lumber, then burned and plowed up the rest with a number of D-9 Caterpillars. There were bodies and pieces of bodies strewn everywhere, some hanging from surviving trees.

Sergeant Mick barked some short commands. The three squads deployed along the edge of Armageddon. We held our weapons at the ready should anyone mysteriously return from the dead.

Every square inch of the territory I scanned was a new revelation in horror, like the indiscriminating brain playing old newsreels of the cleanup of Nazi concentration camps. Several yards to my left front, a completely burnt corpse clutched its bosom as though it were cold. A tiny light flickered inside the skull through the eye socket. The flesh was burned away from the mouth, and it grinned like a lifeless jack-o'-lantern.

It struck a cord. This wasn't real, it was a giant mural. A cynical, surrealistic depiction of man's hatred of man, so detailed that it transcended the immediate imagination. Hope for the future was already dead in the present.

The partially charred corpse of a pregnant woman lay against some rocks. Grass, weeds, and brush had been burned away, and it looked as though she had climbed next to the rocks as a last resort. A burned-away blouse revealed a tiny unblemished foot protruding from a rupture in the side of her abdomen.

It was still. Welcome to the new world somewhere between earth and hell.

When input to the brain becomes too intense or too complex, the entire system shifts a gear, and the index cards are reshuffled and reprogrammed superficially to a different level. The overused dog-eared cards are bundled up and carried to the back, and a crisp new set of cards are popped into the hopper. A whole new program and set of values are initiated, based very loosely on the previous one.

The idea of a thirty-minute lunch break was not disturbing in the midst of this human garbage dump. Picnicking at a community cremation? Maybe Aldous Huxley would have understood. It was just a job; better them than us. Maybe we'd find more after lunch. The programming system works fine unless one of the cards gets jammed and mutilated within the system. Pass the salt, please!

There was mumbling and mild dissension when it was learned that the company was moving out and heading in another direction on a new assignment; there would be no pawing through the ashes to look for souvenirs. The ever-sought-after souvenir was the fighting man's only personal, tangible evidence that he had, indeed, endured the horrendous nightmare. As the years passed the old cards were again bundled up and stacked in the rear of the warehouse, and sometimes inadvertently labeled "fantasy." The souvenir sometimes acts as the key to the warehouse, since most of the men do not want to forget the horrors of death, dying, and destruction that are part of combat. This syndrome can be a practical mechanism in later years in appreciating one's life, when it was so nearly taken in the past.

I was aware of the subtle changes in my mental state, or lack of mental articulation. Complex issues and problems were becoming too simplified. There was a gleam of hope in the fact that I was aware of these changes. The fight to remain alive was one problem; the fight to remain human was quite another. I needed a letter from earth badly.

Wonderful thoughts of home and the faces of people became all too hazy. I labored to fill my head with positive thoughts. Fond memories were trying to get a carnival going under my steel pot. Starting with the most primitive needs, I was standing in my mother's kitchen in front of the sink, drinking as much sheer ice-water as I could hold, and purposefully wasting a lot of it for the pure thrill. And a feminine creature and ice cream are near the top of the list.

CHAPTER TWENTY-FIVE

I stepped out of the cab and gave the Kamikazi driver too many yen. They drove as though their lives depended upon it, instead of their livelihood. Their passengers' lives were depending on it, for sure.

A soft, unimposing rain fell on the bamboo-wood framed, corrugated-tin-roof village outside Camp Hanson Marine Base. I hiked the collar of my green raingear issue to keep the starch of my crisp khakis from running down the furrow in my back.

A mixture of mild sewage and Oriental and American rock music permeated the air along the dirt main street. It was still early evening, and there were only a few local villagers strolling the street while a few shopkeepers closed up. Several MPs strolled slowly down the other side of the street. I instinctively reached up to see if I had remembered my tie, and if my cover was on my head properly. I believed the horror stories of MPs in Okinawa. They would crack your head open for being slightly out of uniform.

At a quick glance one could tell that this bustling metropolis was not hurting for bars or pawn shops. Knowing my ex-fire team too well, I headed for the biggest, noisiest club on the strip called—what else—The Coconut Grove. The Beatles were banging out one of their latest through an antique jukebox as I stepped through the door.

"Hey Oggie, over here!"

It was Red, bouncing a plump young Naisan on his lap. Grinning Charlie was doing the swing with a pretty, short girl, in a pretty, short skirt with an inordinately large bosom, who was long on swing. Ed was also on the dance floor doing some outrageous improvisation, somewhere between Kabuki and the Twist. Richard the III was in the corner involved in tense conversation about Chicago or "Let's Make a Deal." All the girls seemed quite young except for the fat, leathery mama-san behind the bar.

"Oggie, get over here. I want to introduce you to my fiancee. This is Suko, and her sister is dancing with The Horn. Oggie here, when he was our leader, was an asshole; but now he's pretty cool!"

She took her hand from the top of his sweaty head and gave me a little wave. I smiled politely and waved back with two fingers. I picked up the highball glass half full of what looked like Hawaiian Punch and took a sniff.

"What are you apes drinking, anyway?"

"Whatever it is, it's working."

I took a sip; it was incredibly mild and sweet.

"Sloe gin, man, the greatest stuff in the world. Let me order you one."

"No thanks, pardner. I think I'll order something else."

I had been adequately warned about this stuff before. It went down like fruit punch and kicked like a plough horse. It was popular among beginning guzzlers. I walked over to the bar and ordered a beer from a character created by Al Capp.

As I turned from the bar and took a pull on the long-necked bottle, Charlie grinned and waved. He attempted to sling his little bushy partner between his legs and bring her back to her feet. With both of them a little short on technique, she landed solidly on her rear end on the floor, bringing him down on top of her. They rolled and laughed. They were hanging on each other, still in hysterics, as they approached.

"How you doing, buddy? I want you to meet Kico. Kico, this is my old buddy, Oggie."

"Charlie, you're a regular Fred Astaire."

"How is the working party?"

"Oh, as wonderful as ever."

"Them bastards are never going to give you any slack, are they?"

"It doesn't look like it. Not for awhile, anyway."

"That's Kico's sister over there picking fleas off of Bo Bo. Let me buy you a drink. I'm glad you could get out, anyway." He turned and called for the mama-san. "What are you drinking?"

"Beer."

"Give me a beer and a JB and water, Mama."

"I see you don't drink cough syrup like the rest."

"No-siree, JB is almost the best there is."

I was already feeling the first beer as Charlie dragged his little bundle of joy back onto the dance floor. As I looked around "The Longbranch," Miss Kitty was pouring four more sloe gins at the bar. I noticed the posters covering nearly every square foot of each wall. United Airlines, Air Canada, the skyline of Manhattan, and a lake in Oregon. That's close to home. The Beatles, Robert Mitchum, and the Flintstones were nailed to the ceiling. Mickey Mouse was irreverently tacked over the men's room door. Then there was the king, Elvis. He was not my king, but my God. Whoever hung all that stuff together must have been a sadist.

I punched a couple of slow Elvis tunes and Charlie's little Miss Bust eased the homesick pangs by rhythmically trying to etch a hot pattern on my chest through her Maidenform bra. The little girls were completely caught up in the western culture with their teeny skirts and frilly blouses, and with us in our starched khakis the atmosphere was somewhere between a junior high school hijinks and a scene out of "From Here to Eternity."

I forgot these were working girls. They were cute, squeaky-clean, and smelled of imaginary lotus blossoms.

I eased around the dance floor to "Love Me Tender." My new partner was not quite as pretty as the others, but she seemed to work harder at the game. She smiled more, batted her eyes more, and held me tighter, as though I might run away. When we turned with the music she rotated her hips slightly to make sure I knew she was there. Her warm breath from make-believe sighs worked on my rusty, forgotten thermostat.

I pretended I was being romanced. I was both delighted and terrified of being dragged away and romped to death. It was becoming embarrassing. The girls in Tijuana are more businesslike. They just grab you by the crotch: "Wanna go, Joe?"

We made another turn and I watched the negotiations around the room intensify; more petting, kissing, rubbing, and eye-batting. The guzzling of a whole one-and-a-half beers crept up on me, combined with waltzing around in circles, and I inadvertently stepped on a dainty foot. She let out a little yelp and stomped away to the bar. Obviously the illusion of business, or romance, had been broken.

I grinned at myself. It is better to have lost at love than never to have loved at all. Remembering a self-styled wit who had told me I wouldn't be able to make out in a whorehouse with a sack full of quarters, I grinned and swaggered over to the bar like Mitchum would have and ordered another beer. My ex-partner was already working on a couple of marines from another outfit.

I had tipped up the last of my beer when a girl walked in from the back room. My stomach did a flip for a moment and my mind forgot whether I was inhaling or exhaling. Some foam from the beer went up my nose, and I nearly sneezed the back of my head out.

She walked over to some tables opposite the bar and sat down. Spiked heels were connected to lovely little legs that were partially covered by a very short dark skirt. She also wore a pink sleeveless blouse with ruffles down the front. She began to play a game with some little pieces that resembled dominoes. Sensing me staring, she looked up and smiled.

I needed another beer. I really didn't but I did. Holding my breath, I hoped one of the other goons wouldn't move in before I got another bottle of courage down. That can't be on the menu, I thought to myself. It's too small, too young, and too gorgeous. I'm gonna burn in hell for my thoughts. Touch that stuff, buddy boy, and her sisters here will claw your eyes out. She had to be at least two years younger than them, or maybe even more. What was I worrying about? I had just turned eighteen years old a few months ago. What's a few months?

I took a couple more pulls on my bottle for courage, straightened my tie, pawed at my almost-nonexistent hair, then got off the stool and walked toward her. I walked in too straight a line and was too polite—a dead give-away for a drunk.

"May I sit?"

She looked up and smiled again. "Of course."

I melted into the chair opposite her. I took another drink from my crutch and asked the all-important question: "Do you work here?"

"Yes!" she replied with enthusiasm.

I felt a great rush come to all my nerve endings. I must be getting drunk. My face felt flushed and I kept both hands on my bottle to disguise nervousness. The thought of even touching such a lovely creature sent a shiver through my whole body. All kinds of primitive erotica raced through my mind.

She brought me back to my senses. "Would you like to learn the game?"

"I'm not very good at games," I replied weakly.

"That's all right. It's an easy game. It is a most ancient game."

I was surprised; it was very much like dominoes. Dots were replaced with characters with a very detailed and intricate design of animals, birds, plants, and patterns. It took a keen eye, good graphic ability, and a special awareness. The object of the game was to detect the flaw in the pattern or character of each tile. Only the tiles that were absolutely identical could be joined.

My enthusiasm for the game was not forthcoming. My entranced, beer-fogged brain was playing another game similar, but life-sized. And from my vantage point, there were no flaws, only exquisite perfection of beauty in the most profound sense of the word. She was an exotic Oriental creature so striking that it transcended the imagination.

She again brought me back from my euphoric, childlike rapture.

"What's your name?"

"You speak very good English."

"You speak very good English also."

We both giggled. I had drunk myself past courage and well into silly.

"Richard, Rich, or Dick." I gestured with my finger. "Never Richie, Ricky, or Dicky."

We giggled again. Then my giggle quickly faded. As

she bent over to pick up a tile that had fallen on the floor, volumes of long straight hair fell down from her shoulders and closely shrouded her face. A tiny, delicate ear protruded from the dark, rich sheen as she grasped the tile. I marveled at the small, youthful but determined breasts that softly caressed the pink material. My stomach flipped again. She was no child.

Self-awareness, doubt, and insecurity crept in beside the alcohol. The beast began to grow hair and the nose on a tongue-tied Cyrano began to grow.

We grinned and staggered out, hanging onto each other as we crawled into the Kamikaze cab and headed for the base. Everyone laughed and yapped about the fun we'd had. About the girls and how much they had to drink. I sat by the window in a bemused state of mind, staring out into the darkness and watching the cardboard village go by.

"Oggie, why didn't you lay that cute little thing you had tonight? She sure was something. I don't think I've ever seen a whore looking like that."

Little Kobi was just a figment of my imagination. I was dizzier than a bat, and hung on to keep my head from banging on the side of the cab.

At two o'clock the next afternoon I walked briskly through the streets of the cardboard village and found, to my amusement, that in the daylight it wasn't cardboard at all. My brain was still a mold of Jello that was much too aware of each stride. My whole body was slightly off time from the beer which collectively couldn't have amounted to more than four bottles. I managed to do the impossible: whistle and grin at the same time.

I had a date. I was hung over, but I still had a date. Somehow, last night, before the world managed to take a ride without me, I had asked Kobi for a date. A real date, not a five-minute wrestle. A dinner maybe, a walk in the park if they had one, and maybe something else.

Was it possible? A relationship with a working girl? She didn't seem to fit the mold. Maybe because of her age she was only allowed to hustle drinks, or maybe she was just there to be looked at. Why did I waste time playing silly games and trying to drink myself into a coma? Why dinner and all the pretense? Why was I beating around the bush? She was just a bar girl.

I stepped through the door of the Coconut Grove with composed anticipation. I just knew I was gonna be stood up. She had said it would be easier to meet here, as it was her day off.

My eyes had to adjust from the bright sunlight. Then I saw her sitting in the same booth where I had left her.

She smiled. "Hi, Richie-san!"

"Hello, Kobi-san. Shall we go?"

She slipped from behind the table and clicked across the floor in gold-colored high heels and a short, bright-red pleated skirt.

"How is your head, Richie-san? You were funny last night."

"My head is perfect," I lied. "Not much in there to hurt. The air gets a little stale sometimes."

She gave me a puzzled look and continued ahead of

me. I was drawn to an interesting gold bracelet on her upper arm. It was a cobra wrapped around her arm three or more times with little ruby eyes. A teenage dragon lady, I thought. Her whole outfit was a bit garish for my taste for a Saturday afternoon. I would have preferred dirty tennis shoes and cut-off jeans.

As she glided toward the door with me in tow, her lovely behind rolled ever so slightly and smoothly. My stomach flipped again. It's not the wrapper but what's in the package.

As we headed down the street she shortened her hold on me and took me by the arm.

"I know a good place. Good saki and good food."

"I've heard of saki, but I've never tried it."

We stopped at a sidewalk stand and I bought her some flowers. She giggled and kept sticking her nose into the bouquet. They looked like some kind of fruit blossoms.

This part of the village was even more shabby than the rest. It was hastily and crudely slapped together. A typical commercial phenomenon that flourishes near any U.S. military facility throughout the world. I was amazed by how well the Kamikaze cabs and bicycles were getting along on the same street with no traffic signs, no rules and regulations that were noticeable or practiced to any degree.

I got yanked into a side door where a dark, sweet, pungent aroma of cooking dominated the darkness. My eyes were still adjusting as we sat at a table and chairs made of wicker in the center of the restaurant. I glanced around quickly at the drab, empty restaurant.

Then my eyes never left her. It could have been a cave and I still would have felt a marvelous glow. Her big, lovely brown eyes danced and glistened.

A tiny, frail old man with just one tooth waited on us. I ordered abalone chow mein; that sounded exotic enough. She ordered something in Japanese.

I wasn't hungry. My body was anguished between hangover and wanting her. My last chance for two weeks. I had duty the next weekend. Also, we could ship out at any time.

Our ancient waiter brought us two tiny glasses of saki. It was hot. We saluted each other, giggled, and sipped. It went down smoothly, but it had an indistinguishable taste. Another sip of the saki and my whole body felt a nice, warm glow. It seemed to settle my stomach, and my appetite came back. Just a case of nerves. A combat marine terrified by a tiny little girl.

Dinner was finally served and it all looked delicious. Hers was a little more green than mine, but other than that they were the same. Hot tea and cookies were served.

"Where do you live, Kobi?"

"Just around the corner."

I nearly bit my tongue when I bit down on a piece of abalone that had the consistency of sautéed basketball but tasted great.

How convenient, I thought. Now all I have to do is get up the guts.

"Where do you live, Richie-san?"

"Seattle, Washington."

"I know where that is. It's straight across. Are you

lonely for home?"

"Yes, I guess so."

"Do you have a girlfriend?"

"Not any more."

"What happened?"

"She got married."

We finished our dinner and a lot of small talk. My mind wasn't really on conversation; it was around the corner in a dimly lit bedroom. The saki seemed to act like a potion.

"Kobi, can we go to your house?" I asked with an almost merciless approach.

"Sure," she smiled.

I squeezed her tiny wasp waist firmly, almost afraid of crushing her like a clumsy child with a kitten. We kissed. Hard mouths wide open, trying to smother each other as tongues danced, teased, and darted back and forth. I slipped both palms down onto her behind and pulled her to me, nearly lifting her off the bedroom floor. She responded immediately by arching her back and rotating her hips slowly.

We relaxed. I bent and kissed her ear close to her throat, and felt the dampness of sweet perspiration from the close stuffiness of the bedroom and the invisible fire we were building. I slipped both hands up under her bra and found the snap hidden by some lace. I slipped a clumsy fingernail under it and it popped. As her bra peeled away my hand followed the smooth curvature of her rib cage. Her small breast nearly filled my hand, surprisingly. It was firm and her nipple so erect it tickled my palm. She shivered when I opened my hand and kissed the nipple.

She took off her shoes and stepped back, then threw her hair forward and pulled her blouse up over her head. With a slip of a hidden button her skirt fell to the floor. I pulled her close again and kissed her hard. She was breathing steadily, audibly, deeply, and her eyes were almost closed. There was a musky, sweet, pungent scent distinctly her own.

I picked her up and laid her on the bed with a devilish smile and two thumbs. She slipped her black lace panties down, revealing a dark bush that could have been hidden by a single silver dollar. I had forgotten to breathe, and my stomach and heart were beyond flipping. She slowly moved her hips invitingly. Her heat building and my nerves frayed, I finally found her and her secret. She sucked in a quivering breath, and as she convulsed slightly and arched her back, I was going crazy.

We were both terribly inexperienced. I panicked, thinking I might lose it before we began. Then we settled down to a rhythm that I could be safe with as little baby sounds came from deep in her throat. Her tiny, powerful hips and thighs helped deepen a strong, heavy beat.

Her eyes rolled wildly in the dim room as if in panic. She rolled her head from side to side and the squeak of spring and slap of flesh quickened. Her moaning and near-whimpering were contagious. We held each other in panic like two children in a high, scary place. She began to move under me in great, forceful lunges, then she let out a clawing screech that scared the hell out of me. Finally she let go and relaxed. She was breathing very hard with her eyes closed. She smiled, and I knew it had been good.

My own body began to quake, and with great compassion and consideration she gave me a few more helpful lunges. I hung onto her, nearly breaking her. Then it came with such force that it left me momentarily paralyzed from the waist down.

She cuddled beside me and I looked into those child-woman eyes. Okinawa would never be the same. In fact, afternoons anywhere would never be the same again.

"Richie-san, you must have forgot. Two dollars, please!"

CHAPTER TWENTY-SIX

To all appearances the first North Vietnamese regiment was completely gutted, but no animal circled or cornered gives up or quits. The more desperate it becomes the more dangerous it is. Humans are no exception. It is a very chancy business to drop your weapon and surrender, only to be shot by one of your comrades or be blown away by a hysterical marine whose twisted philosophy is to not take prisoners. Then there is the gruesome reality of interrogation and torture by the South Vietnamese army. An appendage of the red war machine was dead or dying quickly, but dangerous nerve endings still spasmed out of desperation.

A convoy of amtracks loaded with fresh supplies made a wrong turn and got left in dense jungle without proper cover and support. They fought to the last man. Command had pushed the giant breadboxes too far.

The squad was spared out in a circle in the light jungle waiting for the squad leaders to return. We tinkered with weapons and discussed among ourselves how much ass-kicking we were doing, like halftime at a football game. We all agreed that the special team deserved the Heisman Trophy.

Daniels came rattling and huffing through the jungle from the direction of the CP. He unslung his M-14, dropped to his knees, and called us around. He could hardly catch his breath.

"There's a chopper down about three miles from here to the north, and our squad's been elected to get to it before you-know-who. There's gonna be a chopper waiting for us about a mile down the beach. The beach is only two hundred yards in that direction." He pointed with his rifle.

I was completely and thoroughly confused. I thought the beach was the other way, but I had forgotten this was a jagged peninsula.

"Okay. The fastest way for us to get our chopper and get to the downed one is for the company to use the beach. When we move out we're gonna spread out at five-yard intervals and run like hell."

"A whole company running down the beach? That's crazy!" Anderson yelled.

"Don't I know it," Daniels said. "Move out."

Two days ago, we had fought like hell to get out of the water onto the beach and into the jungle; now we were running down the beach like it was Malibu. When we got to the edge of the jungle, everyone was reluctant to hit the white sand again.

It was like standing at the hatch of a plane waiting to take your first or second jump.

When we finally got on the beach we were at a full gallop. An entire company huffing and puffing, taking John Wayne's beach again.

I was so tired when the inevitable happened that it seemed like it had taken ten times longer to find cover than usual. It took four more strides than usual to find a depression in the sand instead of dropping like a rock. I would have been left up on the top of a small sand dune with no cover. The smart thing would have been to drop in place and dig like hell.

I was so exhausted that I no longer cared; what was going to happen, was going to happen. Funny how the pop of a round hitting the soft sand and a bit landing in my face changed my mind. You skinny, greasy, mindless little bastards, you're not getting me!

The entire company crawled on its belly closer to the jungle's edge for as much cover as we could find. There were probably no more than four or five guys out there keeping a whole company at bay. We were wasting our ammo on enemy we couldn't see, and with the sea at our backs we had no place to go. I smelled another Silver Star for somebody.

I kept my head down and my face practically buried in the sand. I dropped a few M-79 rounds in their direction and fantasized squashing someone.

After about forty-five minutes of company sunbathing, the cavalry came. A little slow at two-and-a-half times the speed of sound. A Phantom dropped altitude and leveled off before it trimmed the tree line. It made an empty pass to see where the bad guys were in relationship to the good guys, then turned out over the water. We could tell by the color of the pod on its underbelly that he was packing five hundred pounds of our favorite apple jelly.

As he made his turn to straighten out and make the second run, the entire beach looked like it had been invaded by a massive colony of giant sea turtles. Hyperkinetic sea turtles that threw sand every which way and finally dug a hole like they were irreparably late for one of Mother's Nature's deadlines.

I scratched and flayed with both hands and feet. We all prayed that the hot jelly was on target. I could hear the Phantom screaming toward us. I raised my head from the sand like a busy gopher. It was frightening; he was flying so close to the jungle that the wings were nipping off branches and small tree tops.

I felt the air and ground shock of everything evaporating in the target area, then felt the heat on the back of my hands and neck. As far as I could tell, they were right on target. At least there was nothing burning on the beach.

The Phantom made another turn and came back, flying low over the water just off the beach. He tipped his wings in a show of victory and "glad to be of service." We cheered him and waved.

The jungle burned, and to our surprise two of Ho Chi Minh's finest strolled out of it with their hands in the air. Out of reflex, Corporal Daniels gave the order not to shoot. A couple of men stepped out and herded them in at rifle point and forced them to spread-eagle on their bellies to check for weapons and ID.

I couldn't get over how small, young, and frightened they were as they lay in the sand in their sawed-off black pajamas. I wasn't afraid of them and I didn't feel superior toward them. Although I knew they had killed a lot of marines, I still had empathy for them. They were terrified. I knew, as did they, that they were living dead. They would probably die at the hands of some rear-echelon liaison punk who had never seen combat but could tell the folks back home he had seen the enemy and did what was right.

We stood around them, waiting for the company commander to show up and give us orders on what to do with them. We still had a mission.

One of the prisoners made a sign for some water. I took out my canteen and put it to his mouth. Without the slightest warning, Simms stepped up and gave the other one a butt stroke on the head. Corporal Anderson and I grabbed him and threw him to the ground.

"They're prisoners of war, asshole!" I yelled. "Nobody's gonna maltreat them." I looked around at a lot of faces and made my point perfectly clear. "Take your goddamn frustrations out on the gooks that are out there, still armed and able to kill you."

Still down in the sand on his back, Simms growled like a cornered alley cat almost under his breath. "I'll get even with you, Oggie Doggie. I don't know who in the hell you think you are."

I stepped closer to him and bent over so he wouldn't miss a syllable, and smiled. "Any time you want to learn another lesson in manners, just let me know."

When I stood up and turned around, Anderson had lit up a cigarette for both prisoners. Peeling the hide of a five-year-old child with a sharp knife just to make him scream could hardly be equated with butt-stroking a bound prisoner; but I, or we, were fighting for that tiny shred of morality, that tiny particle of humanity.

After our unexpected beach party and barbecue we were all grinning again. Maybe it was the cool breeze blowing in from the hatch, or the fact that we didn't have to hump the sand or the jungle for awhile. I sat directly across from the hatch and the door gunner, and watched the jungle go by at about a thousand feet. There were no flak gear aboard the chopper. We were too tired to sit on our helmets to keep our asses from getting shot off, and too tired to look up at the top of the fuselage for spots of sunlight that appeared magically.

Corporal Daniels was sitting to my right. He put his helmet to mine, cupped his mouth in his hand, and yelled over the roar of the engines. "I'm going to put you up for lance corporal again. You deserve it."

I smiled and gave him a thumbs-up of appreciation. I was grateful he was trying. Back at the air base I had marched down to the CP to take the test and had scored in the upper ten percent of the entire battalion, but Sergeant Nick had rejected it. I didn't care much; I was getting short. I only had weeks to go in this hellhole anyway.

I kept having nightmares that red tape would keep me here for the duration of the war. There were no more rumors of enormous extensions, but I was nervous just the same because of my short time left. I had learned to live with and accept the dangers of combat, and had helped others to do the same. Inside, I had grown up, but I had also grown old. Outwardly, I kept up the front of having my guts well enough intact to get the job done, but inwardly I was becoming old and senile. I had been in Vietnam longer than anyone here. My odds were being used up. The idea of having only a few weeks to go had reduced me to a terrified old man of nineteen years. My fantasies had really started to bother me. I believed the Vietcong had stepped up the program to get me personally before I went home. I had embarrassed them by getting away from them too many times.

The door gunner was searching and traversing the ground below. I thought again how neat it would be to have his job and not have to hump the ground. He flew back to safety every night.

Then daydreaming turned to shock and horror right before my eyes. With a blink of an eye the gunner had been blown backward away from his gun. He hung upside down, dangling from his seat strap. Blood gushed from the center of his chest like a restricted garden hose. We looked on, helpless with horror. He flopped in spasms, and blood gushed up the side of the fuselage and ran down the deck. Still in shock, I watched some fool along the bench pick up his boots so they wouldn't get dirty. We looked at each other, still stunned.

I came to my senses and undid my seat strap, stood up, and unfastened the gunner, letting his body slide gently to the deck. We were flying naked, without any armaments. My next movements didn't seem to be coming from any constructive thought, but were mechanical movements. While I was on my hands and knees with the gunner, Daniels had taken position at the M-60, opened it up, and let it do its thing.

I took off my helmet, threw it on the deck, and slipped the gunner's helmet off his head. The rest of the squad was squeezing toward the hatch, opening up the M-14s. Any little thing to add to our survival. No one could see a thing—just fire like hell.

I placed the flyer's communications helmet on my head, bent the mouthpiece back into place in front of my lips, and with the other hand traced the lines from the helmet that had the male plug at the end. I found the female plug on the wall of the fuselage and shoved the male plug into it.

The ammo belt on the M-60 was running dangerously low. I patted somebody on the shoulder, and he looked up. It was Simms. I pointed to a can of ammo underneath a seat and he knew what I meant. He scrambled for it.

"Skipper, this is PFC Ogden. Your crew chief is dead. What do you want us to do?"

"Oh, no!" There was a pause.

He rattled off orders fast. "Ogden, our ETA is about forty seconds. We're going into a hot LZ. You stay aboard and man the gun and radio. I want every man out in three seconds. We're gonna make a bounce landing and that's all. Repeat, I want every man out in three seconds."

I relayed the message to Daniels, who let me take his place at the gun. He screamed orders to the squad.

The chopper hit the ground hard and bounced, knocking everybody down, but they scrambled and jumped. I helped Daniels shove men out. He hit the ground on his belly last and rolled over and gave me "thumbs up."

I yelled into the mike. "They're out. Let's go, sir." Good-bye, fellows. Keep your asses down.

The engines screamed and we lifted off immediately. I leaned on the trigger. I was having a lot of trouble staying on the seat. I was too short, so I crawled up on my knees. I kept firing aft along the tail, trying to keep our group in sight so I wouldn't hit any of them.

A huge whapping sound shook the entire bird like a giant machete had taken several whacks at it, leaving gaping holes in the fuselage. A shiver went through me. I held my bowels while sweat poured from under the helmet, blinding me. Then I found myself laughing out loud like an idiot. This was the job I had wanted so badly. My knees kept slipping off the seat as the ship began to vibrate even more.

We had gained some altitude and it looked like we might be out of danger. But just when I thought there was a glimmer of hope, the engine began to miss badly. Black smoke passed the fuselage and some drifted in, filling the inside compartment. All hope went out the hatch when the engine quit completely. A strange calm came over me and I took my finger off the trigger.

A solemn voice came over the radio. "What's your name again back there?"

"Ogden, sir."

"Well, Ogden, it's just you and me. The captain bought it, and we're going down. I'm gonna autorotate to give us some help."

He was going to turn the rotor blades loose on the shaft so they would spin by themselves and give us some lift and help with the impact.

"This is Lieutenant Torres. You did a hell of a job back there, partner. If we get out of this I wanna buy you a beer."

"Thanks, lieutenant. Now it's your turn. Give her hell."

I didn't feel like talking any more, but the silence was eerie this high in the sky. I disengaged the wires from the wall. The only thing I could think of was to crawl up into the tail section. I couldn't believe how calm and relaxed I was; I just wanted a place to lay down. Going in at such a steep angle, I knew there was no hope. I had to pull myself along the deck, grabbing onto the struts that held up the benches.

I reached the tiny end of the tail section and curled up into a ball. It was silent except for the wind rushing past the hatch. I closed my eyes. The nightmare was going to be over. It wouldn't hurt any more.

I was the tiny four-year-old child who walked away from home and got lost out in the bus intersection and was nearly hit by cars several times before I was finally rescued and brought back home. I was back in my room, safe under the blankets. No more horror, no more anguish, no more fear. Peace at last.

I woke up to some bright lights on a table of sheets. Standing over me was a clean, smiling face connected to a body wrapped in a white smock which was dotted with faded bloodstains.

"Welcome back to the world. We thought you were going to sleep all the way through it and get paid, too."

I had one hell of a headache. "What happened?"

"Oh, you just got a little bump on your head. But that's pretty good, considering you got shot out of the sky like a turkey. You crashed in a helicopter and were overlooked by a Vietcong patrol. Fortunately, you were found by one of our patrols. During the impact, the tail section broke off and sailed away while you were napping, and landed some distance from the wreckage."

He kept grinning.

"Ever think of going into the air wing? You came down without a scratch and only a bump on the head. That's more than I can say for the rest of them. Incidentally, you have been pulled from the game and sent to the showers. You will probably be home for Christmas."

I smiled back as it began to register.

"Keep smiling and I'll put you back in the game. They're hurting for smiling faces."

I didn't ask further about the Vietcong patrol.

I had lost so much weight that I looked like a young

Frank Sinatra in a Santa Claus suit in my dress greens. I had a window seat in a 707 as it sat on the runway in Danang. There were so many different emotions going through my head. I was dizzy and my stomach was turning, only this time for joy. But I was still scared. A thousand Vietcong could break through the jungle toward the plane at any second. How come we were not moving?

My heart leaped when we began to roll. A pretty stewardess tapped me on the shoulder to get my attention.

"Please fasten your seat belt."

She was a brunette with big blue eyes and lovely round cheeks on both ends. Whoever put us in such quarters with such sweet-smelling loveliness when we were right out of the jungle was an unwitting sadist.

The plane began to pick up speed, and I watched the last glimpses of hell race by the window. As the plane lifted off the runway, my knuckles went white helping it up over the jungle. I kept pulling harder on the armrest until my arms shook from the strain. Although I had great confidence in this 707, which was made at home, there could still be little bastards down there in the jungle with rockets that could bring it down.

When we were high over the jungle out of range, I realized I was still trying to help the plane. My eyes clouded up and tears ran down my cheeks, dripping off my chin onto my tie.

My eyes were still out of focus with tears when I looked across the aisle and saw the professor smiling . . a ghost that will haunt me for the rest of my life.

Biographical Note

Richard E. Ogden is a contributing writer and consultant to Boston Publishing, and Time Life Books, Inc. on the historical, widely acclaimed series, "The Vietnam Experience." He was a special delegate to the United States Congress, and was invited to address Congressional hearings in the House of Representatives on veterans' affairs. He is also an actor, stuntman, and technical adviser in Hollywood, California.

THE BEST IN ADVENTURE FROM ZEBRA